PENGUIN BOOKS

THE WIRE IN THE BLOOD

Val McDermid grew up in a Scottish mining community then read English at Oxford. She was a journalist for sixteen years, spending the last three years as Northern Bureau Chief of a national Sunday tabloid. She is now a full-time writer and lives in south Manchester.

Val McDermid has written five crime novels featuring Kate Brannigan, the third of which, *Crack Down*, was shortlisted for CWA's Gold Dagger Award and the Anthony Award. She has also written a non-fiction book, *A Suitable Job for a Woman*, lifting the lid on the world of female private detectives, and five novels featuring journalist sleuth Lindsay Gordon.

The Mermaids Singing, which introduced clinical psychologist Tony Hill, won the 1995 CWA Gold Dagger Award for Best Crime Novel of the Year.

THE WIRE IN THE BLOOD

Val McDermid

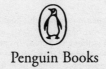

Penguin Books

PENGUIN BOOKS
Published by the Penguin Group
Penguin Books Canada Ltd, 10 Alcorn Avenue, Toronto,
Ontario, Canada M4V 3B2
Penguin Books Ltd, 27 Wrights Lane, London W8 5TZ, England
Penguin Putnam Inc., 375 Hudson Street, New York,
New York 10014, U.S.A.
Penguin Books Australia Ltd, Ringwood, Victoria, Australia
Penguin Books (NZ) Ltd, cnr Rosedale and Airborne Roads, Albany,
Auckland 1310, New Zealand

Penguin Books Ltd, Registered Offices:
Harmondsworth, Middlesex, England

First published by HarperCollins*Publishers*, 1997
First published in Canada, 1998
Published in Penguin Books, 1999
10 9 8 7 6 5 4 3 2 1

Publisher's note: This book is a work of fiction. Names, characters, places and incidents either are the product of the author's imagination or are used fictitiously, and any resemblance to actual persons living or dead, events, or locales is entirely coincidental.

Manufactured in Canada.

Canadian Cataloguing in Publication Data

McDermid, Val
The wire in the blood

ISBN 0-14-027548-7

I. Title

PR6063.C37W57 1999 823'.914 C97-932661-3

British Library Cataloguing in Publication Data Available

Visit Penguin Canada's web site at **www.penguin.ca**

ACKNOWLEDGEMENTS

It's hard to imagine how I could have written this book without a lot of help from several key people. For their specialist knowledge and willingness to give so freely of their expertise, I'd like to thank Sheila Radford, Dr Mike Berry, Jai Penna, Paula Tyler and Dr Sue Black. I owe an apology to Edwina and Lesley, who ran around like headless chickens researching something that was cut in the rewrites. Without Jim and Simon at Thornton Electronics, Mac and Manda, I would almost certainly have had a complete nervous breakdown when the hard disk crashed. But the perseverance and perspicacity of three women in particular got me through to the end. For that reason, this book is for:

Julia, Lisanne and Brigid

With love

The trilling wire in the blood
Sings below inveterate scars
Appeasing long forgotten wars.

Four Quartets,
Burnt Norton
T. S. Eliot

PROLOGUE

Murder was like magic, he thought. The quickness of his hand always deceived the eye, and that was how it was going to stay. He was like the postman delivering to a house where afterwards they would swear there had been no callers. This was the knowledge that was lodged in his being like a pacemaker in a heart patient. Without the power of his magic he'd be dead. Or as good as.

He knew just from looking at her that she would be the next. Even before the eye contact, he knew. There had always been a very particular combination that spelled perfection in his thesaurus of the senses. Innocence and ripeness, mink-dark hair, eyes that danced. He'd never been wrong yet. It was an instinct that kept him alive. Or as good as.

He watched her watching him, and under the urgent mutter of the crowd, he heard echoing in his head the music. '*Jack and Jill went up the hill to fetch a pail of water. Jack fell down and broke his crown . . .* ' The chiming tune swelled and burst then battered his brain like a spring tide against a breakwater. And Jill? What about Jill? Oh, he knew what happened to Jill. Over and over again, repetitious as the barbaric nursery rhyme. But it was never enough. He had never quite been satisfied that the punishment had fit the crime.

And so there had to be a next one. And there he was, watching her watching him sending her messages with his eyes. Messages that said, 'I've noticed you. Find your way to me and I'll notice you some more.' And she read him. She read him, loud and clear. She was so obvious; life hadn't scarred her expectations with static yet. A knowing smile quirked the corners of her mouth and she took the first step on the long and, for him, exciting journey of exploration and pain. The pain, as far as he was concerned, was

I

not quite the only necessity but it was certainly one of them.

She worked her way towards him. Their routes varied, he'd noticed. Some direct, bold; some meandering, wary in case they'd misread what they thought his eyes were telling them. This one favoured the spiral path, circling ever inward as if her feet were tracing the inside of a giant nautilus shell, a miniature Guggenheim Gallery compacted into two dimensions. Her step was measured, determined, her eyes never wavering from him, as if there were no one else between, neither obstacle nor distraction. Even when she was behind his back, he could feel her stare, which was precisely how he thought it should be.

It was an approach that told him something about her. She wanted to savour this encounter. She wanted to see him from every possible angle, to imprint him on her memory forever, because she thought this would be her only chance for so detailed a scrutiny. If anyone had told her what the future truly held, she'd have fainted with the thrill of it.

At last, her decaying orbit brought her within his grasp. Only the immediate circle of admirers stood between them, one or two deep. He locked on to her eyes, injected charm into his gaze and, with a polite nod to those around him, he took a step towards her. The bodies parted obediently as he said, 'Delightful to have met you, do excuse me?'

Uncertainty flitted across her face. Was she supposed to move, like them, or should she stay in the ambit of his mesmerizing stare? It was no contest; it never was. She was captivated, the reality of this evening outstripping her every fantasy. 'Hello,' he said. 'And what's your name?'

She was momentarily speechless, never so close to fame, dazzled by that spectacular dental display all for her benefit. My, what big teeth you've got, he thought. All the better to eat her with.

'Donna,' she finally stuttered. 'Donna Doyle.'

'That's a beautiful name,' he said softly. The smile he won in response was as brilliant as his own. Sometimes, it all felt too easy. People heard what they wanted to hear, especially when what they were hearing sounded like their dream come true. Total suspension of disbelief, that's what he achieved every time. They came to these events expecting Jacko Vance and everyone connected to the great man to be exactly what was projected on TV. By association, any-one who was part of the celebrity's entourage was gilded with the same brush. People were so accustomed to Vance's open sincerity, so familiar with his very public probity, it never crossed their minds to look for the catch. Why should it, when Vance had a popular image that made Good King Wenceslas look like Scrooge? The punters listened to the words and they heard Jack and the Beanstalk – from the little seed Vance or his minions planted, they pictured the burgeoning flower of a life at the top of the tree right alongside his.

In that respect, Donna Doyle was just like all the others. She could have been working from a script he'd written for her. Having moved her strategically into a corner, he made as if to hand her a signed photograph of Vance the megastar. Then he did a double take so exquisitely natural it could have been part of De Niro's repertoire. 'My God,' he breathed. 'Of course. Of course!' The exclamation was the verbal equivalent of smiting himself on the forehead with the heel of his hand.

Caught with her fingers inches from his as she reached out to take what had been so nearly offered, she frowned, not understanding. 'What?'

He made a twisted little *moue* of self-disparagement. 'Ignore me. I'm sorry, I'm sure you've got much more interesting plans for your future than anything we superficial programme makers could come up with.' The first time he'd tried the line, hands sweating, blood thudding in his ears, he'd thought it was so corny it couldn't fool a drunk one sip from catatonia. But he had been right to go with his instincts, even when they had led him down the path of the criminally naff. That first one, just like this next one, had grasped instantly that something was being offered to her that hadn't been on the agenda for the insignificant others he'd been talking to earlier.

'What do you mean?' Breathless, tentative, not wanting to admit she already believed in case she'd misunderstood and left herself open to the hot shaming flush of her misapprehension.

He gave the faintest of shrugs, one that hardly disturbed the smooth fall of his immaculate suiting. 'Forget it,' he said with a slight, almost imperceptible shake of the head, disappointment in the sad cast of his eye, the absence of his gleaming smile.

'No, tell me.' Now there was an edge of desperation, because everybody wanted to be a star, no matter what they said. Was he really going to snatch away that half-glimpsed magic carpet ride that could lift her out of her despised life into his world?

A quick glance to either side, making sure he wasn't overheard, then his voice was both soft and intense. 'A new project we're working on. You've got the look. You'd be perfect. As soon as I looked at you properly, I knew you were the one.' A regretful smile. 'Now, at least I have your image to carry in my head while we interview the hundreds of hopefuls the agents send along to us. Maybe we'll get lucky . . .' His voice trailed off, his eyes liquid and bereft as the puppy left behind in the holiday kennels.

'Couldn't I . . . I mean, well . . .' Donna's face lit up with hope, then amazement at her forwardness, then disappointment as she talked herself out of it without saying another word.

His smile grew indulgent. An adult would have identified it as condescending, but she was too young to recognize when she was being patronized. 'I don't think so. It would be taking an enormous risk. A project like this, at so delicate a stage . . . Just a word in the wrong ear could wreck it commercially. And you've no professional experience, have you?'

That tantalizing peep at what could have been her possible future uncapped a volcano of turbulent hope, words tumbling over each other like rocks in the lava flow. Prizes for karaoke at the youth club, a great dancer according to everybody, the Nurse in her form's reading of *Romeo and Juliet*. He'd imagined schools would have had more sense than to stir the tumultuous waters of adolescent desire with inflammatory drama like that, but he'd been wrong. They'd never learned, teachers. Just like their charges. The kids might assimilate the causes of the First World War but they never grasped that clichés got that way because they reflected reality. Better the devil you know. Don't take sweets from strangers.

Those warnings might never have set Donna Doyle's eardrum vibrating if her present expression of urgent eagerness was anything to go by. He grinned and said, 'All right! You've convinced me!' He lowered his head and held her gaze. Now his voice was conspiratorial. 'But can you keep a secret?'

She nodded as if her life depended on it. She couldn't have known that it did. 'Oh, yes,' Donna said, dark blue eyes sparkling, lips apart, little pink tongue flickering between them. He knew her mouth was growing dry. He also knew that she possessed other orifices where the opposite phenomenon was happening.

He gave her a considering, calculated stare, an obvious appraisal that she met with apprehension and desire mingling like Scotch and water. 'I wonder . . .' he said, his voice almost a sigh. 'Can you meet me tomorrow morning? Nine o'clock?'

A momentary frown, then her face cleared, determination in her eyes. 'Yes,' she said, school dismissed as irrelevant. 'Yes, I can. Whereabout?'

'Do you know the Plaza Hotel?' He had to hurry now. People were starting to move towards him, desperate to recruit his influence to their cause.

She nodded.

'They have an underground car park. You get into it from Beamish Street. I'll be waiting there on level two. And not a word to anyone, is that clear? Not your mum, not your dad, not your best friend, not even the family dog.' She giggled. 'Can you do that?' He gave her the curiously intimate look of the television professional, the one that convinces the mentally troubled that newsreaders are in love with them.

'Level two? Nine o'clock?' Donna checked, determined not to screw up her one chance of escape from the humdrum. She could never have realized that by the end of the week she'd be weeping and screaming and begging for humdrum. She'd be willing to sell what remained of her immortal soul for humdrum. But even if someone had told her that then, she would not have comprehended. Right then, the dazzle and the dream of what he could offer was her complete universe. What could be a finer prospect?

'And not a word, promise?'

'I promise,' she said solemnly. 'Cross my heart and hope to die.'

PART ONE

Tony Hill lay in bed and watched a long strip of cloud slide across a sky the colour of duck eggs. If anything had sold him on this narrow back-to-back terraced house, it was the attic bedroom with its strange angles and the pair of skylights that gave him something to look at when sleep was elusive. A new house, a new city, a new start, but still it was hard to lose consciousness for eight hours at a stretch.

It wasn't surprising that he hadn't slept well. Today was the first day of the rest of his life, he reminded himself with a wry smile that scrunched the skin round his deep-set blue eyes into a nest of wrinkles that not even his best friend could call laughter lines. He'd never laughed enough for that. And making murder his business had made sure he never would.

Work was always the perfect excuse, of course. For two years, he'd been toiling on behalf of the Home Office on a feasibility study to see whether it would be useful or possible to create a national task force of trained psychological profilers, a hit squad capable of moving in on complex cases and working with the investigative teams to improve the rate and speed of clean-up. It had been a job that had required all the clinical and diplomatic skills he'd developed over years of working as a psychologist in secure mental hospitals.

It had kept him off the wards, but it had exposed him to other dangers. The danger of boredom, for example. Tired of being stuck behind a desk or in endless meetings, he'd allowed himself to be seduced away from the job in hand by the tantalizing offer of involvement in a case that even from a distance had appeared to be something very special. Not in his wildest nightmares could he have imagined just how exceptional it could be. Nor how destructive.

He clenched his eyes momentarily against the memories that always stalked on the edge of his consciousness, waiting for him to drop his guard and let them in. That was another reason why he slept badly. The thought of what his dreams could do to him was no enticement to drift away and hand control over to his subconscious.

The cloud slipped out of sight like a slow-moving fish and Tony rolled out of bed, padding downstairs to the kitchen. He poured water into the bottom section of the coffee pot, filled the mid-section with a darkly fragrant roast from the freezer, screwed on the empty top section and set it on the gas. He thought of Carol Jordan, as he did probably one morning in three when he made the coffee. She'd given him the heavy aluminium Italian pot when he'd come home from hospital after the case was over. 'You're not going to be walking to the café for a while,' she'd said. 'At least this way you can get a decent espresso at home.'

It had been months now since he'd seen Carol. They'd not even taken the opportunity to celebrate her promotion to detective chief inspector, which showed just how far apart they'd grown. Initially, after his release from hospital, she'd come to visit whenever the hectic pace of her job would allow. Gradually, they'd both come to realize that every time they were together, the spectre of the investigation rose between them, obscuring and overshadowing whatever else might be possible for them. He understood that Carol was better equipped than most to interpret what she saw in him. He simply couldn't face the risk of opening up to someone who might reject him when she realized how he had been infected by his work.

If that happened, he doubted his capacity to function. And if he couldn't function, he couldn't do his job. And that was too important to let go. What he did saved people's lives. He was good at it, probably one of the best there had ever been because he truly understood the dark side. To risk the work would be the most irresponsible thing he could ever do, especially now when the whole future of the newly created National Offender Profiling Task Force lay in his hands.

What some people perceived as sacrifices were really dividends, he told himself firmly as he poured out his coffee. He was permitted to do the one thing he did supremely well, and they paid him money for it. A tired smile crossed his face. God, but he was lucky.

Shaz Bowman understood perfectly why people commit murder. The revelation had nothing to do with the move to a new city or the job that had brought her there, but everything to do with the cowboy plumbers who had installed the water supply when the former Victorian mill-owner's mansion had been converted into self-contained apartments. The builders had done a thoughtful job, preserving original features and avoiding partitions that wrecked the fine proportions of the spacious rooms. To the naked eye, Shaz's flat had been perfect, right down to the French windows leading to the back garden that was her exclusive domain.

Years of shared student dives with sticky carpets and scummy bathtubs, followed by a police section house and a preposterously expensive rented bedsit in West London had left Shaz desperate for the opportunity to check out whether house-proud was an adjective she could live with. The move north had provided her first afford-able chance. But the idyll had shattered the first morning she had to rise early for work.

Bleary-eyed and semi-conscious, she'd run the shower long enough to get the temperature right. She stepped under the powerful stream of water, lifting her hands above her head in a strangely reverent gesture. Her groan of pleasure turned abruptly to a scream as the water switched from amniotic warmth to a scalding scatter of hypodermic stings. She hurled herself clear of the shower cubicle, twisting her knee as she slipped on the bathroom floor, cursing with a fluency she owed to her three years in the Met.

Speechless, she stared at the plume of steam in the corner of the bathroom where she had stood moments before. Then, as abruptly, the steam dissipated. Cautiously, she extended a hand under the water. The temperature was back where it should be. Inch by tenta-tive inch, she moved under the stream of water. Letting out her unconsciously held breath, she reached for the shampoo. She'd got as far as the halo of white lather when the icy needles of winter rain cascaded on her bare shoulders. This time, her breath went inwards, taking enough shampoo with it to add a coughing retch to the morning's sound effects.

It didn't take much to work out that her ordeal was the result of someone else's synchronous ablutions. She was supposed to be a detective, after all. But understanding didn't make her any happier. The first day of the new job and instead of feeling calm and grounded after a long, soothing shower, she was furious and frustrated, her nerves jangling, the muscles in the nape of her neck tightening with the promise of a headache. 'Great,' she growled, fighting back tears that had more to do with emotion than the shampoo in them.

Shaz advanced on the shower once again and turned it off with a vicious twist of the wrist. Mouth compressed into a thin line, she started running a bath. Tranquillity was no longer an option for the day, but she still had to get the suds out of her hair so she wouldn't arrive in the squad room of the brand new task force looking like something no self-respecting cat would have bothered to drag in. It was going to be unnerving enough without having to worry about what she looked like.

As she crouched in the bath, dunking her head forward into the water, Shaz tried to restore her earlier mood of exhilarated anticipation. 'You're lucky to be here, girl,' she told herself. 'All those dickheads who applied and you didn't even have to fill in the form, you got chosen. Hand-picked, elite. All that shit work paid off, all that taking the crap with a smile. The canteen cowboys going nowhere fast, they're the ones having to swallow the shit now. Not like you, Detective Constable Shaz Bowman. National Offender Profiling Task Force Officer Bowman.' As if that wasn't enough, she'd be working alongside the acknowledged master of that arcane blend of instinct and experience. Dr Tony Hill, BSc (London), DPhil (Oxon), the profiler's profiler, author of the definitive British textbook on serial offenders. If Shaz had been a woman given to hero-worship, Tony Hill would have been right up there in the pantheon of her personal gods. As it was, the opportunity to pick his brains and learn his craft was one that she'd cheerfully have made sacrifices for. But she hadn't had to give up anything. It had been dropped right into her lap.

By the time she was towelling her cap of short dark hair, considering the chance of a lifetime that lay ahead of her had tamed her anger though not her nerves. Shaz forced herself to focus on the day ahead. Dropping the towel carelessly over the side of the bath, she stared into the mirror, ignoring the blurt of freckles across her cheekbones and the bridge of her small soft nose, passing over the straight line of lips too slim to promise much sensuality and focusing on the feature that everyone else noticed first about her.

Her eyes were extraordinary. Dark blue irises were shot through with striations of an intense, paler shade that seemed to catch the light like the facets of a sapphire. In interrogation, they were irresistible. The eyes had it. That intense blue stare fixed people like superglue. Shaz had a feeling that it had made her last boss so uncomfortable he'd been delighted at the prospect of shipping her out in spite of an arrest and conviction record that would have been remarkable in an experienced CID officer, never mind the rookie of the shift.

She'd only met her new boss once. Somehow, she didn't think Tony Hill was going to be quite so much of a pushover. And who knew what he'd see if he slid under those cold blue defences? With a shiver of anxiety, Shaz turned away from the remorseless stare of the mirror and chewed the skin on the side of her thumb.

Detective Chief Inspector Carol Jordan slipped the original out of the photocopier, picked up the copy from the tray and crossed the open-plan CID room to her office with nothing more revelatory than a genial, 'Morning, lads,' to the two early bird detectives already at their desks. She presumed they were only there at this hour because they were trying to make an impression on her. Sad boys.

She shut her door firmly behind her and crossed to her desk. The original crime report went back into the overnight file and onwards into her out tray. The photostat joined four similar previous overnight despatches in a folder that lived in her briefcase when it wasn't sitting on her desk. Five, she decided, was critical mass. Time for action. She glanced at her watch. But not quite yet.

The only other item that cluttered the desk now was a lengthy memo from the Home Office. In the dry civil service language that could render Tarantino dull, it announced the formal launch of the National Offender Profiling Task Force. 'Under the supervision of Commander Paul Bishop, the task force will be led by Home Office clinical psychologist and Senior Profiler Dr Tony Hill. Initially, the task force will consist of a further six experienced detectives seconded to work with Dr Hill and Commander Bishop under Home Office guidelines.'

Carol sighed. 'It could have been me. Oh yeah, it could have been me,' she sang softly. She hadn't been formally invited. But she knew all she'd have had to do was ask. Tony Hill had wanted her on the squad. He'd seen her work at close quarters and he'd told her more than once that she had the right cast of mind to help him make the new task force effective. But it wasn't that simple. The one case they'd worked together had been personally devastating as well as difficult for both of them. And her feelings for Tony Hill were still too complicated for her to relish the prospect of becoming his right-hand woman in other cases that might become as emotionally draining and intellectually challenging as their first encounter.

Nevertheless, she'd been tempted. Then this had come along. Early promotion in a newly created force wasn't an opportunity she felt she could afford to miss. The irony was that this chance had emerged from the same serial killer hunt. John Brandon had been the Assistant Chief Constable at Bradfield who'd had the nerve to bring in Tony Hill and to appoint Carol liaison officer. And when he was promoted to Chief Constable of the new force, he wanted her on board. His timing couldn't have been better, she thought, a faint pang of regret surfacing in spite of herself. She stood up and took the three steps that were all she needed to cross her office and stare down at the docks below where people moved around purposefully doing she knew not what.

Carol had learned the Job first with the Met in London and then with Bradfield Metropolitan Police, both leviathans fuelled by the perpetual adrenaline high of inner city crime. But now she was out on the edge of England with East Yorkshire Police where, as her brother Michael had wryly pointed out, the force's acronym was almost identical to the traditional Yorkshire yokel greeting of 'Ey-up'. Here, the DCI's job didn't involve juggling murder inquiries, drive-by shootings, gang wars, armed robberies and high-profile drug deals.

In the towns and villages of East Yorkshire, there wasn't any shortage of crime. But it was all low-level stuff. Her inspectors and sergeants were more than capable of dealing with it, even in the small cities of Holm and Traskham and the North Sea port of Seaford where she was based. Her junior officers didn't want her running around on their tails. After all, what did a city girl like her know about sheep rustling? Or counterfeit cargo lading bills? Besides which, they all knew perfectly well that when the new DCI turned up on the job, she wasn't so much interested in finding out what was going down as she was in sussing out who was up to scratch and who was busking it, who might be on the sauce and who might be on the take. And they were right. It was taking longer than she'd anticipated, but she was gradually assembling a picture of what her team was like and who was capable of what.

Carol sighed again, rumpling her shaggy blonde hair with the fingers of one hand. It was an uphill struggle, not least because most of the blunt Yorkshiremen she was working with were fighting a lifetime's conditioning to take a woman guv'nor seriously. Not for the first time, she wondered if ambition had shoved her into a drastic mistake and backed her flourishing career into a cul-de-sac.

She shrugged and turned away from the window, then pulled out the file from her briefcase again. She might have opted to turn her back on the profiling task force, but working with Tony Hill had already taught her a few tricks. She knew what a serial offender's signature looked like. She just hoped she didn't need a team of specialists to track one down.

One half of the double doors swung open momentarily ahead of the other. A woman with a face instantly recognizable in 78 per cent of UK homes (according to the latest audience survey) and high heels that shouted the praises of legs which could have modelled pantyhose strode into the make-up department, glancing over her shoulder and saying, '. . . which gives me nothing to work off, so tell Trevor to swap two and four on the running order, OK?'

Betsy Thorne followed her, nodding calmly. She looked far too wholesome to be anything in TV, dark hair with irregular strands of silver swept back in a blue velvet Alice band from a face that was somehow quintessentially English; the intelligent eyes of a sheepdog, the bones of a thoroughbred racehorse and the complexion of a Cox's Orange Pippin. 'No problem,' she said, her voice every degree as warm and caressing as her companion's. She made a note on the clipboard she was carrying.

Micky Morgan, presenter and only permissible star of *Midday with Morgan*, the flagship two-hour lunchtime news magazine programme of the independent networks, carried straight ahead to what was clearly her usual chair. She settled in, pushed her honey blonde hair back and gave her face a quick critical scrutiny in the glass as the make-up artist swathed her in a protective gown. 'Marla, you're back!' Micky exclaimed, delight in her voice and eyes in equal measure. 'Thank God. I'm praying you've been out of the country so you didn't have to look at what they do to me when you're not here. I absolutely forbid you to go on holiday again!'

Marla smiled. 'Still full of shit, Micky.'

'It's what they pay her for,' Betsy said, perching on the counter by the mirror.

'Can't get the staff these days,' Micky said through stiff lips as Marla started to smooth foundation over her skin. 'Zit coming up on the right temple,' she added.

'Premenstrual?' Marla asked.

'I thought I was the only one who could spot that a mile off,' Betsy drawled.

'It's the skin. The elasticity changes,' Marla said absently, completely absorbed in her task. .

'*Talking Point*,' Micky said. 'Run it past me again, Bets.' She closed her eyes to concentrate and Marla seized the chance to work on her eyelids.

Betsy consulted her clipboard. 'In the wake of the latest revelations that yet another junior minister has been caught in the wrong bed by the tabloids, we ask, "What makes a woman want to be a mistress?"' She ran through the guests for the item while Micky listened attentively. Betsy came to the final interviewee and smiled. 'You'll enjoy this: Dorien Simmonds, your favourite novelist. The professional mistress, putting the case that actually being a mistress is not only marvellous fun but a positive social service to all those put-upon wives who have to endure marital sex long after he bores them senseless.'

Micky chuckled. 'Brilliant. Good old Dorien. Is there anything, do you suppose, that Dorien wouldn't do to sell a book?'

'She's just jealous,' Marla said. 'Lips, please, Micky.'

'Jealous?' Betsy asked mildly.

'If Dorien Simmonds had a husband like Micky's, she wouldn't be flying the flag for mistresses,' Marla said firmly. 'She's just pig sick that she'll never land a catch like Jacko. Mind you, who isn't?'

'Mmmm,' Micky purred.

'Mmmm,' Betsy agreed.

It had taken years for the publicity machine to carve the pairing of Micky Morgan and Jacko Vance as firmly into the nation's consciousness as fish and chips or Lennon and McCartney. The celebrity marriage made in ratings heaven, it could never be dissolved. Even the gossip columnists had given up trying.

The irony was that it had been fear of newspaper gossip that had brought them together in the first place. Meeting Betsy had turned Micky's life on its head at a time when her career had started curving towards the heights. To climb as far and as fast as Micky meant collecting an interesting selection of enemies ranging from the poisonously envious to the rivals who'd been edged out of the limelight they thought was theirs of right. Since there was little to fault Micky on professionally, they'd homed in on the personal. Back in the early eighties, lesbian chic hadn't been invented. For women even more than men, being gay was still one of the quickest routes to the P45. Within a few months of abandoning her formerly straight life by falling in love with Betsy, Micky understood what a hunted animal feels like.

Her solution had been radical and extremely successful. Micky had Jacko to thank for that. She had been and still was lucky to have him, she thought as she looked approvingly at her reflection in the make-up mirror.

Perfect.

Tony Hill looked around the room at the team he had hand-picked and felt a moment's pity. They thought they were walking into this grave new world with their eyes open. Coppers never thought of themselves as innocents abroad. They were too streetwise. They'd seen it all, done it all, got pissed and thrown up on the T-shirt. Tony was here to instruct half a dozen cops who already thought they knew it all that there were unimaginable horrors out there that would make them wake up screaming in the night and teach them to pray. Not for forgiveness, but for healing. He knew only too well that whatever they thought, none of them had made a genuinely informed choice when they'd opted for the National Offender Profiling Task Force.

None of them except, perhaps, Paul Bishop. When the Home Office had given the profiling project the green light, Tony had called in every favour he could claim and a few he couldn't to make sure the police figurehead was someone who knew the gravity of what he was taking on. He'd dangled Paul Bishop's name in front of the politicians like a carrot in front of a reluctant mule, reminding them of how well Paul performed in front of the cameras. Even then it had been touch and go till he'd pointed out that even

London's cynical hacks showed a bit of respect for the man who'd headed the successful hunts for the predators they'd dubbed the Railcard Rapist and the Metroland Murderer. After those investigations, there was no question in Tony's mind that Paul knew exactly the kind of nightmares that lay ahead.

On the other hand, the rewards were extraordinary. When it worked, when their work actually put someone away, these police officers would know a high unlike any other they'd ever experienced. It was a powerful feeling, to know your endeavours had helped put a killer away. It was even more gratifying to realize how many lives you might have saved because you shone a light down the right path for your colleagues to go down. It was exhilarating, even though it was tempered with the knowledge of what the perpetrator had already done. Somehow, he had to convey that satisfaction to them as well.

Paul Bishop was talking now, welcoming them to the task force and outlining the training programme he and Tony had thrashed out between them. 'We're going to take you through the process of profiling, giving you the background information you need to start developing the skill for yourself,' he said. It was a crash course in psychology, inevitably superficial, but covering the basics. If they'd chosen wisely, their apprentices would go off in their own preferred directions, reading more widely, tracking down other specialists and building up their own expertise in particular areas of the profiling craft that interested them.

Tony looked around at his new colleagues. All CID-trained, all but one a graduate. A sergeant and five constables, two of them women. Eager eyes, notepads open, pens at the ready. They were smart, this lot. They knew that if they did well here and the unit prospered, they could go all the way to the top on the strength of it.

His steady gaze ranged over them. Part of him wished Carol Jordan was among them, sharing her sharp perceptions and shrewd analyses, tossing in the occasional grenade of humour to lighten the grimness. But his sensible head knew there would be more than enough problems ahead without that complication.

If he had to put money on any of them turning into the kind of star that would stop him missing Carol's abilities, he'd go for the one with the eyes that blazed cold fire. Sharon Bowman. Like all the best hunters, she'd kill if she had to.

Just like he'd done himself.

Tony pushed the thought away and concentrated on Paul's words, waiting for the signal. When Paul nodded, Tony took over smoothly. 'The FBI take two years to train their operatives in offender profiling,' he said, leaning back in his chair in a deliberate attitude of relaxed calm. 'We do things differently over here.' A note of acid in the voice. 'We'll be accepting our first cases in six weeks. In three months' time, the Home Office expects us to be running a full case-load. What you've got to do inside that time frame is assimilate a mountain of theory, learn a series of protocols as long as your arm, develop total familiarity with the computer software we've had specially written for the task force, and cultivate an instinctive understanding of those among us who are, as we clinicians put it, totally fucked up.' He grinned unexpectedly at their serious faces. 'Any questions?'

'Is it too late to resign?' Bowman's electric eyes sparkled humour that was missing from her deadpan tones.

'The only resignations they accept are the ones certified by the pathologist.' The wry response came from Simon McNeill. Psychology graduate from Glasgow, four years' service with Strathclyde Police, Tony reminded himself, reassuring himself that he could recall names and backgrounds without too much effort.

'Correct,' he said.

'What about insanity?' another voice from the group asked.

'Far too useful a tool for us to let you slip from our grasp,' Tony told him. 'I'm glad you brought that up, actually, Sharon. It gives me the perfect lead into what I want to talk about first today.' His eyes moved from face to face, waiting until his seriousness was mirrored in each of their faces. A man accustomed to assuming whatever personality and demeanour would be acceptable, he shouldn't have been surprised at how easy it was to manipulate them, but he was. If he did his job properly, it would be far harder to achieve in a couple of months' time.

Once they were settled and concentrating, he tossed his folder of notes on to the table attached to the arm of his chair and ignored them. 'Isolation,' he said. 'Alienation. The hardest things to deal with. Human beings are gregarious. We're herd animals. We hunt in packs, we celebrate in packs. Take away human contact from someone and their behaviour distorts. You're going to learn a lot about that over the coming months and years.' He had their attention now. Time for the killer blow.

'I'm not talking about serial offenders. I'm talking about you. You're all police officers with CID experience. You're successful cops, you've fitted in, you've made the system work for you. That's why you're here. You're used to the camaraderie of team work, you're accustomed to a support system that backs you up. When you get a result, you've always had a drinking squad to share the victory with. When it's all gone up in smoke, that same squad comes out and commiserates with you. It's a bit like a family, only it's a family without the big brother that picks on you and the auntie that asks when you're going to get married.' He noted the nods and twinges of facial expression that indicated agreement. As he'd expected, there were fewer from the women than the men.

He paused for a moment and leaned forward. 'You've just been collectively bereaved. Your families are dead and you can never, never go home any more. This is the only home you have, this is your only family.' He had them now, gripped tighter than any thriller had ever held them. The Bowman woman's right eyebrow twitched up into an astonished arc, but other than that, they were motionless.

'The best profilers have probably got more in common with serial killers than with the rest of the human race. Because killers have to be good profilers, too. A killer profiles his victims. He has to learn how to look at a shopping precinct full of people and pick out the one person who will work as a victim for him. He picks the wrong person and it's good night, Vienna. So he can't afford to make mistakes any more than we can. Like us, he kicks off consciously sorting by set criteria, but gradually, if he's good, it gets to be an instinct. And that's how good I want you all to be.'

For a moment, his perfect control slipped as images crowded unbidden to the front of his mind. He was the best, he knew that now. But he'd paid a high price to discover that. The idea that payment might come due again was something he managed to reject as long as he was sober. It was no accident that Tony had scarcely had a drink for the best part of a year.

Collecting himself, Tony cleared his throat and straightened in his seat. 'Very soon, your lives are going to change. Your priorities will shift like Los Angeles in an earthquake. Believe me, when you spend your days and nights projecting yourself inside a mind that's programmed to kill until death or incarceration prevents it, you suddenly find a lot of things that used to seem important are completely irrelevant. It's hard to get worked up about the unemployment figures when you've been contemplating the activities of somebody who's taken more people off the register in the last six months than the government has.' His cynical smile gave them the cue to relax the muscles that had been taut for the past few minutes.

'People who have not done this kind of work have no notion of what it is like. Every day, you review the evidence, raking through it for that elusive clue you missed the last forty-seven times. You watch helplessly as your hot leads turn out colder than a junkie's heart. You want to shake the witnesses who saw the killer but don't remember anything about him because nobody told them in advance that one of the people who would fill up with petrol in their service station one night three months ago was a multiple murderer. Some detective who thinks what you're doing is a bag of crap sees no reason why your life shouldn't be as fucking miserable as his, so he gives out your phone number to husbands, wives, lovers, children, parents, siblings, all of them people who want a crumb of hope from you.

'And as if that isn't enough, the media gets on your back. And then the killer does it again.'

Leon Jackson, who'd made it out of Liverpool's black ghetto to the Met via an Oxford scholarship, lit a cigarette. The snap of his lighter had the other two smokers reaching for their own. 'Sounds cool,' he said, dropping one arm over the back of his chair. Tony couldn't help the pang of pity. Harder they come, the bigger the fall.

'Arctic,' Tony said. 'So, that's how people outside the Job see you. What about your former colleagues? When you come up against the ones you left behind, believe me, they're going to start noticing you've gone a bit weird. You're not one of the gang any more, and they'll start avoiding you because you smell wrong. Then when you're working a case, you're going to be transplanted into an alien environment and there will be people there who don't want you on the case. Inevitably.' He leaned forward again, hunched against the chill wind of memory. 'And they won't be afraid to let you know it.'

Tony read superiority in Leon's sneer. Being black, he reasoned, Leon probably figured he'd had a taste of that already and rejection could therefore hold no fears for him. What he almost certainly didn't realize was that his bosses had needed a black success story. They'd have made that clear to the officers who controlled the culture, so the chances were that no one had really pushed Leon half as hard as he thought they had. 'And don't think the brass will back you when the shit comes down,' Tony continued. 'They won't. They'll love you for about two days, then when you haven't solved their headaches, they'll start to hate you. The longer it takes to resolve the serial offences, the worse it becomes. And the other detectives avoid you because you've got a contagious disease called failure. The truth might be out there, but you haven't got it, and until you do, you're a leper.

'Oh, and by the way,' he added, almost as an afterthought, 'when they do nail the bastard thanks to your hard work, they won't even invite you to the party.'

The silence was so intense he could hear the hiss of burning tobacco as Leon inhaled. Tony got to his feet and shoved his springy black hair back from his forehead. 'You probably think I'm exaggerating. Believe me, I'm barely scratching the surface of how bad this job will make you feel. If you don't think it's for you, if you're having doubts about your decision, now's the time to walk away. Nobody will reproach you. No blame, no shame. Just have a word with Commander Bishop.' He looked at his watch. 'Coffee break. Ten minutes.'

He picked up his folder and carefully didn't look at them as they pushed back chairs and made a ragged progress to the door and the coffee station in the largest of the three rooms they'd been grudgingly granted by a police service already strapped for accommodation for their own officers. When at last he looked up, Shaz Bowman stood leaning against the wall by the door, waiting.

'Second thoughts, Sharon?' he asked.

'I hate being called Sharon,' she said. 'People who want a response go for Shaz. I just wanted to say it's not only profilers that get treated like shit. There's nothing you said just now that sounds any worse than what women deal with all the time in this job.'

'So I've been told,' Tony said, thinking inevitably of Carol Jordan. 'If it's true, you lot should have a head start in this game.'

Shaz grinned and pushed off from the wall, satisfied. 'Just watch,' she said, swivelling on the balls of her feet and moving through the door on feet as silent and springy as a jungle cat.

*   *   *

Jacko Vance leaned forward across the flimsy table and frowned. He pointed to the open desk diary. 'You see, Bill? I'm already committed to running the half-marathon on the Sunday. And then after that, we're filming Monday and Tuesday, I'm doing a club opening in Lincoln on Tuesday night – you're coming to that, by the way, aren't you?' Bill nodded, and Jacko continued. 'I've got meetings lined up Wednesday back to back and I've got to drive back up to Northumberland for my volunteer shift. I just don't see how we can accommodate them.' He threw himself back against the striped tweed of the production caravan's comfortless sofa bench with a sigh.

'That's the whole point, Jacko,' his producer said calmly, stirring the skimmed milk into the two coffees he was making in the kitchen area. Bill Ritchie had been producing *Vance's Visits* for long enough to know there was little point in trying to change his star's mind once it was made up. But this time, he was under sufficient pressure from his bosses to try. 'This documentary short's *supposed* to make you look busy, to say, "Here's this amazing guy, busy professional life, yet *he* finds time to work for charity, so why aren't you?"' He brought the coffees to the table.

'I'm sorry, Bill, but it's not on.' Jacko picked up his coffee and winced at its scalding heat. Hastily, he put it down again. 'When are we going to get a proper coffee maker in here?'

'If it's anything to do with me, never,' Bill said with a mock-severe scowl. 'The lousy coffee's the one thing guaranteed to divert you from whatever you're going on about.'

Jacko shook his head ruefully, acknowledging he'd been caught out. 'OK. But I'm still not doing it. For one, I don't want a camera crew dogging my heels any more than I already have to put up with. For two, I don't do charity work so I can show off about it on prime-time telethons. For three, the poor sick bastards I spend my nights with are terminally ill people who do not need a hand-held camera shoved down their emaciated throats. I'll happily do something else for the telethon, maybe something with Micky, but I'm not having the people I work with exploited just so we can guilt-trip a few more grand out of the viewers.'

Bill spread his hands in defeat. 'Fine by me. Do you want to tell them or will I?'

'Would you, Bill? Save me the aggravation?' Jacko's smile was bright as a shaft of sunlight from a thundercloud, promising as the hour before a first date. It was imprinted on his audience like a race memory. Women made love to their husbands with more gusto because Jacko's sexually inviting eyes and kissable mouth were flickering across the inside of their eyelids. Adolescent girls found their vague erotic longings suddenly focused. Old ladies doted on him, without connecting the subsequent feelings of unfulfilled sadness.

Men liked him too, but not because they found him sexy. Men liked Jacko Vance because he was, in spite of everything, one of the lads. A British, Commonwealth, and European gold medallist and holder of the world javelin record, Olympic gold had seemed like an inevitability for the darling of the back pages. Then one night, driving back from an athletics meeting in Gateshead, Jacko drove into a dense bank of fog on the A1. He wasn't the only one.

The morning news bulletins put the figures at between twenty-seven and thirty-five vehicles in the multiple pile-up. The big story wasn't the six dead, however. The big story was the tragic heroism of Jacko Vance, British athletics' golden boy. In spite of suffering multiple lacerations and three broken ribs in the initial impact, Jacko had crawled out of his mangled motor and rescued two children from the back of a car seconds before it burst into flames. Depositing them on the hard shoulder, he'd gone back into the tangled metal and attempted to free a lorry driver pinioned between his steering wheel and the buckled door of his cab.

The creaking of stressed metal turned to a shriek as accumulated pressures built up on the lorry and the roof caved in. The driver didn't stand a chance. Neither did Jacko Vance's throwing arm. It took the firemen three agonizing hours to cut him free from the crushing weight of metal that had smashed his flesh to raw meat and his bones to splinters. Worse, he was conscious for most of it. Trained athletes knew all about pushing through the pain barrier.

The news of his George Cross came the day after the medics fitted his first prosthesis. It was small consolation for the loss of the dream that had been the core of his life for a dozen years. But bitterness didn't cloud his natural shrewdness. He knew how fickle the media could be. He still smarted at the memory of the headlines when he'd blown his first attempt at the European title. JACK SPLAT! had been the kindest stab at the heart of the man who only the day before had been JACK OF HEARTS.

He knew he had to capitalize on his glory quickly or he'd soon be another yesterday's hero, early fodder for the 'Where Are They Now?' column. So he called in a few favours, renewed his acquaintance with Bill Ritchie and ended up commentating on the very Olympics where he should have mounted the rostrum. It had been a start. Simultaneously, he'd worked to establish his reputation as a tireless worker for charity, a man who would never allow his fame to stand in the way of helping people less fortunate than himself.

Now, he was bigger than all the fools who'd been so ready to write him off. He'd charmed and chatted his way to the front of the sports presenters' ranks in a slash and burn operation of such devious ruthlessness that some of his victims still didn't realize they'd been calculatedly chopped off at the knees. Once he'd consolidated that role, he'd presented a chat show that had topped the light entertainment ratings for three years. When the fourth year saw it drop to third place, he dumped the format and launched *Vance's Visits*.

The show claimed to be spontaneous. In fact, Jacko's arrival in the midst of what his publicity called 'ordinary people living ordinary lives' was invariably orchestrated with all the advance planning of a royal visit but none of the attendant publicity. Otherwise he'd have attracted bigger crowds than any of the discredited House of Windsor. Especially if he'd turned up with the wife.

And still it wasn't enough.

Carol bought the coffees. It was a privilege of rank. She thought about refusing to shell out for the chocolate biscuits on the basis that nobody needed three KitKats to get through a meeting with their DCI. But she knew it would be misinterpreted, so she grinned and bore the expense. She led the troops she'd chosen with care to a quiet corner cut off from the rest of the canteen by an array of plastic parlour palms. Detective Sergeant Tommy Taylor, Detective Constable Lee Whitbread and Detective Constable Di Earnshaw had all impressed her with their intelligence and determination. She might yet be proved wrong, but these three officers were her private bet for the pick of Seaford Central's CID.

'I'm not going to attempt to pretend this is a social chat so we can get to know each other better,' she announced, sharing the biscuits out among the three of them. Di Earnshaw watched her, eyes like currants in a suet pudding, hating the way her new boss managed to look elegant in a linen suit with more creases than a dosser's when she just looked lumpy in her perfectly pressed chain-store skirt and jacket.

'Thank Christ for that,' Tommy said, a grin slowly spreading. 'I was beginning to worry in case we'd got a guv'nor who didn't understand the importance of Tetley's Bitter to a well-run CID.'

Carol's answering smile was wry. 'It's Bradfield I came from, remember?'

'That's why we were worried, ma'am,' Tommy replied.

Lee snorted with suppressed laughter, turned it into a cough and spluttered, 'Sorry, ma'am.'

'You will be,' Carol said pleasantly. 'I've got a task for you three. I've been taking a good look at the overnights since I got here, and I'm a bit concerned about the high incidence of unexplained fires and query arsons that we've got on our ground. I spotted five query arsons in the last month and when I made some checks with uniform, I found out there have been another half-dozen unexplained outbreaks of fire.'

'You always get that kind of thing round the docks,' Tommy said, casually shrugging big shoulders inside a baggy silk blouson that had gone out of fashion a couple of years previously.

'I appreciate that, but I'm wondering if there's a bit more to it than that. Agreed, a couple of the smaller blazes are obvious routine cock-ups, but I'm wondering if there's something else going on here.' Carol left it dangling to see who would pick it up.

'A firebug, you mean, ma'am?' It was Di Earnshaw, the voice pleasant but the expression bordering on the insolent.

'A serial arsonist, yes.'

There was a momentary silence. Carol reckoned she knew what they were thinking. The East Yorkshire force might be a new entity, but these officers had worked this patch under the old regime. They were in with the bricks, whereas she was the new kid in town, desperate to shine at their expense. And they weren't sure whether to roll with it or try to derail her. Somehow she had to persuade them that she was the star they should be hitching their wagons to. 'There's a pattern,' she said. 'Empty premises, early hours of the morning. Schools, light industrial units, warehouses. Nothing too big, nowhere there might be a night watchman to put the mockers on it. But serious nevertheless. Big fires, all of them.

They've caused a lot of damage and the insurance companies must be hurting more than they like.'

'Nobody's said owt about an arsonist on the rampage,' Tommy remarked calmly. 'Usually, the firemen tip us the wink if they think there's something a bit not right on the go.'

'Either that or the local rag gives us a load of earache,' Lee chipped in through a mouthful of his second KitKat. Lean as a whippet in spite of the biscuits and the three sugars in his coffee, Carol noted. One to watch for high-strung hyperactivity.

'Call me picky, but I prefer it when we're setting the agenda, not the local hacks or the fire service,' Carol said coolly. 'Arson isn't a Mickey Mouse crime. Like murder, it has terrible consequences. And like murder, you've got a stack of potential motives. Fraud, the destruction of evidence, the elimination of competition, revenge and cover-up, at the "logical" end of the spectrum. And at the screwed-up end, we have the ones who do it for kicks and sexual gratification. Like serial killers, they nearly always have their own internal logic that they mistake for something that makes sense to the rest of us.

'Fortunately for us, serial murder is a lot less common than serial arson. Insurers reckon a quarter of all the fires in the UK have been set deliberately. Imagine if a quarter of all deaths were murder.'

Taylor looked bored. Lee Whitbread stared blankly at her, his hand halfway to the cigarette packet in front of him. Di Earnshaw was the only one who appeared interested in making a contribution. 'I've heard it said that the incidence of arson is an index of the economic prosperity of a country. The more arson there is, the worse the economy is doing. Well, there's plenty unemployed round here,' she said with the air of someone who expects to be ignored.

'And that's something we should bear in mind,' Carol said, nodding with approval. 'Now, this is what I want. A careful trawl through the overnights for CID and uniform for the last six months to see what we come up with. I want the victims re-interviewed to check if there are any obvious common factors, like the same insurance company. Sort it out among yourselves. I'll be having a chat with the fire chief before the four of us reconvene in ... shall we say three days? Fine. Any questions?'

'I could do the fire chief, ma'am,' Di Earnshaw said eagerly. 'I've had dealings with him before.'

'Thanks for the offer, Di, but the sooner I make his acquaintance, the happier I'll feel.'

Di Earnshaw's lips seemed to shrink inwards in disapproval, but she merely nodded.

'You want us to drop our other cases?' Tommy asked.

Carol's smile was sharp as an ice pick. She'd never had a soft spot for chancers. 'Oh, please, Sergeant,' she sighed. 'I know what your case-load is. Like I said at the start of this conversation, it's Bradfield I came from. Seaford might not be the big city, but that's no reason for us to operate at village bobby pace.'

She stood up, taking in the shock in their faces. 'I didn't come here to fall out with people. But I will if I have to. If you think I'm a hard bastard to work for, watch me. However hard you work, you'll see me matching it. I'd like us to be a team. But we have to play my rules.'

Then she was gone. Tommy Taylor scratched his jaw. 'That's us told, then. Still think she's shaggable, Lee?'

Di Earnshaw's thin mouth pursed. 'Not unless you like singing falsetto.'

'I don't think you'd feel a lot like singing,' Lee said. 'Anybody want that last KitKat?'

Shaz rubbed her eyes and turned away from the computer screen. She'd come in early so she could squeeze in a quick revision of the previous day's software familiarization. Finding Tony at work on one of the other terminals had been a bonus. He'd looked astonished to see her walk through the door just after seven. 'I thought I was the only workaholic insomniac around here,' he'd greeted her.

'I'm crap on computers,' she'd said gruffly, trying to cover her satisfaction at having him to herself. 'I've always needed to work twice as hard to keep up.'

Tony's eyebrows had jumped. Cops didn't generally admit weaknesses to an outsider. Either Shaz Bowman was even more unusual than he'd initially appreciated or else he was finally losing his alien status. 'I thought everybody under thirty was a wizard on these,' he said mildly.

'Sorry to disappoint you. I was behind the door when the anoraks were being handed out,' Shaz replied. She settled in front of her screen and pushed up the sleeves of her cotton sweater. 'First remember your password,' she muttered, wondering what he thought of her.

Two forces seethed under Shaz Bowman's calm surface, taking it in turns to drive her. On the one hand, fear of failure gnawed at her, undermining everything she was and all she achieved. When she looked in the mirror, she never saw her good points, only the thinness of her lips and the lack of definition in her nose. When she reviewed her accomplishments, she saw only the places where she had fallen short, the heights she had failed to scale. The countervailing force was her ambition. Somehow, ever since she'd first begun to formulate the ambitions that drove her, those goals had restored her damaged self-confidence and shored up her vulnerabilities before they could cripple her. When her ambition threatened to tip her over into arrogance, somehow the fear would kick in at the crucial point, keeping her human.

The setting up of the task force had coincided so perfectly with the direction of her dreams, she couldn't help but feel the hand of fate in it. That didn't mean that she could let up, however. Shaz's long-term career plan meant she had to shine brighter than anyone else in this task force. One of her tactics for achieving that was to pick Tony Hill's brains like a master locksmith, extracting every scrap of knowledge she could scavenge there while simultaneously worming her way inside his defences so that when she needed his help, he'd be willing to provide it. As part of her approach, and because she was terrified that otherwise she'd fall behind and make a fool of herself in a group that she was convinced were all better than her, she was covertly taping all the group sessions, listening to them over and over again whenever she could. And now, luck had dropped a bonus opportunity into her lap.

So Shaz frowned and stared at the screen, working her way through the lengthy process of filling out an offence report then setting in motion its comparison against the details of all the previous crimes held in the computer's memory banks. When Tony had slipped out of his seat, she'd vaguely registered the movement, but forced herself to carry on working. The last thing she wanted was for him to think she was trying to ingratiate herself.

The intensity of the concentration she imposed upon herself was sufficient for her not to notice when he came back in through the door behind her desk until her subconscious registered a faint masculine smell which it identified as his. It took all her willpower not to react. Instead, she carried on striking keys until his hand cleared the edge of her peripheral vision and placed a carton of coffee topped with a Danish on the desk beside her. 'Time for a break?'

So she'd rubbed her eyes and abandoned the screen. 'Thanks,' she said.

'You're welcome. Anything you're not clear about? I'll take you through it, if you want.'

Still she held back. Don't snatch at it, she cautioned herself. She didn't want to use up her credit with Tony Hill until she absolutely had to, and preferably not before she'd been able to offer him something helpful in return. 'It's not that I don't understand it,' she said. 'It's just that I don't trust it.'

Tony smiled, enjoying her defensive stubbornness. 'One of those kids who demanded empirical proof that two and two were always going to be four?'

A prick of delight that she'd entertained him, quickly stifled. Shaz moved the Danish and opened the coffee. 'I've always been in love with proof. Why do you think I became a cop?'

Tony's smile was lopsided and knowing. 'I could speculate. It's quite a proving ground you've chosen here.'

'Not really. The ground's already been broken. The Americans have been doing it for so long they've not only got manuals, they've got movies about it. It's just taken us forever to catch on, as per usual. But you're one of the ones who forced the issue, so there's nothing left for us to prove.' Shaz took a huge bite of her Danish, nodding in quiet approval as she tasted the apricot glaze on the flaky pastry.

'Don't you believe it,' Tony said wryly, moving back to his own terminal. 'The backlash has only just started. It's taken long enough to get the police to accept we can provide useful help, but already the media hacks who were treating us profilers like gods a couple of years ago are jumping all over our shortcomings. They oversold us, so now they have to blame us for not living up to a set of expectations they created in the first place.'

'I don't know,' Shaz said. 'The public only remember the big successes. That case you did in Bradfield last year. The profile was right on the button. The police knew exactly where to go looking when it came to the crunch.' Oblivious to the permafrost that had settled over Tony's face, Shaz continued enthusiastically. 'Are you going to do a session on that? We've all heard the grapevine version, but there's next to nothing in the literature, even though it's obvious you did a textbook job on the profile.'

'We won't be covering that case,' he said flatly.

Shaz looked up sharply and realized where her eagerness had beached her. She'd blown it this time, in spades. 'I'm sorry,' she said quietly. 'I get carried away, and tact and diplomacy, they're history. I wasn't thinking.' Thick git, she berated herself silently. If he'd had the therapy he would have needed after that particular nightmare, the last thing he'd want would be to expose the details to avid prurience, even if it was masquerading as legitimate scientific interest.

'You don't have to apologize, Shaz,' Tony said wearily. 'You're right, it is a key case. The reason we won't be covering it is that I can't talk about it without feeling like a freak. You'll all have to forgive me. Maybe one day you'll catch a case that leaves you feeling the same way. For your sake, I sincerely hope not.' He looked down at his Danish as if it were an alien artefact and pushed it to one side, appetite dead as the past was supposed to be.

Shaz wished she could rerun the tape, pick up the conversation at the point where he'd put the coffee down on her desk and there was still the possibility of using the moment to build a bridge. 'I'm really sorry, Dr Hill,' she said inadequately.

He looked up and forced a thin smile. 'Truly, Shaz, there's no need. And can we drop the "Dr Hill" bit? I meant to bring it up during yesterday's session, but it slipped my mind. I don't want you all feeling that I'm the teacher and you're the class. At the moment, I'm the group leader simply because I've been doing this for a while. Before long, we'll all be working side by side, and there's no point in having barriers between us. So it's Tony from now on in, OK?'

'You got it, Tony.' Shaz searched for the message in his eyes and his words and, satisfied it contained genuine forgiveness, wolfed the rest of her Danish and returned to her screen. She couldn't do it while he was here, but next time she was in the computer room alone, she intended to use her Internet access to pull up the newspaper archives and check out all the reports of the Bradfield serial killer case. She'd read most of them at the time, but that had been before she'd met Tony Hill and everything had changed. Now, she had a special interest. By the time she was finished, she'd know enough about Tony Hill's most public profile to write the book that, for reasons she still couldn't understand, had never been written. After all, she was a detective, wasn't she?

Carol Jordan fiddled with the complicated chrome coffee maker, a housewarming present from her brother Michael when she'd moved to Seaford. She'd been luckier than most people caught in the housing market slump. She hadn't had far to look for a buyer for her half of the warehouse flat she and Michael owned; the barrister he'd recently been sharing his bedroom with had been so eager to buy her out that Carol had begun to wonder if she'd been even more of a gooseberry than she'd imagined.

Now she had this low stone cottage on the side of the hill that rose above the estuary almost directly opposite Seaford; a place of her own. Well, almost, she corrected herself, reminded by the hard skull head-butting her shin. 'OK, Nelson,' she said, stooping to scratch the black cat's ears. 'I hear what you're saying.' While the coffee brewed, she scooped out a bowl of cat food to a rapture of purring followed by the sloppy sound of Nelson inhaling his breakfast. She walked through to the living room to enjoy the panorama of the estuary and the improbably slender arc of the suspension bridge. Gazing out across the misty river where the bridge appeared to float without connection to the land, she planned her coming encounter with the fire chief. Nelson walked in, tail erect, and jumped without pause straight on to the window sill where he stretched out, arching his head back towards Carol and demanding affection. Carol stroked his dense fur and said, 'I only get one chance to convince this guy that I know arse from elbow, Nelson. I need him on my side. God knows, I need somebody on my side.'

Nelson batted her hand with his paw, as if responding directly to her words. Carol swallowed the rest of her coffee and got to her feet in a movement as smooth as the cat's. One of the advantages she'd soon found with a DCI's office hours was that she actually managed to use her gym membership more than once a month, and she was already feeling the benefit in firmer muscle tone and better aerobic fitness. It would have been a bonus to have someone to share it with, but that wasn't why she did it. She did it for herself, because it made her feel good. She took pride in her body, revelling in its strength and mobility.

An hour later, enduring the tour of the central fire station, she was glad of her fitness as she struggled to keep pace with the long legs of the local chief of operations, Jim Pendlebury. 'You seem to be better organized here than CID ever manages,' Carol said, as they finally made it to his office. 'You'll have to share the secret of your efficiency.'

'We've had so much cost-cutting, we've really had to streamline everything we do,' he told her. 'We used to have all our stations staffed round the clock with a complement of full-time officers, but it really wasn't cost effective. I know a lot of the lads grumbled about it, but a couple of years back we shifted to a mix of part-time and full-time officers. It took a few months to shake down, but it's been a huge advantage to me in management terms.'

Carol pulled a face. 'Not a solution that would work for us.'

Pendlebury shrugged. 'I don't know. You could have a core staff who dealt with the routine stuff and a hit squad that you used as and when you needed them.'

'That's sort of what we have already,' Carol said drily. 'The core staff is called the night shift and the hit squad are the day teams. Unfortunately, it never gets quiet enough to stand any of them down.'

With part of her mind, Carol added to her mental profile of the fire chief as they spoke. In conversation, his straight dark eyebrows crinkled and jutted above his blue-grey eyes. Considering how much time he must spend flying a desk, his skin looked surprisingly weathered, the creases round his eyes showing white when he wasn't smiling or frowning. Probably a part-time sailor or estuary fisherman, she guessed. As he dipped his head to acknowledge something she'd said, she could see a few silver hairs straggling among his dark curls. So, probably a few years the far side of thirty, Carol thought, revising her initial estimate. She had a habit of analysing new acquaintances in terms of how their description would read on a police bulletin. She'd never actually had to produce a photofit of someone she'd encountered, but she was confident her practice would have made her the best possible witness for the police artist to work with.

'Now you've seen the operation, I take it you're a bit more willing to accept that when we say a fire's a query arson, we're not talking absolute rubbish?' Pendlebury's tone was light, but his eyes challenged hers.

'I never doubted what you were telling us,' she said calmly. 'What

I doubted was whether we were taking it as seriously as we should.'
She snapped open the locks on her briefcase and took out her file.
'I'd like to go through the details on these incidents with you, if
you can spare me the time.'

He cocked his head to one side. 'Are you saying what I think
you're saying?'

'Now that I've seen the way you run your operation, I can't
believe the idea of a serial arsonist hasn't already crossed your
mind.'

He tugged at the lobe of one ear, sizing her up. Finally, he said,
'I was wondering when one of your lot would notice.'

Carol breathed out hard through her nose. 'It might have been
helpful if we'd been given a nudge in the right direction. You are
the experts, after all.'

'Your predecessor didn't think so,' Pendlebury said. He might as
well have been commenting on the price of fish. All of the enthusiasm he'd shown earlier for his job had vanished behind an impassive
mask, leaving Carol to draw her own conclusions. They didn't make
a pretty picture.

She placed the file on Pendlebury's desk and flipped it open. 'That
was then. This is now. Are you telling me you've got query arsons
that predate this one?'

He glanced down at the top sheet in the file and snorted. 'How
far back would you like to start?'

Tony Hill sat alone at his desk, ostensibly preparing for the following day's seminar with the task force officers. But his thoughts were
far away from those details. He was thinking about the psychopathic minds out there, already set in the moulds that would gener-
ate pain and misery for people they didn't even know yet.

There had long been a theory among psychologists that discounted the existence of evil, ascribing the worst excesses of the
most sociopathic abductors, torturers and killers to a linked series
of circumstances and events in their past that culminated in one
final stress-laden event that catapulted them over the edge of what
civilized society would tolerate. But that had never entirely satisfied
Tony. It begged the question of why some people with almost
identical backgrounds of abuse and deprivation went on not to
become psychopaths but to lead useful, fruitful lives, integrated into
society.

Now the scientists were talking about a genetic answer, a fracture in the DNA code that might explain this divergence. Somehow, Tony found that answer too pat. It seemed as much of a cop-out as the old-fashioned notion that some men were simply evil and that was that. It evaded responsibility in a way he found repugnant.

It was an issue that had always held particular resonance for him. He knew the reason he was so good at what he did. It was because for so many of the steps down the road that his prey had taken, he had walked in their footprints. But at some point he could never quite identify there had come a parting of the ways. Where they became hunters at first hand, he became a hunter at second hand, tracking them down once they had crossed the line. Yet his life still held echoes of theirs. The fantasies that drove them were about sex and death; his fantasies about sex and death were called profiling. They were chillingly close.

It sometimes seemed chicken and egg to Tony. Had his impotence started because he was afraid the unfettered expression of his sexuality might lead to violence and death? Or had his knowledge of how often the sexual urge led to killing worked on his body to make him sexually inadequate? He doubted he would ever know. However the circuit worked, it was undeniable that his work had profoundly affected his life.

For no apparent reason, he recalled the spark of uncomplicated enthusiasm he'd seen in Shaz Bowman's eyes. He could remember feeling that way too, before his fascination had been tempered by exposure to the horrors humans could inflict upon each other. Maybe he could use what he knew to give his team better armour than he'd had. If he achieved nothing else with them, that alone would be worthwhile.

In another part of the city, Shaz clicked her mouse button and closed down her software. On autopilot, she switched off her computer and stared unseeingly as the screen faded to black. When she'd decided to explore the resources of the Internet as her first stop on the road to disinterring Tony Hill's past, she'd expected to come across a handful of references and, if she was lucky, a set of cuttings in one of the newspaper archives.

Instead, when she'd input 'Tony, Hill, Bradfield, killer' as key words in the search engine, she'd stumbled upon a darkside treasure trove of references to the case that had put his face on the front pages a year before. There was a grisly handful of websites entirely devoted to serial killers which incorporated Tony's headline case. Elsewhere, journalists and commentators had posted their articles on that specific case on their personal websites. There was even a perverse rogues' gallery, a montage of photographs of the faces of the world's most notorious serial killers. Tony's target, the so-called Queer Killer, featured in more than one guise in the bizarre exhibit.

Shaz had downloaded everything she could find and had spent the rest of the evening reading it. What had started out as an academic exercise to figure out what made Tony Hill tick had left her sick at heart.

The facts were not in dispute. The naked bodies of four men had been dumped in gay cruising areas of Bradfield. The victims had been tortured before death with a cruelty that was almost beyond comprehension. After death, they had been sexually mutilated, washed clean and abandoned like trash.

As a last resort, Tony had been brought in as a consultant, working with Detective Inspector Carol Jordan to develop a profile. They were moving close to their target when hunter became hunted. The killer wanted Tony for a human sacrifice. Captured and trussed, he was on the point of becoming victim number five, the torture engine in place, his body screaming in pain. He was saved in the nick of time not by the arrival of the cavalry but by his own verbal skills, honed over years of working with mentally disturbed offenders. But to claim his life, he'd had to kill his captor.

As she'd read, Shaz's heart had filled with horror, her eyes with tears. Cursed with enough imagination to create a picture of the hell Tony had lived through, she found herself sucked into the nightmare of that final showdown where the roles of killer and victim were irrevocably reversed. The scenario made her shudder with fear and trepidation.

How had he begun to live with that? she marvelled. How did he sleep? How could he close his eyes and not be assailed with images beyond most people's imagination or tolerance? Little wonder that he wasn't prepared to use his own past to teach them how to manage their futures. The miracle was that he was still willing to practise a craft that must have pushed him to the edge of madness.

And how would she have coped if she'd been the one in his shoes?

Shaz dropped her head into her hands and, for the first time since she'd heard of the task force, asked herself if she hadn't perhaps made a terrible mistake.

Betsy mixed a drink for the journalist. Heavy on the gin, light on the tonic, a quarter of a lemon squeezed so that the tartness of the juice would cut the oily sweetness of the gin and disguise its potency. One of the principal reasons that Micky's image had survived untainted by scandal was Betsy's insistence that they trust no one outside the trio that held their secret close. Suzy Joseph might be all smiles and charm, filling the airy sitting room with the tinkle of her laugh and the smoke from her menthol cigarettes, but she was still a journalist. Even if she represented the most accommodating and sycophantic of the colour magazines, Betsy knew that among her drinking cronies there would be more than one tabloid hack ready to dip a hand in a pocket for the right piece of gossip. So Suzy would be plied generously with drink today. By the time she came to sit down to lunch with Jacko and Micky, her sharp eyes would be blurred round the edges.

Betsy perched on the arm of a sofa whose squashy cushions engulfed the anorectically thin journalist. She could keep an eye on her easily from there, while Suzy would have to make a deliberate and obvious shift of position to get Betsy in her line of sight. That also made it possible for Betsy to signal caution to Micky without being seen. 'This is such a lovely room,' Suzy gushed. 'So light, so cool. You don't often see something so tasteful, so elegant, so – *appropriate*. And believe me, I've been in more of these Holland Park mansions than the local estate agents!' She twisted round awkwardly and said to Betsy in the same tones she'd have used to a waiter, 'You have made sure the caterers have all they need?'

Betsy nodded. 'Everything's under control. They were delighted with the kitchen.'

'I'm sure they were.' Suzy was back with Micky, Betsy dismissed again. 'Did you design the dining room yourself, Micky? So stylish! So very, very *you*! So perfect for *Junket with Joseph*.' She leaned forward to stub out her cigarette, giving Betsy an unwanted view of a creped cleavage that fake tan and expensive body treatments couldn't entirely disguise.

Being commended on her taste by a woman who could without any indication of shame wear a brash scarlet and black Moschino suit designed for someone twenty years younger and an entirely different shape was a double-edged compliment, Micky felt. But she simply smiled again and said, 'Actually, it was mostly Betsy's inspiration. She's the one with the taste round here. I just tell her what I want the ambience to be like, and she sorts it out.'

Suzy's reflexive smile held no warmth. Another wasted opening; nothing quotable there, it seemed to say. Before she could try again, Jacko strode into the room, his broad shoulders in their perfect tailoring thrusting forward so he appeared like a flying wedge. He ignored Suzy's fluttering twitters and made straight for Micky, descending upon her with one enveloping arm, hugging her close, though not actually kissing. 'Sweetheart,' he said, his professional, public voice carrying the thrum of a cello chord. 'I'm sorry I'm late.' He half-turned and leaned back against the sofa, giving Suzy the full benefit of his perfectly groomed smile. 'You must be Suzy,' he said. 'We're thrilled to have you here with us today.'

Suzy lit up like Christmas. 'I'm thrilled to be here,' she gushed, her breathy voice losing its veneer and revealing the unmistakable West Midlands intonation she'd devoted herself to burying. The effect Jacko still had on women never ceased to astonish Betsy. He could turn the sourest bitch Barsac sweet. Even the tired cynicism of Suzy Joseph, a woman who had the same relationship to celebrity as beetles to dung, wasn't sufficient armour against his charm. '*Junket with Joseph* doesn't often give me the chance to spend time with people I genuinely admire,' she added.

'Thank you,' Jacko said, all smiles. 'Betsy, should we be heading through to the dining room?'

She glanced at the clock. 'That would be helpful,' she said. 'The caterer wants to start serving round about now.' Jacko jumped to his feet and waited attentively for Micky to get up and move towards the door. He ushered Suzy ahead of him too, turning back to roll his eyes upwards in an expression of bored horror for Betsy's benefit. Stifling a giggle, she followed them to the dining-room door, saw them seated and left them to it. Sometimes there were distinct benefits in not being the official consort, she reminded herself as she settled down with her bread and cheese and *The World at One*.

There was no such relief for Micky, who had to pretend she didn't even notice Suzy's vapid flirting with her husband. Micky tuned out the boring ritual dance going on next to her and concentrated on freeing the last morsels of lobster from a claw.

A change in Suzy's tone alerted her that the conversation had shifted a gear. Time for work, Micky realized. 'Of course, I've read in the cuttings how you two got together,' Suzy was saying, her hand covering Jacko's real one. She wouldn't have been so quick to pat the other, Micky reflected grimly. 'But I need to hear it from your own lips.'

Here we go, Micky thought. The first part of the recital was always hers. 'We met in hospital,' she began.

By the middle of the second week, the task force office felt like home to the entire team. It was no accident that all six of the junior officers chosen for the squad were single and unattached, according both to their records and the unofficial background checks that Commander Paul Bishop had pursued in canteens and police clubs up and down the country. Tony had deliberately wanted a group of people who, uprooted from their former lives, would be thrown together and forced to develop team spirit. That at least was something he seemed to have got right, he thought, looking around the seminar room where six heads were bowed over a set of photocopied police files he'd prepared for them.

Already, they had started to form alliances, and so far they'd done well to avoid the personality clashes that could split a group beyond salvaging. Interestingly, the associations were flexible, not fixed in rigid pairs. Although some affinities were stronger than others, there was no attempt to make any of them exclusive.

Shaz was the one exception, as far as Tony could tell. It wasn't that there was a problem between her and the others. It was more that she held herself apart from the easy intimacy that was growing between the rest. She joined in the jokes, took part in the communal brainstorming, but somehow there was always distance between her and her fellows. He sensed in her a passion for success that the rest of the squad lacked. They were ambitious, no denying that, but with Shaz it went deeper. She was driven, her need burning inside her and consuming any trace of frivolity. She was always first there in the mornings and last out at night, eagerly snatching any opportunity to get Tony to expand on whatever he'd been talking about last. But her very need for success made her correspondingly more vulnerable to failure. What he recognized as a desperate desire for approval was a blade that could be used against her with devastating effect. If she didn't learn to drop her defences so she could use her empathy, she'd never achieve her potential as a profiler. It was his job to find a way of making her feel she could relax her vigilance without risking too much damage.

At that moment, Shaz looked up, her eyes direct on his. There was no embarrassment, no awkwardness. She simply stared for a moment then returned to what she was reading. It was as if she had raided his memory banks for a missing piece of information and, having found it, had logged off again. Slightly unnerved, Tony cleared his throat. 'Four separate incidents of sexual assault and rape. Any comments?'

The group had moved beyond awkward silences and polite hanging back to give others a chance. In what was becoming an established pattern, Leon Jackson dived straight in. 'I think the strongest link is in the victims. I read somewhere that serial rapists tend to rape within their own age group, and all these women were in their mid-twenties. Plus they all have short blonde hair and they all took time and trouble to stay fit. You got two joggers, one hockey player, one rower. They all did sports where it wouldn't be hard for a weirdo stalker to watch them without attracting any attention.'

'Thanks, Leon. Any other comments?'

Simon, already the devil's advocate designate of the group, weighed in, his Glasgow accent and habit of staring out from under his heavy dark eyebrows multiplying the aggression factor. 'You could argue that that's because the kind of woman who indulges in these kind of sports is exactly the sort that's confident enough to be out in risky places on her own, convinced it's never going to happen to her. It could easily be two, three or even four attackers. In which case, bringing in a profiler is going to be a total waste of time.'

Shaz shook her head. 'It's not just the victims,' she stated firmly. 'If you read their evidence, in each case their eyes were covered during the attack. In each case, they mention that their assailant verbally abused them continually while he was actually assaulting them. That's more than sheer coincidence.'

Simon wasn't ready to give up. 'Come on, Shaz,' he protested. 'Any bloke who's so powerless he needs to resort to rape to feel good about himself is going to need to talk himself up to it. And as for their eyes being covered – there's nothing in common there except with the first and third where he used their own headbands. Look –' he waved the papers – 'case number two, he pulled her

T-shirt over her head and tied a knot in it. Case number four, the rapist had a roll of packing tape that he wound round her head. Way different.' He sat back, a good-natured grin defusing the force of his words.

Tony grinned. 'The perfectly contrived lead into the next subject. Thanks, Simon. Today, I'm going to hand out your first assignment, the preamble to which is the beginner's guide to signature versus MO. Anybody know what I'm talking about?'

Kay Hallam, the other woman on the team, raised her hand half a dozen inches and looked questioningly at Tony. He nodded. She tucked her light brown hair behind her ears in a gesture he'd come to recognize as Kay's keynote mechanism for looking feminine and vulnerable to defuse criticism, particularly when she was about to make a point she was absolutely sure of. 'MO is dynamic, signature is static,' she said.

'That's one way of putting it,' Tony said. 'However, it's probably a bit too technical for the plods among us,' he added with a grin, pointing his finger one by one at the other five. He pushed back his chair and started moving restlessly round the room as he talked. 'MO means *modus operandi*. Latin. The way of doing. When we use it in a criminal context, we mean the series of actions that the perpetrator committed in the process of achieving his goal, the crime. In the early days of profiling, police officers, and to a large degree psychologists, were very literal about their idea of a serial offender. It was somebody who did pretty much the same things every time to achieve pretty much the same results. Except that they usually showed escalation, moving, say, from assaulting a prostitute to beating a woman's brains out with a hammer.

'As we discovered more, though, we realized we weren't the only ones capable of learning from our mistakes. We were dealing with criminals who were intelligent and imaginative enough to do exactly the same. That meant we had to get our heads round the idea that the MO was something that could change quite drastically from one offence to the next because the offender found that a particular course of action wasn't very effective. So he'd adapt. His first murder could be a strangulation, but maybe our killer feels that took too long, was too noisy, frightened him too much, stressed him rather than allowing him to enjoy his fulfilment. Next time out, he smashes her skull in with a crowbar. Too messy. So number three, he stabs. And the investigators write them off as three separate killings because the MO looks so different.

'What doesn't change is what we call, for the sake of giving it a name, the signature. The sig, for short.' Tony stopped pacing and leaned against the window sill. 'The sig doesn't change because it's the *raison d'etre* of the offence. It's what gives the perpetrator his sense of satisfaction.

'So what does this signature consist of? Well, it's all the bits of behaviour that exceed what is actually necessary to commit the crime. The ritual of the offence. To satisfy the perpetrator, the signature elements have to be acted out every time he goes out on a mission, and they have to be performed in the same style every time. Examples of signature in a killer might be things like: does he strip the victim? Does he make a neat pile of the victim's clothes? Does he use cosmetics on the victim after death? Is he having sex with the victim postmortem? Is he performing some kind of ritualistic mutilation like cutting off their breasts or penises or ears?'

Simon looked faintly queasy. Tony wondered how many murder victims he'd seen so far. He would have to grow a thicker skin or else be prepared to put up with the jibes of colleagues who would enjoy watching the profiler lose his lunch over another vitiated victim. 'A serial offender must accomplish signature activities to fulfil himself, to make the act meaningful,' Tony continued. 'It's about meeting a variety of needs – to dominate, to inflict pain, to provoke distinct responses, to achieve sexual release. The means can vary, but the end remains constant.'

He took a deep breath and tried to keep his mind off the very particular variations he'd seen at first hand. 'For a killer whose pleasure comes from inflicting pain and hearing victims scream, it's immaterial whether he . . .' his voice faltered as irresistible images climbed into his head. 'Whether he . . .' They were all looking at him now and he desperately struggled to look momentarily distracted rather than shipwrecked. 'Whether he . . . ties them up and cuts them, or whether he . . .'

'Whether he whips them with wire,' Shaz said, her voice casual, her expression reassuring.

'Exactly,' Tony said, recovering fast. 'Nice to see you've got such a tender imagination, Shaz.'

'Typical woman, eh?' Simon said with a grunt of laughter.

Shaz looked faintly embarrassed. Before the joke could escalate,

Tony continued. 'So you might have two bodies whose physical conditions are very different. But when you examine the scenario, things have been done that were additional to the act of killing and the ultimate gratification has been the same. That's your signature.'

He paused, his control firmly in place again, and looked around, checking he was taking them all with him. One of the men looked dubious. 'At its most simplistic,' he said, 'think about petty criminals. You've got a burglar who steals videos. That's all he goes for, just videos, because he's got a fence who gives him a good deal. He robs terraced houses, going in through the back yard. But then he reads in the local paper that the police are warning people about the video thief who comes in through the back yard, and they're setting up neighbourhood watch teams to keep a special eye on back alleys. So he abandons his terraced houses and instead he goes for between-the-wars semis and gets in through the side windows in the downstairs hall. He's changed his MO. But he still only nicks the videos. That's his signature.'

The doubter's face cleared. Now he'd grasped it. Gratified, Tony picked up a stack of papers divided into six bundles. 'So we have to learn to be inclusive when we're considering the possibility of a serial offender. Think "linking through similarity", rather than "discounting through difference".'

He stood up again and walked around among their work tables, gearing himself up to the crucial part of the session. 'Some senior police officers and profilers have a hypothesis that's more confidential than the secrets of the Masonic square,' he said, capturing their attention again. 'We believe there could be as many as half a dozen undetected serial killers who have been operating in Britain over the past ten years. Some could have claimed upwards of ten victims. Thanks to the motorway network and the historic reluctance of police forces to exchange information, nobody has sat down and made the crucial connections. Once we're up and running, this will be something we'll be considering as and when we have time and staff available to look at it.' Raised eyebrows and muttering filled his momentary pause.

'So what we're doing here is a dummy run,' Tony explained. 'Thirty missing teenagers. They're all real cases, culled from a dozen forces over the last seven years. You've got a week to examine the cases in your spare time. Then you'll have the chance to present your own theories as to whether any of them have sufficient common factors to give us grounds for suspicion that they might be the work of a serial offender.' He handed them each a bundle of photostats, giving them a few moments to flick through.

'I should emphasize that this is merely an exercise,' he cautioned them, walking back to his seat. 'There's no reason to suppose that any of these girls or lads has been abducted or killed. Some of them may well be dead now, but that's probably got more to do with the attrition of life on the street than foul play. The common factor that links them is that none of these kids were regarded by their families as the kind who would run away. The families all claimed the missing teenagers were happy at home, there had been no serious arguments and there were no significant problems with school. Although one or two of them had some history of involvement with the police or social services, there weren't any current difficulties at the time of the disappearances. However, none of the missing kids subsequently made contact with home. In spite of that, it's likely that most of them made for London and the bright lights.'

He took a deep breath and turned to face them. 'But there could be another scenario lurking in there. If there is, it'll be our job to find it.'

Excitement started like a slow burn in Shaz's gut, powerful enough to dim the memories of what she'd read about Tony's last close encounter with a killer. This was her first chance. If there were undiscovered murder victims out there, she would find them. More than that, she would be their advocate. And their avenger.

Criminals are often caught by accident. He knew that; he'd seen programmes about it on the TV. Dennis Nilsen, killer of fifteen homeless young men, found out because human flesh blocked the drains; Peter Sutcliffe, the Yorkshire Ripper, despatcher of thirteen women, nicked because he'd stolen a set of number plates to disguise his car; Ted Bundy, necrophiliac murderer of as many as forty young women, finally arrested for speeding past a police car at night with no lights. This knowledge didn't frighten him, but it added an extra *frisson* to the adrenaline buzz that inevitably accompanied his fire-setting. His motives might be very different from theirs, but the risk was almost as great. The once soft leather driving gloves were always damp with his nervous sweat.

Somewhere around one in the morning, he parked his car in a carefully chosen spot. He never left it on a residential street, understanding the insomnia of the elderly and the late-night revels of the young. Instead, he chose the car parks of DIY stores, the waste ground beside factories, the forecourts of garages closed for the night. Secondhand car pitches were best; nobody noticed an extra car there for an hour or two in the small hours.

He never carried a holdall either, sensing it to be suspicious at that time of night. A policeman spotting him would have no cause to think he'd been out burgling. And even if a bored night-beat bobby fancied the diversion of getting him to turn out his pockets, there wouldn't be much to arouse suspicion. A length of string, an old-fashioned cigarette lighter with a brass case, a packet of cigarettes with two or three missing, a dog-eared book of matches with a couple remaining, yesterday's newspaper, a Swiss Army knife, a crumpled oil-stained handkerchief, a small but powerful torch. If that was grounds for arrest, the cells would be full every night.

He walked the route he'd memorized, staying close to the walls as he moved silently down empty streets, his blank-soled bowling shoes making no sound. After a few minutes, he came to a narrow alley which led to the blind side of a small industrial estate he'd had his eye on for a while. It had originally been a ropeworks and consisted of a group of four turn-of-the-century brick buildings which had recently been converted to their present uses. An auto electrician's sat next to an upholstery workshop, opposite a plumbing supplier and a bakery that made biscuits from a recipe allegedly as old as the York Mystery plays. He reckoned anyone who got away with charging such ridiculous prices for a poxy packet of gritty biscuits deserved to have their factory razed to the ground, but there wasn't enough flammable material there for his needs.

Tonight, the upholstery workshop was going to go up like a Roman candle.

Later, he'd thrill to the sight of yellow and crimson flames thrusting their long spikes into the plumes of grey and brown smoke billowing up from the blazing cloth and the wooden floors and beams of the elderly building. But for now, he had to get inside.

He'd made his preparations earlier that day, dropping a carrier bag into a rubbish bin by the side door of the workshop. Now he retrieved it and took out the sink plunger and the tube of superglue. He walked round the outside of the building until he was outside the toilet window, where he stuck the plunger to the window. He waited a few minutes to be certain the contact adhesive had hardened, then he gripped the plunger with both hands, braced himself and gave a sharp tug. The glass broke with a tiny tinkle, the fragments falling on the outside of the window, just as they would if it had exploded from the heat. He tapped the plunger smartly against the wall to shatter the circle of glass, leaving only a thin ring still glued to the rubber. That didn't worry him; there would be no reason for any forensic expert to reconstruct the window and reveal a missing circle of glass at the heart of the shards. That done, he was inside within a few minutes. There was, he knew, no burglar alarm.

He took out the torch and flipped it quickly on and off to check his position, then emerged into the corridor that led along the back of the main work space. At the end, he recalled, were a couple of large cardboard boxes of scrap material that local handicraft hobbyists bought for coppers. No reason for fire investigators to doubt it was a place where workers might hang out for a fly fag.

It was a matter of moments to construct his incendiary device. First he opened up the cigarette lighter and rubbed the string with the wadding which he'd previously saturated with lighter fluid. Then he put the string at the centre of a bundle of half a dozen cigarettes held loosely together with an elastic band. He placed his incendiary so that the string fuse lay along the edge of the nearest cardboard box, then laid the oily handkerchief beside it with some crumpled newspaper. Finally, he lit the cigarettes. They would burn halfway down before the string ignited. That in its turn would take a little while to get the boxes of fabric smouldering. But by the time they'd caught hold, there wouldn't be any stopping his fire. It was going to be some blaze.

He'd been saving this one up, knowing it would be a beauty. Rewarding, in more ways than one.

Betsy checked her watch. Ten minutes more, then she would break up Suzy Joseph's junket with a fictitious appointment for Micky. If Jacko wanted to carry on charming, that was up to him. She suspected he'd rather seize the opportunity to escape. He'd have finished filming the latest *Vance's Visit* the night before, so he'd be off on one of his charity stints at one of the specialist hospitals where he worked as a volunteer counsellor and support worker. He'd be gone by mid-afternoon, leaving her and Micky to a peaceful house and a weekend alone.

'Between Jacko and the Princess of Wales, you get no peace these days when you've got a terminal illness,' she said out loud. 'I'm the lucky one,' she went on, moving from bureau to filing cabinet as she cleared her desk in preparation for a guilt-free weekend. 'I don't have to listen to the Authorized Version for the millionth time.' She imitated Jacko's upbeat, dramatic intonation. '"I was lying there, contemplating the wreck of my dreams, convinced I had nothing left to live for. Then, out of the depths of my depression, I saw a vision."' Betsy made the sweeping gesture she'd seen Jacko deploy so often with his living arm. '"This very vision of loveliness, in fact. There, by my hospital bed stood the one thing I'd seen since the accident that made me realize life might memories be worth living."'

It was a tale that bore almost no relationship to the reality Betsy had lived through. She remembered Micky's first encounter with Jacko, but not because it had been the earth-shaking collision of two stars recognizing their counterparts. Betsy's memories were very different and far less romantic.

It was the first time Micky had been the lead outside broadcast reporter on the main evening news bulletin. She'd been bringing millions of eager viewers the first exclusive interview with Jacko Vance, hero of the hottest human story on the networks. Betsy had watched the broadcast at home alone, thrilled to see her lover the cynosure of ten million pairs of eyes, hugging herself in delight.

The exhilaration hadn't lasted long. They'd been celebrating together in the flickering glow of the video replay when the phone had interrupted their pleasure. Betsy had answered, her voice exuberant with happiness. The journalist who greeted her as Micky's girlfriend drained all the joy from her. In spite of Betsy's frostily vehement denials and Micky's scornful ridicule, both women knew their relationship was poised on the edge of the worst kind of tabloid exposure.

The patient campaign Micky had gone on to wage against the sneak tactics of the hacks was as carefully planned and as ruthlessly executed as any career move she'd ever made. Every night, two separate pairs of bedroom curtains would be closed and lights turned on behind them. The lamps would go off at staggered intervals, the one in the spare room controlled by a timer that Betsy adjusted to a different hour each night. Every morning, the curtains would be drawn back at diverse times, each pair by the same hands that had closed them. The only places the two women embraced were behind closed curtains out of the line of sight of the window, or in the hallway, which was invisible from outside. If both left the house at the same time, they parted at the bottom of the steps with a cheerful wave and no bodily contact.

Giving the presumed watchers nothing to chew on would have been enough to make most people feel secure. But Micky preferred a more proactive approach. If the tabloids wanted a story, she'd make sure they had one. It would simply have to be a more exciting, more credible and more sexy story than the one they thought they had. She cared far too much for Betsy to take chances with her lover's peace of mind or their relationship.

The morning after the ominous phone call, Micky had a spare hour. She drove to the hospital where Jacko was a patient and charmed her way past the nurses. Jacko seemed pleased to see her, and not only because she came armed with the gift of a miniature AM/FM radio complete with earphones. Although he was still taking strong medication for his pain, he was alert and receptive to any distraction from the tedium of life in his side ward. She spent half an hour chatting lightly about everything except the accident and the amputation, then left, leaning over to give him a friendly peck on the forehead. It had been no hardship; to her surprise, she'd found herself warming to Jacko. He wasn't the arrogant macho man she'd expected, based on her past experience with male sporting heroes. Nor, even more surprisingly, was he wallowing in self-pity. Micky's visits might have started out as cynical self-interest, but within a very short space of time she was sucked in, first by her respect for his stoicism, then by an unexpected pleasure in his company. He might be more interested in himself than in her, but at least he managed to be entertaining and witty with it.

Five days and four visits later, Jacko asked the question she'd been waiting for. 'Why do you keep visiting me?'

Micky shrugged. 'I like you?'

Jacko's eyebrows rose and fell, as if to say, 'That's not enough.'

She sighed and made a conscious effort to hold his speculative gaze. 'I have always been cursed with an imagination. And I understand the drive to be successful. I've worked my socks off to get where I am. I've made sacrifices and I've sometimes had to treat people in a way that, in other circumstances, I'd be ashamed of. But getting to where I want to be is the most important thing in

48

my life. I can imagine how I would feel if a chain of circumstances outside my control cost me my goal. I guess what I feel for you is empathy.'

'Meaning what?' he asked, his face giving nothing away.

'Sympathy without pity?'

He nodded, as if satisfied. 'The nurse reckoned it was because you fancied me. I knew she was wrong.'

Micky shrugged. It was all going so much better than she'd anticipated. 'Don't disillusion her. People distrust motives they can't understand.'

'You're so right,' he said, an edge of bitterness in his voice that she hadn't heard there before, in spite of the ample reason. 'But understanding doesn't always make it possible to accept something.'

There was more, much more behind his words. But Micky knew when to leave well alone. There would be plenty of opportunity to broach that subject again. When she left that day, she was careful to make sure the nurse saw her kiss him goodbye. If this story was to be credible, it needed to leak out, not be broadcast. And from her own journalistic experience, gossip spread through a hospital faster than legionnaire's disease. From there to the wider community only took one carrier.

When she arrived a week later, Jacko seemed remote. Micky sensed violent emotions barely held in check, but couldn't be sure what those feelings were. Eventually, tired of conducting a monologue rather than a conversation, she said, 'Are you going to tell me or are you just going to let your blood pressure rise till you have a stroke?'

For the first time that afternoon, he looked directly into her face. Momentarily, she thought he was in the grip of fever, then she realized it was a fury so powerful that she couldn't imagine how he could contain it. He was so angry he could barely speak, she realized as she watched him struggle to find the words. At last, he conquered his rage by sheer effort of will and said, 'My fucking so-called fiancee,' he growled.

'Jillie?' Micky hoped she'd got the name right. They'd met briefly one afternoon as Micky had been leaving. She had the impression of a slender dark-haired beauty who managed sultry rather than tarty by an inch.

'Bitch,' he hissed, the tendons on his neck tensing like cords beneath the tanned skin.

'What's happened, Jacko?'

He closed his eyes and breathed deeply, his wide chest expanding and emphasizing the asymmetry of his once perfect upper body. 'Dumped me,' he managed at last, his voice thick with anger.

'No,' Micky breathed. 'Oh, Jacko.' She reached out and touched the tight fist with her fingers. She could actually feel the pulse beating in his flesh, so tightly was his hand clenched. His rage was phenomenal, Micky thought, yet his control seemed in no real danger of slipping.

'Says she can't cope with it.' He gave a grating bark of cynical laughter. 'She can't cope with it? How the fuck does she think it is for me?'

'I'm sorry,' Micky said inadequately.

'I saw it in her face, the first time she visited after the accident. No, I knew before that. I knew because she didn't come near me that first day. It took her two days to get her arse in here.' His voice was harsh and guttural, the heavy words falling like blocks of stone. 'When she did come, she couldn't stand the sight of me. It was all over her face. I repelled her. All she could see was what I wasn't any more.' He pulled his fist away and pounded it on the bed.

'More fool her.'

His eyes opened and he glared at her. 'Don't you start. All I need is one more silly bitch patronizing me. I've had that fucking nurse with her artificial cheerfulness all over me. Just don't!'

Micky didn't flinch. She'd won too many confrontations with news editors for that. 'You should learn to recognize respect when you see it,' she flared back at him. 'I'm sorry Jillie hasn't got what it takes to see you through, but you're better off finding that out now than further down the road.'

Jacko looked astonished. For years now, the only person who'd spoken to him with anything except nervous deference was his trainer. 'What?' he squawked, his anger displaced by baffled astonishment.

Micky continued regardless of his response. 'What you have to decide now is how you're going to play it.'

'What?'

'It's not going to stay a secret between the two of you, is it? From what you said, the nurse already knows. So by tea-time, it's going to be, "Hold the front page." If you want, you can settle for being an object of pity – hero dumped by girlfriend because he's not a proper man any more. You'll get the sympathy vote, and a fair chunk of the Great British Public will spit on Jillie in the street. Alternatively, you can get your retaliation in first and come out on top.'

Jacko's mouth was open, but for a moment no words came. At last, he said in a low voice that fellow members of the Olympic squad would have recognized as a signal for flak jackets, 'Go on.'

'It's up to you. It depends whether you want people to see you as a victim or a victor.'

Micky's level stare felt as much of a challenge as anything that had ever faced him on the field of competition. 'What do you think?' he snarled.

'I'm telling you, man, this is the *sticks*,' Leon said, waving a chicken pakora in a sweeping gesture that seemed to include not only the restaurant but most of the West Riding of Yorkshire as well.

'You've obviously never been to Greenock on a Saturday night,' Simon said drily. 'Believe me, Leon, that makes Leeds look positively cosmopolitan.'

'*Nothing* could make this place cosmopolitan,' Leon protested.

'It's not that bad,' Kay said. 'It's very good for shopping.' Even outside the classroom, Shaz noticed, Kay slipped straight into the conciliatory role, smoothing down her hair as she smoothed down the rough edges in the conversations.

Simon groaned theatrically. 'Oh please, Kay, don't feel you need to glide effortlessly into bland womanly stuff. Go on, make my night, tell me how terrific Leeds is for body-piercing.'

Kay poked her tongue out at him.

'If you don't leave Kay alone, us women might well consider piercing some treasured part of your anatomy with this beer bottle,' Shaz said sweetly, brandishing her Kingfisher.

Simon put his hands up. 'OK. I'll behave, just as long as you promise not to beat me with a chapati.'

There was a moment's silence while the four police officers attacked their starters. The Saturday night curry looked like becoming a regular feature for the quartet, the other two preferring to return to their former home turf rather than explore their new base. When Simon had first suggested it, Shaz hadn't been sure if she wanted to bond that closely with her colleagues. But Simon had been persuasive, and besides, Commander Bishop had been ear-wigging and she wanted to avoid a black mark for being unco-operative. So she'd agreed and, to her surprise, she'd enjoyed herself, even though she had made her excuses and left before the nightclub excursion that had followed. Now, three weeks into the Job, she found she was actually looking forward to their night out, and not just for the food.

Leon was first to clear his plate, as usual. 'What I'm saying is, it's primitive up here.'

'I don't know,' Shaz protested. 'They've got plenty of good curry houses, the property's cheap enough for me to afford something bigger than a rabbit hutch, and if you want to go from one part of the city centre to another, you can walk instead of sitting on the tube for an hour.'

'And the countryside. Don't forget how easy it is to get out into the countryside,' Kay added.

Leon leaned back in his seat, groaning and rolling his eyes extravagantly like a terrible caricature of a Black and White Minstrel. 'Heathcliff,' he warbled in falsetto.

'She's right,' Simon said. 'God, you're such a cliché, Leon. You should get off the city streets, get some fresh air into your lungs. What about coming out tomorrow for a walk? I really fancy seeing if Ilkley Moor lives up to the song.'

Shaz laughed. 'What? You want to walk about without a hat and see if you catch your death of cold?'

The others joined in her laughter. 'See, man, it's primitive, like I said. Nothing to do but walk about on your own two feet. And shit, Simon, I'm not the one that's a cliché. You know I've been stopped driving home three times since I moved here? Even the Met got a bit more racially enlightened than thinking every black man with a decent set of wheels has to be a drug dealer,' Leon said bitterly.

'They're not stopping you because you're black,' Shaz retorted as he paused to light a cigarette.

'No?' Leon exhaled.

'No, they're stopping you for being in possession of an offensive weapon.'

'What do you mean?'

'That suit, babe. Any sharper and you'd cut yourself getting dressed. You're wearing a blade, of course they're going to stop

52

you.' Shaz held out her hand for Leon to give her five and, amid the hoots of laughter from the other two, he made a rueful face and hit her hand.

'Not as sharp as you, Shaz,' Simon said. She wondered if it was only the heat of the spices that was responsible for the scarlet flush across his normally pale cheekbones.

'Speaking of sharp,' Kay chipped in as their main courses arrived, 'you can't get anything past Tony Hill, can you?'

'He's smart, all right,' Simon agreed, sweeping his wavy dark hair back from his sweating forehead. 'I just wish he'd loosen up a bit. It's like there's a wall there that you get right up to but you can't see over.'

'I'll tell you why that is,' Shaz said, suddenly serious. 'Bradfield. The Queer Killer.'

'That's the one he did that went well and truly pear-shaped, yeah?' Leon asked.

'That's right.'

'It was all hushed up, wasn't it?' Kay said, her intent face reminding Shaz of a small furry animal, cute but with hidden teeth. 'The papers hinted at all sorts of stuff, but they never went into much detail.'

'Believe me,' Shaz said, looking at her half-chicken and wishing she'd gone for something vegetarian, 'you wouldn't want to know the details. If you want to know the whole story, check out the Internet. They weren't constrained by technicalities like good taste or requests from the authorities to keep things under wraps. I'm telling you, if you can read what Tony Hill went through without having second thoughts about what we're doing, you're a fuck of a sight braver than I am.'

There was a moment's silence. Then Simon leaned forward and said confidingly, 'You're going to tell us, aren't you, Shaz?'

He always arrived fifteen minutes ahead of the agreed time because he knew she'd be early. It didn't matter which she he'd chosen, she'd turn up ahead of schedule because she was convinced he was Rumpelstiltskin, the man who could spin twenty-four-carat gold out of the dry straw of her life.

Donna Doyle – no longer the next one but rather the latest one – was no different from the others. As her silhouette appeared against the dim light of the car park, he could hear the clumsy childish music crashing in his head. *'Jack and Jill went up the hill, to fetch a pail of water . . .'*

He shook his head to clear his ears, like a snorkeller surfacing from a coral reef. He watched her approach, moving cautiously between the expensive cars, glancing from side to side, a slight frown creasing her forehead, as if she couldn't work out why her antennae weren't pointing her to his precise position. He could see she'd done her best to look good; the school skirt that had obviously been folded over at the waist to show off shapely legs, the school blouse open one button further than parent or teacher would ever have allowed in public, the blazer over one shoulder, hanging thus to obscure the backpack of school supplies. The make-up was heavier than the night before, its excess weight catapulting her straight into middle age. And her hair glinted glossy black, the swing of the short bob catching the dull gleam of the car park lights.

When Donna was almost level, he pushed open the passenger door of the car. The sudden interior light made her jump even as she registered his shockingly handsome profile cutting a dark line through the bright rectangle. He spoke through his already lowered window. 'Come and sit with me while I tell you what all this is about,' he said conversationally.

Donna hesitated fractionally, but she was too familiar with the open candour of his public face to pause properly for reflection. She slid into the seat next to him and he made sure she saw him carefully not looking at the expanse of thigh her moves had revealed. For the time being, chastity was the best policy. Her smile was coquettish yet innocent as she said, 'When I woke up this morning, I wondered if I'd dreamed it all.'

His answering smile was indulgent. 'I feel like that all the time,' he said, building another course of bricks on the false foundation of fake rapport. 'I wondered if you'd have second thoughts. There are so many things you could do with your life that would be a greater contribution to society than being on TV. Believe me, I know.'

'But you do those things too,' she said earnestly. 'All that charity work. It's being famous makes it possible for TV stars to raise so much money. People pay money to see them. They wouldn't be shelling out otherwise. I want to be able to do that. To be like them.'

The impossible dream. Or rather, nightmare. She could never have been like him, though she had no notion of the real reason why. People like him were so rare it was almost an argument for the existence of God. He smiled benevolently, like the Pope from the Vatican balcony. It pushed all the right buttons. 'Well, perhaps I can help you make a start,' he told her. And Donna believed him.

He had her there, alone, co-operative, in his car, in an underground car park. What could have been easier than to whisk her away to his destination?

Only a fool would think like that, he'd realized long ago, and he was no fool. For a start, the car park wasn't exactly empty. Businessmen and women were checking out of the hotel, stowing suit carriers into executive saloons and reversing out of tight spots. They noticed a lot more than anyone would expect. For another thing, it was broad daylight outside, a city centre festooned with traffic lights where people sat with nothing better to do than pick their noses and stare slack-jawed at the inhabitants of the next car. First, they'd register the car. A silver Mercedes, smart enough to catch the eye and the admiration. Or, of course, the envy. Then they'd clock the flowing letters along the front wing that announced,

Cars for Vance's Visits supplied by Morrigan Mercedes of Cheshire. Alerted to the possible proximity of celebrity, they'd peer through the tinted windows, trying to identify the driver and passenger. They weren't going to forget that in a hurry, especially if they glimpsed an attractive teenager in the passenger seat. When her photograph appeared in the local paper, they'd remember, no question.

And finally, he'd got a busy day ahead. There was no space in his schedule for delivering her to a place where he could exact what was due. No point in drawing attention to himself by failing to keep appointments, not turning up for the public appearances that were so carefully constructed to give *Vance's Visits* maximum exposure for minimal effort. Donna would have to wait. For both of them, it would be the sweeter for the anticipation. Well, for him, at least. For her, it wouldn't be long before reality turned her breathless expectation into a sick joke.

So he whetted her appetite and kept her on the leash. 'I couldn't believe it when I saw you last night. You'd be absolutely perfect as the co-host. With a two-handed show, we need contrast. Dark-haired Donna, fair-haired Jacko. Petite Donna, hulking great brute Jacko.' He grinned, she giggled. 'What we're working on is a new game show involving parent and child teams. But the teams don't know they're in the show until we turn up to whisk them off. A total surprise, like *This is Your Life*. That's part of the reason why we need to be so sure that whoever I end up working with is absolutely trustworthy. Total discretion, that's the key.'

'I can keep my mouth shut,' Donna said earnestly. 'Honest. I never told a living soul about coming here to meet you. My mate that was at the opening last night with me, when she asked what we were talking about for so long, I just said I was asking whether you had any advice for me if I wanted to break into TV.'

'And did I?' he demanded.

She smiled, beguiling and seductive. 'I told her you said I should get some qualifications behind me before I made any decisions about a career. She doesn't know enough about you to realize you'd never come out with all that boring shit that I get off my mum.'

'Good thinking,' he told her appreciatively. 'I can promise you I'll never be boring, that's for sure. Now, the problem I've got is that I'm desperately busy for the next couple of days. But I've got Friday morning free, and I can easily set up some screen tests for you. We've got a rehearsal studio up in the north-east and we can work there.'

Her lips parted, her eyes glowed in the dimness of the car interior. 'You mean it? I can be on telly?'

'No promises, but you look the part and you've got a beautiful voice.' He shifted in his seat so he could fix her with a direct gaze. 'All I need to prove to myself is that you really can keep a secret.'

'I told you,' Donna replied, consternation on her face. 'I've said nothing to anybody.'

'But can you keep that up? Can you stay silent until Thursday night?' He put his hand inside his jacket and produced a rail ticket. 'This is a train ticket for Five Walls Halt in Northumberland. On Thursday, you catch the 3.25 Newcastle train from the station here, then at Newcastle, you change to the 7.50 for Carlisle. When you come out of the station, there's a car park on the left. I'll be waiting there in a Land Rover. I can't get out to meet you on the platform because of commercial confidentiality, but I'll be there in the car park, I promise. We'll put you up for the night, then first thing in the morning, you do the screen test.'

'But my mum'll panic if I stay out all night and she doesn't know where I am,' she protested reluctantly.

'You can phone her as soon as we get to the studio complex,' he told her, his voice rich in reassurance. 'Let's face it, she probably wouldn't let you take the screen test if she knew, would she? I bet she doesn't think working in TV is a proper job, does she?'

As usual, he'd calculated to perfection. Donna knew her ambitious mother wouldn't want her to throw her university prospects away to be a game-show bimbo. Her worried look disappeared and she peered up at him from under her eyebrows. 'I won't say a word,' she promised solemnly.

'Good girl. I hope you mean that. All it takes is one wrong word and a whole project can crash. That costs money, and it costs people's jobs too. You might say something in confidence to your best friend, but she'll tell her sister, and her sister will tell her boyfriend, and the boyfriend will tell his best mate over a frame of snooker, and the best mate's sister-in-law just happens to be a reporter. Or a rival TV company executive. And the show's dead. And your big chance goes with it. Let me tell you something. At the start of your career, you only get one bite of the cherry. You screw up, and no one will ever hire you again. You have to have a lot of success under your belt before the TV bosses forgive a bit of failure.' He leaned forward and rested a hand on her arm as he spoke, invading her space and making her feel the sexual thrill of his dangerous edge.

'I understand,' Donna said with all the intensity of a fourteen-year-old who thought she was really a grown-up and couldn't understand why the adults wouldn't admit her into their conspiracy. The promise of an entrée into that world was what made her so ready to swallow something as preposterous as his set-up.

'I can rely on you?'

She nodded. 'I won't let you down. Not with this or anything else.' The sexual innuendo was unmistakable. She was probably still a virgin, he reckoned. Something about her avidity told him so. She was offering herself up to him, a vestal sacrifice.

He leaned closer and kissed the soft, eager mouth that instantly opened under his primly closed lips. He drew back, smiling to soften her obvious disappointment. He always left them wanting more. It was the oldest showbiz cliché in the world. But it worked every time.

Carol wiped up the remaining traces of chicken jalfrezi with the last chunk of nan bread and savoured the final mouthful. 'That', she said reverently, 'was to die for.'

'There's more,' Maggie Brandon said, pushing the heavy casserole dish towards her.

'I'd have to wear it,' Carol groaned. 'There's no room inside.'

'You can take some home with you,' Maggie told her. 'I know the kind of daft hours you'll be working. Cooking's the last thing you'll have time for. When John was made up to DCI, I considered asking his Chief Constable if the family could move into the cells at Scargill Street since that seemed to be the only way his kids would ever get to see him.'

John Brandon, Chief Constable of East Yorkshire Police, shook his head and said affectionately, 'She's a terrible liar, my wife. She only says these things to guilt-trip you into working so hard there'll be nothing left for me to worry about in your whole division.'

Maggie snorted. 'As if! How do you think he ended up looking like that, eh?'

Carol gave Brandon a shrewd look. It was a good question. If ever a man had been born with a graveyard face, it was Brandon. His countenance was all verticals, long and narrow; lines in his hollow cheeks, lines between his brows, aquiline nose, iron-grey hair straight as the grid line on a map. Tall and thin, with the beginnings of a stoop, all he needed was a scythe to audition for Death. She considered her options. It might be 'John' tonight, but on Monday morning it would be back to, 'Mr Brandon, *sir*.' Better not push her informal relationship with the boss too far. 'And there was me thinking it was marriage,' she said innocently.

Maggie roared with laughter. 'Diplomatic as well as quick, eh?'

she got out at last, reaching across to pat her husband's shoulder. 'You did well to get Carol to abandon the fleshpots of Bradfield for the back of beyond, my love.'

'Speaking of which, how are you settling in?' Carol asked.

'Well, this is a police house,' Maggie told her, waving a hand at the brilliant white walls and paintwork, a depressing contrast to the hand-marbled paintwork Carol remembered from their Bradfield dining room. 'But it'll have to do us. We've rented out the house in Bradfield, you know? John's only got another five years till he has his thirty in, and we want to go back there. It's where our roots are, where our friends are. And the kids will all be out of school by then, so it's not like they'll be uprooted again.'

'What Maggie isn't saying is that she feels a bit like a Victorian missionary among the Hottentots,' Brandon said.

'Well, you've got to admit, East Yorkshire's a bit different from Bradfield. Plenty of scenery, but there's not a decent theatre within half an hour's drive of here. There seems to be only one bookshop on the whole patch that sells more than the bestsellers. And as for opera – you can forget it!' Maggie protested, getting to her feet and gathering the empty plates.

'Don't you feel happier about the kids growing up away from the influence of the inner city? Out of the reaches of the drug lords?' Carol asked.

Maggie shook her head. 'They're so insular round here, Carol. Back in Bradfield, the kids had friends from all kinds of backgrounds – Asian, Chinese, Afro-Caribbean. Even one Vietnamese lad. Out here, you stick to your own. There's nothing to do except hang around on street corners. Frankly, I'd take a chance on them having the sense to stay out of trouble in the inner city as a trade-off for all the opportunities they had in Bradfield. This country living is well over-rated.' She marched through to the kitchen.

'Sorry,' Carol said. 'Didn't realize it was such a sore point.'

Brandon shrugged. 'You know Maggie. She likes to get it off her chest. Give it a few more months, she'll be running the village, happy as a pig. The kids like it well enough. How about you? What's the cottage like?'

'I love it. The couple I bought it from did an immaculate restoration job.'

'I'm surprised they were selling it, then.'

'Divorce,' Carol said succinctly.

'Ah.'

'I think they were both more upset about losing the cottage than the marriage. You and Maggie will have to come over for a meal.'

'If you ever find the time to shop,' Maggie said darkly, walking back in with a large cafetiere.

'Well, worst comes to worst, I'll send Nelson out to bring us a rabbit back.'

'He's enjoying the opportunities for murder that living in the country offers?' Maggie asked drily.

'He thinks he's died and gone to feline heaven. You might crave the inner city, but he's turned into a country boy overnight.'

Maggie poured coffee for John and Carol, then said, 'I'm going to leave you pair to it, if you don't mind. I know you're dying to talk shop and I promised Karen I'd pick her up after the pictures in Seaford. There's enough coffee there to keep you both awake till dawn, and if you feel peckish in a bit, there's home-made cheese-cake in the fridge. But Andy's due back around ten, so you'd better help yourself before then. I swear that lad's got worms. That or hollow legs.' She swooped down on Brandon and gave him an affectionate peck on the cheek. 'Enjoy yourselves.'

Unable to resist the feeling that she'd been set up by professionals, Carol took a sip of her coffee and waited. When it came, Brandon's question was hardly a surprise. 'So how are you settling in on the ground?' His voice was casual, but his eyes were watchful.

'Obviously, they're wary of me. Not only am I a woman, which on the evolutionary scale in East Yorkshire comes somewhere between a ferret and a whippet, but I'm also the Chief Constable's nark. Brought in from the big city to crack the whip,' she said ironically.

'I was afraid you'd get lumbered with that,' Brandon said. 'But you must have known how it would be when you took the job on.'

Carol shrugged. 'It's not come as a surprise. But there's been rather less of it than I anticipated. Maybe they're all still on their best behaviour, but I think the Seaford Central Division CID are a not bad crew. Because they were stuck out in the boondocks before the reorganization and nobody was paying much attention, they've got a bit lazy, a bit sloppy. I suspect one or two might be spending a bit more than they're earning, but I don't think there's any deep-rooted, systemic corruption.'

Brandon nodded, satisfied. Trusting Carol Jordan's judgement had been a steep learning curve for him, and he'd known instinctively she was the one senior officer he wanted to tempt away from Bradfield. With her setting the tone in Seaford, word would spread through other divisions and the CID culture would adapt accordingly, given time. Time and a certain amount of stick which Brandon wasn't afraid to apply. 'Anything on the books that's causing you a problem?'

Carol finished her coffee and poured herself another cup, offering the pot to Brandon, who refused with a shake of the head. She frowned in thought, gathering her arsenal of information. 'There is something,' she said. 'Since we're talking informally?'

Brandon nodded.

'Well, I noticed going through the overnights that there seemed to be a positive spate of unexplained fires and query arsons. All at night, all in unoccupied premises like schools, factories, cafés, warehouses. None of them very big in itself, but taken together, you're looking at a lot of damage. I put a team together to re-interview the previous victims, see if we could find any connection – financially or insurance-wise. Zilch. But I went myself to talk to the local fire chief, and he produced a series of incidents going back about four months. None of the fires could be absolutely, positively put down as arson, but circumstantially, he reckons there have been something between six and a dozen possible deliberate fires per month on his patch,' Carol said.

'A serial arsonist?' Brandon said softly.

'It's hard to imagine another interpretation,' Carol agreed.

'And you want to do what, exactly?'

'I want to catch him,' she said with a grin.

'Well, what else?' Brandon smiled. 'Did you have something specific in mind?' he continued mildly.

'I want to carry on working with the team I've already got on it, and I want to do a profile.'

Brandon frowned. 'Bring someone in?'

'No,' Carol said sharply. 'There's not really enough evidence to justify the expense. I think I can take a pretty good stab at it myself.'

Brandon looked impassively at Carol. 'You're not a psychologist.'

'No, but I learned a lot last year, working with Tony Hill. And since then, I've read everything about profiling I could find.'

'You should have applied for the National Task Force,' Brandon said, keeping his eyes fixed on her.

Carol felt her skin burn. She hoped the wine and the coffee would account for her heightened colour. 'I don't think they were looking for officers of my rank,' she said. 'Apart from Commander Bishop, there's no one above the rank of sergeant. Besides, I prefer to work a patch, get to know the people and the ground.'

'They're due to be up and running a full case-load in a few weeks,' Brandon continued implacably. 'Maybe they'd welcome something like this to cut their teeth on before then.'

'Maybe they would,' Carol said. 'But it's my case. And I'm not ready to let it go.'

'Fine,' Brandon said, interested that Carol had already developed such fierce possessiveness about the work of the East Yorkshire force. 'But keep me posted, yes?'

'Of course,' Carol said. Her sense of relief, she told herself, was entirely because she would now have the chance to cover herself and her team in glory when they cracked the case. Deep down, though, she knew she was lying.

Sleeping in what the estate agent had referred to as the guest bedroom of Shaz's flat would have been beyond most people, particularly if they were the sort who needed to read a few pages before they could nod off. While the bookcase in the living room contained an innocuous mix of middlebrow middle-of-the-road modern fiction, the shelves in the room Shaz thought of as her study held only hard-core horror, most of it masquerading as textbooks. There were a few novels by pathologists of psychopathy and anatomists of agony like Barbara Vine and Thomas Harris, but most of Shaz's working library was both stranger and more brutal than fiction ever dared to be. If there had been a vocational course for serial killers, her library would have comprised the set books.

The lowest shelves held those items which mildly embarrassed her – pulp true-crime biographies of notorious serial killers with lurid nicknames, sensational accounts of careers that had robbed hundreds of people of their trust and their lives. Arranged above these were the more respectable versions of those same lives, portentous renderings that provided thoughtful revelations and insights sociological, psychological and sometimes illogical.

Next, at eye-level for anyone sitting at the table that held Shaz's notepads and laptop, were the battle stories of the veterans of the war against serial offenders. Since it was the best part of twenty years since the infancy of offender profiling, the pioneers had been trickling into retirement for a few years now, each determined to augment his pension with graphic accounts of his contribution to the latest soft science with the case histories of his notable successes and a passing gloss over his failures. They were, thus far, all men.

Above these autobiographies was the serious stuff; books with titles like *The Psychopathology of Sexual Homicide*, *Crime Scene Analysis* and *Serial Rape: A Clinical Study*. The top shelf gave the only indications that she aspired to be hunter rather than hunted, with its selection of legal texts, including a couple of guides to the Police and Criminal Evidence Act. It was a comprehensive collection and Shaz hadn't amassed it in the mere couple of months since she'd won her place on the task force; it had been years in the building, helping her prepare for the day she'd always been convinced would come, when she'd be called upon to bring her very own notorious killer to book. If textual familiarity alone caught criminals, Shaz would have had the best arrest record in the country.

She had begged off the nightclub run following the curry in spite of the blandishments of the other three. It wasn't just that she had never been a great one for clubbing. Tonight, her spare room was infinitely more tempting than anything a DJ or a barman had to offer. The truth was, she'd been in a ferment all evening, eager to get back to her computer and to finish the comparisons she'd begun to run through her database that afternoon. In the three days since Tony had set their assignment, Shaz had spent every spare moment working her way through the thirty sketchy sets of case notes. At last, the opportunity had come to put into practice all the theories and tricks of the trade she'd picked up in her reading. She'd read the papers from start to finish, not once, but three times. Not until she was fairly sure she had them well differentiated in her head did she approach her computer.

The database Shaz used hadn't represented the leading edge of software development way back when she'd copied it from a fellow student, and now it was practically a candidate for display in a computing museum. But while it might not have all the latest bells and whistles, it was more than capable of performing what she needed. It displayed the material clearly, it allowed her to create her own categories and criteria for sorting the information, and she found its procedures in tune with her instincts and logic and thus easy to use. She'd been inputting data since early that morning, so focused on her work that she hadn't even left the screen to cook lunch, settling instead for a banana and half a packet of digestive biscuits, upending her laptop afterwards to remove the crumbs from the keyboard.

Now, back in front of her screen, stripped of her glad rags and scrubbed clean of her make-up, Shaz was happy. The mouse pointer flickered as fingers clicked on buttons, summoning up menus that interested her far more than anything on offer at the restaurant. She sorted the so-called runaways by age and printed out the results. She followed the same steps for geographical area, physical type, previous police contact, various permutations on their domestic situation, drink and drugs experience, known sexual contacts and interests. Not that the investigating officers had been much concerned with their hobbies.

Shaz pored over the print-outs, reading them individually then spreading them over the desktop so she could more readily compare notes. As she gazed at the printed lists, the slow burn of excitement began in the pit of her stomach. She scrutinized them one more time, double-checking against the photographs in the files to make sure she wasn't willing something into existence that wasn't there. 'Oh, you beauty,' Shaz exclaimed softly, letting out a long sigh.

She closed her eyes and took a deep breath. When she looked again, it was still there. A cluster of seven girls. First, the positive similarities. They all had bobbed dark hair and blue eyes. They were all fourteen or fifteen years old, between 5'2" and 5'4" tall. They had all lived at home with one or both parents. In each case, their friends and family had told the police they were baffled at the girl's disappearance, convinced that she had no real reason to run away. In every instance, the girls had taken almost nothing with them, though in each case, at least one change of clothes appeared to have gone missing with them, which was the main reason why the police hadn't seriously considered them as possible victims of abduction or murder. Reinforcing that view were the times of the disappearances. In each case, the girl concerned had set off for school as usual but had never arrived. She'd also given a false explanation of where she'd be spending the evening. And, although this couldn't be quantified in a way the computer could digest, they were all of a similar type. There was a flirtatious sensuality in their looks, a knowing quality in the way they embraced the camera that indicated they had left childhood innocence behind. They were sexy, whether they knew it or not.

Next, the negative similarities. None of the seven had ever been in care. None had ever been in trouble with the police. Friends admitted to a bit of recreational drinking, maybe even the occasional joint or even a dab of speed. But no significant drug usage. In none of the seven cases was there any hint that the girls might have been engaged in prostitution or the victims of sexual abuse.

There were problems with the cluster, of course. Three had current boyfriends, four did not. The geographical locations were unconnected – Sunderland was the furthest north, Exmouth the most southerly point. In between were Swindon, Grantham, Tamworth, Wigan and Halifax. The reports also spanned six years. The intervals between the disappearances were not constant, nor did they seem to diminish as time went by, which Shaz would have expected if she were really dealing with the victims of a serial killer.

On the other hand, there might be girls she didn't know about yet.

When Shaz woke early that Sunday morning, she tried to will herself back to sleep. She knew there was only one thing she could do that would advance her search for connections among her theoretical victim cluster and that single task wasn't one that could be hurried. When she'd gone to bed around midnight, she'd promised herself she would achieve it with a lunchtime phone call. But lying wide awake with a racing brain at quarter to seven, she knew she couldn't hold out that long.

Irritated by her inability to make progress except at someone else's hands, she threw back the covers. Half an hour later, she was accelerating up the long incline where the M1 began.

Showering, dressing and swallowing a coffee with the radio news in the background had kept thought at arm's length. Now that the empty black three-lane strip stretched out before her, she couldn't hide behind distraction. The radio presenter's voice wasn't enough on its own. Not even Tony Hill's words of wisdom could hold her today. Impatiently, Shaz pushed a cassette of operatic arias into the stereo and gave up the pretence of concentration. For the next two and a half hours, she had nothing to do but run memories through her mind like old movies on a rainy Sunday.

It was almost ten when she drove down the ramp to the Barbican complex's underground car park. She was pleased to see the car park attendant clearly remembered her, as she'd hoped, though he looked startled to see her face smiling uncertainly round the door of his office. 'Hello, stranger,' he said cheerfully. 'We've not seen you around for a long time.'

'I've moved up to Leeds,' she said, carefully avoiding any hint of how recent her move had been. It had been more than eighteen months since she'd last been here, but the reasons for that were nobody's business but hers.

'Chris didn't say to expect you,' the car park attendant said, getting up from his seat and walking towards her. Shaz backed out of the booth and down the steps as he followed her.

'It was all a bit last-minute,' she said noncommittally, opening her car door.

That seemed to satisfy the attendant. 'Are you here overnight?' he asked, frowning as he scanned the car park for an appropriate space.

'No, I'm not planning on staying long,' Shaz said firmly, starting her engine and crawling down the aisles of cars, following the attendant and slotting the car into the space he indicated.

'I'll let you into the block,' he said as she joined him. 'What's it like up in the frozen north, then?'

Shaz smiled. 'The football's better,' was all she said as he pulled back the massive glass and metal door and waved her inside. Just as well I'm not a terrorist sleeper, she thought as she waited for the lift.

On the third floor, she stopped halfway along the carpeted corridor. Taking a deep breath, she pressed the doorbell. In the silence that followed, she breathed out through her nostrils in a slow steady stream, trying to contain the nervousness that was turning her stomach into a Jacuzzi. When she'd almost given up hope, she heard the faint whisper of footfalls. Then the heavy door inched open.

Tousled chestnut hair, bleary brown eyes with dark smudges under them and frown lines between, a snub nose and a yawn half-stifled behind a square hand with blunt, well-manicured fingers appeared in the gap.

For once, Shaz's narrow smile made it as far as her eyes. The blaze of warmth melted Chris Devine, and not for the first time. The hand dropped away from the mouth, but the lips remained parted. Astonishment came first, then delight, then consternation. 'Any chance of a cup of coffee?' Shaz asked.

Chris stepped back uncertainly, pulling the door wide. 'You'd better come in,' she said.

Nothing worth having had ever come easy. He told himself that at regular intervals through two days of torment, though it was not a lesson he was ever likely to forget. His childhood had been scarred with oppressive discipline, any rebelliousness or frivolity stifled by force. He had learned not to show the currents that moved under the surface, to present a bland and acceptable face to whatever adversity people threw in his teeth. Other men might have revealed some traces of the seething excitement that swirled inside whenever he thought of Donna Doyle, but not him. He was too practised at dissemblement. No one ever noticed his mind was ranging through entirely different territory, detached from his surroundings, entirely elsewhere. It was a trait that in the past had saved him pain; now it kept him safe.

In his head he was with her, wondering if she was keeping her promise, imagining the excitement burning in her veins. He thought of her as a changed being, charged with the secret weapon of knowledge, convinced she had the edge on every tabloid astrologer because she knew for sure what her future held.

Of course, hers could not be the same vision as his, he realized that. It would have been hard to imagine two more disparate fantasies, so far apart on the continuum that there could exist no single uniting factor. Apart from orgasm.

Imagining her imagining a false future had its own *frisson* of delight that cohabited and alternated with the sliver of fear that she would not keep her word, that even as he played computer games with the stricken inhabitants of a children's cancer ward, Donna was huddled in a corner of the school cloakroom revealing her secret to her best friend. That was the gamble he took every time. And every time, he'd judged the roll of the dice perfectly. Not once had anyone come looking for him. Well, not in the investigative sense. There had been one time when the distraught parents of a missing teenage girl asked for a TV appeal because, wherever she'd run off to, their daughter would never miss her weekly fix of *Vance's Visits*. Sweet irony, so delicious he'd grown hard for months afterwards just thinking about it. He could hardly have told them that the only way they were ever going to talk to their daughter again was via a medium, could he?

For two nights running, he went to sleep in the early hours and woke at dawn tangled in damp sheets, his pulse racing and his eyes wide open. Whatever the evaporated dream, it robbed him of further sleep, leaving him to prowl the confined spaces of his hotel room, alternately exulting and fretting.

But nothing lasted forever. Thursday evening found him in his Northumberland retreat. Only fifteen minutes' drive from the centre of the city, it was nevertheless as isolated as a Highland croft. Formerly a tiny Methodist chapel that could never have held more than a couple of dozen, it had been bought when it was reduced to four bulging walls and a sagging roof. A team of local builders happy to have the cash in hand renovated it to very particular specifications, never doubting the reasons they were given for the desired features.

He savoured the preparations for his visitor. The sheets were clean, the clothes laid out. The phone was switched off, the answering machine turned down low, the fax shut away inside a drawer. The fibre optics might sing all night with calls for him, but he wouldn't be hearing them till morning. The table was covered with linen so white it seemed to glow in the dark. On it, crystal, silver and porcelain were arranged in traditional patterns. Red rosebuds in an engraved crystal vase, candles splendid in simple Georgian silver. Donna would be captivated. Of course, she wouldn't realize that it would be the last time she'd ever use cutlery.

He looked around, checking everything was as it should be. The chains and leather straps were all out of sight, the silken gag tucked away, the carpentry bench innocent of tools except for the permanently mounted vice. He had designed the workbench himself, all the tools arrayed on a solid piece of wood like the drop leaf of a table attached to the far end of the bench at ninety degrees to the work surface.

One last glance at his watch. Time to drive the Land Rover across the rutted field track to the empty B-road that would take him to Five Walls Halt with its isolated railway station. He lit the candles and smiled with sheer pleasure, confident now that she would have kept faith and silence alike.

Won't you come into my parlour, said the spider to the fly?

Tim Coughlan had finally had his prayers answered. He'd found the perfect spot. The loading bay was slightly less wide than the factory proper, leaving a recess about seven feet square at one end. At first glance, it looked as if the alcove was blocked off by flattened cardboard cartons stacked on their ends. If anyone had bothered to look more closely, they would have noticed that the cartons weren't tightly packed and that, with a little effort, it wouldn't be too hard to squeeze between them. Anyone inclined to investigate further would have found Tim Coughlan's bedsit, containing a stained and greasy sleeping bag and two carrier bags. The first bag contained one clean T-shirt, one clean pair of socks and one clean pair of underpants. The other held one dirty T-shirt, one dirty pair of socks, one dirty pair of boxer shorts and a pair of shapeless cords that might once have been dark brown but were now the colour of seabirds after the oil slick has trapped them.

Tim slouched in a corner of his space, the sleeping bag scrunched into a cushion beneath his bony buttocks. He was eating chips and curry sauce from a polystyrene container. He had the best part of a litre of cider left to wash it down and send him to sleep. He needed something on the cold nights to carry him forward into oblivion.

It had taken long months living rough on the streets before he'd emerged on the other side of the heroin haze that had robbed him of his life. He'd dropped so low that even drugs were above his reach. That, ironically, was what had saved him. Shivering through cold turkey in a Christmas charity shelter, he'd finally turned the corner. He'd started selling the *Big Issue* on street corners. He'd managed to put together enough cash to buy clothes from charity shops that looked like poverty rather than hopeless homelessness.

And he'd managed to find work on the docks. It was casual, poorly paid, cash in hand, the black economy at its gloomiest. But it was a start. And that was when he'd found his spot in the loading bay of an assembly plant too strapped for cash to afford a night watchman.

Since then, he'd managed to save nearly three hundred pounds, stashed in the building society account that was probably his only extant connection to his past. Soon, he'd have enough for the deposit and a month's rent on a proper place to live and enough to spare to feed himself while the dole dragged their feet over his claim.

Tim had hit bottom and nearly drowned. Soon, he was convinced, he'd be ready to swim back up to the daylight. He screwed up the chip container and tossed it into the corner. Then he opened the cider bottle and tipped the contents down his throat in a long series of quick gulps. The notion of savouring it never occurred to him. There was no reason why it should.

Opportunity had seldom knocked at Jacko Vance's door. Mostly, he'd gripped it by the throat and dragged it kicking and screaming to centre stage. He'd realized while he was still a child that the only way he was ever going to come by some luck was if he managed to make it himself. His mother, plagued by a kind of post-natal depression that had made him repugnant to her, had ignored him as far as possible. She hadn't actually been cruel, simply absent in any meaningful sense. His father had been the one who paid attention, most often of a negative sort.

He hadn't long been at school when the handsome child with the floppy blond hair, the hollow cheeks and the huge baffled eyes had realized that there was a point in having dreams, that things could be made to happen. His little-boy-lost appearance worked on some teachers like a blowtorch on an icicle. It didn't take him long to work out that he could manipulate them into playing accessories in his own particular power game. It didn't erase what happened at home, but it gave him an arena where he began to understand the pleasure of power.

Although he traded on his looks, Jacko never relied solely on the power of his charm. It was as if he had a built-in understanding that there would be those who needed different weaponry if they were to succumb. Since he'd had the work ethic instilled into him from the moment he had begun to comprehend the messages of speech, it was never a hardship to him to work for his effect. The sports field was the obvious place for him to focus, since he had a certain natural talent and it offered a wider arena to shine in than the narrow stage of the classroom. It was also an area where effort paid off visibly and spectacularly.

Inevitably, the elements of his behaviour that endeared him to those who had power alienated his contemporaries. Nobody ever loved a teacher's pet. He fought the obligatory fights, winning some and losing a few. When he did lose, he never forgot. Sometimes it took years, but he found ways to exact some sort of satisfactory revenge. Often, the victim of his vengeance never knew Jacko was behind his ultimate humiliation, but sometimes he did.

Everyone on the council estate where he'd grown up remembered how he'd got his own back on Danny Boy Ferguson. Danny Boy had been the bane of Jacko's life between the ages of ten and twelve, picking on him mercilessly. Finally, when Jacko had flown at him in a rage, Danny Boy had smashed him to the ground with one hand held ostentatiously above his head. Jacko's broken nose had healed without trace, but his black rage burned behind the charm that the adults saw.

When Jacko won his first junior British championship, he became an overnight hero on the estate. No one from there had ever had their picture in the national papers before, not even Liam Gascoigne when he dropped that concrete slab on Gladstone Sanders from the tenth floor. It wasn't hard to persuade Danny Boy's girlfriend Kimberley to come up west with him for a night on the town.

He'd wined and dined her for a week, then dumped her. That Sunday night in the local, just as Danny Boy was working up to his fifth pint, Jacko slipped the landlord fifty quid to broadcast over the pub's PA system the tape he'd secretly recorded of Kimberley telling him in graphic detail what a lousy fuck Danny Boy was.

When Micky Morgan had started visiting him in hospital, he'd recognized a kindred spirit. He wasn't sure what she wanted, but he had a strong feeling she wanted something. The day Jillie dumped him and Micky offered to help him out, he became certain.

Five minutes after she walked out of the ward, he hired the private eye. The man was good; the answers came even faster than he'd expected. By the time he read her handiwork in the headlines that screamed across all the tabloids, he understood Micky's motives and knew how best he could use her.

JACK THE LAD LETS LOVE GO! HEARTBREAK HERO! LOVE TORMENT OF TRAGIC JACK! He smiled and read on.

> Britain's bravest man has revealed he's making the greatest sacrifice of all.
>
> Days after he lost his Olympic dream saving the lives of two toddlers, Jacko Vance has broken his engagement to his childhood sweetheart Jillie Woodrow.
>
> Heartbroken Jacko, speaking from the hospital bed where he is recovering from the amputation of his javelin-throwing arm, said, 'I'm setting her free. I'm no longer the man she agreed to marry. It's not fair to expect her to carry on as before. I can't offer her the life we'd expected to have, and the most important thing to me is her happiness.
>
> 'I know she's upset now, but in the long run, she'll come to see I'm doing the right thing.'

Now Jillie could never deny his version of events without making herself look a complete bitch.

Jacko bided his time, playing along with Micky's proffered friendship. Then, when he deemed the moment was right, he struck like a rattler. 'OK, so when's payback day?' he asked, his eyes holding hers.

'Payback day?' she echoed, puzzled.

'The story of my love sacrifice,' he said, larding his words with heavy irony. 'Don't they call tales like that a nine-day wonder?'

'They do,' Micky said, continuing to arrange the flowers she'd brought in the tall vase she'd charmed from the nurse.

'Well, it's ten days now since the media broke the news. Jacko and Jillie are officially no longer headline material. I was wondering when I'd get the account for payment due.' His voice was mild, but looking into his eyes was like staring into a frozen puddle on high moorland.

Micky shook her head and perched on the edge of the bed, her face composed. But he knew her mind was racing, calculating how best to handle him. 'I'm not sure what you mean,' she stalled.

Jacko's smile was laced with condescension. 'Come on, Micky. I wasn't born yesterday. The world you work in, you've got to be a piranha. Favours don't get done in your circles without the full understanding that payback day is lurking somewhere in the background.'

He watched her consider lying and reject it; he waited while she considered the truth and rejected that, too. 'I'll settle for having one in the bank,' she tried.

'That's the way you want to play it, OK,' he said nonchalantly. His left hand suddenly snaked out and seized her wrist. 'But I'd have thought you and your girlfriend were in pretty dire need as of now.'

His large hand encircled her wrist. The sculpted muscles of his forearm stood out in strong relief, a shocking reminder of what he'd lost. The grip wasn't tight against her flesh, but she sensed it was unbreakable as the bracelet of a handcuff. Micky looked up from her wrist to his implacable face and he saw a momentary clutch of fear as she wondered what lay behind his impenetrable eyes. He made his face relax into a ghost of a smile and the instant passed. He saw himself reflected in her eyes, not a trace of sinister showing now. 'What a strange thing to say,' she said.

'It's not just journalists who have contacts,' Jacko said contemptuously. 'When you started taking an interest in me, I returned the compliment. Her name's Betsy Thorne, you've been together more than a year. She acts as your PA but she is also your lover. For Christmas you bought her a Bulova watch from a Bond Street jeweller's. Two weekends ago you shared a twin room overnight at a country house hotel near Oxford. You send her flowers on the twenty-third of each month. I could go on.'

'Circumstantial,' Micky said. Her voice was cool; the skin under his grip felt like a burning ring of flesh. 'And none of your business.'

'It's not the tabloids' business either, is it? But they're digging, Micky. It's only a matter of time. You know that.'

'They can't find what isn't there to be found,' she said, slipping into obstinacy as if it were a tailored blazer.

'They'll find it,' Jacko promised her. 'Which is where I might be able to help.'

'Supposing I did need help . . . what form would your help take?'

He released her wrist. Rather than pull her arm to her and rub it, Micky let it lie where he dropped it. 'Economists say good money drives out bad. It's like that with journalists. You should know. Give them a better story and they'll abandon their sordid little fishing expedition.'

'I won't argue with that. What did you have in mind?'

'What about, "Hospital romance for hero Jacko and TV journo?"' He raised one eyebrow. Micky wondered if he'd practised the gesture before the mirror in adolescence.

'What's in it for you?' she asked, after a moment when they'd each stared appraisingly at the other, as if measuring for romantic congruence.

'Peace and quiet,' Jacko said. 'You have no idea how many women there are out there who want to save me.'

'Maybe one of them would be the right one.'

Jacko laughed, a dry, bitter sound. 'It's the Groucho Marx principle, isn't it? Not wanting to be a member of any club that would let me in. A woman who's demented enough to think that, a) I need saving and b) that she's the person for the job is by definition the world's worst woman for me. No, Micky, what I need is camouflage. So that when I get out of here – which should be quite soon – I can go about my life without every brain-dead bimbo in Britain thinking I'm her chance at the big time. I don't want someone who feels sorry for me. Until somebody I choose comes along, I could use the erogenous equivalent of a bulletproof vest. Fancy the job?'

Now it was his turn to guess what was really happening behind her eyes. Micky was back in control of herself, maintaining the air of bland interest that would later stand her in good stead as the housebound nation's favourite interviewer. 'I don't do ironing,' was all she said.

'I've always wondered what a PA did,' Jacko said, his smile as wry as his tone.

'You better not let Betsy hear you say that.'

'Deal?'

Jacko covered her hand with his. 'Deal,' she said, turning her hand over and clasping his fingers in hers.

The stench hit Carol as soon as she opened her car door. There was nothing quite as disgusting as barbecued human flesh, and once smelled, it could never be erased from the memory. Trying not to gag too obviously, she walked the short distance to where Jim Pendlebury appeared to be conducting an impromptu press conference under the fire brigade's portable arc lights. She'd spotted the journalists as soon as her driver had turned into the car park, and she'd asked to be dropped nearby, well away from the phalanx of scarlet engines where fire officers were still spraying a smouldering warehouse with water. High above his colleagues, one man on a cherry picker sent a soaring arc of water above their heads on to the flaking remains of the roof. Milling around behind the fire brigade were half a dozen uniformed police officers. One or two watched Carol's arrival with vague interest, but soon turned back to the more absorbing vista of the fag end of the fire.

Carol hung back as Pendlebury gave brief and noncommittal answers for the benefit of local radio and press. Once they realized they would get nothing much out of the fire chief at that stage, they dispersed. If any of them paid attention to the blonde in the trench coat, they probably assumed she was another reporter. Only the crime reporters had met Carol so far, and it was too early for this to have graduated from a news headline into a crime story. As soon as the night-shift news reporters called in that the factory fire was not only fatal but also suspected arson, the jackals on the crime beat would have their morning assignments on a plate. One or two of them might even be turfed out of bed as unceremoniously as she had been.

Pendlebury greeted Carol with a grim smile. 'The smell of hell,' he said.

'Unmistakably.'

'Thanks for turning out.'

'Thanks for tipping me off. Otherwise I'd have known nothing about it till I got into the office and read the overnights. And then I'd have missed the joys of a fresh crime scene,' she said wryly.

'Well, after our little chat the other day, I knew this one would be right up your street.'

'You think it's our serial arsonist?'

'I wouldn't have phoned you at home at half past three in the morning if I hadn't been pretty sure,' he said.

'So what have we got?'

'Want to have a look?'

'In a minute. First, I'd appreciate a verbal briefing while I'm in a position to concentrate on what you're saying rather than on what my stomach's doing.'

Pendlebury looked slightly surprised, as if he expected her to take such horrors in her stride. 'Right,' he said, sounding disconcerted. 'We got the call just after two, from one of your patrol cars, actually. They'd been cruising and saw the flames. We had two units here within seven minutes, but the place was well ablaze. Another three tenders were here inside the half-hour, but there was no way we were going to save the building.'

'And the body?'

'As soon as they had the fire damped down at this end of the warehouse – which took about half an hour – the officers became aware of the smell. That was when they called me out. I'm on permanent stand-by for all fatal fires. Your lads called in CID, and I called you.'

'So where is the body?'

Pendlebury pointed to one side of the building. 'As far as we can tell, it was in the corner of the loading bay. There seems to have been a kind of alcove at one end. Looking at the ash, there was probably a load of cardboard stashed at the front of it. We've not been able to get in yet, it's still too hot and too chancy in terms of walls coming down, but from what we can see and what we can smell, I'd say the body's behind or underneath all that wet ash down the back of that recess.'

'There's no doubt in your mind that there's definitely a body in there?' Carol was grasping at straws, and she knew it.

'There's only one thing that smells like roast human, and that's roast human,' Pendlebury said bluntly. 'Besides, I think you can just about see the outline of the body. Come on, I'll show you.'

A couple of minutes later, Carol stood by Pendlebury's side at what he claimed was a safe distance from the smoking ruin. It felt uncomfortably warm to her, but she had learned when to trust the expertise of others during her years in the force. To have hung back would have been insulting. As Pendlebury pointed out the contours of the blackened forms the fire and water had left at the end of the loading bay, she found herself irresistibly forming the same conclusion as the fire chief.

'When can the scene-of-crime people start work?' she asked dully.

Pendlebury pulled a face. 'Later this morning?'

She nodded. 'I'll make sure the team's on stand-by.' She turned away. 'This is exactly what I didn't want to happen,' she said, half to herself.

'It was bound to happen sooner or later. Law of averages,' Pendlebury said lightly, falling into step with her as she walked back towards her car.

'We should have been all over this arsonist ages ago,' Carol said, angrily searching through her pockets for a tissue to wipe the wet ash from her trainers. 'It's sloppy policing. He should have been nabbed by now. It's our fault that he's still on the loose to kill people.'

'You're not being fair on yourself,' Pendlebury protested. 'You've only been here five minutes, and you picked up on it right away. You mustn't blame yourself.'

Carol looked up from her attempts at cleaning her shoes and scowled. 'I'm not blaming myself, though maybe we could have put a bit more effort into the case. I'm saying that somewhere along the line the police on this patch have let down the people they're supposed to serve. And maybe you should have been a bit more forceful about making the point to my predecessor that you thought you had a firebug.'

Pendlebury looked shocked. He couldn't remember the last time he'd been criticized to his face by a member of another emergency service. 'I think you're a bit out of order, Chief Inspector,' he said, made pompous by his outrage.

'I'm sorry you feel like that,' Carol said stiffly, standing up and straightening her shoulders. 'But if we're going to have a productive working relationship, there's no room for cosiness at the expense of honesty. I expect you to tell me if we're not keeping our end of the deal. And when I see things I don't like, I'll call them. I don't want to fall out with you about this. I want to catch this guy. But we're not going to make any progress if we all stand around saying it can't be helped that some poor bastard is lying there dead.'

For a moment, they glared at each other, Pendlebury uncertain how to deal with her fiery determination. Then he spread his hands in a conciliatory gesture. 'I'm sorry. You're right. I shouldn't have taken no for an answer.'

Carol smiled and thrust out her hand. 'Let's both try and get it right from now in, OK?'

They shook on it. 'Deal,' he said. 'I'll talk to you later, when the forensics team have been all over it.'

As she drove off, Carol had room for only one thought. She had a serial arsonist who had now become a killer on her patch. Catching him was the only show in town. By the time the forensics team had something positive to tell her, she intended to have a draft profile. By the time the inquest opened, she meant to have a suspect in custody. If John Brandon had thought she was driven when they'd worked together in Bradfield, he was in for a surprise. Carol Jordan was out to prove a lot of points to a lot of people. And if she felt discouraged along the way, the stink that clung to her nostrils would be impetus enough to get her moving again.

Shaz turned over and looked at the clock. Twenty minutes to seven. Only ten minutes since she'd looked at it last. She wasn't going to fall asleep again, not now. If she was honest, she thought as she got out of bed and made for the bathroom, she probably wasn't going to sleep properly until Chris had delivered on her promise.

Asking the favour had been less awkward than she'd expected, Shaz reflected as she sat on the loo and leaned over to turn on the bath taps. Time seemed to have smoothed the rough edges of her relationship with Detective Sergeant Devine until it was back where it had been before misunderstandings and false moves had abraded it to a series of painful snags.

From the start of Shaz's career in the Met, Chris Devine had represented everything Shaz aspired to. There had been only two women in CID at the station where Shaz was based in West London, and Chris was the higher ranking. It was obvious why. She was a good cop with one of the best arrest records in the division. Rock solid in a crisis, hard working, imaginative and incorruptible, she also demonstrably possessed a brain and a sense of humour. Even more importantly, she could be one of the lads without ever letting anyone forget she was a woman.

Shaz had studied her like a specimen under a microscope. Where Chris was, she wanted to be, and she wanted that same respect. Already she'd seen too many women officers dismissed as plonks or slits, and she was determined that would never happen to her. Shaz knew that as a brand new uniformed constable, she was an insignificant dot somewhere in Chris's peripheral vision, but somehow she insinuated herself into the older woman's consciousness until, whenever they were in the station taking refs at the same time, they could invariably be found in a corner of the canteen drinking brutally strong tea and talking shop.

The very day Shaz became eligible for a CID aide posting, she'd submitted her name. Chris's recommendation was enough to swing it and, a few weeks later, Shaz found herself on her first night-shift stakeout with Chris. It took her rather longer to realize that Chris was gay, and had been working on the assumption that Shaz's hot pursuit was sexual rather than professional. The night her sergeant kissed her had been the worst moment of her police career.

For an instant, she'd almost gone along with it, so deep-rooted was her ambition. Then reality had clicked in. Shaz might not have been much good at forming relationships, but she knew enough about herself to be clear that it was very definitely men rather than women that she wasn't connecting with. She'd recoiled from Chris's embrace more vigorously than from a sawn-off shotgun. The aftermath was something neither Shaz nor Chris could recall without an uncomfortable mixture of emotions; humiliation, embarrassment, anger and betrayal. The sensible option would probably have been for one of them to seek a transfer, but Chris wasn't prepared to abandon a patch she knew like her own back garden, and Shaz was too stubborn to give up her first best chance at making it on to a permanent CID appointment.

So they'd established an awkward armistice that allowed them to stay on the same team, though whenever they could avoid working shift together, they did. Six months before Shaz's move to Leeds, Chris had been promoted and transferred to New Scotland Yard. They hadn't spoken from that day until Shaz had fetched up on Chris's doorstep looking for a favour.

Shaz chopped fresh fruit into her muesli and reflected that it had been easier than she'd expected to swallow her pride and ask Chris for help, possibly because Chris had been wrong-footed by the presence in her flat – and, clearly, her bed – of a fingerprint technician Shaz remembered from Notting Hill Gate. When Shaz had explained what she wanted, Chris had agreed immediately, understanding exactly why Shaz was so eager to push far beyond what her course leader expected from his officers. And, again as if fate had taken a hand in Shaz's life, it happened that Chris was off duty the following day, so garnering Shaz's information in the minimal time available would be simple.

As she absently shovelled breakfast into her mouth, she imagined Chris spending her day in the national newspaper archives at Colindale, copying page after page of local papers until she'd covered the period surrounding each of the seven disappearances that had captured Shaz's imagination. Shaz ran her empty cereal bowl under the hot tap with happy anticipation swelling inside. She couldn't say why she was so certain, but she was convinced that the first steps on her journey of proof would be waymarked in the local press.

She'd never been wrong so far. Except, of course, about Chris. But that, she told herself, had been different.

'The kind of cases we'll be working are the ones that leave most police officers feeling edgy. That's because the perpetrators are dancing to a different beat from the rest of us,' Tony looked around, double-checking that they were listening to him rather than shuffling through their papers. Leon looked as if he'd rather be somewhere else, but Tony had grown accustomed to his affectations and no longer took them at face value. Satisfied, he continued. 'Knowing you're dealing with someone who has manufactured their own set of rules is a very unsettling experience for anyone, even trained police officers. Because we come in from the outside to make sense of the bizarre, there's a tendency to lump us as part of the problem rather than the solution, so it's important that the first thing we concentrate on is building a rapport with the investigating officers. You've all come here from CID work – any ideas about the sort of thing that might work?'

Simon jumped straight in. 'Take them out for a pint?' he suggested. The others groaned and catcalled at his predictability.

Tony's smile came nowhere near his eyes. 'Chances are they'll have half a dozen good excuses why they can't come to the pub with you. Any other ideas?'

Shaz raised her pen. 'Work your socks off. If they see you're a grafter, they'll give you some respect.'

'Either that or think you're brown-nosing the bosses,' Leon sneered.

'It's not a bad idea,' Tony said, 'though Leon does have a point. If you're going to go down that road, you also need to demonstrate a complete contempt for everyone over the rank of DCI, which can be wearing, not to say counterproductive.' They laughed. 'What does the trick for me is incredibly simple.' He gave them a last questioning look. 'No? How about flattery?'

A couple nodded sagely. Leon's lip curled and he snorted. 'More brown-nosing.'

'I prefer to think of it as one technique among many in the arsenal of the profiler. I don't use it for personal advancement; I use it for the benefit of the casework,' Tony corrected him mildly. 'I have a mantra that I trot out at every available opportunity.' He shifted his position slightly, but that small change altered his body language from comfortable authority to subordinate. His smile was self-deprecating. 'Of course,' he said ingratiatingly, 'I don't solve murders. It's bobbies that do that.' Then, just as swiftly, he returned to his previous posture. 'It works for me. It might not work for you. But it's never going to do any harm to tell the investigating officers how much you respect their work and how you're just a tiny cog that might make their machine work better.' He paused for a moment. 'You have to tell them this at least five times a day.' They were all grinning now.

'Once you've done that, there's a reasonable chance they'll give you the information you need to draw up your profile. If you can't be bothered making the effort, they're likely to hold as much back as they can get away with because they see you as a rival for the glory of solving a high-profile case. So. You've got the investigating officers on your side, and you've got your evidence. It's time to work on the profile. First you assess probabilities.'

He stood up and began to prowl round the perimeter of the room, like a big cat checking the limits of its domain. 'Probability is the only god of the profiler. To abandon probability for the alternative demands the strongest evidence. The downside of that is that there will be times when you end up with so much egg on your face you'll look like an omelette on legs.'

Already, he could feel his heart rate increasing and still he hadn't said a word about the case. 'I had that experience myself on the last major case I worked. We were dealing with a serial killer of young men. I had all the information that was available to the police, thanks to a brilliant liaison officer. On the basis of the evidence, I drew up a profile. The liaison officer made a couple of suggestions based on her instincts. One of those suggestions was an interesting idea I hadn't thought of because I didn't know as much about information technology as she did. But equally, because it was something only a small proportion of the population would know about, I assigned it a moderately low probability. Normally, that would mean the investigation team would assign it low priority, but they were stuck for leads, so they pursued it. It turned out she'd been right, but in itself it didn't move the investigation much further forward.'

His hands were clammy with perspiration, but now he was actually confronting the details that still shredded his nights, his stomach had stopped clenching. It was less effort than he'd expected to continue his analysis. 'Her other suggestion I discounted out of hand because it was completely off the wall. It ran counter to everything I knew about serial killers.' Tony met their curious stares. His tension had transmitted itself to the entire squad and they sat silent and motionless, waiting for what would come next.

'My disregard for her suggestion nearly cost me my life,' he said simply, reaching his seat and sitting down again. He looked around the room, surprised he could speak so levelly. 'And you know something? I was right to ignore her. Because, on a scale of one to a hundred, her proposition was so unlikely it wouldn't even register.'

As soon as the formal confirmation of the body in the blaze came through, Carol called a meeting of her team. This time, there were no chocolate biscuits. 'I expect you've all heard this morning's news,' she said flatly as they arranged themselves around her office, Tommy Taylor straddling the only chair apart from Carol's on the basis that he was the sergeant. He might have been brought up never to sit while women were standing, but he'd long since stopped thinking of Di Earnshaw as a woman.

'Aye,' he said.

'Poor bugger,' Lee Whitbread chimed in.

'Poor bugger nothing,' Tommy protested. 'He shouldn't have been there, should he?'

Repelled but not surprised, Carol said, 'Whether he should or shouldn't have been there, he's dead, and we're supposed to be looking for the person who killed him.' Tommy looked mutinous, folding his arms across the chair back and planting his feet more firmly on the floor, but Carol refused to respond to the challenge. 'Arson's always a time bomb,' she continued. 'And this time it's gone off right in our faces. Today has not been the proudest day of my career to date. So what have you got for me?'

Lee, leaning against the filing cabinet, shifted his shoulders. 'I went through all the back files for the last six months. Leastways, all I could get my hands on,' he corrected himself. 'I found quite a few incidents like you told us to look for, some off night-shift CID reports, some off the uniform lads. I was planning on getting them collated on paper today.'

'Di and me, we've been re-interviewing the victims, like you said. There doesn't seem to be any linking factor that we've come across so far,' Tommy said, his voice distant following Carol's snub.

'A variety of insurance companies, that kind of thing,' Di amplified.

'What about a racial motive?' Carol asked.

'Some Asian victims, but not what you'd call enough to make it look significant,' Di said.

'Have we spoken to the insurers themselves yet?'

Di looked at Tommy and Lee stared out of the window. Tommy cleared his throat. 'It was on Di's list for today. First chance she's had.'

Unimpressed, Carol shook her head. 'Right. Here's what we do next. I've had some experience in offender profiling . . .' She stopped when Tommy muttered something. 'I'm sorry, Sergeant Taylor, did you have a contribution?'

Confidence restored, Tommy grinned insolently back at Carol. 'I said, "We'd heard," ma'am.'

For a moment, Carol said nothing, merely staring him down. It was situations like this that could make the job degenerate into a misery if they weren't handled right. So far, it was only cheeky disrespect. But if she let it go, it would quickly slide into full-scale insubordination. When she spoke, her voice was quiet but chill. 'Sergeant, I can't think why you have this burning ambition to go back into uniform and play at community policing, but I'll be more than happy to oblige you if CID work continues not to be to your taste.'

Lee's mouth twitched in spite of himself; Di Earnshaw's dark eyes narrowed, waiting for the explosion that never came. Tommy pushed his shirtsleeves above his elbows, looked Carol straight in the eye and said, 'Reckon I'd better show you what I'm made of then, Guv.'

Carol nodded. 'You better had, Tommy. Now, I'm going to work on a profile, but to make that anything more than a bit of an academic exercise, I'm going to need a lot of raw data. Since we can't find any evidence of linkage between the victims, I'm going to stick my neck out and say we've got a thrill seeker rather than a torch for hire. Which means we're looking for a young adult male. He's probably unemployed, likely to be single and still living with his parents. I'm not going to go into all the psychobabble about social inadequacy and all that right now. What we need to look for is someone with a record of police contact for petty nuisance offences, vandalism, substance abuse, that sort of thing. Maybe minor sex offences. Peeping Tom, exposing himself. He's not going to be a mugger, a burglar, a thief, a fly boy. He's going to be a sad bastard. In and out of minor bother since he was a pre-teen. He probably doesn't have a car, so we need to look at the geography of the fires; chances are if you drew a line linking the outermost fires, he'll live inside its boundaries. He'll probably have watched all the fires from a vantage point, so have a think about where that might have been and who might have witnessed him there.

'You know the ground. It's your job to bring me suspects that we can match against my profile. Lee, I want you to talk to the collator and see who uniform know that fits those criteria. I'll get going on a fuller profile and Tommy and Di will do the routine work-up on the crime itself, liaising with forensics and organizing a door-to-door in the area. Hell, I don't have to tell you how to run a murder inquiry . . .'

A knock at the door interrupted Carol's flow. 'Come in,' she called.

The door opened on John Brandon. It was, Carol realized, a measure of how far she had to go before she'd be accepted into the East Yorkshire force that no one had stuck a head round the door to warn her the chief was on his way. She jumped to her feet, Tommy nearly toppled in his hurry to get out of his chair and Lee cracked his elbow on the filing cabinet pushing himself upright. Only Di Earnshaw was already in place, standing against the back wall with her arms folded across her chest. 'Sorry to interrupt, DCI Jordan,' Brandon said pleasantly. 'A word?'

'Certainly, sir. We're pretty much finished here. You three know what we're after, I'll leave you to it.' Carol's smile managed to dismiss as well as encourage and the three junior officers edged out of the office with barely a backward glance.

Brandon waved Carol to her seat as he folded his long body into the guest chair. 'This fatal fire at Wardlaw's,' he began without formalities.

Carol nodded. 'I was out there earlier.'

'So I heard. One of your series then, I take it?'

'I think so. It's got all the hallmarks of it. I'm waiting to hear from the fire investigators, but Jim Pendlebury, the fire chief, reckons it's got generic similarities to the earlier incidents we'd identified.'

Brandon chewed one side of his lower lip. It was the first time Carol had ever seen him look anything other than completely composed. He breathed heavily through his nose and said, 'I know we talked about this before and you were convinced that you could handle it. I'm not saying that you can't, because I think you're a bloody good detective, Carol. But I want Tony Hill to take a look at this.'

'There's really no need,' Carol said, feeling heat spreading up her chest and into her neck. 'Certainly not at this stage.'

Brandon's gloomy bloodhound face seemed to grow even longer. 'It's no slur on your competence,' he said.

'I'm bound to say that's what it looks like from here,' Carol said, trying not to sound as mutinous as she felt, forcing herself to remember how angry Tommy Taylor's earlier impertinence had made her feel. 'Sir, we've barely started our own inquiries. It may well be that we'll have this whole thing wrapped up in a matter of days. There can't be that many potential suspects in Seaford who fit the serial arsonist profile.'

Brandon shifted in his chair, as if struggling to find an appropriate arrangement for his long legs. 'I find myself in a slightly awkward position here, Carol. I've never been happy with the "theirs not to reason why" approach to command. I've always thought things run better when my officers understand why I issue the orders I do rather than having to rely on blind obedience. On the other hand, for operational reasons, sometimes things have to be taken on trust. And when other units outside my command are involved, even when I think there's no earthly reason for confidentiality, I have to respect what they ask for. If you follow me?' He raised his eyebrows in an anxious question. If any of his officers could read between so oblique a set of lines, it would be Carol Jordan.

Carol frowned as she digested Brandon's words. 'So, hypothetically,' she eventually said, taking her time to think through what she was saying, 'if a new unit was being set up with a specialist area of responsibility, and they wanted a sympathetic force to let them use one of their cases as a sort of guinea pig, even if you thought the officer in charge had a right to know what the score was, you'd be obliged to go along with their demand for confidentiality as to the real reason why they were being handed the case? That sort of thing, sir?'

Brandon smiled gratefully. 'Speaking purely hypothetically, yes.'

There was no answering smile. 'This wouldn't be an appropriate occasion for such an experiment, in my opinion.' She paused. 'Sir.'

Brandon looked surprised. 'Why not?' he asked.

Carol thought for a moment. Few fast-track graduates climbed the greasy pole as fast as she'd done, particularly women. John Brandon's patronage had given her more than she could ever have expected. And she couldn't even be certain if her real reasons for reluctance were the ones she was about to voice. Nevertheless, she'd stuck her neck out this far and she'd never been a quitter. 'We're a new force,' she said carefully. 'I've only just arrived to work with a group of people who have been a team for a long time. I'm trying to build up a working relationship that will allow us to protect and serve our community. I can't do that if I'm stripped of the first major case that's crossed my desk since I got here.'

'No one's talking about taking the case away from you, Chief Inspector,' Brandon said, reflecting Carol's formality. 'We're talking about using the new task force on a consultancy basis.'

'It'll look like you've no confidence in me,' Carol insisted.

'That's nonsense. If I had no confidence in your abilities, why on earth would I have appointed you to a promoted post?'

Carol shook her head in disbelief. He really didn't get it. 'I'm sure the canteen cowboys won't have any trouble coming up with ideas on that score, sir,' she said bitterly.

Brandon's eyes widened as he grasped her meaning. 'You think they ... That can't be ... It's ridiculous! I never heard anything so absurd!'

'If you say so, sir.' Carol managed a twisted smile and ran a hand through her shaggy blonde hair. 'I didn't think I looked that rough.'

Brandon shook his head in disbelief. 'It never occurred to me that people would misinterpret your promotion. You're self-evidently such a good copper.' He sighed and chewed his lip again. 'Now I'm in an even worse position than I was when I walked in.' He looked up at her and made a decision.

'I'm going to speak off the record. Paul Bishop has been having liaison problems with the local brass in Leeds. They've made it clear they don't want his team on their ground and they won't let him near any of their crimes. He needs a real case for his officers to learn their trade, and for obvious reasons, he doesn't want some high-profile serial killer or rapist. He rang me because we're next door to him and he asked me to keep an eye out for something that might do for his squad to cut their teeth on before they're officially available to catch cases from every Tom, Dick and Harry. To be perfectly honest, I was going to offer them your serial arsonist even before it turned fatal.'

Carol tried to keep her anger out of her face. It was always the way. Just when you thought you'd got them house-trained, they reverted to Neanderthal. 'It's a murder now. You don't get much more high profile than that,' she said. 'For my own self-respect, never mind the respect of my team, I need to head the investigation. I do not need to be seen to be hanging on the coat-tails of the National Offender Profiling Task Force,' she continued coldly. 'If I'd thought sending in visiting firemen was the best way to police serious crime, I'd have applied to join them. I can't believe you'd undermine me like this. Sir.' The last word came out like a expletive.

Brandon's method of dealing with threatened insubordination was very different from Carol's. A man in his position had little need of veiled threats; he could afford to be more creative. 'I have no intention of undermining any of my officers, DCI Jordan. That's why you will be the only officer who has direct dealings with the task force. You will go to them in Leeds, they will not come on our ground. I will make it clear to Commander Bishop that his officers will discuss the case with no other officer of the East York-shire force. I trust you will find that satisfactory?'

Carol couldn't help feeling a grudging respect for the speed with which her chief had thought on his feet. 'You've made your orders perfectly clear,' she said, leaning back in resignation.

Relieved that the crisis had been resolved without anything that would have been embarrassing to report back to Maggie, Brandon got to his feet with a relaxed smile. 'Thanks, Carol. I appreciate it. Funny, I could have sworn you'd have jumped at the chance to work with Tony Hill again. The two of you hit it off so well when you worked liaison on the Bradfield murders.'

She coaxed her muscles to conjure up a smile from memory and hoped it would pass for the real thing. 'My reluctance was nothing to do with Dr Hill,' she said, wondering whether Brandon would believe her when she couldn't even convince herself.

'I'll let them know you'll be in touch.' Brandon closed the door on his way out, a courtesy Carol was profoundly grateful for.

'I can hardly wait,' she said grimly to the empty room.

*　　*　　*

Shaz bounced through the door of the police station where the task force was based and grinned at the uniformed officer behind the desk with cheerful expectation. 'DC Bowman,' she said. 'NOP task force. There should be a package for me?'

The constable looked sceptical. 'Here?'

'That's right.' She glanced at her watch. 'It was supposed to be sent by overnight courier. For delivery by nine a.m. And since my watch says it's ten past . . .'

'Then you owe somebody a bollocking, because there's nowt here for you, love,' the constable said, incapable of keeping the satisfaction out of his voice. It wasn't often he had the chance to score a point against a task force outsider *and* patronize a woman in a single go.

'You sure?' Shaz asked, trying not to show the consternation that she knew would only increase his smugness.

'I've got my reading badge, love. Trust me, I'm a bobby. There's no package here for you.' Bored now, he ostentatiously turned away and pretended to be interested in a pile of paperwork.

Fizzing with frustration, her good mood history, Shaz bypassed the bank of lifts and jogged up the five flights of stairs to the task force operations room. 'Never trust someone else, never trust someone else,' pounded in her head in sync with her feet on the stairs and the blood in her ears. She marched straight into the room that held their computer terminals and threw herself into her chair, barely managing to grunt a greeting to Simon, the only other occupant of the room. Shaz grabbed her phone and punched in Chris's home number. 'Bugger!' she muttered when the answering machine picked up. She yanked her personal organizer out of her bag and keyed in Chris's name. Her index finger stabbed out the direct line at New Scotland Yard. The phone was answered on the second ring. 'Devine.'

'It's Shaz.'

'Whatever it is you're after, the answer's no, doll. I don't think I'm ever going to get the dust and ink out from under my fingernails after yesterday's little exercise. Definitely a non-starter on the "fun things to do with your day off" list.'

'I really appreciate it, you know that. Only . . .'

Chris groaned. 'What, Shaz?'

'The stuff hasn't arrived.'

Chris snorted. 'That all? Listen, by the time I'd got finished –

which I have to tell you I only managed by flashing the old warrant card and roping the staff in – it was too late to get an overnight delivery. Best they could do was by noon. So you should get it some time this morning. All right?'

'It'll have to be,' Shaz said, aware she was being ungracious, but unable to care.

'Relax, doll. It's never the end of the world. You're going to give yourself an ulcer,' Chris told her.

'I've got to present my case tomorrow afternoon,' Shaz pointed out.

Chris laughed. 'So what's the problem? 'King hell, Shaz, that Yorkshire air's slowing you up. Time was, you were greased lightning. You got a whole night to turn it around. Don't tell me you're getting soft.'

'I do like the odd bit of sleep between dusk and dawn,' Shaz said.

'Just as well you and me never got it together, then, isn't it? Gimme a call if you haven't got the stuff by the middle of the afternoon, all right, doll? Just hang loose. Nobody's going to die.'

'I flaming hope not,' Shaz said to a dead line.

'Problems?' Simon asked, plonking himself down next to her and pushing a mug of coffee towards her.

Shaz shrugged, reaching for the brew. 'Just some stuff I wanted to check out before we report back on the exercise tomorrow.'

Simon's interest suddenly expanded beyond the erotic possibilities of a fling with Shaz. 'You on to something?' he asked, trying for nonchalant and failing.

Shaz's grin was evil. 'You mean you haven't spotted the cluster?'

'Course I have. Saw it right away, no messing,' he said, clearly blustering.

'Right. So you also found the external link?' Shaz enjoyed the momentary blankness that crossed Simon's milk-pale face before he regained command. She snorted with laughter. 'Good try, Simon.'

He shook his head. 'All right, Shaz, you win. Will you tell me what you've got if I buy you dinner tonight?'

'I'll tell you what I've got tomorrow afternoon, same time as I tell everybody else. But if the offer's genuine and not just a bribe, I'd say yes to a drink before we go for the curry on Saturday night.'

Simon thrust out his hand. 'Deal, DC Bowman.' Shaz took his hand and matched his grip.

The prospect of a pre-dinner drink with Simon, enticing though it was, couldn't distract Shaz from the anticipation of her parcel. At coffee break, she was at the front counter before the others had even brewed up. For the rest of the morning, as Paul Bishop took them through the application of a profile to a suspect list, Shaz, normally the most attentive of students, fidgeted like a four-year-old at the opera. As soon as they broke for lunch, Shaz was off down the stairs like a greyhound out of a trap.

This time, her prayers were answered. A cardboard archive box sealed with what looked like an entire roll of packing tape sat on the front counter. 'Any longer and I'd have phoned the bomb disposal squad to get rid of it,' the desk officer said. 'We're a police station, not a post office.'

'Just as well. You'd never stand the pace.' Shaz swept the box off the counter and marched out to the car park with it. She opened the boot of her car and snatched a quick look at her watch. She reckoned she had about ten minutes to spare before her absence from the communal lunch table would excite comment. Hastily, she ripped at the packing tape with her fingernails, managing to unpick it enough to force the lid open.

Her heart sank. The box was almost brimful of photocopies. For a brief moment, she wondered if she couldn't just ignore her hunch. Then she thought of the seven teenage girls, their faces smiling up at her with all the expectation that, however many disappointments life might hold, at least they'd have a life. This wasn't just an exercise. Somewhere out there was a cold-hearted killer. And the only person who seemed to be aware of it was Shaz Bowman. Even if it did take all night, she owed them that effort at the very least.

Seeing him again face to face, Carol was stuck by the realization that it was pain that lurked behind Tony Hill's face. All the time she'd known him, she'd never recognized what underpinned his intensity. She'd always assumed that he was like her, driven only by the desire to capture and understand, fired by a passion to elucidate, haunted by the things he'd seen, heard and done. Now, distance had allowed her to comprehend what she had failed to see before, and she found herself wondering how different her behaviour towards him would have been had she really grasped what was going on behind his dark and troubled eyes.

Of course, he'd arranged it so that they would not be alone when they first encountered each other after the intervening months. Paul Bishop had been despatched to greet her when she'd arrived at the task force base in Leeds, smothering her in the charm that had made him such a media darling. His gallantry didn't extend to offering to carry her two briefcases heavy with case files, and Carol noticed with amusement that he couldn't pass a reflective surface without checking his appearance for imperfection, now smoothing an eyebrow, now straightening broad shoulders in a uniform that had plainly been made to measure. 'I can't tell you how thrilled I am to meet you,' he said. 'John Brandon's best and brightest. Some accolade in itself, never mind your track record. That speaks for itself, of course. Did John mention we'd been at staff college together? What a copper that man is, and what a talent spotter.' His enthusiasm was infectious and Carol found herself responding to his flattery in spite of her best intentions.

'I've always enjoyed working with Mr Brandon,' she said. 'How are things bedding down with the task force?'

'Oh, you'll see all that for yourself,' he said dismissively, ushering her into the lift. 'Of course, Tony's been singing your praises to the heavens. What a joy you are to work with, what a delightful colleague, how bright, how easy to deal with.' He grinned down at her. 'And the rest.'

Now Carol knew he was a bullshitter. She had no doubt as to Tony's professional respect for her, but she knew him well enough to be certain he would never have spoken about her in personal terms. His ingrained reticence would have taken far greater subtlety and skill to penetrate than Paul Bishop clearly possessed. Tony would never talk about Carol because to do so, he'd have to talk about the case that had brought them together. And that would mean revealing far more about both of them than any stranger had a right to know. He'd have had to explain how she'd fallen for him and how his sexual inadequacies forced him to reject her, how any hope of them ever getting together had been the last victim of the murderous psychopath they'd tracked. She felt in her bones that he would never have told another living soul these things, and if there was one thing that raised her above her colleagues, it was her instinct. 'Mmm,' she said noncommittally. 'I've always admired Dr Hill's professionalism.' Bishop brushed against her hip as he pushed the button for the fifth floor. If I'd been a man, Carol thought, he'd just have told me which floor to go for.

'It's a real bonus for us that you've worked with Tony before,' Bishop continued, eyeing his hair in the brushed metal doors. 'Our new trainees will be able to learn a lot from watching how you divide up the process, how you communicate, what you both need from each other.'

'"You know my methods, Watson,"' Carol parodied wryly.

Bishop looked momentarily puzzled, then his face cleared. 'Ah, yes.' The lift opened. 'This way. We're going to have coffee together, just the three of us, then you and Tony can work through the initial contact interview with the students looking on.' He strode down the corridor and held a door open for her, standing back while she entered what looked like a scaled-down scruffy school staff-room.

Across the room, Tony Hill swung round, coffee filter in one hand, spoon in the other. His eyes widened at the sight of Carol and she felt a slow smile spread irresistibly across her face. 'Tony,' she said, managing to keep her voice formal. 'How nice to see you.'

'Carol,' he greeted her, dropping the teaspoon on the table with a clatter. 'You look . . . well. You look well.'

She'd have been lying if she'd said the same to him. He was still pale, though she'd seen him paler. The dark smudges under his eyes were less like bruises than they'd been the last time the two of them had stared at each other, but they were still the badges of someone to whom eight hours' sleep was the impossible dream. His eyes had lost some of the strain she'd grown accustomed to seeing there after their one memorable case had finally been resolved, but he still looked tense. Regardless, she wanted to kiss him.

Instead, she placed her briefcases on the long coffee table and said, 'Any chance of a brew, then?'

'Strong, black, no sugar?' Tony checked with the hint of a smile.

'You must have made an impression,' Bishop said, striding past Carol and dropping into one of the sagging chairs, carefully lifting the knees of his trousers to avoid bagging them. 'He can't remember from one day to the next how I like mine.'

'When we worked together before, it was the kind of situation where every detail is engraved on your brain forever,' Carol said repressively.

Tony flashed her a quick look of gratitude then turned away to brew up. 'Thanks for sending the case files over,' he said against the wheezing of the elderly electric kettle. 'I've had them copied and the team have had them to study overnight.'

'Fine. How do you want to play this?' Carol asked.

'I thought we could go into live role-play,' Tony said, still with his back to them as he made the coffee. 'Sit across a table from each other and run through the case file exactly the way we would do it for real.' He half-turned with a tentative smile and a spasm ran across Carol's stomach.

Get a grip, she told herself angrily. Even if he could, he wouldn't want you. Remember? 'That sounds fine,' she heard herself say. 'How were you planning on involving the trainees?'

Tony juggled the three hot mugs in his broad square hands and managed to get them on to the coffee table without spilling much on the tobacco brown carpet. 'Specially chosen to hide the stains,' he muttered, frowning in concentration.

'There's half a dozen of them,' Bishop said. 'So it's not feasible to let them each have a crack at you, even if you were willing to give up that much of your time. They'll watch you and Tony work through the case files. Then, if they have any questions about that part of the process, they'll ask them. After you've gone, Tony will work with them on the drawing up of a profile, which will be passed back to you in a matter of days. What we're hoping is that when you develop a suspect to the point of arresting and charging, you'll liaise with Tony on interview strategies and allow us access to the taped interviews afterwards.' His smile said he wasn't accustomed to being refused.

'That may not be possible,' Carol said cautiously, not completely sure of her position. 'You may have to wait until after a trial to have access to the interview tapes, and then only if the interviewee agrees. I'll need to take advice on that.'

Tiny movements of muscle beneath the skin stripped Bishop's face of its bonhomie. 'My impression from Mr Brandon was that we weren't being slavish about formalities on this one,' he said briskly.

'I'm the investigating officer here, Commander. This is not a classroom exercise. It's an inquiry into an unlawful death and it's my intention to get a conviction if that's appropriate. I will take absolutely no risk that could cost me a successful prosecution. I don't leave windows open for smart defence counsel.'

'She's right,' Tony said unexpectedly. 'We get carried away with ourselves here. It's heady stuff, you know, Paul. The bottom line is, Carol has to make the case against this arsonist stand up in court, and we can't expect her to go along with anything that might interfere with that.'

'Fine,' Bishop said curtly. Ignoring his coffee, he stood up and headed for the door. 'I'll leave you to it. I've got some phone calls I need to get out of the way if I'm going to sit in on your session. See you later, DCI Jordan.'

Carol grinned. 'Would five get me ten that he'll be on the phone to John Brandon before his backside hits the chair?'

Tony shook his head, eyes glinting with amusement. 'Probably not, actually. Paul doesn't like being crossed, but he keeps his powder dry for the battles that matter.'

'Not like me, rushing in where angels fear to tread, eh?'

Tony met her gaze and recognized the goodwill there. 'Nobody's quite like you, Carol. I was genuinely sorry that you didn't want to join the team here.'

She twitched one shoulder in a shrug. 'Not my kind of policing, Tony. Sure, I like the big cases, but I don't like living in limbo.'

Her words hung between them, freighted with more meaning than any casual bystander could have read. Tony looked away and cleared his throat. 'All the more reason why I'm pleased to have the chance to work this case with you. If we'd already been up and running, I don't expect you'd have come running to us with what looks on the face of it to be a fairly straightforward serial arson that's turned nasty almost by accident. So it's a bonus for the squad that they're going to get to see someone as good as you at work.'

'You know, all I've had since this task force was mentioned in connection with my case is enough flattery to choke a politician,' Carol said, trying to cover her gratification with a sardonic tone.

'When did I ever offer you flattery?' Tony said simply.

Again, Carol's stomach clenched. 'Maybe it's not such a good idea,' she said. 'Having an officer like me along, I mean. You should have given them a reality check and wheeled in one of the cavemen,' she added, struggling to keep her smile in place.

Tony laughed in delight. 'Can you imagine? Great session that would be.' He dropped his voice and broadened his Yorkshire accent. 'Right bloody load of crap this is. You want me to go round asking me suspects if they pissed the bed when they were kids?'

'I'd forgotten you were from round here,' Carol said.

'I hadn't,' Tony said. 'Back in the West Riding, last place on earth I ever wanted to be. But I wanted the task force, and the Home Office were adamant we had to be based outside London. God forbid we should do anything sensible like billet the profiling squad with the intelligence unit. How are you finding it out in the primeval ooze of Seaford?'

Carol shrugged. 'Life among the dinosaurs? Ask me in six months.' She glanced at her watch. 'What time are we due to kick off?'

'Couple of minutes.'

'Fancy catching up over lunch?' She'd practised the casual tone half a hundred times on the motorway coming over to Leeds.

'I can't.' He looked genuinely sorry. 'We eat together in the squad. But I was going to ask you . . .'

'Yes?' Careful, Carol, not too eager!

'Are you in a hurry to get back?'

'No, no rush.' Her heart singing, yes, yes, he's going to ask me to dinner.

'Only, I wondered if you'd like to sit in on the afternoon session?'

'Right.' Her voice bright, her hopes squashed, the light in her eyes dulled. 'Any particular reason?'

'I set them an exercise last week. They're supposed to produce their conclusions today and I thought it might be helpful to have your response to their analyses.'

'Fine.'

Tony took a shallow breath and said, 'Plus, I thought we could maybe have a drink afterwards?'

Apprehension and anticipation had pitched Shaz on an adrenaline high. Even though she'd only squeezed three hours' sleep out of the night, she was buzzing like a raver on an amphetamine high. She'd attacked the photocopied newspapers the minute she'd got home, laying them out in piles on her living-room carpet and pausing only to phone for a pizza. So engrossed was she that she didn't even notice when they sent her a ten-inch Margarita and charged her for a twelve-inch with everything on.

By one in the morning, she'd eliminated everything except the entertainments ads and the sports pages. Her earlier conviction that the external link that would prove her contention was lurking in the local papers was starting to look less like a solid hunch than a desperate clutching at straws. Stretching her stiff back and rubbing her gritty eyes, Shaz got to her feet and staggered through to the kitchen to brew another Thermos of coffee.

Refuelled, she returned to her task, deciding to go for the sports pages first. Maybe the same visiting football team with its loyal supporters? Or a player who had moved from club to club and then become a manager? Maybe a local golf championship that attracted outsiders, or a series of bridge trophies? Eliminating all the sporting possibilities took another couple of hours, and left Shaz jittery with exhaustion, caffeine and a looming fear of failure.

When the connection finally emerged, her first response was that she was hallucinating. It was so outrageous an idea she couldn't take it seriously. She caught herself giggling nervously, like a child who hasn't yet learned the appropriate response to the pain of others. 'This is crazy,' she said softly, double-checking through all seven sets of newspapers to confirm she wasn't seeing things. She lurched stiffly to her feet, trying to loosen her cramped muscles, and staggered through to the bedroom, stripping her clothes off as she went. It was too much to take in at half past three in the morning. Setting her alarm for half past six, Shaz fell face down on the bed where sleep hit her like a truck colliding with a motorway bridge.

Shaz dreamed about television game shows where the winner got to choose how they'd be killed. When the alarm clock went off, she dreamed it was a buzzer on an electric chair. Still groggy from sleep, her memory of what she'd unearthed in the newspapers felt like an extension of the nightmare. She pushed the duvet back and tiptoed through to the living room as if normal footfalls would scare her discovery away.

There were seven ragged piles of photocopies. On the top of each pile was a page from the entertainment section. Each page contained either an advertisement for a personal appearance or a featured interview with the same man. However she cut it, it looked as if one of the nation's darlings was somehow tied in to the disappearance and presumed murder of at least seven teenage girls.

And now she was going to have to share her revelation.

It wasn't difficult to set tongues wagging, Micky had soon discovered. Whenever she visited the rehabilitation unit where Jacko was learning how to use his artificial arm, they made a point of closing the door of his room and sitting close together so that when they were interrupted by a physio or a nurse, they could spring apart and appear embarrassed.

At work, she would phone him when the surrounding desks were occupied and she was almost certain to be overheard. The conversations would swing between animated hilarity, with his name dropped in at regular intervals, and the low, intimate tones her colleagues would unimaginatively associate only with lovers.

Finally, to move things up a gear, it was time for scandal and drama. Micky chose a friend on a middle-market tabloid. Three days later, the paper splashed with PERVERT TARGETS JACKO'S NEW LOVE.

Lifesaving hero Jacko Vance's new girlfriend has become the target of a terrifying campaign of vandalism and hate mail.

Since the start of their whirlwind romance, TV journalist Micky Morgan has had

* paint thrown over her car
* dead mice and birds posted through her letter box
* a vicious series of poison pen letters sent to her home.

The couple met when she interviewed the world record-holding javelin star in hospital after the motorway pile-up where Jacko's tragic heroism cost him his lower right arm and his Olympic dream. They had been trying to keep their affair under wraps.

But we can exclusively reveal that their secret has leaked to someone who bears a grudge against attractive blonde Micky, 25, a popular reporter on *Six O'Clock World*.

Last night, at her West London home, Micky said, 'It's been a nightmare. We've no idea who's behind it. I just wish they'd stop.

'We've been keeping our relationship to ourselves because we wanted to get to know each other better without the glare of publicity. We're very much in love. The private man is even more exciting than the person the public sees.

'He's brave and he's beautiful. How could I not be madly in love? All we want now is for this heartless campaign to end.'

A spokesman for Jacko, who is undergoing intensive rehabilitation and physiotherapy at London's exclusive Martingale Clinic, said, 'Jacko is obviously disgusted that anyone should treat Micky like this. She's the most wonderful woman he's ever met. Whoever is behind this better hope the police catch them before he does.'

Jacko, who ended his engagement to (*Continued on page* 4)

The press coverage was hectic for a couple of weeks, then it slowly died away, resurfacing every now and again whenever something happened to either of the alleged lovers. Jacko's emergence from rehab into his old life; his hiring as a TV sports presenter; Micky's new job as an interviewer on breakfast television; Jacko's voluntary work with the terminally ill; all of these and more refreshed interest in their supposed affair. They soon learned it was necessary for them to be seen together somewhere public and high profile at least once a week to avoid speculation in the gossip columns. Often, knowing they were being followed, Jacko ended up spending the night under the same roof as the two women after he and Micky had been clubbing or charity working. After nearly a year of this, Micky summoned Jacko to a powwow over dinner with Betsy.

Her lover's culinary skills had not deserted her since the years she had spent catering for boardroom lunches. As he swallowed the last morsel, Jacko gave the two women his most wolfish grin. 'It must be bad,' he said, 'if it took something that good to soften me up.'

Betsy smiled demurely. 'You haven't had the sticky toffee pudding with home-made hazelnut ice cream yet.'

Jacko pretended to be shocked. 'If I was a police officer, you could be arrested for an offer like that.'

'We do have a proposition for you,' Micky said.

'Something tells me you're not talking three in a bed,' he said, rocking gently on the back legs of the chair.

'You might try and sound a little disappointed,' Betsy said drily. 'The idea that we're so unappealing is bad for what the Americans so charmingly call our self-esteem.'

Jacko's smile reminded Micky disturbingly of Jack Nicholson. 'Betsy, my dear, if you knew what I like to do with my women, you'd be profoundly grateful for my lack of interest.'

'Actually, our ignorance on that very point is one of the factors that has made us reluctant to put our proposal to you before now,' Betsy said, briskly clearing the plates and carrying them through to the small kitchen.

'I'm intrigued now,' Jacko said, tipping forward with a slight thump and leaning his prosthetic arm on the table. He held Micky's eyes in a glittering stare. 'Spill the beans, Micky.'

Betsy appeared in the kitchen doorway and leaned against the jamb. 'It's awfully time consuming, this silly business of you and Micky having to go out enjoying yourselves. I don't mind in the slightest that she's out with you. It's just that we'd both rather spend what limited time we can spare together.'

'You want to call the whole thing off?' Jacko frowned.

'Quite the opposite,' Betsy said, sitting down at the table again and placing her hand over Micky's. 'We rather thought it might be a good idea if the two of you were to get married.'

He looked astonished. Micky thought she had never seen a more genuine expression cross Jacko Vance's carefully controlled features. 'Married,' he echoed. It wasn't a question.

Shaz looked around the seminar room again, assessing her audience, hoping she wasn't about to make a complete fool of herself. She tried to second-guess where the objections would come from and what they'd be. Simon would pick holes on principle, she knew that. Leon would tilt his chair back and smoke, the ghost of a sneer on his mouth, then find some load-bearing prop in her argument and demolish it. Kay would cavil and quibble over details, never seeing the big picture. Tony, she hoped, would be quietly impressed with her brilliance in spotting the cluster and her diligence in pursuing it to a demonstrable external connection. Her groundwork would be the trigger for a major inquiry and when the dust finally settled, her future would be sealed. The woman who nailed the celebrity serial killer. She'd be a legend in squad rooms up and down the country. She'd be in a position to pick her billet.

Carol Jordan was the wild card. A morning watching her work with Tony hadn't provided nearly enough raw material for accurate conjecture about her response to Shaz's theory. To leave as little to chance as possible, she'd have to hang back and let a couple of her colleagues go first so she could watch Carol carefully while they presented their reports.

Leon went first. Shaz was surprised by the brevity of his report, and she didn't think she was the only one. He said that while there were clearly similarities between certain of the cases, given the number of teenage runaways recorded annually it was hard to argue that there was any statistical significance in that. He had, seemingly grudgingly, chosen four girls from the West Country, including one of Shaz's cluster. The connecting factor he'd identified was that all four were reported to have harboured ambitions to become models. He suggested they might have been abducted by one or more pornographers under the pretext of offering them the opportunity to become photographers' models then suckered into a life of blue movies and sex for sale.

A short silence was followed by a few apathetic comments from the room. Then Carol said coolly, 'And how long did you spend on this analysis, Mr Jackson?'

Leon's eyebrows descended. 'There wasn't a lot to analyse,' he said belligerently. 'I did what it took.'

'If I were the investigating officer who had handed this material to you, I would be rather underwhelmed by something so superficial,' Carol said. 'I'd feel disappointed, short-changed, and I'd have a pretty low opinion of a specialist unit which produced nothing of more significance than one of my own officers could have provided in an afternoon's work.'

Leon's mouth opened in astonishment. Neither Tony nor Bishop had ever been so openly critical of anyone's work. Before he could respond, Tony cut in. 'DCI Jordan's right, Leon. It's not good enough. We're supposed to be an elite squad, and we're not going to make any friends if we don't treat every assignment as something serious and worthy of our attention. It doesn't matter if we think a group of cases are Mickey Mouse. To the investigating officers, they're important. To the victims, they're important.'

'This was just an exercise,' Leon protested. 'There isn't an investigating officer. It's just playtime. You can't get worked up about that!' The whine in his voice said, 'It's not fair!' louder than the actual words.

'As I understand it, every one of these cases is real,' Carol said quietly. 'Every one of those kids is on the missing list. Some of them are almost certainly dead. The pain of uncertainty can often be more damaging than knowledge of the truth. If we ignore people's pain, we deserve their contempt.'

Shaz watched Tony's impassive face incline in a tiny acknowledgement of Carol's words, then followed his eyes across to Leon, who had compressed his mouth into a thin line, half-turning in his seat so he didn't have to look at Carol. 'Right,' said Tony. 'We've established that DCI Jordan doesn't do polite. Who's next for the high jump?'

Shaz could barely contain her impatience during Kay's report, a pedestrian but painstakingly thorough analysis that forged several possible groups with an assortment of linkages. One was identical to Shaz's own cluster, but it was given no extra weight compared to the others. When the recital drew to a close, Tony looked happier. 'A thorough piece of work,' he said, the unspoken 'but' hanging in the air like a relay baton.

Carol picked up the challenge. 'Yes, but it sounds like you're sitting on the fence. An investigating officer wants information presented in a way that underpins specific initiatives. So you need to prioritize your conclusions. "This is quite likely, this is less likely, this is tenuous, this is frankly improbable." That lets the officers on the ground structure their inquiries in the most productive way.'

'In fairness, it's hard to do that in the vacuum of a classroom exercise,' Tony added. 'But we should always attempt to do it. Any ideas regarding the order of priority we should be looking at here?'

Shaz barely contributed to the vigorous discussion that followed. She was too nervous about what lay ahead to care about the impression she might be making. A couple of times, she caught a stray look of inquiry from Carol Jordan, and responded with some innocuous comment.

Then, suddenly, it was her turn. Shaz cleared her throat and assembled her papers in front of her. 'Although there are several superficial similarities that pull together a variety of potential groupings, closer analysis reveals that there is one strong cluster linked by a nexus of common factors,' she began firmly. 'What I intend to show this afternoon is that this cluster is further linked by a significant common external factor and the irresistible conclusion is that the members of this cluster are the victims of a single serial killer.'

She looked up, hearing a gasp from Kay and a guffaw from Leon. Tony looked startled, but Carol Jordan was leaning forward, chin on her fists, gripped. Shaz allowed a small smile to twitch one corner of her mouth. 'I'm not making this up, I promise you,' she said, distributing stapled pages of photocopies around the table.

'Seven cases,' she said. 'The first page you have in front of you is a table listing the common features in these seven disappearances. One of those key connections, in my view, is that all seven girls took a change of clothes with them. But they didn't go for the kind of things you'd choose if you were planning on running away and living on the streets. In every case, what they went missing with was their "best" gear, the fashion outfits they'd have worn if they were going out on a special date, not trainers for walking the streets and ski jackets for staying warm at night. I know teenagers aren't always sensible when it comes to what they wear, but remember, our sample weren't irresponsible, out of control, wild-child girls.'

She glanced up and was gratified to see that Tony was now as rapt as Carol Jordan. 'In each case, they didn't turn up for school and had lied in advance about what they were doing afterwards to give themselves a clear run of about twelve hours. Only one of them had ever come to the notice of the police or social services and that was for shoplifting when she was twelve. They weren't delinquent, they didn't do drink or drugs to any significant degree.

'Now, if you turn to page two, you'll see I've laid out their photographs scaled down to the same size. Don't you think there's a remarkable physical similarity?' Shaz paused for effect.

'That's eerie,' Simon muttered. 'I can't believe I didn't see that.'

'It's more than physical,' Carol said, sounding faintly bemused. 'There's a look they've all got. Something . . . almost sexual.'

'They're dying to become former virgins,' Leon told the room. 'That's what it is. Unmistakable.'

'Whatever it is,' Shaz interrupted, 'they've all got it. The cases are geographically scattered, the time frame is six years at irregular intervals, but the victims look practically interchangeable. Now, that's strong evidence in itself. But Tony's taught us that we should also be looking for external connectors; factors outside the victim's control or influence that are common. Factors that link to the killer, not the victim.

'I asked myself where I might find the relevant external link that would tie together my cluster of putative victims.' Shaz picked up another pile of stapled photocopies and passed them round. 'Local newspapers. I trawled the local papers for two weeks either side of each disappearance. And in the early hours of this morning, I found what I was looking for. You've got it in front of you. Just before each one of these girls died, the same very public personality was in their home town. And each and every one of them, let's not forget, went off with the one and only outfit they'd have chosen from their wardrobes if they were planning on impressing a man.'

The murmur of disbelief was already rising around her as the enormity of Shaz's suggestion hit them. 'That's right,' she said. 'I couldn't believe it either. I mean, who's going to believe the nation's favourite sporting hero and TV personality is a serial killer? And who's going to authorize an investigation of Jacko Vance?'

The soft whimper seemed to be swallowed by the chill darkness. Donna Doyle had never felt more frightened in her short life. She'd never realized that fear could act like an anaesthetic, apprehension dulling excruciating agony to a throbbing ache. What had already happened had been terrible enough. But not knowing what the future held was almost worse.

It had all started so well. She'd kept the secret, in spite of the way it kept bubbling up inside her, almost seeming to press against her lips and demand release. But she knew he'd meant what he'd said about the importance of confidentiality, and this was too good a chance to miss. Excitement at her new prospects had buoyed her up, allowing her to stifle her awareness that what she was doing would cause uproar at home. She rationalized her failure to inform her mother of her plans by telling herself that when everything worked out as she dreamed, there would be so much joy that the trouble would be forgotten. Deep down, she knew that was a lie, but she couldn't bear to let that knowledge interfere with her elation.

Bunking off school had been easy. She'd set off as usual, then, instead of turning in down the road leading to school, she'd carried on into the town centre where she'd dodged into the public lavatories and changed into the clothes she'd carefully folded into her school backpack instead of books. Her best outfit, she knew, making her look older than she was, making her look like the young women she saw on MTV, cool as fuck. In the dim light of the toilet, she applied her make-up and pouted at the mirror. God, she looked good. But would it be good enough for him?

He'd picked her out when she wasn't even dressed up to the nines, she reminded herself. He'd seen her star quality. Dressed like this, she'd knock him dead. Wouldn't she?

The memory of that nonchalant self-confidence was like a sick joke to Donna now, lying in pain and fear in the dark. But at the time it had been more than enough to get her through the day. She'd caught a bus into Manchester, hanging back until it was about to leave, making sure there wasn't one of the neighbours or her mother's boring friends on board. Then she'd run upstairs, sitting at the back so she could see who got on and off.

Having a few hours in Manchester on a weekday on her own was almost adventure enough in itself. She browsed the department stores, played the fruit machines in the video arcades, bought a couple of lottery scratch cards in a newsagent near the station and told herself that winning ten straight off wasn't just a result, it was an omen. By the time she boarded the train, she was irrepressibly high, more than capable of ignoring the nerves that still fluttered annoyingly in her stomach when she thought of what her mum was going to say.

Changing trains wasn't quite so much fun. It was growing dark, and she couldn't understand a word anyone on Newcastle station tannoy said. They didn't sound like Jimmy Nail or Kevin Whately off the telly. They sounded like aliens. Somehow, she managed to find the right platform for Five Walls Halt and nervously boarded the train, aware that she was among strangers with curious faces who eyed her short skirt and dramatic make-up with predatory eyes. Donna's imagination began to work overtime, translating weary commuters into stalkers and mad axemen.

It had been a relief to get off the train and find him waiting in the car park, just like he'd said. And it had been lovely. He'd said all the right things, reassuring her and convincing her she'd done the right thing. He was lovely, she told herself, not a bit like she expected someone off the telly to be.

As they'd driven down narrow country roads, he'd explained that they wouldn't be able to do the screen test until morning, but that he hoped she'd have dinner with him. He said he had a cottage, that she could stay overnight, there was a spare room, which would save him having to drive after he'd had a glass or two of wine. If she didn't mind, of course. Otherwise, he could take her to a hotel.

The part of her that had been well brought up and drilled to wariness wanted to go instantly to a hotel where she could phone her mother and reveal that she was safe and well. But it wasn't an enticing prospect, a night in a lonely room in a strange place where she knew no one, with no company except the TV and her mum complaining down the phone line. The other voice in her head, the tempting adventurous voice, told her she'd never have a chance like this to make her mark. Having him to herself for a whole evening would be the perfect opportunity to impress him so much that the screen test would be a formality.

The voice she stifled through a mixture of apprehension and anticipation pointed out that there might never be a more propitious time to lose her virginity.

'Staying with you'd be great,' she said.

He smiled, briefly turning his eyes away from the road. 'I promise we'll have fun,' he said.

And he hadn't been lying. Not to begin with, anyway. The food had been wonderful, like the really expensive stuff from Marks and Spencer that her mum always said they couldn't afford. And they'd had wine. Lots of different kinds. Champagne to start with, then white wine with the starters, then red with the main course and a sticky aromatic golden one with the pudding. She'd had no idea there were so many different-tasting ones. He'd been lovely, all through dinner. He'd been funny and flirty and full of stories that made her smile and hug herself inside because she was learning all these secrets about telly people.

And he seemed to find her entertaining, too. He was always asking her what she thought, what she felt, who she liked on TV and who she hated. He was interested, staring deep into her eyes and really paying attention, like men were supposed to when they fancied you, not like the lads she'd gone out with from school who were only interested in football and how far you'd let them go. It was obvious he fancied her. But he wasn't slobbering all over her like some dirty old man. He was considerate, treating her like she was a person. With all the conversation, phoning her mum had been the last thing on her mind.

By the end of the meal, she'd been pleasantly woozy. Not drunk, not like at Emma Lomas's party when she'd had five bottles of extra-strong cider and thrown up for hours. Just a bit blurred round the edges, filled with happiness and desire to feel his warm flesh against hers, to bury her face in the citrus and woody smell of his cologne, to make her fantasies reality.

When he got up to make coffee, she followed, a little unsteady on her feet, conscious of the giddiness that made the room sway gently but not unpleasantly. She came up behind him and slipped her arms round his waist. 'I think you're gorgeous,' she said. 'Fantastic.'

He'd turned and let her lean into him, burying his face in her hair and nuzzling her ear. 'You're very special,' he murmured. 'Very special.'

She felt his erection hard against her stomach. For a moment, a thrill of fear squirmed through her, then his lips were on hers and she was lost to the sensation of what felt like her first kiss. They kissed for what seemed like a lifetime, a dizzying parade of colours spinning behind her eyes as arousal sent her blood charging through her veins.

Almost without her realizing, he moved her gradually round so that her back was against the workbench and he was facing her, still kissing, his tongue darting in and out of her mouth. Suddenly, without warning, his hand clamped over her wrist and yanked her arm to one side. Donna felt cold metal against her flesh and her eyes jerked open. At the same moment, their mouths parted.

Baffled, she looked at her arm, not understanding why it was pinned between the two faces of a big steel vice. He stepped back and quickly spun the handle so the jaws closed on the flushed flesh of her naked arm. Vainly, she tried to pull away. But there was no escape. She was trapped by the arm, pinioned to the workbench vice. 'What are you doing?' she squealed. All her face revealed was hurt puzzlement. It was too soon for fear.

His face was blank. An impassive mask had replaced the interest and affection she'd seen there all evening. 'You're all the same, aren't you?' he said dispassionately. 'You're all out for what you can get.'

'What are you talking about?' Donna entreated him. 'Let me go, this isn't funny. It hurts.' With her free arm, she reached across her body towards the handle of the vice. He raised his arm and smashed her in the face with a backhanded swipe that sent her reeling.

'You do as you're told, you treacherous bitch,' he said, still sounding calm.

Donna tasted blood. A rending sob broke from her throat. 'I don't understand,' she stuttered. 'What did I do wrong?'

'You throw yourself at me because you think I'll get you what you want. You tell me you love me. But if you woke up tomorrow and I couldn't give you what you wanted, you'd throw yourself at the next meal ticket that walked past.' He leaned against her, pressing his body to hers, his weight preventing her from making another attempt at releasing the vice.

'I don't know what you're on about,' Donna whined. 'I never ... Aagh!' Her voice rose in a yell of pain as he turned the vice tighter. Pain shot up her arm as muscle and bone were compacted, the edges of the vice cutting deep and cruel into the tissue of her arm. As her scream subsided into tearful entreaty, he half-turned so that his weight was still on her free arm and tore her dress from top to bottom with one powerful wrench.

Now she was really afraid. She couldn't understand why he was doing this. All she'd wanted was to love him, to be chosen by him to appear on the telly. It wasn't supposed to be like this. It was supposed to be romantic and tender and beautiful, but this was senseless and stupid and she couldn't believe how much her arm was hurting and all she wanted was for it to stop.

He'd barely begun. Within moments, her knickers were in a torn heap at her feet, deep welts in her side where the fabric had bitten into her skin before the seams had finally yielded to his force. Shaking with sobs, her voice a mumbling of meaningless pleadings, she had no resources left to resist as he unzipped his trousers and thrust his cock into her.

It wasn't the pain of losing her virginity that Donna remembered. It was the agony that coursed through her when he bore down on the vice in rhythm with the thrusting of his hips into hers. The breaking of her hymen went unnoticed among the splintering of the bones of her wrist and forearm and the pulverizing of her flesh between the blank metal plates.

As she lay in the dark, she was glad only that she'd passed out then. She didn't know where she was or how she'd got there. All she knew was that she was blessedly alone. And that was enough. For now, that was enough.

Tony walked down Briggate, hands thrust deep into his jacket pockets against the cold, swerving to avoid the last straggles of shoppers and the weary-footed sales assistants making for the bus stops. He deserved a drink. It had been a difficult afternoon. For a time it had looked as if the group spirit nurtured from day one was about to become a memory as differences of opinion escalated into argument then teetered on the edge of hurling abuse.

The first response to Shaz's dramatic hypothesis had been stunned silence. Then Leon had slapped his leg and rocked to and fro on his chair. 'Shazza, baby,' he yelled. 'You are more full of shit than a sewage farm, but you are the best value in town! All right, baby, way to go!'

'Hang on a minute, Leon,' Simon objected. 'You're quick off the mark to slap the girl down. What if she's right?'

'Oh, yeah,' Leon drawled contemptuously. 'Like Jacko Vance is *obviously* a psychopathic serial killer. You've only got to watch him on the telly. Or read about him in the tabloids. Yeah, Jack the Lad, marriage made in heaven, England's glory, the hero who sacrificed his arm and his Olympic medal so that others might live. Very Jeffrey Dahmer, very Peter Sutcliffe. Not.'

Tony had kept half an eye on Shaz during Leon's outburst, noticing the apparent darkening of her eyes and the tense line of her mouth. She couldn't handle mockery the way she dealt with straightforward criticism, he realized. As Leon paused for breath, Tony jumped in with a dose of irony. 'I just love the cut and thrust of intellectual debate,' he said. 'So, Leon, how about you stop showing off and provide us with some cogent argument against the case that Shaz is making?'

Leon scowled, unable as usual to disguise his emotions. Hiding behind the lighting of a cigarette, he mumbled something.

'Can you let us have that again?' Carol interjected sweetly.

'I said, I didn't think Jacko Vance's personality fit our general terms of reference for serial offenders,' he repeated.

'How do you know that?' Kay cut in. 'All we ever see of Jacko Vance is the image manufactured by the media. Some serial killers have been superficially charming and manipulative. Like Ted Bundy. If you're going to be a top athlete, you have to develop phenomenal self-control. Maybe that's what we're seeing with Jacko Vance. A totally synthetic front covering up a psychopathic personality.'

'Spot on,' Simon said vigorously.

'But he's been married a dozen years or more. Would his wife have stayed with him if he was a psychopath? I mean, he couldn't maintain the mask permanently,' someone objected.

'Sonia Sutcliffe always asserted she was totally unaware that her husband went out topping prostitutes the way some men go to football matches. And Rosemary West still claims she had no idea Fred was using bodies for foundations under their patio extension,' Carol pointed out.

'Yeah, and think about it,' Simon urged, 'couples with jobs like Micky Morgan and Jacko Vance, they're not like the rest of us. Half the time Jacko's on the road doing *Vance's Visits*. Then there's all his hospital voluntary work. And Micky must be in the studio at the crack of sparrowfart getting prepared for her programme. They probably see less of each other than coppers see of their kids.'

'It's an interesting point,' Tony said, cutting across a couple of loud interjections. 'What do you think, Shaz? It's your theory, after all.'

Shaz's jaw was set mutinously. 'I don't hear anybody arguing against my identification of the cluster as a significant entity,' she started.

'We-ell,' Kay said. 'I'm wondering how significant it really is. I mean, I pulled together several clusters that maybe are just as validly connected. The girls who the police thought might have been sexually abused, for example.'

'No,' Shaz said firmly. 'Not with as many linking factors as this group. It's worth saying again that some of the things that connect them are unusual features, unusual enough for investigating officers to make a particular note of them. Like taking their best clothes with them.' Tony was pleased to see she was undaunted by this latest example of Kay's constant nit-picking.

Her rebuttal didn't win her a reprieve, however. 'Of course you'd note that,' Leon chipped in, never squashed for long. 'It's the single factor that indicates you're looking at a runaway rather than the victim of a serial killer. You didn't make a note of it, you'd be a pretty crap detective.'

'Like the one who didn't even notice the cluster in the first place?' Shaz demanded belligerently.

Leon cast his eyes upwards and stubbed out his cigarette. 'You women, when you get an idea in your heads . . .'

'Christ, you talk shite sometimes,' Simon said. 'If we could just get back to what this is supposed to be about . . . I'm wondering how much of a coincidence it is that Vance visited those towns. I mean, we don't know how many public appearances he does in the average week. It maybe that he's constantly on the road, in which case it wouldn't mean a lot.'

'Exactly,' Kay backed him up. 'Did you check the local newspapers for the missing kids who aren't in your cluster to see if Vance turned up there as well?'

Shaz's pursed lips gave the answer before she even opened her mouth. 'I didn't have the chance,' she admitted reluctantly. 'Maybe you'd like to take on that little task, Kay?'

'If it was a real operation, you'd have to follow up Kay's suggestion,' Carol pointed out. 'But you would have the bodies and time to do it, which you didn't have here. I must say, I'm impressed with what you have achieved with the limited time and resources available.' Shaz's shoulders squared at Carol's praise, but as the DCI continued, she looked wary. 'However, even if it's a genuine connection, it's too much of a leap in the dark to point the finger straight at Jacko Vance. If these disappearances and presumed murders are connected to his appearances, it's much more likely that the perpetrator is a member of Jacko's entourage or even a member of the public who has an initiating stressor in his past that connects to Vance. At its most obvious, perhaps he was rejected by a woman who was a big fan of Jacko's. These would be my first areas of interest, before I came to the assumption that Jacko himself was involved.'

'It's a point of view,' Shaz said, momentarily mortified that she'd been so carried away with her headline-grabbing theory that she hadn't considered that possibility. It was the nearest Tony had ever seen her come to a concession. 'But you think the cluster is worth pursuing?'

Carol had looked desperately at Tony. 'I . . . uh . . .'

Coming to her rescue, he'd said, 'This was only ever going to be an exercise, Shaz. We've got no authority to take any of these cases any further.'

She looked devastated. 'But there's a cluster here. Seven suspicious disappearances. Those girls, they've got families.'

Leon butted in again, sarcasm back in full working order. 'C'mon, Shazza. Get them synapses working. We're supposed to be clearing things up for the plods on the street, not finding more work for them to do. D'you really think anybody's going to thank us for stirring up a load of aggro over a theory that's dead easy to dismiss out of hand as the product of the fevered minds of a bunch of rookies on a special squad that nobody much wants on the job anyway?'

'Fine,' Shaz said bitterly. 'Let's just forget I spoke, eh? So whose turn is it to be shot down in flames next? Simon? We going to get the benefit of your words of wisdom now?'

Tony had taken Shaz's seeming capitulation as a signal to move on. The other team members' analyses had been considerably less controversial, which had allowed him to demonstrate useful tips and pitfalls in data sifting and the developing of conclusions from raw material. As the afternoon had worn on, he'd noticed Shaz slowly recover from the combative reception her ideas had been given. Gradually, she had ceased to look desolate, moving through crestfallen to an air of stubborn determination that he found slightly worrying. Some time in the next few days, he'd have to make time to have a word with her, to point out the quality of much of her analysis and explain the importance of keeping apparently wild conclusions private until she could back them up with something more solid than a hunch.

He turned off the main street into the narrow alley that housed Whitelocks pub, an old-fashioned relic that had somehow survived the years when the city centre died at half past five. If he was honest, the last thing he felt like was a drink with Carol. The history between them meant theirs could never be entirely easy encounters, and tonight he had something he ought to tell her that she wouldn't want to hear.

At the bar, he ordered a pint of bitter and found a quiet table in the far corner. He'd never been one to shirk his obligations. But Shaz's failure to consider one of Jacko Vance's fans or a member of his entourage as a possibility had reminded him of the importance of waiting for data before exposing theories to the harsh scrutiny of others. Just for once, Tony thought he'd take his own mental advice to Shaz and say nothing of his ideas until he too had more evidence.

It had taken Carol half an hour to escape from the probing questions of the two women task force officers. She had the distinct feeling that if she hadn't taken so very definite a leave, the one with the eyes, Shaz, would have pinned her to the wall until she'd sucked her dry of every piece of pertinent information, and a fair amount of impertinent. By the time she pushed open the etched glass door of the pub, she was convinced he'd have given up on her and left.

She saw his wave of greeting as soon as she approached the bar. He was sitting in a wood-panelled nook at the far end of the room, the remains of a pint of bitter in front of him. 'Same again?' she mouthed, making the universal gesture of a hand tipping a glass.

Tony placed one index finger across the top of the other to form a T. Carol grinned. Moments later, she placed a straight glass of Tetley's in front of Tony and sat down opposite him with her own half-pint. 'Driving,' she said succinctly.

'I took the bus. Cheers,' he added, raising his glass.

'Cheers. It's good to see you.'

'And you.'

Carol's answering smile was wry. 'I wonder if there'll ever come a time when you and I can sit opposite each other and not feel there's a third person at the table?' She couldn't help it. It was like a scab she was impelled to pick, always convinced that this time it wouldn't draw blood.

He looked away. 'Actually,' he said, 'you're about the only person who doesn't make me feel like that. Thanks for coming today. I know it probably wasn't the way you would have chosen to reopen our . . .'

'Acquaintance?' Carol said, unable to avoid a sour note.

'Friendship?'

It was her turn to look away. 'I hope so,' she said. 'I hope friendship.' It was less than the truth and they both knew it, but it served its purpose. Carol found a frail smile. 'An interesting bunch, your baby profilers.'

'They are, aren't they? I suppose you saw what they've all got in common?'

'If ambition was illegal they'd all be doing life. In the next cell to Paul Bishop.'

Tony nearly choked on his mouthful of beer, spraying the table and narrowly missing Carol's cream twill jacket. 'I see you haven't lost your killer instinct,' he spluttered.

'What's to be coy about? You can't miss it. High octane aspiration. It fills the room like testosterone in a nightclub. Doesn't it worry you that they all see the task force as a stepping stone in their brilliant careers?'

Tony shook his head. 'No. Maybe half of them will use it as a springboard to what they perceive as greater things. The other half think that's what they're doing, but actually they're going to fall in love with profiling and they're never going to want to do anything else.'

'Name names.'

'Simon, the lad from Glasgow. He's got that sceptical turn of mind that takes nothing on trust. Dave, the sergeant. He likes the idea that it's methodical and logical yet it still has space for flair. But the real star is going to be Shaz. She doesn't know it yet, but she's been bitten by the bug. Don't you think?'

She nodded. 'She's an obsessive workaholic and she can't wait to get to grips with the screwed-up minds out there on the street.' She cocked her head to one side. 'Know what?'

'What?'

'She reminded me of you.'

Tony looked like he couldn't decide whether to be offended or amused and settled for puzzled. 'How odd,' he said. 'She reminded *me* of you.'

'What!' Carol exclaimed, startled.

'This afternoon's presentation. The basic work was solid. The cluster she'd identified is definitely worth consideration as a phenomenon.' He spread his hands and opened his eyes wide. 'To jump from that to the conclusion that Jacko Vance is a serial killer was a leap of imagination unrivalled since your virtuoso performance in the Bradfield case!'

Carol couldn't help laughing at his histrionics. 'But I was right,' she protested.

'You may have been right in *fact*, but you broke all the laws of logic and probability to get there.'

'Maybe Shaz is right. And maybe we're just better at profiling than the boys,' Carol teased.

Tony grunted. 'I wouldn't deny the possibility that girls are better at this,' he said. 'But I can't believe you think Shaz is right.'

Carol pulled a face. 'Six months down the road, she'll be mortified she even suggested it.'

'Knowing cops, one of that bunch will probably set her up with a face-to-face on *Vance's Visits*.'

Carol shuddered. 'I can see it now. Jacko Vance nailed to the wall by those extraordinary eyes, Shaz saying, "And where were you on the night of 17th January 1993?"' When they'd both stopped laughing, she added, 'I'll be fascinated to see what she comes up with for my serial arsonist.'

'Mmm,' Tony said.

She raised her glass in a toast. 'To the mumbo jumbo squad.'

'May we be a long time in heaven before the devil notices we're gone,' he responded wryly and drained his glass. 'Another?'

Carol looked at her watch consideringly. It wasn't that she had to be anywhere; she wanted a moment to decide whether it was better to leave things on this pleasant footing or stay for another drink with the risk they might end up putting the distance back between each other. Deciding not to chance it, she shook her head regretfully. 'No can do, I'm afraid. I want to catch the night-shift CID team before they all disappear into the twilight zone.' She swallowed the last half-inch of beer and stood up. 'I'm glad we had the chance for a chat.'

'Me too. Come back on Monday, we'll have something for you then.'

'Great.'

'Drive safely,' he said as she turned to go.

She half-turned. 'I will. And you take care.'

Then she was gone. Tony sat for a while staring into his empty glass considering why someone might set fires without the pay-off of a sexual thrill. When the glimmer of an idea crept into his mind, he got up and walked alone through the echoing streets.

*   *   *

It wasn't the laughter of Shaz's colleagues that smarted like shampoo in her eyes. It wasn't even Carol Jordan's metaphorical pat on the head. It was Tony's sympathy. Instead of being bowled over by the quality of her work and the incisiveness of her insights, Tony had been kind. She hadn't wanted to hear that it took courage to stick her neck out, that she'd shown real initiative but that she'd fallen into the trap of getting carried away by coincidence. It would have been easier if he'd been dismissive or even patronizing, but the fellow-feeling in his compassion was too obvious for her to hide her crushing disappointment in anger. He'd even told a couple of stories against himself about mistaken conclusions he'd leapt to in his early efforts at profiling.

It was a generosity of spirit that Shaz had no equipment to deal with. The only, and accidental, child of a couple so devoted to each other that the emotional needs of their daughter barely impinged, she had learned to get by without expectations of tenderness or indulgence. She'd been told off for misbehaving, praised absentmindedly for success, but mostly, she'd been ignored. Her driven ambition had its roots in a childhood where she'd worked desperately hard to win the recognition from her parents that she craved. Instead, her teachers had offered approval, and their off-handed professional assessments had been the only generosity she'd learned to feel at ease with. Now, genuine personal kindness left her baffled and uncomfortable. She could handle Carol Jordan's businesslike appreciation of her work, but Tony's sympathy unsettled her and fired her to do something that would render it redundant.

The morning after the debacle, she endured the chaffing of her colleagues, even managing to join in their banter rather than fixing them with her chill blue stare and stripping their self-confidence to the bone. Underneath the affable surface, though, her mind was churning, thoughts revolving in an attempt to find a way forward that would show she was right.

Trawling the missing persons records in a bid to find other cases that fit the pattern was out of the question. Shaz knew from her days on the beat that somewhere in the region of a quarter of a million people went missing every year, nearly a hundred thousand of them under eighteen. Many of them simply walked away from the pressures of jobs they hated and families who offered them nothing. Others ran from lives grown intolerable. Some were seduced by promises of streets paved with gold. And a few were snatched unwilling from their familiar worlds and plunged into hell. But it was almost impossible to tell which category individuals fell into by a swift scrutiny of the report summary. Even if she could have persuaded her doubting colleagues to join the search, to unearth other possible victims of Shaz's serial killer would take far more resources than they had available.

When Tony announced that the afternoon would be devoted to private study, Shaz felt the itch of her impatience ease. Now she could at least *do* something. Rejecting Simon's suggestion of a pub lunch, she made straight for the city's biggest bookshop. Minutes later, she was standing by the till with a copy of *Jack on the Box: the Unauthorized Version* by Tosh Barnes, a Fleet Street columnist known for his vitriolic pen, and *Lionheart: the True Story of a Hero* by Micky Morgan, an updated version of the account she'd first written shortly after their marriage. Tony had suggested that even if Shaz was right about the link, the killer would be more likely to be one of Vance's entourage than the man himself. The books might help either to eliminate him or to provide corroborative support for her theory.

A short bus ride and she was home. Popping the top on a can of Diet Coke, she sat down at her desk and plunged straight into his wife's adoring take on Jacko Vance's brilliant career. Great athlete, selfless hero, indomitable fighter, peerless broadcaster, tireless charity worker and sublime husband. As she forced herself through the hagiography, Shaz started to think it might actually be a pleasure to demolish so revoltingly perfect a figure. If her first assumption was right, he didn't so much have feet of clay as an entirely false facade.

It was a relief to reach the end, even though that meant facing the question she'd been pushing to the back of her mind. It was the classic misgiving of serial killer inquiries: how could the wife not know? Even leading such busy lives independent of each other, how could Micky Morgan share her bed and her existence with an abductor and murderer of adolescent girls and not sense something in his head was twisted out of true? And if she knew, or even suspected, how could she sit in front of the cameras day after day interviewing life's victims and victors without a flicker of anything other than professional compassion and composure?

It was a question that had no answer. Unless Tony had been right and it wasn't Jacko himself but a fan or a team member.

Suppressing these misgivings, Shaz turned to *Jack on the Box* which proved to be merely an irreverent version of the same myth. Only the anecdotes were different, revealing nothing more sinister than that when he was wearing his professional hat, Jacko Vance was a perfectionist with a corrosive line in invective that could strip even TV's hardest cases of their protective armour. It was hardly a signpost to a homicidal maniac.

But for someone searching for elements that would fit the identikit notion of a serial killer, there were hints and clues that suggested she might not be completely deluded. There were certainly more factors than the average person would exhibit and, in her book, that kept Jacko Vance in the prime suspect slot thus far. It might well be someone else around him, but so far the research she had done had provided nothing to contradict her original theory.

Shaz had made notes as she worked her way through both books. At the end of her initial research, she booted up the laptop and opened a file she'd developed earlier in the profiling course. Headed *Organized Offender Checklist*, it was exactly what it said: a list of potential indicators to reveal to an investigator whether a suspect was a serious contender. She made a copy of the file; then, using her notes for guidance, occasionally referring back to the books, Shaz worked her way down the inventory. When she'd finished, she almost purred with satisfaction. She wasn't crazy after all. This was something Tony Hill wouldn't be able to ignore when it formed Part One of the new dossier she planned to present him with. She printed it out and smiled in satisfaction as she double-checked it.

Shaz was particularly pleased with the concluding paragraph. Concise, to the point, but telling the readers who knew what to look for all they needed to know, she thought. She wished she could get her hands on the newspaper cuttings about Vance and Micky Morgan, particularly the tabloids and the gossip columns. But to put in a formal request to any of the newspaper libraries would set too many alarm bells ringing. On a story this big, she couldn't even dare trust a personal contact.

She considered whether to present Tony with this fresh analysis. In her heart, she knew there wasn't enough to change his mind. But someone was killing young girls and on the balance of probabilities, given how long it had been going on and how many indicators lurked in his background, she reckoned Jacko Vance was her man. Somewhere, there was something that would expose his weakness, and she was going to find it.

The desk sergeant tipped the second spoonful of sugar into his mug of black tea and stirred it languidly, staring at the sluggish whirlpool it produced as if willing it to do something interesting enough to divert him from the pile of paperwork stacked beside him on the desk. The swirling slowed then stilled. Nothing else happened. With a sigh that started in the pit of his stomach, he picked up the first file and opened it.

The reprieve came two pages into the report. His hand shot out to the phone as if it was attached by elastic suddenly released. 'Glossop Police, Sergeant Stone,' he said cheerfully.

The voice on the phone was staccato with nerves, control barely in place. It was a woman, not young, not old, Peter Stone registered automatically as he pulled a pile of scrap paper towards him. 'It's my daughter,' the woman said. 'Donna. She's not come home. She's only fourteen. She never went to her friend's. I don't know where she is. Help me! You've got to help me!' The pitch rose to a frightened squeak.

'I understand how upsetting this is for you,' Stone said stolidly. Himself a father of daughters, he refused to allow his imagination to run riot over the possible disasters that could befall them. Otherwise he'd never have slept again. 'I'll need a few details so we can set about being of some assistance.' His formality was deliberate, a calculated attempt to slow things down and instil calmness in his frantic caller. 'Your name is . . . ?'

'Doyle. Pauline Doyle. My daughter's Donna. Donna Theresa Doyle. We live up Corunna Street. Number 15 Corunna Street. Just the two of us. Her dad's dead, see? He took a brain haemorrhage three years ago, dropped down dead, just like that. What's happened to my Donna?' Tears shook her voice. Stone could hear sniffs and sobs despite her best efforts to stay coherent.

'What I'm going to do, Mrs Doyle, I'm going to send somebody round to take a statement from you. Meantime, can you just tell me how long Donna's been missing?'

'I don't know,' Pauline Doyle wailed. 'She left the house this morning to go to school and said she was going for her tea to her pal Dawn's house. They had some science project they were working on together. When she wasn't home by ten, I rang Dawn's mum and she told me Donna hadn't been there and Dawn said she wasn't in school all day.'

Stone glanced at the clock. Quarter past eleven. That meant the girl had been somewhere other than where she was supposed to be for the best part of fifteen hours. Not officially time to worry yet, but a dozen years in the Job had given him an instinct for the significant. 'You hadn't had words, had you?' he asked gently.

'No-o-o-o,' Mrs Doyle wept. She hiccupped and Stone could hear her breathe deeply to calm her voice. 'She's all I've got,' she said, her voice soft and piteous.

'There could be a simple explanation. It's not uncommon with young girls, going missing overnight. Now, I want you to put the kettle on and brew a pot of tea, because there'll be a couple of officers with you within ten minutes, OK?'

'Thank you.' Forlorn, Pauline Doyle replaced the phone and stared bleakly at the photograph on top of the television set. Donna smiled back at her, a flirtatious, knowing smile that said she was nudging the borderline between child and woman. Her mother stuffed her hand between her teeth to avoid crying out, then stumbled to her feet and went through to the fluorescent brilliance of the kitchen.

At that point, Donna Doyle had been alive and well and slightly drunk.

Once the decision had been taken, all that remained were details. First, the official proposal, arranged for maximum effect during the annual fund-raising telethon that garnered millions for children's charities. Jacko went down on one knee in front of eight million viewers and asked Micky to marry him. She looked suitably stunned, then moved. With tears in her eyes, she said yes. Like every other aspect of their marriage, there was nothing about the whole process that couldn't be screened before the watershed.

The wedding took place in a register office, of course, but that was no reason not to splurge on a party that would keep the gossip column inches flowing for days. Jacko's agent and Betsy were the witnesses, each acting as a kind of unofficial minder to make sure neither member of the wedding drank champagne to the destruction of discretion. Then, afterwards, the honeymoon. A private island in the Seychelles, Betsy and Micky in one cottage, Jacko in the other. On several occasions they spotted him on the beach, with a different woman each time, but no one apart from Jacko himself ever joined them for a meal and they were never introduced to any of his partners.

On the last night, the three had dinner together under the Indian Ocean moon. 'Your friends gone, then?' Betsy had asked, emboldened by the fifth glass of champagne.

'Not friends,' Jacko said carefully. His mouth twisted in a strange smile. 'Not even personal assistants, I'm afraid. I don't sleep with friends. Sex is something I keep in the realm of transactions. After the accident, after Jillie, I told myself I was never ever going to put myself in a position where anybody could take anything that mattered from me again.'

'That's sad,' Micky said. 'You lose a lot by not being prepared to take risks.'

His eyes seemed to glaze over, like a tinted-glass limo window rising to obscure its inhabitant. It was a look she was certain was never seen by his public, nor even the terminally ill and permanently damaged that he gave his time and energy to reassure so potently. If the powers that be had ever seen that darkness behind his eyes, they'd have made sure he never came within a hundred miles of the sick and dying. All the world got was the charm. Come to that, it was mostly all she ever got. But either he willingly let her see more, or else he wasn't aware that she knew him so well. Even Betsy told her she was exaggerating when she spoke of the darkness battened down inside her husband. Only Micky knew she wasn't.

Jacko looked unsmiling into his wife's eyes and said, 'I take plenty of risks, Micky. I just minimize the possibility of damage. Take this marriage. It's a risk, but I wouldn't have taken it unless I'd been certain it was safer for me because you have a lot more to lose than I do if it's ever exposed as a sham.'

'Maybe so,' Micky acknowledged with a tip of her glass. 'But I think it's sad to cut yourself off from the possibility of love, which is what you've done ever since you split with Jillie and started playing games with me.'

'This isn't a game,' Jacko said, his face closed and intense. 'But if you're worried about me lacking nourishment, don't be. I take responsibility for my own needs. And I promise my solutions will never embarrass you. I am the king of deniability.' He put his left hand over his heart and smiled solemnly.

The words had always haunted Micky, though he had never given her reason to throw them in his face. But sometimes, when she saw expressions cross his eyes that reminded her of the first time she'd seen his contained fury in that sterile hospital room, she wondered what exactly there might be lurking in Jacko's secret world that would require denial. Murder, however, would never have made it to the list.

The trouble with working alone was that you just couldn't cover the ground, Shaz had realized after a fitful night's sleep. There weren't enough hours in the day, she didn't have the authority to make full background inquiries, she had no access to the information network of the bobbies who worked the patches where Jacko Vance had grown up or lived since. There was no one to gossip with. If she was going to make any progress worth speaking of, there was only one possible route to go.

She'd have to stir things up. And that meant calling in more favours. She picked up the phone and rang Chris Devine's number. The answering machine picked up on the third ring. It was a relief not to have to explain the whole seemingly insane enterprise to Chris. When she heard the beep, she said, 'Chris? It's Shaz. Thanks for your help the other day. It was so useful, I need another favour. Any chance you could get me a home number for Jacko Vance? I'll be at home all evening. You're a star, thanks.'

'Hang on,' Chris's voice cut across hers. Shaz jumped and almost knocked her coffee cup to the floor. 'Hello?' she said. 'Chris?'

'I was in the shower. What are you up to?' Chris's voice was more affectionate than Shaz reckoned she deserved.

'I want to set up an interview with Jacko Vance, and I haven't got a number for him.'

'Is there some problem with official channels, doll?'

Shaz cleared her throat. 'It's not exactly an official inquiry.'

'You're going to have to do better than that. Has this got something to do with the half-dozen trees I had to murder to do the last favour you asked for?'

'Sort of. The exercise I told you about? Well, it's thrown up what looks like a genuine cluster. I think there's a real serial killer out there doing teenage girls. And it's connected to Jacko Vance.'

'Jacko Vance? *The* Jacko Vance? *Vance's Visits* Jacko Vance? What's he got to do with a serial killer?'

'That's what I'm trying to find out. Only we're not supposed to be doing this for real yet, so nobody's prepared to take any action unless I can come up with something more concrete.'

'Hang on a minute, doll. Back up a bit, to where you said it's connected to Jacko. How d'you mean, "connected"?' Chris was starting to sound worried, Shaz thought. Time for a bit of back-pedalling. Time also to adopt the less dramatic suggestion of her colleagues.

'It could be something and nothing. Only, this cluster I spotted: he was doing a personal appearance in each of the girls' home towns a couple of days before they went walkabout. It's an odd coincidence, and I'm thinking maybe it's someone in his entourage or some psycho fan of his who has it in for girls who maybe come on too strong to Jacko or something.'

'So, let me get this right. You want to front up Jacko Vance to see if he's noticed any revolving-eyed maniacs hanging around his gigs? And you want to do this unofficial?' Chris's voice mixed incredulity and concern.

'That's about the size of it, yeah.'

'You're off your head, Bowman.'

'I thought that was part of my charm.'

''King hell, doll, charm won't get you out of the shit if you put a foot wrong on this one.'

'Tell me something I don't know. Are you going to help me or not?'

There was a long silence. Shaz let it stretch, even though her nerves were stretching to breaking point with it. Finally, Chris caved in. 'If I don't, you'll just go somewhere else, won't you?'

'I have to, Chris. If I'm right, somebody's killing kids. I can't ignore that.'

'It's if you're wrong I'm worried about, doll. You want me to come with you, give you a bit of back-up, make it look more official?'

It was tempting. 'I don't think so,' Shaz said slowly. 'If I end up going down in flames, I don't want to take you with me. But there is something you could do.'

Chris groaned. 'Not if it involves a library.'

'You could cover my back. I'll probably need to give a ring-back number. People like him, they don't take anything on trust. Only, we can't take phone calls on the course because we're always in lectures or group sessions or whatever. If I could use your office number, at least he's going to be getting a police phone if he calls back to check me out.'

'You got it,' Chris sighed. 'Give me five minutes.'

Shaz endured the wait stoically. There were times when she envied smokers, though not enough to start. She stared at the second hand of her watch, tightening her lips as it swept into the sixth minute. When the phone rang, she grabbed it before the end of the first peal.

'Got a pen?' Chris said.

'Yeah.'

'Here you go, then.' She recited the supposedly secret unlisted number she'd wheedled out of the desk officer at Notting Hill police station. 'You didn't get it from me.'

'Thanks, Chris. I owe you.'

'More than you'll ever pay, unfortunately,' Chris said ruefully. 'Hang loose, doll. Talk to you soon.'

'I'll keep you posted. Bye.' Shaz contemplated the piece of paper with a quiet smile of triumph. Here I come, ready or not, she thought, reaching for the phone again. Half past eight wasn't too early to call.

The number rang out a couple of times, then an automated voice told Shaz, 'Your call is being diverted.' A series of clicks, a hollow sound, then the distinctive warble of a mobile phone ringing. 'Hello?' The answering voice was instantly recognizable. Shaz found it disconcerting to have what normally came from the TV issuing from her phone, especially since it wasn't the voice she expected.

'Ms Morgan?' she asked tentatively.

'Speaking. Who is this?'

'I'm Detective Constable Sharon Bowman of the Metropolitan Police. I'm sorry to trouble you, but I need to speak to your husband.'

'I'm afraid he's not at home just now. Nor am I. You've actually come through on the wrong line. This is my personal line. His is a different number.'

Shaz felt a blush creeping up her neck. 'I'm sorry to have disturbed you.'

'No problem. Is it something I can help you with, officer?'

'I don't think so, Ms Morgan. Unless you could possibly give me a number where I can reach him?'

Micky hesitated. 'I'd rather not, if you don't mind. I could pass a message on, if that would do?'

It would have to, Shaz thought grimly. The rich really did do things differently. Just as well she'd already made the arrangement with Chris. 'I think he might have some background information relating to an inquiry we're pursuing. I realize he's a very busy man, but I can meet him any time tomorrow, wherever and whenever suits him. Now, I'm going to be out of the office for the rest of the day, so if he could ring this number . . .' she dictated Chris's direct line. 'And ask to speak to Sergeant Devine. He can make the arrangements with her.'

Micky read the number back to her. 'That right? Tomorrow?

Fine, DC Bowman, I'll pass the message on to him.'

'Sorry to have intruded,' Shaz said gruffly.

The familiar chuckle came down the line. 'Think nothing of it. I'm always delighted to help the police. But you'll know that, if you ever see the programme.'

It was so obviously an opening that Shaz couldn't resist. 'It's a terrific show. I watch you whenever I can.'

'Flattery will always get your messages delivered,' Micky said, her voice as seductive as it always managed to be at noon.

'I look forward to hearing from Mr Vance,' Shaz said. She'd never meant anything more in her life.

Pauline Doyle stared at the empty frame on top of the television. The officers who had visited her the night of Donna's disappearance had taken the photograph to have some copies made. They'd seemed concerned about Donna, asking a lot of questions about her friends and her school, whether she had a boyfriend, what she liked to do on a weekend. When they'd eventually left with the photo and a description of Donna, she felt they'd helped her keep hysteria at bay. All her instincts were to run through the midnight streets crying her daughter's name, but the composed responses of the two uniformed officers who had filled her kitchen had soothed her, made her understand this was not the time to act on irrational impulses. 'Best stop here,' the older man had said. 'If she tries to phone home, you don't want her missing you. Leave it to us to look for her. We're the experts, we know what we're about.'

The woman who'd come the following morning had undermined those reassurances. She'd persuaded Pauline to do a detailed audit of Donna's possessions. When they'd established the absence of Donna's favourite dance outfit – a short black Lycra skirt, a body-hugging black-and-white striped T-shirt with a scoop neck and black patent leather Doc Marten's – the detective had visibly relaxed. Pauline understood why. In the eyes of the police, the missing clothes meant just another teenage runaway. They could relax now, stop worrying about their earlier assumption that they might well be looking for a body.

How could she explain in a way that they'd understand? How could she make them see that Donna had neither need nor reason to run away? She hadn't fallen out with Pauline. Quite the opposite. They were close, closer than most women managed to stay to their teenage daughters. Bernard's death had driven them to each other for comfort and they'd continued to share their confidences. Pauline clenched her eyes shut and sent a fierce supplication to the Virgin she'd lost faith in years before. The police wouldn't listen; what harm could it do to pray?

The dawn came up on her left-hand side to road noise and the sound of her own voice. All the way down the M1, Shaz practised the interview. She'd always envied lawyers the comfort of only asking questions to which they knew the answers. To face a professional without role-playing and exploring every possible response would have been madness, so she drove on automatic pilot, rehearsing her questions and the imagined replies. By the time she arrived in West London, she was as ready as she'd ever be. Either he'd let something slip, which she doubted he'd be amateur enough to do, or else she'd panic him into some subsequent action that would confirm everything she'd worked out for herself. Or she might be wrong and the others right and he might simply point her in the direction of a fanatical devotee that he'd spotted with the putative victims. It would be an anti-climax, but one she could live with if it saved lives and put a killer behind bars.

That she might be putting herself at risk never seriously occurred to her in spite of Chris Devine's warnings. At twenty-four, Shaz had no intimations of mortality. Even three years in the police, with the occasional assaults and regular dangers, hadn't dented her sense of invincibility. Besides, people who lived in Holland Park mansions didn't attack police officers. Especially not when it was their wife who'd made the appointment.

Early as usual, Shaz ignored the instructions to park on their drive that had been passed on to her. Instead, she found a meter in Notting Hill and walked down into Holland Park, strolling down the street where they lived. Carefully counting the numbers, Shaz identified the house belonging to Jacko and Micky. It was hard to believe that somewhere so huge in the heart of Central London was still dedicated to only one household, but Shaz knew from her background reading that this was no mansion split into flats. It was all for Jacko and Micky, the only live-in staff, Micky's long-standing personal assistant Betsy Thorne. Gobsmacking, Shaz thought as she passed the wedding cake white house with its flawless facade. She couldn't see much of the garden, shielded from the world by tall, clipped variegated laurel hedges, but the section beyond the electronic gates appeared to be as immaculate as an exhibit at the Chelsea Flower Show. Shaz felt a momentary doubt in the pit of her stomach. How could she suspect the tenant of such a jewel of the hideous crimes her imagination had constructed? People like this didn't do things like that, did they?

Biting her lip in anger at her lack of self-belief, Shaz turned on her heel and marched back to her car, determination building with the very rhythm of her stride. He was a criminal and when she'd finished with him, the whole world would know it. It took her less than five minutes to drive back to the house and turn into the gateway. She wound down her window and pressed the speaker box. 'DC Bowman to see Mr Vance,' she said firmly.

The gates swung open with a low electric hum and Shaz advanced into what she couldn't help thinking of as enemy territory. Not sure where to leave her car, she opted to avoid blocking the double garage and followed the drive round to the other side of the house, past a Range Rover parked by the front steps, and stopped alongside a silver Mercedes convertible. She turned off the engine and sat for a moment, gathering her energies and focusing on her objective. 'Just do it,' she finally said, her voice low and tough.

She ran up the steps to the front door and pushed the bell. Almost instantaneously, the door swung open and Micky Morgan's face smiled down at her, familiar as family. 'Detective Constable Bowman,' she said, stepping back and waving Shaz inside. 'Come in. I was just leaving.' Micky extended an arm to one side, indicating a middle-aged woman with grey-streaked hair pulled loosely back in a heavy plait. 'This is Betsy Thorne, my PA. We're off to catch Le Shuttle.'

'An overnight break in Le Touquet,' Betsy amplified.

'Lots of seafood and a flutter in the casino,' Micky added, reaching over to take a leather holdall from Betsy. 'Jacko's expecting you. He's just finishing a phone call. If you take that first door on the left, he'll be with you in a minute.'

Shaz finally managed to get a word in. 'Thanks,' she said. Micky and Betsy hovered on the doorstep, till Shaz realized they weren't going to close the door until they were certain she was in the correct place. With an awkward smile, Shaz nodded and walked through the open door Micky had indicated. Only when she'd disappeared from sight did she hear the front door closing. Moving to the window, she saw the women climb into the Range Rover.

'DC Bowman?'

Shaz whirled around. She hadn't heard anyone enter. Across the room, smaller in life than he appeared on TV, Jacko Vance smiled. Fuelled by her imagination, Shaz saw the grin of the panther just before its prey becomes a carcass. She wondered if she was face to face with her first serial killer. If so, she hoped he didn't realize he was seeing Nemesis.

Her eyes were extraordinary. From behind, she'd looked so average. Brown hair brushing the collar of a tailored dark navy blazer over blue jeans and tan deck shoes. Nothing you'd glance at twice in a crowded bar. But when he startled her into turning round, the blaze of her blue eyes converted her into an entirely different creature. Vance felt a tingle of apprehension coupled with a strange sense of satisfaction. Whatever she was after, this woman wasn't a nobody. She was an adversary. 'Sorry to keep you waiting,' he said, his voice the familiar TV caress.

'I was early,' she said neutrally.

Vance walked towards her, stopping when there was about six feet between them. 'Have a seat, officer,' he said, indicating the sofa behind her.

'Thanks,' Shaz said, ignoring his instruction and moving instead to the very armchair he'd planned to occupy. He'd chosen it because the seat was higher and the light was behind it. He'd intended to place her at a disadvantage, but she'd turned the tables. Irritation stung him like an insect bite and rather than sitting down himself, he moved over to the fireplace and leaned against the ornately carved overmantel. He stared across at her, his silence demanding that she open the bidding.

'I appreciate you making the time to see me,' she said after a long moment. 'I realize how busy you are.'

'You didn't leave me much option. Besides, I'm always happy to be of assistance to the police. Your Deputy Commissioner could fill you in on the details of the number of times I've helped police charities.' The smile never left his voice but didn't make it to his eyes.

The blue stare didn't blink. 'I'm sure he could, sir.'

'Which reminds me. Your warrant card?' Vance didn't move, forcing Shaz to get up and cross the room once she'd taken out the wallet that contained her police credentials. 'I can't believe we'd be so careless,' Vance said conversationally as she approached. 'Letting a stranger across the door without checking she was who she claimed to be.' He gave her Metropolitan Police warrant card a perfunctory glance. 'There's another one, isn't there?'

'I'm sorry? This is the only card Metropolitan Police officers are issued with. It's our ID,' Shaz said, face giving nothing away of the alarm bells ringing in her head, telling her he knew too much and she should clear out while the going was good.

Vance's lips seemed to shrink as his smile became more vulpine. Time to show her who held the cards, he decided. 'But you're not with the Met any longer, are you, DC Bowman? You see, you're not the only one who's done their homework. You have done your homework?'

'I am still an officer of the Metropolitan Police,' Shaz said firmly. 'Anyone who has told you different is mistaken, sir.'

He pounced. 'But you're not based in the Met's area, are you? You're on attachment to a special unit. Why don't you show me your current ID so that I know you are who you say you are and we can get down to business?' Careful, he told himself, don't get carried away just because you're so much smarter than her. You don't know yet what she's doing here. He shrugged winningly, his eyebrows lifting. 'I don't mean to be difficult, but a man in my position can't be too careful.'

Shaz looked him up and down, her face a mask. 'That's very true,' she said, producing her National Profiling Task Force ID, complete with photograph. He reached out for it, but she moved it out of his grasp.

'I've not seen one of those before,' he said chattily, hiding his frustration at not being able to glimpse more than a logo and the word 'profiling', which had leapt out like a burning brand. 'The profiling task force we've all read so much about, eh? Once you're actually up and running, you should get one of your experienced officers to go on my wife's programme, tell the people what's being done to protect them.' Now she'd know he knew she was an absolute beginner.

'That wouldn't be my decision, sir.' Shaz deliberately turned her back on him and walked back to the chair. 'Now, if we could get down to business?'

'Of course.' He spread his left arm in an expansive gesture without making a move towards a chair. 'I'm at your disposal, DC Bowman. Perhaps we could start with you telling me exactly what this is all about.'

'We've reopened the cases of a group of missing teenage girls,' Shaz said, opening the folder she was carrying. 'Initially, we have identified seven cases with strong similarities. The cases cover a period of six years, and we will be expanding our inquiries to see whether there are other cases with common features that we haven't pinpointed yet.'

'I don't quite see what I . . .' Vance frowned convincingly. 'Teenage girls?'

'Fourteen- and fifteen-year-olds,' Shaz said firmly. 'I can't go into the precise details that have linked these cases, but we have grounds for believing they may be connected.'

'You mean, they're not just run-of-the-mill runaways?' he asked, sounding perplexed.

'We have reason to believe their disappearances were planned by a third party,' Shaz said cautiously, never shifting her eyes from his face. The intensity of her gaze made him uncomfortable. He wanted to edge away from her stare, to fidget his way out of her eyeline. But he forced himself to keep his pose casual.

'Kidnapped, is that what you're saying?'

Her eyebrows and a slight movement of her head indicated a shrug. 'I'm not in a position to release any more information,' she said with a sudden smile.

'Fine, but you're still not making much sense. What has a bunch of missing teenagers got to do with me?' He made his voice sound a little edgy. It wasn't hard to do; there was plenty of nervous tension buzzing in his veins to draw on.

Shaz flipped open her folder and drew out a sheaf of photocopied photographs. 'In every case, a couple of days before the girls disappeared, you'd made a public appearance or taken part in a charity event in the towns where they lived. We have reason to believe that each of the girls attended the occasion.'

He could feel the red tide rising up his neck. He was powerless to stop the flush of anger as it climbed into his face. It was an effort to keep himself calm and his voice level. 'Hundreds of people come to my events,' he said evenly, his voice a fraction husky to his ears. 'Statistically, some of them must go missing. All the time.'

Shaz cocked her head, as if she'd also picked up on a change in his tone. She looked like a hunting dog who's just had the faintest whiff of what might possibly be a rabbit. 'I know. I'm sorry we have to bother you with this. It's just that my boss thinks there's an outside possibility that either someone in your entourage or possibly someone who's got an unhealthy interest in you might conceivably be involved in the disappearance of those girls.'

'You mean, you think I've got a stalker who's capturing my fans?' This time, he found it wasn't hard to sound incredulous. As a cover story, it was ridiculous. An imbecile could see that the person she was really interested in wasn't some crazy, nor a member of his entourage. It was him. He could tell by her eyes, obsessively fixed on him, recording his every move, noticing the faint sheen of sweat he could feel on his forehead. And her talk of a boss was just as evidently a bluff. She was a lone wolf, like him. He could smell it on her.

Shaz nodded. 'It could be. Transference, the psychologists call it. Like John Hinckley. Remember him? The guy who shot Ronald Reagan because he wanted Jodie Foster to take notice of him?' Her voice was pleasant, friendly, carefully pitched so he wouldn't feel threatened. He hated her for thinking so simple a technique would slip past him unnoticed.

'This is bizarre,' he said, pushing off from the mantelpiece and striding to and fro on the hearth rug, a hand-knotted silk Bokhara that he'd chosen himself. Staring down at the grey and cream intricacies under his feet calmed him until he was able to meet the woman's intense eyes again. 'It's absurd. If it wasn't so appalling a suggestion, it would be funny. And I still don't see what it has to do with me.'

'It's simple, sir,' Shaz said soothingly.

Feeling patronized, Vance stopped in his tracks and scowled. 'What?' he demanded, charm disintegrating by the second.

'All I want you to do is to look at some photographs and tell me if you noticed the girls for any reason. Maybe they were particularly pushy with you, and someone wanted to punish them. Maybe you noticed one of your staff chatting them up. Or maybe you never spotted any of them. Just a couple of minutes of your time, then

I'm out of here,' Shaz coaxed. She leaned forward and spread the photocopies over a kilim-covered footstool the size of a coffee table.

He moved towards her, transfixed by the photographs that she'd arranged to face him. Only a fraction of his work, that was all she'd captured. But every single smiling stare was one he'd destroyed.

Vance forced a laugh. 'Seven faces out of thousands? Sorry, DC Bowman, you've been wasting your time. I've never seen any of them before.'

'Look again,' she said. 'Are you absolutely certain?' There was an edge in her voice that hadn't been there before, sharp and excited. He dragged his eyes away from the pale reflections of the living flesh he'd punished and met Shaz Bowman's implacable eyes. She knew. She might not have the proof yet, but he knew she knew now. He also knew she wouldn't stop until she had destroyed him. It had come down to dog eat dog, and she had no chance. Not handicapped by the law.

He shook his head, a sorrowful smile on his lips. 'I'm positive. I've never clapped eyes on any of them before.'

Without even looking, Shaz pushed the middle picture closer to him. 'You made an appeal in a national tabloid for Tiffany Thompson to call her parents,' she said without inflexion.

'My God,' he exclaimed, forcing his features into an expression of happy astonishment. 'Do you know, I'd completely forgotten about that? You're right, of course, I see it now.'

Her attention was all on his face as he spoke. In a swift movement, he swung his prosthesis round in a short arc and smashed it violently into the side of her head. Her eyes showed a momentary shock, then panic. As she fell out of the chair, her forehead smacked into the footstool. By the time she crashed to the floor, she was unconscious.

Vance wasted no time. He raced down to the cellar where he grabbed a reel of hi-fi speaker wire and a pack of latex gloves. Within minutes, Shaz was trussed like a hog-tied steer on the polished parquet. Then he ran up to the top floor and opened his wardrobe, scrabbling around on the floor until he found what he was looking for. Back downstairs, he covered Shaz's head with the soft flannel bag that his new leather briefcase had come in. Then he wrapped a few lengths of wire round her neck, tight enough to be uncomfortable but not so that it would constrict her breathing. He wanted her dead, but not yet. Not here, and not accidentally.

As soon as he was sure that she wasn't going to be able to break free, he picked up her shoulder bag and sat down with it on the sofa, gathering the photocopies and the file they'd come from on the way. Meticulously, he began to go through everything, starting with the file. The abstracts of the police reports he skimmed over, knowing he would have the opportunity to look at them in more detail later. When he came to the analysis Shaz had presented to her colleagues, he took his time, weighing and calculating how dangerous to him it might prove. Not very, he decided. The photocopies of the newspaper clippings about his visits to the places in question were meaningless; for every one connected to a disappearance, he could produce twenty that weren't. Putting that aside, he picked up the organized offender checklist. Reading her conclusion so angered him that he jumped to his feet and gave the unconscious detective a couple of savage kicks in the stomach. 'Fuck do you know, bitch?' he shouted angrily. He wished he could see her eyes now. They wouldn't be judging him, they'd be begging him for mercy.

Furious, he stuffed the papers back in the file along with the photocopies. He'd have to study them more carefully, but there wasn't time now. He'd been right to nip this in the bud before anyone else paid attention to this bitch's allegations. He turned to her roomy shoulder bag and pulled out a spiral-bound notebook. A quick flick through the pages revealed nothing of interest except Micky's phone number and their address. Since he wasn't going to be able to deny she'd been here, that had better stay. But he tore out a handful of pages after the last entry, making it look as if someone had ripped out details pertaining to a subsequent appointment, then replaced it in the bag.

Next out was the microcassette recorder, the tape still turning. He stopped the machine and removed the tape, placing it with the blank sheets of paper on one side. He ignored the Ian Rankin paperback and pulled out a filofax. Under that day's date, the only entry read, 'JV 9.30'. He considered adding another cryptic entry and settled for the single letter 'T' underneath her appointment with him. Let them think about that. Inside the front cover, he found what he was looking for. 'If found, return to S. Bowman, Flat 1, 17 Hyde Park Hill, Headingley, Leeds. REWARD.' His fingers groped around the bottom of the bag. No keys.

Vance stuffed everything back into the shoulder bag, picked up the file and crossed to Shaz. He patted her down until he found a bunch of keys in her trouser pocket. Smiling, he went upstairs to his office and found a padded envelope big enough for the file. He addressed it to his Northumberland retreat, stamped it and sealed Shaz's research inside.

A quick glance at his watch told him it was barely half past ten. He went through to his bedroom and changed into jeans, one of the few short-sleeved T-shirts he possessed, and a denim jacket. He picked up a holdall from the back of the fitted wardrobes that ran deep under the eaves. He took out a Nike baseball cap that was attached to a professional quality wig of collar-length salt-and-pepper hair and put it on. The effect was remarkable. When he added a pair of aviator glasses with clear lenses and a pair of foam pads to fill out his hollow cheeks, the transformation was complete. The only giveaway was his prosthetic arm. And Jacko had the perfect answer to that.

He let himself out of the house, careful to lock up behind himself, and opened Shaz's car. He took a careful note of the seat position, then climbed in and adjusted it to suit his longer legs. He spent a few minutes familiarizing himself with the controls, making sure he was going to be able to manage the stick shift and steer at the same time. Then he set off, stopping only to drop the padded envelope in a pillar box in Ladbroke Grove. As he hit the approach ramp to the M1 shortly after eleven o'clock, he allowed himself a small, private smile. Shaz Bowman was going to be very sorry she'd ever crossed him. But not for long.

The first pain was a scream of cramp in her left leg, penetrating her muzzy unconsciousness like a serrated knife across a knuckle. The instinctive attempt at stretching and flexing the muscle triggered a slash of agony around her wrists. It made no sense to a disorientated mind that had started to throb like a thumb hit with a hammer. Shaz forced her eyes open, but the blackness didn't go away. Then she registered the damp material against her face. It was some sort of hood, made of thick fabric with a soft nap. It covered her whole head, fastening tightly round her throat, making it hard to swallow.

Gradually, she made sense of her position. She was lying on her side on a hard surface, her hands fastened behind her back with some sort of ligature that bit cruelly into the flesh of her wrists. Her feet were also fastened at the ankle, and both sets of bonds were linked to allow minimal movement. Anything adventurous like stretching her legs or trying to shift her spot cost too much in pain. She had no idea how small or how large her area of confinement was, nor any desire to explore once she had experienced the torment of attempting to turn over.

She had no idea how long she'd been unconscious. The last thing she could remember was Jacko Vance's laughing face looming over her, as if he didn't have a care in the world, secure in the certainty that no one would ever take this pipsqueak detective seriously. No, that wasn't quite right. Something else tugged at her memory. Shaz tried the deep breathing of relaxation techniques and tried to picture what she'd seen. The memory stirred and took shape. Out on the edge of her peripheral vision, his right arm rising, then swinging down savagely like a club. That was the last thing she could remember.

With the memory came terror, sharper than any of her physical afflictions. Nobody knew where she was except Chris, who wasn't expecting to hear from her anyway. She hadn't told anyone else, not even Simon. She hadn't been able to face their mockery, however friendly. Now the fear of being laughed at was going to cost her her life. Shaz was under no illusion about that. She'd asked Jacko Vance questions that made him realize she knew he was a serial killer and he hadn't panicked as she'd believed he would. Instead, he'd worked out for himself that she was a maverick. That although her deductions were a threat to him, he could win himself a stay of execution by getting rid of her, the renegade cop in hot pursuit of a solo hunch. Removing Shaz would, at worst, buy him time to cover his tracks or even leave the country.

Shaz felt a wave of sweat drench her skin. There was no question about it. She was going to die. The only question was how.

She'd been right. And being right was going to kill her.

Pauline Doyle was desperate. The police refused to regard Donna's disappearance as anything other than a typical teenage runaway. 'She'll have gone to London, probably. There's no point in us looking for her round here,' one of the uniformed officers she'd mithered at the counter of the police station had said in exasperation one night.

Pauline might shout from the rooftops that someone had stolen her daughter, but the evidence of the missing outfit was more than enough to convince overworked cops that Donna Doyle was just another teenager bored with home and convinced the streets somewhere were paved with gold. You only had to look at her photograph, that knowing smile, to understand she was nothing like as innocent as her poor misguided mother wanted to believe.

With the police showing no interest beyond a routine posting of Donna on the missing list, Pauline was stymied. Not for her the passionate television appeals for the missing daughter, not with the absence of official backing. Even the local paper wasn't interested, though the women's editor toyed with the idea of running a feature on teenage runaways. But like the police, when she saw Donna's photograph, she thought again. There was something about Donna that defied any attempt to portray her as an innocent abroad, seduced by chaste dreams. Something about the line of her mouth, the tilt of her chin said that she had crossed the line. The women's editor reckoned Donna Doyle was the sort of Lolita that would make most women want to put blinkers on their husbands.

Her frustration spilling over into nightly storms of tears, Pauline decided the time had come to take matters into her own hands. Her job in the estate agency wasn't particularly well paid. It was enough to feed and clothe her and Donna and to keep a roof over their heads, but not much more than that. There was still a couple of thousand left over from Bernard's insurance. Pauline had been saving that for when Donna went off to university, knowing how tight things would be then.

But if Donna didn't come back, there would be no point in saving it for university, Pauline reasoned. Better then to spend the money to try and get her home and let higher education fend for itself. So Pauline took Donna's photograph to the local print shop and had them make up thousands of flyers with her daughter's image occupying the whole of one side. The text on the reverse read, 'HAVE YOU SEEN THIS GIRL? Donna Doyle went missing on Thursday 11th October. She was last seen at quarter past eight in the morning, on her way to Glossop Girls Grammar. She was wearing school uniform of maroon skirt, maroon cardigan, white open-necked blouse. Her shoes were black Kickers, and she had a black anorak. She was carrying a black Nike backpack. If you saw her at any time after that, please contact her mother, Pauline Doyle.' It gave the address in Corunna Street, and telephone numbers at home and the agency.

Pauline took a week off work and stuffed the leaflets through letterboxes from dawn till dusk. She started in the town centre, thrusting the reproductions of Donna's face at anyone who would take them, and gradually worked her way out into suburban streets, not noticing the steepness of the hills she climbed or the blisters that swelled inside her shoes.

No one phoned.

While Shaz Bowman was lying on his hard floor in London, conscious only of fear and pain, Jacko Vance was exploring her domain. He'd made good time to Leeds, stopping only to fill up with petrol and visit the disabled toilet at the motorway services. He'd wanted to use its sanitary disposal unit to get rid of the tape he'd unravelled from Shaz's microcassette. In the car park, he'd crushed the casing underfoot, leaving the fragments to scatter in the blustery wind that swept across the Midlands.

Finding Shaz's home had been made even easier by her recently purchased *A to Z*, which conveniently had the street circled in blue biro. He parked the car round the corner and forced himself to combat his twitching nerves by strolling slowly down the street, empty except for a couple of small boys playing cricket on the opposite pavement. He turned in at the gate of number 17 and tried one of the two Yale keys in the heavy Victorian front door. That he got it right first time convinced him that the gods really were on his side.

He found himself in a gloomy hallway, lit only by two thin lancet windows on either side of the door. Peering into the murk, he saw a wide and graceful staircase rising ahead of him. There seemed to be one ground-floor flat on either side. He chose the left-hand side, and was proved right again. Breathing more easily now, convinced everything was going his way, Vance let himself into the flat. He wasn't planning on staying long, just enough to scout out the lie of the land, so he moved swiftly through the rooms. As soon as he saw the living room, he realized that Shaz could not possibly have chosen a flat better suited to his purpose. The French windows led out on to a garden surrounded by high walls, shaded by tall fruit trees. At the end, he could discern the outlines of a wooden door in the brick wall.

Only one thing remained to be done. He slipped off his jacket and unfastened his prosthesis. From the holdall, he took an object he'd persuaded the props department to make for him a couple of years back, supposedly as a practical joke. Using the fittings from one of his previous artificial arms, an earlier model now discarded, they'd built a plaster cast with disturbingly realistic fingertips protruding from the end. Once it was fitted, especially with a jacket over it and a sling holding it in place, it looked exactly like a broken arm. When he was satisfied he'd arranged it correctly, Vance re-packed the holdall, took a deep breath and decided it was time to go.

He let himself out of the French windows, pushing them to behind him, then strode confidently down the gravel path to the gate. He could feel the hair on his neck prickling under the wig, wondering if there were eyes behind any of the windows at his back, eyes that would remember what they'd seen once his handiwork was over and exposed to the public gaze. In a bid for reassurance, he reminded himself that any description they could come up with would sound nothing like Jacko Vance.

He unbolted the back gate, convinced that no one would fasten it again before he returned. He found himself in a narrow lane that ran between two sets of walled back gardens and led out on to one of the main roads that ran down towards the city centre. Walking to the station took the best part of an hour, but he had barely ten minutes to wait for a London train. He was back in Holland Park and restored to Jacko Vance by half past seven.

Before he made his final preparations, he slammed a twelve-inch pizza into the oven. It wasn't his usual idea of Saturday night dinner, but the carbohydrate should stop his stomach turning somersaults. Tension always hit him in the gut. Whenever the fever of anticipation had him in its grasp, he'd have to endure cramps and clenches, knots and nausea. He'd learned early on in his days as a live sports commentator that the only way to stop the churning and grumbling was to stodge out in advance. What worked for TV worked just as well for murder, he'd soon discovered. Now, he always ate before he picked up his targets. And of course, he always ate with them before the act itself.

While the pizza was cooking, he loaded his Mercedes. Exertion was easier on an empty stomach. Now everything was ready for Shaz Bowman's final performance. All he had to do was get her on stage.

Donna Doyle was also alone. But, deranged by agony, she lacked the luxury of introspection. The first time she'd woken from broken sleep, she'd felt strong enough to explore her prison. Her fear was still overwhelming, but it was no longer paralysing. Wherever she was, it was dark as a grave and had the dank smell of the tiny coal cellar at home. She used her good arm to help her gain a sense of where she was and what was around her. She was, she realized, lying on a plastic-covered mattress. Her fingers explored the edges and felt cold tiles. Not as smooth as the ceramic ones in the bathroom at home, more like the glazed terracotta on Sarah Dyson's mum's conservatory steps.

The wall behind her was rough stone. She struggled to her feet, realizing properly for the first time that her legs were shackled. She bent and let her fingers trace the outline of an iron cuff round each ankle. They were attached to a heavy chain. One-handed, it was impossible to gauge how long it was. Four hesitant steps along one wall brought her to a corner. She turned through ninety degrees and moved on. Two steps and her shin crashed painfully against something solid. It didn't take long both by touch and smell to identify it as a chemical toilet. Pathetically grateful, Donna subsided on to it and emptied her bladder.

That only reminded her of how thirsty she was. Hunger she wasn't too sure about, but thirst was definitely a problem. She stood up and carried on along the wall for another few feet before the chain round her ankles brought her up short. The jerk sent a spasm of pain shooting from her arm into her neck and head, and she gasped. Slowly, bent like an old woman, she retraced her steps and moved past the other end of the mattress, her hand brushing the wall.

Within a few feet, the questions of food and drink were answered. A stiff metal tap produced a surge of icy water which she drank thirstily, falling to her knees to get her head right underneath the flow. As she did, she knocked something over beyond her. Her thirst slaked, she groped blindly for whatever she'd bumped into. Probing fingers found four boxes, all large and light. She shook them and heard the familiar rustle of cornflakes.

An hour of investigation later and she was forced to realize that was it. Four boxes of cornflakes – she'd tested each one – and as much freezing water as she could drink. She'd tried running the water over her shattered arm, but the pain had made her head reel. This was it. The bastard had left her chained up like a dog. Left her to die?

She sat back on her heels and keened like a bereft mother.

But that had been a couple of endless days ago. Now, delirious with pain, she moaned and gibbered, occasionally passing out, occasionally drifting exhausted into tormented sleep. If she'd been able to comprehend the state she was in, Donna wouldn't have wanted to live.

The car stopped. Shaz slid irresistibly forward into the bulwark separating the narrow confines of the boot from the back seat, crushing her wrists and shoulders again. She tried to strain upwards to bang her head on the lid in a desperate bid to attract someone's attention, but all she achieved was a fresh wave of pain. She tried not to sob, afraid that if mucus blocked her nose, she'd suffocate, unable to breathe through the gag that Vance had tied over the hood before he'd rolled her agonizingly across hard floors, over a carpeted area and down a short flight of steps, then hoisted her into the boot of the car. She had been horribly amazed at the strength and dexterity of this one-armed man.

Shaz breathed as deeply as she could; too far and her chest expansion made her stiff shoulder muscles protest. Only sheer willpower kept her from gagging at the stench of her own urine. Let's see you get rid of that from your boot carpet, she thought triumphantly; she couldn't do anything to save her life, but she was still determined to seize every opportunity to prevent Jacko Vance from walking away from his crimes. If SOCO ever got this far, a piss-stained carpet would make their day.

Abruptly the muffled music stopped. Ever since they'd set off, he'd listened to hits of the sixties. Shaz had forced herself to pay attention and had counted the tracks. At an average of three minutes a song, she reckoned they'd been driving for somewhere around three hours of what had felt like motorway after the first twenty minutes or so. That probably meant the north; heading west would have taken them on to the motorway more quickly. Of course, it was possible that he could have confused her by driving a circuit round the M25, orbiting London until he'd laid a completely false trail. Shaz didn't think so; she doubted whether he felt any need to mislead her. She wasn't going to be alive to tell anyone, after all.

It was probably dark by now; she'd lain bound in the house for what felt like several hours before Vance had returned to deal with her. If they were in the depths of the country, there would be no one to see or hear her. Somehow, she thought that was probably Vance's plan. He must have taken his victims somewhere isolated to escape detection. She could think of no reason why he'd treat her differently.

A car door closed with a soft thud and a faint click. Then a metallic sound closer to hand and the soft hydraulic sigh of a boot opening. 'God, you stink,' Vance said contemptuously, dragging her carelessly forward.

'Listen,' he continued, sounding closer. 'I'm going to free your feet. I'm going to cut them free. The knife is very, very sharp. Mostly I use it to joint meat. If you take my meaning.' His voice was almost a whisper, his hot breath penetrating the hood next to her ear. Shaz felt another ripple of nausea. 'If you try to run, I'll gut you like a pig on a butcher's hook. There's nowhere to run to, see? We're in the middle of nowhere.'

Shaz's ears told her different. To her surprise, there was the rumble of traffic not far off, the underlying mutter of city life. If she had half a chance, she'd take it.

She felt the cold blade of the knife briefly against the skin of her ankle, then her feet were miraculously free. For a second, she thought she could kick out then make a run for it. Then her circulation reasserted itself and spasms of excruciating pins and needles squeezed a moan from the dry mouth behind the unyielding gag. Before the cramp could pass, Shaz felt herself hauled over the edge of the boot. She collapsed in an uncoordinated heap before he slammed the boot shut and yanked her to her feet. He half-dragged, half-carried her through a gap or a gateway where she bashed her shoulder on the wall, then down a path and up a couple of steps. Then he pushed her sharply and she crashed to a carpeted floor, her legs still useless rubbery handicaps.

Even through the haze of disorientation and pain, the closing of the door and the rattle of curtains being drawn sounded strangely familiar to Shaz. A fresh dread seized her and she began to shiver uncontrollably, losing control of her bladder for the second time in the past hour.

'God, you're a disgusting bitch,' Vance sneered. Again she felt herself irresistibly hauled upwards. This time she was dumped unceremoniously in a hard, upright chair. Before she could adjust to the fresh pain in her shoulders and arms, she felt a new restraint being fastened to her leg, attaching it to the chair like a broken limb to a splint. In a desperate bid for freedom, she forced her other leg to kick out, rejoicing in the jarring connection with Vance's body, exulting in his cry of surprised pain.

The blow to her jaw snapped her head back with a crack that sent waves of sick pain down her spine. 'You fucking stupid cow,' was all he said before he grabbed her other leg and forced it against the chair while he bound them tightly together.

She felt his legs between her knees. The warmth of his body was almost the worst suffering she'd had to endure so far. He raised her arms agonizingly and forced them back down over the back of the chair to hold her irresistibly upright. Then the hood was pulled away from her flesh and she heard the whisper of a razor-sharp blade through cloth. Blinking at the sudden appalling brightness, Shaz's stomach was gripped with a cold cramp as she discovered her worst fear was a reality. She was sitting in her own living room, strapped to one of the four dining chairs she'd bought only ten days before in Ikea.

Vance pressed his body against hers as he cut the hood away just above the gag, leaving her able to see and hear properly, but incapable of any noise other than a muffled grunt. He stepped back, giving her breast a cruel tweak with his artificial hand as he went.

He stood staring at her, flicking the blade of the butcher's filleting knife against the table edge. Shaz thought she had never seen a more arrogant human being. His pose, his expression, everything reeked of self-important righteousness. 'You really fucked up my weekend,' he said witheringly. 'Believe me, this is not how I planned to spend Saturday night. Dressing up in fucking surgical greens and latex in some shitty flat in Leeds is not my idea of a good time, bitch.' He shook his head pityingly. 'You're going to pay, Detective Bowman. You're going to pay for being a stupid little fuck.'

He put the knife down and fumbled under his top. Shaz glimpsed a bum bag as he unzipped it and took out a CD-ROM. Without another word he walked out of the room. Shaz heard the familiar hum then clatter as first her computer then her printer were switched on. Straining her ears, she fancied she heard the clicking of the mouse and the sound of keys being struck. Then, unmistakably, the vibrating thrum of paper loading and printing.

When he returned, he carried a single sheet of paper which he held in front of her face. She recognized the print-out of an illustrated encyclopaedia article. She didn't have to read the words to understand the symbolism of the line drawing at the top of the page. 'You know what this is?' he demanded.

Shaz just stared at him, her eyes bloodshot but still arresting. She was determined not to give in to him on any level.

'It's a teaching aid, student detective Bowman. It's the three wise monkeys. See no evil, hear no evil, speak no evil. You should have taken that as your class motto. You should have stayed away from me. You should have kept your nose out of my business. You won't be doing that again.'

He let the paper flutter to the floor. Suddenly he lunged forward, hands pushing her head back. Then his prosthetic thumb was over her eyeball, pushing down and out, rending muscles, ripping the hollow globe free from its moorings. The scream was only inside Shaz's head. But it was loud enough to carry her over into blessed unconsciousness.

Jacko Vance studied his handiwork and saw that it was good. Because his usual killings were fuelled by a completely different set of needs, he'd never contemplated them in a purely aesthetic light before. But this was a work of art, laden with symbolism. He wondered if anyone would be smart enough to read the message he'd left and, having read it, to heed it. Somehow, he doubted it.

He leaned forward and made a slight adjustment to the angle of the sheet of paper in her lap. Then, satisfied, he allowed himself the luxury of a smile. All he had to do now was to make sure she'd left no messages behind. He began to search the flat methodically, inch by inch, including the waste bins. He was used to the company of corpses, so the presence of Shaz's remains caused him no stress. He was so relaxed as he meticulously searched her kitchen that he actually caught himself singing softly as he worked.

In the room she'd made her office, he found more than he'd bargained for. A box of photocopies of newspapers, a pad of rough notes, files on the hard disk of her laptop and back-ups on floppy disk, print-outs of various drafts of the analysis he'd found earlier in the file she'd brought to his house. What was even worse was that much of the print-out didn't seem to have any matching files on the computer. There were copies on floppy disk, but not on the hard disk. It was a nightmare. When he spotted the modem, he almost panicked. The reason the files weren't on her hard disk was that they were somewhere else, presumably on some National Profiling Task Force computer. And there was no way he could access that. His only hope was that Shaz Bowman had been as paranoid with her computer files as she seemed to have been about sharing her showdown with a colleague. Either way, there was nothing he could do about it now. He'd get rid of every trace there was here and just have to hope that nobody would go looking in her computer files at work. If the Luddite cops he knew were anything to judge by, it would never occur to them that she might have techie tendencies. Besides, she wasn't supposed to be working cases, was she? Not according to the contacts he'd so cautiously and entirely naturally exploited to find out what he had about her before their meeting. There was no reason why anyone should connect so bizarre a death to her profiling training.

But how was he going to deal with all this *stuff*? He couldn't take the material with him in case a chance encounter with a traffic cop led to a search of his car. Equally, he couldn't leave it behind, pointing a giant finger of blame in his direction. He wasn't singing now.

He crouched in one corner of the office, thinking furiously. He couldn't burn it. It would take too long and the smell would be bound to attract the attention of her neighbours. The last thing he needed was the fire brigade. He couldn't flush it down the toilet; it would block the drains in no time at all unless he tore it into tiny fragments, and that would take till dawn and beyond. He couldn't even dig a hole in the garden and bury it, since the discovery of the bitch's body would only be the starting point for a massively thorough investigation, beginning with the immediate environs of the body.

In the end, the only solution he could come up with left no choice but to take all the incriminating evidence with him. It was a scary thought, but he kept telling himself that luck and the gods were with him, that he'd been untouchable up to now because he took every precaution humanly possible and left only a fraction of the risk to a benevolent fate.

Vance loaded a couple of bin liners with the material and staggered out to the car with them, every step an effort. He had been working on ditching Detective Constable Shaz Bowman for something like fifteen or sixteen hours, and he was running out of mental and physical energy. He never used drugs when he was working; the false sense of power and capability they induced were certain steps to fallibility and stupid mistakes. But just this once, he wished he had a neatly folded paper packet of cocaine in his pocket. A couple of lines of charlie and he'd be flying through the tasks that remained instead of dragging his weary body down this bloody gravel path through the arse end of Leeds.

With a small groan of relief, he dropped the second bin liner in the boot. He paused momentarily, wrinkling his nose in disgust. Leaning forward and sniffing, he confirmed his suspicion. The bitch had pissed in his car, soaking the carpet. One more item to dispose of, he thought, glad he had a ready solution to the problem. He stripped off his surgical greens and gloves and pushed them into the spare-tyre well then gently closed the lid with a soft snap of metal. 'Goodbye, DC Bowman,' he muttered as he lowered himself wearily into the driving seat. The clock on the dashboard told him it was nearly half past two. Provided he wasn't stopped by the cops for being in possession of a smart motor in the small hours of the morning, he'd be at his destination by half past four. The only difficulty would be fighting his instinct to hammer the pedal to the metal so he could put as much distance between him and his achievement as possible. With one hand sweating and the other as cool as the night air, he drove out of the city and headed north.

He made it ten minutes ahead of schedule. The maintenance area of the Royal Newcastle Infirmary was deserted, as he knew it would be until the Sunday morning skeleton shift arrived at six. Vance backed his car into a space in the service bay right next to the double doors that led through to the incinerators that dealt with the hospital's surgical waste. Often when he'd finished his voluntary work with the patients, he'd come down here to have a brew and a gossip with the service staff. They were proud to count a celebrity like Jacko Vance as a friend, and they'd been more than honoured to provide him with his own smart card to admit him to the maintenance sectors so he could come and go at will. They'd even known him to come down on his own in the middle of the night when there was no one else around and help them out by getting stuck in to the incineration work himself, stoking the furnace with the sealed bags of waste that came down from clinics, wards and operating theatres.

It never occurred to them that he added his own fuel to the flames.

That was one of the many reasons why Jacko Vance never feared discovery. He was no Fred West with bodies underpinning the foundations of his home. When he'd finished taking his pleasure with his victims, they disappeared forever in the fierce disintegrating heat of the RNI's incinerator. For an appliance that routinely swallowed the waste of an entire city hospital, two bin bags full of Shaz Bowman's research would be a mere *amuse bouche*. He'd be in and out in twenty minutes. Then the end would be in sight. He could fall into his favourite bed, the one at the heart of his killing floor, ignore all the other distractions and sleep the sleep of the just.

PART TWO

'Anybody know where Bowman is?' Paul Bishop asked impatiently, looking at his watch for the fifth time in two minutes. Five blank faces stared back at him.

'Gotta be dead, hasn't she?' Leon grinned. 'Never late, not Shazza baby.'

'Ha ha, Jackson,' Bishop said sarcastically. 'Be a good boy and call down to the front desk, see if they've taken a message from her.'

Leon tipped his chair forward on to all four feet and slouched out of the door, the wide shoulders of his sharply tapering jacket managing to make his six feet of skinniness look challenging. Bishop started drumming his fingers on the edge of the video remote control. If he didn't get this session kicked off soon, he'd be running late. He had a series of scene-of-crime videos to get through then a meeting with a Home Office minister scheduled for lunch. Bloody Bowman. Why did she have to be late today of all days? He'd give her till Jackson got back and then he was forging ahead with the session. Too bad if she missed something crucial.

Simon spoke softly to Kay. 'Have you spoken to Shaz since Friday?'

Kay shook her head, her light brown hair falling like a curtain across one cheek to create the image of a fieldmouse peering through winter grasses. 'I left a message when she didn't turn up for the curry, but she didn't get back to me. I was half-expecting to see her at the women's swim last night, but she wasn't there either. Mind, it wasn't a firm arrangement or anything.'

Before Simon could say anything more, Leon returned. 'Not a dicky bird from her,' he announced. 'She's not rung in sick or anything.'

Bishop tutted. 'Well, we'll just have to manage without her.' He briefed them on the morning's programme, then pressed 'play' on the video.

The aftermath of uncontrolled violence and viciousness that unfolded before them made little impact on Simon. Nor did he have much to contribute to the discussion afterwards. He couldn't get Shaz's absence out of his head. He'd gone round to her flat to pick her up on Saturday night for their pre-curry drink, as they'd agreed. But when he'd rung the bell, there had been no reply. He'd been early, admittedly, so, thinking she might have been deafened by the shower or the hair dryer, he'd walked back to the main road and found a phone box. He'd let her number ring out until the call was automatically disconnected, then he'd tried twice more. Unable to believe she'd stood him up without a word, he'd walked back up the hill to the flat and tried the doorbell again.

He knew which ground-floor flat was Shaz's – he'd given her a lift home after they'd all been out for a drink one evening and, already wistfully hoping he might pluck up the courage to ask her out, he'd lingered long enough to see which set of lights came on. So, just by looking, he could see that the curtains were closed across the deep bay of the master bedroom at the front of the house although it wasn't long dark. As far as he was concerned, that meant she'd been getting ready to go out. Though not, it appeared, with him. He was about to give up and go to the pub alone to drown his humiliation in Tetley's when he noticed the narrow passage running down the side of the house. Not giving himself time to wonder whether he was either justified or wise, he slipped down the ginnel, through the wrought-iron gate and into the gloomy darkness of the back garden.

He rounded the corner of the house and almost tripped over a short flight of steps leading up from the garden to a pair of French windows. 'For fuck's sake,' he muttered angrily, catching himself before he pitched headlong. He peered through the glass, cupping his hand round his eyes against the stray beams of light from the next-door house. He could see dim shapes of furniture against a faint glow that appeared to be coming from another room opening off the hall. But there was no sign of life. Suddenly a light snapped on from the floor above, casting an irregular rectangle of light right next to Simon.

Instantly aware that he must appear more like burglar than

policeman to any casual observer, he'd slid back into the darkness against the wall and returned to the street, hoping he'd managed to avoid anyone's attention. The last thing he needed were jibes from the local uniforms about the Peeping Toms of the profiling squad. Baffled by Shaz's apparent rebuff, he'd walked miserably down to the Sheesh Mahal to meet Leon and Kay for the agreed meal. He wasn't in the mood to join in their speculation that Shaz had had a better offer, concentrating instead on getting as much Kingfisher lager down his throat as he could.

Now, on Monday morning, he was seriously worried. It was one thing standing him up. Let's face it, she could probably do a lot better than him without trying too hard. But to miss a training session was completely out of character. Oblivious to Paul Bishop's words of wisdom, Simon sat and fretted, a pair of frown lines dividing his dark brows. As soon as the screech of chairs on floor announced the end of the session, he went in search of Tony Hill.

He found the psychologist in the canteen, sitting at the table the profiling squad had made their own. 'Can you spare a minute, Tony?' he asked, his dark intense expression almost a mirror image of his tutor's.

'Sure. Pull up a coffee and join me.'

Simon looked uncertainly over his shoulder. 'It's just that the others'll be down any minute, and . . . well, it's a bit . . . you know, sort of private.'

Tony picked up his own coffee and the file he'd been reading. 'We'll grab one of the interview rooms for a minute.'

Simon followed him down the corridor to the first witness interview room without a red light showing. The air smelled of sweat, stale cigarettes and, obscurely, burnt sugar. Tony straddled one of the chairs and watched Simon pace for a moment before he leaned into one corner of the room. 'It's Shaz,' Simon said. 'I'm worried about her. She didn't turn up this morning and she didn't phone in or anything.'

Tony knew without being told there was more to it than that. It was his job to find out what. 'I agree, it's not like her. She's very conscientious. But something could have come up unexpectedly. A family problem, perhaps?'

One corner of Simon's mouth twitched downwards. 'I suppose so,' he conceded reluctantly. 'But she would have phoned somebody if that's what it was. She's not just conscientious, she's obsessive. You know that.'

'Maybe she's had an accident.'

Simon pounced. 'Exactly. My point exactly. We should be worried about her, shouldn't we?'

Tony shrugged. 'If she has had an accident, we'll hear about it soon enough. Either she'll call us or else someone else will.'

Simon clenched his teeth. He was going to have to explain why it was more urgent than that. 'If she's had an accident, I don't think it was this morning. We had a sort of date on Saturday night. Leon and Kay and me and Shaz, we've taken to going out on a Saturday night for a curry and a few bevvies. But I'd arranged to have a drink with Shaz first, just the two of us. I was supposed to meet her at her flat.' Once he'd started, the words poured out of him. 'When I turned up, there was no sign of her. I thought she'd had second thoughts. Bottled out, whatever. But now it's Monday, and she's not turned up. I think something's happened to her, and whatever it is, it's not trivial. She could have had an accident at home. She could have slipped in the shower and hit her head. Or outside. She could be lying in hospital somewhere and nobody knows who she is. Don't you think we should do something about it? We're supposed to be a team, are we not?'

A dreadful premonition shimmered at the edge of Tony's mind. Simon was right. Two days was too long for a woman like Shaz Bowman to drop out of sight when that meant letting down a colleague and missing work. He got to his feet. 'Have you tried ringing her?' he asked.

'Loads of times. Her answering machine's not on, either. That's why I thought maybe she'd had an accident in the house. You know? I thought, she might've switched the machine off when she came in, and then something happened and . . . I don't know,' he added impatiently. 'This is really embarrassing, you know? I feel like a teenager. Making a fuss about nothing.' He shrugged away from the wall and crossed to the door.

Tony put a hand on Simon's arm. 'I think you're right. You've got a policeman's instinct for when something doesn't smell right. It's one of the reasons you're on this squad. Come on, let's go round to Shaz's flat and see what we can see.'

In the car, Simon leaned forward in his seat as if willing them forward. Realizing any attempt at conversation would be futile,

Tony concentrated on following the young officer's terse directions. They pulled up outside Shaz's flat and Simon was on the pavement before Tony could even turn off the engine. 'The curtains are still drawn,' Simon said urgently as soon as Tony joined him on the doorstep. 'That's her bedroom on the left. The curtains were drawn on Saturday night when I was here.' He pushed the bell marked 'Flat 1: Bowman'. They could both hear the irritating buzz from within.

'At least we know the bell's working,' Tony said. He stepped back and looked up at the imposing villa, its York stone blackened by a century of the internal combustion engine.

'You can get round the back,' Simon said, finally releasing the bell push. Without waiting for a response, he was off down the ginnel. Tony followed him, but not quickly enough. As he reached the corner, he heard a wail like an agonized cat in the night. He emerged in time to see Simon reel back from a pair of French windows like a man struck in the face. The young policeman sank to his knees and emptied his guts on the grass, groaning incoherently.

Shocked, Tony took a few hesitant steps forward. As he came level with the steps leading up to the windows, the sight that had stripped Simon McNeill of his manhood turned his stomach to ice. Beyond thought, beyond emotion, Tony stared through the glass at something that looked more like a pastiche of a Bacon painting executed by a psychopath than it did a human being. At first, it was more than he could grasp.

When realization came a moment later, he'd have sold his soul for that previous incomprehension.

It was not the first mutilated corpse Tony had ever faced. But it was the first time he'd had any personal connection to a victim. Momentarily, he put a hand over his eyes, massaging his eyebrows with thumb and forefinger. This wasn't the time to mourn. There were things he could do for Shaz Bowman that no one else was capable of, and crawling round on the grass like a wounded puppy wasn't one of them.

Taking a deep breath, he turned to Simon and said, 'Call this in. Then go round the front and secure the scene there.'

Simon looked up at him beseechingly, his baffled pain impossible to ignore. 'That's Shaz?'

Tony nodded. 'That's Shaz. Simon, do as I say. Call this in. Go round the front. It's important. We need to get other officers here, now. Do it.' He waited until Simon stumbled to his feet and reeled towards the ginnel like a drunk. Then he turned back and stared through the glass at the ruination of Shaz Bowman. He longed to be closer, to move round her body and take in the horrific details of what had been done to her. But he knew too much about crime scene contamination even to consider it.

He made do with what he could see. It would have been more than enough for most people, but for Tony it was a tantalizing partial picture. The first thing he had to do was to stop thinking of this shell as Shaz Bowman. He must be detached, analytical and clear-headed if he was to be any use at all to the investigating officers. Looking again at the body in the chair, he found it wasn't so hard to distance himself from memories of Shaz. The deformed freakish head that faced him bore so little resemblance to anything human.

He could see dark holes where her startling eyes had last looked out at him. Gouged out, he guessed, judging by what looked like threads and strings trailing from the wounds. Blood had flowed and dried round the black orifices, making the hideous mask of her face even more grotesque. Her mouth looked like a mass of plastic in a dozen hues of purple and pink.

There were no ears. Her hair stuck out in spikes above and behind where the ears should have been, held in place by the dried blood that had sprayed and flowed over them.

His eyes moved down to her lap. A sheet of paper was propped up against her chest. Tony was too far away to make out the words, but he could distinguish the line drawing easily. The three wise monkeys. A shiver shook him from head to foot. It was too early to tell, but from what he could see, there was no sign of any sexual assault. Coupled with the deadly calculation of the three wise monkeys, Tony read the scene. This was no sex killing. Shaz hadn't caught the chance attention of some psychopathic stranger. This was an execution.

'You didn't do this for pleasure,' he said softly to himself. 'You wanted to teach her a lesson. You wanted to teach all of us a lesson. You're telling us you're better than us. You're showing off, thumbing your nose at us because you're convinced we'll never find anything to incriminate you. And you're telling us to keep our noses out of your business. You're an arrogant bastard, aren't you?'

The scene before him told Tony things it would never reveal to a police officer trained to look only for the physical clues. To the psychologist, it revealed a mind that was incisive and decisive. This was a cold-blooded killing, not a frenzied, sexually motivated attack. To Tony, that suggested that the killer had identified Shaz Bowman as a threat. Then he'd acted on it. Brutally, coldly and methodically. Even before the SOCOs arrived, Tony could have told them they would find no significant material clues to the identity of this perpetrator. The solution to this crime lay in the mind, not the forensic lab. 'You're good,' Tony murmured. 'But I'm going to be better.'

When the sirens tore the silence into shreds and uniformed feet pounded down the ginnel, Tony was still standing at the windows, memorizing the scene, drinking in every detail so it would be there later when he needed it. Then and only then he walked round to the front of the house to offer what consolation he could to Simon.

'Hardly bloody urgent,' the police surgeon grumbled, opening his bag and pulling out a pair of latex gloves. 'State she's in, an hour's neither here nor there. Not like doctoring the living, is it? Bloody pager, bane of my bloody life.'

Tony resisted the impulse to hit the chubby doctor. 'She was a police officer,' he said sharply.

The doctor flashed him a shrewd look. 'We've not met, have we? You new here?'

'Dr Hill works for the Home Office,' the local DI said. Tony had already forgotten the man's name. 'He runs this new profiling task force you'll have heard about. The lass was one of his trainees.'

'Aye, well, she'll get the same treatment from me as a Yorkshire lass would,' the doctor said drily, turning back to his grim task.

Tony was standing outside the now open French windows, looking in on the crime scene where a photographer and a team of SOCOs worked their way round the room. He could not take his eyes off the wreckage of Shaz Bowman. No matter how hard he tried, he could not avoid the occasional flashback image of what she had been. It heightened his resolve, but it was a provocation he could well have done without.

Worse for Simon, he thought bitterly. He'd been taken, putty-skinned and trembling, back to police HQ to give a statement about Saturday night. Tony knew enough about the workings of the official mind to realize that the murder squad were probably treating him as their current prime suspect. He was going to have to do something about that sooner rather than later.

The DI whose name he couldn't remember walked down the steps and stood behind him. 'Helluva mess,' he said.

'She was a good officer,' Tony told him.

'We'll get the bastard,' the DI said confidently. 'Don't you worry about that.'

'I want to help.'

The DI raised one eyebrow. 'Not my decision,' he said. 'It's not a serial killer, you know. We've never seen owt like this on our patch.'

Tony fought to suppress his frustration. 'Inspector, this is not a first-time killing. Whoever did this is an expert. He might not have killed on your patch or used this precise method before, but this is not the product of amateur night out.'

Before the inspector could respond, they were interrupted. The police surgeon had finished his grisly work. 'Well, Colin,' he said, walking over to them, 'She's definitely dead.'

With a quick sidelong glance, the policeman said, 'Spare us the gallows humour for once, Doc. Any idea when?'

'Ask your pathologist, Inspector Wharton,' the doctor said huffily.

'I will. But in the meantime, can you give me a ballpark figure?'

The doctor peeled off his gloves with a snap of latex. 'Monday lunchtime . . . let me see . . . Some time between seven o'clock Saturday night and four o'clock Sunday morning, depending on whether the heating was on and how long for.'

DI Colin Wharton sighed. 'That's a bloody big window of opportunity. Can't you get it tighter than that?'

'I'm a doctor, not bloody Mystic Meg,' he said caustically. 'And I'm going back to my game of golf, if you don't mind. You'll have my report in the morning.'

Tony impulsively put a hand on his arm. 'Doctor, I could use some help here. I know it's not really your place to say, but you've obviously developed a lot of expertise in this kind of thing.' When in doubt, flatter. 'The injuries . . . Do you know if she was still alive, or are they postmortem?'

The doctor pursed full red lips and stared back consideringly at Shaz's body. He looked like a small boy puckering up for his maiden aunt, calculating how much of a tip it was going to earn him. 'A mixture of both,' he said finally. 'I reckon the eyes both went while she was still alive. I think she must have been gagged or she'd have screamed the place down. She probably passed out then, a combination of shock and pain. Whatever was poured down her throat was very caustic and that's what killed her. The total disintegration of her respiratory tract, that's what they'll find when they open her up. I'd stake my pension on it. Looking at the amount of blood, I'd reckon the ears came off more or less as she was dying. They're neatly cut off, though. No trial attempts like you usually get with any kind of mutilation. He must have one hell of a sharp knife and a lot of nerve. If he was trying to make sure she'd end up like them three wise monkeys, he went the right way about it.' He nodded to the two men. 'I'll be off, then. Leave you to it. Good luck finding him. You've got a right nutter here.' He waddled off round the side of the house.

'That bastard's got the worst bedside manner in the whole West Riding,' Colin Wharton said in disgust. 'Sorry about that.'

Tony shook his head. 'What's the point in dressing up something as brutal as that in fancy words? Nothing alters the fact that somebody took Shaz Bowman apart and made sure we knew why.'

'What?' Wharton demanded. 'Have I missed something here? What d'you mean, we know why? I don't bloody know why.'

'You saw the drawing, didn't you? The three wise monkeys. See no evil, hear no evil, speak no evil. The killer destroyed her eyes, her ears, her mouth. Doesn't that say something to you?'

Wharton shrugged. 'Either the boyfriend's the killer, in which case he's a certifiable nutter and it doesn't matter what screwed-up shite was going round his head. Or else it was some other nutter who's got it in for coppers because he thinks we stick our noses into things that we'd be better off leaving alone.'

'You don't think it could be a killer who specifically had it in for Shaz because she was sticking her nose in somewhere it didn't belong?' Tony suggested.

'I don't see how it could be,' Wharton said dismissively. 'She's never worked any cases up here, has she? You lot aren't catching live ones yet, so she's not had the chance to get up some local nutter's nose.'

'Even though we're not catching new cases, we've been working on some genuine old ones. Shaz came up with a theory the other day about a previously unidentified serial killer . . .'

'The Jacko Vance story?' Wharton couldn't stop the snigger. 'We've all had a good laugh about that one.'

Tony's face tightened. 'You shouldn't have heard anything about it. Who let that out of the bag?'

'Nay, Doc, I'm not for dropping anybody else in it. Besides, you know there are no secrets in a nick. That were too good a joke to keep a secret. Jacko Vance, serial killer. It'll be the Queen Mum next!' He spluttered with laughter and clapped Tony indulgently on the shoulder. 'Face it, Doc, chances are you picked a wrong 'un when you co-opted the boyfriend. You don't need me to tell you that nine times out of ten we never end up looking beyond whoever the stiff's been shagging.' He raised a speculative eyebrow. 'Not to mention the person who finds the body.'

Tony snorted derisively. 'You'll be wasting your time if you try pinning it on Simon McNeill. He hasn't done this.'

Wharton turned to face Tony, pulling a Marlboro out of its pack with his teeth. He caught it in his lips and lit it with a throwaway lighter. 'I heard you lecture once, Doc,' he said. 'Over in Manchester. You said the best hunters were the ones who were most like the prey. Two sides of the same coin, you said. I reckon you were right. Only, one of your hunters has gone native on you.'

Jacko flapped a dismissive hand at his PA and hit a button on the remote control. His wife's face filled the king-size TV screen as she handed her audience over to the newsroom for the midday head-lines. Still nothing. The longer the better, he couldn't help thinking. The less accurate the pathologist could be about the time of death, the further it could be distanced from the stupid cow's visit to his home. As he killed the TV picture and turned to the script in front of him, he wondered momentarily what it must be like to have the sort of life where no one would notice you'd been lying dead for a couple of days. It was never likely to happen to him, he thought, self-satisfied as ever. It had been a very long time since he'd been that insignificant in anyone's life.

Even his mother would have noticed if he'd disappeared. She might well have been delighted at the prospect, but she'd have at least noticed. He wondered how Donna Doyle's mother was reacting to the disappearance of her daughter. He'd seen nothing on the news, but there was no reason why she should cause more of a stir than any of the others.

He'd made them pay, all of them, for what had been done to him. He knew he couldn't take it out on the one who deserved it; it would be too obvious, the finger pointing straight at him. But he could find surrogate Jillies all over the place, looking just as ripe and delicious as she'd been when he'd first pinned her to the ground and felt her virginity surrender to his power. He could make them understand what he'd been through, feel what he'd felt in ways that the treacherous bitch had never comprehended. His girls could never abandon him; he was the one with power over life and death. And he could make them discharge her debt over and over again.

Once, he had believed that there would come an occasion when these surrogate deaths would have purged him for good. But the catharsis never lasted. Always, the need came creeping back.

Lucky he'd got it off to such a fine art, really. All those years, all those deaths, and only one off-the-wall maverick cop had ever suspected.

Jacko smiled a very private smile, one his fans never saw. The means of payment had had to be different for Shaz Bowman. But they'd been satisfying, nonetheless. It made him wonder if it might not be the time to ring a few changes.

It never did to become a slave to routine.

Frustration drove Tony up the stairs two at a time. No one would let him near Simon. Colin Wharton was stonewalling, claiming he didn't have the authority to allow Tony to collaborate on the investigation. Paul Bishop was out of the building at one of his interminable and ever-convenient meetings, and the Divisional Chief Superintendent was allegedly too busy to see Tony.

He threw open the door of the seminar room, expecting to see the four remaining members of his task force engaged in some meaningful activity. Instead, Carol Jordan looked up from the file of papers in front of her. 'I was beginning to think I'd got the day wrong,' she said.

'Ah, Carol,' Tony sighed, subsiding into the nearest chair. 'I completely forgot you were coming back this afternoon.'

'Looks like you weren't the only one,' she said drily, gesturing at the remaining empty seats. 'Where's the rest of the team? Playing truant?'

'Nobody's told you, have they?' Tony said, looking up at her with angry eyes in a pained face.

'What's happened?' she asked, her chest constricting. What had happened now to drill more anguish into him?

'You remember Shaz Bowman?'

Carol nodded with a rueful smile. 'Ambition on legs. Blazing blue eyes, uses her ears and mouth in the correct proportion of two to one.'

Tony winced. 'Not any more she doesn't.'

'What's happened to her?' The concern in Carol's voice was still more for Tony than for Shaz.

He swallowed and closed his eyes, summoning the picture of her death and forcing all emotion out of his voice. 'A psychopath happened to her. Somebody who thought it would be entertaining to gouge out those blazing blue eyes and chop off those wide-open ears and pour something so corrosive into that smart mouth that it ended up looking like multicoloured bubble gum. She's dead, Carol. Shaz Bowman is dead.'

Carol's face opened in incredulous horror. 'No,' she breathed. She was silent for a long moment. 'That's terrible,' she finally said. 'So much life in her.'

'She was the best of the bunch. Desperate to be the best. And she wasn't arrogant with it. She could work with the others without making it obvious that she was the racehorse among the donkeys. What he did to her, it went straight to the heart of who she was.'

'Why?' As she had done so often in their previous case, Carol picked the important question.

'He left her with a computer print-out. A drawing and an encyclopaedia entry about the three wise monkeys,' Tony said.

Understanding flashed into Carol's eyes, followed swiftly by a confused frown. 'You don't seriously think . . . That theory she came out with the other day? It can't be anything to do with that, can it?'

Tony rubbed his forehead with his fingertips. 'I keep coming back to it. What else is there? The only live case we've had anything to do with is your arsonist, and none of them came up with enough to threaten anyone.'

'But Jacko Vance?' Carol shook her head. 'Surely you can't believe that? Grannies from Land's End to John O'Groats dote on him. Half the women I know think he's as sexy as Sean Connery.'

'And you? What do you think?' Tony asked. There was no innuendo in the question.

Carol turned the question over in her mind, making sure she had the right words before she spoke. 'I wouldn't trust him,' she eventually said. 'He's too glossy. Non-stick. Nothing leaves a lasting impact. He'll be charming, sympathetic, warm, understanding. But as soon as he moves on to the next interview, it's like the previous encounter never happened. Having said that . . .'

'You'd never have thought of him as a serial killer,' Tony said flatly. 'Me neither. There are some people in public life that you wouldn't feel overly surprised to see on a fistful of murder charges. Jacko Vance isn't one of them.'

They sat in silence facing each other across the room. 'It might not be him,' Carol said at last. 'What about somebody in his entourage? A driver, a minder, a researcher. One of those hangers-on, what do they call them?'

'Go-fers.'

'Yeah, go-fers, right.'

'But that still doesn't answer your question. Why?' Tony pushed himself to his feet and started pacing out the perimeter of the room. 'I don't see how anything she said in here could conceivably have made it into Jacko Vance's circles. So how did our theoretical killer know she was on to him?'

Carol swung round awkwardly in her chair so she could watch him as he crossed behind her. 'She wanted to be a glory girl, Tony. I don't think she was ready to let it drop. I think she decided to follow up her idea. And one way or another, she alerted the killer.'

Tony reached the corner and stopped. 'Do you know . . .' was all he had time for before the door opened on Detective Chief Superintendent Dougal McCormick. His bulky shoulders almost filled the frame.

An Aberdonian, he resembled one of the black Aberdeen Angus cattle from his native territory: black curls tumbling over a broad forehead, liquid dark eyes always on the lookout for the red rag, wide cheekbones seeming to drag his fleshy nose across his face, full lips always moist. The only incongruity was his voice. Where a deep roar should have rumbled in his chest, a melodious light tenor emerged. 'Dr Hill,' he said, closing the door behind him without looking at it. His eyes flickered in Carol's direction then looked a question at Tony.

'DCS McCormick, this is DCI Carol Jordan from the East Yorkshire force. We're helping her with an arson inquiry,' Tony said.

Carol stood up. 'Pleased to meet you, sir.'

McCormick's nod was almost imperceptible. 'If you'd excuse us, I need a moment with Dr Hill,' he said.

Carol knew when she was being dismissed. 'I'll wait down in the canteen.'

'Dr Hill won't be staying on the premises,' McCormick said. 'You'd do better to wait in the car park.'

Carol's eyes widened, but she simply said, 'Very well, sir. I'll see you outside, Tony.'

As soon as Carol had closed the door behind her, Tony rounded on McCormick. 'And what exactly do you mean by that, Mr McCormick?'

'What I said. This is my division and I'm running a murder inquiry. A police officer has been ... destroyed, and it's my job to find out who's responsible. There's no sign of forcible entry in Sharon Bowman's flat and, by all accounts, she was no fool. So the chances are she knew her killer. And as far as I know at this point in time, the only people Sharon Bowman knew in Leeds were her fellow officers in the task force, and you, Dr Hill.'

'Shaz,' Tony interrupted. 'She hated being called Sharon. Shaz, that's what she was called.'

'Shaz, Sharon, whatever, it makes little difference now.' McCormick brushed the objection aside with all the casual grace of a bull flicking its tail at a fly. 'The point is that you people are the only ones she'd have let in. So I don't want you talking to each other until my murder squad officers have had a chance to interview each and every one of you. Until further notice, this task force is suspended. You will not be authorized to occupy police premises and you are not to communicate with each other. I've already discussed this with Commander Bishop and the Home Office, and we're all agreed that's the appropriate path to go down. Is that clear?'

Tony shook his head. It was all too much. Shaz was dead, horribly dead. And now McCormick wanted to arrest one of the handful of people who might actually be able to provide a way through to her killer. 'You might, by some stretch of the imagination, have authority over the officers in my squad. But I'm not a police officer, McCormick. I don't answer to you. You should be using our talents, not pissing on us. We can help, man, can't you understand that?'

'Help?' McCormick's voice was scornful. 'Help? What were you planning on doing? I've heard some of the daft ideas your lot have come up with. My men are going to be chasing leads, not jokes. Jacko Vance, for heaven's sake. You'll be asking us to arrest Sooty next.'

'We're on the same side,' Tony said, smudges of scarlet rising across his cheekbones.

'Maybe so, but some kinds of help turn out to be more of a hindrance. I want you out of here now, and I don't want you bothering my men. You will report back to this station at ten tomorrow morning so that my officers can interview you formally about Sharon Bowman. Have I made myself clear, Dr Hill?'

'Listen, I can help you here. I understand killers; I know why they do the things they do.'

'It's not hard to work that out. They're sick in the head, that's why.'

'Granted, but they're all sick in the head in their own particular ways,' Tony said. 'This one, for example. I bet he didn't assault her sexually, did he?'

McCormick frowned. 'How did you know about that?'

Tony ran a hand through his hair and spoke passionately. 'I didn't know in the sense of being told. I know because I can read things in a crime scene that your men can't. This wasn't a run-of-the-mill sexual homicide, Superintendent, this was a deliberate message to us that this killer thinks he's so far ahead of us he's never going to be caught. I can help you catch him.'

'Sounds to me like you're more interested in covering up for your own,' McCormick said, shaking his head. 'You've picked up some information at the scene of the crime and turned it into some fancy theory. It'll take more than that to convince me. And I haven't got time to wait till you pick up the next bit of gossip. As far as this station's concerned, you're history. And your bosses at the Home Office agree with me.'

Fury drove Tony's normal tools of flattery and appeasement underground. 'You are making one hell of a mistake, McCormick,' he said, his voice rough with anger.

The big detective gave a snort of laughter, 'I'll take that risk, son.' He gestured with his thumb towards the door. 'Away you go, now.'

Realizing he couldn't win on this battleground, Tony bit down hard on the flesh of his cheek. The flavour of humiliation was the coppery taste of fresh blood. Defiantly, he walked over to his locker and pulled out his briefcase, filling it with the missing person files and the squad's analyses. Snapping the lock shut, he turned on his heel and walked out. On his way through the police station, officers fell silent as he passed. He was thankful that Carol wasn't there to witness his rout. She would never have been able to keep the silence that was his only remaining weapon.

As the front door swung shut behind him, he heard an unidentifiable voice behind him call out, 'Bloody good riddance.'

In a rare moment of lucidity in the ocean of pain, Donna Doyle contemplated her brief life and the foolish trust that had brought her to this place. Regret swelled inside her like a strange tumour, devouring everything it encountered. One mistake, one attempt to follow the rainbow to the pot of gold, one act of faith that was no more preposterous than the one the priest talked about every Sunday, and here she was. Once upon a time, she'd have said she'd do anything for a chance at stardom. Now she knew it wasn't true.

It wasn't fair. It wasn't as if she'd just wanted to be famous for herself. With the fame would have come money, so her mum wouldn't have had to scrimp and save and worry about every penny like she'd had to all the time since Dad had died. Donna had wanted it to be a surprise, a wonderful, wicked, exciting surprise. Now it would never happen. Even if she got out of here, she knew she wasn't going to be a star, not ever. She might be famous for fifteen minutes, like the song said, but not for being a one-armed TV star like Jacko Vance. Even if they found her, she was finished.

They could still find her, she told herself. She wasn't just whistling in the dark, she thought defiantly. They'd be looking for her by now, surely. Her mum would have gone to the police, her picture would be in the papers, maybe even on the telly. People all over the country would see her and search their memory. Somebody would remember her. There had been loads of people on the trains. Half a dozen other passengers had got off with her at Five Walls Halt. At least one of them *must* have noticed her. All dolled up in her best outfit, she knew she looked tasty. Surely the police would be asking questions, working out whose Land Rover she'd got into? Wouldn't they?

She groaned. In her heart, she knew this would be the last place she would lie. Alone in her tomb, Donna Doyle wept.

Tony sat hunched forward in the armchair, staring into the flickering gas flames of the fake hearth. He was still nursing the same glass of Theakston's he'd had since they'd arrived back at Carol's cottage. She'd refused to take no for an answer. He'd had a shock, he needed someone to discuss the case with, and she needed his input on her arsonist. She had a cat to feed, he had none, so logically their destination should be an hour down the motorway to the outskirts of Seaford.

Since they'd arrived, he'd said barely a word. He'd sat with his eyes on the fire and his mind projecting the film of Shaz Bowman's death. Carol had left him alone, taking the chance to throw together a packet of chicken breasts from the freezer, a couple of chopped onions and a jar of ready-made cider and apple sauce. She'd put the result into the oven with a couple of baking potatoes and left it on a low heat while she made up the guest bedroom. She knew there was little point in expecting anything more or less from Tony.

She poured herself a large gin and tonic, adding a couple of chunks of frozen lemon, and returned to the living room. Without saying anything, she tucked her legs under her and let the armchair opposite his swallow her up. Between them, Nelson lay stretched out like a long black hearth rug.

Tony looked up at Carol and managed a faint smile. 'Thanks for the peace and quiet,' he said. 'It has a very welcoming ambience, your cottage.'

'That's one of the reasons why I bought it. That and the view. I'm glad you like it.'

'I . . . I keep imagining it,' he said. 'The process. Tying her up, gagging her. Torturing her with the knowledge that she wasn't going to get out of it alive, not knowing what she knew.'

'Whatever that was.'

He nodded. 'Whatever that was.'

'I suppose it brings it all back to you?' Carol said softly.

He let out a long breath. 'Inevitably,' he said through tight lips. He looked up at her, his keen eyes shining under the jut of his frowning eyebrows. When he spoke again, his voice was a brisk contrast, indicating he wanted to escape the memories that were sometimes almost as bad as the experience itself. 'Carol, you're a detective. You heard Shaz's presentation, you were one of the ones who passed judgement on it. Imagine you'd been on the other end of our criticisms. Imagine you're back at the start of your career, with it all to prove. Don't think too hard about this. Give me your gut reaction. What would you do?'

'I'd want to prove you were wrong and I was right.'

'Yes, yes,' Tony acknowledged impatiently. 'That's a given. But what would you *do*? How would you go about it?'

Carol sipped her drink and considered. 'I know what I'd do now. I'd put a small team together – just a sergeant and a couple of DCs – and blitz every one of those cases. I'd go back and talk to friends, family. Check out whether the missing girls were Jacko Vance fans, whether they'd gone to the event he was appearing at. If they did, who they went with. What their companions noticed.'

'Shaz didn't have either the time or the team for that kind of operation. Think back to what it was like when you were young and hungry,' Tony urged.

'As to what I'd have done then . . . Given no resources, you have to fall back on your own assets.'

Tony gave her an encouraging nod. 'Meaning?'

'Smart mouth, fancy footwork. You know you're right, that's the bottom line. You know the truth is out there waiting for the proof to go round it. Me? I'd shake the tree and see what falls out.'

'So you'd do what, specifically?'

'These days, I'd probably drop some poison in the ear of a friendly journalist and plant a story that would mean something more to our killer than it would to the casual reader. But I haven't seen any signs that Shaz had those kind of contacts or, if she did, that she used them. What I'd probably have done in her shoes, if I'd had the bottle, would have been to set up a meeting with the man himself.'

Tony sat back in his chair and took a long swallow of beer. 'I'm glad you said that. It's the sort of idea I'm always reluctant to bring out into the open in case your lot starts laughing because no self-respecting police officer would dream of doing something so risky either to life or career.'

'You think she made contact with Jacko Vance?'

He nodded.

'And you think that whatever she said to him . . .'

'Or to someone around him,' Tony interrupted. 'It might not be Vance. It might be his manager or his minder or even his wife. But yes, I think she said something to someone in that group of people and she made a killer afraid.'

'Whoever it was didn't waste much time.'

'He didn't waste time and he's clearly got a lot of nerve to kill her in her own living room. To risk a cry, a scream, the noise of furniture being knocked over, anything untoward in a house split into flats.'

Carol sipped her drink, savouring the growing edge of lemon as the frozen fruit thawed completely. 'And he had to get her there in the first place.'

Tony looked puzzled. 'What makes you say that?'

'She'd never have agreed to meet someone she suspected was a serial killer in her own home. Not even with the hubris of youth. That would be like inviting a fox into the henhouse. And if he turned up there later, after the official interview, she'd hit the panic button, not let him in. No, Tony, she was already his prisoner by the time she got home.'

It was such flashes of insight backed with impeccable logic that had made Carol Jordan such a joy to work with before, Tony remembered. 'You're right, of course. Thank you.' He toasted her mutely with his glass. Now he knew where to start. He finished his beer and said, 'Any chance of another one? Then I think we need to talk about your little problem.'

Carol uncurled herself from the chair and stretched like Nelson. 'You sure you don't want to talk some more about Shaz?' Tony's expression of distaste told her all she needed to know. She went through to the kitchen for another beer.

'I'll save it for your West Yorkshire colleagues tomorrow morning. If you haven't heard from me by teatime, you'd better make sure I've got a decent brief,' he called after her.

When she was settled again in the armchair, he dragged his brooding eyes away from the fire and pulled a couple of sheets of lined paper from his briefcase. 'At the tail end of the week, I got the squad to work on their idea of a profile for you. They had a day to work up an individual profile, then on Friday, they collaborated on a joint effort. I've got a copy of it with me, I'll show you later.'

'Terrific. I didn't want to say anything before, but I've been working on a profile of my own. It'll be interesting to see how they compare.' She tried to keep her voice light, but Tony heard the desire for his praise, nevertheless. It made what he had to say all the more awkward. Sometimes he wished he smoked. It would give him something to do with his hands and mouth at times like this.

Instead, he ran a hand over his face. 'Carol, I have to tell you that I suspect you've all been wasting your time.'

Unconsciously, her chin jutted forward. 'Meaning what?' The words were more aggressive than the tone.

'Meaning that I don't think your fires fit into any known category.'

'You mean they're not arson?'

Before he could answer, a heavy knock reverberated through the cottage. Startled, Carol spilled a few drops of her drink. 'Are you expecting visitors?' Tony asked, turning to the dark window behind him to see if anything penetrated the darkness outside.

'No,' she said, jumping to her feet and moving across the room to the heavy wooden door that opened into the small stone porch. As she unlatched the door, a chill gust of wind filled the room with a cold waft of estuary silt. Carol looked surprised. Beyond her, Tony glimpsed the outline of a large male shape. 'Jim,' she exclaimed. 'I wasn't expecting you.'

'I tried to ring you this afternoon and I kept getting the runaround from Sergeant Taylor. So I thought I might as well head on up here and see if I could run you to earth.' As Carol stepped back, Pendlebury followed her in. 'Oh, I'm sorry – you've got company.'

'No, your timing couldn't be better,' she said, waving him towards the fire. 'This is Dr Tony Hill from the Home Office. We're just talking about the arson case. Tony, this is Jim Pendlebury, the fire chief in Seaford.'

Tony ceded his hand into the bone-grinding grip of a competitive handshake. 'Pleased to meet you,' he said mildly, refusing the invitation to joust.

'Tony is in charge of the new National Offender Profiling Task Force in Leeds,' Carol said.

'Tough job.' Pendlebury thrust his hands into the deep pockets of the fashionably oversized mac he was wearing. They emerged with a bottle of Australian Shiraz on the end of each. 'Housewarming present. Now we can all discuss our firebug with a bit of lubrication.'

Carol fetched glasses and corkscrew and poured wine for herself and Pendlebury, Tony waving his glass to indicate he'd stick with the beer. 'So, Tony, what have your baby boffins got to tell us?' Pendlebury asked, stretching his long legs out in front of him, forcing Nelson to move to one side. The cat gave him a malevolent glare and curled into a ball beside Carol's chair.

'Nothing Carol couldn't work out for herself, I imagine. The problem is that I suspect what they've done is irrelevant.'

Pendlebury's laugh sounded too loud in the confines of the cottage. 'Am I hearing things?' he said. 'A profiler admitting it's all a load of bollocks? Carol, have you got the tape running?'

Wondering how many more times he would have to smile politely while his life's work was denigrated, Tony let Pendlebury wind down before he spoke. 'Would you use a screwdriver to drive a fence post into the ground?'

Pendlebury cocked his head to one side. 'You're saying profiling is the wrong tool for the job?'

'That's exactly what I'm saying. Profiling works on certain crimes where the motivation is psychopathic to some degree.'

'Meaning?' Pendlebury asked, drawing his legs up and leaning forward, his interest wholly engaged, his face sceptical.

'Do you want the thirty-second version or the full lecture?'

'You'd better give me the idiot's guide, me being a mere fireman.'

Tony ran a hand through his thick dark hair, a reflex that always left him looking like a cartoon mad scientist. 'OK. Most crimes in this country are committed either for gain or in the heat of the moment, or under the influence of drink or drugs. Or a combination of all of the above. The crime is a means to an end – acquiring cash or drugs, gaining revenge, putting a halt to unacceptable behaviour.

'A handful of crimes have their roots in stranger soil. They grow from an inner psychological compulsion on the part of the criminal. Something drives him – and it's almost always a him – to perform certain acts that are an end in themselves. The criminal act can be as petty as stealing women's underwear from washing lines. It can be as serious as serial murder. Serial arson is one such crime.

'And if what we were dealing with here was serial arson, I'd be the first to defend the value of a psychological profile. But as I was saying to Carol just before you arrived, I don't think you've got your common or garden thrill-seeking firebug in Seaford. It's not a torch for hire either. What you've got here is a beast of a different colour altogether. More of a hybrid.'

Pendlebury looked unconvinced. 'Want to tell us what you mean by that?'

'I'd be happy to,' Tony said, leaning back and cradling his glass in his linked fingers. 'Let's eliminate the hired arsonist for a start. While it's true that a handful of the fires have probably been an answer to the building owner's prayers, in the vast majority of cases, there seems to be no financial gain. Mostly, we're looking at massive inconvenience and, in a few cases, positive damage to the businesses or sections of the community affected. They're not grudge fires either – different insurance companies, no reason why anyone would have it in for such a wide spectrum of buildings. There's no common link at all, except that the fires were all set at night and up until the last one, they took place in deserted premises. So, no reason to think there is a professional torch for hire behind the blazes. Agreed?'

Carol bent over to pick up the wine and refill her glass. 'You'll get no argument from me.'

'What if there was a mixture of motives behind the hiring? What if he was hired sometimes for gain, sometimes for grudge?' Pendlebury stubbornly asked.

'Still leaves too many unaccounted for,' Carol said. 'My team ruled out a torch for hire almost from the start. So, Tony, why isn't it some emotional retard doing it for kicks?'

'I could be wrong,' he said.

'Oh, yeah. Your track record is littered with mistakes,' Carol said ironically.

'Thank you. Here's why I don't think it's some nutter. All these fires have been carefully set. In most cases, there have been almost no forensic traces, just the identification of the seat of the fire and some indication of lighter fuel and ignition trails. Mostly there's no sign of forced entry either. If there hadn't been such a spate of these fires over a relatively short period of time, chances are most of them would have been written off as accidents or carelessness. That would point to a professional torch, except that we've already written that off for other reasons.' He picked up the papers he'd dropped by his chair earlier and gave his notes a quick glance.

'So we've got someone who's controlled and organized, which firebugs almost never are. He brings stuff with him and also uses available materials. He knows what he's doing, yet there's no sign of him having graduated to this from small-scale fires in rubbish tips, garden sheds, building sites.

'Then you've got to consider that most firebugs are sexually motivated. When they set fires, they often masturbate or urinate or defecate at the sites. There have been no traces of that, nor of any pornographic materials. If he doesn't wank at the fire site, he probably does it at the vantage point where he watches the fire from. Again, there are no reports from outraged members of the public of anyone exposing themselves in the vicinities of the fires. So, another negative.'

'What about timing?' Carol interrupted. 'He's doing it more often than he was when he started out. Isn't that typical of a serial offender?'

'Yeah, it's in all the books about serial killers,' Pendlebury added.

'It's less true of firebugs,' Tony said. 'Especially the ones who go in for the more serious arson attacks like this. The gaps are unpredictable. They can go weeks, months or even years without a big blaze. But within the series, you do get sprees, so yes, the timing of these fires might support the idea that you're looking at a serial offender. But I'm not trying to suggest that these fires are the work of several individuals. I think it's one person. I just don't believe he's a thrill seeker.'

'So what are you saying?' Carol said.

'Whoever is setting these fires is not a psychopath. I believe he has a conventional criminal motive for what he's doing.'

'So what is this so-called motive?' Pendlebury asked suspiciously.

'That's what we don't know yet.'

Pendlebury snorted. 'Minor detail.'

'Actually, in a sense it is, Jim,' Carol chipped in. 'Because once we've established that it's not a psychopath operating on unique and personal logic, we should be able to apply reasoning to uncover what's behind the fires. And once we've done that . . . well, it's just a matter of solid coppering.'

A look of disgruntled annoyance had settled over Jim Pendlebury's face like an occluded cold front on the weather map. 'Well, I can't think of any reason for setting these fires unless you get a kick out of them.'

'Oh, I don't know,' Tony said casually, starting almost to enjoy himself.

'Share it then, Sherlock,' Carol urged him.

'Could be a security firm coming round in the wake of the fires offering cut-rate night watchmen. Could be a fire-alarm or sprinkler-system company facing hard times. Or . . .' his voice tailed off and he cast a look of speculation at the fire chief.

'What?'

'Jim, do you employ any part-time firemen?'

Pendlebury looked horrified. Then he took in the half-smile twitching the corner of Tony's mouth and misread it completely. The fire chief visibly relaxed and grinned. 'You're at the wind-up,' he said, wagging a finger at Tony.

'If you say so,' Tony said. 'But do you? Just as a matter of curiosity?'

The fireman's eyes showed uncertainty and suspicion. 'We do, yes.'

'Maybe tomorrow you could let me have their names?' Carol asked.

Pendlebury's head thrust forward and he stared intently into Carol's closed face. His broad shoulders seemed to expand as he clenched his fists. 'My God,' he said wonderingly. 'You really mean it, don't you, Carol?'

'We can't afford to ignore any possibilities,' she said calmly. 'This is not personal, Jim. But Tony has opened up a valid line of inquiry. I'd be derelict in my duty if I didn't follow it through.'

'Derelict in your duty?' Pendlebury got to his feet. 'If my fire crews were derelict in their duty, there wouldn't be a building in this city left standing. My people put their lives on the line every time this nutter has a night on the town. And you sit there and suggest one of them might be behind it?'

Carol stood up and faced him. 'I'd feel just the same if it was a question of a bent copper. No one's accusing anyone at this stage. I've worked with Tony before, and I'd stake my career that he doesn't make mischievous or ill-considered suggestions. Why don't you sit down and have another glass of wine?' She put a hand on his arm and smiled. 'Come on, there's no need for us to fall out.'

Slowly Pendlebury relaxed and gingerly lowered himself back into his chair. He allowed Carol to top up his glass and even managed a half-smile at Tony. 'I'm very protective of my officers,' he said.

Tony, impressed at Carol's smooth handling of a potentially explosive situation, had shrugged. 'They're lucky to have you,' was all he said.

Somehow, the three of them managed to shift the conversation on to the more neutral territory of how Carol was settling in at East Yorkshire. The fire chief slipped into professional Yorkshireman mode, keeping everyone happy with a series of anecdotes. For Tony, it was a blessed rescue from thoughts of Shaz Bowman's last hours.

Later, in the small hours and the loneliness of Carol's spare room, there was no distraction to damp down the flames of imagination. As he pushed away the nightmare vision of her distorted and devastated face, he promised Shaz Bowman that he would expose the man who had done this to her. No matter what the price.

And Tony Hill was a man who knew all about paying the ferryman.

Jacko Vance sat in his soundproofed and electronically shielded projection room at the top of the house, behind locked doors. Obsessively, he replayed the tape he'd spliced together from his recordings of the late evening news bulletins on a variety of channels, terrestrial and satellite. What they all had in common was the news of Shaz Bowman's death. Her blue eyes blazed at him again from the screen time after time, an exciting contrast to his last memory of her.

They wouldn't be showing pictures of her like that. Not even after the watershed. Not even with an X-certificate.

He wondered how Donna Doyle was feeling. There had been nothing on TV about her. They all thought they had star quality, but the truth was none of them raised the faintest flicker of interest in anyone except him. For him, they were perfect, the ultimate representation of his ideal woman. He loved their pliancy, their willingness to believe exactly what he wanted them to believe. And the perfection of the moment when they realized this encounter was not about sex and fame but pain and death. He loved that look in their eyes.

When he saw that translation from adoration to alarm, their faces seemed to lose all individuality. They no longer merely resembled Jillie, they became her. It made the punishment so easy and so perfectly right.

What also made it appropriate was the unfairness. Almost all of his girls spoke about their families with affection. It might be shrouded behind a veil of adolescent frustration and exasperation, but it was obvious as he listened to them that their mothers or fathers or siblings cared about them even though their sluttish readiness to do whatever he wanted demonstrated they didn't merit that concern. He'd deserved their lives, and what had he got?

Anger surged through him, but like a thermostat, self-control cut in and tamped the fires down. This was not an appropriate time or place for that energy, he reminded himself. His anger could be channelled in a variety of useful directions; ranting pointlessly about what he had been deprived of wasn't one of them.

He took a series of deep breaths and forced his emotions into another mould. Satisfaction. That's what he ought to be feeling. Satisfaction at a job well done, a danger neutralized.

> Little Jack Horner
> Sat in the corner
> Eating his pudding and pie.
> He put in his thumb
> And pulled out a plum
> And said, "What a good boy am I!"

Vance giggled softly. He'd put in his thumbs and pulled out the glistening plum of Shaz Bowman's eyes and felt the silent scream vibrating in his very core. It had been easier than he'd expected. It took surprisingly little force to pop an eye free from its roots.

The only pity of it was that you couldn't then see her expression when you poured the acid in or sliced the ears off. He didn't anticipate any need for there to be a next time, but if there were, he'd have to think carefully about the order of the ceremony.

Sighing with satisfaction, he rewound the tape.

If Micky hadn't been such a purist about her morning routine, they might have heard about Shaz's death on the radio news or seen it on satellite TV. But Micky insisted on no exposure to the day's news until she was behind the closed door of her office at the studios. So they breakfasted to Mozart and drove in to Wagner. No one from the programme was ever foolish enough to thrust a tabloid at Micky as she strode from car parking slot to her desk. Not twice, anyway.

So, because their early morning start forced them to bed before the late bulletins that had alerted Jacko, it was Betsy who had the first shock of recognition at Shaz's picture. Even dulled by newsprint, her blue eyes were still the first thing that demanded notice. 'My God,' Betsy breathed, moving round behind Micky's desk the better to examine the front pages.

'What is it?' Micky said without pausing in the habitual process of removing her jacket, placing it on a hanger and checking it critically for creases.

'Look, Micky.' Betsy thrust the *Daily Mail* towards her. 'Isn't that the policewoman who came to the house on Saturday? Just as we were leaving?'

Micky registered the thick black type before she took in the photograph. SLAUGHTERED, it read. Her eyes moved to Shaz Bowman's smiling face underneath the peak of a Metropolitan Police cap. 'There can't be two of them,' she said. She sat down heavily on one of the visitors' armchairs that faced her desk and read the melodramatic copy that provided Shaz's epitaph. Words like 'nightmare', 'gory', 'blood-soaked', 'agony' and 'gruesome' leapt out to ambush her. She felt strangely queasy.

In a television career that had spanned war zones, massacres and individual tragedy, no one in Micky's life had ever been touched personally by any of the catastrophes she had reported. Even a connection as tangential as hers to Shaz Bowman was all the more shocking because it had no precedent. 'Jesus,' she said, stretching the syllables. She looked up at Betsy, who read the shock in her face. 'She was in our house on Saturday morning. According to this, they think she was murdered late Saturday or early Sunday. We spoke to her. And within hours, she was dead. What are we going to do, Bets?'

Betsy moved round the desk and crouched beside Micky, hands flat on her thighs, staring up into her face. 'We're going to do nothing,' she said. 'It's not up to us to do anything. She came to see Jacko, not us. She's nothing to do with us.'

Micky looked appalled. 'We can't do *nothing*,' she protested. 'Whoever killed her, they must have hooked up with her after she left our house. At the very least, it lets the police know she was alive and well and walking around of her own free will in London on Saturday morning. We can't ignore it, Bets.'

'Sweetheart, take a deep breath and think about what you're saying. This isn't any old murder victim. She was a police officer. That means her colleagues are not going to be satisfied with a one-page statement saying she came to the house and we left. They're going to be stripping our lives down to the bone, on the off chance that there's something there they should know about. You know and I know that we just won't stand up to that kind of scrutiny. I say, leave it to Jacko. I'll give him a call and tell him to say we'd gone before she arrived. It's simplest that way.'

Micky pushed herself back violently. The chair slid along the carpet and Betsy almost toppled forward. Micky jumped to her feet and started pacing agitatedly. 'And what happens if they start questioning the neighbours and there's some nosy old biddy who remembers DC Bowman arriving and then us leaving? Anyway, I was the one who spoke to her in the first place. I made the appointment. What if she jotted that down in her notebook? What if she even taped the call, for God's sake? I can't believe you think we should just shut up about it.'

Betsy struggled to her feet, her chin tipped back to reveal a stubborn set to her firm jaw. 'If you'd stop being such a bloody drama queen, you'd see I'm talking sense,' she said in a low, angry voice. She'd spent too long providing the advice that Micky routinely acted upon to abandon the role now it had become so crucial. 'No good will come of it,' she added ominously.

Micky stopped by the desk and picked up the phone. 'I'm ringing Jacko,' she said, glancing at her watch. 'He won't be up yet. At least I can break the news more gently than the tabloids.'

'Good. Maybe he'll talk some sense into you,' Betsy said caustically.

'I'm not calling for permission, Betsy. I'm calling to tell him I'm about to phone the police.' As she punched in her husband's private number, Micky looked sadly at her lover. 'God, I can't believe you're running so scared that you'd kid yourself you can walk away from doing the right thing.'

'It's called love,' Betsy said bitterly, turning away to hide the tears of anger and humiliation that had sprung without warning.

'No, Betsy. It's called fear ... Hello, Jacko? It's me. Listen, I've got some terrible news for you ...'

Betsy turned her head and watched Micky's mobile face with its frame of silky blonde hair. It was a sight that had given her pleasure beyond dreams of avarice over the years. All she felt now was an unreasonable, unfathomable sense of impending disaster.

Jacko leaned back on his pillows and considered what he'd just heard. He'd been in two minds whether to call the police himself. On the one hand, it argued for his innocence, since, for all he knew, nobody outside his household knew DC Bowman had been anywhere near him. On the other hand, it made him look a little too eager to be involved in a high-profile murder inquiry. And one of the things everyone who had read a book on psychopathic killers knew was that the murderer often tried to insert himself into the investigation.

Leaving it to Micky was somehow much safer. It demonstrated his innocence at second hand; she was his devoted wife, crammed with public probity and therefore to be trusted in her account of events. He knew it was safe to assume she'd go straight to the police as soon as she saw Shaz's picture, which would be well before his normal rising time, so there would be no question of him having known and said nothing. Because, of course, officer, he'd been too busy to watch the evening news the previous day. Why, sometimes he barely had time to watch his own show, never mind his wife's!

What he had to do now was to work out his strategy. There would be no question of him having to schlepp up to Leeds to talk to the investigating plods; the police would come to him, he felt sure. If he was proved wrong, he wouldn't call in any favours just yet. He'd play along, the magnanimous man with nothing to hide. Of course you can have an autograph for your wife, officer.

The important thing now was to plan. Imagine every contingency and work out in advance how best to deal with it. Planning was the secret of his success. It was a lesson he'd almost had to learn the hard way. The first time, he'd not really worked out the eventualities ahead of time. He'd been intoxicated by the possibilities he saw opening in front of him, and he'd not realized how necessary it was to project all the conceivable outcomes and work out how to deal with them. He'd not had the Northumberland cottage then, relying foolishly on a tumbledown walkers' hut that he remembered from hill-walking expeditions in his youth.

He'd thought no one would be using the place in the dead of winter and knew he could drive right up to it on an old drovers' track. Because he dared not leave her alive, he'd had to finish her off the night he'd taken her there. But it had been almost dawn by the time she'd taken her last breath. Shaken and exhausted by the effort of confining her, carrying the heavy vice that would crush her arm to a bloody pulp, then killing her with a wicked ligature made from a guitar string (symbolic, if he'd but considered it, of another of the accomplishments he'd lost), the planned burial had been beyond him. He decided to leave her where she was and come back the following night to deal with the carcass.

Jacko sucked his breath in at the memory. He'd been on the main road, only a couple of miles from the turn-off to the track, when the local news bulletin announced that the body of a young woman had been discovered by a group of ramblers within the past hour. The shock had nearly sent the Land Rover off the road.

Somehow, he'd controlled himself and driven home in a lather of clammy sweat. Amazingly, he hadn't left sufficient forensic traces for there to be any trail leading back to him. He was never questioned. As far as he knew, he was never even considered. The previous connection was so minimal as to be insignificant.

He'd learned three crucial things from that experience. Firstly, he needed to find a way to make it last so he could savour her suffering as she went through what he'd endured.

Secondly, he didn't actually enjoy the act of killing. He liked what led up to it, the agony and the terror, and he loved the sense of control that having been responsible for taking a life gave him, but despatching a strong, healthy young woman was no fun. Far too much like hard work, he had decided. He didn't much mind whether they died of septicaemia or despair, he preferred it when he didn't have to do it himself.

And thirdly, he needed a place of safety, both metaphorically and literally. Micky, Northumberland and the voluntary work with the terminally ill had been the tripartite answer. For the six months it had taken to put that answer together, he'd simply had to be patient. It hadn't been easy, but it had made the next one all the more sweet.

He wasn't about to give up on that sweet and secret pleasure just because Shaz Bowman had thought she was smarter than him. All it would take was a little bit of planning.

Jacko closed his eyes and considered.

Carol took a deep breath and knocked on the door. A familiar voice told her to come in and she walked into Jim Pendlebury's office as if there had never been a moment's tension between them. 'Morning, Jim,' she said briskly.

'Carol,' he said. 'Come with some news for me?'

She sat down opposite him, shaking her head. 'I've come for the list of part-time firemen we spoke about last night.'

His eyes widened. 'You're not still entertaining that daft idea in the cold light of morning?' he said scornfully. 'I thought you must just be humouring your guest.'

'When it comes to criminal investigation, I'd back Tony Hill's ideas over yours any time.'

'You expect me to sit back and help you turn my men into scapegoats?' he said, his voice low. 'When they're the ones who stand at risk every time we get a call-out?'

Carol sighed in vexation. 'I'm trying to put an end to that risk. Not just for your firefighters, but for the poor sods like Tim Coughlan who don't even know they're taking a chance. Don't you understand that? This isn't a witch-hunt. I'm not out to frame the innocent. If you think that's what I'm about, then you certainly don't know enough about me to have the right to turn up at my home unannounced and uninvited and expect to cross the threshold ever again.'

Long seconds dragged past while they stared each other down. Finally, Pendlebury shook his head in resignation, his mouth a thin line. 'I'll give you the list,' he said, loathing every word. 'But you won't find your arsonist on it.'

'I hope not,' she said calmly. 'I know you don't believe me, but I don't want this to be one of yours, any more than I enjoy the prospect of uncovering police corruption. It undermines all of us. But I can't ignore the possibility now it's been pointed out to me so convincingly.'

He turned away and walked his chair over to a filing cabinet. He pulled out the bottom drawer and took out a sheet of paper. With a flick of the wrist, he floated it across the desk to her. All it contained were the names, addresses and telephone numbers of Seaford's twelve part-time fire officers.

'Thank you,' Carol said. 'I appreciate this.' She half-turned to go, then looked back as if struck by an afterthought. 'One thing, Jim. These fires. Do they all come under one division or are they more spread out?'

He pursed his lips. 'They're all on Seaford Central's patch. If they hadn't been, you wouldn't be walking out the door with that bit of paper.'

It confirmed what she'd already thought. 'I figured it might be something like that,' she said, her voice offering armistice. 'Believe me, Jim, there'd be nobody happier than me if all your lads check out.'

He looked away. 'They will do. I know those lads. I've trusted my life to them. Your psychologist – he knows nothing about it.'

Carol walked to the door. As she opened it, she looked back. He was staring intensely at her. 'We'll see, Jim.'

The steel-capped heels of her brown boots clattered on the stairs as she ran down to the anonymous security of her car. The pain of Jim Pendlebury's conviction that she would scapegoat a fellow member of the emergency services cut deep. 'Damn it,' Carol said, slamming the door closed behind her and jabbing the key angrily at the ignition. 'Damn it all to hell.'

Working on the principle that any psychologist worth his salt would see straight through any attempts at manipulation, they'd clearly decided to dispense with finesse. They had, however, paid Tony the compliment of rank. Detective Chief Superintendent McCormick and Detective Inspector Colin Wharton rubbed shoulders at the narrow table in the interview room. The tape was running. They hadn't even bothered with the spurious reassurance that it was for his benefit.

They'd run through the discovery of the body first, their questions clearly directed at tripping him up in his assertion that he'd never been to Shaz's flat before and had no idea which windows were hers. Now they were moving into areas for which there was less obvious justification. Tony was not unprepared. He'd fully expected to be given a hard time. For one thing, he wasn't actually a cop, so if they were looking for a scapegoat, he'd be a preferable choice to one of his team. Add to that the local force's resentment at having to hand over space and resources to a bunch of outsiders led by a Home Office boffin they regarded as one step away from a leader of Satanic rituals, and he was inevitably on a hiding to nothing. With this in mind, he'd been running alternative scenarios on the projection screen inside his head almost before his eyes had opened. Concern about the interview had preoccupied him through breakfast, in spite of Carol's best efforts to reassure him that it would be no more than routine.

On the train back to Leeds he had stared out of the window without registering anything except that he had to find a way to convince his interrogators that they should be looking outside Shaz's circle of friends and colleagues for whoever had done this to her. Now he was faced with the reality, he wished he'd caught a train to London instead. Already the muscles in his shoulders were cramped into tight knots. He could actually feel the creeping rigidity climbing up the back of his neck and into his scalp. He was going to have one hell of a headache.

'Take us right back to the beginning,' McCormick said brusquely.

'When did you first meet DC Bowman?' Wharton demanded. At least they weren't playing 'nice cop, nasty cop'. They were both comfortably displaying their true colours as oppressive aggressors.

'Commander Bishop and I interviewed her in London about eight weeks ago. The exact date is in our office diary.' His voice was blank and even, kept so by willpower alone. Only a Voice Stress Analyser could have detected the micro-tremors skittering beneath the surface. Luckily for Tony, the technology hadn't penetrated that far.

'You interviewed her together?' McCormick with the question this time.

'Yes. Following the interview, Commander Bishop withdrew and I administered some psychological tests. Then DC Bowman left and I did not see her again until the start of the task force's training period.'

'How long were you alone with Bowman?' McCormick again. Wharton was leaning back in his seat, fixing Tony with a professional blend of speculation, contempt and suspicion.

'It takes about an hour to carry out the tests.'

'Long enough to get to know somebody, then.'

Tony shook his head. 'There's no time for casual conversation. In fact, that would be counter-productive. We were aiming to keep the selection process as objective as possible.'

'And the decision to take Bowman on the squad was unanimous?'

Tony hesitated for a moment. If they hadn't already talked to Paul Bishop, they would. There was no point in any diversion from the truth. 'Paul had some reservations. He thought she was too intense. I argued that we needed some diversity on the team. So he agreed to Shaz and I conceded on one of his choices that I was less enthusiastic about.'

'Which one was that?' McCormick asked.

Tony was too smart to walk into that one. 'You'd better ask Paul about that.'

Wharton suddenly leaned forward, thrusting his heavy blunt features towards Tony. 'Find her attractive, did you?'

'What kind of question is that?'

'About as straightforward as you can get. Yes or no. Did you find the lass attractive? Did you fancy her?'

Tony paused momentarily, assembling his careful response. 'I registered that her looks would have made her appealing to a lot of men, yes. I was not myself sexually attracted to her.'

Wharton sneered. 'How could you tell? From what I've heard, you don't respond like most red-blooded blokes, do you?'

Tony flinched as if he'd been struck. A tremor ran through his taut muscles and his stomach grew turbulent. The inquiry that had inevitably followed the case he'd worked with Carol Jordan the year before had had to be told of his sexual problems. He had been promised absolute confidentiality, and if the reactions of the police officers he had encountered since were anything to go by, he had been granted that. Now, overnight, Shaz Bowman's death seemed to have stripped him of that right. He wondered momentarily where they'd gained their information, hoping this didn't mean his impotence would now be common gossip. 'My relationship with Shaz Bowman was purely professional,' he said, forcing his voice to stay calm. 'My personal life has nothing to do with this inquiry whatsoever.'

'That's for us to decide,' McCormick stated baldly.

Without pausing, Wharton continued. 'You say your relationship was purely professional. But we have statements that indicate you spent more time with Bowman than you did with other members of the squad. Officers would arrive of a morning to find the two of you deep in conversation. She would stay behind at the end of group sessions for a word in private. A very close relationship seems to have sprung up between you.'

'There was nothing untoward between Shaz and me. I've always been an early starter in the morning. Check it out with anyone who's ever worked with me. Shaz was having some problems mastering the computer software we're using so she came in beforehand to put in some extra time. And yes, she did stay behind after group sessions with questions, but that was because she was fascinated with the work, not for any seedy ulterior motive. If your murder inquiry had taught you anything at all about Shaz Bowman, you'd know the only thing she was in love with was the Job.' He took a deep breath.

There was a long moment's silence. Then McCormick said, 'Where were you on Saturday?'

Tony shook his head, mystified. 'You're wasting your time with this. You should be using us to catch the killer, not trying to make it look like one of us is guilty. We should be talking about the meaning of what this killer did to Shaz, why he left the picture of the three wise monkeys on the body, why there was no sexual interference with the body nor any forensic traces.'

McCormick's eyes narrowed. 'I'm interested that you're so definite about the absence of forensic traces. Now how would you happen to know that?'

Tony groaned. 'I don't *know* it. But I did see the body and the scene of crime. From my experience of psychopathic killers, I reckoned it was the most likely scenario.'

'A police officer or someone who works closely with the police would recognize the significance of forensic evidence,' McCormick said cannily.

'Everybody who has a TV set or who can read recognizes the significance of forensic evidence,' Tony countered.

'But they don't all know how to erase all traces of their presence like people who are accustomed to watching SOCOs avoiding the contamination of evidence at a crime scene, do they?'

'So you're saying there was no forensic evidence?' Tony challenged, latching on to the one piece of information that seemed significant.

'I didn't say that, no,' McCormick retorted triumphantly.

'Whoever killed Sharon Bowman probably thinks they didn't leave a trace. But they'd be wrong.'

Tony's mind raced. It couldn't be finger or shoe prints; that would be completely at odds with the organized precision of this killer. It might be hairs or fibres. Hair would only be useful if they had a serious suspect to match it against. Fibres, on the other hand, could be tracked down by a forensic expert. He hoped West Yorkshire used the best. 'Good,' was all he said. McCormick scowled.

Wharton opened a folder and placed a sheet of paper in front of Tony. 'For the tape, I am showing Dr Hill a photostat of DC Bowman's diary for the week of her death. There are two entries for the day she was murdered. JV, nine thirty. And the letter T. I put it to you, Dr Hill, that you had arranged to meet Shaz Bowman on Saturday. That you did in fact meet her on Saturday.'

Tony ran a hand through his hair. The confirmation of Carol's idea that Shaz would have confronted Vance with what she knew gave him no satisfaction. 'Inspector, I made no such arrangement. The last time I saw Shaz alive was at the end of the working day on Friday. What I was doing on Saturday could not be less relevant to this inquiry.'

McCormick leaned forward and spoke softly. 'I'm not so sure about that. T for Tony. She could have been meeting you. She could have met you out of office hours away from the squad room, and the boyfriend could have found out about it and let it wind him up. Maybe he confronted her with it and she admitted she fancied you more than she fancied him?'

Tony's lip twitched in contempt. 'Is that the best you can come up with? That's pathetic, McCormick. I've had patients who came up with more credible fantasies. Surely you must recognize that the crucial thing here is the diary entry that says JV, nine thirty? Shaz may have *intended* talking to me after that interview, but she never made it. If you're interested in what the killer was doing on Saturday, you really should be checking out Jacko Vance and his entourage.' As soon as the name was out of his mouth, Tony knew he'd blown it. McCormick shook his head pityingly and Wharton jumped to his feet, his chair shrieking on the cheap vinyl flooring.

'Jacko Vance tries to *save* lives, not take them. You're the one with the track record here,' Wharton shouted. 'You've already killed somebody, haven't you, Dr Hill? And as you psychologists are always telling us, once the taboo's breached, it's gone for good.

Once a killer ... Fill in the blanks, Doctor. Fill in the fucking blanks.'

Tony closed his eyes. His chest hurt, as if a punch to the diaphragm had robbed him of air. All the progress he'd made over the past year was stripped away and again he smelled sweat and blood, felt them slick on his hands, heard the screams ripped from his own throat, tasted the Judas kiss. His eyes snapped open and he looked at Wharton and McCormick with a hatred he'd forgotten he was capable of. 'That's it,' he said, standing up. 'Next time you want to talk to me, you'll have to arrest me. And you'd better make sure my lawyer's on the premises when you do.'

Only his desire not to give them the satisfaction held him together as he marched out of the interview room, through the police station and out into the fresh air. No one made any move to stop him. He set off across the car park, desperate to make it to the street before his stomach lost its battle with breakfast. Just as he reached the kerb, a car pulled up beside him and the passenger window descended. Simon McNeill's dark head loomed towards him. 'Want a lift?'

Tony recoiled as if from a blow. 'No ... I ... No thanks.'

'Come on,' Simon urged. 'I've been waiting for you. They kept me in half the night. They'll try and pin this on me given half a chance. We need to find out who killed Shaz before they decide it's time to make an arrest.'

Tony leaned into the car. 'Simon, listen very carefully to me. You're right that they want it to be one of us. I'm not sure they'd go so far as to manufacture evidence against anybody. But I don't intend to sit back and wait and see if that happens. I intend to find out who's behind this, and I can't have you along. It's dangerous enough going up against a man who's capable of what this guy did to Shaz. It'll be hard enough for me to watch my own back without having to watch yours as well. You might be a great detective, but when it comes to going head to head with psychopaths like this, you're an absolute beginner. So do us both a favour. Please. Go home. Deal with your loss. Don't try to be a hero, Simon. I don't want to bury another one of you.'

Simon looked as if he wanted to burst into tears and thump Tony. 'I'm not a child. I'm a trained detective. I've worked on murder squads. I cared about her. You can't shut me out. You can't stop me nailing this bastard.'

A long sigh. 'No, I can't. But Shaz was a trained detective. She'd worked on murders. She knew she was rattling a killer's cage. And she still got demolished. Not just killed, but annihilated. It's not conventional police methods that are going to sort this out, Simon. I've done this once before. Believe me, I know what it's like and I wouldn't wish it on another living soul. Go home, Simon.'

With a screech of rubber on asphalt, Simon's car streaked away from the kerb. Tony watched it take the next left far too fast, the rear spoiler fishtailing out of sight. He hoped it would be the biggest risk Simon had to take until Shaz's killer was dealt with. He knew a traffic accident would be the least of his own worries.

There was something to be said for delirium. When feverish sweat ran down her face and added another layer to the sour staleness that covered her sticky skin, it meant she could escape into hallucinations that were infinitely preferable to reality.

Donna Doyle lay huddled against the wall, holding on to the chimeras of childhood memory as if they could somehow save her. One year, her mum and dad had taken her to the Valentine Fair at Leeds. Candyfloss, hot dogs and onions, the blurry kaleidoscope of lights on the waltzer, the sparkling jeweller's window of the city spread beneath her from the top of the Ferris wheel as they swung gently in the cold night air, the neon glow of the fair like a carpet at their feet.

Her dad had won her a big teddy bear, electric pink fun fur with a goofy grin stitched across its white face. It had been the last present he'd given her before he died. It was all his fault, Donna thought, snivelling. If he hadn't gone and died, none of this would have happened. They wouldn't have been poor and she wouldn't have had to think about being a telly star, she could have listened to her mum and stuck in at school and gone to university.

Tears crept out of the corners of her eyes and she beat her left fist against the wall. 'I hate you,' she cried, screaming at the wavering image of a thin-faced man who had adored his daughter. 'I hate you, you bastard!'

At least the incoherent sobs tired her out, letting her consciousness slide mercifully from her again.

The brashness that characterized Leon's performance among his peers was gone. Instead, he was locked behind the blank insolent face he'd seen on too many young blacks, both in custody and on the street. His street. He might have the warrant card that said he was one of them, but he had enough smarts to know that the two Yorkshiremen sitting across the interview room table were still The Man.

'So, Leon,' Wharton was saying in seemingly expansive mode, 'what you're telling us squares with what we've already heard from DC Hallam. The pair of you met at four o'clock and went tenpin bowling. Then you went for a drink in the Cardigan Arms, after which you met Simon McNeill for a curry.' He smiled encouragingly.

'So neither of you two killed Shaz Bowman,' McCormick said. Leon had him figured for a racist, his pink slab of a face showing no rapport, his eyes hard and cold, his wet mouth permanently a mere twitch away from a sneer.

'None of us killed Shaz, man,' Leon said, deliberately drawing out the last word. 'She was one of us. Maybe we've not been a team for long, but we know how to stick together. You're wasting your time on us.'

'We've got to go through the motions, lad, you know that,' Wharton said. 'You're going to be a profiler, you know that over ninety per cent of murders are committed by families or lovers. Now, when Simon turned up, how did he seem?'

'I don't know what you mean.'

'OK. Did he seem agitated, wound up, in a state?'

Leon shook his head. 'None of that, no. He was a bit quiet, but

I put that down to Shaz not being there. I reckoned he fancied her, and he was disappointed when she didn't show.'

'What made you think he fancied her?'

Leon spread his hands. 'Stuff. You know? The way he tried to impress her. The way he was always checking her out. The way he'd always be bringing her into the conversation. The way a man does when he's interested, know what I mean?'

'Did you think she was interested in him?'

'I don't reckon Shaz was too interested in anybody. Not in the shagging sense. She was too obsessed with the Job to be bothered with it, if you ask me. I don't think Simon was going to drop lucky and get his leg over. Not unless he had something she wanted bad, like the inside track on a serial killer.'

'Did he say he'd been round her house?' McCormick interjected.

'He never mentioned it, no. But you wouldn't, would you? I mean, if you thought a woman had just stood you up, you wouldn't be telling people about it. Not saying anything isn't strange behaviour. Saying something, setting yourself up for having the piss taken out of you all round the squad room, now that would be strange.' Leon lit a cigarette and gave McCormick the blank-eyed stare again.

'What was he wearing?' Wharton asked.

Leon frowned with the effort of recollection. 'Leather jacket, bottle green polo shirt, black jeans, black Docs.'

'Not a flannel shirt?'

Leon shook his head. 'Not when we met him. Why? You found some flannel fibres on her clothes?'

'Not her clothes,' Wharton said. 'We think she was –'

'I don't think we'll be going into details about the forensic evidence just now,' McCormick interrupted firmly. 'Weren't you worried when DC Bowman didn't show up for this big night out?'

Leon shrugged and blew out a stream of smoke. 'Not worried, no. Kay figured she'd got a better offer. Me, I thought she probably had her head in her computer, doing her homework.'

'Bit of a teacher's pet, was she?' Wharton asked, sympathy to the fore again.

'Nah. She was just a grafter, that's all. Look, shouldn't you be out there catching the bastard who did this, instead of wasting your time with us? You're not going to find her killer in the task force. We signed up to solve shit like this, not commit it, man.'

Wharton nodded. 'So the sooner we get this over, the better. We need your help here, Leon. You're a trained detective, but you've also got trained instincts, or else you wouldn't be on this task force. Give us the benefit of your insights. What do you make of Tony Hill? I mean, you do know that he didn't want you on the task force, don't you?'

Tony stared at the dark blue screen. McCormick and Wharton might have barred him from the task squad offices, but either they didn't know about the group's networked computer system or they had no idea how to exclude him from it. The set-up was straightforward. It had to be; the people using it were less computer literate than the average seven-year-old. All the PCs in the office were linked via a central processing and storage unit. A modem connection made it possible for any of the team who was working off site to plug straight into their personal data store as well as any of the general material that was available to everyone. For security reasons, they each had personal logins as well as individual passwords. The trainees had all been instructed to change their passwords weekly to avoid possible leaks. Whether any of them bothered was a moot point.

What none of the squad knew was that Tony had a list of every individual login. In effect, he could dial up the office computer and pretend to be any of them, with the machine none the wiser. Of course, without the password, he wouldn't get very far with the private material, but he'd be in the system.

As soon as he'd returned home from his interview, he'd switched on his home computer. First, he'd called up Shaz's application form and test responses, all scanned in as soon as she'd been accepted for the squad. He printed them out, along with the progress reports that both he and Paul Bishop had compiled.

Then he signed off as himself and signed in as Shaz. Now, the best part of two hours and a pot of coffee later, he was no further forward. He'd tried everything he could think of. SHAZ, SHARON, BOWMAN, ROBIN, HOOD, WILLIAM, TELL, ARCHER, AMBRIDGE . . . He'd run through every character he could think of from the eponymous radio soap opera. He'd tried her parents' names, every town, city, institution and street name mentioned in her CV. He'd even attempted the obvious JACKO, VANCE and the less obvious MICKY, MORGAN. And still he was staring at a screen that said, 'Welcome to the National Offender Profiling Task Force. Please type in your password now: – '. The cursor had been flashing so long the only thing he could say with total certainty was that he had no epileptic tendencies.

He stood up and prowled round the room. He didn't have an idea to bless himself with. 'Enough,' he muttered in exasperation. He lifted his jacket from the chair where he'd thrown it and shrugged it on. A walk down to the shop for the evening paper, that might clear his head. 'Don't fool yourself,' he muttered as he opened his front door. 'You just want to see what those pillocks have told the latest press conference.'

He walked down the path bisecting two flower beds where grimy rose bushes fought a rearguard action against urban enemies both human and industrial. As he turned into the street, he noticed a couple of men in a nondescript saloon car opposite. One was scrambling out of the passenger seat to the accompaniment of the engine being over-enthusiastically started. Shocked, Tony recognized all the hallmarks of an amateurish stakeout. Surely they couldn't be wasting their human resources keeping tabs on him?

At the corner, he stopped to look in the window of Bric'n'Brac, a junk shop with sad pretensions. Its proud owner kept the glass clean, which allowed Tony to take a look over his shoulder and across the street. The man who'd jumped out of the car was over there, loitering by the bus stop, pretending to read the timetable. It was an activity that marked him out as a stranger more than almost anything else could have done; the locals knew the anarchic practices of the rival bus companies too well to regard the timetable as anything other than a bad joke.

Tony walked on to the corner. Under the cloak of crossing the road, he threw a look over his shoulder. The car had turned round and was creeping down his street about fifty yards behind him. There was no doubt about it. If these were the best the local force had to offer, Shaz Bowman's killer didn't have much to worry about.

Despairing of his supposed colleagues, Tony bought an evening paper from the local newsagent and walked slowly home, reading as he went. At least the police weren't publicly saying anything to attract ridicule. In fact, they weren't saying anything much at all. Either they were playing things very close to their chest, or they had nothing to play with. He knew which he believed was the case.

Once inside, under the guise of drawing a curtain across to protect his computer screen from the bright sun, he checked for his watchers. They were both back in the car, parked in the same spot as before. What were they waiting for? What did they expect him to do?

If it wasn't so appalling in its potential consequences, it would be funny, he thought as he grabbed the phone and dialled Paul Bishop's mobile. When Bishop answered, Tony dived straight in. 'Paul? You're not going to believe this. McCormick and Wharton have got it into their heads that someone connected to the task force killed Shaz, since we're the only people up here she knew.'

'I know,' Bishop said, sounding depressed. 'But what can I do? It's their inquiry. If it makes you feel any better, I do know they've been in touch with her old division, asking them to check out if there were any villains down there who might have had enough of a grudge against her to follow her up here. So far, no joy. But her old CID sergeant has apparently been in touch to say she acted as intermediary to set up a meeting between Jacko Vance and Bowman on Saturday morning. It looks as if she was determined to pursue that wild idea of hers about the teenage girls.'

Tony let out a sigh of relief. 'Well, thank God for that. Now maybe they'll begin to take us seriously. I mean, they have to be asking at the very least why Vance hasn't come forward and revealed this himself, given that Shaz's picture has been all over the papers.'

'It's not quite that simple,' Bishop said. 'Vance's wife actually rang in within minutes of the other call to say Bowman had come to the house on Saturday morning. She said her husband hadn't seen the papers yet. So no one's actually hiding anything.'

'But they are at least going to talk to him?'

'I'm sure they will.'

'So they'll have to treat him as a suspect.'

Tony heard Bishop exhale. 'Who knows? The trouble is, Tony, I can make gentle suggestions, but I've no authority to stop them running this their own sweet way.'

'I was told that you'd agreed with them that the squad should effectively be suspended,' Tony pointed out. 'You didn't have to go along with that, surely.'

'Come on, Tony, you know how difficult the politics of the task force are. The Home Office is adamant that we don't cause problems on the ground. It was a small concession. The squad hasn't been disbanded. Nobody's being reassigned to their old units. We're just out of the operational loop until this case is either resolved or out of the headlines. Try and treat it like a sabbatical.'

Exasperated, Tony got to the initial point of his call. 'It's a pretty strange sabbatical that includes a stakeout straight out of the Keystone Cops on my doorstep.'

'You're joking?'

'I wish I was. I walked out of my interview with them this morning after they accused me of being their best bet because I'm already a killer. And now I've got Beavis and Butthead on my tail. This is intolerable, Paul.'

He could hear Bishop take a deep breath. 'I agree, but we're just going to have to roll with the punches until they get bored with us and start running a proper investigation.'

'I don't think so, Paul,' Tony said, his voice clipped and authoritative. 'One of my team is dead and they won't let us help find out who killed her. They're quick enough to remind me that I'm not one of them, I'm an outsider. Well, that cuts both ways. If you can't persuade them to get out of my face, I will be holding a press conference of my own tomorrow. And I promise, you won't like it any more than Wharton and McCormick will. It's time to pull some strings, Paul.'

'I hear you, Tony,' Bishop sighed. 'Leave it with me.'

Tony dropped the phone back into its cradle and pulled the curtain back. He switched on his desk lamp and stood in front of the window staring mutinously out at his watchers. He reviewed the information Paul Bishop had given him and related it to what he had learned at the crime scene. This killer was angry because Shaz had stuck her nose into his business. That indicated that she had been right in her supposition that there was at large a serial killer of teenage girls. Something she had done had panicked the murderer into making her his next target. The only thing she had apparently done that was connected to her theory was to visit Jacko Vance within hours of her death.

He knew now that Shaz Bowman's killer could not be some crazed fan of Vance's. There was no way for even the most dedicated stalker to find out in the short interval before her murder who Shaz was or the reason for her visit to Vance's house.

He had to find out more about the encounter between Shaz and

Vance. If the killer was one of his entourage, it was possible he'd been present. But if Vance had been alone when Shaz confronted him, the finger pointed only at him. Even if he'd picked up the phone the minute she'd left and reported her suspicions to someone else, there was no way such a third party could have picked up Shaz's trail, discovered where she lived, or persuaded her to open her door to him in the time available.

As he reached this conclusion, his watchers departed. Tony threw his jacket down and dropped like a stone into the chair facing the screen. It was a small victory, but it renewed his appetite for the struggle. Now he had to find the proof to demonstrate that Shaz had been right and it had killed her. What would Shaz Bowman have used as a password? A fictional hero? Warshawski and Scarpetta were too long. KINSEY, MILLHONE, MORSE, WEXFORD, DALZIEL, HOLMES, MARPLE, POIROT all failed. A fictional villain? MORIARTY, HANNIBAL, LECTER. Still nothing.

Normally, the sound of a car pulling up outside wouldn't have penetrated his concentration. But after the day he'd had, the stilling of the engine sounded louder than an alarm buzzer. He looked out and his heart sank again. The last three people he wanted to see piled out of a familiar scarlet Ford. Mob-handed, Leon Jackson, Kay Hallam and Simon McNeill crowded up the path, sheepishly acknowledging his scowl through the window. With a groan, he got up and unlocked the door, turning straight on his heel and walking back down the hall to his study.

They followed him, crowding into the small room and, without waiting to be asked, finding places to settle; Simon on the window sill, Leon leaning elegantly against a filing cupboard, Kay in the armchair in the opposite corner. Tony swivelled round in his chair and glared, trying not to acknowledge the resignation he felt. 'Now I understand why people confess to crimes they haven't committed,' he said, only half-joking. They were impressive in spite of their youth and their uncertainty.

'You wouldn't take me seriously, so I brought in reinforcements,' Simon said. He looked too pale to be conscious, Tony registered, noticing for the first time a dusting of freckles across the bridge of his nose.

'That McCormick and Wharton, they've got it in for us,' Leon burst out. 'I've been in there all afternoon, with them doing kissy faces, "Come on, Leon, you can tell us what you really think about

Tony Hill and Simon McNeill." Man, they are two sick fuckers, let me tell you. "McNeill fancied Bowman, but she was in love with Hill, so he killed her out of jealousy, what do you reckon? Or Hill wanted to get into Bowman's knickers but she was more interested in a date with McNeill and he killed her in a fit of jealous rage." More bullshit than a farmyard, made me sick.' He pulled his cigarettes out, then paused. 'Is this OK?'

Tony nodded, pointing to a lopsided Christmas cactus on a shelf. 'Just use the saucer.'

Kay leaned forward in her chair, elbows on knees. 'It's like they can't see past the end of their noses. And while they're trying to find evidence against you, they're not looking anywhere else. Least of all at what Shaz was digging into. They think her theory about a serial killer preying on teenagers is the sort of stupid thing us girls come up with because we've got our hormones in a twist. Well, we figured that if they won't do what needs to be done, we better had.'

'Do I get a word in edgeways?' Tony said.

'Be our guest,' Leon said, with an expansive gesture.

'I appreciate how you feel. And it does you credit. But this isn't a classroom exercise. It's not, "Five Go Hunting a Psychopath." This is the most dangerous game, in both senses of the word. The last time I got involved with a serial killer, it nearly cost me my own life. And, with great respect to your talents as police officers, I knew a hell of a lot more than all three of you rolled into one. I'm not prepared to take the responsibility of having you working with me off the books.' He ran a hand through his hair.

'We know it's the real thing, Tony,' Kay protested. 'And we know you're the best. That's why we've come to you. But we can do stuff you can't. We've got warrant cards. You don't. Strange cops only trust other cops. They won't trust you.'

'So if you won't help us, we'll just have to do the best we can without you,' Simon said, his mouth set in a stubborn line.

The shrill insistence of the phone came as a relief. Tony's hand closed over the receiver. 'Hello?' he said cautiously, eyeing the other three as if they were an unexploded bomb.

'It's me,' Carol said. 'I just called to see how you'd got on.'

'I'd rather tell you face to face,' he said briskly.

'You can't talk just now?'

'I'm in the middle of something. Can we meet later?'

'My cottage? Half past six?'

'Better make it seven,' he said. 'I've got a lot to do here before I can get away.'

'I'll be there. Safe journey.'

'Thanks.' He gently replaced the phone. He closed his eyes momentarily. He hadn't realized how isolated he'd been feeling. It was the existence of police officers like Carol, and the stubborn belief that one day they'd be in the majority, that made his job bearable. He opened his eyes again to find the three junior members of his squad staring avidly at him. The ghost of an idea was taking shape at the back of his mind. 'What about the other two?' he stalled. 'Saw sense, did they?'

Leon breathed smoke. 'Got no bottle. They're frightened to rock the boat in case their promotion prospects get drowned.'

'Who gives a shit about promotion when someone like Shaz gets killed and nobody cares enough to catch the killer? Who'd want to be a copper on that kind of force?' Simon spat.

'I'm sorry,' Tony said. 'The answer's still no.'

'Fine,' Kay said. Her smile could have cut steak. 'In that case, we'll move on to Plan B. The sit-in. We're staying on your case till you come on board. Where you go, we go. Twenty-four hours a day. Three of us, one of you.'

'Not good odds.' Leon lit a fresh cigarette while the embers of the previous stub still glowed.

Tony sighed. 'OK. You won't listen to me. Maybe you'll listen to somebody who really knows the score.'

The dashboard clock said it was just after seven; the radio played the theme from *The Archers*, revealing the clock was three minutes slow. Tony's car jounced up the rough track from the road, his suspension giving its age away. He rounded the last bend and saw with satisfaction that the lights were on in Carol's cottage.

She was framed in the doorway as he closed the car door behind himself. He couldn't remember the last time he'd felt so glad to be walking into someone else's company, someone else's territory. The only sign that his companions were completely unexpected was the slight lift of her eyebrows.

'Kettle's on, beer's cold,' she greeted them, offering Tony a gentle squeeze of the arm. 'Is this your bodyguard?'

'Not as such. I am currently being held hostage,' he said drily, following her indoors. His squad didn't wait for an invitation. They were right there on his heels. 'You remember Kay, Leon and Simon? They're going to hang round my neck like millstones until I agree to work with them on uncovering who killed Shaz.' In the living room, he gestured with his thumb towards the sofa and chairs. The threesome sat. 'I was hoping you would help me talk them out of it.'

Carol shook her head, acting bemused. 'They *want* to work with you on a live case? God, the rumour mill must have deteriorated one hell of a lot recently.'

'Coffee first,' Tony said, lifting a hand and placing it lightly on her shoulder, steering her towards the kitchen.

'Coming up.'

He closed the door behind them. 'I'm sorry for landing you with this. But they wouldn't listen to me. The problem is that West Yorkshire are acting like Simon's the prime suspect and I'm a close second. And this lot are not going to lie down and take that. But you know what it's like when you're working a serial killer case and it gets personal. They don't have the experience to handle this. Vance or someone close to him has already killed the best and brightest of them. I don't want any more deaths on my conscience.'

Carol spooned coffee into the filter and switched it on as he spoke. 'You're absolutely right,' she said. 'However ... unless I misjudge them completely, they're going to pursue this anyway. The best way to make sure you don't lose another one is to take control. And the way to do that is to work with them. Set them all the drudge jobs, the runaround background inquiries that baby detectives cut their teeth on. Anything dodgy, anything we think is dangerous or needs expert interrogation techniques, we'll sort out.'

'"We?"'

Carol clapped the palm of her hand to her forehead and grimaced. 'Why do I feel like I've just been suckered?' She punched his arm. 'Put some sugar and milk and mugs on a tray and take it through before I get seriously cross.'

He did as he was told, feeling strangely gratified that he had moved from the Lone Ranger to team captain in the space of a few hours. By the time Carol brought the coffee through, he'd shared the new deal with a self-satisfied team.

He opened his laptop on the stripped pine dining table, jacked the modem into the phone line, and plugged the transformer into the nearest power point. As the others arranged themselves so they could see the screen, Carol asked Tony, 'How bad was the interview?'

'I walked out in the end,' he said succinctly as he watched the machine boot up. 'It was what you might call hostile. When it comes to, "Hey, lads, hey," they don't really think I'm on the same side, you see. But they're saving the prime suspect slot for Simon. He had the bad luck to get Shaz to agree to a date on the very night she was killed. But I'm probably second favourite in the book that some smart-arse on the murder team will be running.' He looked up and Carol could see the hurt behind the assumed self-possession.

'Stupid bastards,' Carol said, putting his mug of coffee next to the computer. 'But then, they are Yorkshiremen. I can't believe they're not using you lot.'

Leon gave a bark of mirthless laughter. 'Tell us about it. You let people smoke in here?'

Carol glanced at him, taking in the fingers beating a silent tattoo on his thigh. Better that the tobacco combusted than he did. 'You'll find a saucer in the cupboard above the kettle,' she said. 'Only in this room, please.' As he left, she took over his chair and settled down next to Tony, watching the screen change as his fingers hit the keys.

Tony worked his way into the task force computer system with Shaz's login. He pointed to the flashing cursor. 'This is what I've been racking my brains over all afternoon. I can get on to the system as Shaz, but I can't figure out her password.' He ran through the attempts he'd made, ticking the categories off on his fingers. Leon, Kay and Simon started throwing out their own suggestions based on what they knew of their late colleague.

Carol listened carefully, left hand teasing the tendrils of blonde hair on the back of her neck. When Tony and the other three had run out of steam and ideas, she said, 'Missed the obvious, didn't you? Who did Shaz look up to? What did she want to be?'

'Running Scotland Yard? You think I should try famous Met Commissioners?'

Carol reached over and pulled the laptop within touch-typing range. 'Famous profilers.' She typed in RESSLER, DOUGLAS, LEYTON. Nothing happened. A rueful quirk of the lips, then she typed TONYHILL. The screen went momentarily blank, then a menu appeared. 'Fuck, I wish I'd taken a bet on it,' she said wryly. Around her, the trainee profilers applauded, Leon wolf-whistling and whooping.

Tony shook his head, astonished. 'What do I have to do to get you on the national squad?' he asked. 'You're wasted in ordinary CID work at your rank. All that admin when you should be harnessing that inspiration to catch pychopaths.'

'Right,' Carol said sarcastically, pushing the laptop back towards him. 'If I'm so good, how come I didn't work out that my arsonist was a crook, not a crazy?'

'Because you were working alone. That's never the best way to operate when you're dealing with psychological analysis. I think profilers should work in pairs, detective and psychologist, complementary skills.' He took the cursor down to the 'File directory' option and hit ENTER.

The quality of their meeting of minds was not a conversation Carol wanted to have, especially not in company as sharp as the present one. Deftly, she moved the subject forward, bringing Leon, Kay and Simon up to speed with Tony's theory that the arsonist was a part-time fireman with a conventional criminal motive.

'But what *is* the motive?' Kay asked. 'That's the important bit, isn't it?'

'If it's criminal, you always want to know who benefits,' Leon pointed out. 'And since there's no common ownership or insurance, maybe it's somebody high up in the fire service who doesn't want any more cutbacks.'

Tony looked up from the file names he was scrolling through. 'Nice idea,' he said. 'Devious, though. And as a proponent of Occam's Razor, I'm going to go for the most straightforward theory. Debt,' he said and turned his eyes back to the screen.

'Debt?' Carol's voice was full of doubt.

'That's right.' He swung round to face her. 'Somebody who owes money all over the place, somebody with a credit rating that's fallen through the floor. His house has been repossessed or it's on the point of it, he's got a stack of county court judgements against him and he's robbing Peter to pay Paul.'

'But a night callout is, what? Fifty, a hundred quid max, depending on how long they're out there? You surely don't think somebody would put his liberty, his mates' lives, at risk for that sort of cash!' Simon protested.

Tony shrugged. 'If you're up against the wall, perpetually juggling creditors, an extra hundred quid a week can make all the difference to staying in one piece and having your legs broken, your car snatched, your electricity cut off, the bank putting you into bankruptcy. You pay twenty quid off one debt, fifty off another, a tenner here, a fiver there. You show willing. It keeps everybody off your back. The courts are reluctant to take drastic steps if you can show you're really trying. Any sensible person knows that it's only postponing the evil hour, but when you're in debt up to your eyeballs, you stop thinking straight. You get into this self-deluding fantasy that if you can just get over this hump, you'll be heading towards getting straight again. Nobody cons themselves better than a bad debtor. I've seen pathetic idiots who owe the best part of twenty grand to a loan shark still employing a cleaning lady and a gardener because getting rid of them would be an admission that their lives were totally out of control. Look for somebody who's teetering on the brink of insolvency, Carol.'

Already back in communion with the computer screen, he muttered, 'Let me see ... MISPER.001. That'll be the report she did for the squad, wouldn't you think?'

'Seems likely. And MISPERJV.001 could be her Jacko Vance inquiries.'

'Let's take a look.' Tony opened the file. Shaz's words spilled down the screen, giving him a strange sense of communing with the dead. It was as if those extraordinary blue eyes were hovering behind his head, fixing him with their inexorable stare. 'My God,' he whispered. 'She wasn't playing games.'

Leon peered over his shoulder. 'Fuck,' he breathed. 'You fucking witch, Shazza.' It summed up everyone's feelings perfectly as they stared at Shaz's briefing from beyond the grave.

ORGANIZED OFFENDER CHECKLIST

Jacko Vance
Re: MISPER cluster

High birth order
　　Only child.

Father's work stable
　　Civil engineer – often away from home for prolonged
　　periods on long-term contracts.

Absent father
  See above.

Parental discipline perceived as inconsistent
  See above; also, mother appears to have suffered post-natal depression, rejected JV and later treated v. strictly.

Higher than average IQ
  Regarded as bright by teachers but never did as well as expected academically; poor exam performer.

Skilled occupation, work history uneven
  First as a champion javelin thrower then as TV presenter; perfectionist, prone to temper tantrums and firing junior members of team; if not for medal-winning prowess/popularity with TV audience, would have lost several contracts over the years because of arrogant and overbearing behaviour.

Socially adept; may be gregarious and good talker, but can't connect emotionally
  See above; relates very well to members of the public on superficial level; however, one of reasons why his marriage is perceived as so successful is that he appears to have no intimate relationships with either gender outside that relationship.

Living with partner
  Wife, Micky, been together for twelve years. A very public marriage, the golden couple of UK TV. However, often away from home both on business and on extensive charity work.

Controlled mood during commission of crime
  Unknown: but Vance is known in the business for coolness under pressure.

Use of alcohol or drugs during commission of crime
  Unknown. No history of drink problem, some hint that there may have been a problem with painkiller addiction following accident in which Vance lost his arm.

Mobile; car in good condition

Vance has a silver Mercedes convertible and a Land Rover. Both are automatics and have been adapted for his disability.

Follows crimes in the media

He's perfectly placed to do this – he has direct access to all areas of the media. He numbers many journalists among his circle of acquaintance.

Victims share common characteristics

Yes – see appendix A on original cluster of seven victims.

Unsuspicious demeanour

Millions of people would trust him with their lives or their daughters. In a poll four years ago, he was voted the third most trustworthy person in Britain after the Queen and the Bishop of Liverpool.

Looks average

Impossible to comment objectively. The gloss of celebrity, grooming and an expensive wardrobe makes it hard to judge beyond the facade.

Mental illness in immediate family

Nothing known; mother died eight years ago, cancer.

Alcohol or drugs problem in immediate family

Nothing known.

Parents with criminal records

Nothing known.

Emotional abuse

Mother reportedly told him he was ugly and clumsy, 'just like your father'. Mother appeared to blame him for his father's absences.

Sexually dysfunctional – incapable of mature, consensual relationship with another adult

Nothing to support this: marriage very public. No indications that MM unhappy with marriage or has lover. ??? Check newspaper gossip columns ??? Check with uniforms on local patrol – any signs ???

Cool, distant mother; very little touching or emotional warmth as child
  Implied in both books.

Egocentric world view
  All the evidence – even from MM's adoring account – supports this.

Beaten as child
  MM recalls him speaking of his father coming home from trip and thrashing him for failing eleven-plus; otherwise, nothing known.

Witnessed sexually stressful situation as child, e.g. marital rape, mother engaged in prostitution
  Nothing known

Parents separated in childhood or early adolescence
  Parents divorced when he was twelve. According to MM book, his obsession with athletics was bid to gain father's attention.

Autoerotic adolescence
  Nothing known.

Rape fantasies
  Nothing known.

Obsession with pornography
  Nothing known.

Voyeuristic tendencies
  Nothing specific known; but cf. *Vance's Visits*, the ultimate poke-your-nose-in television.

Aware his sexual/emotional relationships are abnormal and resents it
  Nothing known.

Obsessive
  Attested to by work colleagues and rivals alike.

Irrational phobias
  Nothing known.

Chronic liar
  Several instances of him 'remaking' past incidents; compare two books.

Initiating stressor?

Jacko Vance's first girlfriend was Jillie Woodrow. He was unsuccessful with girls before her, and by the time they got together, he was almost sixteen and she was just fourteen. Apart from his obsessive sports training, she was his only interest. They had a relationship that was exclusive, compulsive and consuming. He appears to have been a dominating influence upon her. They were engaged as soon as she turned sixteen, opposed by her parents and his mother; he was no longer in touch with his father by this time. After the accident when he lost his arm, MM's account claims he set Jillie free since he was no longer the man she'd contracted to marry; TB's version is that she had been looking for a way out of the claustrophobic relationship for some time and fixed on his accident as a way out, claiming she was repelled by his injury and the prospect of living with a man with a prosthesis. MM and Vance got together shortly afterwards. Just before they married, Jillie did a 'kiss and tell' with the *News of the World* revealing that Vance had forced her to indulge in sado-masochistic rituals, tying her up to have sex in spite of her protests that it frightened her. Vance tried to prevent the story's publication, denying it vigorously. He failed to get an injunction, but never sued for libel, claiming that he couldn't afford the legal process. (Probably true at that stage in career.) Either the end of the relationship with Jillie in such stressful circumstances or her subsequent revelations could have been a powerful enough stressor to trigger off the first in Vance's series of crimes.

'Oh, shit,' Carol said as she reached the end of Shaz's analysis. 'You really have to wonder, don't you?'

'You think Jacko Vance could be a serial killer?' Kay asked.

'Shaz thought so. And I think she might have been right,' Tony said grimly.

'There's something bothering me about this,' Simon said. Encouraged by a questioning look from Tony he continued. 'If Vance is a sociopath, how come he saved those kids and tried to rescue that lorry driver in the accident where he lost his arm? Why did he not just leave them to it?'

'Good point,' Tony said. 'You know I hate to theorize ahead of the data, but looking at what we know so far, I'd say Jacko spent most of his formative years desperate for attention and approval. When the accident happened, he automatically went down the road that would make him look good in other people's eyes. It's not uncommon for what looks like heroism to be a desperate craving for glory. I think that's what happened there. If you still think we're barking up the wrong tree, let me tell you about a conversation I had with Commander Bishop this afternoon.' He told them about Shaz's appointment with Vance and the conclusions he'd drawn from that.

'You're going to have to let McCormick and Wharton know about this file,' Carol said.

'I don't feel much like it, the way they treated me.'

'You want them to put Shaz's killer away, don't you?'

'I want Shaz's killer put away,' Tony said firmly. 'I just don't think those two have the imagination to deal with the information. Think about it, Carol. If I tell them what we've found here, first off, they won't want to believe it. They'll think we've tinkered with her files. I can just imagine the interview with Vance. He slipped effortlessly into the broad Yorkshire of his childhood. 'A'right, Mr Vance, we're sorry to trouble tha, but we think the lass here last Saturday thought tha were a serial killer. Daft, tha knows, but seeing as 'ow she got herself murdered that night, we thought we'd better come and 'ave a word. 'Appen tha might've seen summat, some weirdo following her, like.'

'They're not that bad, surely,' Carol protested, spluttering with laughter in spite of herself.

'You ask me, he's being generous,' Leon muttered.

'They're not going to go in and *interrogate* Jacko Vance,' Simon said. 'They're going to be overawed, they're going to be on his side. All they'll do is mark his card.'

'And Jack the Lad is a clever bastard,' Tony continued. 'Now he knows they know about Shaz's visit, he'll be the biggest Goody Two Shoes on legs. So there's part of me that thinks, no, don't tell them.'

There was a long silence. Then Simon said, 'So what now?'

Tony had taken a notepad from the laptop bag and started scribbling. 'If we're going to do this, we've got to do it right. Which means I act as controller and co-ordinator. Carol, is there a local takeaway that delivers?'

She snorted with derision. 'Out here? Do me a favour. There's bread, cheese, salami, tuna, salad stuff. Give me a hand, team. we'll throw some butties together while our leader cogitates.'

When they returned fifteen minutes later with mounds of sandwiches and a mixing bowl filled with crisps, Tony was ready for them. Sprawled round the room with bottles of beer and plates of food, they listened while he explained what he wanted them to do.

'I think we're all agreed that on the balance of probabilities, Shaz was killed because of the work she'd done since she came to Leeds. There's no indication that she had any kind of personally threatening experiences up to that point. So we take as our starting point the assumption that Shaz Bowman correctly identified the existence of an as yet unknown serial killer of teenage girls.' He raised his eyebrows in a question and noted four nods.

'The external connector in these cases concerned Jacko Vance. Shaz assumed him to be the killer, though we shouldn't fail to consider that our target could conceivably be someone in his entourage. Me, I'm inclined to go for Vance.'

'Good old Occam,' Simon muttered wryly.

'Not just on the least complicated principle,' Tony said. 'My view is coloured by the length of time these killings apparently cover. I don't know if there's anyone who has been professionally close to Vance for that long. Even if they had, I'm not convinced that they would have the charisma to lure young women into what looks superficially like a runaway bid.

'So, we've got Shaz's profile of Vance. It's inevitably superficial. She only had access to what was in the public domain that she could get her hands on readily. That seems to have consisted mainly of two biographies, one written by his wife, the other by a showbiz hack. We need to dig a lot deeper than that before we can check whether this man is a serious possible for the series of killings we're postulating. This is an unusual job for us profilers. Usually we're making deductions from crime to offender. This time, we're going from putative offender to hypothetical murders. I don't feel entirely confident about it, if I'm honest. It's fresh territory for me. So we need to be very careful before we put our heads anywhere near the parapet.' More nods. Leon stood up and moved across to the doorway so he could smoke without polluting everyone else's food.

'We get the message,' Leon drawled. 'Our missions, should we choose to accept them, are . . . ?'

'We need to track down his fiancee, Jillie Woodrow. The person responsible for interviewing Jillie should also carry out a general investigation into his early life – family, neighbours, school friends, teachers, any local bobbies still on the payroll or recently retired. Simon, are you up for that?'

Simon looked apprehensive. 'What exactly do I do?'

Tony signalled to Carol with his eyes. 'Find out everything you possibly can about Jacko,' she said. 'Deep background. If you want a cover story for everyone except Jillie, say we're investigating threats against him and we think the reason may lie deep in his past. People love a bit of melodrama. With Jillie, that won't work. It might be worth hinting that you're investigating allegations made against Jacko by a prostitute, perhaps imply that you suspect they're malicious lies?'

'OK. Any ideas how I find her, given that I haven't got access to the PNC?'

'I'll get to that in a minute,' Tony said. 'Leon, I want you to start digging into what was going on in his life around the time of the accident where he lost his arm. That and his early TV career. See if you can find his old trainer, the first people he worked with when he was starting out in sports' broadcasting. Athletes on the British team with him, that sort of thing. OK?'

'Just watch me,' Leon said, cold and serious for once. 'You won't be sorry you asked me, man.'

'Kay, your job is to go round the parents of the girls Shaz identified in her cluster and re-interview them. All the usual misper stuff, plus anything and everything you can pull out about Jacko Vance.'

'The local lads should be more than happy to hand off their case files to you,' Carol put in. 'They'll be so delighted that somebody else is prepared to take responsibility for such a no-hoper, they'll probably give you the freedom of the nick.'

'All of which DCI Jordan here will set up for you in advance,' Tony continued. 'She will be your facilitator, the one who speaks to ranking officers in other police stations around the country and gets you the information that will kick-start your inquiries. Stuff like where Jillie Woodrow is now, what happened to Vance's coach, which victim's parents have moved to Scunthorpe.'

Carol stared open-mouthed for a long moment. Leon, Simon and Kay looked on with the delight of adolescents watching grown-ups on the verge of behaving badly. 'Fine,' she eventually said, her voice loaded with sarcasm. 'I have so little to do at work, it'll be a pleasure fitting it in. So, Tony, what are you going to be up to while the rest of the squad are doing all the hard graft?'

He reached for a sandwich, checked the filling, then looked up with a smile that appeared entirely free from guile. 'I'm going to shake the tree,' he said.

Detective Inspector Colin Wharton looked like a refugee from one of those dreadfully predictable gritty northern cops-and-robbers dramas that the networks churned out to fill the gap between the late news and bedtime, Micky thought. Once handsome in a craggy way, too much drink and junk food had blurred his features and shrouded his blue eyes in heavy pouches. She imagined him on a second marriage which would be in trouble; the kids from his first marriage would be the teenagers from hell; and he'd have a vague but worrying recurring pain somewhere in his internal organs. She crossed her legs demurely and gave him the smile that had reassured a thousand studio guests. She just knew he'd be a complete sucker for it. Him and Detective Constable Sidekick, who looked one step away from asking for her autograph.

She glanced at her watch. 'Jacko should be back any minute. It'll be the traffic. Same with Betsy. My personal assistant.'

'You mentioned that,' Wharton said. 'If it's all the same to you, we might as well get started. We can talk to Ms Thorne and Mr Vance when they get here.' He consulted a folder spread across his tightly trousered lap. 'I'm told you spoke to DC Bowman the day before she died. How did that come about?'

'We've got two phone lines – one for me and one for Jacko. They're ex-directory, very private. Only a handful of people have the numbers. I switch mine over to the mobile when I'm out and DC Bowman came through on that. It must have been about half past eight on Friday morning – I was with one of my researchers at the time, she could probably confirm that.' Realizing she was wallowing in inconsequentiality, too obvious a marker for nervousness, Micky paused for a moment.

'But it wasn't your researcher?' Wharton prompted her.

'No. It was a voice I didn't recognize. She said she was Detective

Constable Sharon Bowman from the Metropolitan Police and she wanted to arrange an appointment with Jacko. My husband.'

Wharton nodded encouragingly. 'And you said?'

'I told her she'd come through on my line and she apologized and said she'd been told this was his private number. She asked if he was there, and when I said he was away she said could she leave a message. I don't normally act as Jacko's secretary, but since she was with the police and I didn't know what it was about, I thought it would be best just to make a note of what she wanted and pass it on to him.' She smiled, aiming for the self-deprecating air of a woman unsure of herself faced with authority. It was a blatant performance, but Wharton didn't seem to notice.

'Sensible approach, Ms Morgan,' he said. 'What was the message?'

'She said it was merely a formality, a routine matter, but she'd like to interview him in connection with a case she was working on. Because of her other commitments, she said it would have to be Saturday, but she'd happily fit in with his arrangements. The time and place would be up to him. And she left a number where he could get back to her.'

'Do you still have that number?' Wharton asked, just another standard question.

Micky picked up a notepad and held it out to him. 'As you see, we start a fresh page for each day. It's a catch-all – phone messages, programme ideas, domestic bits and pieces.' She handed it over, pointing to a few lines near the top of the page.

Wharton read, 'Det. Con. Sharon Bowman. Jacko. i/v ???Saturday??? you name time + place. 307 4676 Sgt. Devine.' That confirmed the telephone statement Chris Devine had already given them, but Wharton wanted to double-check. 'This number . . . is it London?'

Micky nodded. 'Yes. 0171. Same code as ours, that's why I didn't bother writing it down. Well, it would be, wouldn't it? She was with the Met.'

'She was on secondment to a unit in Leeds,' he said heavily. 'That's why she was living there, Ms Morgan.'

'Oh God, of course,' she said hollowly. 'Do you know, for some reason that just hadn't registered. How odd.'

'Indeed,' Wharton said. 'So, you passed the message on to your husband and that was that?' he said.

'I left the message on his voice mail. He mentioned later that he'd arranged for her to come to the house on Saturday morning. He knew I wouldn't mind since Betsy and I were going off on Le Shuttle on a freebie. Perks of the job.' She gave him the full-beam smile again. Wharton wondered sourly why the women in his life never managed to look so gratified when they spoke to him.

Before he could ask the next question, he heard footfalls on the parquet floor of the hall. He half-turned as the door opened behind him. His first impression of Jacko Vance was a sense of tremendous energy contained within expensive tailoring. There was something irresistibly watchable about him, even doing something as banal as crossing the room and extending his left hand in a gesture of welcome. 'Inspector Wharton, I presume,' Vance said warmly, affecting not to notice the policeman's fluster as he half-rose, reached out with the wrong hand then clumsily shifted his papers and grabbed at the proffered hand in an awkward shake. 'I'm Jacko Vance,' he said, pretending a humility Micky recognized as false as her own. 'Desperate business, this.' Vance turned away from the detective, nodding a friendly greeting at the hovering constable and dropped on to the sofa next to his wife. He patted her thigh. 'All right, Micky?' His voice dripped the same concern he always showed the terminally ill.

'We've just been going over DC Bowman's phone call,' she said.

'Right. Sorry I'm late. Got held up in traffic in the West End,' he said, his mouth curling upwards in a familiar self-deprecating smile. 'So, what can I tell you, officer?'

'Ms Morgan passed a message on to you from DC Bowman, is that right?'

'Absolutely,' Vance said confidently. 'I called the number she'd left and spoke to a detective sergeant whose name I have completely forgotten. I said that if DC Bowman came to the house on Saturday morning between half past nine and noon, I would see her then.'

'Very generous, a busy man like yourself,' Wharton said.

Vance raised his eyebrows. 'I always try to help the authorities when I can. It didn't inconvenience me in any way. All I had planned for the day was to catch up on some personal paperwork then drive up to my cottage in Northumberland in time for an early night. I was running a charity half-marathon at Sunderland on Sunday, you see.' He leaned back negligently, fully expecting his throwaway line to be noted, believed and filed away in support of his innocence.

'What time did DC Bowman arrive?' Wharton asked.

Vance pulled a face and turned to Micky. 'What time was it? You were just leaving, weren't you?'

'That's right,' she confirmed. 'Must have been around half past nine. Betsy could probably tell you more exactly. She's the only one in the house with any sense of time.' She smiled wryly, amazed at how ready this policeman was to accept that two major TV personalities who anchored key programmes couldn't measure time instinctively to the last half-minute. 'We more or less passed on the doorstep. Jacko was on the phone upstairs, so I pointed her in here, and we were off.'

'I didn't keep her waiting more than a couple of minutes,' Vance continued seamlessly. 'She apologized for interrupting my weekend, but I explained that in this job, we don't really have weekends. We take time for ourselves when we can, don't we, darling?' He gazed adoringly at her, slipping his arm round her shoulders.

'Not often enough,' Micky sighed.

Wharton cleared his throat and said, 'Can you tell me what it was DC Bowman wanted to talk to you about?'

'You mean, you don't know?' Micky demanded, the dormant news reporter inside her springing into action. 'A police officer comes all the way from Yorkshire to London to interview someone with as high a profile as Jacko, and you don't know what it was in aid of?' She looked astonished, leaning forward, forearms on thighs, hands spread open.

Wharton shifted in his seat and stared fixedly at a point on the wall between the two long windows. 'DC Bowman was attached to a new unit. Strictly speaking, she should not have been on operational duties at present. We think we know what she was working on, but as yet we have no independent corroboration of that. It'd help us a lot if Mr Vance could just tell us what transpired between the two of them on Saturday morning.' He breathed out heavily through his nose and shot them a quick look that mingled embarrassment and pleading.

'No problem,' Vance said easily. 'DC Bowman was very apologetic about invading my privacy with her questions, but she said she was working on a series of missing teenage girls. She thought they had been lured away from home by the same individual. It appeared that some of these girls had been at one of my public appearances shortly before they dropped out of sight and she wondered if some nutter was targeting my fans. She said she wanted to show me pictures of the girls, just in case I'd noticed them talking to a particular person.'

'One of your entourage, you mean?' Wharton prompted, proud of knowing the right word.

Vance laughed, a rich baritone laugh. 'I'm sorry to disappoint you, Inspector, but I don't exactly have an entourage. When I'm doing the programme, I have a team who work very closely with me. Sometimes when I'm doing PAs – public appearances, that is – my producer or my researcher will come along to keep me company and provide a bit of back-up. But that apart, anything I spend on minders or whatever comes out of my pocket. And since most of the work I do involves earning cash for charities as well, it seems crazy to spend any more than is absolutely necessary. So, as I explained to DC Bowman, there are no loyal retainers. What there is, however, is a hard core of devotees. There are, I suppose, a couple of dozen fans who turn up regularly at virtually every event I do. Strange people, but I'd always considered them harmless.'

'It's a mark of celebrity,' Micky said matter-of-factly. 'If you don't have your retinue of attendant weirdos, you're nobody. Badly dressed men in anoraks and women in polyester slacks and acrylic cardies. All of them with dreadful haircuts. Not the sort your average teenage girl would run off with, take it from me.'

'Which is pretty much what I told DC Bowman,' Vance continued. They were so smooth, so natural, he thought. Maybe it was about time they made some programmes together. He made a mental note to explore the idea with his producer. 'She showed me a few photographs of the girls she was concerned about, but none of them rang any bells.' His shrug was disarming. 'Not surprising. I can sign upwards of three hundred autographs at a PA. Well, I say sign ... scrawl would be more like it.' He looked ruefully at his prosthetic hand. 'Writing's one of the many things I can't do properly any more.'

There was a moment's silence. To Wharton it felt as long as Remembrance Sunday. He searched around for a meaningful question. 'How did DC Bowman respond, sir? To your lack of recognition, I mean.'

'She seemed disappointed,' Vance said. 'But she admitted it had always been a long shot. I said I was sorry not to have been more help, and she left. That must have been around ... oh, half past ten, thereabouts?'

'So she was here for about an hour? That seems quite a long time for a few questions,' Wharton said, punctilious rather than suspicious.

'It does, doesn't it?' Vance agreed. 'But I did keep her waiting a few minutes, then I made us both some coffee, we did the usual small talk. People always want to know behind-the-scenes gossip about *Vance's Visits*. Then I had to go through all the photographs. I took my time. Missing girls is too serious a subject to take lightly. I mean, no contact with their families after all this time – years, in some cases, according to DC Bowman – chances are they could have been murdered. It merited my attention.'

'Quite so, sir,' Wharton said heavily, wishing he hadn't bothered asking. 'I don't suppose she mentioned any plans she might have for the rest of the day?'

Vance shook his head. 'Sorry, Inspector. I had the impression she had another appointment, but she didn't say where or with whom.'

'What gave you that impression, sir?' Wharton looked up, for the first time feeling he might be doing more than going through the motions.

Vance frowned for a moment, as if thinking. 'After I'd finished with the photographs, I offered to make fresh coffee. But she looked at her watch and seemed startled. As if she hadn't realized the time. She said she had to be going, she'd no idea we'd been talking for so long. She was out the door within minutes.'

Wharton closed his notebook. 'As I think I should be too, sir. I very much appreciate both of you taking the time to talk to me. If there's anything else, which I very much doubt, I'll be in touch.' He rose and gave his junior officer a 'let's go' jerk of the head.

'You don't need to speak to Betsy?' Micky asked. 'She shouldn't be long.'

'I don't think that'll be necessary,' Wharton said. 'Frankly, I think DC Bowman's visit here was almost certainly nothing to do with her death. We just have to tie up the loose ends.'

Vance crossed to the door and opened it to usher them out. 'A shame you have to be dragged down here when the real work's waiting for you in Yorkshire,' he said, his sympathetic smile adding weight to the commiseration in his voice.

Micky said goodbye and watched from the window as Vance saw the police officers off the premises. She wasn't sure what her husband was hiding. But she knew him well enough to know that what she had just heard was only a distant relative of the truth, the whole truth and nothing but the truth.

When he walked back into the room, she was leaning against the fireplace. 'Are you going to tell me what you didn't tell them?' she asked, her eyes giving him the shrewd appraisal that could always penetrate his glossy surface.

Vance grinned. 'You're a witch, Micky. Yes, I'll tell you what I didn't tell them. I did recognize one of the girls whose picture Bowman showed me.'

Micky's eyes widened. 'You did? How come? Where from?'

'No need to panic,' he said scornfully. 'It's perfectly innocent. When she went missing, her parents contacted us. Said she was my biggest fan, blah, blah, blah, never missed a show, blah, blah, blah. Wanted us to put out an appeal for her to contact them.'

'And did you?'

'Course not. It wouldn't fit the format of the programme at all. Somebody from the office sent them a sympathetic letter and we got one of the tabloids to run a story saying, "Jacko begs runaway to phone home".'

'So why didn't you tell Wharton? If you did something for the press, there'll be cuttings somewhere! They could dig them out and then you'll be in deep shit.'

'How? They don't even know what Bowman was doing, which doesn't sound like they've got her files, does it? Look, Mick, I never met the girl. I never spoke to her. But if I tell DI Plod I recognized her ... shit, Mick, you know the police are the leakiest sieve in town. Next thing you know, it'll be "Jacko in murder quiz" splashed all over the front pages. No thanks. I can do without it. They can't connect me to a single one of Bowman's runaways. The king of deniability, remember?'

Micky shook her head, admiring his chutzpah in spite of herself. 'More like Teflon Man,' she said. 'I've got to hand it to you, Jacko. When it comes to playing the audience like a fiddle, even I can't hold a candle to you.'

He crossed to her and kissed her cheek. 'Never try to bullshit a bullshitter.'

*　　*　　*

Carol walked next morning into her office to find her crew had wrong-footed her by being there ahead of her. Tommy Taylor sprawled in the chair opposite hers, legs wide apart to emphasize his masculinity. Lee had the window cracked open, blowing his smoke out to join the traffic fumes. Di was in her usual position leaning against the wall, arms folded over her badly fitting suit. Carol itched to drag her kicking and screaming to the January sales to kit the woman out in clothes that would both fit and flatter her instead of the expensive and nasty stuff she chose now.

Carol made straight for her bastion behind the desk, flipping open her briefcase as she sat. 'Right,' she said. 'Our serial arsonist.'

'Crunchy nut cornflake,' Lee said.

'Actually, not,' Carol said. 'Apparently, our firebug is as sane as you or me. Well, me, anyway, since I can't speak for you three. According to a psychologist whose judgement I trust implicitly, we're not dealing with a psychopath. The man who's setting these fires has a straightforward criminal motive. And that points to Jim Pendlebury's part-timers.' The three stared at her as if she'd suddenly slipped into Swedish.

'You what?' Lee managed to speak first.

Carol distributed copies of the list the fire chief had given her. 'I want deep background checks into these men. Particular attention to financial details. And I don't want them to get so much as a sniff that we're interested.'

Tommy Taylor found his voice. 'You're accusing *firemen*?'

'I think you'll find we're supposed to call them firefighters these days,' Carol said mildly. 'I'm not accusing anybody yet, Sergeant. I'm trying to gather enough information on which we can base a decision.'

'Firemen *die* in fires,' Di Earnshaw sniped mutinously. 'They get injured, they inhale smoke. Why would a fireman set fires? He'd have to be a real sicko, and you just said this bloke isn't. Surely that's a contradiction in terms?'

'He's not sick,' Carol said firmly. 'Desperate, maybe, but he's not suffering from a mental illness. We're looking for someone who's so deep in debt he's lost sight of anything except how to get out of it. It's not that he wants to put his mates at risk; he's just not allowing himself to include them in the equation.'

Taylor shook his head sceptically. 'It's a helluva slur on the fire service,' he protested.

'No more so than outside inquiries into allegations of police corruption. And we all know that happens.' Carol's voice was dry. She shuffled the case papers back into her briefcase then looked up at them. 'You lot still here?'

Lee tossed his cigarette into the street below in an eloquent gesture and pushed himself into a slouching walk to the door. 'I'm on it,' he said.

Taylor stood up and ostentatiously rearranged the outward evidence of his gender. 'Aye,' he said, following Lee and indicating to Di Earnshaw that she should follow.

'Softly, softly,' Carol said to the retreating backs.

If spines could speak, Di Earnshaw's would have uttered a fluent 'Fuck off.' The door closed behind them and Carol leaned back in her chair, one hand massaging the tight knots at the base of her skull. It was going to be a very long day.

Tony reached for the phone automatically, mumbling, 'Tony Hill here, can you hang on a minute,' before finishing the sentence he was typing into his computer. He looked at the receiver in his hand as if not quite certain how it had arrived there. 'Yes, sorry, Tony Hill speaking.'

'This is DI Wharton.' His voice was neutral.

'Why?' Tony asked.

'What?' Wharton stumbled, wrong-footed.

'I asked why you were calling. What's so strange about that?'

'Aye, right. Well, I'm calling out of courtesy,' Wharton said with a brusqueness that contradicted his words.

'That's novel.'

'There's no need to get clever. My boss would have no problem with bringing you in for another visit.'

'He'd have to take that up with my lawyer. You've had your one free shot. So what was this courtesy you wanted to extend me?'

'We had a telephone call from Micky Morgan, the TV presenter who, as you may or may not know, is Mrs Jacko Vance. She volunteered the information that Bowman visited their house in London on Saturday morning to interview her husband. So we took a trip down there and spoke to Mr Vance ourselves. And he's in the clear. Bowman might have made a fool of herself in front of your little clique, but she wasn't daft enough to repeat her nonsense to the man himself. Turns out all she wanted to ask was if he'd seen anybody at his events stalking these missing girls. And he hadn't. Not surprising, when you consider how many faces pass his in a week. So you see, Dr Hill, he's clean. They came to us, we didn't go to them.'

'And that's it? Jacko Vance told you he'd waved goodbye to Shaz Bowman on the doorstep and that's good enough for you?'

'We've no reason to think otherwise,' Wharton said stiffly.

'The last person to see her alive? Aren't they usually worth a look?'

'Not when they have no known connection to the victim, a reputation for probity that's never been challenged and they said goodbye twelve hours before the crime was committed,' Wharton said, his voice laced with acid. 'Especially when they're a registered disabled, one-armed person who's supposed to have overwhelmed a highly trained, able-bodied police officer.'

'Can I ask one question?'

'You can ask.'

'Was there a witness to this interview or did Vance see Shaz alone?'

'His wife let her into the house, but she left them to it. Bowman saw him alone. But that doesn't automatically mean he's lying, you know. I've been in this game a long time. I can tell when folk are telling me lies. Face it, Doctor, you're well off target. I can't say I blame you for trying to divert us, but we're sticking with the people that she knew.'

'Thanks for letting me know.' Not trusting himself to say more, Tony dropped the phone back into its cradle. The blindness of the human animal never ceased to amaze him. It wasn't that Wharton was a stupid man; he was simply, in spite of years in the police service, conditioned to the belief that men like Jacko Vance could not be violent criminals.

In a way, Wharton's call was what he had been waiting for. The police could not avenge Shaz Bowman and vindicate his own work. It was up to him now, and there was a mordant satisfaction in that. Besides, Wharton's answer to his question had confirmed Vance as prime suspect in Tony's eyes. It had to be him. Tony had already eliminated a psychotic fan; now he could eliminate the members of Vance's entourage. If no one else had witnessed the interview, no one else could have picked up Shaz's trail after she left the house.

Picking up the phone again, Tony called the number he'd

obtained earlier from Directory Enquiries, anticipating this moment. When the switchboard answered, he said, 'Can you put me through to the *Midday with Morgan* production office?' Then he leaned back to wait, a grim little smile curving his lips.

John Brandon fiddled with the handle of his coffee cup. 'I don't like it, Carol,' he admitted. She opened her mouth to respond and he lifted a finger to silence her. 'Oh, I know you're no more fond of the idea than I am. It's still a big step, pointing the finger at the fire service. I only hope we're not making a terrible mistake here.'

'Tony Hill's been right before,' she reminded him. 'And when you look at his analysis, it makes sense the way nothing else does.'

Brandon shook his head despairingly, looking more like a world-weary undertaker than ever. 'I know. It's such a depressing thought, though. To put so many lives at risk for so little. At least when coppers go bent, people don't usually end up dead.' He sipped his coffee. The aroma wafted across the desk to Carol, making her mouth water. Normally he offered her a cup; it was a measure of how shocked he was by her report that she wasn't sharing the fragrant brew. 'Ah well,' he said. 'Keep me informed of what your team comes up with. I'd appreciate advance notice of an arrest.'

'No problem. There was one other thing, sir?'

'Was that the bad news or the good news?'

'I think it was the bad news. Depending on what you think of the other matter, sir.' Carol's smile held no cheer.

The Chief Constable sighed and half-turned in his swivel chair to stare out across the estuary. As usual, the boss had the best view, Carol thought irrelevantly as an ocean-going trawler slid from one window to the next. 'Let's hear it, then,' he said.

'It also concerns Tony Hill,' she said. 'You know about the murder on his squad?'

'Hellish business,' Brandon said accurately. 'The worst thing that can happen in this job is losing an officer. But losing one like that . . . It's your biggest nightmare.'

'Especially if you've got memories like Tony Hill's to draw on.'

'You're not wrong.' He looked shrewdly across at her. 'Apart from our natural compassion, how does this engage us?'

'Officially, not at all.'

'But unofficially?'

'Tony's having some problems with West Yorkshire. They appear to be treating him and his profiling trainees as their principal suspects instead of an effective resource. Tony feels they've dismissed other avenues for arbitrary reasons, and he's determined that Shaz Bowman's killer shouldn't escape simply because the investigating officers are taking a blinkered approach.'

A smile escaped and spread across Brandon's face. 'Those his words?'

Carol's answering smile was complicit. 'Not verbatim, sir. I didn't take a contemporaneous note.'

'I can see why he feels the need to take action,' Brandon said cautiously. 'Any investigator would have the same reaction. But we have rules in the police service that prevent officers investigating crimes where they have a personal interest. Those rules exist for the very good reason that crimes close to home distort an officer's judgement. Are you sure it wouldn't be best to let West Yorkshire get on with this in their own way?'

'Not if it means leaving a psychopath on the streets,' Carol said firmly. 'There's nothing wrong that I can see with the way Tony's mind's working.'

'You still haven't explained what this has to do with us.'

'He needs help. He's working with some of his task force officers, but they're all currently on suspension, so they don't have access to any official channels. Plus he needs input from an experienced police officer to counterbalance his viewpoint. He can't get that from West Yorkshire. All they want to do is find a reason to stick him or one of his team behind bars.'

'They never wanted to host that unit in the first place,' Brandon said. 'It's not surprising they see this as an excuse to shoot it down in flames. Nevertheless, it is their case and they're not looking to us for assistance.'

'No, but Tony is. And I feel I owe him, sir. All I'd be doing is a little background digging to provide his team with raw materials like names and addresses. I intend to give him what help I can. I'd prefer to do it with your blessing.'

'When you say help . . . ?'

'I won't be treading on West Yorkshire's heels. The angle Tony's interested in is miles away from their inquiries. They won't know I'm there. I'm not going to drop you in a jurisdictional wrangle.'

Brandon swallowed the last of his coffee and pushed the cup away from him. 'Damn right, you're not. Carol, do what you've got to do. But you're doing it off the books. This conversation never happened, and if it all comes on top, I never met you before.'

She grinned and got to her feet. 'Thank you, sir.'

'Stay out of trouble, Chief Inspector,' he said gruffly, dismissing her with a flutter of his fingers. As she opened the door to leave, he added, 'If you need my help, you have my number.'

It was a promise Carol hoped she'd never have to collect on.

Sunderland was the furthest north, Exmouth the most southerly point. In between were Swindon, Grantham, Tamworth, Wigan and Halifax. In each place, a teenage girl's disappearance had snagged Shaz Bowman's attention. Kay Hallam knew that somehow she had to squeeze fresh juice from those investigations that would shore up the edifice of circumstantial evidence Tony was building against Jacko Vance. It wasn't an easy assignment. Years had passed and with them the sharpness of memory. Doing it single-handed wasn't the best option either. In an ideal world, there would be two of them, taking a couple of weeks to complete the task, conducting interviews with brains that weren't exhausted from driving the length and breadth of the country.

No such luxury. Not that she wanted to hang around. Whoever had killed Shaz didn't deserve a minute longer at liberty than they'd already had. It was tough enough sitting on her hands while she waited for the results of DCI Jordan hammering the phones. Now there was a role model, Kay thought as she prowled from room to room of her terraced Victorian artisan's cottage. Whatever Carol Jordan had done, she'd obviously done it right. 'If you want to be successful, hang around with successful people and copy what they do,' Kay recited, a familiar mantra from one of her American self-improvement tapes.

The call came at lunchtime. Carol had spoken to all of the CID divisions who had dealt with the missing girls. In three cases, she'd even managed to contact the investigating officer, though investigation was probably too exalted a word for the cursory inquiries into missing teenage girls who didn't appear to want to be found. She had arranged for Kay to survey the slender files, and she'd contrived to elicit addresses and phone numbers for the distraught parents.

Kay put the phone down and studied a road atlas. She reckoned she could do Halifax in the afternoon and Wigan that evening.

Then down the motorway to the Midlands and an overnight motel. Breakfast at Tamworth then hammer down to Exmouth for late afternoon. Back up the motorway to overnight at Swindon, then cross-country to Grantham. A stop the following day in Leeds to report to Tony, then she could finish off in Sunderland. It sounded like the road movie from hell. Even Thelma and Louise got it more glamorous than this, she thought.

But then, unlike some of her colleagues, she'd never expected it to be glamorous. Hard graft, job security and a decent pay cheque were all Kay had ever supposed she'd get from the police. The gratification of detective work had come as a surprise. And she was good at it, thanks to an eye for detail that her less appreciative colleagues called anal. Profiling seemed like the ideal area for using her observational skills to the full. She hadn't imagined her first case would be so close to home, or how personal it would feel. Nobody deserved what Shaz Bowman had endured, and nobody deserved to get away with it.

That was the thought Kay held on to as she hacked her way round the network of motorways that crisscrossed England. She noticed that all of her destinations were either close by one of those motorways or to one of the other major arterial roads peppered with fast-food joints tacked on to petrol stations. She wondered if there were any significance in that. Did Vance arrange to meet his victims at service areas they could easily scrounge a lift to? It was almost the only fresh thing to come out of two days' work, she thought grimly. That and the faintest ghostly glimmering of a pattern. But the stories of the parents were depressingly similar, and distressingly short on significant detail, certainly where Vance was concerned. She'd managed to talk to a couple of friends of missing girls, and they'd been scarcely more helpful. It wasn't that they didn't want to help; Kay was the sort of interviewer people always talked to. Her mousey insignificance belied her intelligence; she was no threat to women and made men feel protective. No, it wasn't that they were holding back, it was simply that there wasn't much to be said. Yes, the missing girls were daft on Jacko, yes, they'd been to events where he was present and yes, they were really excited about it. But nothing more than that flimsy gleaning.

By Grantham, she was operating on automatic pilot. Two nights in motels with the beds too soft and the constant high zip, zing and zoom of all-night traffic diluted but not deleted by double glazing was no recipe for a productive interview, but it was better than no sleep at all, she scolded herself as she yawned expansively before ringing the doorbell.

Kenny and Denise Burton didn't seem to notice her exhaustion. It had been two years, seven months and three days since Stacey had walked out of the front door and never returned and the shadows under their eyes indicated neither had had a decent night's sleep since. They were like twins; both short, burly with pale, indoor skin and puffy fingers. Looking at the wall of photographs of their slim, bright-eyed daughter, it was hard to believe in genetics as a science. They sat in a living room that was a monument to the expression 'a place for everything and everything in its place'. There were a lot of places in the cramped room; corner display cabinets, alcoves shelved to accommodate knickknacks without number, a feature fireplace with built-in niches. It was a claustrophobic, timidly conventional room. With the two bars of the electric fire throwing out dusty heat, Kay could hardly breathe. It was no wonder Stacey hadn't been reluctant to leave.

'She was a lovely girl,' Denise said wistfully. It was a refrain Kay had come to hate, hiding as it did every useful element of an adolescent girl's personality. It also reminded her discouragingly of her own mother, forever obliterating the reality of Kay's identity behind the anodyne phrase.

'Not like some,' Kenny said darkly, smoothing his greying hair back over the bald patch threatening to burst through like a cartoon bump on the head. 'She was told to be in by ten, by ten she'd be in.'

'She'd never have gone off of her own free will,' Denise said, the next line in the litany perfectly timed, perfectly placed. 'She had no reason to. She must have been abducted. There's no other explanation.'

Kay avoided the painfully obvious one. 'I'd like to ask some questions about the days before Stacey disappeared,' she said. 'Apart from going to school, did she go out at all that week?'

Kenny and Denise didn't pause for thought. In counterpoint, they said, 'She went to the pictures.'

'With Kerry.'

'The weekend before she was taken.'

'Tom Cruise.'

'She loves Tom Cruise.' The defiant present tense.

'She went out on the Monday as well.'

'We wouldn't normally allow her out on a school night.'

'But this was special.'

'Jacko Vance.'

'Her hero, he is.'

'Opening a fun pub in town, he was.'

'We wouldn't normally have allowed her into a pub.'

'What with her only being fourteen.'

'But Kerry's mum was taking them, so we thought it would be all right.'

'And it was.'

'She was home right on time, right when Kerry's mum said they'd be.'

'Full of it, our Stacey was. She got a signed photo.'

'Personally signed. To her personally.'

'She had that with her. When she went.' There was a pause while Kenny and Denise swallowed their grief.

Kay took advantage. 'How did she seem after their night out?'

'She was very excited, wasn't she, Kenny? It was like a dream come true to her, talking to Jacko Vance.'

'She actually got to talk to him?' Kay forced herself to sound nonchalant. The faint pattern she'd discerned was growing stronger with each interview.

'Like a moonstruck calf she was, after,' Stacey's father confirmed.

'She'd always wanted to go on the television.' The counterpoint was back.

'Your people reckoned she'd run off to London to try and break into showbiz,' Kenny said contemptuously. 'No way. Not Stacey. She was far too sensible. She agreed with us. Stay at school, get her A-levels, then we'd see.'

'She could have been on the television,' Denise wistful now.

'She had the looks.'

Kay cut in before they could get off and running again. 'Did she say what she'd talked about with Jacko Vance?'

'Just that he was really friendly,' Denise said. 'I don't think he said anything in particular to her, did he, Kenny?'

'He hasn't got time to take a personal interest. A busy man. Dozens of people, no, hundreds of people want him to sign an autograph, exchange a few words, pose for a picture.'

The words hung in the air like the afterimage of sparklers. 'Pose for a picture?' Kay said faintly. 'Did Stacey have her picture taken with him?'

They nodded in sync. 'Kerry's mum took it.'

'Could I see it?' Kay's heart was suddenly thudding like a drum, her palms sweating in the stuffy room.

Kenny pulled an embossed album from under a coffee table stained a colour unknown in nature. With practised hand, he turned swiftly to the last page. There, blown up to ten by eight was a fuzzy snapshot of a cluster of people surrounding Jacko Vance. The angle was skewed, the faces blurred, as if seen through a heat haze. But the girl standing next to Jacko Vance, the one he was unquestionably talking to, his hand on her shoulder, his head inclined towards her, the girl looking up with the adoring look of a new puppy was without a shadow of a doubt Stacey Burton.

It had been harder than Wharton had expected to talk to Detective Sergeant Chris Devine. When he'd rung her office, he'd discovered she'd signed up for a couple of days' compassionate leave following her initial telephone statement to the murder inquiry. It was the first time Wharton had encountered anyone who seemed to be genuinely grieving for Shaz Bowman; he'd not been the officer charged with breaking the news to her devastated parents.

By the time Chris had returned the message on her answering machine, Wharton was already in London interviewing Vance and his wife. It had been easy to arrange to meet at her flat afterwards.

The hard-nosed copper in him had warmed to Chris Devine immediately she'd opened her door and greeted them with, 'I sincerely hope you're going to nail the bastard who did this.' He wasn't bothered by the array of artistic photographs of beautiful women that covered the walls of her flat. He'd worked with dykes before and on balance he thought they were a damn sight less disruptive than most of the straight women on the force. His sidekick was less sanguine, carefully choosing to sit facing the wall of glass that looked out from the modern block of flats to the ancient church left incongruously standing at the heart of the Barbican complex.

'I hope so, too,' he'd said, perching on the lumpy futon sofa and wondering fleetingly how people ever slept on the things.

'You've been to see Jacko Vance?' Chris said almost before she was settled in the big wing chair opposite him.

'We interviewed him and his wife yesterday. He confirmed what you'd already told us about the appointment DC Bowman kept with him on the day she died.'

She nodded, pushing her thick chestnut hair away from her face. 'I had Vance down as the type that would keep a note of everything.'

'So what was all that about?' Wharton asked. 'Why were you helping DC Bowman maintain the illusion that she was a Met officer?'

The frown line between her eyes deepened. 'I'm sorry?'

'Your direct line in the CID office was left as a contact number for DC Bowman. The impression it gave was that she was still a Met officer.'

'She *was* still a Met officer,' Chris pointed out. 'But there was nothing sinister in giving my number as a contact. During their training period, the profiling squad officers can't take phone calls in working hours. Shaz asked if I'd sort it, that's all.'

'Why you, Sergeant? Why not the desk officer where she was stationed? Why not leave her home number and ask him to call in the evening?' There was nothing hostile in Wharton's manner; he was genuinely interested in the answer.

'I suppose because we were already in contact over the case,' Chris said, feeling irritation rise inside her but giving no outward sign. Her years in the police had left her with the tendency to see innuendo in everything and the ability not to show her reaction.

'You were? In what respect?'

Chris's turned her head and her dark eyes looked over Wharton's shoulder to the sky beyond. 'She'd already asked for my help. She needed some newspapers photocopied and I went out to Colindale to do it for her.'

'You were responsible for that parcel?'

'I was, yes.'

'I've heard about that. Must have been hundreds of pages, box that size and weight. That's a lot of work for an officer as busy as you must be,' Wharton said, starting to lean a little now he suspected there might be more going on here than met the eye.

'I did it in my own time. OK, Inspector?'

'That's a lot of time to give up for a junior officer,' Wharton suggested.

Chris's mouth tightened momentarily. With her snub nose, she had more than a passing resemblance to Grumpy from the Seven Dwarves. 'Shaz and I were partners on the night shift for a long time. We were friends as well as colleagues. She was probably the most talented young officer I've ever worked with and frankly, Mr Wharton, I don't see how questioning why I was happy to give up my day off to help her is going to help you put her killer away.'

Wharton shrugged. 'Background. You never know.'

'I know, believe me. You should be asking about Jacko Vance.'

In spite of himself, Wharton couldn't help an ironic grin. 'Don't tell me you fell for that as well?'

'If you mean, do I go along with Shaz's theory that Jacko Vance was killing teenage girls, the answer is, I don't know. I've not had the chance to review her evidence. But what I do know is that Vance arranged with me that she should come to his house early on Saturday and she was dead by the next morning. Now, the way we work things down here is we get very interested in the last known person to see a murder victim alive, and according to Shaz's mum, you don't seem to have any record of anyone seeing her after she left Vance's house. That would make me very interested in Jacko Vance. What are the profiling squad saying about it?'

'I'm sure you'll appreciate that until we can conclusively rule out her immediate colleagues from our inquiries, we can't use them to investigate the case.'

Chris's mouth fell open. 'You're not using Tony Hill?'

'We think she may have known her killer, and the only people she knew in Leeds were the ones she was working with. You're an experienced detective. You must see that we can't risk contaminating the inquiry by taking any of them into our confidence.'

'You've got the most talented profiler in the country in the palm of your hand, a man who actually knew the victim and knew what she was working on, and you're ignoring him? Is there some reason you don't want to catch Shaz's killer? I bet Tony Hill doesn't think you should be letting Jacko Vance off the hook.'

Wharton smiled indulgently. 'I can understand you getting a bit emotional about this case.' Chris seethed inside but said nothing as he continued. 'But I can assure you, I've spoken to Mr Vance and there's nothing to suggest that he had anything to do with the murder. According to him, all DC Bowman was interested in was whether he'd spotted any of her so-called cluster of missing girls in the company of any regular attenders at his events. He said he hadn't and that was that.'

'And you take his word for it? Just like that?'

Wharton shrugged. 'Like I said, why wouldn't we? Where's the evidence to suggest anything suspicious?'

Chris stood up abruptly and picked up a packet of cigarettes from a corner table. She lit up and turned back to face Wharton. 'He is the last person that we know who saw her,' she said, her voice harsh.

Wharton's smile was meant to placate but only enraged. 'We don't know that, with respect. She'd written the letter "T" in her diary beneath the appointment with Vance. As if she was going on somewhere else. You wouldn't know who "T" is, would you, Sergeant?'

A deep inhalation of smoke, a long exhalation, then Chris said, 'I can't think of anyone. Sorry.'

'You don't think it might refer to Tony Hill?'

She shrugged. 'It could, I suppose. It could mean almost anything. She could have been going to the Trocadero to play laser games, for all I know. She never said anything about any other plans to me.'

'She didn't come here?'

Chris frowned. 'Why would she?'

'You said you were friends. She was in London. I'd have thought she'd have popped in, especially with you being so helpful and all.' There was a tougher element in Wharton's voice and his jaw thrust outward.

'She didn't come here.' Chris's mouth clamped shut.

Sensing a weak spot, Wharton pushed harder. 'Why was that, Sergeant? Did she prefer to keep a bit of distance between you? Especially now she'd got herself a boyfriend?'

Chris walked briskly to the door and opened it. 'Goodbye, Inspector Wharton.'

'That's a very interesting response, Sergeant Devine,' Wharton said, taking his time getting to his feet and checking that his junior officer was still taking notes.

'If you want to insult Shaz's memory and my intelligence, you're not doing it in my home. Next time, make it formal. Sir.' She leaned against the door, watching them walk down the hall to the lifts. 'Arsehole,' she muttered under her breath. Then she let the heavy door swing shut and crossed to the phone where she rang an old flame in the Home Office. 'Dee? It's Chris. Hey, doll, I need a favour. You've got a psychologist on the payroll, geezer called Tony Hill. I need a personal number . . .'

Jimmy Linden had noticed the young black man even before he'd reached his seat in the sixth row of the empty stand. Years of working with promising young athletes had developed his instinct for spotting strangers. It wasn't only sex perverts you had to be on the lookout for. The drug pushers were just as dangerous with their promises of steroid magic. And Jimmy's youngsters were the very ones most prone to falling for their promises. Anyone who wanted to be the best at javelin, hammer, shot or discus needed the kind of muscle that anabolic steroids could provide a lot more easily than training.

No, it never hurt to keep a weather eye out for strangers, especially here at Meadowbank Stadium where he coached the Scottish junior squad, the pick of the bunch, all of them desperate for that edge that would make them a champion. Jimmy looked up again at the stranger. He looked in pretty good shape, though if he'd ever had dreams of being a contender, he should have knocked those fags on the head a long time ago.

As the session drew to a close and the young athletes climbed into their tracksuits, Jimmy spotted the stranger getting up and disappearing down the stairway. When he emerged trackside moments later, demonstrating he had some official reason for being there, Jimmy felt the muscles in the back of his neck relax slightly, the first sign he'd had that they'd been tense. Old age was creeping up at a gallop, he thought wryly. Used to be he was that close to his body that not a nerve fluttered without him knowing about it.

Before he could follow the sweating bodies into the changing rooms, the stranger stepped in front of him and flashed a warrant card. It was too fast for Jimmy to suss which force he belonged to, but he knew what the card was. 'Detective Constable Jackson,' the man said. 'I'm sorry to bother you at work, but I could use half an hour of your time.'

Jimmy tutted, his whippet face narrowing in displeasure. 'You'll not find any drugs with this lot,' he said. 'I run a clean team, and they all know it.'

Leon shook his head and smiled. 'It's nothing to do with your squad. I just need to pick your brains about some ancient history, that's all.' There was no trace of the smart-mouthed jive talk he used on his fellow profilers.

'What kind of ancient history?'

Leon noticed Jimmy's eyes flickering after his disciples and realized the trainer still had things he wanted to say to them. Hastily, he said, 'It's nothing to worry about, honestly. Look, I noticed a half-decent café just down the road. Why don't you meet me there when you're done here and we can have a chat?'

'Aye, OK,' Jimmy said grudgingly. Half an hour later he was facing Leon over a mug of tea and a plate piled with the sort of bakery products that earned Scotland its nickname of the Land O'Cakes. He must be one hell of a coach, Leon thought as the little man wolfed down a coconut-covered snowball. All the successful throwing jocks Leon had ever known were big blokes, broad in the shoulder and heavy through the thighs. But Jimmy Linden resembled a medieval ascetic, the classic long-distance runner, one of those creatures of bone and sinew who stride easily across the finishing line at marathons, eyes on the middle distance, looking as if the only thing they could want was the next twenty-six miles.

'So what's this all about?' Jimmy said, wiping his mouth with surprising daintiness on a proper monogrammed cotton handkerchief pulled from the sleeve of his sweatshirt.

'For reasons that will become obvious, I can't go into too much detail. We're investigating a case that may have its roots deep in the past. I thought you might be able to give me some pointers.'

'About what? All I know anything about is athletics, son.'

Leon nodded and watched a meringue disappear. 'I'm going back now a dozen or more years ago.'

'When I was based down south? Before I came back up here?'

'That's right. You coached Jacko Vance,' Leon said.

A shadow passed across Jimmy's face. Then he cocked his head to one side and said, 'You're not telling me somebody's putting the black on Jacko and thinking they'll get away with it?' Amusement lit up his watery blue eyes.

Leon winked. 'You didn't hear that from me, Mr Linden.'

'It's Jimmy, son, everybody calls me Jimmy. So, Jacko Vance, eh? What can I tell you about the boy wonder?'

'Anything you can remember.'

'How long have you got?'

Leon's smile was tinged with grimness. He hadn't forgotten why he was in Edinburgh. 'As long as it takes, Jimmy.'

'Let me see. He won the British under-fifteen title when he was only thirteen. I was coaching the national squad at the time and I said as soon as I saw him throw that he was the best chance of an Olympic gold that we'd had in a generation.' He shook his head. 'I wasn't wrong. Poor bugger. Nobody deserves to watch the event they should be winning when they're trying to learn how to use an artificial limb.' Leon understood the implied but unspoken, 'not even Jacko Vance'.

'He never considered doing the disabled games?' Leon asked.

Jimmy snorted derisively. 'Jacko? That would have meant admitting he was disabled.'

'So you became his coach when he was thirteen?'

'That's right. He was a worker, I'll say that for him. He was lucky, living in London, because he had good access to me and to the facilities, and by Christ, he made the most of it. I used to ask him, did he not have a home to go to?'

'And what did he say to that?'

'Ach, he'd just shrug. I got the impression that his mother wasn't bothered what he was doing as long as he was out from under her feet. She was away from his father by then, of course. Separated, divorced, whatever.'

'Did his parents not come along, then?'

Jimmy shook his head. 'Never saw the mother. Not a once. His dad came to one meeting. I think it was the time he was going for the British junior record, but he blew it. I mind his dad took the piss out of him good style. I took him to one side and told him if he couldn't back his boy up, he wasn't welcome.'

'How did he take that?'

Jimmy took a gulp of tea and said, 'Ach, stupid bastard called me a bum boy. I just told him to fuck right off, and that was the last we saw of him.'

Leon made a mental note. He knew Tony would be interested in this. As he saw it, the young Jacko had been desperate for attention. His mother was indifferent, his father absent and his whole being was focused on his sporting achievement in the hope that somehow that would win him approval. 'So, was he lonely, Jacko?' He lit a cigarette, ignoring the disapproving look on the coach's narrow face.

Jimmy considered the question. 'He could mess about with the best of them, but he wasn't really one of the lads, know what I mean? He was too dedicated. He couldn't loosen up enough. Not that he was a loner. No, he always had Jillie in tow, hanging around him, telling him he was wonderful.'

'So they were devoted to each other?'

'She was devoted to him. He was devoted to himself, but he liked the adoration. Unconditional, like you get from a collie dog. Mind you, even Jillie got the hump sometimes. I moved heaven and earth to keep that pair together. Whenever she got fed up with taking the back seat to his training or competitions, I used to bolster her up with how great she'd feel when he stood there on the Olympic rostrum picking up the gold. I'd say, most girls, the only gold they ever got was a poxy wedding ring, but she was going to get a gold medal.'

'And that was enough, was it?'

Jimmy shrugged, wafting Leon's smoke away with one hand. 'To be honest, it got so that was the only thing that kept her going. When he started competing on the senior circuit, and Jillie was that wee bit older, she started taking notice of the way the other lads treated their girls. And Jacko didn't stand up too well to the comparison. If he hadn't have lost his arm, she might just have put up with it for the acclaim and the cash that went with it, because athletes were just about starting to make megabucks around then and the writing was on the wall for more to come. But as soon as she decided he wasn't going to be a cash machine or a household name, she got shot of him.'

Leon was on full alert. 'I thought he dumped her? Didn't I read at the time that he broke off the engagement because he wasn't the man she'd signed up for and it wasn't fair to tie her down? Something like that?'

Jimmy's mouth curled into a contemptuous smile. 'So you fell for that load of toffee? That was just the story Jacko leaked to the press, to make him look like the big man instead of the sad bastard who'd been dumped.'

So Shaz might well have been right, Leon thought. Circumstance had piled two traumatic stressors right on top of each other. First Vance had lost his arm and his future. Then he had lost the one person who had believed in him as a human being rather than as a throwing machine. It would take a strong man to survive that unscathed; a warped one would need to take revenge against a world that had done this to him. Leon stubbed out his cigarette and said, 'Did he tell you the truth?'

'No. Jillie did. I was the one drove her to the hospital that day. And I saw Jacko after she told him.'

'How did he take it?'

Jimmy's eyes dripped contempt. 'Oh, just like a man. He told me she was a heartless bitch who was only after one thing. I told him he didn't have to give in to his injuries, that he could train for the disabled games and that it was just as well he found out the truth about Jillie now. He told me to fuck off and never come near him again. And that was the last time I saw him.'

'You didn't go back to the hospital?'

The trainer's face was bleak. 'I went every day for a week. He wouldn't see me. Refused point-blank. He didn't seem to realize I had lost my dreams, too. Anyway, I got the chance of this job back in Scotland round about then, so I came back here and started all over again.'

'Were you surprised when he popped up as a television celebrity?'

'I can't say I was, no. He needs somebody telling him he's wonderful, that one. I've often wondered if all those millions of viewers are ever enough, if he's still as desperate to be adored as he was back then. He could never see any value in himself that wasn't reflected in other folks' eyes.' Jimmy shook his head and signalled for another cup of tea. 'I suppose you want to know if he had any enemies and what his deep dark secrets were?'

An hour later, Leon knew that what Jimmy Linden had told them at the start of their conversation was the stuff that had mattered. Just as well, he realized as he sat in the car afterwards. For some reason, his miniature tape recorder had failed to turn over automatically and had only recorded the first half of their chat. Feeling well pleased with himself nevertheless, Leon set out on the long journey south, wondering who'd done best so far. He knew it wasn't a competition. He'd liked Shaz enough to do it for her sake. But he was sufficiently human to realize that if he performed well out on the street, it would do him no harm. Especially since he now understood that as far as Tony Hill was concerned, he had more than a little to prove.

It wasn't difficult to spot the sports stadium and leisure-centre complex. Spotlit against the dark Malvern Hills, it was visible for miles from the motorway. Once he'd turned off on to minor roads and a rash of mini-roundabouts, however, Tony was glad he'd called in advance for directions. The centre was too recently built for most locals to know where it was, so the anonymous voice that had given explicit guidance over the phone was clearly used to the process.

As it turned out, he'd have arrived safely if he'd simply followed any other car heading in the same direction. The car park was already crowded when he reached it, and he had to park a few hundred yards away from the main entrance with its banner proclaiming, 'Grand Opening Gala – with Special Guests Jacko Vance and Stars from the England Squad'. Footballers for the lads, Jacko for the women, he thought as he walked briskly across the Tarmac, grateful for the bulk of the stadium acting as a buffer against the chill night wind.

He joined the throng of eager people thrusting through the turnstiles, casting a practised eye along the staff checking tickets. He chose a middle-aged woman who looked competent and motherly, and squeezed through the press of bodies to present himself at her window. He slipped his Home Office credentials out of his pocket and showed them to her, arranging his face into a rueful, harried expression. 'Dr Hill, Home Office, sports research group. I was supposed to have a VIP pass, but it didn't arrive. I don't suppose . . . ?'

The woman frowned momentarily. She gave him a swift appraisal, reckoning whether he was up to something, realizing the queue behind him was building up, finally deciding it was someone else's problem if he was, she pressed the release button to let him through. 'You want the directors' suite. Round to the right, second floor.'

Tony let the natural movement of the crowd carry him forward into the vast echoing area under the grandstand, then edged to one side to study the giant map of the stadium cunningly laid out on the underside of the tiered seating. Whoever had designed it had been aware of the three-dimensional surface it would be reproduced on, and it somehow managed to be clear from whatever angle it was viewed. According to the programme he'd just bought, there would be live music in the main arena, followed by a demonstration five-a-side football match featuring England squad players, then an Irish dance spectacular. For those who had shelled out an extra fifty pounds or won one of the contests run by the local TV, radio and newspapers, there would be a chance to meet the celebrities. And that was where he needed to be.

He slid through the crowd, calculating his moves so he upset no one on his route to the executive lift. The lobby was cordoned off with heavy crimson ropes. A security guard wearing a belt loaded with enough equipment to stock a hardware store stared balefully out from under a cap worn low like a guardsman. Tony knew it was nothing more than bravado. He flashed his credentials at the guard, moving purposefully as if the last thing he expected was to be challenged. The man took a step backwards and said, 'Wait a minute.'

Tony was already at the lift, pressing the call button. 'It's OK,' he said. 'Home Office. We like to turn up when they least expect us. Got to keep an eye on things, you know.' He winked and stepped into the car. 'Don't want another Hillsborough, do we?' The doors slid closed on the bemused face of the guard.

After that, it was easy. Out of the lifts, down the hall, in through the open double doors, a glass of something straw-coloured and fizzy from the nearest waistcoated flunkey and he was established. Tony took in the long windows that ran the length of the opposite wall, looking down on the all-weather pitch. He could just see a team of majorettes strutting their stuff down below. A thin crowd bunched around the edges of the room. At the far end, over by the window, Jacko Vance stood at the centre of a cluster of middle-aged women and a few men. His hair gleamed in the refracted light from the spotlights over the pitch, his eyes shone in the soft lighting of the executive suite. Even though he'd already glad-handed his way through two charity appearances that day, his body language was still warm, welcoming, his smile treating everyone as a welcome equal. He looked like a god dealing with his worshippers without condescension. Tony gave a thin smile. The third event since he'd gone out on the prowl for Jacko, and every time he'd struck gold. It was almost as if there were a connection, an invisible fibre optic linking the hunter and the prey. This time, though, he'd make certain those roles were never reversed. Once had been enough for that.

Tony moved to one side and made his way up the room, using the legitimate guests as cover. After a few minutes, he had travelled the length of the room, occupying a corner opposite Vance but slightly behind him. His eyes moved regularly from side to side, scanning the area immediately around the TV star, never lingering for long, but never leaving Vance unattended for more than a moment.

He didn't have long to wait. A young woman with slicked back blonde hair, John Lennon glasses and a scarlet cupid's bow bounced into the room clutching a bag emblazoned with SHOUT! FM, checking over her shoulder to see that her charges were still firmly in tow. Following in a ragged line came three adolescent girls overdressed and overpainted, a couple of youths with more spots than charm and an elderly woman whose hair was so rigidly set it appeared the rollers were still bound into it. Three paces behind slouched a nerd in a gilet with a dozen bulging pockets, a pair of battered SLR cameras hanging negligently round his neck. The winners of some moronic phone-in competition, Tony guessed. He could think of one question they wouldn't have been asked: How many teenagers has Jacko Vance murdered? It would take a year or two after he'd finished his work for that to filter down into the trivia quiz books.

The bouncy blonde approached where Vance was holding court. Tony could see Vance look up at her then dismissively abandon her for the middle-aged woman in the turquoise sari he'd been charming previously. The blonde lunged through the inner circle round Jacko, only to be headed off by the woman Tony had noticed running interference for Jacko the first time he'd staked him out. Their heads huddled together, then the PA nodded and touched Vance on the elbow. As he turned, his professional gaze slid round the room and caught Tony. The sweep of his eyes paused momentarily, then continued, nothing else in his expression changing.

The blonde's competition winners were ushered into the presence of their idol. He smiled down on them, charm personified. He chatted, signed autographs, shook hands, pecked cheeks and posed for photographs. Every thirty seconds, his eyes lost their focus and glanced unerringly at where Tony stood leaning against the wall, sipping fake champagne, his pose and his expression reeking assurance and confidence.

As the competition winners reached the end of their audience, Tony moved away from his vantage point and headed for the little group, still standing near Vance, their expressions ranging from ecstasy to an affected nonchalance, depending on how cool they felt the need to be. All bonhomie, Tony insinuated himself into their group, his expression a model of openness and geniality. 'I'm sorry to butt in on you,' he said. 'But I think you might be able to help me. My name's Tony Hill and I'm a psychological profiler. You know how stars like Jacko are always being plagued by stalkers? Well, I'm working with a team of crack police officers on ways to find out who those stalkers are before they start causing real problems. What we're trying to do is to come up with a psychological profile of the perfect fan, the good supporter. Someone like you, the sort of fan any celebrity would be glad to have on their side. We need to do this so we can get what's called a control profile. All we need is a short interview with you. Half an hour, tops. We come to your place or you come to us, we pay you £25, and you get the comfort of knowing you might have stopped the next Mark Chapman.' He loved the way their faces always changed when he mentioned the money.

Tony took out the pre-printed name and address slips from his inside pocket. 'How about it? Painless anonymous questionnaire, you help us save a life and you earn yourself £25. Just fill in your name and address on one of these and one of my researchers will be in touch.' Out came the handsome embossed National Offender Profiling Task Force business cards. 'This is who I am.' He handed them out. By now, all except one of the youths had their hands out for a form. 'There we go,' he said, providing them with pens.

He looked across at Vance. His face was still smiling, his mouth forming words, his hands patting an elbow here, a shoulder there. But his eyes were on Tony; dark, questioning, hostile.

The house was nothing special, Simon thought as he parked the car. A three-bedroomed dormer bungalow on a thirty-year-old development that was well on course to disprove the adage that life begins at forty. She'd have done a lot better if she and Jacko had stayed together. She certainly wouldn't have ended up in a town like Wellingborough where a night out at the DIY superstore was most people's idea of a good time.

He was amazed at the speed with which Carol Jordan had come up with Jillie Woodrow's whereabouts, particularly since she was three years into her second marriage. 'Don't ask,' Carol had said when he'd complimented her, admitting it would have taken him days to make that much progress. He remembered Tony Hill mentioning something to Carol about her brother in the computer industry and wondered if their shoestring task force had just added data burglary to its irregularities.

He sat in the car and looked across the narrow street at the house belonging to Jillie and Jeff Lewis. It looked spick and span and relentlessly suburban with its perfectly trimmed lawn and borders filled with neatly equidistant hebes and heathers. There was a year-old Metro on the drive and net curtains across the picture window. If Jillie Lewis's attention had been caught by the sound of his engine, she could be watching him and he'd have no idea at all.

This was almost certainly going to be the most crucial interview of his career to date, Simon thought, gearing himself up for the task. He had no clear idea of what he was going to ask, but if Jillie Lewis had information that would nail Jacko Vance for the murder of Shaz Bowman, he was determined to prise it out of her, one way or another. He hadn't had the chance to find out whether he would ever have been allowed to owe Shaz more than a colleague would. But even that was more than debt enough for him. Simon got out of the car and pulled on the jacket of his Marks and Spencer suit. Straightening his tie and his shoulders, he took a deep breath and walked up the path.

The door opened seconds after his ring, stopped short by a flimsy chain that he could have been past in seconds if he'd had a mind to. For a brief, mad moment, he wondered whether this was the cleaner or the nanny. The woman who faced him across the door-step bore no superficial resemblance to the old newspaper photo-graphs of Jillie Woodrow, nor to the teenage girls on the missing list. Her hair was a streaked blonde urchin cut rather than the dark bob he'd expected, and she'd lost every vestige of puppy fat, being skinny to the point where, if he were her husband, Simon would be surreptitiously reading up on anorexia. He was about to make his apologies when he recognized the eyes. The expression had hardened, there were lines starting to show at the edges, but these were Jillie Woodrow's dark blue soulful eyes. 'Mrs Lewis?' he asked.

The woman nodded. 'Who are you?' Simon presented his warrant card and she gasped, 'Jeff?'

Quickly Simon reassured her. 'It's nothing to do with your hus-band. I'm currently attached to a special investigations unit in Leeds, but my home force is Strathclyde. I don't have any local connection.'

'Leeds? I've never been to Leeds.' When she frowned, discontent was written across her face like an advertising hoarding.

Simon smiled. 'Lucky you. There have been times lately when I've wished I could say the same thing. Mrs Lewis, this is a very awkward situation and it would be a lot easier for me to explain it inside with a cup of coffee than it is on the doorstep. Can I come in?'

She looked uncertain, making a show of checking her watch. 'I'm supposed to be at work,' she said, carefully not saying when.

'I wouldn't be here if it wasn't important,' Simon said, his apologetic smile displaying the charm that had been one of the assets that had taken him this far in his career.

'I suppose you'd better come in, then,' she said, slipping the chain off and stepping back. He walked into a hall that looked as if it belonged to a show house. Spotless, tasteless and immaculate, it led into a kitchen that no one appeared ever to have cooked in. Jillie led the way and gestured to the circular table crammed into one corner. 'You better have a seat,' she muttered as she picked up a kettle, dark green to match the tiles along the splashback of the sink. 'Coffee, then?'

'Please,' Simon said, wedging himself behind the table. 'Milk, no sugar.'

'I suppose you think you're sweet enough,' Jillie said sourly, taking a jar of cheap instant from the cupboard and spooning it into two china mugs. 'I suppose this is something to do with Jacko Vance, is it?'

Simon tried not to reveal how taken aback he was. 'What makes you say that?'

Jillie turned and leaned against the worktop, crossing her jean-clad legs and folding her arms protectively over her chest. 'What else would it be? Jeff's an honest hard-working salesman, I'm a part-time data processor. We don't know any criminals. The only thing I've ever done that anybody outside these four walls would be interested in was being Jacko Vance's girlfriend. The only person I've ever had anything to do with who would interest some special investigation unit is Jacko bloody Vance, come back to flaming haunt me again.' It was a defiant outburst and she concluded it by turning her back on him and managing to make vicious the act of pouring two coffees.

Not quite sure where to go next, Simon said, 'I'm sorry. It's clearly a sensitive subject.'

Jillie dumped the coffee in front of him. Given the pristine kitchen, he was surprised she didn't run for a cloth when it slopped on the pine tabletop. Instead, she retreated back against the work-top, clutching her coffee like a child with a hot-water bottle. 'I've got nothing to say about Jacko Vance. You've had a wasted journey from Leeds. Still, I suppose you get good mileage since it's the taxpayers that foot the bill and not some skinflint company.'

Her bitterness seemed to have infected the coffee, Simon thought ruefully, sipping the brew to give himself time to think of a reply. 'It's a serious inquiry,' he said. 'We could use your help.'

She banged her mug down on the worktop. 'Look. I don't care what he says. It's not me that's pestering him. I had this up to the back teeth just after I first married Jeff. I had cops round half a dozen times. Was I sending Jacko anonymous letters? Was I making abusive phone calls to his wife? Did I parcel up dog turds and post them to his office? Well, the answer's the same now as it was then. If you think I'm the only person Jacko Vance has upset in his selfish journey to the top of the greasy pole, you have got a serious imagination deficiency.' She stopped short and glared at him. 'I don't do blackmail, either. You can check. Every penny in and out of this house is accounted for. I've had that accusation to contend with, and that's a load of flaming rubbish as well.' She shook her head. 'I can't believe that *pig*,' she fumed.

Simon held his hands up in a placatory gesture. 'Whoa, wait a minute. I think you've got hold of the wrong end of the stick here. I didn't come to see you because Jacko made a complaint. Sure, I want to talk to you about Jacko, but I'm only interested in what he's done, not what he says you've done. Honest!'

She gave him a sharp look. 'What?'

Uneasy that he might have gone too far, Simon said, 'As I said, this is all very sensitive. Jacko Vance's name has come up in an inquiry and my job is to make some background checks. Without alerting Mr Vance to our interest, if you take my point.' He hoped he didn't look as nervous as he felt. Whatever he'd expected, it hadn't been this.

'You're investigating Jacko?' Jillie sounded incredulous but had started to look almost cheerful.

Simon shifted in his chair. 'Like I said, his name has come up in connection with a serious matter . . .'

Jillie punched her thigh. 'Yes! And not before bloody time. Don't tell me, let me guess. He hurt some poor bloody woman too much and didn't terrify her enough to make her keep her mouth shut, is that it?'

Simon sensed the interview spiralling out of his control. All he could do was cling on with his fingernails and hope he wouldn't get shaken off somewhere along the way. 'What makes you say that?' he asked.

'It was bound to happen some day,' she said, all but gleeful. 'So, what do you want to know?'

By the time he got home, Tony's eyes were gritty with staring at too many night motorway miles. He hadn't intended to check his answering machine, but the flashing light caught his eye as he passed the door of his study. Wearily, he hit the playback button. 'Hi. My name's Chris Devine. Detective Sergeant Chris Devine. I was Shaz Bowman's CID partner in London for a while. She used me to set up her appointment with Jacko Vance. Give me a call whenever you get in. Doesn't matter how late it is.'

He grabbed a pen and scribbled the number, reaching for the phone as soon as the message clicked off. The phone rang half a dozen times, then was picked up. 'Is that Chris Devine?' he said to the silence.

'Is that Tony Hill?' The voice was pure South London.

'You left a message on my machine. About Shaz?'

'Yeah. Listen, I've had them turnips from West Yorkshire down here, and they told me they're not working with you. Is that right?'

He liked a person who didn't waste time. 'They feel it would compromise the integrity of their investigation to involve me or any of Shaz's other immediate colleagues,' he said caustically.

'Bollocks,' she said in disgust. 'They haven't got a fucking clue, pardon my French. So are you running your own investigation, or what?'

It was like being pinned to the wall by a very large weight, Tony thought. 'I'm obviously very keen to see Shaz's killer caught,' he tried.

'So what are you doing about it?'

'Why do you ask?' he parried.

'To see if you need an extra pair of hands, of course,' she said, exasperated. 'Shaz was a great kid, and she was gonna be a great cop. Now, either Jacko Vance topped her for reasons we don't entirely know yet, or somebody else did. Either way, the trail starts at his front door, no?'

'You're right,' Tony said. Now he knew what cement felt like under a steamroller.

'And you're working the case?'

'In a manner of speaking.'

Her sigh sounded like something from the Shipping Forecast. 'Well, in a manner of speaking, I could help. What do you need from me?'

Tony's mind raced. 'I'm a bit stalled on leverage where Vance and his wife are concerned. Something that might help me put a bit of a wedge between them might help.'

'Like, Micky Morgan's really a dyke?'

'That sort of thing, yes.'

'You mean that's not enough?' Chris demanded.

'That's for real?'

She snorted. 'Course it's for real. They're so far in the closet you'd take them for a pair of winter coats, but they're coke.'

'Coke?'

'The real thing. She's been with Betsy for donkey's years. Way before she even met Jacko.'

'Betsy Thorne? Her PA?'

'PA, bollocks. Lover, more like. Betsy had a good little catering business with her ex, then she met Micky Morgan and it was wham, bam, thank you, ma'am. They used to go to a couple of very discreet places in the early days. Then they disappeared off the scene and, next thing you know, she pops up as Jacko Vance's tottie. But Betsy's still right there in the picture. See, Micky was on the up and up, and there were rumours that the tabloids were going to nail her for being a dyke.'

'How do you know all this?' Tony said faintly.

'How do you think? Christ, twelve, fifteen years ago, you didn't stay in this job if you were out. We used to go to the same places. Places where everybody was in the same boat so nobody ever shopped anybody else. Take it from me, whoever Jacko Vance is shagging, it's not his wife. Tell you the truth, that's what made me think Shaz was maybe on to something.'

'Did you tell Shaz about this?'

'I hadn't thought about Micky Morgan from one year's end to the next. It only came to me after I set up the interview. I was gonna let Shaz know when she belled me to tell me how she'd got on with Jacko. So no, I never got round to telling her. Is this any use to you?'

'Chris, it's fabulous. You're fabulous.'

'That's what they all say, babe. So, you want me to help, or what?'

'I think you already have.'

When Carol walked into her domain, the threesome were already there in their accustomed places, a trickle of smoke curling out of the corner of her window from Lee's cigarette. She sensed the smoking was meant as a challenge. But although she'd never smoked – or perhaps for that very reason – the faint tang of cigarettes was something that seldom troubled her. Carol found the energy for a smile and tried not to slump when her backside hit the chair. 'So, what have we got?'

Tommy Taylor rested his left ankle on his right knee and squirmed lower in the chair. Carol didn't envy him the lower back pain he was storing up for later years. He tossed a file negligently on to her desk. As it slithered towards her, the edges of the papers inside spilled out. 'We know more about this lot's finances than their wives do.'

'From what I hear about Yorkshire, that's not saying much,' Carol said. Tommy and Lee Whitbread grinned. Di Earnshaw's dour expression didn't crack.

'By heck, ma'am, I think that might just be a sexist remark,' Lee said.

'So sue me. What have we got?'

'It's all in the file,' Tommy said, jerking a thumb towards her.

'Summarize.'

'Di?' Tommy said. 'You're the wizard with words.'

Di unfolded her arms and thrust her hands into the pockets of an olive green jacket that made her look ripe for throwing up. 'Mr Pendlebury wasn't very keen, but he did authorize us to gain access to payroll information which provided us with bank details, addresses and dates of birth for our suspects. With that information we were able to check county court judgements . . .'

'And a little bird helped us with some commercial credit checking,' Lee chipped in.

'But we don't talk about that,' Tommy said repressively.

Carol said, 'Can we edit out the stand-up and cut to the chase?'

Di's lips pursed in their now familiar disapproval. 'Two candidates stand out. Alan Brinkley and Raymond Watson. They're both heavily in debt, as you'll see. Both local men. Watson's single, Brinkley's wed about a year since. They're both on the edge of having their houses repossessed, both got CCJs against them, both juggling Peter to pay Paul. These fires have been a bit of a blessing for the pair of them.'

'It's an ill wind,' Taylor added.

Carol opened the file and took out the sheets relating to the two men. 'Good work. You did well to get this much detail.'

Lee shrugged. 'When you get down to it, Seaford's a big village. Favours owed, favours paid.'

'As long as we don't cross the line when it comes to wages day,' Carol said.

'Don't you trust us, ma'am?' Tommy drawled.

'Give me five good reasons why I should.'

'So, d'you want us to pull them in for questioning?' Lee asked.

Carol considered for a moment. What she actually wanted was to consult with Tony, but she didn't want them to know their guv'nor wasn't able to make her own decisions. 'I'll get back to you when I've had a chance to go through these in more detail. There might be more fruitful options than trying to sweat it out of them.'

'We could try for a search warrant.' Lee again, the eager beaver of the team.

'We'll discuss it again in the morning,' Carol promised. She watched them leave, then shoved the file into her bulging briefcase. Time for a quick tour of the squad room, making sure the rest of the CID were doing what they were supposed to be doing with the cases dominating the stacks of paper on their desks. She hoped no one expected inspiration. Perspiration was about all she had left to offer.

She was about to walk through the door when the phone rang. 'DCI Jordan,' she said.

'Brandon here.'

'Sir?'

'I've just been speaking to a colleague over in West Yorkshire. In the course of our chat, we got round to talking about their officer murder. He mentioned that their prime suspect seems to have done a runner. Some chap called Simon McNeill. He said they'd probably be putting out an internal bulletin tomorrow morning asking other forces to keep a lookout for McNeill and detain him if they find him.'

'Ah.'

'I thought you might be interested,' Brandon said airily. 'With our patch being next door to theirs.'

'Absolutely, sir. As soon as I get the official notice, I'll be sure to mention it to the squad.'

'Not that I expect he'll turn up here.'

'Mmm. Thank you, sir.' Carol gingerly replaced the receiver. 'Oh, shit,' she said softly.

Tony licked his finger and smoothed down a couple of unruly hairs in his left eyebrow. He studied himself critically in the mirror that was, apart from a pair of orange polypropylene bucket chairs, the only furnishing in a room little bigger than a cupboard where he had been asked to wait. He thought he looked appropriately serious in his one decent suit even if Carol had told him it made him look like a time-warped professional footballer. But not even she could fault his dove grey shirt and dark magenta tie, he decided.

The door opened to reveal the calm-faced woman who had introduced herself as Micky's PA but whom he'd identified, thanks to Chris, as Micky's lover Betsy. 'Everything all right?' she asked.

'I'm fine.'

'Good.' Her voice was warm and encouraging, like the best type of primary school teacher. Her smile, however, was perfunctory, Tony realized, her mind clearly elsewhere. 'Now, this is quite unusual for us, because normally Micky likes to come completely fresh to her guests. But because . . . well, because she feels *involved*, however tangentially, with your tragic loss, she wants to have a few words with you ahead of time. I take it you have no objection?'

There was something about that steely upper class voice that left no possible room for demurral. Lucky Micky, he thought, to have such a lioness at the gates. 'I'd be delighted,' he said, quite truthfully.

'Good. She'll be along in a few minutes. Is there anything you need? Some coffee? Mineral water?'

'Does the coffee come from a machine?' he asked.

The smile this time was genuine. 'I'm afraid so. Indistinguishable from the tea, the hot chocolate and the chicken soup.'

'I'll pass, then.'

The head disappeared and the door snicked shut. His stomach fluttered apprehensively. Public displays always stressed him. But today there was the additional tension of his campaign to unsettle Jacko Vance to the point where he would make a mistake. Staking out Vance's personal appearances was only the opening shot across the bows. Insinuating himself into the heart of Vance's wife's TV programme was an incremental upping of the stakes. There was no point in trying to kid himself otherwise.

He cleared his throat nervously and compulsively rechecked his appearance in the mirror. The door opened without warning and suddenly Micky Morgan was in the room. Tony forced himself to turn slowly to face her. 'Hello, Ms Morgan,' he said, extending a hand.

'Dr Hill,' Micky said. Her handshake was swift, cool and firm. 'Thanks for coming on the programme.'

'My pleasure. There's so much misunderstanding about what we do, I always welcome the chance to set the record straight. Especially since we're in the news again for all the wrong reasons.' He deliberately dropped his eyes momentarily.

'Quite. I was genuinely sorry to hear about Detective Constable Bowman. I only met her very briefly, but she struck me as being very sharp, very focused. As well as being very beautiful, of course.'

Tony nodded. 'She'll be missed. She was one of the best young officers I've ever had the privilege of working with.'

'I can imagine that. It's a terrible thing for police officers to lose one of their own.'

'There's always a lot of anger flying around, covering up for the fact that they tend to feel a death in the family is a reflection of their competence, that somehow they should have been able to prevent it if they'd only been doing their jobs properly. And in this instance, I share that guilt.'

'I'm sure there was nothing you could have done to prevent it,' Micky said, impulsively putting a hand on his arm. 'When I told my husband you were coming on the programme, he said the same thing, and he's got even less reason to feel responsible.'

'No reason at all,' Tony said, surprised he could sound so sincere. 'Even though we're now coming round to thinking that her killer may have made contact with her in London rather than in Leeds.

In fact, I was hoping you might give me the chance to put out an appeal for witnesses?'

Micky's hand flew to her throat in a curiously vulnerable gesture. 'You don't think she was stalked from our house, do you?'

'There's no reason to think that,' he said hastily.

'No?'

'No.'

'Thanks for the reassurance.' She took a deep breath and pushed her blonde hair back from her face. 'Now, the interview. I'm going to ask about why the unit was set up, how it's constituted, what sort of offences you'll be covering and when the task force will go into action. Then I'll move on to Sharon . . .'

'Shaz,' Tony interrupted. 'Call her Shaz. She hated being called Sharon.'

Micky nodded. 'Shaz. I'll move on to Shaz, which will give you the chance to ask for any help you want to solicit. Is that OK? Is there anything else you particularly want the opportunity to say?'

'I'm sure I'll be able to get the message across,' he said.

She reached for the door handle. 'Betsy, my PA – you spoke to her earlier – she'll come and fetch you shortly before we go on air. You'll be the last item before we break for the news bulletin.'

'Thanks,' he said, wanting to say something to build a bridge between them but not knowing what that might be. She would be his best way under Jacko Vance's defences if he could only find a way to manipulate her into unconsciously helping him.

'You're welcome,' Micky said. Then she was gone, leaving nothing behind her but the faint scent of cosmetics. He'd only have one more chance to get her on his side. He hoped he'd make a better job of it.

It had better be worth it, Vance thought. He'd cancelled lunch cooked personally by Marco Pierre White for this, and the notoriously temperamental chef would make him suffer for it. He locked his office door and closed the blinds. His secretary knew better than to put any calls through, and neither his producer nor his PA knew he was still in the building. Whatever *Midday with Morgan* revealed, there would be no one to see his reaction.

He threw himself on to the long leather sofa that dominated one side of the room and put his feet up. His face a mask of petulance, he turned on the giant TV screen with the remote control just as the familiar titles started to roll. He had nothing to fear, he knew that. Whatever Shaz Bowman had thought she'd known, she hadn't been able to convince her colleagues. He'd already dealt with the police. They'd eaten out of his hand, and rightly so. Some academic psychologist doling out half-baked theories could hardly threaten him without the backing of the plod. Nevertheless, being careful had kept him safe until now, and he wasn't about to give in to the temptation towards arrogance that such a successful career might breed.

He'd been able to glean some information about Tony Hill from his sources, though not as much as he would have liked. Again, he had been careful to keep the questions casual, taking pains not to have his inquiries arouse curiosity. What he'd learned had pricked his interest. He'd been behind the controversial Home Office study that had led to the setting up of the profiling task force that Shaz Bowman had aspired to. He'd been involved in a serial killer hunt in Bradfield where he'd ended up with blood on his hands because he hadn't been smart enough. And there were murmurings that there was something borderline perverse about his sexuality. That had really got Vance's adrenaline pumping, but it was the one angle he simply had to leave alone or risk his source wondering exactly what his concern was with the psychologist.

Fascinated though Vance was with his speculations about Tony, his thoughts were no competition for the TV screen. His attraction to the glamour of television had never waned in all his years on the performing end of the camera. He loved the medium, but most of all, he loved live TV with all its high-wire risks. Even though he ought to have been wondering how to neutralize Tony Hill if that became necessary, he couldn't resist Micky. Familiarity had bred respect rather than contempt for her professional skills and her talent. She really was one of the best. He'd spotted that right from the word go, recognized that she was one to have on his side. That he'd been able to keep her there so effectively had been a huge bonus.

She'd been good back then, but she'd improved, no doubt about that. Confidence had been part of that, Betsy another part. Her lover had shown her how to submerge the rougher edges of aggression beneath a surface of unruffled, gently probing interest. Most of Micky Morgan's victims didn't even realize how effectively they'd been filleted till someone played the tape back to them afterwards.

If there was any ruffling of Tony Hill's surface to be done, a live interview with Micky would do it. He'd hinted to her that there might be darkness lurking behind her guest's facade. Now it was up to her.

He watched the first fifty minutes of the programme with a connoisseur's eye, assessing and appraising the performance of his wife and her colleagues. That Midlands reporter was going to have to go, he decided. He'd have to tell Micky. Vance hated journalists who brought the same breathless urgency to stories of distant wars, cabinet reshuffles and soap opera plots. It revealed a lack of empathy most successful hacks learned to hide early on.

It was strange, he thought, how he'd never felt the slightest twinge of sexual desire for his wife. True, she wasn't his type, but even so, he'd periodically found women attractive who didn't conform to his blueprint of desire. Never Micky, however. Not even on those rare occasions when he'd glimpsed her naked. It was probably as well, given the basis of their relationship. One glimmer of what he really wanted from the female of the species and Micky would be history. And he definitely didn't want that. Particularly not now.

'And after the break,' Micky said with that intimate warmth he suspected of causing erections among unemployed youths throughout the land, 'I'll be talking to a man who spends his days inside the heads of serial offenders. Psychological profiler Dr Tony Hill reveals the inside secrets of the new national police task force. And we pay tribute to the officer who has already tragically lost her life in that battle. All that, and the news on the hour, after the break.'

As the adverts took over, Vance pressed the record button on the video remote. He swung his feet to the floor and leaned forward, intent on the screen. The last commercial faded to the logo of *Midday with Morgan* and his wife was smiling out at him as if he were the only light of her life. 'Welcome back,' Micky said. 'My guest now is the distinguished clinical psychologist Dr Tony Hill. Nice to have you with us, Tony.'

The director switched to a two-shot, giving Vance his first sight of Shaz Bowman's boss. The colour drained from his cheeks then raced back in a dark flush. He'd thought Tony Hill was going to be a stranger. But he knew the man on the screen. He'd spotted him first three gigs ago at the sponsored sequence dancing competition. Lurking on the fringes, talking to some of the regulars. He'd initially written him off as the latest addition to the sad squad of his camp followers. But the night before, at the sports centre, when he'd spotted him handing business cards out to the others, he'd wondered. He'd planned to send someone over to check him out, but it had slipped his mind. Now, here was the stranger, sitting on a sofa talking to Vance's wife in front of millions of viewers.

This was no routine nutter. This was no dumbshit plod. This was Shaz Bowman's boss. This might just also be an adversary.

'How has the tragic death of one of your trainees affected the squad?' Micky asked solicitously, her eyes glistening perfectly to convey heartfelt sympathy as she leaned forward.

Tony's eyes slid away from hers, the pain obvious. 'It's been a shocking blow,' he said. 'Shaz Bowman was one of the brightest officers it's ever been my privilege to work with. She had a real flair for offender profiling work, and she'll be impossible to replace. But we're determined that her killer will be caught.'

'Are you working closely with the investigating officers on the case?' Micky asked. His response to what she'd thought was a routine question was interesting. His eyebrows flashed up and his eyes widened momentarily.

'Everyone on the profiling task force is doing all they can to help,' he said quickly. 'And it's possible that your viewers could also help us.'

She was impressed with the speed of his recovery. She doubted if one in a thousand of her viewers had even noticed the blip. 'How is that, Tony?'

'As you know, Shaz Bowman was murdered in her flat in Leeds. However, we have reason to believe this wasn't a random killing. Indeed, her murderer may not even be a local man. Shaz was in London on Saturday morning, about twelve hours before she was murdered. We don't know where she went or who she saw after about ten thirty on Saturday morning. It's possible that her killer made contact with her that early in the day.'

'You mean it could have been a stalker?'

'I think it's possible that she was followed back to Leeds from London.'

That wasn't quite the same thing, but Micky knew she didn't have time to quibble. 'And you hope someone witnessed this?'

Tony nodded and stared directly into the camera with the red light showing. She could see his sincerity on the monitor in front of her. God, he was a natural, all nervousness gone as he made his impassioned appeal. 'We're looking for anyone who saw Shaz Bowman after half past ten on Saturday morning. She was very distinctive-looking. She had particularly bright blue eyes, very noticeable. You may have seen her alone or with her killer, perhaps filling her car with petrol – she drove a black Volkswagen Golf. Or possibly in one of the motorway service areas between London and Leeds. You may have noticed someone taking an unusual amount of interest in her. If so, we need to hear from you.'

'We have the number of the Leeds incident room,' Micky cut in as it appeared on a ribbon across the foot of the monitor screen. She and Tony disappeared to be replaced by a head and shoulders shot of Shaz grinning at the camera. 'If you saw Shaz Bowman on Saturday, no matter how briefly, call the police and let them know.'

'We want to catch him before he kills again,' Tony added.

'So don't be afraid to call West Yorkshire Police or even your local police station if you can help. Tony, thanks for coming in and talking to us.' Her smile shifted to the camera because her director was bellowing from the control room. 'And now, over to the news-room for the lunchtime bulletin.'

Micky leaned back and let out her breath in an explosive sigh. 'Thanks, Tony,' she said, unclipping her mike and leaning forward so their knees touched in the angle of the sofa.

'It's me that should be thanking you,' he said in a rush as Betsy strode efficiently towards them. She reached over his shoulder to unfasten his mike.

'I'll see you out,' Betsy said.

Micky jumped to her feet. 'It's been fascinating,' she said. 'I wish we could have had longer.'

Grabbing the chance, Tony said, 'We could have dinner.'

'Yes, I'd like that,' Micky said, sounding surprised at herself. 'Are you free this evening?'

'Yes. Yes, I am.'

'Let's make it this evening, then. Is six thirty OK? I need to eat early, working this show.'

'I'll book a table.'

'No need. Betsy'll see to it, won't you, Bets?'

There was a flicker of indulgent amusement in the woman's face, Tony thought. Almost immediately, the professional mask was back. 'No problem. But I need to get Dr Hill off set, Micky,' she said, with an apologetic smile at him.

'OK. See you later, Tony.' She watched Betsy hustle him away, savouring the anticipation of picking the brains of someone really interesting for a change. The demented bleating in her earpiece brought her back to the cold reality of getting the rest of the programme out of the way. 'We go straight to the classroom anarchy piece, yeah?' she said peering up at the control booth, her mind back on her job, Shaz Bowman already a memory.

Carol stared out of her office window at the port below. It was cold enough to get rid of the casual strollers. Everyone out there was brisk, even the dog walkers. She hoped her detectives were following their example. She dialled the hotel number Tony had left her. She was as eager to hear about his TV appearance as she was to pass on her own news. She didn't have to listen to the 'Cuckoo Waltz' for long. 'Hello?' she heard him say.

'*Midday with Morgan* was great, Tony. What did you think? Did you see Jack the Lad?'

'No, I didn't see him, but I liked her more than I expected to. She's a good interviewer. Lulls you into a false sense of security then sticks in a couple of awkward questions. I managed to make the points I wanted to make, though.'

'So Vance wasn't around?'

'Not at the studios, no. But she said she'd told him I was going to be on, so I wouldn't take any bets on Jack the Lad having missed today's programme.'

'Do you think she has any idea?'

'That we suspect her husband?' He sounded surprised at the question.

'That her husband's a serial killer.' He was a little slow tonight, Carol thought. Normally he read any conversation as if he'd seen the script in advance.

'I don't think she has the faintest notion. I doubt she'd be with him if she did.' He sounded unusually positive. It wasn't like Tony to categorize things as black or white.

'He really is a smooth operator.'

'As silk. Now we have to sit back and see how much more it takes to unsettle him. Starting with tonight. I'm taking his wife out to dinner.'

Carol couldn't help the pang of jealousy, but she kept her voice even. She'd had plenty of practice with Tony. 'Really? How did you manage that?'

'I think she's genuinely interested in the profiling,' he said. 'Let's hope I can dig some information out of her that we can use.'

'If anyone can, you can. Tony, I think we've got a problem. With Simon.' Briefly, she relayed her conversation with John Brandon. 'What do you think? Should we persuade him to turn himself in?'

'I think we leave it up to him. If you're comfortable with that? Given that he might well be sitting in your living room again before all of this is over.'

'I don't expect it to be a problem,' Carol said slowly. 'It's only an internal bulletin we're talking about here. It's not as if there's going to be a nationwide manhunt with his picture splashed across the papers. Well, not for a couple of days yet, anyway. If it runs into next week and he's not been home or in contact with his friends and family, it might get more serious, in which case we'd have to persuade him to come in from the cold.'

'You're assuming he won't meekly walk into police HQ in Leeds?'

Carol snorted derisively. 'What do you think?'

'I think he's got too much invested in what we're doing. And speaking of which, how have the team been doing?'

She filled him in on Kay's grand tour of the grieving. When she came to the photograph she'd pried from the unwilling hands of Kenny and Denise Burton, Carol heard a sharp intake of breath.

'The zealots,' he said.

'I'm sorry?'

'Zealots. Fanatics. Jacko Vance's disciples. I've been to three of his public appearances so far, and there's a few obsessives who show up every time. Just three or four of them. I noticed them right away.'

'You ever end up on the dole, you could get a job as a spotter for Neighbourhood Watch,' she said. 'You could call it Nutter Watch.'

He laughed. 'The point is, two of them were taking photos.'

'Gotcha?'

'Could be. Could very well be. This is very, very good. This might just give us the edge. He's clever, Carol. He's the best I've ever seen, ever heard about, ever read about. Somehow, we've got to be better.' His voice was soft but keen, charged with determination.

'We are. There are five of us. He only ever sees things from one angle.'

'You're so right. I'll talk to you tomorrow, OK?'

She could sense his eagerness to be active, to be gone. She couldn't blame him. Micky Morgan would be a real challenge to his skills and Tony was a man who adored a challenge. Whether he obtained fresh information from her or merely used their dinner date to set the cat among Jacko Vance's pigeons, he would be more effective than anyone else she could think of. But she couldn't let him go just yet. 'There's one more thing . . . the arsonist?'

'Oh God, yes, of course, I'm sorry. Any progress?'

She outlined the discoveries of her team, giving a thumbnail sketch of the two suspects. 'I'm not sure at this stage whether to bring them both in for questioning and try for a search warrant for their homes, or set up surveillance. I thought I'd run it past you.'

'How do they spend their money?'

'Brinkley and his wife go in for conspicuous consumption. New cars, household goods, store credit cards. Watson looks like a gambler. He raises cash any way he can and passes it on to the bookies.'

Tony said nothing for a moment. She pictured him frowning, a hand running through his thick black hair, his deep-set eyes dark and distant as his mind moved over the question. 'If I was Watson, I'd bet on Brinkley,' he said eventually.

'How so?'

'If Watson is truly a compulsive gambler, he's convinced it's the next bet, the next lottery ticket that will solve all his problems. He's a believer. Brinkley hasn't got that conviction. He thinks if he can just keep ahead of the game, cut down on spending, find some extra cash, he can get out of this mess by some conventional route. That's my reading of it. But whether I'm right or wrong, bringing them in for questioning isn't going to get you a result. It might stop the fires, but nobody will ever be charged with them. A search warrant won't help either, from what you've told me about how the fires are started. I know it's not the answer you want to hear, but surveillance is your best chance of a conviction. And you need to cover both of them in case I've got it wrong.'

Carol groaned. 'I knew you were going to say that,' she complained. 'Surveillance. A copper's favourite job. A budgetary nightmare.'

'At least you only have to cover the hours of darkness. And he's operating frequently, so it's not going to last for long.'

'That's supposed to make me feel better?'

'It's the best I can manage.'

'OK. Not your fault. Thanks for your help, Tony. Off you go and enjoy dinner. I'm going home to a frozen pizza and, hopefully, updates from Simon and Leon. And, please God, an early night. Sleep . . .' The last word sounded like a caress.

Tony laughed. 'Enjoy it.'

'Oh, I will,' she promised fervently. 'And Tony – good luck.'

'In the absence of miracles, I'll settle for that.'

The click of his receiver going down sliced off any chance of her telling him the other thing she'd initiated that day. She couldn't work out exactly why she'd felt impelled to do it, but her instinct told her it was important. And past experience had taught her painfully that her instinct was sometimes far more reliable than logic. Something had niggled at the back of her mind until, in the midst of all the other tasks for the day, she'd found time to send a query out to all the other police forces in the country. Detective Chief Inspector Carol Jordan of East Yorkshire Police wanted to hear about any recent reports of teenage girls inexplicably missing from home.

'Mike McGowan? That's him, over in the corner booth, duck,' the barmaid said, gesturing with her thumb.

'What does he drink?' Leon asked. But the barmaid had already moved on to another customer. The pub was moderately busy, occupied almost completely by men. In a small East Midlands town like this, there were clear distinctions between pubs where men went to spend their time with women and ones where they went to avoid that necessity. The giveaway here was the large board outside advertising 'All day satellite sport, giant screens'.

Leon sipped his lager shandy and took a moment to watch Mike McGowan. Jimmy Linden had offered his name as the media expert on Jacko Vance. 'Like me, Mike spotted him early on and he wrote a lot about him over the years,' he'd said. When Leon had contacted McGowan's old paper in London, he'd discovered that the journalist had been made redundant three years before. Divorced, his children grown and scattered round the country, there had been nothing to keep McGowan in the expensive capital, so he'd returned to the Nottinghamshire town where he'd grown up.

The ex-reporter looked more like a caricature of an Oxbridge don than any national newspaperman Leon had ever seen. Even sitting down, he was clearly tall. A mop of grey-blond hair cut in a heavy fringe that flopped over his eyes, big tortoiseshell glasses and pink and white skin gave him the same boyish looks that Alan Bennett and David Hockney turned into trademarks. His jacket was the sort of ancient tweed that takes fifteen years to look wearable then lasts another twenty without any sign of attrition. Beneath it he wore a grey flannel shirt and a striped tie with a narrow tight knot. He sat alone in the narrow corner booth, staring up studiously at a 56-inch TV screen where two teams were playing basketball. As Leon watched, McGowan tapped the bowl of a pipe against the ashtray, automatically cleaning and filling it without taking his eyes from the screen.

When Leon loomed up next to him, he still didn't take his eyes off the basketball. 'Mike McGowan?'

'That's me. And who are you?' he said, local vowels as distinctive as the barmaid's shattering the illusion of lofty academe.

'Leon Jackson.'

McGowan threw him a quick look of assessment. 'Any relation to Billy Boy Jackson?'

Astounded, Leon almost crossed himself. 'He was my uncle,' he blurted out.

'You've got the same shaped head. I should know. I was ringside the night Marty Pyeman fractured your uncle's skull. That's not what you've come to see me about, though, is it?' The quick glance this time was shrewd.

'Can I get you a drink, Mr McGowan?'

The journalist shook his head. 'I don't come here for the drink. I come for the sport. My pension's crap. I can't afford a satellite subscription or a screen like this. I was at school with the landlord's dad, so he doesn't bother that I make a single pint last the best part of the day. Sit down and tell me what you're after.'

Leon obeyed, taking out his warrant card. He tried to snap it shut and away, but McGowan was faster. 'Metropolitan Police,' he mused. 'Now what would a London bobby with a Liverpool accent be doing with a retired hack in darkest Nottinghamshire?'

'Jimmy Linden said you might be able to help me,' Leon said.

'Jimmy Linden? Now there's a name from the past.' He closed the warrant card and slid it across to Leon. 'So what's your interest in Jacko Vance?'

Leon shook his head admiringly. 'I never said I had an interest in the man. But if that's who you want to talk about, be my guest.'

'My, they're teaching them subtlety these days,' McGowan said acidly, striking a match and applying it to his pipe. He sucked and expelled a cloud of blue smoke that swallowed whole the feeble spiral from Leon's cigarette. 'What's Jacko supposed to have done? Whatever it is, I bet you never manage to nick him for it.'

Leon remained silent. It nearly killed him, but he managed it. This clever old bastard wasn't going to put one over on him, he thought, almost convincing himself.

'I haven't seen Jacko in years,' McGowan finally said. 'He's not that keen on faces who remember what he was like when he had all his limbs. He hates being reminded of what he lost.'

'You'd think what he's got now would be compensation,' Leon said. 'Great job, more money than any reasonable geezer could spend, gorgeous wife, house the size of a stately home. I mean, how many Olympic gold medallists got a better deal than that?'

McGowan slowly shook his head. 'Nothing can compensate a man who thinks he's a god for the discovery of his vulnerability. That lass of his was lucky she got out from under. She'd have been the obvious choice when it came to making somebody pay for what the gods had done to Jacko Vance.'

'Jimmy said you knew more about Jacko than anybody else.'

'Only superficially. I followed his career, I interviewed him. I probably caught a few glimpses behind the mask, but I wouldn't say I knew him. I can't think of anybody that did. Really, there's nothing I want to say about Jacko Vance that I haven't already put in writing.'

McGowan breathed out another plume of smoke. Leon thought it smelled like Black Forest gateau, all cherries and chocolate. He couldn't imagine wanting to smoke a pudding. 'Jimmy also said that you kept cuttings files on the athletes that really interested you.'

'My, you did get a lot out of old Jimmy. He must have taken to you in a big way. Mind you, he's always had a lot of respect for black athletes. He reckoned they had to work twice as hard as anybody else to get their start. I suppose he reckoned it was probably much the same in the police.'

'Or maybe I'm just a good interviewer,' Leon said drily. 'Any chance of you letting me take a look at your cuttings?'

'Any in particular, Detective?' McGowan teased.

'I'd be guided by you as to what was interesting, sir.'

McGowan, his eyes firmly on the basketball, said, 'A career as long as mine, it'd be hard to pick out particular highlights.'

'I'm sure you could manage it.'

'This finishes in ten minutes. Perhaps you'd care to come back and look at my files?'

Half an hour later, Leon was sitting in a room in McGowan's two-bedroomed terrace that managed to be both spartan and cluttered. The only furniture was a battered leather swivel chair that looked as if it had seen service in the Spanish Civil War, and a scarred and scratched gun-metal grey desk. All four walls were covered with industrial metal shelving and packed with shoeboxes, each with a label stuck to the outer edge. 'This is incredible,' he said.

'I always promised myself that when I retired, I'd write a book,' McGowan said. 'Amazing how we delude ourselves. I used to travel the world covering the top sporting events. Now my world's shrunk to the satellite screens in the Dog and Gun. You'd think I'd be depressed. But the funny thing is, I'm not. I've never been so bloody contented all my born days. It's reminded me that what I always liked best about sport was watching it. Freedom without responsibility, that's what I've got now.'

'A dangerous mixture,' Leon said.

'A liberating mixture. Three years ago, you turning up would have had me sniffing a story. I'd not have rested until I'd found out what was going on. Now, it's hard to imagine how I could care less. I'm more excited about the Vegas fight on Saturday than I could ever be about anything Jacko Vance has said or done.' He pointed to a shelf. 'Jacko Vance. Fifteen shoeboxes full. Enjoy yourself, lad. I've got an appointment with a tennis match at the Dog and Gun. If you're gone before I get back, just pull the front door closed behind you.'

When Mike McGowan returned just before midnight, Leon was still working his way systematically through the cuttings. The journalist brought him a mug of instant coffee and said, 'I hope they're paying you overtime, lad.'

'More of a labour of love, you might say,' Leon said wryly.

269

'Yours or your boss's?'

Leon thought for a moment. 'One of my mates. Call it a debt of honour.'

'The only kind worth paying. I'll leave you to it. Try not to slam the door behind you when you go.'

Leon was half aware of the sounds of someone getting ready for bed: floorboards creaking, plumbing grumbling, a toilet flushing. Then silence apart from the whisper of yellowed newsprint.

It was almost two when he found what he thought he might just be looking for. There was only one cutting, a fleeting mention. But it was a start. When he let himself out into the dark and empty street, Leon Jackson was whistling.

Her eyes were as candid as any he could remember. She pushed the last morsel of the smoked duck on to her fork, speared a final mange tout and said, 'But surely it has an effect on you, spending so much time and energy getting inside such twisted logic?'

Tony took longer than he needed to finish his mouthful of polenta. 'You learn to build Chinese walls,' he said at last. 'You know but you don't know. You feel but you don't feel. I imagine it's similar to being a news journalist. How do you sleep at night after you've been out reporting on something like the Dunblane massacre or the Lockerbie bombing?'

'Yes, but we're always outside the event. You have to get inside or you fail, surely?'

'You're not always outside the event, though, are you? When you met Jacko, the story invaded your life. You must have had to build walls between what you knew of the man personally and what you reported to the world. When his ex-girlfriend was doing her kiss-and-tell revelations with the tabloids, you can't have looked at that as just another story. Didn't it affect the way you viewed your world?' he said, seizing the first chance he'd had to get her talking about her husband.

Micky pushed her hair back from her face. Twelve years on, he could see the contempt for Jillie Woodrow hadn't grown less. 'What a bitch,' she muttered. 'But Jacko said it was mostly fiction, and I believe him. So it didn't really get under my defences.'

The arrival of the waiter let her off the hook and he cleared their plates in silence. Then, alone again, Tony repeated the question.

'You're the psychologist,' she parried, reaching into her bag and producing a pack of Marlboro. 'Do you mind if I . . . ?'

He shook his head. 'I didn't realize you did.'

'Only after dinner. A maximum of five a day,' she said, a droll twist to her mouth. 'The control freak's control freak, that's me.'

The expression gave him a jolt. The one and only time he'd used the expression, he'd been talking about a compulsive killer who had almost robbed him of his own life. To hear it from her lips was dislocating and strange.

'You look like you've seen a ghost,' she said, inhaling her first mouthful of smoke with an air of sensuous pleasure.

'Just a stray memory,' he said. 'There are a lot of very bizarre resonances kicking around inside my head.'

'I bet. Something I've always wondered is how you *know* when you're getting it right in a profile.' She inhaled deeply and blew pale filtered smoke down her nostrils, an expression of interest on her face.

He gave her an appraising look. It was now or never. 'The same way any of us work out anything about people. A mixture of knowledge and experience. Plus knowing the right question to ask.'

'Such as?'

The interest was so genuine he almost felt guilty for what he was about to do to their pleasant evening. 'Doesn't Jacko mind that Betsy's in love with you?'

Her face froze and her pupils dilated in a panic reflex. After a long moment she swallowed and managed a faint laugh. 'If you were trying to wrong-foot me, you certainly succeeded.' It was one of the best recoveries he'd ever seen, but he hadn't imagined the confession in her eyes.

'I'm no danger to you,' he said softly. 'Confidentiality is second nature to me. But I'm not a fool either. You and Jacko, it's as fake as a nine-bob note. Betsy was there first. Oh, there were rumours. But you and Jacko had the most public courtship since Charles and Diana. It killed the gossip.'

'Why are you bringing this up?' she asked.

'We're both here because we're curious. I've answered all the questions you asked me. You can return the compliment, or not.' His smile was, he hoped, warm.

'God,' she said wonderingly. 'You have got a nerve.'

'How do you think I got to be the best?'

Micky looked speculatively at him, waving away the waiter who was approaching with the dessert menus. 'Bring us another bottle of the Zinfandel,' she said as an afterthought. She leaned forward and spoke softly. 'What do you want to ask?'

'What's in it for Jacko? Surely he's not gay?'

Micky shook her head emphatically. 'Jillie dumped Jacko after his accident because she didn't want to be with a man who wasn't perfect. He swore he would never enter into another sexual relationship where his emotions were engaged. He needed a decoy to keep the women away from him, I needed a man to hide Betsy behind.'

'Mutual benefit.'

'Oh, yes, mutual benefit. And to be fair to Jacko, he's never tried to renege on the deal. I don't know what he does for sex, though I suspect well-paid call girls come into it. Frankly, I don't care as long as he never embarrasses me.' She stubbed out her cigarette and gave him the accomplished frank gaze she normally directed at the camera.

'I'm amazed that someone who's paid to be curious about other people is so lacking in curiosity about her own husband.'

Her smile was ironic. 'If there's one thing that eleven years of marriage to Jacko has taught me, it's that nobody gets to know Jacko. It's not that I think he tells lies,' she said consideringly, 'just that I don't think he tells very much of the truth. Different people get little bits of Jacko's truth, but I don't think anybody gets it all.'

'How do you mean?' Tony picked up the discreetly delivered bottle of wine, refilling Micky's glass and topping up his almost full one.

'I get to see Jacko behaving in public like the perfect, solicitous husband, but I know that's an act. When there's only the three of us around, he's so distant it's hard to believe we've all lived under the same roof for the last dozen years. When he's working he acts like people expect a TV celeb to behave – perfectionist, a bit OTT, yelling at the crew and his PA when things don't get done just so. But with the public, he's Mr Charm. Then, when it comes to raising money, he's a hard-headed businessman. Do you know that for every pound he makes for charity, he earns two for himself?'

Tony shook his head. 'I suppose he'd argue that he's generating funds for the charity they wouldn't get otherwise.'

'And why should he work for free? Right. Me, when I do charity events, I don't even take my expenses. But then there's the other side, the volunteer work he does with people who are terminally ill or severely damaged after accidents. He spends hours by their bedsides, listening, talking, and nobody knows what goes on between them. One time a journalist tried to sneak in a tape recorder to reveal "the secret heart of Jacko Vance". Jacko found out about it and he smashed the tape recorder. He literally stamped it to pieces. They thought he was going to do the same to the journalist, but the guy had the good sense to make his legs do the walking.'

'A man who likes his privacy,' Tony said.

'Oh, he gets plenty of that. He's got a house in Northumberland, out in the middle of nowhere. I've seen it once in twelve years and that was only because Bets and I were driving up to Scotland and we decided to drop in on him. I practically had to force him to make us a cup of tea. I've never felt less welcome in my whole life.' Micky smiled indulgently. 'Yes, you could say that Jacko likes his privacy. But that's OK with me. Better that than hanging around in my face all the time.'

'He can't have been very pleased to have the police poking their noses in, then,' Tony said. 'After Shaz Bowman's visit, I mean.'

'You're not kidding. It was actually me who called the police, you know. The way Betsy and Jacko reacted, you'd think I'd shopped them on a murder rap. It was a nightmare, trying to make the pair of them see that we couldn't ignore the fact that this poor woman had been at the house not long before she was murdered.'

'Just as well one of you has a sense of duty,' Tony said drily.

'Well, yes. Besides, at least one other person knew she was coming to the house – that other police officer that Jacko spoke to. It wasn't as if we could hope to keep it to ourselves.'

'I feel so guilty about Shaz,' Tony said, half-turning away. 'I knew she was worrying away at some theory of her own, but I didn't think she'd take action on it without clearing it with me.'

'You mean you don't know what she was working on either?' Micky said incredulously. 'The cops who came to the house didn't seem to have much of a clue, but I thought you'd be sure to know.'

Tony shrugged. 'Not really. I know she had some idea that there was a serial killer preying on teenage girls and that he might be a celebrity stalker as well. But I didn't have the details. It was only supposed to be a training exercise, not the real thing.'

Micky shivered and emptied her glass. 'Can we change the subject? It's bad for the digestion, talking about murder.'

For once, he wasn't about to argue. The gamble had paid off handsomely. And he'd never been greedy. 'OK. Tell me how you got the Agriculture Minister to admit his involvement with that biotechnology company.'

Carol stared down the three mutinous faces opposite her. 'I know nobody likes stakeout work. But that's the way we're going to catch our man. At least the intervals between his outings are pretty short, so the chances are we're going to get lucky within a few days. Now, this is the way I want it to work. We're going to do it single-handed. I realize that makes it tougher, but you know what budgets are like. I've spoken to uniform and they've agreed to let us have some bodies to cover during daylight hours. Each night at ten, two of you will pick up the surveillance. You'll each work two nights on and one off. You will each use the other as back-up if it looks like we've got something going off. We start today. The first watchers are out there now. Any questions?'

'What if we get clocked?' Lee asked.

'We don't get clocked,' Carol said. 'But if the unthinkable happens, you pull off, call your oppo and swap targets at the first opportune moment. I appreciate this is a tough operation with such a low body count. But I have every confidence that you can pull this off. Don't disappoint me, please.'

'Ma'am?' Di said.

'Yes?'

'If we're really that tight on staffing levels, why don't we prioritize our two suspects and focus on the most likely with all our resources?'

It was an awkward question, and an intelligent one. It was one Carol herself had debated with Nelson over breakfast that morning. It had taken her mind off a growing fear that was coming to obsess her. 'Good question,' she said now. 'I considered it myself. Then I thought, what if we go for the wrong candidate and we only find that out after another fatal fire?' She let the question hang in the air. 'So I decided it was probably better in terms of public policy to opt for thin cover over both suspects.'

Di nodded. 'Fair enough. I just wondered.'

'Right. Sort out the rota among yourselves, and knock off now until ten. Keep me posted. Anything happens, I'm only a phone call away. Don't keep me in the dark.'

'When you say only a phone call away, ma'am . . .' Tommy drawled suggestively.

'I want to be there when you make an arrest.'

'Aye, that's what I thought you meant.'

His feigned disappointment was aimed at annoying her, she knew. Determined not to show he'd succeeded, Carol smiled sweetly. 'Believe me, Tommy, you should be grateful for that. Now get out of here and let me get some work done.' Her hand was on the phone before she'd finished speaking. She hit the first number on a list in front of her, tapping her pad with a pencil as Seaford's finest trooped out with all the brio of a snail on Valium. 'Close the door behind you, please,' she called. 'Hello? Force control? This is DCI Jordan from East Yorkshire. I need to talk to someone about Mispers . . . I sent out an information request about teenage girls . . .'

Tony eased the car on to the slip road, wondering whether he'd enjoy driving more if he had one of those ultimate driving machines he saw in all the glossy adverts instead of a clapped out old Vauxhall. Somehow, he doubted it. But that wasn't what he was supposed to be thinking about as his windscreen wipers slapped the slanting Yorkshire rain away to reveal a distant prospect of Bradford. At the ring road, he followed the achingly precise instructions he'd been given and eventually pulled up outside a terraced house whose obsessive neatness was matched only by the military precision of its single flower bed. Even the curtains appeared to have been drawn back so that exactly the same amount of lining showed at each side of the window.

The doorbell was a nasty insistent buzz. It opened to reveal a man Tony had spotted at every Jacko Vance event he'd attended. He'd persuaded him and a couple of other camera-toting enthusiasts to part with names and addresses on the pretext that he was doing a study of the phenomenon of fame as seen through the eyes of the fans rather than the famous. It was meaningless drivel, but it made them feel important enough to be co-operative.

Philip Hawsley was first, for no better reason than living nearest. As he followed him into a preternaturally tidy front room that smelled of furniture polish and air freshener, and looked like a heritage museum recreation of lower middle class life in 1962, Tony registered all the signs of the obsessive compulsive. Hawsley, who could have been any age between thirty and fifty, constantly ran his fingers over the buttons of his beige cardigan to check they were all in place. He studied his fingernails at least once a minute to ensure they hadn't grown dirty since he last looked. His greying hair was cropped in a short, military style and his shoes were polished to mirror radiance. He invited Tony to sit, pointing out the chair he wanted him to occupy, and offered no refreshment, sitting down very precisely opposite the psychologist, ankles and knees pressed firmly together.

'Quite a collection,' Tony said, glancing round the room. An entire wall was given over to shelves of video tapes, each labelled with a date and name of a programme. Even from where he was sitting, he could see the vast majority were *Vance's Visits*. A laminated wall unit held a series of albums and scrapbooks. Half a dozen books sat on a shelf above the unit. Pride of place went to a large framed colour photograph sitting on the wall-mounted gas fire. It showed Hawsley shaking hands with Jacko Vance.

'A small tribute, but mine own,' Hawsley said in a prissily camp voice. Tony could imagine all too vividly how he would have been teased as an adolescent. 'We're the same age, you know. To the very day. I feel our fates are inextricably linked. We're like two sides of the same coin. Jacko is the public face and I am the private.'

'It must have taken years to amass all this material,' Tony said.

'I've dedicated myself to maintaining the archive,' Hawsley said primly. 'I like to think I have a better overview of Jacko's life than he does himself. When you're so busy living it, you don't have time to sit and reflect on it the way I do. His bravery, his common touch, his warmth, his compassion. He's the complete man of our time. It's one of life's little paradoxes that he had to lose part of himself to gain that pre-eminence.'

'I couldn't agree more,' Tony said, naturally falling back into the conversational techniques that years of working with the mentally ill had delivered into his repertoire. 'He's an inspiration, is Jacko.' He sat back and let Hawsley's adulation flow over him, pretending to fascination when what he felt was disgust for this killer who disguised himself so well that the innocent and ill fell for his every pretence. Eventually, after Hawsley had relaxed enough to inch back from the edge of his chair into an approximation of comfort, Tony said, 'I'd love to see your photograph albums.'

The crucial dates were carved on his memory. 'For the purposes of our study, we're going to be looking at precise points in people's careers,' Tony said as Hawsley opened the cabinet and started taking down albums. Every time Tony mentioned a month and year, Hawsley chose a particular volume and laid it on the coffee table in front of Tony, open at the appropriate pages. Jacko Vance was clearly a busy man, doing between five and twenty appearances a month, many of them related to charity fund-raising, often for the hospital in Newcastle where he did volunteer work.

Hawsley's memory for detail when it related to his idol was phenomenal, a mixed blessing for Tony. On the plus side, it gave him plenty of time to scrutinize the images before him; the minus side of the equation was that his droning voice came close to sending Tony into a hypnotic trance. Soon, however, Tony felt a quiver of excitement that snapped him back to full attentiveness. There, just two days before the first of Shaz Bowman's cluster of teenage girls had disappeared for good, was Jacko Vance opening a hospice in Swindon. In the second of Hawsley's four photographs of the event, Tony saw a face he'd memorized, right next to Jacko Vance's gleaming head. Debra Cressey. Fourteen when she vanished. Two days earlier, gazing up adoringly at Jacko Vance as he signed an autograph, she'd looked like a girl in paradise.

Two hours later, Tony had identified another missing girl next to Vance, this time apparently in conversation with her. A third possibility was straining upwards on tiptoe to steal a kiss from a laughing Vance. But her head was half-turned from the camera, making it hard to be certain. Now all he had to do was to extract the photographs from Hawsley. 'I wonder if I could borrow some of these photographs?' he asked.

Hawsley shook his head vigorously, looking deeply shocked. 'Of course not,' he said. 'It's vital that the integrity of the archive is maintained. What if I were called on and there were missing items from the inventory? No, Dr Hill, I'm afraid that's completely out of the question.'

'What about negatives? Do you still have them?'

Clearly offended, Hawsley said, 'Of course I do. What kind of sloppy operation do you think I'm running here?' He rose and opened the cupboard in the wall unit. Negative storage boxes were stacked on the shelves, each as obsessively labelled as the videos. Tony shuddered inwardly, imagining the painstaking listing of every negative in the box. Not so much anal retentive as banal retentive.

'Well, could I borrow the negatives so I can have them copied?' he asked, determinedly keeping the edge of exasperation out of his voice.

'I can't let them out of my possession,' Hawsley said stubbornly. 'They're significant.'

It took another fifteen minutes to find the acceptable compromise. He drove Philip Hawsley and his precious negatives to the local photographic shop where Tony paid an extortionate sum to have prints made of the relevant photographs while they waited. Then he drove Philip Hawsley home so he could replace the negatives in their proper place before their companions noticed they'd gone.

Driving down the motorway to the next name on his list, he allowed himself a short moment of triumphalism. 'We're going to get you, Jack the Lad,' he said. 'We are going to get you.'

All Simon McNeill really knew about Tottenham was that they had a second-rate football team and they killed a copper during a riot some time in the eighties when he'd still been at school. He didn't expect the natives to be friendly, so it was no surprise when his appearance at the local electoral roll office was greeted with less than rapture. When he explained what he wanted, the stick insect in a suit behind the counter cast his eyes heavenwards and sighed. 'You'll have to do it yourself,' he said grudgingly. 'I haven't the staff to spare, especially with no notice at all.' He showed Simon into the dusty archives, gave him a ten second run-down on the filing system and left him to it.

The results of his search were not encouraging. The street where Jacko Vance had grown up had consisted of about forty houses back in the sixties. By 1975, twenty-two of the houses had disappeared, replaced, presumably, by a block of flats called Shirley Williams House. The eighteen remaining houses revealed a steady turnover of registered electors, few people seeming to remain for more than a couple of years, particularly during the grim poll tax years of the mid-eighties. Only one name remained constant throughout. Simon pinched the bridge of his nose to ease the beginning headache. He hoped Tony Hill was right, that all this would bring them closer to nailing Shaz's killer. The image of her face rose painfully before him, her startling blue eyes bright with laughter. It was almost more than he could bear. No time to brood, he told himself as he shrugged back into his leather jacket and set off to find Harold Adams.

Number 9 Jimson Street was a tiny terraced house in dirty yellow London brick. The little oblong of garden that separated it from the street was choked with empty beer cans, crisp packets and takeaway food containers. A scrawny black cat stared up malevolently as he opened the gate, then sprang for freedom with a chicken bone in its teeth. The street smelled of decay. The desiccated shell who opened the door after much rattling of bolts and turning of locks looked as if he must have already been an old man when Jacko Vance was a boy. Simon's heart sank. 'Mr Adams?' he asked, without much hope of intelligent response.

The old man cocked his head in an effort to defeat his stoop and look Simon in the eye. 'You from the council? I told that woman already, I don't need a home help and I don't want meals on wheels.' His voice sounded like a hinge in desperate need of oil.

'I'm from the police.'

'I never saw anything,' Adams said swiftly, moving to close the door.

'No, wait. It's nothing like that. I want to talk about somebody who lived here years ago: Jacko Vance. I want to talk about Jacko Vance.'

Adams paused. 'You're one of them journalists, aren't you? You're trying to con an old man. I'm going to call the police.'

'I *am* the police,' Simon said, waving his open warrant card in front of faded grey eyes. 'Look.'

'All right, all right, I'm not blind. You lot are always telling us, you can't be too careful. What d'you want to talk about Jacko Vance for? He hasn't lived here for . . . let me see, must be seventeen, eighteen years now.'

'Could I come in and have a chat, maybe?' Simon said, half-hoping Adams would send him off with a flea in his ear.

'I suppose so.' Adams pulled the door wide and stood back to let Simon enter. He caught a whiff of the old man smell of spilled urine and stale biscuits before he turned into the living room. To his surprise, the place was spotless. There wasn't a speck of dust on the screen of the huge TV set, not a mark on the lace-edged arm protectors on the easy chairs, not a smear on the glass of the framed photographs that lined the mantelpiece. Harold Adams was right; he didn't need a home help. Simon waited for the old man to settle in his own chair before he sat down.

'I'm the last one left,' Adams said proudly. 'When we came here in 1947, it was like a big family, this street. Everybody knew everybody's business and, just like a family, they was always falling out. Now, nobody knows anybody, but they still fall out just the same.' When he grinned, Simon thought, his face looked like the skull of a predatory bird whose eyes had somehow survived.

'I bet they do. So you knew the Vance family pretty well?'

Adams sniggered. 'Not much of a family, you ask me. His dad, called himself an engineer, but as far as I could see, all that meant was he had an excuse for disappearing at the drop of a hat for weeks on end. Mind you, it wouldn't surprise me if he earned a bob or two. He was always dressed better than the street, if you get my meaning. Never spent a shilling on the house or the wife and kid that he didn't have to, though.'

'What was she like?'

'Off her head. She had no time for that lad, not even when he was a babe in arms. She'd stick him out the front in his pram and just leave him there for hours. Sometimes she even forgot to take him in when it started raining and my Joan or one of the other women would have to go and knock on her door and tell her. My Joan used to say that some days she was still in her dressing gown at dinner time.'

'Did she drink, then?'

'I never heard that, no. She just didn't like the kid. Cramped her style, I suppose. When he got older, she just let him run wild, then when people went to complain, she'd come down on him like a ton of bricks. I don't know what went on behind closed doors, but sometimes you'd hear that kid sobbing his heart out. Never did no good, mind.'

'How do you mean?'

'He was a nasty piece of work, that Jacko Vance. I don't care what they say about him being a hero and sportsman, he had a nasty streak a mile wide. Oh, he could be all charm when he thought it would get him somewhere. He had all the wives in this street wrapped round his little finger. They were always giving him little treats, letting him watch telly round their house when his mum locked him out.' Adams was enjoying himself. Simon suspected it wasn't often these days that his malice was allowed free rein. He was determined to make the most of it.

'But you knew different?

Adams sniggered again. 'I knew everything that went on in this street. I caught that little bugger Vance once round the back of the lock-up garages off Boulmer Street. He had a cat by the scruff, you know, so it couldn't fight him off. He was dipping its tail in a jar of petrol when I came round the corner. And there was a box of matches on the ground beside him.' The momentary silence was eloquent. 'I made him let the cat go, then I kicked his arse for him, good and proper. I shouldn't think I stopped him, though. Cats were always going missing round here. People used to comment on it. Me, I had my own ideas.'

'Like you said, a nasty piece of work.' It was almost too good to be true. Simon had spent too much time preparing for his assignment in Leeds not to recognize the accepted markers for psychopathy in a background history. Torturing animals was textbook stuff. And this man had seen it first hand. He couldn't have found a better source if he'd searched for weeks.

'He was a bully, an' all. Always picking on the little kids, daring them to do dangerous things, getting them hurt, but he never laid a finger on them himself. It was like he set it up to happen and then stood back and watched. Me and Joan, we were glad our two were grown and gone by then. And by the time the grandkids came along, Vance had discovered he could throw a silly spear further than anybody else. We hardly saw him after that, and good riddance to bad rubbish, if you ask me.'

'You'll not find many people with a bad word to say about that man,' Simon said mildly. 'He saved some lives, you can't argue with that. He does a lot of work for charity. And he gives up his time to work with the terminally ill.'

Adams screwed up his face in a sneer. 'I told you, he likes watching. He probably gets a kick out of knowing they'll be dead soon and he'll still be strutting around like Lord Muck on the telly. I'm telling you, sonny, Jacko Vance is a nasty piece of work. So, what are you after him for?'

Simon smiled. 'I never said I was after him.'

'So what d'you want to go around talking about him for, then?'

Simon winked. 'Now, you know I can't reveal the details of a police investigation, sir. You've been extremely helpful, I will say that much. If I was you, I'd keep an eye on the television for the next few days. With a bit of luck, you'll find out exactly why I came here.' He got to his feet. 'And now, I think I'd better be on my way. My senior officer will be very interested in what you have to say, Mr Adams.'

'I've been waiting years to say it, sonny. Years, I've been waiting.'

Barbara Fenwick had been killed six days before her fifteenth birthday. If she'd lived, she'd have been almost twenty-seven. Her mutilated body had been found in a walker's hut on the moors above the city, strangled. There were signs that she had had sexual intercourse against her will, though there had been no trace of sperm either inside or outside her body. What made the crime unusual was the nature of her injuries. Where most psychopathic killers disfigured the sexual organs of their victims, this killer had crushed the girl's right arm to a bloody pulp, shattering bones and tearing muscle till it was difficult to reconstruct which fragment went where. Even more interestingly, the pathologist had been insistent that the injuries were consistent with the application of increasing pressure rather than a single, terrible impact.

It had made no sense to the investigating officers.

The finders of Barbara's body were in the clear, having been camping and hiking together for the previous six days. Her parents, who had been distraught since her disappearance five days previously, were also under no suspicion. The girl had been alive and well for a couple of days after they had reported her missing and her stepfather had been in the company of his wife and at least one police officer ever since. The parents had said all along that their daughter was happy at home, that she would never have run away, that she must have been abducted. The police had been sceptical, pointing out that Barbara's best clothes were missing and that she had told her parents a lie about her movements following school the day she disappeared. Added to that, she'd bunked off school, and not for the first time.

It had made no sense to the investigating officers.

Barbara Fenwick hadn't been a wild, troublesome teenager. She wasn't known to the police, her friends denied she drank more than the occasional can of sweet cider and no one thought she'd ever experimented with drugs or sex. Her last boyfriend, who had chucked her a month before to go out with someone else, said they'd never gone all the way and he thought in spite of her sexy looks she was probably, like him, a virgin. She'd been doing reasonably well at school and had ambitions to train as a nursery nurse.

The last reliable sighting of her had been on the local bus to Manchester on the morning of her disappearance. She'd told the neighbour who had spotted her that she was going to the Dental Hospital for an appointment to do with her wisdom teeth. Her mother said Barbara didn't have any sign of wisdom teeth, a fact borne out by the pathologist.

It had made no sense to the investigating officers.

There had been nothing in her behaviour to suggest a girl about to go off the rails. She'd been out to a disco with a bunch of friends on the Saturday night before her disappearance. Jacko Vance had been there, making a celebrity appearance, signing autographs for charity. Her friends said she'd had a great night.

None of this had made any sense to the investigating officers.

But it made a lot of sense to Leon Jackson.

The stone slab was so well engineered that it didn't even make the sinister grating sound of a horror film. When a small electrical current applied pressure to a particular, precise point, it simply pivoted silently through 180 degrees to reveal the steps that led to the small crypt that no one would any longer suspect existed beneath the converted chapel. Jacko Vance flipped the switch that flooded the crypt with harsh fluorescent light and descended.

The first thing he noticed was the smell, hitting him before his head was far enough underground to be able to see the creature that had once been Donna Doyle. The putrefaction of pulverized flesh mingled with the stale smell of unwashed fevered skin and the acrid reek of the chemical toilet. He felt his stomach turn, but told himself he'd smelled worse in the terminal ward as gangrene devoured the bodies of people who had already had as much amputated as could reasonably be excised. It was a lie, but one that stiffened his sinews.

At the bottom of the steps, he stood and stared at the pathetic creature pressing herself against the cold stone wall as if she expected to be able to push her way through it and so escape him. 'God, you're disgusting,' he said contemptuously, taking in her matted hair, foul wounds and the dirt she'd gathered bumping into things in the dark.

He'd left her boxes of breakfast cereal and she had water from the tap on the rising main. There was no excuse for her to be in this state; she could have made an effort to clean herself up instead of sitting on the mattress in her own filth, he thought. The leg irons allowed her enough freedom of movement for that, and the pain from her arm hadn't been enough to stop her from eating, judging by the open packets lying around her. He was glad he'd opted for a plastic-covered mattress so he could hose off her disgusting presence when he'd finished with her.

'Look at yourself,' he sneered, swaggering across the room towards her, unbuttoning his jacket and tossing it over a chair that was well out of her reach. 'Why should I want anything to do with a mess like you?'

The whimpering noise that came from Donna's bruised lips was wordless. With her undamaged hand, she grabbed at the blanket in a poignant attempt to cover her nakedness. In one swift step, Jacko was towering over her, yanking the rough woollen cover away from her. With his prosthetic arm, he smashed her across the face and she fell back on the mattress, tears spilling and mingling with the blood and mucus from her nose.

Vance stepped back and spat at her. Coolly, he stripped himself, folding his clothes and placing them neatly on the chair. He was hot and hard, ready for what he'd come there for. He'd had to wait longer than usual, longer than he'd wanted because of that inconvenient bitch Bowman. After the discovery of her body he hadn't dared come near the place until he'd seen off the police, wary of attracting their notice. And even if Tony Hill thought he had something on him, there was no proof and no one to pay him any attention. It was safe to come back for another dose of what made life worth living, the sweet allotment of vengeance, the savour of suffering.

He dropped to his knees on the mattress, forcing the teenager's legs apart with a rough hand, relishing her protests, her futile attempts at prevention, her sad little cries of repudiation. As he thrust into her, he let his full weight fall on her injured arm.

Donna Doyle finally produced a coherent sound. The scream that echoed round the grim little crypt was, unequivocally, 'No!'

Carol yanked open the door and practically dragged Tony into the cottage. 'We were beginning to wonder if you'd got lost,' she said, marching ahead of him to the dining table where a wide-mouthed Thermos of soup sat next to a couple of loaves of olive bread and a selection of cheeses.

'Accident on the motorway,' he said, dropping a folder on to the table and sinking into a chair. He looked disoriented and sounded preoccupied.

Carol poured two mugs of soup and passed one to Tony. 'I need to talk to you before the others get here. Tony, this isn't just an academic exercise any more. I think he took another one a few days before he killed Shaz.'

Suddenly she had all his attention. Whatever had been on his mind when he'd walked through the door was thrust aside and his dark blue eyes burned into hers. 'Evidence?' he demanded.

'I had a hunch, so I put out a Misper request nationwide. I got a call this afternoon from Derbyshire. Donna Doyle. Aged fourteen. From Glossop. About five miles from the end of the M57.' Carol gave him a copy of the fax the local CID had sent her. 'The mother put this flyer together because the police weren't terribly worried. The usual pattern, you see. She left the house to go to school in the morning, with an excuse for not being home until late. Her best clothes were missing. Premeditated runaway, case not so much closed as discreetly ignored. But I had a chat with the WPC who interviewed the mother before they lost interest. I didn't lead her; she volunteered that a couple of nights before she went missing, Donna had been out with one of her friends at a charity do where Jacko Vance was the guest of honour.'

'Shit,' Tony exhaled. 'Carol, depending on what he does with them, she could still be alive.'

'I didn't even want to think it.'

'It's possible. If he keeps them before he kills them – and we know a lot of serial offenders do that for the power charge it gives them – chances are he won't have risked going near her since he murdered Shaz. Christ, we've got to find a way to locate his killing ground. And soon.' They looked at each other with the constricting realization that another life could depend on how well they did their jobs. 'He's got a cottage in Northumberland,' Tony said.

'He's not going to be doing it on his own doorstep,' Carol objected.

'Probably not, but I wouldn't mind betting that his killing ground is a short drive from there. What have the team got?' he said grimly.

Carol glanced up at the clock. 'I don't know. They're due here any minute. They were meeting in Leeds and coming on together. They've all checked in, and it sounds like we've hit a lot of pay dirt.'

'Good.' Before he could say more, they both heard the sound of an engine labouring up the hill to the cottage. 'Here comes the cavalry, by the sounds of it.'

Carol opened the door and the trio trooped in, all looking remarkably pleased with themselves. They piled into chairs round the table, pulling off jackets and coats and dumping them on the floor, eager to begin. Tony ran a hand through his hair and said, 'We think he took a girl just before he killed Shaz. She could still be alive.' It gave him no pleasure to watch the light bleed out of their eyes, to see their faces change from the glow of satisfaction to the pinched pale of anxiety. 'Carol?'

Carol relayed the information she'd already given Tony, while he went to the kitchen and poured out the coffee he'd smelled brewing. When he returned, he said, 'We're not going to have the luxury of time to draw out a detailed profile and brainstorm all the elements of it. We're going to have to go hell for leather to get evidence and do what we can to save another life. So. Let's hear how we've all been doing. Kay, why don't you kick off?'

Succinctly, Kay reported on her interviews with the bereft parents. 'The bottom line is that they're all telling the same story. There are no significant discrepancies, either with what they originally told the police, or with each other's version of events. I managed to pick up a photograph of one of the girls with Jacko Vance, and I have established that they all went to events in their local area within a few days of their disappearance. But no stronger connection than that. Sorry.'

'You've nothing to apologize for,' Tony said. 'You did a great job. It can't have been easy, getting this much out of people who are still suffering because their child is on the missing list. The picture is helpful, too, because we can tie that down very specifically. Good job, Kay. Simon?'

'Thanks to Carol, I was able to track down the fiancee who chucked Jacko after his accident. If you remember, Shaz put forward the theory it was that emotional event, coupled with the shock of his accident, that tipped him over the edge into killing. Well, from what I heard, he maybe didn't have that far to fall.

'According to Jillie Woodrow, there was nothing normal about Jacko's bedroom habits. Right from the start of their sex life, he had to be in control. She was supposed to be passive and adoring. He hated her touching him sexually and, on occasion, he actually slapped her for laying hands on him. He became more interested in S&M pornography and wanted her to act out fantasies from magazines and books and from his own imagination. She didn't mind being tied up, she says, and she didn't much mind the spanking or the whipping, but when he started on the hot candle wax and the nipple clamps and the outsize vibrators, she drew the line.' He glanced down at the brief notes he'd made to ensure he got through his report without missing out anything crucial.

'She reckons that somewhere around the time his athletics career took off and he started banking big money, he began going to prostitutes. Nothing seedy, nothing low rent or street corner. From what he let slip, she thinks he had a couple of expensive call girls that he used, women who would either go along with the more extreme stuff that he wanted, or else they'd lay on the kind of lassies that it didn't matter if he messed up. Junkies, that sort of thing. According to Jillie, she was desperate to get out, but she was terrified of how he'd react. Outside the bedroom, he was the perfect partner. Solicitous, kind, generous, but incredibly possessive. So, after the accident, she grabbed the chance with both hands. She figured if she told him while he was in the hospital, he wouldn't be able to react. And he'd be stuck in there long enough to cool down and get over her.' Simon looked up and was surprised by how grim Tony looked.

'And we all know what happened next, don't we?' Tony said. 'Micky Morgan. The marriage of convenience.'

The faces around the table went from incomprehension to shocked amazement as he filled them in on what he'd heard first from Chris Devine and then from Micky herself. 'So we're seeing some fascinatingly aberrant behaviour here,' he said. 'Still hard to stand anything up that a senior officer would stake his arrest record on, but we know now, don't we?' They didn't have to say anything. The answer was in their eyes.

'There's more,' Simon said, launching into Harold Adams's tale.

'Man, the more we find out, the more incredible it is that Jack the Lad is still walking the streets,' Leon sighed, lighting his third cigarette since he'd walked in. 'Wait till you hear what I've dug up.' He passed on the meagre information he'd obtained from Jimmy Linden in a matter of minutes. 'Then he told me about this retired journo, Mike McGowan. This guy has forgotten more about sport than we'll ever know. He's got archives the British Library would kill for. I tell you, it took me half the night to get through the stuff he's got on Jack the Lad. And then I found this.'

With a flourish, Leon produced a brittle clipping and five photocopies of the article. It came from the *Manchester Evening News* and dealt with the murder of Barbara Fenwick. Emphasized in yellow highlighter, one paragraph stood out. '"Barbara was no party girl, according to her friends. Her last Saturday night out was typical. She was one of a group who went to a disco where sports hero Jacko Vance was making a charity appearance." This was just fourteen weeks after the accident,' Leon pointed out.

'He didn't hang about, did he? Got stuck right into the charity work,' Simon said.

'Well, we never doubted that he was driven,' Tony commented. 'So, is there any evidence that Vance actually met this girl?'

'The high point of her night out was getting his autograph.' Leon passed round copies of the summary he'd prepared from the police evidence store. 'They wouldn't let me photocopy the files, so I had to do this. I reckon she was his first victim,' he said confidently.

'And I reckon you're right,' Tony breathed. 'Oh, this is good, Leon, this is really good. He got better after this. My God, those hillwalkers must practically have stumbled over him. Look, it says they saw what they thought was a Land Rover heading off down the track just after they came over the ridge. Jack the Lad got a fright. He realized he needed a proper killing ground, a place where he wasn't going to be disturbed. We think that might be in Northumberland, by the way. Near his cottage. But without more information . . .' He rubbed his hands over his face. 'A twelve-year-old case, though. Where's the evidence?'

Leon looked slightly downcast. 'They don't know. They moved all the unsolved stuff to a new location about five years ago, and all the forensics on this case have either got lost or misfiled. Not that there was much, according to the abstract. No prints, no body fluids. Some tyre tracks, but that's no use a dozen years on.'

'The investigating officers. That's who we need to talk to. But before we discuss what comes next, I'd better tell you what I've come up with. It's pretty meagre compared to the huge strides you three have taken, but it does give us a handy chunk of circumstantial evidence.' Tony opened his folder and fanned out an array of photographs. 'I've done the rounds of the zealots. I have to say it was very like being back working in a secure mental hospital. At the risk of baffling you with professional jargon, they're all a few bricks short of a wall. However, after enduring the histories of their assorted obsessions with Jacko Vance, what we've got is a selection of photographs of Jacko taken at events where we know our putative victims were also present. Four of the pics put him next or near to one of our missing girls. In another five or six, it's possible that the girl in the picture is one of ours, but by no means certain without computer enhancement.' He leaned over and began carving himself a chunk of bread.

'With Kay's pick-ups, that makes five. We've got an overlap,' Carol said.

'I don't suppose it's enough to start an official investigation?' Tony asked without hope. He started to slice some cheese.

Carol pulled a face. 'The trouble is, there's no connection to my patch. If one of these girls had disappeared from East Yorkshire, I'd be willing to have a go at getting something moving, but I can't find one. Even so, I don't know where we could take any investigation. All we've got is highly circumstantial; it's nowhere near enough to bring him in for questioning, never mind a search warrant.'

'So you don't reckon we could convince West Yorkshire to take another look at Vance, even with this much?' Kay asked.

Simon snorted. 'Are you kidding? Given what they think about me? Every time I see a cop car on the road, I start sweating. Anything we come up with is tainted because they're convinced I'm the killer and you're protecting me. I don't think they're going to believe a word we say.'

'Point taken,' Kay said.

'What we need is a witness who saw him with Shaz after she's supposed to have left his house. Ideally, someone who saw them in Leeds,' Leon suggested.

'Ideally, a bishop of the Church of England,' Carol said cynically. 'Don't forget, it has to be somebody whose word would stand up against the people's champion.'

The hand that was cutting the cheese slipped and Tony sliced the edge off his index finger. He jumped to his feet, blood dripping from the wound. 'Shit, fuck and God damn it,' he exploded. He thrust his finger into his mouth and sucked.

Carol grabbed the paper napkin wrapped round the Thermos to catch drips and bandaged it round his finger, gripping it tightly. 'Klutz,' she said briskly.

'It was your fault,' he said, subsiding into the chair.

'My fault?'

'What you said. About unimpeachable witnesses.'

'Yes?'

'The camera doesn't lie, right?'

'Depends if it's digital or not,' Carol said ironically.

'Don't be difficult. I'm talking cameras that are already used to convict criminals.'

'What?'

'Motorway cameras, Carol. Motorway cameras.'

Leon snorted in derision. 'Don't tell us you've fallen for that one?'

'What?' Tony said, puzzled.

'Great myths of our time number forty-seven. Motorway cameras catch villains. Not.' Leon leaned back in his chair, his cynical swagger full on.

'What do you mean? I've seen those programmes on TV, police videos of car chases. And what about all those speeding convictions on the back of still photographs from the motorway cameras?' Tony demanded indignantly.

Carol sighed. 'The cameras operate perfectly. But only in certain situations. That's what Leon's getting at. The still cameras only snap vehicles travelling well in excess of the speed limit. They're not going to flicker a shutter at much under ninety. And the videos are only actually turned on if there's an incident in progress or a traffic-flow problem. The rest of the time, they're just not running. And even when they are, you'd need state-of-the-art enhancement software to get anything convincing from them.'

'Wouldn't your brother know somebody?' Simon asked. 'I thought he was some sort of computer whizz kid.'

'Well, yes, but we haven't got anything to show him yet, and we're not likely to have,' Carol objected.

'But I thought when Manchester city centre got blown to bits by the IRA, the police backtracked the route the bombers' van took using the motorway cameras?' Tony said persistent to the last.

Kay shook her head. 'They thought they might have been able to pick it up on the photos of the speeders, but there wasn't enough detail . . .' Her voice tailed off and her face lit up.

'What is it?' Carol asked.

'Private CCTV videos,' she breathed. 'Remember? Greater Manchester Police put out an appeal for any garages or food outlets with CCTV surveillance on possible routes to submit their recordings. We won't get Vance or Shaz on motorway surveillance, but we'll get them wherever they stopped for petrol. Logically, Shaz would have filled up before she left Leeds. She'd have got all the way to London, but she'd not have made it all the way back on a single tank. And the chances are, she would have used a motorway service area rather than come off the motorway just for petrol.'

'And you lot can get access to these tapes?'

Carol groaned. 'It won't be access that's the problem. Most companies are happy to co-operate. Usually they don't even bother asking what it's all in aid of. It's the prospect of all those hours of jerky video. I'm getting a migraine just at the thought of it.'

Tony cleared his throat. 'Actually, Carol, I was going to suggest that you come with me to talk to the police officers who investigated Barbara Fenwick's murder.' He gave an apologetic smile to the other three. Simon and Kay looked merely disappointed, but Leon looked mutinous. 'I'm sorry, but this needs a senior officer to look good. And it needs to be small scale. We don't want to give these guys the hump. We want to avoid giving the impression that they did a lousy job and we're the crack troops coming in to clear up the mess. This is one for me and Carol. What I'd like you to do is divide up the motorway and check out all these service station cameras.' Now all three looked deeply fed up. 'I'd do it myself if I could,' Tony said sympathetically. 'But this is one for the warrant card.'

Inarticulate grumbling came from round the table. 'We know,' Simon said scathingly.

'And Donna Doyle might still be alive,' Carol pointed out.

The trio of detective constables stared at each other, eyes dark and serious. Leon nodded slowly. 'And even if she isn't, the next one is.'

One of the first lessons Tony Hill had learned as a profiler was that preparation was never wasted. It was hard for him and Carol to work up enthusiasm in the stacks of a dusty police document store, but they both knew how important it was to stay alert as they combed the files. The drudgery of poring over every available piece of information was as vital to painting an accurate picture of a killer as the flair that some people seemed naturally to bring to the job. Plodding alone never made a good profiler, but neither did flashy charisma. He'd been happy to be proved wrong about Leon. His superficial approach to the training exercise had confirmed all Tony's prejudices about his peacock display. But either he'd learned from the humiliation of being shown up in front of the rest of the team or else he was one of the ones who could only ever do it for real. Either way, Tony thought as he and Carol ploughed the identical furrow a day later, he couldn't fault the job he'd done.

At the end of a couple of hours, they leaned back in their seats almost simultaneously. 'Looks like Leon didn't miss a thing,' Tony said.

'Looks that way. But if we're going to talk to the man who ran the case, we needed to know that for ourselves.'

'I really appreciate your help in this, Carol,' he said quietly, knocking the papers into a neat pile. 'You didn't have to stick your neck out.'

One corner of her mouth twisted in what might have been a smile or a trace of pain. 'I did, you know,' was all she said. What she didn't say was that they both knew she would never be able to turn her back on his need, personal or professional. And that she also knew the feeling was mutual, provided they both stayed within the limits they seemed to have evolved to keep themselves whole.

'You're sure you can spare the time away from your arson investigation?' he asked, understanding what lay unspoken.

She stacked papers in a file box. 'If anything's going to happen, it'll happen at night. That may be the price you have to pay for crashing in my spare room.'

'I think I can just about afford that,' he said wryly. He followed her back to the counter where they returned the files to a uniformed PC who looked like his thirty was approaching but not fast enough for him.

Carol gave him her best smile. 'The officer in charge of this inquiry – Detective Superintendent Scott? I take it he's retired now?'

'Finished up ten years ago,' the man said, hefting the heavy boxes and heading for the distant shelves where they had come from.

'I don't suppose you know where I could find him?' Carol called to his retreating back.

His voice floated back, muffled by the shelves. 'He lives out Buxton way. Place called Countess Sterndale. There's only three houses.'

It took a few minutes to obtain directions to Countess Sterndale, which didn't appear on their map, and another thirty-five to drive there. 'He wasn't lying, then,' Tony said at the end of the single-track road that concluded in a tree-lined loop round a circle of grass. A battered Queen Anne manor house faced them and over to their left was a pair of long, low cottages with heavy slate roofs and thick limestone walls. 'Which one, d'you reckon?'

Carol shrugged. 'Not the manor, unless he was on the take. Eeny meeny, miny mo . . .' She pointed to the right-hand cottage.

As they walked across the grass, Tony said, 'You take the lead. He'll open up more easily to a copper than a mumbo jumbo man.'

'Even though I'm a woman?' Carol asked ironically.

'You have a point. Play it as it lays.' He opened a smartly painted gate which swung back silently. The path was herringbone brick, not a single weed in the interstices. Tony raised the black iron knocker and let it fall. The sound echoed behind the door. As it died away, heavy footsteps approached and the door opened to reveal a broad man with iron grey hair brilliantined in a side parting and a toothbrush moustache. He looked like a forties matinee idol put out to grass, Carol thought, stifling a smile. 'I'm sorry to trouble you, but we're looking for ex-Detective Superintendent Scott,' she said.

'I'm Gordon Scott,' he said. 'And you are?'

This was where it got difficult. 'DCI Carol Jordan, sir. East Yorkshire Police. And this is Dr Tony Hill from the National Profiling Task Force.' To her surprise, Scott's face lit up with delight.

'Is this to do with Barbara Fenwick?' he said eagerly.

Dismayed, Carol looked helplessly at Tony. 'What makes you say that?' he asked.

A laugh rumbled in his chest. 'I might have been out of the game for ten years, but when three people in two days turn up to look at the files of my only unsolved murder, somebody picks up the phone. Come in, come in.' He ushered them into a comfortable sitting room, ducking to avoid cracking his head on the door frame. The room felt lived in, with magazines and books in unruly piles by the pair of armchairs that faced each other across the beamed fireplace. Scott waved them into the chairs. 'How about a drink? My wife's off doing the shopping in Buxton, but I can just about manage tea. Or a beer?'

'A beer would be great,' Tony said, reluctant to wait while Scott brewed tea. Carol nodded agreement and moments later he returned with three cans of Boddington's.

Scott moved a large ginger cat and settled his bulky frame in the window seat, reducing the light in the room by at least half. He popped the top of his beer, but before he drank, he launched into speech. 'I was that glad when I heard you were looking at Barbara Fenwick's murder. I worried at that case for the best part of two years. It kept me awake nights. I'll never forget the look on her mother's face when I arrived with the news we'd found the body. It still haunts me. I always thought the answer was out there, we just didn't have what it took to get it. So when I got the call and I heard it was the profiling task force ... well, I have to say, my hopes have been raised. What's drawn you to Barbara?'

Tony decided to take advantage of Scott's enthusiasm and offer him frankness. 'This is a somewhat unorthodox investigation,' he began. 'You may have read about the murder of one of my squad.'

Scott nodded his big head sadly. 'Aye, I saw. You have my sympathies.'

'What you won't have read is that she was working on a theory that there is an unsuspected serial killer of teenage girls on the loose and that he's been doing it for a long time. It started off as a classroom exercise, but Shaz couldn't sit on it. My team and I think that's why she was killed. Unfortunately, West Yorkshire Police don't agree. The main reason for that is the person Shaz put in the frame.' He glanced at Carol, ready for some seemingly official back-up.

'There is a significant amount of circumstantial evidence that points to Jacko Vance,' she said baldly.

Scott's eyebrows climbed. 'The telly man?' He let out a soft whistle and his hand went automatically to the cat, stroking its head rhythmically. 'I'm not surprised they didn't want to know. So how does this connect to Barbara Fenwick?'

Carol outlined how Leon's researches had turned up the clipping that had brought them to Gordon Scott's case files. When she had finished, Tony said, 'What we hoped was that there was stuff that never made it on to paper. I know from working with Carol what it's like on a murder squad. You have a feeling in your water, hunches that you never confide to anybody except your partner, never mind put in a memo. We wondered what the gut feelings were among the officers who actually worked the case.'

Scott took a long draught of beer. 'Of course you did. And quite right, too. The trouble is, there's bugger all I can tell you. A couple of times, we got the wrong smell off some of the nonces we had in for questioning, but it was always something else that they were wound up about. To be honest, the gut feeling on our team was total frustration. We just could not get a handle on the bugger. He seemed to have come out of nowhere and vanished the same way. We ended up convinced it was someone from off our patch who'd stumbled across the girl when she was doing a routine bunk off school. And that would sort of fit in with your idea, wouldn't it?'

'Broadly, except that we think he sets it up a lot more carefully than that,' Tony said. 'Oh well, it was worth a try.'

'Sir, there didn't seem to be a lot of forensic evidence,' Carol prompted.

'No. That set us back a bit. Truth to tell, I'd no experience of a sex offender who took that kind of forensic care. Mostly they're hot-headed, spur of the moment, leave all sorts of traces, go home covered in mud and blood. But there was almost nothing to work off. The only distinctive thing was the crushed arm, according to the pathologist. She wouldn't stick her neck out on paper, but she had this notion that the girl's arm had been crushed in a vice.'

The thought of such cold-blooded torture sent a shiver of unwelcome echoes through Tony's stomach. 'Ah,' he said.

Scott struck his forehead with the heel of his hand. 'Of course! Vance lost his arm, didn't he? He was going for the Olympics and he lost his arm. Perfect sense, why didn't we think of something like that at the time? God, what an idiot I am!'

'There's no reason why you should have considered it,' Tony said, wishing he meant it, wondering how many lives might have been saved if a psychologist had been brought in all those years ago.

'Is the pathologist still working?' Carol asked, as ever straight to the point.

'She's a professor now at one of the London teaching hospitals. I've got her card somewhere,' Scott said, getting to his feet and lumbering out of the room. 'God, why didn't I think more about the arm?'

'It's not his fault, Tony,' Carol said.

'I know. I sometimes wonder how many more people have to die before everybody recognizes psychologists aren't just witch doctors,' he said. 'Listen, Carol, in the interests of speed, I think we should get Chris Devine to follow up on this pathologist. She's desperate to help, and she's got the experience to know the kind of things she should be looking for. What do you say?'

'I think that's a good idea. To tell you the truth, I was dreading telling you that I couldn't go to London now. I need to be around tonight in case the arsonist decides to have a go.'

He smiled. 'I remembered.' It was probably the first time in his career as a profiler that something outside the case obsessing him had impinged. That was the trouble with working with Carol Jordan. She affected him in ways no one else ever had. When he didn't see her, he could conveniently forget that. Working this closely, it was impossible to ignore. He gave her a grave smile. 'I'm too scared of upsetting John Brandon to let you chance blowing the arson collar,' he lied.

'I know.' She detected the lie, but did not show it. It was neither the time nor the place for some kinds of truth.

Kay had lost count. She couldn't remember if this was the seventh or the eighth set of videos she'd inspected. Having drawn the short straw in the division of the sites, she'd set off on the M1 from Leeds before dawn and driven all the way to London. Then she turned the car round and retraced her journey, stopping at every service area she came to. Now it was late afternoon and she was sitting in yet another scruffy office, stuffy with stale sweat and smoke, watching jerky images dancing in front of her as she fast-forwarded through the tapes. She was awash with bad coffee, her mouth still slimy and fat-flavoured from the long ago breakfast at Scratchwood Services. Her eyes were gritty and tired, and she wished she was anywhere else.

At least they'd managed to narrow the time frame down. They reckoned the earliest Shaz or Vance could possibly have hit the first northbound services on the motorway was eleven in the morning, the latest seven at night. Adjusting the times forward for each service area wasn't difficult.

The tapes took much less running time than real time, since, rather than taping continuously, the cameras only took a certain number of still frames per second. Even so, she'd spent hours working her way through the recordings, fast-forwarding until she saw either a black Volkswagen Golf or one of the cars registered to Jacko Vance – a silver Mercedes convertible or a Land Rover. The Golf was common enough to cause frequent pauses, the other cars turning up less often.

She thought she was faster now than when she'd started. Her eyes were in tune with what she was searching for, though she feared she was beginning to flag and worried that might make her miss something crucial. Forcing herself to concentrate, Kay flicked forward until the familiar black pram-like shape of another Golf appeared. She slowed to normal speed, then almost at once she registered that the driver was a male with grey hair sticking out from under a baseball cap rather than either of her expected targets so her finger moved towards the fast-forward button. Then, suddenly, it swerved to the pause button as she noticed that there was something odd about the man.

But the first thing that struck her on closer scrutiny had nothing to do with the person who'd climbed out of the driver's seat and headed for the petrol pump. What Kay spotted was quite different. Although the car was sitting at an awkward angle to the pumps, she could make out the last two letters of the number plate. They were identical to the final digits of Shaz's registration.

'Ah, shit,' she breathed softly. She rewound the tape and watched it again. This time she identified what had caught her eye about the driver. He was awkwardly left-handed, to the point where he hardly used his right arm at all. Just as Jacko Vance would inevitably be if he were using equipment that wasn't specially designed to accommodate his disability.

Kay studied the tape a few more times. It wasn't easy to make out the man's features, but she wouldn't mind betting that Carol Jordan would know someone who could help them over that particular hurdle. Before the night was over, they'd have something on Jacko Vance that even a team of highly paid defence lawyers wouldn't be able to get him out of. And it would be down to her, the best tribute she could pay to a woman who had been on the way to becoming a friend.

She flipped open her mobile phone and called Carol. 'Carol? It's Kay. I think I might have something your brother would like to see . . .'

It wasn't that Chris Devine objected to pathologists having a day off. What pissed her off royally was that this particular pathologist spent her free time sitting in the pouring rain in the middle of nowhere waiting for a glimpse of some bloody stupid bird that was supposed to be in Norway but had managed to get lost. There was nothing clever about getting lost, Chris muttered as she felt more rain slide between her neck and her collar. Bloody Essex, she thought bitterly.

She sheltered from the gusting easterly so she could take another look at the rough map the bird warden had sketched out for her. She couldn't be far away now. Why did these bloody hides have to be so inconspicuous? Why didn't they just make them look like her nan's house? She had more bloody birds in her back garden than Chris had seen all afternoon on the marshes. The birds were too flaming sensible to come out on a day like this, she grumbled as she stuffed the map back in her pocket and set off round the edge of the copse.

She almost missed the hide, so well was it camouflaged. Chris pulled back the wooden door and forced the scowl from her face. 'Sorry to butt in,' she said to the three people cramped inside, grateful that her head at least was out of the wind. 'Is one of you Professor Stewart?' She hoped she was in the right place; it was impossible to tell even genders inside waxed jackets, woolly scarves and thermal hats.

A gloved hand rose. 'I'm Liz Stewart,' one of the figures said. 'What's going on?'

Chris sighed with relief. 'Detective Sergeant Devine, Metropolitan Police. I wonder if I could have a word?'

The woman shook her head. 'I'm not on call,' she said, her Scottish accent growing stronger in indignation.

'I appreciate that. But it is rather urgent.' Chris unobtrusively edged the door wider so the wind could whip inside the rickety structure.

'Oh, for God's sake, Liz, go and see what the woman wants,' an irritated male voice said from under one of the other hats. 'We're not going to see anything worthwhile at all if you two stand there screaming like fishwives.'

The grudging professor squeezed past the other two and followed Chris outside. 'There's some shelter under the trees,' Professor Stewart said, pushing past her and scrambling through the undergrowth until they were out of reach of most of the weather. In the clearing, Chris could see she was a sharp-featured forty-something with clear amber eyes like a hawk. 'Now, what is all this about?' she demanded.

'You worked a case twelve years ago. An unsolved murder of a teenage girl in Manchester, Barbara Fenwick. Do you remember it?'

'The girl with the crushed arm?'

'That's the one. The case has cropped up in connection with another investigation. We think we're looking at a serial killer, and it's possible that Barbara Fenwick is the only one of his victims where the body's turned up. Which makes your postmortem pretty significant.'

'Which it will still be on Monday morning,' the professor said briskly.

'Yeah, but the girl we think he's holding might not make it that long,' Chris said.

'Ah. You'd better fire away then, Sergeant.'

'Retired Superintendent Scott told my colleagues that you had thought, but didn't put in your report, that the arm looked like it might have been crushed deliberately in something like a vice rather than accidentally, is that right?'

'That was my opinion, but it was only speculation. Not the sort of fanciful thing I'd put in a formal postmortem report unless I had considerably stronger grounds for my belief,' she said repressively.

'But if you were pressed, you'd say that?'

'If I were asked directly if it were possible, yes, I'd have to agree.'

'Was there anything else you didn't write down because it was "fanciful"?' Chris asked.

'Not that I can think of.'

'I know you said you didn't put it in your formal report, but would you have put something in your notes to that effect?'

'Oh yes,' the professor said, as if it were the most natural thing in the world. 'That way, if it became important later, the prosecution could introduce it more readily.'

Chris closed her eyes momentarily in a short prayer. 'And have you still got your notes?'

'Of course. In fact, I've got something even better than that.'

The cafe of the motorway services at Hartshead Moor on the M62 had never been anyone's idea of a good Saturday night out, which made it perfect for their purposes. The ad hoc investigative team was now augmented by Chris Devine, who had slotted in as if she'd always been there. Already, it seemed she and Carol were about to sign up as blood sisters, both because of their common experiences in the Job and because they were the nearest thing the team had to senior officers.

The group had colonized a distant corner with no prospect of being overheard or disturbed since it was right on the border of the smoking area. Leon, dispirited at drawing a blank, was buoyed up by Kay's results. But Simon's face was showing signs of strain inevitable in a man whose name was on the wanted list, turned on by the very group who had given him a sense of community. Tony wondered how long the younger man could stand it without his judgement slipping dangerously.

Carol cut into his thoughts. 'I've arranged for Kay to meet a friend of my brother who can enhance these pictures for us, to cut the margin of doubt to the bone.'

'You're not coming along?' Kay asked, looking slightly worried.

'Carol has responsibilities in East Yorkshire tonight,' Tony said. 'Is that a problem, Kay?'

She looked embarrassed. 'Not a problem, not as such. It's just

'... well, I don't know this bloke, and he's doing this as a favour, right?'

'That's right,' Carol said. 'Michael says he owes him.'

'It's just that ... well, if I want to push a bit harder, you know, if I don't think he's going to the max because he can't be bothered, or it's going to cost too much, I can't actually lean on him the way Carol could.'

'She's got a point,' Chris affirmed from the smoking table she was occupying with Leon. 'She's not even the one who's asked for the favour. And it's Saturday night. Even computer nerds must have something better to do than a favour for somebody who can't be bothered to turn up in person. That'll be how it looks. I think Carol should be there.'

Carol stirred her sludgy coffee. 'You're right. I can't fault your logic. But I can't afford to be off my patch tonight.' She glanced at her watch and made rapid calculations.

'No, Carol,' Tony said hopelessly, knowing already he was wasting his breath.

'If we left now ... we could be there by nine ... I could be back in Seaford by one at the latest. And nothing ever happens before then ...' Coming to a decision, Carol grabbed her coat and bag. 'All right. Come on, Kay, we're off.' As they walked towards the door with Kay scrambling to catch up, Carol turned. 'Chris – good hunting.'

'So what do we do now?' Leon demanded aggressively, lighting another cigarette from the butt of the one he'd been smoking. 'I feel like I've wasted a whole day fucking about with motorway cameras. I want to be doing something worthwhile, you know?'

Tony was glad Chris Devine had come to join them; he had a feeling he was going to have to rely on her experience now the others were starting to fray round the edges. 'Nobody's been wasting their time, Leon. We've come a long way today,' he said calmly. 'We need to build on that. The information Chris has got from the pathologist is a big step forward. But on its own, it's still not worth a whole lot. He profiles right. Everything we learn about him puts another tick in the box. But we're still in the realms of supposition.'

'Even with a victim with a crushed right arm?' Simon asked incredulously. 'Come on, that's got to be a clincher. What more do we need, for God's sake?'

'Given the kind of lawyers Jack the Lad is going to be able to afford, we'd be laughed out of court – always supposing we got that far,' Tony said. 'I'm sorry, but that's the way it is.'

'The crushed arm is good stuff,' Chris said. 'But it's not a lot of use as an isolated case. What we need is something to compare it with. Only so far there haven't been any bodies, right?' The others nodded. 'But you reckon he'd got another one just before Shaz fronted him up? Well then, chances are he'd started on her but he hadn't finished. So we find her, we tie her to him, and we've got him. Anything wrong with that?'

'No, except we don't know where he keeps them before he kills them,' Tony said.

'Course we don't. Or do we?'

If they'd been dogs, their ears would have pricked up. 'Go on,' Tony encouraged her.

'The great thing about being a dyke my age is that when I was getting into the scene, everyone who had a job was in the closet. Now, half the women I used to drink with are bosses all over the shop. One of them just happens be a partner in the agency that handles Jacko's publicity.' She pulled out a sheaf of fax paper from inside her jacket. 'Jacko's schedule for the last six weeks. Now, unless he's Superman or his wife is in on this, there's only one area of the country he could possibly be keeping this kid.' She leaned back and watched them cotton on to what had leapt out at her.

Tony ran his hand through his hair. 'I know he's got a cottage up there. But it's a huge area. How can we narrow it down?'

'He could be using his own place,' Leon said.

'Yeah,' Simon butted in eagerly. 'Let's get up there, take a look at this hideaway.'

'I don't know,' Chris said. 'He's been so careful about everything else, I can't believe he'd do something so risky.'

'Where's the risk?' Tony demanded. 'He brings the girls there under cover of darkness, they're never seen or heard from again. There's never a trace of the bodies. But Jack the Lad does volunteer work at the hospital in Newcastle. They must have an incinerator. He's always pushing the image of himself as being a man with the common touch. I'd guess he regularly pops down to the boiler room, having a natter with the lads. And if he helps them load the incinerator from time to time, well, who's going to notice the extra bag of body parts?'

A chilled silence fell over the group. Tony scratched the stubble on his chin. 'I should have worked this out before now. He's a control freak. The only killing ground he'd trust would be one he had total control over.'

'So let's go.' Simon said, pushing his cup away and reaching for his jacket.

'No,' Tony said firmly. 'Simon, this is not the time for Action Man tactics. We need to plan carefully here. We can't just go charging in mob-handed and hope what we find justifies the action. His lawyers would make mincemeat of us. We need to have a strategy.'

'That's easy for you to say, man,' Leon said. 'You're not the one the cops are looking to arrest. You can sleep in your own bed at night. Simon needs this to be sorted.'

'All right, all right,' Chris said mildly. 'It wouldn't hurt to do a trawl locally with pictures of Donna Doyle. Looking at his time-table, she must have got there under her own steam. I bet he sends them up on the train or the coach. We need to blitz the bus terminal and the train station, talk to the staff. And the locals. If there's a small local station near to Jack the Lad's hideaway, somebody might have seen her getting off the train.'

Simon stood up, dark eyes burning. 'So what are we waiting for?'

'No point in hitting it before morning,' Chris said.

'It's a two and a half hour drive from here. We're not doing anything better, are we? Let's go now, find a cheap hotel and get cracking first thing in the morning. You up for it, Leon?'

Leon stubbed out his cigarette. 'Long as I don't have to go in your car. What're you driving, Chris?'

'You wouldn't like my music. We'll take all the cars. OK, Tony?'

'OK. Provided you stay well away from his house. I have your word on that, Chris?'

'You got my word, Tony.'

'That go for you two? Bearing in mind Chris is technically your senior officer?'

Leon scowled but gave a grudging nod. Simon, too, conceded. 'OK. I probably shouldn't be making the decisions anyway.'

'What've you got planned, Tony?' Chris asked.

'I'm going home to draw up a full profile based on all we know now. I can't say I blame you for wanting to hare off up the A1, but if Carol and Kay come back with the goods, I'm proposing we go to West Yorkshire first thing in the morning and persuade them to make this official. So, nothing except local inquiries until we've spoken. OK?'

Chris nodded sombrely. 'Trust me, Tony. Shaz meant too much to me to risk fucking this up.'

If she'd been trying to take the gung-ho madness out of the two male officers' eyes, she succeeded. Even Leon stopped bouncing on the balls of his feet. 'I hadn't forgotten that,' Tony said. 'Or how much she wanted to catch Jack the Lad.'

'I know,' Chris said. 'Fucking mad bitch, she'd have loved this.'

Once upon a time she'd understood most of what there was to know about computers, Carol thought wistfully. Back around 1989, she was almost as much of a whizz with CP/M and DOS as her brother. But she'd gone into the police force and it had eaten up her life. While she'd been getting to grips with the Police and Criminal Evidence Act, Michael had been assimilating software and hardware that often moved forward on a daily basis. Now she was the one-eyed woman in the kingdom of 20/20 vision. She knew enough to crunch numbers and process words, to retrieve lost files from limbo and to rewrite boot files so that a reluctant machine could be persuaded to talk to its user. But ten minutes with her brother and his mate Donny and she knew that, these days, this was the culinary equivalent of being able to boil a kettle. From the look on Kay's face, it wasn't any better for her. It was just as well she'd come along, Carol thought. At least she had enough knowledge to know when the boys were spinning off into a world of their own and the authority to drag them back to the job in hand.

The two men sitting in front of a computer screen the size of a pub TV muttered to each other incomprehensibly about video drivers, local buses and smart caches. Carol knew what the words meant, but she couldn't connect them to anything they were doing with keyboard and mouse. Donny, Michael had told her, was the best man in the north when it came to computer-enhancing photographs or video stills. And he just happened to work in the same building where Michael's software company had its suite of offices. And, in spite of Chris's convictions, he was so devoid of a life that he was thrilled to be dragged away from *The X Files* and a microwave dinner to show off his toys.

Carol and Kay looked over their shoulders at the screen. Donny had already done everything he could with the number plate, yielding confirmation of the last two letters and a strong probability of a match with the third. Now he was working on the driver. He'd already tweaked and twiddled with some full-length shots of the man, pronouncing himself finally satisfied with one and printing out a couple of colour copies for the two women to pore over. The more Carol looked, the more convinced she was that under the Nike baseball cap and behind the aviator glasses, Jacko Vance was peeking out at her. 'What do you think?' she asked Kay.

'I don't know if you'd pick him out of a line-up, but if you know who you're looking for, I think you can tell it's him.'

Now, without any prompting from them, Donny was working on a head and shoulders of the man who'd filled the Golf with petrol at lunchtime on the Saturday Shaz Bowman died. It was hard to find a good shot to work with because the peak of the cap shaded his face most of the time when he wasn't actually bending over the fuel tank. Only by advancing one frame at a time did Donny finally come up with a single shot where the man in the cap glanced swiftly up at the pump to check how much petrol he'd taken.

Watching Donny painstakingly improve the quality of the picture was agonizing. Carol couldn't keep her eyes off her watch, gripped with the knowledge that she should be elsewhere and if anything happened in Seaford she'd be in deep shit. The minutes crawled by while the powerful processor drove a search through the computer's massive memory for the next best alternative to the pixels on the screen. Although it was making more calculations per second than the human brain could comfortably comprehend, the computer seemed to Carol to take forever. At last, Donny turned away from the screen and pushed his own baseball cap back on his head. 'Best you're going to get,' he said. 'Funny, he looks familiar. Is he supposed to?'

'Can you print me off half a dozen copies?' Carol said. She felt mean ignoring his good-natured question, but it wasn't the time or place to tell Donny that, apart from cheeks that were undeniably too chubby, the face he'd recreated was that of the nation's favourite TV personality.

Michael was either quicker on the uptake or more familiar with the medium. 'He looks like Jacko Vance, that's what's got you confused, Donny,' he said innocently.

'Yeah, right, that dickhead,' Donny said, swinging round in his chair and blinking at the women. 'Fucking hell, shame it's not him you're going to arrest. You'd be doing the world a favour, getting that shit he does off the box. Sorry I couldn't get a better head shot, but there wasn't a lot to go on. Where did you say you got the tape from?'

'M1 services. Watford Gap,' Kay said.

'Yeah, right. Pity you weren't looking for your man in Leeds.'

'Leeds?' Carol leapt on the word. 'Why Leeds?'

'Cos that's where the state-of-the-art CCTV development company is. Seesee Visions. They are the total business. They think civil liberties is that posh but polite department store in London.' He laughed at his own bad joke. 'Double wicked fuckers, they are. You can't miss them. That sodding great smoked glass monolith just after the end of the motorway. You want somebody coming off the M1 at Leeds, they've got it taped.'

'What do you mean, somebody coming off at Leeds?' Carol's fingers were twitching with the desire to grab Donny by the shirt and make him get to the point.

Donny cast his eyes upwards as if he were tired of dealing with mental defectives. 'Right. History lesson. Nineteenth-century Britain. Little pockets of mains water supply, gas providers, railway companies. Gradually, they all linked up to make national utilities. With me so far?'

'And there's me thinking nerds knew nothing about the Victorian era apart from Charles Babbage,' Carol snapped. 'OK, Donny, we did the Industrial Revolution at school. Can we get to CCTV?'

'OK, OK, be chill. CCTV is kind of like the baby utilities were then. But soon it won't be. Soon we're going to have all these inner-city systems linking up with private security systems and motorway cameras and we're going to have a national network of CCTV. And these systems will be so finely tuned that they can recognize you or your wheels and if you're not supposed to be some place, then the big fuck-off security guards are gonna remove you. Like if you're a convicted shoplifter and Marks and Sparks don't want you hanging out in their food hall, or you're a known perv and your local launderette doesn't want you in there ogling the knickers –' He made a throat-cutting gesture.

'So what exactly has all this got to do with the M1?'

'Seesee Vision are the masters of the universe when it comes to leading-edge techno. And they test all their new gear on the traffic flow off the M1. Their stuff is so well developed they can give you a high-res picture of the drivers and the front-seat passengers, never mind baby stuff like number plates.' Donny shook his head in wonder. 'I went for a job there, but I didn't like it. You could tell it was seagull city.'

'Seagull city?' Carol asked faintly.

'The bosses fly in, do a lot of screaming, grab everything worth having, crap over everybody and fly out again. Not my scene.'

'Do you think they'd co-operate with me?'

'They'd wet their pants. They're desperate to make a big impression on your lot. When this national network finally creaks into being, they want to be in the driving seat. The company of choice.'

Carol looked at her watch. It was after ten. She should be heading back to Seaford, on the spot if her team had to swing into action. Besides, no one in authority would be at Seesee Vision at this time of night.

Donny spotted her glance and read her mind. 'There'll be somebody there this time of night, if that's what you're wondering. Give them a bell. You got nothing to lose.'

But Donna Doyle might, Carol thought, catching Kay's pleading look. And besides, Leeds was halfway between Manchester and Seaford. Her team were grown-ups. It wouldn't be the first time they'd had to think for themselves.

First, the victims. It was always the place to start. The problem here was to convince anyone that there were victims. It was always possible that they were wrong, Tony realized. They so badly wanted Shaz to have been right, they so desperately needed to be instrumental in putting a stop to the person who had killed her that they might all be deluding themselves about the value of the material they had uncovered. It was almost conceivable that the circumstantial evidence piling up against Jacko Vance was just that and no more.

But that way madness lay. Madness and the prospect of poor Simon being arrested as soon as he crossed the threshold of his own home. 'The victims,' Tony said. He stared at the laptop screen and started to type.

THE CASE FOR A SERIAL OFFENDER

The first known victim in this putative cluster is Barbara Fenwick whose murder took place twelve years ago (see attached summary prepared by DC Leon Jackson for crime details). We can say with some degree of certainty that this was the first killing by this perpetrator since there is no previous record of this signature behaviour, namely the pulverizing of the lower right arm. This is clearly signature behaviour; there is no need to inflict such an injury in order to commit sexual assault and murder. It is extraneous, it is ritualistic and therefore it is safe to assume that it has particular significance for this offender. Given the ceremonial nature of this signature behaviour, it is likely that he has used the same implement to produce these injuries in all his killings; other victims could therefore be expected to display very similar disfigurement.

There is at least one other indication that this was a first murder. The killer had chosen what he thought was a sufficiently isolated and safe place to carry out his crime undisturbed, but he was in fact almost caught in the act. This will have frightened him considerably and he will have taken immediate steps to secure his future killing grounds. That he was successful in this is shown by the fact that no bodies have been recovered from his subsequent victims.

In the absence of bodies, what possible grounds can there be for assuming a serial offender?

He paused and referred back to the list of common features that Shaz had presented to the profiling team what felt like an age ago. The least he could do was make sure the work she'd left wasn't wasted. With a few changes and additions, he typed in the list then continued.

While two or three common features are to be expected with any such grouping, the number and congruence we can identify here is of far too high a level to be coincidental. Of particular importance is the degree of physical similarity between the victims. They could be sisters.

Perhaps more significantly, they could also be sisters of a woman called Jillie Woodrow as she looked fifteen or sixteen years ago, when she first became the earliest known lover of Jacko Vance, our prime suspect. It is not coincidence, in my opinion, that Vance was robbed of a brilliant athletic career when he lost his lower right arm in an accident that crushed it beyond hope of restoration.

Further, the date of the killing of Barbara Fenwick was

a mere fourteen weeks after Jacko Vance's accident. For much of that time, he was in hospital recovering from his injuries and subsequently undergoing extensive physiotherapy. It was during this hospitalization that Jillie Woodrow took the opportunity to terminate what had become an increasingly oppressive and unwelcome relationship (see appended notes of interview with JW, conducted by DC Simon McNeill). The combined stress of these two events would be sufficient to trigger a sexual homicide in one who was predisposed to realize his sociopathic responses in violent behaviour.

He has never released his sexual impulses in a normal fashion since. His extremely high-profile marriage is a sham, his wife being a lesbian whose 'personal assistant' is in fact her lover and has been since before the wedding took place. Vance and his wife have never had sexual intercourse and his wife assumes he uses 'high-class call girls' to provide him with a sexual outlet. There is no suggestion that she has any suspicion of his homicidal activities.

When Vance's early life is set against the criteria that experience has demonstrated are common features among homicidally active sociopaths, a remarkable degree of commonality is obvious. We have witness interviews that attest to a difficult relationship with a rejecting mother, an often absent father whom the subject was desperate to impress, bullying of younger children, cruelty to animals and sadistic, controlling sexual behaviour, and evidence of powerful and perverse sexual fantasies. His sporting prowess can be identified as a massive overcompensation for the worthlessness he felt in every other area of his life, and the loss of that prowess as a devastating blow to his extremely fragile self-esteem.

In those circumstances, women would be the obvious victim gender. He would perceive his mother and subsequently his fiancée as having emasculated him. But he is far too intelligent to vent his rage on the obvious targets, and so he has assumed a series of surrogates. These are girls who bear a strong resemblance to Jillie Woodrow at the age when he first seduced her.

It should be borne in mind that captured serial killers have in the main been above average intelligence, in some cases well above. We should not therefore be surprised that uncaught and unsuspected serial offenders exist who are using their greater intelligence more effectively. Jacko Vance is, in my opinion, an example of this principle in action.

He leaned back in his chair. So much for the psychology. He'd have to draw up a more detailed table of corresponding preconditions, but that wouldn't take long. Added to the hard evidence he hoped Carol and Kay would produce that night, he felt sure that there was enough material to make certain that within twelve hours, West Yorkshire would have started to take Jacko Vance seriously.

Detective Sergeant Tommy Taylor knew a pile of crap when he saw it. And surveilling part-time firemen was the biggest pile of crap he'd seen in a very long time. He'd spent the night before watching Raymond Watson, which in effect meant watching Raymond Watson's house. It wasn't as if it was packed with architectural detail to keep the mind active. A bog-standard terraced house with a pocket handkerchief front garden that boasted a tired rose bush contorted by the north-east winds into a shape some modern sculptors would have given their eye teeth to achieve. Flaked paintwork, scabby varnish on the front door.

Watson had come home at eleven the night before, after the last race at the dog track. There was no meeting tonight, so he'd arrived home just after seven, according to the seconded uniforms who'd been keeping an eye out in their mufti. Since then, nothing. Unless you counted putting out the milk bottles as a major event.

The lights had gone off about ten minutes after that. An hour later, there was no sign of life anywhere. The back streets of Seaford weren't noted for their liveliness after midnight. The only thing that was going to get Raymond Watson out of his kip now was a major fire, Taylor reckoned. He grunted and shifted in the car seat, scratching his balls and sniffing his fingers afterwards. Bored shitless, he flicked the switch on his personal radio and called Di Earnshaw. 'Owt happening your end?' he asked.

'Negative,' came the reply.

'If Control come through to you with news of a fire that our lads are getting called out on, give me a shout on the PR, OK?'

'Why? Are you leaving the car on foot pursuit?' She sounded eager. Probably as bored as him, excited by the thought of some action even at second hand.

'Negative,' Taylor said. 'I need to stretch my legs. These fucking sardine tins weren't built for the likes of me. Like I said, anything doing, give me a shout. Over and out.'

He turned the key in the ignition. The engine coughed to life, sounding freakishly noisy in the quiet side street. Bollocks to Carol Jordan's daft ideas. Less than a mile away there was a club that kept late doors, catering mainly for the sailors off the foreign ships. There was a pint there with Tommy Taylor's name on it, unless he was very much mistaken. It was time he checked out the possibility.

Carol and Kay followed the security guard down blindingly white corridors. He opened a door and stood back, waving them into a large, dimly lit room. Computer monitors occupied almost every horizontal surface. A young woman in jeans and a polo shirt, hair dyed platinum blonde and cut flat to her head, glanced over her shoulder, registered the new arrivals and turned back to the screen she'd been engrossed in. Fingers tapped keys and the display changed. Carol caught movement in her peripheral vision and turned her head. A tall man in a suit that screamed money was perched on the edge of a computer desk over to one side. What she'd caught was him unfolding his arms and dropping his hands in preparation for rising to greet them.

He took a step towards them, pushing a persistent cowlick of mid-brown hair out of his eyes. If he was going for boyish, Carol thought, he'd missed it by about a generation. 'Detective Chief Inspector Jordan,' he said, clearly relishing the bass resonance of his voice. 'And Detective Constable Hallam. Welcome to the future.'

God help me, Carol thought. 'You must be Philip Jarvis,' she said, forcing a smile. 'I'm impressed and grateful that you were prepared to help me out at this time of night.'

'Time waits for no man,' he said, as proudly as if he'd coined the phrase. 'Or woman, come to that. We recognize the importance of your work and, like you, we operate twenty-four hours a day. We are, after all, in the same business, the business of crime prevention and, when that fails us, catching those responsible.'

'Mmm,' Carol murmured noncommittally. It was clearly a prepared speech that placed no reliance on a response.

Jarvis smiled benevolently, revealing the sort of brilliant white dental work more common in New York than Yorkshire. 'This is the viewing room,' he said with a sweep of his arm, undaunted by the obviousness of his statement. 'It's fed either from our fully automated library or by live feeds from the many cameras we have being road-tested on the site. The operator chooses the source and summons the images he or she wants to look at.'

He ushered Carol and Kay forward until they were standing behind the woman. Close up, Carol could see her skin was older than her face, faded to unhealthy by the lack of natural light and the radiation from the monitors. 'This is Gina,' Jarvis announced. He made her sound like royalty. 'When you told me the date and time period you were interested in and the vehicle index numbers that you wanted to know about, I got Gina on to it right away.'

'As I said, I really appreciate this. Have you had any luck?'

'Luck doesn't enter into it, Chief Inspector,' Jarvis said with throwaway arrogance. 'Not with a leading-edge system like ours. Gina?'

Gina tore her eyes from the screen and pushed off with her feet, spinning round to face them, grabbing a sheet of paper from the desk. 'Seventeen minutes past two on the afternoon in question.' Her voice was clipped and efficient. 'The black Volkswagen Golf left the M1 heading for the city centre. Then, at eleven thirty-two p.m., the silver Mercedes convertible did exactly the same thing. We can supply timed and dated tapes and still photographs of both events.'

'Is it possible to identify the drivers of either vehicle?' Kay asked, trying to keep the excitement out of her voice and failing. Gina flicked an interested eyebrow upwards and stared.

'Obviously, the daytime shots pose fewer problems in that respect,' Jarvis butted in. 'But we're using very high-end experimental media with the night filming at present, and with our computer enhancement technology, it would be possible to come up with surprisingly good images.'

'If you knew who it was you were looking at, you would be able to recognize them. If you were planning on doing a "does anyone know this man" on *Crimewatch UK*, you might have one or two problems,' Gina qualified.

'You say this system's experimental. How well do you think this evidence would stand up in court?' Carol asked.

'One hundred per cent on the vehicles. More like a seventy-five per cent chance on the drivers,' Gina said.

'Come on now, Gina, let's not be so pessimistic. It depends, like so much evidence, on how it's presented to the jury,' Jarvis protested. 'I'd happily testify that I'd stake my reputation on the reliability of the system.'

'And you're a qualified expert witness, are you, sir?' Carol asked. She wasn't trying to put him on the spot, but time was short and she needed to know how firm was her ground.

'I'm not, no, but some of my colleagues are.'

'Like me,' Gina said. 'Look, Ms Jordan, why don't you look at what we've got and see if that isn't enough to help you get the corroborative evidence so it won't depend on what a jury thinks about our technology?'

When she left half an hour later, Kay was clutching a bundle of video tape and laser-printed stills that both women knew in their bones would corner Jacko Vance. If Donna Doyle remained alive, they were her last best hope. Carol could hardly wait to tell Tony. She looked at her watch when she got back to the car. Half past midnight. She knew he'd want to see what she had, but she needed to get back to Seaford. And Kay could always take the material over to him now. Carol stood by her car, undecided.

To hell with it, she thought. She really wanted to talk over the evidence with Tony. He'd only get one shot at McCormick and Wharton and she needed to make sure he'd prepared a case that would speak directly to a copper's idea of evidence.

She had her mobile if they really needed her, after all.

Detective Constable Di Earnshaw pushed her shoulders hard back against the car seat, thrusting her pelvis forward in a vain attempt to loosen her stiff spine and find a comfortable position in the unmarked CID car. She wished she'd been able to bring her own little Citroën whose seat seemed moulded to her contours. Whoever had designed the police Vauxhall had obviously been a hell of a lot narrower in the hips and longer in the leg than she had any hope of ever achieving.

At least the discomfort kept her awake. There was a kind of spiteful pride in Di's determination to stay on the job. She was as convinced as Tommy Taylor that these stakeouts were a total waste of time and money, but she reckoned there were more subtle and effective ways of demonstrating that to the powers that be than skiving off. She knew her sergeant well enough by now to have a pretty shrewd idea of how he was passing the weary hours as night crawled relentlessly toward dawn. If Carol Jordan found out, he'd be back in uniform so fast he wouldn't know what had hit him. CID was such a gossip factory, she was bound to find out sooner or later. If not on this job, then on another, perhaps one that actually counted.

Di wouldn't dream of doing anything so obvious to undermine Jordan's authority. More in sorrow than in anger, that would be her line. The pitying smiles behind Jordan's back, the back-stabbing, 'I shouldn't really say this, but . . .' at every opportunity. Make it look like every cock-up emanated from Jordan's orders, every success from the troops' initiatives. There was almost nothing as destructive as constant undermining. She should know. She'd experienced plenty of it in her years with the East Yorkshire Police.

She yawned. Nothing was going to happen. Alan Brinkley was tucked up in bed with his wife inside their pretentious modern box on a so-called executive development with ideas above its station. Never mind that it would be easier to keep clean and maintained, Di preferred her little trawlerman's terraced cottage down by the old docks, even though they were now a tourist trap heritage centre. She loved the cobbled streets and the salt on the air, the sense that generations of Yorkshirewomen had stood on those doorsteps and scanned the horizon for their men. She should be so lucky, she thought with a moment's self-hatred.

She checked her watch against the clock on the dashboard. In the ten minutes that had passed since she'd last done it, the two had managed to remain precisely five seconds out of sync. Yawning, she switched on her small portable radio. Hopefully the phone-in she personally called prole-speak would be over and the DJ would be playing some decent sounds. Just as Gloria Gaynor stridently revealed that as long as she knew how to love, she knew she'd stay alive, soft light abruptly appeared behind the four frosted glass panels of the mock-Georgian fanlight in the Brinkleys' front door. Di grabbed the steering wheel tightly and sat up hurriedly. Was this it? Or was it insomnia pushing someone towards a cup of tea?

Just as suddenly as it had appeared, the light vanished. Di slumped back with a sigh, then from under the garage door, a thin rope of brightness stretched across the driveway. Startled, she punched the off button on the radio and wound down the car window, letting the raw night air flood her airways and sharpen her senses. Yes, there it was. The unmistakable cough of a car engine.

Within moments, the garage door shuddered upwards and the car rolled forward on to the drive. It was Brinkley's car, no mistake. Or rather, it was the car on which Brinkley had only ever paid three hire-purchase instalments and which would be snatched back just as soon as the repo men figured out how to grab it without actually breaking into Brinkley's garage. As she watched, Brinkley himself got out of the car and walked back to the garage, reaching inside presumably to hit the button that closed the door behind him.

'Oh boy,' Di Earnshaw said, winding up her window. She pressed the record button on her personal microcassette recorder and said excitedly, 'Alan Brinkley is now leaving his home by car at one twenty-seven a.m.' Dropping the tape machine on the seat beside her, she grabbed the personal radio that was meant to keep her in close touch with Tommy Taylor. 'This is Tango Charlie. Tango Alpha, do you read me? Over.' She started her engine, careful to avoid the reflex of turning on her lights. Brinkley had pulled off the drive now and was driving out of the cul-de-sac, signalling a right turn. She eased her foot off the clutch, still driving without lights, and picked him up on the winding avenue that ran through the housing development and out to the main road.

She clicked the radio as she drove, repeating her message to her sergeant. 'Tango Charlie to Tango Alpha. Subject on the move, do you read me? Tango Alpha, do you read me? Over.' At the main road, Brinkley turned left. She counted to five, then switched on her lights and turned after him. He was heading for the city centre three miles away, keeping his speed steady, just above the limit. Not so careful he'd be pulled on suspicion of over-cautious drunk driving, not so fast he'd attract a tug for speeding. 'Tango Charlie to Tango Alpha.' She swore silently at her errant boss. She needed back-up and he wasn't there. She thought about calling in to control, but they'd only send a troop of patrol cars that would scare off any arsonist for three counties.

'Oh, shit,' she complained as Brinkley turned off the main road into the dimly lit streets of a small industrial estate. It looked very much as if this was it. Turning off her lights again, she followed cautiously. As the high walls of the units closed around her, she decided she had to call for uniformed back-up. She turned up the volume on her police radio and picked up the mike. 'Delta Three to control, over?'

There was a crackle of static, then nothing. Her heart sank as she realized she was in one of a handful of radio shadows that peppered the city centre. She might as well have been in a black hole for all the chance she had of raising back-up. There was nothing else for it. She was on her own.

Donna Doyle no longer felt any pain. She was swimming through a warm soup of delirium, revisiting memories through a distorting lens. Her dad was still alive, alive and throwing her up into the air in the park where the trees waved at her. Their branches turned into arms and Donna was in the centre of a ring of friends playing party games. Everything was bigger than usual, because she was only six and things always loomed larger when you were little. The colours bled into each other and it was Well Dressing week, the carnival floats melting over the streets like jellies left out in the sun.

And there she was at the heart of the parade, on a dais in a pick-up truck covered in crepe-paper flowers that swelled big as cabbage roses in her fevered derangement. She was the Rose Princess, radiant in layers of stiff petticoat, the glory of the occasion cancelling out the discomfort of the itchy fabric on the warm summer afternoon and the plastic tiara cutting into the soft flesh behind her ears. Through the misty dislocation between dream and reality Donna wondered why the sun was burning with such tropical fervour that it made her sweat and then shiver.

Outside her consciousness, the swollen, discoloured meat that hung uselessly down by her side continued to decay, sending more poisons into her body, continually shifting the balance between toxicity and survival. The rotting stink and the corrupt flesh were only the outward signs of a deeper putrefaction.

Her eager body couldn't wait for death to begin the business of decomposition.

Getting out of the car to close the garage door, Alan Brinkley had noticed his breath puff white on the night air. It was a bitter one, all right. Winter was gripping tight. Just as well he'd got one earmarked that didn't involve a long walk. The last thing he needed was fingers numbed with cold fumbling about their work. But there was nothing like a good fire to warm a man to the bone, he'd thought with an ironic smile as he revved the car engine to encourage the heater to deliver its scarlet promise of warmth.

His target was a specialist paint factory at the far end of a small industrial estate on the edge of town. For once, he could avoid the walk from his chosen parking spot because the unit next to his goal was a body shop. There were always half a dozen cars parked outside in varying stages of being resprayed or restored after an accident. One more wouldn't be noticeable. Not that there was anyone to notice. He happened to know for a fact that the guard employed to patrol the estate was never there between two and three thirty. Brinkley had watched him often enough to know that the guy was a victim of greedy bosses. He had too many premises to protect and not enough time to keep an eye on them properly.

He turned into the narrow canyon between tall warehouses that led into the estate and nosed slowly down the access road that led to the body shop. He killed the engine and lights then double-checked that none of the items in his kit had slipped out of his pocket. They were all there: the string, the brass cigarette lighter smelling of petrol, the packet of seventeen cigarettes, the dog-eared book of matches, last night's evening paper, his seven-bladed Swiss Army knife and a crumpled oil-stained handkerchief. He leaned across and took the small but powerful torch out of the glovebox. Three deep breaths with eyes closed and he was ready.

He got out of the car and glanced quickly around. His gaze swept over the cars surrounding the body shop. He saw without seeing the nose of a Vauxhall sitting in the shadow of a warehouse just on the curve of the access road. He failed to register that he hadn't passed it moments before since there was no thrum of an engine or blur of lights to alert him. Certain there was nothing else moving in the landscape, he cut across the Tarmac apron to the paint factory. God, this was going to be one hell of a display, he thought with satisfaction. He wouldn't mind betting that when this went, it would take one or two other buildings with it. Another couple of conflagrations like this and Jim Pendlebury was going to have to say, 'Bugger the budget,' and take him on full-time. It wouldn't be enough even to pay off the interest on the debts he and Maureen seemed to have accumulated like fleas on a cat, but it would keep the creditors at bay while he could work out a way to get their heads above water once and for all.

Brinkley shook his head to clear away the clutter of worry and dread that engulfed him whenever he allowed their mountain of debt to cast its shadow over him. He couldn't do this unless his mind was focused, and whenever he thought about the amount he owed, his head swam and he couldn't imagine ever making it out the other side in one piece. He kept telling himself that what he was doing was the only way he had to survive. The dosser who had died had already given up on that struggle long before Brinkley had come on the scene. He would be different. He would survive. So now he had to stifle distractions and concentrate on achieving the right result without getting caught.

Getting caught would defeat the whole purpose. He'd never get the debts paid off then. Maureen would never forgive him getting caught.

Brinkley thrust his hand between the industrial-sized rubbish skip and the wall of the factory, his fingers closing on the bag he'd stowed there earlier. This time, the office window was his best bet for entry. The fact that it was wide open to the eyes of anyone who happened to walk or drive down the access road didn't worry him. None of the units worked a night shift, the security guard wasn't due for another hour and the paint factory was the last building before the dead end of a seven-foot security fence. Nobody would be taking a short cut down here.

It took less than five minutes to get inside, and only another seven for his practised hands to set his standard fuse. The cigarette smoke billowed upwards, to his nostrils the most fragrant aroma around, its sweetness mingling with the chemical smells of the paint that permeated the air of the factory. The paint would go up like a pillar of flame in the desert, Brinkley thought with satisfaction as he backed down the dark corridor, his eyes never leaving the smouldering fuse.

He felt behind him for the open doorway of the office where he'd come in. Instead of empty space, his fingers brushed against warm fabric. Startled, he whirled in his tracks and the glare of a torch hit his eyes like a thrown glass of wine. Blinded, he tried to blink the light away. He struggled to back through the doorway, but, disorientated, stumbled sideways into the wall. The light moved and he heard the door snick shut.

'You're fucking nicked,' a woman's voice said. 'Alan Brinkley, I am arresting you on suspicion of arson . . .'

'No!' he roared like a cornered animal, throwing himself forward at the light. They collided and crashed to the ground in a tangle of limbs and a crash of office furniture. The woman beneath him struggled and wriggled like a furious kitten, but he was heavier and stronger, his upper body developed through years of fire officer's training.

She tried to hit him with the torch, but he easily fended off the blow with his shoulder, sending the light rolling across the floor where it came to rest against a filing cabinet, rocking slightly and throwing a seasick light on the struggle. He could see her face now, her mouth screwed open in a rictus of determination as she tried to break free. If he could see her, she could see him, his panicking mind screamed.

Getting caught would defeat the whole purpose. He'd never get the debts paid off then. Maureen would never forgive him getting caught.

He brought one knee up over her abdomen and leaned on it to crush the air from her lungs. He pushed his forearm against her throat, pinning her to the floor. As her tongue thrust out in a desperate fight for air, he grabbed her hair with his free hand and yanked her head forward against the brace of his forearm. He felt rather than heard something snap. Suddenly she was limp. The fight was over.

He fell away from her, curling on the floor in a foetal crouch. A sob rose in his throat. What had he done? He knew the answer well enough, but he had to repeat the question continually inside his head. He rolled on to his knees, head hanging like a disgraced dog. He couldn't leave her there. They'd find her too soon. She needed to be somewhere else.

A groan dragged from his lips. He forced himself to touch flesh that already felt dead and cold in his imagination. Somehow he hauled the woman's body over his shoulders in the traditional fireman's lift. Staggering to his feet, he lurched through the doorway and back towards the seat of the fire. He carried on beyond the fuse that now smelled harsh, on to where cases of paint tins stood on pallets waiting to be loaded on lorries. The fire would burn hot here, leaving the forensic people little to go on. There would certainly be nothing left to connect him to her. He let the body fall loose-limbed to the floor.

Wiping tears from his eyes, Brinkley turned and ran into the welcoming cold of the night. How had it come to this? How had a few good times, a taste for the good life, brought him to this place? He wanted to fall to the ground and howl like a wolf. But he had to get to his feet, get to the car, answer his pager when it summoned him to the fire station. He had to get through this. Not for his sake but for Maureen's.

Because getting caught would defeat the whole purpose. He'd never get the debts paid off then. Maureen would never forgive him getting caught.

'Shouldn't you be in Seaford?' he'd asked.

'I've got my phone with me. It'll only take me half an hour longer on the motorway than it does from the cottage. And we need to sort out what we've got and what comes next.'

'You'd better come in, then.'

It took Carol longer to read Tony's report than he needed to scan the photographs and watch the videos she'd brought, but he didn't mind that. He kept replaying the tape and shuffling the date-stamped photographs, a tight smile on his lips, fire in his eyes. Eventually, Carol reached the end. The look of complicity they shared told them both that they had been right, and now they could demonstrate a case that could no longer be ignored. 'Good work, Doctor,' Carol said.

'Good work, Detective Chief Inspector,' he echoed.

'Vengeance is mine, saith the profiler.'

He bowed his head in acknowledgement. 'I wish I'd paid more attention when Shaz first raised it. Maybe we could have achieved this without such a high price then.'

Carol reached out impulsively and covered his hand with hers. 'That's ridiculous, Tony. No one would have mounted an investigation on the basis of what she came up with at that classroom session.'

'I didn't mean that, exactly.' He ran his fingers through his hair. 'I meant that I'm supposed to be a psychologist. I should have seen that she wasn't going to let it go. I should have discussed it with her, made her feel that she wasn't being discounted, explored ways we could have taken the matter further without putting her at risk.'

'You might as well say it's Chris Devine's fault,' Carol said briskly. 'She knew Shaz was going to interview him and she let her go alone.'

'And why do you think Chris is spending her valuable time off tearing round Northumberland with Leon and Simon? It's not out of a sense of duty. It's out of a sense of guilt.'

'You can't take responsibility for them all. Shaz was a copper. She should have considered the risk. There was no need for her to go in like she did, so even if you had tried to stop her, she probably wouldn't have paid any attention. Let it go, Tony.'

He lifted his head and read the compassion in her eyes. He gave a rueful nod. 'We need to go official on this now, if we're going to avoid accusations that we're as out of control as Shaz was.'

Carol slipped her hand away from his. 'I'm glad you said that, because I'm starting to feel really edgy about uncovering hard evidence like this without any formal relationship to the investigation and no chain of custody on any of the physical evidence apart from "It was in my handbag, Guv." I keep thinking about the defence counsel making mincemeat out of me on the witness stand. "And so, DCI Jordan, you expect the jury to believe that on this maverick quest for justice – that only you, as opposed to the entire West Yorkshire force, could conduct – you just happened upon the one piece of evidence that links my client to the murder of DC Bowman, a woman he met once for less than an hour? And what is it your brother does again, Ms Jordan? Computer wizard, would that be a fair description? The sort of whizz kid who can make a digital image say anything he wants it to say?" We need to get this under

West Yorkshire's umbrella so they can construct the case properly.'

'I know. There comes a point where you have to stop playing at being the Lone Ranger and we're there now. We need to cover your back as well. In the morning, I'll go straight over to the murder room. How does that sound?'

'It's not that I want to wash my hands of this, Tony,' she said plaintively. 'It's just that we're going to lose it if we don't bring it in.'

He felt a rush of warmth towards her. 'I couldn't have achieved any of this alone. When Jacko Vance faces a jury, it'll be thanks to you coming on board.'

Before she could reply, her phone rang, splitting the closeness between them like an axe in wood. 'Oh, shit,' she said, grabbing the handset and hitting the button. 'DCI Jordan.'

The familiar voice of Jim Pendlebury came down the line. 'We've got what looks like another one, Carol. Paint factory. It's gone up like a torch.'

'I'll be there as soon as I can, Jim. Can you give me a locus?' Without being asked, Tony shoved pencil and paper across to her and she scribbled down directions. 'Thanks,' she said. She ended the call and closed her eyes momentarily. Then she hit the memory buttons and was connected to her communications room. 'This is DCI Jordan. Has there been anything from DS Taylor or DC Earnshaw?'

'Negative, ma'am,' came the anonymous voice. 'They were supposed to be maintaining radio silence unless they had something specific to their stakeouts.'

'Will you see if you can raise them and get them to meet me at the site of the paint factory fire on the Holt Industrial Estate. Thanks. Good night.' She looked at Tony, perplexed. 'It seems we were wrong,' she said.

'The arsonist?'

'He's struck again. But neither Tommy Taylor nor Di Earnshaw radioed in, so it looks as if it was neither of our suspects.' She shook her head. 'Back to square one, I guess. I'd better get over there and see what's going on.'

'Good luck,' Tony said as she pulled on her mac.

'It's you that'll need the luck, talking round Wharton and McCormick,' she said as he followed her down the hall. On the doorstep, she turned and impulsively put a hand on his arm. 'Don't beat yourself up about Shaz.' She leaned into him and kissed his cheek. 'Concentrate on beating up Jack the Lad.'

Then she was gone, leaving nothing behind but a shiver of her scent in the night air.

Above the blur of sodium and neon, it was a clear, starry night. From his eyrie on top of the Holland Park house, Jacko Vance stared out across the London night and imagined the Northumberland stars. There was a loose end, the only possible strand that could unravel and leave him stripped of his protective colouring. It was time for Donna Doyle to die.

He hadn't actually had to kill one for a long time now. It wasn't the killing he enjoyed. It was the process. The disintegration of a human being through the degradation of pain and infection. One had been defiant. She had refused to eat or drink or to use the chemical toilet. She'd been a challenge, but she hadn't lasted long. She had failed to consider the infective possibilities of piss and shit all over the floor. All she'd been thinking about was making herself too disgusting for him to touch, and she'd failed in that, too.

But he'd have to get rid of this particular Jillie soon. Her existence had been worrying him, a constant itch like a fleabite under a waistband. But while the police had been sniffing around after Shaz Bowman's death, he hadn't wanted to make an untoward move. An unscheduled dash for Northumberland would have been suspicious. The swift visit he had made hadn't been long enough to deal with the bitch properly. Then there had been Tony Hill's involvement to consider. Did the man have anything or was he just trying to rattle him into doing precisely the one thing that would expose him?

Either way, she had to go. That she might still be alive was a possibility that put him in mortal danger. He should have disposed of her on the night he killed Bowman, but he'd been afraid that his movements might come under too close scrutiny for comfort. Besides, he'd been too exhausted to have been certain of making a proper job of it.

He'd just have to rely on the invisibility of her hiding place, entombed beneath the stone flags. The only people who knew about the old crypt were the two builders he'd hired to install the perfectly engineered opening. Twelve years before, people had still believed in the nuclear threat. His talk of wanting to create a bomb shelter had gone down as merely eccentric among the locals. It would, he felt certain, be long forgotten.

Nevertheless, she had to go. Not tonight. He was filming early in the morning and he needed what sleep his apprehensions would allow him. But in a day or two, he could slip away overnight and see to the girl.

He'd have to make the most of it. It would have to be a little while before he could indulge himself again. A thought flickered into his mind. If he was ever going to feel safe again, perhaps Tony Hill needed to be taught a lesson more personal than Shaz Bowman. Jacko Vance gazed across the city and wondered if there was a woman in his life. He'd remember to ask his wife in the morning if Hill had said anything over dinner about a partner.

It had been no hardship killing Shaz Bowman. A repetition with Tony Hill's girlfriend could only be easier.

Hands thrust deep into the pockets of her mac, collar turned up against the harsh estuary wind, Carol Jordan stared stonily at the still smoking ruin of the paint factory. Her vigil was already three hours old, but she wasn't ready to leave yet. Fire officers, their distinctive yellow helmets smudged with greasy residue, moved in and out of the fringes of the building. Somewhere inside that creaking shell, some of them were trying to penetrate to the seat of the fire. Carol was beginning to accept that she didn't need the evidence of their eyes to know why Di Earnshaw hadn't responded to the control room's radio messages telling her to come to the fire site.

Di Earnshaw had been there already.

Carol heard a car draw to a halt behind her, but she didn't turn her head. A rustle of the crime scene tapes, then Lee Whitbread moved into her line of sight, proffering a carton of burger joint coffee. 'I thought you could probably do with this,' he said.

She nodded and took the brew wordlessly. 'No news, then?' he asked, his normally eager expression apprehensive.

'Nothing,' she said. She flipped off the polystyrene lid and raised the cup to her lips. The coffee was strong and hot, surprisingly good.

'There's been nothing at the station, neither,' Lee said, cupping his hands round his mouth to light a cigarette. 'I bobbed round her house, just to check, like, that she hadn't knocked off and gone home, but there's no sign. Bedroom curtains are still shut, so maybe she's got her head down and earplugs in?' Like every cop, his occupational pessimism was always tempered with hope when it appeared that a colleague was in line for a police funeral.

Carol couldn't bring herself to share even the fragile hope of earplugs. And if she knew Di Earnshaw wasn't the sort to go on the missing list, Lee must be doubly sure that his fellow DC was out of action for good. 'Have you seen DS Taylor?' she asked.

Lee hid his expression behind his hand as he smoked furiously. 'He says she never called in. He's back at the station, seeing if anything comes up there.'

'I hope he's coming up with something a little more imaginative than that,' Carol said grimly.

Three figures emerged from the dark hulk of the factory and pulled the breathing apparatus from their mouths. One detached himself from the other two and walked towards them. A few feet away from her, Jim Pendlebury came to a halt and pulled off his helmet. 'I can't tell you how sorry I am, Carol.'

Carol's head tilted back, then dropped in a tired nod. 'No doubt, I suppose?'

'There's always room for doubt until they've done the business down the path. lab. But we reckon it's a female, and there's what looks like a melted down radio next to the body.' His voice was soft with sympathy.

She looked up at his compassionate expression. He knew what it was like to lose people he was nominally responsible for. She wished he could tell her how long it would take before she could look herself in the mirror again. 'Can I see her?'

He shook his head. 'It's still too hot in there.'

Carol exhaled, a short, sharp sigh. 'I'll be in my office if anyone wants me.' She dropped the carton of coffee, turned away and ducked under the tapes, hurrying blindly in the direction of her car. Behind her, the coffee pooled on the Tarmac. Lee Whitbread flicked his cigarette butt into it, watching it fizz depressingly before dying. He looked up at Jim Pendlebury. 'Me too. We've got a fucking cop killer to nail now.'

Colin Wharton shuffled the pile of video stills together then leaned across and ejected the tape from the video recorder in the training suite that Tony's team had abandoned what felt like half a lifetime ago. Avoiding Tony's eye, he said, 'It proves nothing. OK, somebody else was driving Shaz Bowman's car back from London. It could be anybody behind that disguise. You hardly see anything of the guy's face, and these computer enhancements . . . *I* don't trust them, and juries are worse. By the time fucking Rumpole the defence brief's finished, they assume anything that's come from a computer's been doctored to make it show what we want it to show.'

'What about the arm? You can't doctor that. Jacko Vance has a prosthesis on his right arm. The man putting the petrol in never uses that arm at all. It's really noticeable,' Tony pressed.

Wharton shrugged. 'There could be all sorts of reasons for that. Could be that the man in question is left-handed. It could be that he'd hurt his arm in a struggle to overpower Bowman. It could even be that he knew about that daft bee Bowman had in her bonnet about Jacko Vance, and he decided to play on that. *Punters* know about video cameras now, Dr Hill. Vance *works* in the business – do you really think he's not going to have thought about cameras?'

Tony ran a hand through his hair, gripping the ends as if he were holding on to his temper. 'You've got Vance coming off the motorway at Leeds in his own wheels at the crucial time. Surely that's too much of a coincidence?'

Wharton shook his head. 'I don't think so. The man has a cottage in Northumberland. He does all that volunteer work up there. OK, the A1 might be the more direct route, but the M1's a faster road, and it's easy enough to pick up the A1 north of the city. He might even have decided he wanted fish and chips at Bryan's on the road,' he added with a pale attempt to lighten the atmosphere.

Tony folded his arms as if this would hold his dark anger inside. 'Why won't you take this seriously?' he asked.

'If Simon McNeill wasn't on the run, we might not assume everything you produce is tainted,' Wharton said angrily.

'Simon has nothing to do with this. He did not murder Shaz Bowman. Jacko Vance did. He is a cold-blooded killer. Everything I know about psychology tells me he killed Shaz Bowman because she threatened to bring his playhouse down about his ears. We've got pictures of him driving her car, she's nowhere in sight. Then in his car, covering the same ground. You've seen the psychological profile I prepared. What more do we have to do to persuade you to at least take a serious look at the man?'

The door behind him opened. DCS Dougal McCormick thrust his massive torso into the room. His face was the dark red of a man who'd had too much drink at lunchtime, a sheen of sweat gleaming on his fleshy cheeks. His light voice had dropped half an octave with the alcohol. 'I thought you were barred from here unless we came for you?' he added, stabbing a finger at Tony.

'I brought you the evidence to make a case against Shaz Bowman's killer,' Tony said, his voice weary now. 'Only Mr Wharton doesn't seem to be able to grasp its significance.'

McCormick shouldered his way into the room. 'Is that right? What have you got to say to that, Colin?'

'There's some very interesting motorway petrol station footage that's been computer-enhanced to show someone else driving Shaz Bowman's motor the afternoon she was killed.' Silently, he spread the pictures out for McCormick to check. The Chief Superintendent screwed up his dark eyes and studied them closely.

'It's Jacko Vance,' Tony insisted. 'He took her car back to Leeds, then made his way back to London before driving north again, presumably with Shaz in the boot.'

'Never mind Jacko Vance,' McCormick said dismissively. 'We've got a witness.'

'A witness?'

'Aye, a witness.'

'A witness to what, exactly?'

'A neighbour who saw your blue-eyed boy Simon McNeill going round the back of Sharon Bowman's flat the night she was killed and didn't see him come back out front again. I've got a team taking his place apart even as we speak. We were looking for him already, but now there'll be a public announcement. Maybe you'd know where we could find him, eh, Dr Hill?'

'You're the ones who disbanded my squad. How would I know where Simon is now?' Tony said, his voice a cold disguise for the frustration boiling inside.

'Ach, well, never mind. We'll be able to put our hand on him sooner or later. I've no doubt my boys will end up with something better to show a court than some videos your girlfriend's brother's tarted up.' Seeing Tony's startled expression, he nodded grimly. 'That's right, we know all about you and DCI Jordan. Do you really think we don't talk to each other in this job?'

'You keep telling me you're interested in evidence, not supposition,' Tony said, hanging on to his self-possession by sheer force of will. 'For the record, DCI Jordan is not now nor has she ever been my girlfriend. And my contention that Vance is the killer does not rely solely on the video evidence. I'm really not trying to teach you how to suck eggs, but at least look at the report I've drawn up. There's solid evidence there.'

McCormick picked the folder up from the table and flicked through it. 'A psychological profile is not what I'd call evidence. Rumour, innuendo, jealous people getting their own back. That's what you're relying on here.'

'His own wife says he's never slept with her. You're not telling me that's regarded as normal behaviour in West Yorkshire?'

'She might have all sorts of reasons for lying to you,' McCormick said dismissively, dropping the report with a soft rustle.

'He met Barbara Fenwick a couple of days before she was abducted and murdered. It's there, in Greater Manchester Police's murder file. One of his first ever charity events after the accident that destroyed his dream. We have photographs of him at later events with other girls who have disappeared and never been heard from again.' Tony's voice was discouraged now. He'd failed to establish a rapport that would have allowed the two policemen to back down and consider what he had to say. Worse than that, he seemed to have alienated McCormick to the point where if he said 'black', McCormick would retort, 'white'.

'A man like that meets hundreds of lassies a week and nothing ever happens to them,' McCormick said, sinking into a chair. 'Look, Dr Hill, I know it's hard to accept that you've had the wool pulled over your eyes, with you being a senior Home Office psychologist. But look at your man McNeill. He was in love with the lassie, and she doesn't seem to have felt the same about him. We've only got his word for it that she was supposed to be meeting him for a drink in advance of their night out with the other two. He was seen going round the back of the house at about the time she could have died. We've got his fingerprints on the glass of the French windows. And now he's done a disappearing act. You've got to admit, it's a hell of a lot more persuasive than a stack of circumstantial evidence against a man who's a national hero. What you're trying to do, Dr Hill, it's understandable. I'd probably feel the same as you if it was one of my officers in the frame. But face it, you made a mistake. You picked a bad apple.'

Tony stood up. 'I'm sorry we can't see eye to eye on this. I'm particularly sorry because I think Jacko Vance is holding another teenage girl prisoner, and she might still be alive. Gentlemen, there are none so blind as those who will not see. I sincerely hope your blindness doesn't cost Donna Doyle her life. Now, if you'll excuse me, I have work to do.'

Wharton and McCormick made no attempt to prevent him leaving. As he reached the door, Wharton said, 'It would better for McNeill if he didn't wait to be arrested.'

'I don't think so, somehow,' Tony said. Out in the car park, he leaned against the car door, head on folded arms. What the hell was left to do? The only senior police officer who believed his flimsy evidence was Carol, and she had no clout with West Yorkshire Police now, that much was clear. The evidence they still needed was the sort that came from TV reconstructions and nationwide press appeals; not resources available to a discredited psychologist, a pair of maverick cops from opposite ends of the country and a ragbag of junior detectives.

Conventional means had failed them. Now it was time to throw away the rule book. He'd done it before and it had saved his life. This time, it might just save someone else's.

Carol stood in the doorway of the squad room, fists on hips, glaring down the room. The news had travelled ahead of her and the only two detectives on the premises were clearly downcast by it. One was typing up notes, the other working bleakly through a wad of paperwork. Neither moved more than their eyes, a quick sidelong glance to register her arrival.

'Where is he?' Carol demanded.

The two detectives flicked their eyes towards each other, mutual understanding and decisions passing instantly between them. The one at the keyboard spoke, keeping his eyes on his work. 'DS Taylor, ma'am?'

'Who else? Where is he? I know he was here earlier, but I want to know where he is now.'

'He went out just after the news came through about Di,' the other man said.

'And where will he be?' Carol wasn't giving an inch. She couldn't afford to. Not for the sake of her future authority, but for her own self-respect. The buck stopped with her, and she had no wish to evade that responsibility. But she needed to understand how her operation had gone so disastrously wrong. Only one man might be able to tell her, and she was determined to find him. 'Come on,' she urged. 'Where?'

The two detectives exchanged another look. This time resignation was the key component. 'Harbourmaster's Club,' the typist said.

'He's in a drinking den at this time of the morning?' she demanded angrily.

'It's not just a bar, it's a club, ma'am. Originally for officers on merchant ships. You can get meals there, or just go in and read the papers and have a cup of coffee.' Carol turned to leave, but the typist continued. 'Ma'am, you can't go there,' he said, his voice urgent.

The look she gave him had induced rapists to confess. 'It's men only,' the young detective stammered. 'They won't let you in.'

'Jesus Christ!' Carol exploded. 'God forbid we should disturb the native customs. All right, Beckham, stop what you're doing and get down the Harbourmaster's Club. I want you and DS Taylor back here within half an hour, or I'll have your warrant card as well as his. Do I make myself clear?'

The file folder closed and Beckham jumped to his feet, brushing past her with an apology as he hurried out. 'I'll be in my office,' Carol growled at the remaining detective. She tried to slam the door behind her, but the hinges were too stiff.

Carol flopped into her chair, not even taking off her mac. Bleak self-reproach settled oppressively, immobilizing her. She stared emptily at the back wall where Di Earnshaw had stood during their briefing, remembering the dead fish stare, the badly fitting suit, the pug-nosed face. They'd never have been friends, Carol knew that instinctively, and in a way that made what had happened worse. Coupled with the guilt of Di Earnshaw's death in her own botched operation, Carol had the guilt of knowing she hadn't liked the woman very much, that if she'd been forced under duress to choose a victim from her command, Di wouldn't have been last on the list.

Carol ran through the case history again, wondering what she could have, should have done differently. Which was the decision that got Di Earnshaw killed? However she cut it, she came back to the same thing every time. She'd not kept a tight enough grip on the investigation, or a close enough eye on junior officers who weren't worried about discrediting her with their sloppy policing. She'd been too busy playing knight-in-shining-armour games with

Tony Hill. Not for the first time, she'd let her emotional response to him interfere with her judgement. This time, the consequences had been fatal.

The peal of her phone cut across her self-flagellation and she grabbed it in the middle of the second ring. Not even a major guilt-trip could stifle her instincts to the point where she could ignore a ringing phone on her office desk. 'DCI Jordan,' she said, her voice dull.

'Guv, it's Lee.' His voice sounded brighter than it had any right to be. Even as negative personality as Di Earnshaw had the right to a little more sorrow from her immediate colleagues.

'What have you got?' Carol asked brusquely, swivelling round in her chair to stare out of the window at the deserted windswept quay.

'I found her car. Tucked away down the side of one of the other warehouses, well out of sight. Guv, she had this little tape recorder. It was lying on the passenger seat, so I got one of the traffic lads to get me into the car. It's all there, name, time, route, destination, the lot. There's more than enough there to nail Brinkley!'

'Good work,' she said dully. Better than nothing, it still wasn't enough to assuage the guilt. Somehow, she knew that when she told Tony that, after all, he'd been right, he wouldn't consider it an acceptable trade-off either. 'Bring it in, Lee.'

She turned to replace the handset to find John Brandon standing in the doorway. Wearily, she started to get up, but he motioned her to stay seated, folding his long limbs into one of the comfortless visitor's chairs. 'A bad business,' he said.

'No one to blame but me,' Carol said. 'I took my eye off the ball. I left my officers to their own devices on an operation they all thought was a waste of time. They weren't taking it seriously, and now Di Earnshaw's dead. I should have stayed on their tails.'

'I'm surprised she was out there without back-up,' Brandon said. The words were censure enough without the look of reproach on his face.

'That wasn't the intention,' Carol said flatly.

'For both our sakes, I hope you can substantiate that.' It wasn't a threat, Carol realized, seeing the warmth of regret in his eyes.

Carol stared unseeing at the scarred wood of her desk top. 'Somehow, I can't get worked up about that now, sir.'

Brandon's voice hardened. 'Well, I suggest you do, Chief Inspector. Di Earnshaw doesn't have the luxury of feeling sorry for herself. All we can do for her now is take her killer off the streets. When can I expect an arrest?'

Stung, Carol jerked her head up and glared at Brandon. 'Just as soon as DC Whitbread gets back here with the evidence, sir.'

'Good.' Brandon got to his feet. 'Once you have a clearer idea what happened out there last night, we'll talk.' The ghost of a smile crossed his eyes. 'You're not to blame, Carol. You can't be on duty twenty-four hours a day.'

Carol stared at the empty doorway after he'd gone, wondering how many years it had taken John Brandon to learn how to let go. Then, weighing up what she knew of the man, she wondered if he ever had, or if he'd simply learned to hide it better.

Leon looked around, bemused. 'I thought Newcastle was supposed to be the last place on earth where men were men and sheep ran scared?'

'You got a problem with a vegetarian pub?' Chris Devine asked mildly.

Simon grinned. 'He only pretends he likes his meat raw.' He sipped his pint experimentally. 'Nothing wrong with the bevvy, though. How did you find out about this place?'

'Don't ask and you won't be embarrassed, babe. Just trust your senior officer, especially when she's a woman. So, how are we doing?' Chris asked. 'I got nowhere showing her picture round the station. Nobody in the buffet or the ticket office or the bookstall remembered seeing her.'

'The bus station was the same,' Simon reported. 'Not a sausage. Except that one of the drivers said, was it not that lass that went missing in Sunderland a couple of years back?' They contemplated the irony glumly.

'I got a sniff,' Leon said. 'I talked to one of the train guards, and he put me on to a cafe where all the drivers and guards go for a brew and a bacon butty on their breaks. I sat down with the guys and flashed the photos. One of them reckoned he was pretty sure he'd seen her on the Carlisle train. He remembered because she double-checked with him what time the train got into Five Walls Halt and that they were running on time.'

'When was this?' Chris asked, offering him an encouraging cigarette.

'He couldn't be sure. But he reckoned it was the week before last.' Leon didn't have to remind them that timetable would fit perfectly with Donna Doyle's disappearance.

'Where's Five Walls Halt?' Simon asked.

'It's somewhere in the middle of nowhere this side of Hexham,' Chris informed him. 'Near Hadrian's Wall. And presumably another four. And don't ask how I know that either, right?'

'So what's at Five Walls Halt that she'd want to get off there?'

Leon looked at Chris. She shrugged. 'I'm only guessing, but I'd say it might be somewhere near Jacko Vance's place in the country. Which, I don't have to tell you, we're not supposed to be going anywhere near.'

'We could go to Five Walls Halt, though,' Leon said.

'Not until you finish that pint, we can't,' Simon prompted.

'Leave the pint,' Chris instructed him. 'She can't have been the only one who got off the train there. If we're going knocking on doors, we don't want to smell like a brewery.' She got to her feet. 'Let's go and discover the beauties of the Northumberland country-side. Did you bring your wellies?'

Leon and Simon exchanged a look of panic. 'Thanks, Chris,' Leon muttered sarcastically as they trailed after her into the soft rain.

Alan Brinkley stood under the shower, the cascade of water almost scalding. The man who made the decisions had finally decreed that the officers who had fought the fierce fire at the paint factory could be stood down and replaced by a smaller crew who would damp down the hot spots and keep their fresh eyes peeled for anything significant among the wreckage. No one in authority was taking any chances now the body had been found.

At the thought of the body, a shudder convulsed Brinkley from head to foot. In spite of the steaming heat, his teeth chattered involuntarily. He wasn't going to think about the body. Normal, he had to be normal. But what was normal? How did he usually behave when there had been a fatal fire? What did he say to Maureen? How many beers did he drink the night after? What did his mates see in his face?

He slumped against the streaming tiles of the shower cubicle, tears falling invisibly from his eyes. Thank God for the privacy of the new fire station, not like the old communal showers they'd had when he'd learned his trade. In the shower now, no one could see him weep.

He couldn't get the smell out of his nostrils, the taste out of his mouth. He knew it was imagination; the chemicals in the paint factory overlaid any hint of incinerated flesh. But it was as real as it had ever been. He didn't even know her name, but he knew what she smelled like, what she tasted like now.

His mouth opened in a silent scream and he pounded with the sides of his fists against the solid wall, making no sound. Behind him, the shower curtain rattled back on its metal hoops. He turned slowly, pressing himself into the corner of the cubicle. He'd seen the man and the woman before, inside the scene-of-crime tapes at the fires. He watched the woman's lips move, heard her voice, but could not process what she was saying.

It didn't matter. He suddenly knew this was the only relief. He slid down the wall into a foetal crouch. He found his voice and started to sob like a damaged child.

Chris Devine was only a few miles out of Newcastle when her mobile rang. 'It's me, Tony. Any joy?'

She filled him in on the limited success of their morning, and in turn he told her about his failure to convince Wharton and McCormick to take him seriously. 'It's a nightmare,' he said. 'We can't afford to hang around indefinitely on this. If Donna Doyle is still alive, every hour could count. Chris, I think the only thing to do is for me to confront him with the evidence and hope we can panic him into a confession or an incriminating move.'

'That's what killed Shaz,' Chris said. Mentioning her name brought the grief back like a physical blow. If she could ignore the bright presence Shaz had been in her life and the darkness of her absence, she could get through this in a fair simulacrum of the normal breezy Chris Devine. But every time Shaz was mentioned by name, it knocked the breath from her. She suspected she wasn't the only one who suffered a reaction; it would explain why Shaz was seldom spoken of directly.

'I wasn't planning on going it alone. I need back-up.'

'What about Carol?'

There was a long silence. 'Carol lost an officer in the night.'

'Ah, shit. Her arsonist?'

'Her arsonist. She's beating herself up because she thinks her involvement in this made her derelict in her duty. She's wrong, as it happens, but there's no way she can walk away from her responsibilities in Seaford today.'

'Sounds like she's got more shit on her plate right now than anyone should ever have to eat. Yeah, forget Carol.'

'I'm going to need you down there, Chris. Can you bear to pull out and go back to London? Now?'

She didn't have to hesitate for a moment. When it came to catching the man who brutalized Shaz Bowman's beautiful face before destroying her soul, there wasn't much Chris would have refused. 'No problem. I'll flag the lads down and tell them.'

'You can tell them Kay's on her way, too. She was waiting for me when I got back from Leeds HQ this morning. I'll call her and tell her to head for Five Walls Halt station. She can meet Simon and Leon there.'

'Thank God there'll be one person there with a bit of common sense,' she said ironically. 'She can keep the lid on Die Hard one and two.'

'Getting a bit gung-ho, are they?'

'There's nothing they'd love more than kicking Jacko Vance's head in. Failing that, they'd settle for his front door.' She spotted a lay-by on the fast dual carriageway and indicated she was going to pull over, checking in her mirror that Simon and Leon were following.

'I was thinking of reserving that pleasure for myself.'

Chris gave a grunt of sardonic laughter. 'Join the queue, babe. I'll call you when I hit the M25.'

The officers in the canteen broke into a ragged round of applause as Carol and Lee Whitbread walked in. Carol nodded a distant acknowledgement, Lee doing better with a wan smile. Two coffees, two doughnuts, her treat, then they were out of there and heading back to the CID room. It would be at least an hour before Alan Brinkley's solicitor could get there, and till then, he was off limits.

Halfway up the stairs, she turned and blocked Lee's way. 'Where was he?'

Lee looked shifty. 'I don't know,' he mumbled. 'Must have been in a radio black spot.'

'Bollocks,' Carol said. 'Come on, Lee. This isn't the time for false loyalty. Di Earnshaw would probably still be alive if Taylor had been watching her back like he was supposed to. It could have been you. Next time it could be. So where was he? Over the side?'

Lee scratched his eyebrow. 'The nights we were on together, he stuck with it till gone midnight. Then he called in and said he were going for a bevvy to Corcoran's.'

'If he'd done that with Di, why would she have been shouting for back-up over the radio?' Carol demanded.

Lee squirmed, his mouth twisting awkwardly. 'He wouldn't have told Di. Not one of the lads, was she?'

Carol closed her eyes momentarily. 'You're telling me I've lost one of my officers because of traditional Yorkshire male chauvinism?' she said incredulously.

Lee dropped his eyes and studied the step he stood on. 'None of us thought owt would happen.'

Carol turned on her heel and marched upstairs, leaving Lee to trail in her wake. This time when she shouldered open the squad-room door, Tommy Taylor jumped to his feet. 'Guv,' he began.

'Chief Inspector to you. My office. Now.' She waited for him to move ahead of her. 'You know something, Taylor? I'm ashamed to work in the same squad as you.' The other detectives in the room suddenly developed total fascination with their routine tasks.

Carol kicked the door shut behind her. 'Don't bother sitting down,' she said, moving behind her desk and dropping into her chair. For this interview, she didn't need artificial aids like standing while her junior officer sat. 'DC Earnshaw is lying in the morgue incinerated because you went on the piss while you were supposed to be working.'

'I never . . .' he began.

Carol simply raised her voice and continued. 'There will be an official inquiry where you can bullshit all you like about radio black spots. By that time, I'll have statements from every drunk in Corcoran's. I am going to bury you, Taylor. Until you're officially drummed out of this force, you're on suspension. Now get out of my squad room and stay away from my officers.'

'I never thought she were at risk,' he said pathetically.

'The reason we get our wages is that we're always at risk,' Carol snapped. 'Now get out of my sight and pray you don't get reinstated because there isn't a cop in East Yorkshire who would piss on you if you were on fire.'

Taylor backed out, carefully closing the door behind him. 'Feel better now?' Carol said under her breath. 'And you're the woman who said she'd never pass the buck.' Her head dropped into her hands. She knew any inquiry would lay little blame at her door. It didn't stop her feeling that Di Earnshaw's blood stained her hands as much as Taylor's. And once the identification was official, she was the one who'd have to break the news to her parents.

At least she wouldn't have to worry about Jacko Vance and Donna Doyle any more. That, thank God, must be someone else's problem by now.

When Chris Devine had talked about knocking on doors, Simon and Leon had pictured a neat little village with two or three streets. Neither of them had considered the area served by a small station halfway between Carlisle and Hexham. Apart from the straggle of houses that made up Five Walls Halt itself, there were farms, smallholdings, outlying pockets of agricultural cottages now colonized by city commuters, holiday homes and cramped council estates snagged improbably in the distant corners of narrow valleys. They'd ended up in a tourist information office buying Ordnance Survey maps.

Once Kay arrived, they split the area among themselves, agreeing to meet back at the station at the end of the afternoon. It was a thankless task, but one that Kay was more successful with than the others. People always talked more to a woman on their doorstep than they ever would to a man. By late afternoon, she'd got two possible sightings of Donna Doyle. Both put her on their regular evening train home, but neither could be certain of the day.

She'd also discovered the location of Jacko Vance's hideaway. One of the doors she'd knocked on had belonged to the roofer who'd replaced the black slate roof of the former chapel only five years before. Her oblique raising of the subject and her gossipy questioning about Vance had left him unsuspicious. He would merely mention down the pub that night that women coppers were just like any other women when it came to being pushovers for a famous name with a nice smile and a big bank balance.

By the time the three reconvened, she had added a few more bits and pieces to her store of knowledge. Vance had bought the place a dozen years before, maybe six months or so after his accident. It hadn't been much more than four walls and a roof, and he'd spent a fair whack of cash on doing it up. When he'd married Micky, the locals had expected them to use it as a weekend cottage, but instead he'd used it more as a retreat; a useful base for the voluntary work he did at the hospital in Newcastle. No one knew why he'd chosen the area. He had no roots or connections to it as far as anyone knew.

Leon and Simon were excited by her information. They had little to offer themselves apart from a couple of dubious sightings of Donna. One put her in the station car park, getting into a vehicle. But the witness couldn't remember the day, the time or the make of the wheels. 'It's no coincidence that witness sounds very like witless,' Leon said. 'We're not getting anywhere with this shit. Let's go over Vance's place.'

'Tony said to stay away,' Simon objected.

'I'm not sure it's a good idea,' Kay agreed.

'What harm can it do? Listen, if he picked up the kid here and took her back to his gaff, chances are somebody local might have seen him. We can't just go back to Leeds now, not knowing this much.'

'We should call Tony first,' Simon said stubbornly.

Leon cast his eyes heavenwards. 'OK,' he sighed. He made great play of getting his phone out and tapping in a number. Neither of the others thought to check it was Tony's number. As the ringing tone continued without interruption, Leon said triumphantly, 'He's not answering, right? So what harm can it do if we go and check it out? Shit, that kid could still be alive, and we're talking about sitting on our butts till Christmas? Come on, we got to *do* something.'

Kay and Simon exchanged a look. Neither wanted to contradict Tony's orders. But equally, they were too infected with the glory of the chase to bear sitting around doing nothing while a young woman's life might be on the line. 'All right,' Kay said. 'But all we do is take a look around. Right?'

'Right,' said Leon enthusiastically.

'I hope so,' Simon said wearily. 'I really hope so.'

Chris Devine sipped a double espresso and drew deeply on another cigarette in an attempt to keep her tiredness at bay. At tea-time on a Sunday, the Shepherd's Bush diner was less lively than a funeral parlour. 'Run it past me again,' she commanded Tony.

'I go to the house. According to your contact's schedule for him,

Vance was supposed to be compering a charity fashion show in Kensington this afternoon, so he's not going to be in Northumberland.'

'Are you sure we shouldn't be hitting his place up there first?' Chris interrupted. 'If Donna Doyle's still alive . . .'

'And if she's not there? We couldn't start poking around without the locals noticing and probably getting straight on the phone to Vance. And then we're completely blown. At the moment, he doesn't know for sure that anybody's close to him. All he knows is that I've been sticking my nose in. That's the only advantage we've got. We have to go straight for the direct confrontation.'

'What if his wife's there? He's not going to risk her hearing anything you might have to say to him about Shaz.'

'If Micky and Betsy are there, he'll make damn sure he gets me out of their way before I get the chance to say a word. In a way, it's safer for me if they are around, since I'm more likely to get out in one piece.'

'I suppose so. You better take me through it, then,' she said, exhaling a cloud of smoke.

'I tell Jacko I've been working independently of the police and I've uncovered important video evidence relating to Shaz Bowman's death that I think he might be able to help us with. He'll let me in because I'm alone and he'll figure he can dispose of me the same way he got rid of Shaz if it emerges that I really am a lone maverick. I show him the enhanced video and the stills and accuse him. You are sitting outside in your car with a radio receiver and a tape recorder picking up everything that's transmitted from the mike in this natty little pen I bought in Tottenham Court Road on the way here.' Tony wiggled the pen in front of Chris's nose.

'You don't seriously think he's going to roll over?'

Tony shook his head. 'I think if he's alone, he'll try to kill me. And that's where you come in like the cavalry, leaping tall buildings with one mighty bound.' His words were light, but his tone was sombre. They looked bleakly at each other.

'So let's do it,' Chris said. 'Let's nail the fucker to a tree.'

It had taken them less than ten minutes to discover it was impossible to stake out Jacko Vance's converted chapel without being as obvious as a wolfhound in a flock of sheep. 'Fuck,' Leon said.

'I don't think he picked somewhere like this by chance,' Simon said, looking around at the bleak hillside opposite the hideaway. On either side of the gravel circle in front of the tall narrow building were fields of sheep held at bay by wire fences. Even in the thickening dusk, it was obvious there was neither human being nor habitation within sight.

'It's funny,' Kay mused. 'Normally, celebs like a bit of privacy. Gates, walls, high hedges. But you must be able to see this place for miles if you walked over the moors.'

'Cuts both ways, man,' Leon said. 'They can see you, but you get plenty of warning when anybody approaches you. Look at that road. Them fucking Romans didn't mess about, did they? Any Picts came looking for trouble, you'd see them soon as they hit the horizon.'

'He likes the kind of privacy where you can't be spied on,' Simon said. 'I reckon that means he's got a lot more to hide than some starlet sucking his toes.'

'And I reckon we ought to check out what it is,' Leon said.

They looked at each other for a long moment. Kay shook her head. Simon said, 'There is no way I'm going to be party to kicking Jacko Vance's door in.'

'Who said anything about kicking his door in?' Leon said. 'Kay, you talked to the guy that put the roof on this place. He say anything about locals that work here? Gardener, cleaner, cook? Anything like that?'

'Oh, yeah, like he's going to have a cleaner on premises where he's stashing murder victims,' Simon scoffed scornfully.

'This guy loves the double bluff,' Leon said. 'He loves putting one over on the stupid old plod. There's nothing would appeal to him more than having some old dear polishing the secret panel when he's got some kid chained up behind it. What did the guy say, Kay?'

'He didn't say anything,' she said. 'But if anybody knows that, chances are it's the nearest neighbour.'

'So who does the best Geordie accent?' Leon demanded, pointing directly at Simon.

'This is not a good idea,' he protested. Ten minutes later, he was knocking at the door of the first dwelling they came to, a large square farmhouse that faced out over the moorland towards Hadrian's Wall less than a mile away. He shifted from one foot to the other.

'Calm down,' Kay said. 'Just flash the warrant card dead fast. They'll never examine it closely.'

'We're going to lose our careers over this,' Simon muttered through clenched teeth.

'I'd rather chance that than let Shaz's killer walk.' Kay's frown changed to a radiant smile as the door opened on a small dark scowling man. It wasn't hard to imagine his Pictish ancestors making Roman lives a misery.

'Aye? What is it?'

They flipped their warrant cards open and closed in unison. The man looked momentarily confused, then resumed his glower. 'DC McNeill from Northumbria Police,' Simon gabbled. 'We've had a report of intruders at Mr Vance's place down the road. We can't obtain entry to the property, and we wondered whether you knew if there was a local keyholder?'

'Did the local man not tell you?' he demanded in an accent Kay found almost incomprehensible.

'Why no,' Simon said, laying on the Newcastle accent. 'We cannot get hold of him, with it being Sunday, like.'

'You want Doreen Elliott. Back down the road past Vance's place, gan down the first turning on the left and her cottage is down the dip. She keeps an eye on the place for him.' The door began to close.

'Thanks,' Simon said weakly.

'Aye,' the man said, shutting the door firmly in their faces.

Half an hour later, they had the keys to Jacko Vance's pied-a-terre in their possession. Unfortunately for them, they also had Mrs Doreen Elliott in the passenger seat of Kay's car, determined to make sure Jacko's precious property didn't come to harm in the clumsy hands of the police. Kay could only hope for the older woman's sake that they didn't find what she feared behind Jacko Vance's heavy wooden front door.

The gate had been released at the mention of his name and Tony walked up the drive, with each step becoming more immersed in the persona he had chosen for the encounter. He wanted Vance to think he was uncertain and capable of being outwitted. He would take control by appearing to be the weaker of the two. It was a risky strategy, but one he felt confident he could handle.

Vance had opened the door wreathed in smiles, greeting him by his first name. Tony could only allow himself to be swept inside, assuming a faintly confused look. 'I'm so sorry, you've missed Micky,' Vance said. 'She's spending the weekend with some friends in the country. But I didn't want you to go off without taking the opportunity to meet you face to face,' he continued as he ushered Tony in. 'Of course, I saw you on my wife's programme the other day, but I've been noticing you at all my events lately. You should have come over and introduced yourself, we could have had a chat before now, saved you coming all the way to London.' He was the model of charm and suavity, his words flowing calm and mollifying.

'Actually, it wasn't Micky I came to see. I wanted to talk to you about Shaz Bowman,' Tony said, trying to appear stiff and awkward.

A momentary look of puzzlement. Then Vance said, 'Ah, yes, the detective who was killed so tragically. Right. I had it in mind that it was something altogether other that you wanted to ... Are you actually working with the police on the case, then?'

'As you'll recall from the interview I did with your wife, I was in charge of the unit Shaz was on attachment to. So, naturally, I have taken a role in the investigation,' Tony said. Hiding behind formality would make Vance feel he was uncomfortable.

Vance's eyebrows rose, his dancing blue eyes teasing as they always seemed to on TV. 'I heard your role in the investigation was on the opposite side of the fence,' he said mildly. 'That you were answering questions rather than asking.'

Vance's inside information, however gleaned, could be turned to his own advantage, Tony realized. In a way, it actually played into the strategy he'd outlined to Chris. 'You have good sources,' he said, trying to sound grudging. 'But I can assure you that although I'm working independently of the police, the evidence I have uncovered will be placed in their hands at the appropriate time.' That planted the idea he was working solo.

'And what has all of this to do with me?' Vance leaned casually against the newel post of the staircase that curved upwards.

'I have some video footage that I think you might be able to cast some light on,' Tony said, patting his jacket pocket.

For the first time since his greeting, Vance looked slightly disconcerted. His face cleared momentarily and the golden boy smile was back. 'Then I suggest you come upstairs with me. I have a room on the top floor that I use for screenings for small and select audiences.' He stepped to one side and with a graceful sweep of his real arm indicated that Tony should climb ahead of him.

Tony mounted the stairs. He told himself it didn't matter which room they were in; Chris could still hear him, and if things turned dangerous, she'd have time enough to mount a rescue. He hoped.

He paused at the landing, but Vance silently directed him up the next flight. 'First door on the right,' he said as they emerged on the top landing, an astonishingly bright area lit by a four-sided pyramid skylight.

The room Tony entered was long and narrow. The far wall was mostly occupied by a video screen. To his left, bolted to the floor, was a tall trolley holding a video recorder and a film projector. Behind it, shelves built round an editing desk were crammed with video tapes and film canisters. A cluster of comfy-looking leather slings on wooden frames completed the furnishings.

The window was what should have made Tony's heart sink. Although it was transparent, it had clearly had some sort of coating applied to it. Had he paid the same attention to his surroundings as he did to their occupants, he'd have noticed the precaution previously in government buildings where things went on that officials didn't want to become common knowledge. The coating made the windows impervious to radio signals, preventing electronic eavesdropping. This, added to the baffles that covered the walls, ensured that the room was to all intents and purposes sealed to the outside world. He could scream all he liked. Chris Devine would no longer be able to hear him.

Chris stared at the Holland Park mansion, wondering what the hell to do. Tony and Vance's voices had been coming through loud and clear then suddenly, nothing. The last thing she'd heard had been Vance saying, 'First door on the right.' It wasn't even enough information to work out which room they were in, since she had no idea which way the staircase turned.

At first, she'd thought there was something wrong with the equipment – a loose wire, a dislodged battery. Terrible seconds raced past as Chris quickly checked what she could. But the reels of tape were still turning, although nothing was coming through on the receiver. She clutched her forehead, trying to figure out what was happening. Certainly there had been no sound of a struggle, no indication that the transmitter had been spotted. It could even be that Tony had turned it off. If, for example, he'd found himself in the kind of environment where electronic feedback might betray him. Vance had spoken of a special viewing room, the kind of place that might just house that sort of sensitive electronic gear.

She could feel herself dithering and hated herself for it. Anything could be happening to Tony. He was in a house with a killer, a man he fully expected to try to murder him.

She could, she supposed, try his mobile. They had agreed she would only use the phone as a last resort. Well, there was nothing else she could attempt in the face of radio silence. She hit the memory button that summoned his number and hit 'send'. Moments of nothing then the familiar three tones followed by the infuriatingly calm female voice intoning, 'I'm sorry. The Vodaphone you are calling has not responded. Please try later.'

'Shit, shit, shit,' Chris hissed. There was nothing else for it. She might blow Tony out of the water, but better that than cost him his life by wavering like this. Chris jumped out of her car and ran up the road towards the Vance mansion.

Oblivious to the danger he had walked into, Tony turned to face Vance. 'Smart set-up,' he said.

Vance couldn't help preening. 'The best money can buy. So, what was it you wanted me to look at?'

Tony handed him the video cassette and watched him slot it into the machine, noticing that here on his home ground Vance's handicap was almost unnoticeable. A jury might find it hard to believe that he could be as awkward as he appeared when filling Shaz Bowman's car with petrol. Tony made a mental note to suggest a restaging of the event for the court's benefit.

'Grab a seat,' Vance said.

Tony chose a chair where he could just see Vance in his peripheral vision. As the tape started to play, Vance used a remote control to dim the lights. Tony readied himself for the next stage of the confrontation. The first section showed the unenhanced sequence of the disguised Vance at the motorway filling station. Barely thirty seconds into the film, Vance made a low sound in the bottom of his throat, almost a growl. As it continued to play, the sound grew in volume and rose in pitch. Tony realized the man was laughing. 'Is that meant to be me?' he eventually squeezed out between laughter, turning his grinning face to Tony.

346

'It is you. You know it, I know it. And soon the rest of the world will know it,' Tony hoped he'd struck the right note, somewhere between bravado and whingeing. As long as Vance was confident he was in control, there was the chance he might make a mistake.

Vance's eyes flicked past him to the screen. In slo-mo, the enhanced video was playing. To anyone who knew who they were looking for, it was hard to resist the resemblance between the man on the video and the one with the remote control. 'Dear, oh dear,' he said sardonically. 'You think anyone's going to build a case on something as obviously doctored as that?'

'There's not just that,' Tony said mildly. 'Keep watching. I like the footage of you arriving back in Leeds to finish the job off.'

Ignoring him, Vance hit the button that stopped the tape. He flipped it out of the player and tossed it back to Tony, all with single-handed smoothness. 'I don't move like that,' he said contemptuously. 'I'd be ashamed of myself if I'd adapted that poorly to my disability.'

'It was an unfamiliar car, a strange situation.'

'You'll have to do better than that.'

Tony threw a copy of his report at Vance. His left hand shot out in a trained reflex and caught it. He opened it at the first page and glanced at it. For a moment, the skin round his mouth and eyes tightened. Tony could sense the sheer force of will that stopped him from a more powerful reaction. 'It's all there,' Tony said. 'A selection of your victims. Photographs of you with them. Their astonishing resemblance to Jillie. The mutilation of Barbara Fenwick. It's all tied in to you.'

Vance lifted his handsome face and shook his head pityingly. 'You haven't got a hope,' he said contemptuously. 'Circumstantial trash. A load of doctored photographs. Have you any idea how many people have their photographs taken with me in a year? The only surprising thing in statistical terms is that more of them don't end up murdered. You're wasting your time, Dr Hill. Just like DC Bowman before you.'

'You can't talk your way out of this, Vance,' Tony said. 'This goes way beyond coincidence. There isn't a jury in the land will fall for that.'

'There isn't a jury in the land that won't contain half a dozen of my fans. If they're told this is a witch-hunt, they'll believe me. If I hear another word of this, I will not only set my lawyers on you

347

but I will also go to the press and tell them about this sad little man who works for the Home Office and is obsessed with my wife. He's deluded, of course, just like all the sad little men who fall in love with an image on the TV screen. He thinks just because she had dinner with him that she'd fall into his arms if I was out of the picture. So he's trying to frame me for a bunch of non-existent serial killings. Let's see who ends up looking like a fool then, Dr Hill.' Gripping the folder under his right upper arm, Vance ripped it across.

'You killed Shaz Bowman,' Tony said. 'You've killed a lot of other girls, but you killed Shaz Bowman and you are not going to walk away from that. You can tear up my report as many times as you like, but we are going to get you.'

'I don't think so. If there was anything like evidence in this folder, there would be a team of senior police officers here. This is fantasy, Dr Hill. You need help.'

Before Tony could respond, a green light started flashing on the wall near the door. Vance strode over and picked up a handset. 'Who is it?' He listened for a moment. 'There's no need for you to come in, Detective. Dr Hill is just leaving.' He replaced the receiver and gave Tony a measured look. 'Well, Dr Hill? Are you? Or do I have to call police officers who will be rather more rational on the subject of DC Bowman than Sergeant Devine?'

Tony got to his feet. 'I'm not giving up on this,' he said.

Vance gave a shout of laughter. 'And my friends at the Home Office thought you had such a promising career. Take my advice, Dr Hill. Go on holiday. Forget about Bowman. Get a life. You've obviously been working too hard.' But his eyes were not laughing. In spite of his experience at presenting a facade for the world, even Jacko Vance could not prevent apprehension leaking out from behind his genial expression.

Tony resisted the impulse to show the jubilation he felt and began to descend the stairs with the air of a man drowned in defeat. He'd achieved almost exactly what he'd expected. It wasn't quite the same goal as he'd revealed to Chris Devine, since he hadn't been sure he could carry it off. Well satisfied, Tony plodded down the hall and through Jacko Vance's front door.

The chapel had been built for a small but passionately devout congregation. It was simple but genuinely beautiful in its proportions,

Kay thought as she stood in the doorway. The conversion to living space had been done tastefully, retaining the sense of airiness. Vance had chosen furnishings with simple, uncluttered lines, the only ornamentation a series of bright gabbeh rugs scattered over the stone flags of the floor. The single room had a galley kitchen, a small dining area and a sitting space with a couple of sofas angled round a big low slate table. At the far end, a raised sleeping gallery had been built. Underneath was what looked like a workbench fitted out with tools. Kay felt the clench of excitement in her stomach as she watched Simon and Leon range through the room, ostensibly looking for signs of the fictitious intruder.

By her side, Doreen Elliott stood foursquare and firm, a squat blunt obelisk of a woman in her fifties with a face as impassive as the massive stones of Hadrian's Wall itself. 'Who did you say reported the intruder?' she demanded, jealously guarding her rights as custodian of Jacko Vance's privacy.

'I don't know exactly,' Kay said. 'I think the call came from a car phone. Someone driving past saw a flickering light inside, like a torch.'

'Must be a quiet night for three of you to come out on something like this.' Her acerbic tone indicated that the local police generally failed to meet her exacting standards.

'We were in the area,' Kay said. 'It was easier to divert us than to send out other officers. Besides,' she added with a confiding smile, 'when it's someone like Jacko Vance involved, well, I suppose we try a bit harder.'

'Hmmph. What do they think they're looking for, that pair?'

Kay looked down the room where Simon seemed to be scanning the floor, lifting the corners of rugs with his toe and peering underneath. Leon was methodically opening kitchen cupboards and drawers, looking, she knew, for any indication that Donna Doyle might have been here.

'Just checking nothing obvious is missing, and there's nowhere for anyone to hide,' she said. Simon had given up on the rugs and moved on to the workbench. She saw his back stiffen as he got closer. His steps changed almost to a prowl and he angled his head all the better to study whatever had caught his attention. He turned to face them, and Kay saw the brightness of discovery in his eyes.

'Looks like Mr Vance is quite into woodwork,' Simon said, gesturing with his head to Leon.

'He makes wooden toys for the bairns in the hospital,' Mrs Elliott said, as proudly as if he were her own son. 'He cannot do enough for them. Never mind the George Cross, they should give him a medal for the hours he puts in with people at death's door. You cannot measure the comfort he gives folk.'

Leon had joined Simon at the workbench. 'Some serious kit here,' he said. 'Man, these chisels are sharp as razors.' His face was sombre and grim. 'And you want to see this vice, Kay. I've never seen anything like it.'

'He needs that to hold the wood,' Mrs Elliott said firmly. 'With his arm the way it is, he cannot manage without it. He calls it his extra pair of hands.'

Tony trudged down Vance's drive, head down, the sound of the slamming door still ringing in his ears. He raised his eyes and caught Chris's anxious look. Giving her a broad wink, he maintained his dejected body language until he was through the electronic gates and back on the street, hidden from the house by the high hedge.

'What the fuck happened in there?' Chris demanded.

'What do you mean? I was just getting into my stride when you butted in,' Tony protested.

'You went off the air. I didn't know what the hell was going on.'

'What do you mean, I went off the air?'

'It just went dead. He said, "First on the right," then total silence. For all I knew, he'd topped you.'

Tony frowned, trying to work out what had happened. 'He must have that room electronically shielded,' he eventually said. 'Of course. The last thing he'd want is anyone doing any snooping round him that he didn't know about. It never crossed my mind.'

Chris cupped her hands against the wind and lit a cigarette. 'Jesus,' she exploded softly in a long stream of smoke. 'Don't ever give me a fright like that again. So what happened? Did he cough? Don't tell me he coughed and we didn't get it on tape?'

Tony shook his head, walking her across the street to where he'd parked his car in full view of Vance's house. He glanced back and was pleased to see his target standing at a window on the top floor looking down at them. 'Get in my car for now, I'll explain,' he said.

He started the engine and drove round the corner. 'He poured scorn on the evidence,' Tony said as he turned into another street, doubling back to get behind where Chris was parked a couple of hundred yards from Vance's gate, out of the line of sight from the house. 'He made it plain that he thought we had nothing on him and that if we didn't call off the dogs he'd come after me.'

'He threatened to kill you?'

'No, he threatened to go to the papers and make an idiot of me.'

'You sound pretty pleased with yourself for somebody that just blew their big showdown,' Chris said. 'I thought he was supposed to either roll over and spill his guts or else try to top you?'

Tony shrugged. 'I didn't really expect him to confess. And if he was going to kill me, I don't think he'd have done it on the spot. He might have convinced Wharton and McCormick that there was nothing sinister about Shaz visiting him before she died, but I think even they would have to pay attention if I was killed after I'd just been to Vance's house. No, what I wanted to do was unsettle him to the point where he starts to worry how well he's covered his tracks.'

'And what good does that do?' She wound the window down an inch to flick her ash clear.

'With a bit of luck, it sets him off like a clockwork mouse, straight for his killing ground. He needs to make sure there's nothing that can incriminate him in the unlikely event that I could ever persuade the police to apply for a search warrant.'

'You think he'll go now?'

'I'm banking on it. According to his schedule, he's got nothing on tomorrow until a meeting at three. After that, the week starts looking horrendous. He's got to go for it now.'

Chris groaned. 'Not the M1 *again*.'

'You up for it?'

'I'm up for it,' she said wearily. 'What's the plan?'

'I go now. He's seen me drive off with you, so he should think the coast's clear. I'll head on up to Northumberland and you try to stay with him when he emerges. We can keep in touch by phone.'

'At least it's dark,' she said. 'Hopefully he won't notice the same headlights in his rear-view mirror.' She opened the door and got out, leaning back in to speak. 'I can't believe I'm doing this. All the bloody way down from Northumberland to London just to turn round and go back there again. We must be demented.'

'No. Just determined.'

He was that, all right, Chris thought as she walked to her car and watched Tony do a three-point turn and return the way he'd come. God, she thought. It was already seven. Five, six hours back to Northumberland. She hoped there wasn't going to be too much action at the other end of the trip because she would be dead on her feet.

She tuned the radio to a golden oldies station and settled down to sing along with the sixties. She didn't have long to harmonize before the gates of Vance's house slid back and the long silver nose of his Mercedes appeared. 'You fucking beauty,' she said, turning on her ignition and rolling forward to keep him in her sights. Holland Park Avenue, then up to join the A40. As they headed out through Acton and Ealing, Chris felt a vague sense of uneasiness. This wasn't just the pretty way to Northumberland. It was perverse. She couldn't believe he was going to drive all the way out west to the orbital M25 just to circle round to the northbound M1.

She stayed close enough not to lose him at the lights, always managing to keep a single car between them. It was hard driving, but at least the streetlights helped. Eventually, the signs for the M25 appeared and Chris prepared to take the slip road even though Vance showed no signs of leaving the carriageway. Probably do a last-minute lane change, she thought, if he thinks he might have a tail.

But he didn't move and it was she who had to do the last-minute rescue, stamping on the accelerator to keep in touch with his tail lights. She only made it because he was driving a scant handful of miles above the limit, like a man who absolutely doesn't want to be stopped for speeding. She grabbed her phone and hit the recall button for Tony's number.

'Tony? It's Chris. Listen, I'm on the M40 heading west tight on Jack the Lad's tail. Wherever he's going, it's not Northumberland.'

The discovery of the vice injected a new urgency into the search. Acutely aware of how bizarre this must seem to Doreen Elliott, Kay desperately tried to distract her with conversation. 'They made a lovely job of converting this place,' she said brightly.

It was clearly the right thing. Mrs Elliott turned to the kitchen and ran a hand along the polished smoothness of the solid wood. 'Our Derek did the kitchen. He wanted no expense spared, like. Everything you could possibly want, all the latest stuff.' She pointed to the cupboard fronts. 'Washer-dryer, dishwasher, fridge, freezer, all tucked away.'

'I'd have thought he'd have brought his wife up with him more often,' Kay tried.

It was clearly the wrong thing. Mrs Elliott frowned. 'Well, he told us they'd be using it as a weekend place. But in the end, she never came. He said she was too much of a city girl. She doesn't like the country, you see. Well, you only have to look at her on that TV programme to see she'd not fit in with the likes of us. Not like Mr Vance.'

'What, she's never been here at all?' Kay tried to sound as if this was news to her. She had half her attention on Simon and Leon, but she was still keeping watch on Mrs Elliott's reactions. 'We're just trying to work out who else might have a key. For security reasons,' she added hastily as the older woman's face grew more slab-like.

'Never seen hide nor hair of her.' Then a smirk. 'That's not to say there's never been a woman's hand on the place. Well, a man's entitled to his compensations if his wife cannot bring herself to share his interests.'

'You've seen him here with other women, then?' Kay asked, aiming for casual.

'Not actually seen him, no, but I come in once a fortnight to give the place a clean, and there's been a couple of times I've unloaded the dishwasher and there's been glasses with lipstick traces. It doesn't always come off in the machine, you see. So putting two and two together, I suppose he's got a girlfriend. But he knows he can rely on us to keep our mouths shut.'

Only because no one's ever asked you, Kay thought cynically. 'As you say, if his wife won't come to a place like this . . .'

'It's a palace,' Mrs Elliott said, doubtless comparing it to the dark kitchen of her own cottage. 'I tell you something: I bet it's the only house in Northumberland with its own private nuclear shelter.'

The words fell into the conversation like a bomb.

'A nuclear shelter?' Kay asked faintly. Simon and Leon froze where they stood like gun dogs on point.

She mistook the stillness of their surprise for doubt. 'Right under our feet,' Mrs Elliott said. 'I'm not making this up, pet.'

*   *   *

Chris had barely finished the call to Tony when she saw the tail lights ahead of her wink to indicate that Vance was about to take the next slip road. Chris followed, leaving her move to the last possible moment. They turned north then, a couple of miles from the motorway, Vance signalled a left turn. At the junction, Chris slowed down and saw something that made her swear like a football supporter.

She switched off her main lights and drove cautiously down the narrow lane on sidelights only. She rounded a bend and there on her left was Jacko Vance's destination.

The private airfield was floodlit. Parked on a strip of Tarmac, Chris saw a dozen small planes standing in front of four hangars. She watched Vance's headlamps cut twin cones through the darkness round the perimeter then be swallowed up in the greater brightness as he drew up behind one of the planes. A man jumped out of the cockpit and waved. Vance got out of his car and walked to the plane, greeting the pilot with a clap on the shoulder.

'Oh, fuck,' Chris said. For the second time in the space of an hour, she had no idea what to do. Vance could have chartered the plane to get him to Northumberland ahead of any possible pursuit. Or he could have chartered it to get him out of the country. A quick flight across the Channel into the open borders of Europe and he could be anywhere by morning. Should she opt for dramatic intervention or leave him to take off?

It was a gamble, and one she didn't want to take responsibility for. Her eyes scanned the airfield, settling on the small control tower that jutted out beyond the furthest hangar. Then she saw Vance and the pilot disappear aboard. Seconds later, the propellers stuttered into life. 'Fuck it,' Chris said and put the car in gear. She raced round the airport perimeter fence and reached the control tower just as the small plane taxied out on to the runway.

She raced inside, startling the man who sat at a plotting desk beside a computer. Chris thrust her warrant card in his face. 'That plane on the runway. Has it filed a flight plan?'

'Yeah, yeah, he has,' the man stammered. 'He's going to Newcastle. Is there some sort of a problem? I mean, I can tell him to abort his take-off if there's a problem. We're always keen to help the police . . .'

'No problem,' Chris said grimly. 'Just forget you ever saw me, OK? No little radio messages saying anybody was interested, OK?'

'No, I mean yes, whatever you say, officer. No messages.'

'And just to make sure,' Chris said, pulling up a chair and giving him the predatory smile that sucked confessions from hard men, 'I'm staying right here.' She pulled out her phone and called Tony. 'Sergeant Devine,' she said. 'Subject is aboard private plane, destination Newcastle. You're going to have to deal with it from here on in. Suggest you organize a reception committee with the troops on the ground at his ultimate destination. OK?'

A bemused Tony stared at the shifting lights ahead of him on the motorway and said, 'Oh, shit, a plane? I take it you can't speak freely?'

'Correct. I'm staying here to make sure subject isn't given a warning by the control tower.'

'Ask him how long it'll take to Newcastle.'

There was a muffled conversation, then Chris came back on the line. 'He says they're flying an Aztec, which should do it in about two and a half to three hours. No chance you can beat the clock.'

'I'll do what I can. And Chris – thanks.' He ended the call and carried on driving on automatic pilot. So, somewhere between two and a half and three hours? Then he'd have to find his way to Five Walls Halt, either by taxi or by hiring a car, which wouldn't be easy at ten o'clock on a Sunday night. Even so, Tony realized Chris was right. There was no way he could possibly arrive at Vance's bolt hole ahead of him.

'Which is why he did it, of course,' he said aloud. Vance was no fool. He would expect Tony to know about his other home and to make for there once he'd stirred things up. What Vance hadn't known was that Tony already had three police profilers in Northumberland. At least, he presumed they were still making inquiries up there, since he'd heard nothing to the contrary. Come to that, he'd heard nothing since mid-afternoon, when he'd checked in with Simon to discover that they were going door-to-door in a bid to trace any sightings of Donna Doyle.

It wasn't enough, though. Three junior CID officers, none from the local force, none with any experience of command. They'd be uncertain, not knowing when or whether to challenge Vance. They wouldn't know when to hang back and when to move. It needed more than any of them had to give. There was only one person who could get there in time and keep Leon, Simon and Kay in check.

She answered on the second ring. 'DCI Jordan.'

'Carol? It's me. How are you doing?'

'Not good. To be honest, I'm grateful for the human contact. I've been feeling like a leper. I'm an outcast from the infantry because they think I'm partly responsible for Di Earnshaw's death. I'm isolated from John Brandon because there will have to be an inquiry which he can't be seen to influence. And I'm out of the loop when it comes to questioning Alan Brinkley in case I compromise the interrogation for personal reasons. And I have to tell you that breaking the news to her parents left me feeling that the Ancient Greeks' method of dealing with bad news must sometimes have been a relief to the messenger.'

'I'm sorry. You must wish now I hadn't dragged you into this Vance business,' he said.

'I don't,' she said firmly. 'Somebody's got to put a stop to Vance, and nobody else would listen to you. I don't blame you for what went wrong in Seaford. That's my responsibility. I shouldn't have tried to do surveillance on a shoestring. I knew you were right and I should have carried that conviction through and demanded the bodies to do the job properly instead of settling for a skeleton crew. If I had, Di Earnshaw would still be alive.'

'You can't know that for sure,' Tony protested. 'Anything could have happened. Her partner could have gone for a piss at the crucial moment, they could have separated to circle the building. If anyone's to blame, it's the sergeant. Not only were they supposed to look out for each other, he was her immediate boss. He owed her a duty of care and he failed her.'

'And what about my duty of care?'

Tony shook his head. 'Oh, Carol, ease up on yourself.'

'I can't. But enough of that. Where are you? And what's happening with Vance?'

'I'm on the M1. It's been a complicated day.' As he hammered on in the outside lane oblivious to anything but the traffic and the woman on the end of the phone, he brought Carol up to speed.

'So now he's somewhere between London and Newcastle?' Carol asked.

'That's right.'

'You're not going to make it in time, are you?'

'No.'

'But I could?'

'Possibly. Probably, if you stuck the blue light on. I can't ask you to, but I . . .'

'There's nothing for me to do here. I'm off duty, and nobody's going to call out the CID leper tonight. I'm better off doing this than sitting here feeling sorry for myself. Get me some directions. I'll call you when I get near Newcastle.' Her voice was stronger and firmer than it had been at the start of the call. Even if he'd wanted to argue, he realized it would have been pointless. She was the woman he'd taken her for, and she wouldn't walk away from a challenge.

'Thanks,' he said simply.

'We're wasting time talking.' Abruptly, the line went dead.

The price of Tony's skill was the empathy he brought to situations like this. He understood precisely what Carol was going through. Very few people ever experienced a justified sense of responsibility for the death of another human being. Everything Carol had been certain of had suddenly shifted on to shaky ground and no one who had not shared a similar experience could help her back to terra firma. But he understood and he cared enough to try. He suspected that his phone call had, serendipitously, been the first step in the right direction. Hoping he was correct, Tony stared into the narrowing tunnel of red lights and carried on driving north.

On the exact location of the entrance to the basement shelter, Mrs Elliott was rather more vague. 'It's under the flags somewhere. He had a couple of lads from Newcastle over to install it so that you cannot see it just by looking.'

The three police officers glared in frustration at the metre-square stone slabs that made up the floor. Then Simon said, 'If you can't see it, how do you get down there?'

'Our Derek said they'd installed an electric motor,' Mrs Elliott said.

'Well, if there's a motor, there's gotta be a switch,' Leon muttered. 'Si, you start on the right-hand side of the door. Kay, you start on the left. I'll go up to the sleeping gallery.' The two men moved away and started flicking switches, but Kay was held back by Mrs Elliott's hand on her sleeve.

'What do you need to find the shelter for?' she asked. 'I thought you said there was supposed to be a prowler? They're not going to be down there.'

Kay dug out her most reassuring smile. 'When we're dealing with a celebrity like Mr Vance, we have to be especially careful. A prowler in his house could be a lot more serious than a straightforward burglar. If someone was stalking him, for example, they could be hiding in waiting for him. So we have to take this extremely seriously.' She covered the woman's hand with her own. 'Why don't we wait outside?'

'What for?'

'If there is someone down there, it could be very dangerous.' Kay's smile felt strained. If Donna Doyle was trapped in the cellar, discovering her would be a revelation that would give even the stolid Doreen Elliott nightmares for the rest of her life, Kay knew. 'It's our job to protect members of the public, you know. How do you think my boss would react if I let you be taken hostage by some nutter with a knife?'

Mrs Elliott let herself be led into the tiny porch with only a single backward glance at Simon and Leon moving round the room snapping switches on and off. 'You think it's a stalker, then?' she asked avidly. 'Up here?'

'It wouldn't necessarily be someone from around here,' Kay said. 'These people are obsessive. They'll follow a celebrity for weeks, months, learning every detail of their life and routine. Have you seen any strangers hanging around?'

'Well, we get the tourists and the hikers, but mostly they're only here for the wall. They don't hang about.'

Before Kay could say more, her phone rang. 'Will you excuse me? I'll only be a minute,' she said, slipping back inside to take the call. 'Hello?'

'Kay? It's Tony. Where are you?'

Oh, shit, she thought. Why me? Why couldn't he have phoned Leon? 'Er . . . we're inside Jacko Vance's house in Northumberland,' she said. Simon glanced across at her, but she waved to him to continue his search.

'What?' Tony exclaimed, outraged.

'I know you said to wait, but we kept thinking about Donna Doyle . . .'

'You broke in?'

'No. We're perfectly entitled to be here. A local woman has a key. We informed her there had been reports of a prowler and she let us in.'

'Well, you'd better get out asap.'

'Tony, she could be here. This place has got a sealed basement. Vance told the builders he wanted a nuclear shelter.'

'A nuclear shelter?' His incredulity was palpable.

'It was a dozen years ago. People still believed Russia was going to nuke us,' Kay reminded him plaintively. 'The point is, she could be down there and we wouldn't hear her, not even standing right above her. We've got to find the door.'

'No. You've got to leave it. He's on his way there. He's chartered a plane, Kay. He's probably coming up there to make sure he's not left any loose ends. Kay, we need to catch him in the act. We need to stake the place out and watch him go down there to an untouched crime scene.'

As he spoke, Kay looked on in amazement as the ground moved only feet away from her. Silently, a single slab tilted and swung open in response to a switch flicked by Simon. As the fetid air escaped, Kay gagged. Recovering herself, she said, 'It's too late for that. We've found the door.'

Simon was already at the opening in the floor, peering down a set of stone steps. His groping hands found a switch and flooded the area with light. A long moment passed then he turned to Kay, his face the colour of putty. 'If that's Tony, you better tell him we've found Donna Doyle, as well.'

He drummed his fingers gently against the arm rest, the only movement in a body still as a lion preparing for the pounce. He didn't even brace himself against the jolts of the pockets of turbulence the small twin-engined plane hit occasionally, but let his body shift with the movement. Once upon a time, he used to bite the nails of his right hand when he was nervous. Losing his arm had been an extreme cure for a bad habit, he was fond of saying wryly in public. Now, he had cultivated stillness, understanding that nervous tics made nothing happen faster or easier. Besides, stillness was much more unsettling for everyone else.

The engine note changed as the pilot prepared to land. Jacko peered out of the window, staring down at the smudge of suburban streetlights through the fine rain. He'd left Tony Hill standing. There was no way he could have beaten the aircraft. And he had no back-up, Jacko knew from his own discreet inquiries, confirmed by what both Micky and Tony himself had admitted.

The wheels hit the runway and jolted him against his seatbelt. A slight swerve, a correction, then they were heading for the flying club hangars at a gentle taxi. They had barely come to a standstill when Jacko had the door open. He jumped to the Tarmac and looked around, his eyes searching for the familiar shape of his Land Rover. Sam Foxwell and his brother were always glad to earn the twenty quid he paid them whenever he needed the Land Rover brought to the airport and when he'd spoken to them from the car phone, they'd promised to have it there for him.

When he couldn't spot it, he felt a shiver of panic. They couldn't have let him down, not tonight of all nights. The pilot interrupted his thoughts, pointing to the side of the hangar in deep shadow. 'If you're looking for your Land Rover, I think it's tucked round there. I noticed it when I was taxi-ing.'

'Cheers.' Jacko dug into his pocket and took a twenty-pound note from his money clip. 'Have a beer on me. See you soon, Keith.'

As he thundered along the narrow Northumberland side roads that were the quickest route to the place he considered his real home, he reviewed what he had to do in the couple of hours' grace he had before Tony Hill could possibly arrive. First, check if the bitch was still alive and if she was, see she didn't stay that way. Then, take the chain saw to her, get her bagged and into the Land Rover. Clean the basement with the high-pressure hose and set off for the hospital. Would he have time? Or should he simply disable the motor that opened the door on its swivel? After all, Hill had no way of knowing about the basement shelter and the local police were not going to mount a search on his say-so, not when it would offend an upstanding local taxpayer like Jacko Vance. And there was no guarantee that Tony Hill would even show up.

Maybe he should just settle for making sure she was dead and leave the clearing up for later. There would be a certain delight in entertaining Tony Hill only feet away from his latest victim. His mouth twisted in an ugly snarl. Donna Doyle would have to be his last victim for a while. Damn the man. Tony Hill should have let sleeping bitches lie. Jacko had plans for Tony Hill, though. One day, when it had all gone quiet and Tony Hill had resigned himself to the fact that he'd failed, that plan would go into action and he'd wish he'd never stuck his nose into someone else's business.

The headlights sliced through the deep darkness of the countryside, breasting the hill that rolled down to his sanctuary. Where there should have been nothing but blackness, light spilled out over the cropped moorland grass and the grey gravel of his drive. Jacko stamped on the brakes and the Land Rover screamed to a jittering halt. What the fuck?

As he sat there, mind racing, adrenaline pumping, a pair of head-lights on full beam crept up behind him, angling across the narrow road so there was no possibility of going backwards. Slowly, Vance took his foot off the brake and let the Land Rover cruise down the hill towards his home. The lights shifted and fell into convoy behind him. As he grew closer, he saw a second car parked diagonally just beyond his gateway, effectively blocking the road beyond.

Vance drove on to his property, the cold grip of fear in his stomach focusing his mind. When he rolled to a halt he jumped out of his vehicle, every inch the outraged householder, and con-fronted the young black man standing in his doorway. 'What the hell's going on?' he demanded.

'I'm afraid I'm going to have to ask you to wait outside, sir,' Leon said deferentially.

'What do you mean? This is my house. Has there been a burglary or what? What's going on? And who the hell are you?'

'I'm Detective Constable Leon Jackson of the Metropolitan Police.' He held out his warrant card for inspection.

Vance switched the charm on. 'You're a long way from home.'

'Pursuing an investigation, sir. It's amazing where a line of inquiry can take us in these days of electronic communications and efficient travel networks.' Leon's voice was impassive, but his eyes never left Vance.

'Look, you know who I am, obviously. You know this is my place. Can't you at least tell me what the hell is going on?'

A horn beeped and Vance turned to see the car that had followed him down the hill stop just outside the gate, blocking the road in the opposite direction. He was hemmed in completely. Jesus, he hoped the bitch was dead. Another young man got out of the car and walked across the gravel. 'Are you from the Metropolitan Police as well?' Vance asked, forcing himself to maintain his professionally beguiling mode.

'No,' Simon said. 'I'm from Strathclyde.'

'*Strathclyde?*' Vance was momentarily confused. He'd taken someone from London few years ago, but he'd never brought any-one down from Scotland. He hated the accent. It reminded him of

Jimmy Linden and all that meant to him. So if there was a cop here from Scotland, they couldn't be tracking the girls. It was going to be fine, he told himself. He could walk away from this.

'That's right, sir. DC Jackson and myself have been working on different aspects of the same case. We were in the area and we had a report from a passing motorist of a prowler here. So we thought we'd better check it out.'

'That's very commendable, officers. Perhaps I could go inside and check to see if anything's missing or broken?' He moved to edge around Leon, but the policeman was too fast for him. He extended his arm, blocking Vance, and shook his head.

'I'm afraid not, sir. It's a crime scene, you see. We need to make sure nothing interferes with it.'

'A crime scene? What on earth has happened?' Concerned, try to sound concerned, he warned himself. This is your house, you're an innocent man and you want to know what's happened on your property.

'I'm afraid there's been a suspicious death,' Simon said coldly.

Jacko made himself take what looked like an involuntary step backwards, covering his face with his hands to make sure no sign of the relief that flooded him was visible to the police. She was dead, hallelujah. A dead woman could never testify. He pasted an expression of worried anxiety on his face and looked up. 'But that's terrible. A death? Here? But who ... How? This is my home. Nobody comes here except me. How can there be someone dead here?'

'That's what we're trying to establish, sir,' Leon said.

'But who is it? A burglar? What?'

'We don't think it was a burglar,' Simon said, trying to keep the lid on the rage he felt face to face with the man who had killed Shaz and who was trying to pretend he had nothing to do with the putrefying mess in his cellar.

'But ... the only person who has keys is Mrs Elliott. Doreen Elliott at Dene Cottage. It's not ... It's not her?'

'No, sir. Mrs Elliott is in excellent health. It was Mrs Elliott who let us in to the property and gave us permission to search. One of our colleagues has taken her home.' There was something in the way the black cop held his stare when he said this that sent a tremor of fear skittering round Vance's nerves. The message coming through loud and clear between the spoken words was the unspoken warning that his first line of defence had crumbled. This was not an illegal entry and search.

'Thank God for that. So who is it?'

'We can't speculate at this point, sir.'

'But you must be able to tell me if it's a man or a woman, surely?'

Simon's lip curled. He could hold back no longer. 'As if you didn't know,' he said, his voice thick with angry contempt. 'You think our heads button up the back?' He turned away, his hands balling into fists.

'What is he talking about?' Vance demanded, moving into the angry mode of the innocent bystander who senses they're about to become snagged up in someone else's trouble.

Leon shrugged and lit a cigarette. 'You tell me,' he said negligently. 'Oh good,' he said, looking over Vance's shoulder. 'Looks like the cavalry.'

The woman emerging from the car that had drawn up behind Simon's didn't look much like the cavalry to Vance. She couldn't have been more than thirty. Even shrugged into an oversized mac, she was clearly slim and pretty, with short blonde hair cut thick and shaggy. 'Good evening, gentlemen,' she said briskly. 'Mr Vance, I'm Detective Chief Inspector Carol Jordan. Would you excuse me for a moment, while I confer with one of my colleagues. Leon, can you keep Mr Vance company for a minute? I want to take a look inside. Simon, a word, please?'

Before he had the chance to say anything, she'd swept Simon inside, managing to open the door so narrowly that Vance had no chance to see within. 'I don't understand what's going on,' Vance said. 'Shouldn't there be scene-of-crimes people here? And uniformed officers?'

Again, Leon shrugged. 'It's not very like the telly, life.' He continued smoking down to the tip then threw his cigarette on the porch step and ground it out.

'Do you mind?' Vance said, pointing. 'This is my house. My doorstep. Just because somebody got themselves killed inside doesn't mean the police can vandalize the place, too.'

Leon raised an eyebrow. 'Frankly, sir, I think that's the least of your worries right now.'

'This is outrageous,' Vance said.

'Me, I find suspicious death enough outrage for one night.'

The door inched open and Simon and Carol re-emerged. The

woman looked sombre, the man faintly sick, Vance thought. Good. She didn't deserve to die pretty, the bitch. 'Chief Inspector, when is someone going to tell me what is going on here?'

He'd been so busy watching her, he hadn't noticed the two men had moved to either side of him in a flanking movement. Carol locked eyes with him, her cold blue stare a match for his. 'Jacko Vance, I am arresting you on suspicion of murder. You do not need to say anything, but I must warn you that it may harm your defence if you do not mention when questioned something which you later rely upon in court. Anything you do say may be given in evidence.'

Disbelief blazed across his face as Simon and Leon closed in on him. Before it had really sunk in that not only was this woman arresting him but these idiots were laying hands on him, a cuff of steel clamped hard over his left wrist. He recovered himself as they tried to manhandle him back towards the Land Rover, convulsing beneath their hands in a desperate attempt to free himself by sheer superiority of strength. But he was off balance, and his feet went from under him on the gravel.

'Don't let him fall,' Carol yelled, and somehow, Leon managed to get under Vance as he hit the ground. Simon hung on grimly to the other end of the handcuffs, yanking Vance's arm back, making him squeal.

'Make my day, shithead,' Simon shouted. 'Give me a reason to give you a taste of what you gave Shaz.' He hauled upwards on Vance's arm, forcing him to struggle to his feet.

Leon scrambled back upright and pushed Vance in the chest. 'You know what would really make me happy? You trying to leg it, that would make me fucking delirious, because then I'd have an excuse for kicking seven colours of shit out of your scumbag body.' He pushed him in the chest again. 'Go on, go for it. Go on, do one.'

Vance stumbled back, as much to escape the venom in Leon's voice as to ease the pain on his arm. He hit the Land Rover with a thud. Simon yanked his arm down and fastened the other end of the handcuffs to the bull bar. He took a deep breath then spat in Vance's face. When he turned to face Carol, there were tears in his eyes. 'He'll not be going anywhere in a hurry,' he croaked.

'You are going to regret this night,' Vance said, his voice low and dangerous.

Carol stepped forward and put a hand on Simon's arm. 'You did well, Simon. Now, unless anybody's got any better ideas, I think it's about time we called the police.'

There was something generic about police stations, Tony thought. The canteens never served salad, the waiting areas always smelled of stale cigarettes in spite of smoking having been banned for years, and the decor never varied. Looking round the interview room in Hexham police station at three in the morning, he realized he could be anywhere from Penzance to Perth. On that gloomy thought, the door opened and Carol came in with two mugs of coffee. 'Strong, black and brewed some time in the last week,' she said, dropping into the chair opposite him.

'What's happening?'

She snorted. 'He's still screaming about wrongful arrest and false imprisonment. I've just given a statement of explanation.'

He stirred his coffee and took in the signs of strain round her eyes. 'Which was?'

'In the area on inquiries, the lads got a report of a possible prowler. They thought it would be quicker to check it out themselves – being into inter-force co-operation – so they found a keyholder who was happy to let them in and gave permission to search,' Carol recited, leaning back and staring sightlessly at the ceiling. 'Concerned about the possibility of a hidden stalker, they opened the basement where they found the dead body of a young white female who answered the description of Donna Doyle, whom they knew to be on the missing list. Since Mr Vance is the only person known to frequent the house, it was clear he must be a suspect in what was obviously a suspicious death. I considered he was a fugitive risk. He was at the scene with a vehicle capable of leaving the road and avoiding pursuit.

'Although my authority does not extend into the force area of Northumbria Police, I am empowered to effect a citizen's arrest. Placing Mr Vance in restraints which caused him minimal discomfort seemed a better alternative than leaving him at large where any movement towards his vehicle might have led to an overreaction on the part of the officers I was working with. Cuffing him to the Land Rover was, in effect, for his own protection.'

By the time she ended her recital, they were both grinning. 'Anyway, the local lads did me the favour of re-arresting him when they got there.'

'What about charging him?'

Carol looked depressed. 'They're waiting for Vance's brief to arrive. But they're running very scared. They've seen your dossier and they've interviewed Kay and Simon and Leon, but they're still wary. It's not over, Tony. Not by a long way. The fat lady hasn't even arrived yet.'

'I just wish that they hadn't opened that cellar. That they'd staked the place out and witnessed him opening it and going down there with Donna's body.'

Carol sighed. 'She hadn't been dead long, did you know?'

'No.'

'The police surgeon thought less than twenty-four hours.' They sat in silence, each wondering what they could have done better or faster, whether more or less orthodoxy could have won them a faster response. Carol broke the uneasy stillness. 'If we can't put Vance away, I don't think I want to be a copper any more.'

'You feel like that because of what happened to Di Earnshaw,' Tony said, laying his hand on her arm.

'I feel like that because Vance is a lethal weapon and if we can't neutralize the likes of him, we're nothing more than glorified traffic wardens,' she said bitterly.

'And if we can?'

She shrugged. 'Then maybe we redeem ourselves for the ones we lose.'

They sat in silence, sipping coffee. Then Tony ran a hand through his hair and said, 'Have they got a good pathologist?'

'I've no idea. Why?'

Before he could answer, the door opened on the worried face of Phil Marshall, the superintendent in charge of the division. 'Dr Hill? Could I have a word?'

'Come in, it's a shop,' Carol muttered.

Marshall closed the door behind him. 'Vance wants to talk to you. Alone. He's happy for the conversation to be taped, but he wants it to be just you and him.'

'What about his brief?' Carol asked.

'He says he just wants Dr Hill and himself. What do you say, Doc? Will you talk to him?'

'We've got nothing to lose, have we?'

Marshall winced. 'From where I'm standing, we've got quite a lot to lose, actually. Frankly, I want evidence to charge Vance with or else I want him out of here within the day. I'm going to no magistrate to ask if I can keep Jacko Vance under lock and key on the basis of what you've given me so far.'

Tony took out his notebook and tore out a sheet of paper, scribbling down a name and number. He handed it to Carol. 'This is who we need to get up here. Can you explain to them while I'm in with Jack the Lad?'

Carol read what he'd written and comprehension lit up her tired eyes. 'Of course.' She reached out and squeezed his hand. 'Good luck.'

Tony nodded, then followed Marshall down the corridor. 'We'll be taping it, of course,' Marshall said. 'We've got to be squeaky clean on this one. He's already talking about suing DCI Jordan.' He stopped outside an interview room and opened the door. He nodded to the uniformed officer in the corner and the man left.

Tony stepped into the room and stared at his adversary. He couldn't believe that there was still no dent in that arrogant exterior, no crack in the charming facade. 'Dr Hill,' Vance said, not a tremor in the professionally smooth voice. 'I wish I could say it was a pleasure, but that would be too much of a lie for anyone to swallow. A bit like your insane accusations.'

'Dr Hill has agreed to talk to you,' Marshall interrupted. 'We will be taping the conversation. I'll leave you now.'

He backed out and Vance waved Tony to a chair. The psychologist shook his head and leaned against the wall, arms folded. 'What did you want me for?' Tony asked. 'A confession?'

'If I wanted confession, I'd have asked for a priest. I wanted to see you face to face to tell you that as soon as I get out of here I will be suing you and DCI Jordan for slander.'

Tony laughed. 'Go ahead. We're neither of us worth a fraction of your annual earnings. You'll be the one who ends up shelling out a fortune in legal costs. Me, I'd relish the opportunity to get you on a witness stand under oath.'

'That's something you'll never achieve.' Vance leaned back in his chair. His eyes were cold, his smile reptilian. 'These trumped-up accusations won't stand up in the cold light of day. What have you got? This dossier of yours with its doctored photographs and circumstantial coincidences. "Here's Jacko Vance on the M1 at Leeds the night Shaz Bowman died." Well, yes, that's because my second home is in Northumberland and that's the best way to get there.' His sonorous voice dripped sarcasm.

'What about, "Here's Jacko Vance with a body in the cellar?"' Or, "Here's a photo of Jacko Vance with the dead girl from his cellar when she was still living, breathing and laughing?"' Tony asked, keeping his voice level and mild. Let Vance get worked up, let him be the one to strain at the leash of his self-control.

Vance's response was a sardonic smile. 'It was your officers who provided the answer to that,' he said. 'They were the ones who raised the possibility of a stalker. It's not so unlikely. Stalkers become obsessed with their targets. I don't find it too hard to imagine a stalker tracking me back to Northumberland. Everybody locally knows Doreen Elliott keeps a set of my keys and, like most of the people round here, she never locks her door if she's only popping next door for a cup of tea, or down to her vegetable garden to dig some potatoes. Child's play to borrow the keys and have a set made.'

As he warmed to his theme, his smile broadened and his body language grew more relaxed. 'It's also common knowledge that I had a nuclear shelter built in the chapel crypt. Slightly embarrassing in these days of détente, but I can live with that,' Vance continued, leaning forward now, his prosthesis resting on the table, his other arm hooked over the back of the chair. 'And let's not forget the very public vendetta with my ex-fiancée who, as you rightly pointed out, bears a strong resemblance to these poor missing girls. I mean, wouldn't you think you were doing me a favour by killing her image if you were obsessed with me?' His grin was positively triumphal.

'And you are, aren't you, Dr Hill? Or rather, as I will take great pleasure in explaining to the world's press, you're obsessed with my wife, I believe. Shaz Bowman's tragic death gave you the opportunity to force your way into our lives and when dear, sweet Micky agreed to have dinner with you, you formed the view that without me, she'd fall into your arms. And your sad delusion has brought us to this point.' He shook his confident head pityingly.

Tony lifted his head and stared into a pair of eyes that could have come from Mars for all the humanity they contained. 'You killed Shaz Bowman. You killed Donna Doyle.'

'You'll never prove that. Since it's a complete fabrication, you'll never prove it,' Vance said with an air of nonchalance. Then he raised one arm and covered first his eyes, then his mouth and finally, stroked his ear. To a casual observer, it was merely the gesture of a tired man. Tony read it instantly as the taunt it was.

He pushed off from the wall and took two long steps across the room. Leaning on his fists, he thrust his face into Vance's personal space. In spite of himself, the TV star craned his head back like a tortoise retreating into its shell. 'You may be right,' Tony said. 'It is entirely possible that we will never nail you for Shaz Bowman or Donna Doyle. But I'll tell you something, Jacko. You weren't always this good. We'll get you for Barbara Fenwick.'

'I have no idea what you're talking about,' Vance said contemptuously.

Tony stood up and slowly began to stroll around the confined space as leisurely as if it were the local park. 'Twelve years ago when you killed Barbara Fenwick there were a lot of things forensic science couldn't do. Take toolmarks, for example. Pretty crude, the comparisons they made back then. But these days, they've got scanning electron microscopes and back-scatter electron microscopes. Don't ask me how they work, but they can compare an injury to an implement and say whether the two match up. Within the next few days, they'll be matching the bones in Donna Doyle's damaged arm to the vice in your house.' He glanced at his watch. 'With a bit of luck, the pathologist will be on her way now. Professor Elizabeth Stewart. I don't know if you've heard of her, but she has a terrific reputation in forensic anthropology as well as pathology. If anyone can find the match between your vice and Donna's injuries, it's Liz Stewart. Now, I realize that doesn't implicate you if we accept the fantasy you've been spinning here.'

He turned slowly to face Vance. 'But it would if the vice matched Barbara Fenwick's bone injuries, wouldn't it? Serial killers often like to use the same weapon for all their murders. But it's hard to imagine a stalker who's followed you around on a killing spree for twelve years and never put a foot wrong, don't you think?'

This time, he saw a flicker of uncertainty in Vance's confident mask. 'What utter rubbish. Just for the sake of argument, even if you got an exhumation order, no Crown Prosecutor is going to push a case that depends on a mark on a piece of bone that's been in the ground for twelve years.'

'I couldn't agree more,' Tony said. 'But you see, the pathologist who did the postmortem on Barbara Fenwick had never seen injuries quite like that. They intrigued her. And she is a university professor. Professor Elizabeth Stewart, actually. She applied to the Home Office to retain Barbara Fenwick's arm so she could use it as a teaching aid. To illustrate the effect on bone and flesh of blunt trauma from compression. Funnily enough, she noticed that there was a slight imperfection on the bottom edge of the implement that inflicted the injuries. A tiny projection of metal that made a mark in bone as distinctive as a fingerprint.' He let the words hang in the air. Vance's eyes never left his face.

'When Professor Stewart moved to London, she left the arm behind. For the last twelve years, Barbara Fenwick's arm has been perfectly preserved in the anatomy department of Manchester University.' Tony smiled gently. 'One solid piece of irrefutable evidence tying you to a weapon used on a murder victim, and suddenly the circumstantial looks very different, don't you think?'

He walked to the door and opened it. 'And by the way – I don't fancy your wife in the slightest. *I've* never been so inadequate that I had to hide behind a lesbian.'

In the corridor, Tony signalled to the uniformed officer by the door that he should go back into the interview room. Then, exhausted by the effort of confronting Vance, he leaned against the wall, sliding down into a squat, elbows on knees and hands over his face.

He was still there ten minutes later when Carol Jordan emerged from the viewing room where she and Marshall had watched the encounter between the hunter and the killer. She crouched in front of him and took his head between her hands. He looked into her face. 'What do you think?' he said anxiously.

'You convinced Phil Marshall,' she said. 'He's spoken to Professor Stewart. She wasn't too thrilled at being woken in the middle of the night, but when Marshall explained what was what, she got really excited. There's a train gets in from London around nine. She'll be on it, with her famous slides of the injury. Marshall's organized someone to go over and collect Barbara Fenwick's arm from Manchester University first thing. If it looks like a match, they'll charge him.'

Tony closed his eyes. 'I just hope he's still using the same vice.'

'Oh, I think you'll find he is,' Carol said eagerly. 'We were watching. You couldn't see from where you were, but when you hit him with Professor Stewart and her preserved arm, his right leg started jittering up and down. He couldn't control it. He's still got the same vice. I'd stake my life on it.'

Tony felt a smile gather the corners of his mouth. 'I think the fat lady just landed.' He put his arms round Carol and stood up, bringing her with him. He held her at arm's length and grinned down at her.

'You did a great job in there. I'm really proud to be on your team.' Her face was solemn, her eyes grave.

Tony dropped his arms and took a deep breath. 'Carol, I've been running away from you for a long time,' he said.

Carol nodded. 'I think I understand why.' She looked down, reluctant to meet his eyes now they were finally having this conversation.

'Oh?'

The muscles along her jaw tightened, then she looked up at him. 'I didn't have blood on my hands. So I could never understand what it feels like to be you. Di Earnshaw's death changed that. And the fact that neither of us could save Donna . . .'

Tony nodded bleakly. 'It's not a comfortable thing to have in common.'

Carol had often visualized a moment like this between them. She had thought she knew what she wanted to happen. Now, she was taken aback to find her responses so different from what she had imagined. She put a hand on his forearm and said, 'It's easier for friends to share than lovers, Tony.'

He gazed at her for a long moment, frowning. He thought of the bodies Jacko Vance had incinerated in the hospital where he gave his time to sit with the dying. He thought of the loss of what Shaz Bowman could have achieved. He thought of all the other deaths that still lay ahead of them both. And he thought of redemption, not through work, but through friendship. His face cleared and he smiled. 'You know, I think you could be right.'

EPILOGUE

Murder was like magic, he thought. The quickness of his hand had always deceived the eye, and that was how it was going to stay. They thought they had him trapped, sewn into a bag and wrapped with chains of guilt. They thought they were lowering him into a tank of proof that would drown him. But he was Houdini. He would burst free when they least expected it.

Jacko Vance lay on the narrow police cell bed, the real arm tucked behind his head. He stared at the ceiling, remembering how he had felt in hospital, the only other place where he'd had no choice about staying put. There had been pockets of despair and impotent anger and he knew those would probably afflict him again before he was free of this place and others like it. But when he'd been in hospital, he'd known he would be free of it all one day and he'd focused all his powerful intelligence on shaping that moment.

True, he'd had Micky's help then. He wondered if he could still rely on her. He thought that as long as he could cast credible doubt, she would stand by him. As soon as it looked like he was going under, she'd be gone. Since he had no intention of letting that happen, he thought he could probably be sure of her.

The evidence was flimsy. But he couldn't deny that Tony Hill was impressive in his command of it. He would be hard to discredit in a courtroom, even if Vance succeeded in planting advance press stories accusing the psychologist of being obsessed with Micky. And there was a risk there. Hill had somehow discovered that Micky was a lesbian. If he leaked that in response to an accusation against him, it would do serious damage both to Micky's credibility and his own image as a man who needed no other woman but his adorable wife.

No, if it came to a court battle, even with a jury of telly addicts,

Vance would be at risk. He had to make certain it never went past a preliminary hearing. He had to destroy the evidence against him, to demonstrate there was no case to answer.

The greatest threat came from the pathologist and her reading of the toolmarks. If he could discredit that, there were only circumstantial details. Together, they weighed heavy, but individually, they could be undermined. The vice was too solid a piece of substantiation to submit to that.

The first step was to cast doubt on whether the arm from the university really belonged to Barbara Fenwick. In a university pathology department, it could not be held under the sort of security of a police evidence room. Anyone could have had access to it over the years. It could even have been replaced with another arm deliberately crushed in his vice by, say, a police officer determined to frame him. Or students could have swapped it in some macabre prank. Yes, a little work there could force a few cracks into the reliability of the preserved arm.

The second step was to prove the vice had not belonged to him when Barbara Fenwick had died. He lay on the hard mattress and racked his brains to find an answer. 'Phyllis,' he eventually murmured, a sly smile creeping across his face. 'Phyllis Gates.'

She'd had terminal cancer. It had started in her left breast then worked its way through her lymphatic system and finally, agonizingly, into her spine. He'd spent several nights by her bedside, sometimes talking, sometimes simply holding her hand in silence. He loved the sense of power that working with the virtual dead gave him. They'd be gone, and he would still be here, on top of the world. Phyllis Gates was long gone, but her twin brother Terry was alive and well. Presumably he was still running his market stall.

Terry sold tools. New and second-hand. Terry credited Vance with the only happiness his sister had known in the last weeks of her life. Terry would walk on hot coals for Vance. Terry would think telling a jury he'd sold the vice to Vance only a couple of years previously was the least he could do to repay the debt.

Vance sat upright, stretching out his arms like a hero accepting the adulation of the crowd. He'd worked it out. He was as good as a free man. Murder was indeed like magic. And one day soon, Tony Hill would find that out for himself. Vance could hardly wait.

Montana
★ MAVERICKS

**Welcome to Whitehorn, Montana—the home of
bold men and daring women. A place where
rich tales of passion and adventure are unfolding
under the Big Sky. Seems that this charming
little town has some mighty big secrets.
And everybody's talking about...**

Homer Gilmore: A harmless hermit, he's been wandering
around Whitehorn for longer than anyone can remember.
And he may be the silent witness to some strange
goings-on. Can anyone believe his stories?
Especially a lawman like...

Officer Rafe "Wolf Boy" Rawlings:
The life of Rafe, dark and brooding, has been one big
question mark. Now the discovery of the mysterious bones
found on the Laughing Horse Reservation could signal the
end to his elusive past. But nobody can help him unravel
the clues, not even...

Winona Cobbs: Wily old Winona, town seer, doesn't have
all the answers. But her mind is filled with images, and her
soul is haunted by visions—of a woman with two faces....

Mary Jo Kincaid: She married a rich man and is sitting
pretty. A relative newcomer, she has a special interest in
Whitehorn's colorful history—especially the old rumors
about the disappearance of...

Lexine Baxter: Turns out she's more than just a name
on a missing person report. This hell-raiser had a wild
history—and an obsession with a lost sapphire mine....

Montana
★ MAVERICKS

LAURIE PAIGE

*The Once and
Future Wife*

Silhouette Books

Published by Silhouette Books
America's Publisher of Contemporary Romance

Special thanks and acknowledgment to Laurie Paige
for her contribution to the Montana Mavericks series.

 SILHOUETTE BOOKS

ISBN-13: 978-0-373-31090-6

Recycling programs
for this product may
not exist in your area.

THE ONCE AND FUTURE WIFE

LAURIE PAIGE

says, "One of the nicest things about writing romances is researching locales, careers and ideas. In the interest of authenticity, most writers will try anything...once." Along with her writing adventures, Laurie has been a NASA engineer, a past president of Romance Writers of America (twice!), a mother and a grandmother (twice, also!). She was a RITA® Award finalist two times for Best Traditional Romance and has won awards from *Romantic Times BOOKreviews* for Best Silhouette Special Edition and Best Silhouette Book. She has also been presented with *Affaire de Coeur*'s Readers' Choice Silver Pen Award for Favorite Contemporary Author. Now living in Northern California, Laurie is looking forward to whatever experiences her next novel will send her on.

To Jill Barnett—for Keegan
To Jane Bonander—for Kerrigan
And to Georgina Devon—for reading
through all of it

One

Tracy Roper parked across the street from the police station. She sat in the car, her hands locked on the steering wheel as she let her gaze drift along the busy avenue, past the mayor's house on the corner; past the Roxy Theater, where she'd gone to summer movies with friends; past the real-estate office where she was to pick up the key to the rental house.

From where she was on Center Avenue, it was only a couple of blocks, then a left turn onto another street and a short drive to the last house on the right before the county-road intersection....

A tremor ran through her as she realized where her thoughts were taking her. Once upon a time she'd lived in that house on Stoney Ridge Road...so long ago it some-times seemed like a dream.

Or a nightmare.

Squeals of laughter reached her through the closed windows of her compact car. She glanced down the block toward the town park, where three children played on the swings. Their mothers sat on the wooden benches that lined the play area, chatting and laughing while they kept an eye on their young charges.

For a minute, Tracy's eyes lingered on a toddler, a busy little boy whose dark hair gleamed with auburn highlights in the morning sun. When he fell in the sand, her heart lurched and her hands tightened in a painful grip.

The child's mother scooped him up in a soothing embrace and dried his tears. Tracy glanced away.

Pulling down the sun visor, she checked her face in the mirror. She looked okay, she decided. Her makeup seemed fresh enough from when she'd put it on at six that morning at her father's house in Missoula.

She'd visited him over the weekend before driving down to Whitehorn to begin her latest task—checking out some bones found on the Laughing Horse Reservation.

The tribal police and the county sheriff's office were in contention over who was in charge of the case, so the federal government had been called in. As a forensic anthropologist for the FBI, she would have full control of the investigation.

Sighing, she admitted she was putting off the moment she would have to face Judd Hensley, the county sheriff—the man who'd been her husband…the father of her child….

She picked up her purse, opened the car door and climbed out into the hot late-June sunshine. The breeze was crisp, blowing off mountains where clouds were gathering for an afternoon rain.

Before she could cross the street, a couple came out of

the station and stood on the steps. She stopped as if struck by lightning.

Judd.

The sun glanced off his shining black hair with its smooth wave brushed back from his forehead. His skin was evenly, darkly tanned. The first time she'd seen him she'd thought he was an Indian.

So long ago…that magical summer when she'd been nineteen and thought all the world was in love. Seventeen years…

He'd been kneeling by the creek when she'd rounded a bend in the trail and spotted him. She'd stopped, surprised, alarmed and fascinated as he scooped up water and drank it from his hand. It had dribbled over his chest and belly.

He'd been buck naked.

She'd thought he was a savage or a character from an ancient fable somehow transported through aeons to this moment. She'd known in an instant that she'd never forget him.

He'd whipped his head around, sensing her presence. His eyes, as dark and alluring as forbidden knowledge, had taken in all aspects of her, including her soul, in one glance. He'd stood and turned in one smooth, sinuous movement.

His body had been fully erect, a symbol of the power and creative force contained within him.

Pagan, she'd thought, spellbound by his special magic.

She'd stood very still, as if in the presence of a mythical creature, not wanting to startle him into disappearing. They'd stared into each other's eyes for an eternity.

Then he'd spoken, his voice a deep rumble of concern and assurance. "Don't be afraid," he'd murmured.

He'd said the same thing two weeks later when they'd made love for the first time…

Laughter broke into her memories.

Judd's teeth gleamed strong and white against his tan while he laughed at something his companion said. The woman—Maris Wyler, Tracy decided, delving into her memories for a name to go with the face—reached up and caressed his cheek before running lightly down the steps and climbing into a truck at the curb.

Tracy watched his gaze follow the truck. The smile that had lingered on his passionately mobile mouth disappeared. A tight-lipped expression took its place. He swung his head in her direction suddenly.

Judd had thought he was prepared to meet Tracy again. It had been years since he'd seen her. The pain had long since subsided into the empty place inside him where nothing could hurt.

But he hadn't counted on this. The impact of seeing her was like getting hit with a slug from a buffalo gun. He tightened one hand into a fist, angered by the reaction that raged through his body. He watched as she left her car and approached the crosswalk.

She wore a golden yellow suit with a blouse printed in random splotches of red, blue and yellow. Her belt, heels and purse were the same shade as the blue in the blouse. Her earrings were blue flowers with golden centers. She looked like Spring personified.

Her hair was light auburn. It gleamed like copper wire in the sun, but he knew its real texture. It was the same shade, the same downy softness, wherever he'd touched it on her body.

A harsh pang of need drove through him like a heat-tempered spear. He knew exactly what she looked like without the city clothes and the makeup that highlighted her green eyes.

The mountain wind made wanton love to her as she paused, her gaze going in one direction, then the other, as she waited for a break in the bustling Monday-morning traffic.

Her skirt, coaxed by the wind, pressed between her thighs, outlining the long slender grace of her legs…legs that had once wrapped sensuously around him, demanding he give himself to her completely, holding nothing back. And he had. God, he had!

She'd taken possession of his heart and soul. She'd wound herself around him until no moment was complete without her. Then she'd rejected him, scorning him as if their marriage had become an abomination, his touch so distasteful she couldn't bear it.

He'd waited, making no demands, ignoring his own pain, knowing they both needed to heal after the death of their son, but their time had never come again. It had been the final grief.

By the time of the divorce, it had been a relief to move out. By then, he'd felt like a dry husk of a man, empty, drained, with nothing left inside to give, even if she had wanted him again.

She never had. She'd left, not returning once during the seven years since the divorce. He forced the unwanted feelings into abeyance. It was better to be empty. Life was easier.

* * *

Tracy crossed the street, her two-inch heels clicking noisily on the pavement. She should have worn flats, but she would have felt short next to Judd's six-feet-plus frame, even though she was a bit over five-seven herself. She needed to feel in control, not like that foolish teenager who'd thought physical attraction was enough to build a life on.

The station steps had an iron railing running down the middle of them. She started up the right side of it. Judd was on the other side. He started down. They met in the middle.

He moved down one more step, so that they stood eye-to-eye. His hand brushed hers on the railing as he paused. A flash of sensation raced across her skin, almost like a pain.

"Hello, Tracy," he said, moving his hand farther up the railing. The other settled below where she gripped the smooth iron like a lifeline. "How are you?"

She stared at their hands, his tanned skin dark next to her paleness. There were tiny black hairs on the backs of his hands. His fingers were well-shaped, long and slender…sensuous.

A strange shiver ran over her, as if she could feel them caressing her, running down her breasts, her ribs, her stomach, her thighs….

With a gasp, she tore her gaze from those hands whose touch she'd once loved more than anything. "Fine," she finally answered. "And you?"

He shrugged. His shoulders were broad. He wore the uniform of the county sheriff well, at ease with the authority it imparted.

The dark brown shirt with the gold-silver-and-black badge that stated his official status hugged his muscular torso with great accuracy. The dark brown stripe up the side of the light brown pants made his legs seem even longer and more powerful.

A sudden memory came to her, sensual and compelling. During the cold Montana winters, he'd always slept close to her, his leg thrown across her thighs, his arm over her waist. Once he'd murmured it was too bad they didn't live at the North Pole so he could hold her close every night of the year.

She felt the warming of her body, the softness creeping inside her, the moist heat forming as she prepared to receive him. She tightened her grip on the railing.

"Are you all right?" he asked.

She looked at him, helpless, haunted by a love she hadn't asked for, hadn't known how to handle, by a passion that wouldn't leave her completely.

A shock of dark hair, a whispered voice behind her at the theater, a graceful movement of a man glimpsed at a distance and it was like a door opening inside her, welcoming the man whose image the hair, the voice or the movement had invoked.

"Yes," she said, gathering herself together. "Of course. I thought I'd check in with you to let you know I was in town."

"What are your plans?"

"Well, I have to pick up the key to the house I rented—"

"I have it. The agent left on a fishing trip. He said he might not make it back if the fish were biting, so he gave me the key last Friday."

"Oh. Well, good." What else was there to say? Her residence while she was here could hardly be kept a secret. "I want to go out to the site where the bones were found as soon as possible."

"Right." He sounded crisp and official. "You have a meeting with the tribal chairman and attorney in the morning. They want to discuss the situation."

"Okay." She could tell Judd didn't like the idea of consulting with the others. If a crime had been committed in the county, he wanted to jump right on the case.

He was a man who took his responsibilities seriously. When they'd suspected she was pregnant that summer many years ago, he'd insisted they marry immediately. "Growing up is hard enough in this day and age without being a bastard in the bargain," he'd said, then grinned. "I don't intend to let you go."

She knew his own youth had been unhappy. His parents, though married and wealthy, had quarreled all the time. When Judd had come out to Montana on a vacation after practicing law with his father for three years, he'd liked the wide, open spaces, the peace he'd found there. That was the summer they'd met.

He'd stayed—against his parents' wishes—and started work as a rookie in the sheriff's department when they married. They'd been deliriously happy that year. At least, she had.

"We'll go to the site after the meeting. You'll need to wear jeans and hiking shoes. It's rough country." He looked at his watch. "Have you had lunch?"

"No, I'd forgotten about it."

He nodded and looked away. "Yeah."

Tracy knew he was recalling the past. He used to tease her about losing herself in whatever she was doing, whether researching forensic techniques or planting a garden. He'd often arrived home to find her buried in a project, no supper on the table, the bed unmade, in spite of her good intentions.

He would always chuckle at her consternation, and they would end up making love. Later, they would prepare the meal together.

Judd had been a patient, forbearing husband. Eight years her senior, he'd been indulgent toward her enthusiastic rush through life. He'd made no demands, except that she welcome his caress....

She turned her back on him and the memories he invoked and headed for her car.

"We'll go by your...house first. Then we'll pick up something to eat and go to my office. I have the reports you requested and the topography maps," he said, easily keeping up with her, his stride long and surefooted.

She wondered at the hesitation before he mentioned her rental house. Was it because he, too, remembered the house they'd built together? It had been small but perfect, set on its own ten acres with woods all around it, next to Route 17.

After the divorce, the house had been sold and the profit split between them. She'd invested her share, unable to bring herself to spend it. It had felt like blood money, spoils from the death of their marriage...and the death of their son.

Judd pulled out of the parking lot in his unmarked county vehicle, which was a black sports utility truck. The only difference between it and others of its kind was the wire-mesh glass that could be rolled up between the driver and the rear seat, and the fact that the rear doors couldn't be opened from inside the vehicle.

Behind him, Tracy eased into the traffic flow and

followed him to Pale Bluff Lane. The rental house was a white, two-bedroom cottage set behind a picket fence. Multiflora roses covered the fence along the side of the driveway.

He stopped in front of the house while Tracy turned into the drive and parked under the carport. He met her at the front door, fished the key out of his pocket and let her precede him into the house. "I, uh, had someone come over and give it a good cleaning on Saturday. It was rather grimy."

"Thank you." She was clearly startled by this news. She looked around the tiny living room. "Oh, this is really nice." Her smile was hesitant, but pleased.

He noticed the way the light from the window reflected in her eyes, turning them from mossy to golden green. He'd liked to make love to her outside, on the grass with the sun streaming over them, her eyes the color of new leaves as she smiled up at him.

When they'd made love like that, he'd carefully shielded her tender skin from the sun with his own body, which tanned easily.

He cursed silently at himself. "I'll bring your stuff in."

"I'll help," she said. "It isn't much."

It wasn't—only a soft-sided suitcase with wheels and a nylon carpetbag with a matching makeup bag. He recognized the latter. She'd asked for them as a Christmas present years ago. He and Thadd had picked them out. He was surprised she still had them, or that she would use them.

But then, two years ago he had repurchased the house they'd shared as man and wife. He wasn't sure why, except it was the only place he'd ever been truly happy. He wondered if she knew….

He doubted she'd ever wanted to know about him after she left town. She'd left the state *and* the country after the divorce.

For a second, the emptiness threatened to fill with the black grief of those days. He trampled it down roughly. Emotion had no place in his life, not anymore.

He suddenly remembered a time from the past. Tracy had turned on him in anger. "Tell me how to stop feeling!" she'd cried. "Our son is dead. Tell me how to stop hurting!"

He'd had no answers for her, no words of comfort. He hadn't wanted to talk about it. The pain was too much. He'd walked out.

Later, knowing he'd failed her, he'd tried to hold her, to make love and erase the bitter hurt, but she'd pushed him away, coldly rejecting him. In that instant it had become clear that she blamed him for their son's death.

He blamed himself. He was the one who'd laughed at her fears. He was the one who'd encouraged Thadd to roam the woods, to watch for animals, to learn the ways of nature.

Their son had been shot through the lungs from a quarter-mile distance with a high-powered rifle. The police had never found whoever had fired the shot. It was doubtful the hunter had even known he'd hit anything, much less an eight-year-old boy tracking a deer.

"That's all," she said. "Judd?"

He blinked, then nodded, pulling himself from the past as if walking across land mines. He willed the emptiness into place.

Carrying the suitcase and carpetbag, he followed her back to the house and into one of the two bedrooms. It looked a hell of a lot better than it had on Friday when, out of curiosity, he'd come over to check the place before Tracy arrived.

At that time the floors, windows, curtains and furniture had been dusty and stained from the last people who'd rented it. Judd had called his cleaning woman for help. Mrs. Johnstone and her son had dashed to the rescue.

It had taken the three of them all day Saturday, but the cottage showed the results in sparkling windows, sweet-smelling curtains, shampooed rugs and furniture and scrubbed floors.

Outside, the son had mowed the yard while Judd had weeded and clipped back the roses. Together they had washed the windows, then the doors and window facings smudged with fingerprints.

A sense of satisfaction hit him. At least the cottage wasn't a disappointment to her.

"Just set them down anywhere," she told him. "I'll freshen up and be with you in a minute."

"Take your time. Change to something more comfortable if you like. We're still casual here in the country." He didn't know why he'd added that little barb. It was just that she looked so damned sophisticated…so damned *untouchable*…in that silk suit.

He placed the luggage on the bed and hurriedly departed. The bed, covered in a white frilly spread with gold-and-pink poppies embroidered all over it, was giving him ideas.

He paced to the back door and gripped the framing as he looked at the clear vista beyond the yard.

Pale Bluff Lane ran across the lip of a limestone outcropping that formed a bluff rising twenty to fifty feet above the lower part of the valley floor, where Highway 191 curved north and ran the length of the county.

His county. His domain and responsibility.

He leaned against the jamb and crossed his arms over his chest, worry forming inside him. Tracy would be officially in charge, but it was going to be his case.

A murder investigation was no place for a woman as delicate as Tracy. Hell, she'd been squeamish over the wild game he and Thadd had brought in for dinner during various hunting seasons.

Actually, it might not be a murder case. That was what she was supposed to tell them. The department needed the who, what, why, where and when of the bones found on the reservation before they would know if they had a case.

"Okay, I'm ready," she said from behind him.

He turned and stopped stone-still. She had changed into slacks that matched the golden yellow suit, but had retained the printed blouse and suit jacket. Her hair was drawn back from her face with a barrette, and she wore tasseled loafers.

She looked like the girl of nineteen he'd first seen on a rarely used hiking trail, watching him drink before he plunged into the cold pool to bathe.

At that time she'd been dressed in jeans, a yellow T-shirt and a long-sleeved, yellow-checked shirt open down the front. She'd driven him to instant arousal then. She did the same now.

"God help me," he muttered, and forced himself to walk out the door before he did the same thing he'd done two weeks after that first meeting—kiss her until she was pliant in his arms.

Tracy nibbled on the chicken sandwich without much enthusiasm. Judd had gone to a fast-food place out on the highway. Now they sat on opposite sides of the desk in his office while he filled her in on the case.

"Last March, George Sweetwater found the bones—"

"George," Tracy interrupted. "I remember him. What was he doing in the woods, especially in that area? It's sacred ground."

"He says he was running his dogs to keep them in trim for the hunting season in the fall."

Tracy had to smile. "He was rabbit hunting," she concluded.

Judd's eyes met hers. He smiled, too. "Out of season," he added. "And without a license."

"He doesn't need a license on tribal ground."

Tracy knew tribal law better than most of the Cheyenne. She had spent every summer since her earliest years on the reservation, helping her father gather oral histories and myths about the tribe.

As a history professor at the university, he'd made Montana Native Americans and pioneers his particular field. He'd been delighted when his daughter had followed in his footsteps—sort of—with her degree in anthropology. That was before she'd gone into forensic science.

"So you're still up on local codes," Judd remarked dryly.

"I reviewed the case with my father."

"How is he?"

"His knee is bothering him some, but he stills walks up the hill every day." She laughed, thinking of the steep hill overlooking the campus in Missoula. "Faster than some of his students. In fact, he loves to challenge the freshman history class to meet him at the top for their first lesson."

Judd's deep chuckle rippled over her, setting up vibrations in some molten inner core that she rarely acknowledged. She wanted no soft, vulnerable places inside her. She didn't want to respond to him in any way.

"I'm sorry about your mother," he said, the smile fading.

Tracy's mother had died in an accident two years ago. Her father had been lonely after that. "Thank you. And your folks?"

"They're fine. My niece graduated from high school."

"Oh, yes. She's eighteen. I'd forgotten."

The cooling breeze from the air conditioner swirled a strand of hair across her mouth. She pushed it back, then refastened the clip that held the thick waves away from her face.

When she finished, she glanced across the desk and caught Judd watching her. The harsh expression on his face stunned her.

Then it was gone, and she wasn't certain what she'd seen. But there for a second, as he'd watched her fix her hair, his expression had been so grim, she thought he must hate her.

"Anyway, George found the bones near a bluff. Apparently someone from the reservation called the FBI before my department was notified," he said, a note of irritation visible when he balled the hamburger wrapper in his fist. He gathered his debris and stuffed it in the white paper bag.

She quickly ate the last of her sandwich and spicy french fries. "Did you examine the bones?"

He snorted. "Are you kidding? I got a glimpse of them, but the tribal police won't let anyone near them. Sara Lewis—you remember her?"

Tracy nodded. She could vaguely remember the younger woman.

"She's curator of the Native American Museum here in

Whitehorn," he continued. "She and some of the tribe think the bones belong to some long-lost ancestors of theirs."

"They might," Tracy reminded him mildly.

He grimaced in disbelief. "Are you ready to look at the officer's reports?"

She nodded. The cool air sighed over her face, a soft, slow caress like that of a lover. She recoiled from the idea.

She'd known some of the old feelings and memories were bound to be stirred by her return to Whitehorn. She just hadn't realized they would be so strong.

But he'd always done that to her, she admitted.

Judd had always made her think of touching and loving and all those other things associated with the male-female attraction from the very first moment they had met. It came as a shock to her that he still did. And that no other man ever had.

While she read the field reports of the people who had made the initial investigation after George had brought the bones into the tribal-police office, Judd returned several telephone calls.

She noted his tone seemed different with other people compared to the one he used with her. When he talked with the mayor, the tension she'd heard earlier was gone. In its place was a relaxed amusement with a sincere undertone— Judd took his responsibilities seriously—as they discussed plans for the county fair scheduled for the next weekend.

When his secretary, Juliet Clarke, came in with some letters for him to sign, Tracy felt a strange jolt of some peculiar emotion, sort of the way she'd felt when she witnessed the caress Maris Wyler had given him.

Judd and the attractive blonde talked quietly. His voice

held a lazy resonance that shivered right down Tracy's spine. He had a way of listening while seeming to stare at the ground or off into space, then looking at the speaker with a slow, sideways glance, his full attention on the person.

It was very appealing to a woman to be the center of that attention, which had a dark, sensual aspect to it that Tracy didn't think Judd even knew about.

Women did. They fell at his feet like trees in the path of a tornado.

When he finished with the letters and the secretary left, he placed another call. He laughed after identifying himself. The other person must have said something very humorous. Tracy thought it was a woman's voice on the other end of the line.

She tried hard not to listen, but Judd's laughter rumbled over her like distant thunder, vibrating right down to her toes. She clenched the report. Against her will, she wondered if he was talking to Maris. He was making plans for the evening.

When he hung up, she laid the brief reports on his desk. "I'd like to see the topos now."

He removed the topography maps from a cabinet and spread them over the cleared surface of the desk. Moving around until he stood beside her, he stretched his arms wide as he opened the rolled map.

"Hold that corner," he requested.

When she did, he used his left hand to point out the location of the crime scene…if there had been a crime. Bones did not necessarily mean murder and mayhem. They might even belong to an animal instead of a person.

His shoulder pressed against hers as she leaned forward

to study the area. A jolt of sensation shot through her. She moved slightly away and sensed his quick look.

When she glanced at him, she witnessed a harshness that hadn't been present when he'd talked to his date for the evening. She stood very still as a storm of emotion swept her in its path.

The moment stretched…became forever….

The secretary knocked and stuck her head in the open doorway. "Sterling is on line two."

Judd moved back around the desk.

Tracy breathed once more. "I have all the information I need. I think I'll go home."

He paused with his hand on the telephone. "I'll drive you in a minute."

"Uh, no, I'd rather walk." She picked up her purse and slipped out of the office. She knew she was running away. She just didn't know from what.

Two

Tracy explored the town before starting home. She compared the stores and buildings with her memories. Some things had changed. Some had not.

Mason's jewelry store had had an antique clock in the window seventeen years ago when she and Judd had married. It had been there when she'd left town seven years ago. It was there still. However, the name on the sign indicated the son was now the jeweler. She assumed the older Mason had retired.

A new supermarket occupied a corner, but she couldn't recall what had been there before it. She walked to the house, drove back in the rental car and bought groceries.

The sun was beginning to set when she returned to the cottage. The sky was gilded in shades of rose, gold and lavender when she finished putting her groceries away and arranging the kitchen. She unpacked the clothing she'd brought.

Sitting at the table, drinking a cold soda, she listened to the sigh of the wind through the pines. The only sound in the house was the steady *drip-drip* of the faucet.

She tried to turn it off and failed. She made a mental note to pick up a washer at the hardware store and replace the worn one.

After that, she changed from her good clothes into old, much-worn jeans, a blue T-shirt and a nylon Windbreaker with blue sleeves and interesting splashes of primary colors on the rest. She thought of eating, but decided she wasn't hungry.

Leaving the house, she wandered across the backyard to the rocky outcropping that overlooked the highway down below. Cars whipped past fairly steadily. It wasn't like city or freeway traffic in California, where she now lived, but the road was busy for a small town in southern Montana.

Yellowstone traffic, she decided. Families on vacation, going to see Old Faithful geyser, or maybe they'd already been to the park and were heading on up to the Lewis and Clark National Forest to camp and fish.

She leaned against a tree and gave a shaky sigh. Darkness seemed to fill her soul. She'd talked with a psychologist a couple of years ago. The woman had told her she needed to face the past and come to terms with her grief before she could get on with her life. Tracy had thought the doctor crazy.

Now she wasn't so sure. Returning was harder than she'd expected. Emotions she'd buried in her work were stirring, and she couldn't seem to stop them.

She spotted a vehicle on the highway that reminded her

of Judd's unmarked sports truck. Was he with his date now? Did he take her to his place after dinner? Or did he go to hers? Was he getting on with his life as the doctor had told her to do?

Tracy squeezed her eyes tightly shut, unable to bear the thought of him making love to another woman.

She felt lost and confused and unable to cope.

All this on the first day back in town, she mused, trying to mock her emotions. She trembled to think of the coming days with Judd. He would want to be in on every detail of her investigation.

Maybe she could solve the case quickly and go back to where it was safe. In California, they only had earthquakes, mud slides and wildfires to deal with.

Restless, she walked north along the bluff. The sky was an interesting watercolor of lavender fading into blue fading into deep purple-blue. When the path angled back to the lane, she followed it without question.

Almost in a trance she turned left on Silver Creek Road, then right on Stoney Ridge. In another few minutes, she stood in front of the rustic rail fence along the front of the house she and Judd had built. Honesty forced her to admit he'd done most of the work, but she'd loved helping.

They had worked so hard that fall, getting the outside done so they could finish the inside during the winter. Later, it had been nip and tuck to see which occurred first— completing the house or having the child that spring.

Judd had put the final touches on the nursery three weeks before Thadd had been born.

She gripped the log railing with both hands as she stared at the house. It had natural stone halfway up the sides, then split redwood logs the rest of the way. Wide, double-paned windows framed views of the woods on all sides.

The steep pitch of the roof allowed two rooms upstairs, one as a guest bedroom, the other for storage of all the treasures families collected and couldn't bear to throw out.

She wondered if the same family lived there. No one seemed to be home. There were no lights inside that she could detect.

Walking along the fence, she stopped by the front gate, which stood open. A red-and-white soccer ball lay by the road. She picked it up and studied it as if she'd never seen one before.

Finally, her chest tight and achy, she tossed the ball gently toward the house so that it came to rest by the two steps leading down from the front porch. She thrust her hands into her pockets and quickly walked down the street.

Instead of returning home, she headed for the main part of town. She realized she was hungry.

Crossing the street, she went to the Hip Hop Café. The small eating place hadn't been there eight years ago. It wouldn't bring back any painful memories. She pushed open the door and went in.

The café was a jumble of used tables and chairs that were bright and colorful. The place had a vibrant charm that must make it popular—along with its good food, going by the delicious aromas. A jukebox sat in a corner. Two samplers decorated the walls, among various other things. The first person she saw was Lily Mae Wheeler, widow, divorcée, town gossip. Tracy hesitated, but it was too late to turn around and skedaddle back to the cottage.

"Well, bless my soul! Would you look what the cat

dragged in?" Lily Mae demanded of no one in particular. "Tracy Hensley."

When Lily Mae pushed out a chair with her three-inch-spike heeled sandal, Tracy had no choice but to join her.

"When did you get into town, hon?"

"Today. Around noon," Tracy answered.

"I'd heard you were coming—oh, here's my dinner." She picked up her purse to make room for the dinner plate. "Melissa, were you in town when Tracy lived here? About five, six years ago, wasn't it, Tracy?"

Since Lily Mae didn't leave anyone time to answer questions, Tracy and the other woman spoke at once.

"It was seven years ago when I left—"

"I wasn't here then—"

They both stopped, then smiled at each other. Lily Mae broke right in. "Melissa Avery, this is Tracy Hensley."

"Roper," Tracy corrected. "Tracy Roper. I decided to use my maiden name after the divorce."

Melissa frowned thoughtfully. "I remember. You were married to the sheriff. Your little boy…" She trailed off, embarrassed at bringing up the subject.

"It's all right," Tracy said quickly. "I'm glad to meet you."

"Tracy is a famous FBI agent," Lily Mae put in.

Melissa expressed an interest in what she did.

"Actually, I'm a consultant on special cases," Tracy explained. "I also work at archeology digs as an anthropologist for the University of California sometimes, although forensic investigations are taking more of my time."

"I'm fascinated," Melissa told her, "but I have to get back to work. We're shorthanded tonight, so I'm helping wait tables. I'll bring you a menu in a sec." She hurried away.

"You two should be friends," Lily Mae announced. "You're both hardworking and independent as hell. Now tell me what you've been doing since I saw your father last spring."

Tracy told Lily Mae of her doings after she ordered a salad special. It was nice to know some people never changed, she mused while they ate and talked. The gay divorcée had once had an eye for Dr. Roper, but he had seen no one but his wife.

Tracy worried briefly over him getting hooked now by the voluptuous woman, who preferred to call herself a widow.

Maybe that wouldn't be so bad. Her father, a workaholic like herself, had buried himself in his book project this past year.

Lily Mae, with her bleached hair, outrageous earrings, loud laughter and come-hither glances, might be good for him. She was good-hearted, and might introduce some fun into his life—a spark of unpredictability. Heaven knew, one could never tell what the woman would say or do next.

Tracy controlled an urge to giggle at the idea of staid Professor Roper being tugged through life by Lily Mae.

"So I told her she should try spanking his bottom and that would put a stop to those tantrums," Lily Mae said, ending another story while Tracy finished her meal. The hoop earrings with two-inch parrots sitting in the hoops swung to and fro.

Lily Mae was in her fifties. She'd never had children, and her marriages hadn't lasted all that long.

Tracy realized the woman was lonely. She'd adopted the residents of the town and county as her extended family, thus she felt quite free to give out advice on any subject to anyone. A wry affection warmed Tracy's heart for the talkative widow.

"I guess you heard about Maris Wyler, didn't you?" Lily Mae asked over fresh blackberry cobbler and ice cream.

Tracy's heart leapt to her throat. "Maris?" she said cautiously. She didn't want to hear of an engagement. It was none of her business what Judd did in his private life, but…she didn't want to hear about it.

"She up and married some drifter that came through, a rodeo rider just like that good-for-nothing husband of hers who got himself killed. The man showed up claiming Ray had died owing him some money. Which was probably true."

"So…Maris is married to—to this other man?"

The parrots swung wildly as Lily Mae nodded. "She just had a baby a few months ago—his name is Clay. I always thought Maris had a head on her shoulders, but you know what passion can do to a person."

Tracy felt a rush of heat to her face. She bent over her cobbler and scooped up the last bites. When she looked up, Lily Mae was studying her curiously.

"She and Judd went out some for a year or more, but nothing ever came of it. Sometimes a person can't get over that first love. Your father is that kind, I think."

A flash of mutual understanding passed between them. Tracy touched Lily Mae's hand in sympathy. The widow, for all her bright clothes, jewelry and painted face, had more depth to her than appeared on the surface.

During the rest of the meal, they chatted about the town and its various problems. It was dark and surprisingly late when Tracy refused a ride from Lily Mae and started home.

As she passed the mayor's house, she heard the familiar gravelly rumble of a deep voice. She ducked her head and tried to hurry. She didn't want to see Judd and his date saying good-night to the mayor and his wife.

"Tracy," he called out before she could get more than three-fourths of the way past the mansion.

She stopped and turned. Judd stood alone on the paved driveway next to the house. He was dressed in a suit and tie. Her heart knocked hard against her ribs.

"Hello," she managed to say in a nonchalant voice. She looked at him, then away.

His face wore a frown when he came to her at the end of the sweeping drive. "What are you doing out after dark?"

She bristled at his tone. "Is there a curfew you didn't tell me about?"

That brought him up short. "Of course not," he said in a more reasonable manner. "It's just…it's after nine. Not many people wander around a small town this late."

She didn't owe him an explanation, but she found herself giving one anyway. "I went to the café for dinner. Lily Mae Wheeler was there—"

His muted groan brought a stop to the words. "Say no more. She talked your ear off for three hours."

"Well, two," Tracy admitted.

"Get in. I'll drive you home." He motioned to a low-slung sporty-looking car at the curb.

"This is yours?"

"Yeah."

His direct gaze challenged her to make something of it. They had never been able to afford a new car, much less a luxury vehicle such as this, during their marriage, but they had teased each other about the one they would buy "when our ship comes in."

The plans they had made...so many dreams and hopes...so many bright promises for the future...

"Trace?" he said, shortening her name as he used to. He held the car door open for her.

She got in, feeling very uncertain about the wisdom of this. She hadn't felt this self-conscious the first time they'd made love, there on a grassy meadow with the June sun pouring over their entwined bodies.

It took less than five minutes to get to her house. He sat in the car after turning off the engine. "You didn't leave the porch light on."

"Uh, no. I didn't expect to be gone so long. I mean, I was just out for a walk. I'd thought I might go to town for dinner, but I wasn't sure." She stopped the incoherent chatter.

For some reason, it was more difficult to talk to him knowing he wasn't involved with Maris.

That didn't mean he wasn't involved with someone else.

She realized it must have been the mayor's wife on the phone earlier that day, inviting him to dinner. Tracy wondered if there had been an extra woman at the table for him. She shied away from the thought. It was none of her business.

"Look," he said harshly, "I don't know if we can work together if you're going to act as if you suspect my motives every time I speak to you."

"I don't know what you mean."

"Don't you?" he snapped. He swung his head around to glare at her in the dim glow cast by a streetlight on the corner. "Admit you didn't want me to come to the house this morning.

Admit you didn't want to have lunch with me. Hell, you didn't want to come into my office to review the case."

"Judd—"

"Do you hate me that much?"

She gasped, stunned by the question. "I—I don't hate you at all." She stumbled over her denial.

He faced forward, staring out into the darkness behind the cottage. Trees were visible as a darker outline against the dark sky. A sliver of moon hung above their branches.

When he said nothing more, she ventured, "All right. I admit I was reluctant to see you. I think having a few misgivings would be the natural order of things, considering our past. It was bound to be awkward…this first meeting. It brought back memories."

"Yes," he said. "God, yes."

The silence, the dark, the close confinement of the sports car crept over her like a warm cape.

"You'd better go in," he said.

She didn't want to go into the house, not alone. She didn't think she could bear the silence.

Besides, she felt they might be on the verge of discovering something important about each other and about their time together before. Perhaps it *was* time she faced the past. "Would you like some coffee?" she heard herself ask.

He frowned as if he were going to refuse, then nodded. When he climbed out, she did the same. He removed his jacket and tie and tossed them onto the seat. They went into the dark house.

"You should leave some lights on when you go out," he told her. "A lamp on an electronic timer is a good idea."

"I will." She turned on lights as they made their way to

the kitchen. Once there, she started a pot of coffee. She noticed her hands were trembling when she stripped off her Windbreaker.

"Coffee cake?" she offered.

"No, thanks. I had dessert at the mayor's house. He's already started his goodwill campaign to win reelection." The irony in Judd's tone made her smile.

"Is anyone thinking of running against him?"

"Not that I know of."

"What about you?"

"What about me?" He gave her a puzzled glance, his expression once more guarded.

"You'd make a good mayor. You're well known for your honesty. You get along with the city council."

He gave an amused snort: "I don't like the kind of politicking it takes to get elected. Even as sheriff, I find I can't always say exactly what I think."

"Yes, you're a man of few words," she said wryly.

She considered this statement. Judd *had* been a quiet man, especially about his feelings. Perhaps she should have pushed him to talk to her. Perhaps she should have made him listen when she'd wanted to explain her feelings. Perhaps... But it was too late now. As the Cheyenne said, the path of life is a one-way road.

She poured the coffee and took it to the table. He held her chair for her. He'd always been gallant. It was one of the things that had attracted her to him from the first. He was gentle with women and children, at ease with his fellow men.

When his hand brushed her shoulder, she felt a leap in her pulse rate. It was scary, the things he could still make her feel, or was that part of once having been as close as earth and air?

He sat opposite her. They drank the steaming coffee. He opened his shirt collar and rolled his sleeves back. She tried to think of something innocuous to discuss, but nothing came to mind. She wanted him, she realized.

"Why did you come back?" he asked suddenly. He sounded angry. "Why now, after all this time?"

She swallowed as emotion gathered in her throat. They'd met in June. Seventeen years...

"Frank Many Horses asked for me," she finally said. "He wanted someone who would understand tribal ways and respect their ancestors and their customs."

He studied her, as if wondering whether this was the truth, his dark gaze so penetrating it made her wonder at her decision to accept the case. Since she worked as a special agent, on a consulting basis only, she could have refused.

"I saw your father last summer," Judd mentioned. "He said you were buried in your work. He was worried about you."

This was news to her. "Why?" she asked in surprise.

"He thought you didn't have a life outside of your studies. He said you didn't go out much."

"Oh." She licked her lips. Her mouth seemed to have dried up. Little sensations spiraled off inside her. "Well, I have been busy. However, I do see friends occasionally."

"Friends?" Judd questioned. His gaze seemed sharper.

"I do go out," she said firmly. "Some."

The clock in the living room ticked off the seconds as he silently absorbed this information.

Judd knew he should leave. It was dangerous to stay here in this quiet house with Tracy. She was the only female he'd ever met who could make him forget his good intentions. Hell, she made him forget the basic instincts of self-preservation.

"Some," he repeated, hot anger going through him at the thought of the men who might have touched her. He fought the rising hunger in himself, the conviction someplace inside him that this woman belonged to him.

Not anymore, he reminded himself ruthlessly. Somehow that bright flaming passion had used itself up, like the fuel of the sun, burning itself out in a fury of intense heat.

A man would be a fool to trust those feelings again. When he'd first seen her, some gut instinct had said she was his. He'd believed it then; he knew better now.

He stood abruptly.

She did, too.

Her green eyes widened as she gazed into his. He knew what she saw. She'd always been able to read him like the front page of a newspaper when it came to passion. He cursed himself for wanting her, for thinking he needed her. He didn't.

He didn't need anyone. Hadn't the last seven years proven that—eight if he counted the final, devastating year of their marriage before it fell apart? "I'd better go."

She nodded.

Neither of them moved.

Her lips parted as if she would speak, but she didn't.

He moved toward her. "One day," he murmured. "One day, and I already wonder what you would taste like, how you would react to my touch if we were to kiss."

"I—I...me, too."

Her confession threw him further off balance. He'd expected her to deny the attraction. He'd wanted her to.

Now the admission lingered in the air between them like gunpowder that might explode at any moment.

Slowly, he reached out. He almost wished she would disappear, the way a mirage would when a person tried to grab it.

She didn't vanish.

Instead, with a sigh, she settled into his arms when he enclosed her in an embrace. Some part of him wondered what he was doing. An experiment, he decided. It was an experiment. But he had no idea what he was trying to prove.

And then it didn't matter. His lips met hers. She made a little choked sound in her throat. He held her tighter.

The kiss burned through him, driving out everything but the need for her, fed by eight long years of starvation.

She moved her head from side to side, as if trying to deny the kiss. He slipped his hands into her hair, which felt cool on the surface, but was warm, so warm, underneath. He held her face up to his. She stopped the restless movement and stared at him.

"You mustn't," she whispered.

"Don't tell me no," he growled. It wasn't what he wanted to hear from her. He wanted acquiescence, acceptance...*response*.

Tracy thought she might faint, she was so light-headed. When he framed her face with his long, sensuous fingers, she felt the tremor in them and was afraid for both of them.

They were becoming enmeshed in something neither could control. She knew she should push him away, but her hands spread over his chest. The warmth of his skin under the white shirt radiated into her cold fingers.

It seemed she'd been cold a long time.

"No," she said, but it was a whimper of need.

His hands tugged at her T-shirt, pulling it from her jeans. Then they slipped under the material and caressed her back. His hands were large compared to her slenderness. They felt strong and capable on her flesh. And gentle...so gentle.

She'd instinctively trusted him and his touch from the first moment they'd met. It was like that all over again.

"Touch me," he growled low in her ear, his mouth raining hot kisses all over her face.

She obeyed mindlessly, reaching for the shirt buttons, opening them, pushing his shirt aside so she could reach the bare flesh underneath. She pressed her nose into the rough diamond of wiry hairs on his chest and inhaled deeply.

Judd groaned helplessly. When she touched her lips to his chest, the caress was as hot as a branding iron. He wrapped his arms around her, lifting her from the floor, bringing her into searing contact from lips to chest to stomach to thighs.

He placed her on the counter. She opened her legs, letting him come close, tacitly giving him permission to explore further, whether she knew it or not.

His heart leapt like a jackhammer in his chest, and for the briefest second he wondered what he was doing. And then her tongue touched his nipple, causing flames to shoot through him, burning out all other thoughts.

Tracy felt the spasm that went through Judd and experienced the wild thrill of triumph. He still went crazy in her arms. As she did in his.

He pushed her T-shirt up and unfastened her bra. The cool night air hit her breasts, then was gone, shut out by his hands as he cupped her against his palms.

His lips sought hers when she lifted her head. She saw his eyes close, felt his breath blow across her mouth, and then his mouth was on hers, demanding, exploring, seeking the passion that she'd thought was dead.

She felt his hands move, pulling his shirt free, brushing it to either side, then the controlled weight of his chest settled against hers. Flesh against flesh. Hot and wonderful and wild.

A throb started between her thighs as the hard length of his arousal pressed there. He moved against her, again…and again.

Once during the embrace—after a minute or an aeon, she wasn't sure which—he said her name against her mouth, and his lips trembled on hers before he slipped his tongue inside.

The smooth thrust of it was a wanton replay of the many times their bodies had plunged together until she'd cried out in ecstasy.

A moan tore its way out of her, from deep inside where she was vulnerable, where emptiness demanded fulfillment, where love dwelled, all alone and in darkness.

She turned her head, her breath panting from her body. She was afraid to feel this passion, afraid of what feelings might come after…:

"Trace," he said.

There was no choice. She had to look at him.

He shook his head, and she knew he, too, was fighting the needs that drove them. She looked away.

He eased her bra into place, his hands shaking as badly as hers, and pulled her T-shirt down over her bare skin. Then he fastened his shirt.

"I'm sorry," he said.

That surprised her. "It was both of us," she insisted, taking her share of the blame.

She put her hands on the counter, preparing to jump down. He caught her by the waist and lifted her, setting her on her feet and making sure she was steady before he let her go.

"You're shaking," he said. "So am I."

He gave a snort of laughter. The bitterness of it cut into her. She didn't know what to say. Everything was confused.

"We overreacted to the tension," she finally offered by way of explanation. It was the best she could come up with.

"Tension? That's a new name for it."

She pressed her fingertips to her temples, where a headache now throbbed mercilessly. "Don't," she pleaded. "Let's forget it happened. It's late, and we were…our defenses were down."

He spun away from her. "Why the hell does it have to be you?" he demanded. He tucked his shirt into his dress slacks.

The harshness had returned to his face, and he looked ready to destroy something. With a low curse, he reached out and twisted the faucet handle. The steady dripping stopped.

The inane thought came to her that she probably wouldn't be able to turn it back on.

"I'll fix it," Judd said. He looked around the kitchen, but apparently didn't see anything to vent his fury on. He rubbed a hand over his face and pressed his fingers against his eyes.

Tracy realized how very tired and vulnerable he looked. She felt the same. Her throat was tight and achy now. She feared she might cry at any moment. She swallowed a couple of times. The feeling passed, but the terrible sorrow lingered inside her. She felt sorry for both of them.

"I'm going now." He dropped his hand from his eyes and studied her. "Will you be all right?"

"Yes."

"Maybe we'll solve the case soon, and you can leave."

She nodded, too weary to answer. They walked to the door.

He paused before going out into the night. "I'm sorry," he murmured again, so low the words might have been the sighing of the wind.

Three

Judd held the door for her the next morning when he came by. She climbed into the truck. He didn't touch her. She was grateful for that. They were both subdued, careful of each other. It was just as well. They had to maintain a distance.

During the night she had made up her mind to ignore the storm signals between her and Judd. She wasn't nineteen anymore. She could control herself. After all, she'd had no trouble doing so in the presence of some very attractive men in California.

After a few minutes of stilted conversation they gave up talking. Tracy watched the passing scenery. In less than an hour they arrived at the reservation. Judd drove along the main road to the tribal headquarters.

At the council offices, they went inside and were directed to the conference room. A carved wooden box sat on the conference table. Sara Lewis, who, according to

Judd, worked at the Native American Museum, stood on the other side of the table.

Tracy smiled and nodded to the younger woman, who returned her greeting cautiously.

A few elders of the tribe stood around to observe what would take place. At the end of the room was the tribal chairman, Frank Many Horses. The attorney, Jackson Hawk, also a tribal leader, was with him.

"Jackson!" Tracy exclaimed in pleased surprise. He was the same age as she was. They had played together when they'd both been free of the demands of education—she from public school in Missoula, he from the BIA boarding school he'd been forced to attend. "I heard you had returned."

Jackson was as tall as Judd. His hair and eyes were black as obsidian. He wore braids tied with rawhide strips which to her looked perfectly natural with his suit and tie. His jutting nose and prominent cheekbones proclaimed his Cheyenne ancestry.

He'd gone to college on a basketball scholarship and earned his law degree after that. His lithe body proved his athletic skill; his alert gaze indicated his mental acuity.

The attorney came to her, his smile bright and warm. His welcome lifted her spirits, which needed all the help they could get, she admitted ruefully.

"Tracy, daughter of the professor who goes around asking personal questions," he teased. His smile disappeared. "Now you're here to ask your own questions."

"Yes. Do you have the bones?"

He nodded. "My uncle wishes to speak with you."

Jackson took her arm and led her to the old man, who stood at the back of the room by the council table. Judd fell into step behind them. Tracy noted the way his gaze darted from her to Jackson, as if he were assessing the situation between them.

The tribal attorney introduced her to Uncle Frank as if she hadn't known the old man all her life.

She stood quietly, waiting for him to speak. When he did, she realized he was much older than he'd seemed the last time she had talked to him. A second heart attack had taken away some of the inner strength she had always associated with him.

The thought made her sad, as if a way of life would go with the passing of the man.

"How are you?" he asked.

"Fine."

"Your father?"

"He sends you greetings. He has to finish the book with the new oral histories this summer. He'll bring you a copy, he said."

The thick brows, almost white now, pulled together. "Good," he said. "That's good." He looked around as if tired.

A young tribal policeman pulled a chair into position. "Here, Uncle," he said, using the honorary title. "You must rest. Dr. Hunter said we were to make sure you do."

"Kane," the elder snorted. "He's an old woman."

Tracy saw the old man was pleased at the care.

When he was seated, he motioned for the young man to bring a chair for her. When she faced him, their chairs placed so that their knees almost touched, he spoke again. "Kane needs to find a wife, as his cousin has had the good fortune to do." He looked at his nephew in affection.

"Jackson?" Tracy inquired.

"Yes. Just last week." The attorney smiled. For a second she glimpsed the quiet joy in his eyes. He gestured toward his uncle. "He's turned into a matchmaker in his old age."

Her eyes were drawn to where Judd had taken up a position against the wall while he waited for the greetings to be over and for them to get down to real business. She couldn't tell if he was impatient with the proceedings or merely resigned.

"I wish you happiness," she said softly.

Jackson nodded his thanks.

"You know the story of the bones?" Uncle Frank asked.

She waited a few seconds before answering in order to give the question and her response the consideration they deserved. Her summers on the reservation had taught her it wasn't polite to jump into speech without prior thought.

"I've been told a little. Would you tell me again so that I may have the facts clear in my mind?"

Uncle Frank recounted the story she had learned from the initial report to the FBI and from Judd. The sequence of events was the same. After the tribal elder fell silent, she thanked him. She waited, then asked to see the evidence.

"It isn't proper for the remains of ancestors to be despoiled by the white methods," he said, giving her a frown that would have sent her scurrying if she'd still been a child.

"The forensic investigation," Jackson clarified.

Tracy gazed at the floor while she reflected on this. "No test will be undertaken without tribal permission," she promised.

Nearby, she felt the movement as Judd stirred in surprise at this rescinding of authority. She touched her finger to her lips to bid him be silent, then faced the tribal chairman squarely.

Uncle Frank studied her until she thought he was searching out every lie she'd ever spoken. He nodded.

A wave of relief swept over her. She wasn't going to have to be the pushy representative of the federal government.

"Now come and let us talk heart-to-heart," Uncle Frank said, standing and opening his arms. She went into them for a warm hug that had her fighting the sting of tears all of a sudden. "You and Jackson begged many a treat of fry bread and honey at my house when you were young. You'll come soon and share a meal with us?"

"I'd love to."

There was some chatter now in the background. She glanced at Judd. He was more impassive than the most stereotyped Indian in any movie she'd ever seen.

She and the tribal elder talked about her career since she'd left town years ago. She'd finished her master's degree and done field work with the world's foremost forensic anthropologist for three years, traveling all over the world.

"This living with old bones doesn't bother you?" Uncle Frank inquired over coffee. The box on the table wasn't referred to during the conversation.

"No. I find it fascinating to try and figure out ancient people's lives—how they might have lived, what they did for food and medicines." She paused. "How they died."

He nodded and sat silently for a long minute. "Jackson, open the box," he said.

Tracy felt a beat of excitement. Finding old bones was like a treasure hunt for her. She loved to study the past.

Because it was safer?

She ignored the inner question and went to the table. Jackson slid the box in front of her. He unlocked it, then

carefully lifted the top off. The silence in the room was that
of a held breath. She looked inside while the handsome
attorney laid the top to one side.

The first thing that caught her eye was a deep scratch in
one of the bones, which were the skeletal remains of an arm
and part of a hand. The scratch gleamed white against the
brown-stained surface surrounding it.

She glanced behind her, to where Judd still leaned against
the wall. His mouth relaxed just a bit, not enough to call it
a smile. Jackson's tightened as the three exchanged glances
that admitted what the two men had suspected from the first.

"These aren't old bones," she said.

The truck jolted over a road that grew increasingly
rougher. Tracy grasped the door handle and the seat edge
in an effort to keep from bouncing.

When the road became a logging or hunting trail winding
upward through some thick woods, Judd slowed down.

It didn't take a forensic expert to know he was in a foul
mood. He hadn't spoken two words since they'd left the
council house and started for the site where the bones had
been found.

The road ended abruptly near a bluff—a limestone-and-
shale cliff ranging from ten to a hundred feet high, with the
Beartooth Creek running at its base.

The creek separated the Kincaid ranch from the reservation, ending in Lovers Lake on the ranch. It was near the
lake that she had first seen Judd that summer long ago.

She brushed the thought impatiently from her mind.
She had a job to do. She leaned forward to change from
her sandals to socks and hiking shoes.

The land angled steeply upward from the small open meadow where they stopped. The trees and brush were thicker in the section on the other side of the clearing, she noted.

The sacred woods. Uncle Frank had given her permission to explore the area.

Judd parked beside a tribal police car and a marked sheriff's-department truck. Tracy jumped out before Judd could come around to help her.

Hooking her purse strap over her shoulder, she headed toward the bright yellow police tape attached to the trees. Judd caught her by the elbow.

"This way," he said. He let her go and started off at an angle to the road. He ducked under the tape and held it up for her, his face expressionless as he waited.

She quickly followed, irritated at his cool assumption of authority. "I want to circle the site before homing in on the place the bones were found."

That's the way forensic investigations were conducted—start at the outer perimeter and spiral in. Leave the site by retracing the same path. That way the investigator ran the least risk of ruining the evidence, if any was present and assuming it hadn't already been trampled by others who'd been there before her. Judd knew this as well as she.

"That's what we're doing," he said tersely. He let her take the lead, but directed her by voice as they walked the site.

She examined the lay of the land, the types of vegetation and the rock formations as they worked their way to the bluff, then up along its spine and finally down into the center of the woods. They met a tribal policeman and a deputy from Judd's department there.

Judd introduced her to the two men. She spoke briefly to them, her gaze going to the marked area in the dirt. Moving carefully, she circled the small yellow flags attached to stiff wires pushed into the ground. She finally stopped and stooped to inspect the bones uncovered in the dirt.

"George Sweetwater took the bones he found from the site. Those were the ones you saw at the council house," Judd explained, dropping to his haunches on the opposite side of the markers. "We found the tribal police going over the area when we got here. They had discovered the rest of the bones belonging to the hand—"

"How do you know these belong to the bones in the box?"

"It was an assumption," he said curtly.

She nodded and continued to study the site. She could tell it grated on Judd to be fighting over a motley bunch of bones like two opposing packs of dogs. He was also stifled in getting on with the investigation by the impasse with the tribal council.

It wasn't like him to let his temper show, though. At least, it wasn't like the man she'd once known.

During the years of their marriage, she'd rarely seen him let his emotions get the better of him, not even at their son's funeral. Neither had she.

In the face of his stoicism, she'd held her grief inside. Sometimes she'd wondered if they might not have made it if they'd cried in each other's arms.

Last night, after he'd left, she'd felt like crying, although she hadn't. That episode in his arms had been an aberration on both their parts, she decided, one driven by passion, not emotion.

She sighed, stood and studied the rising slope above them.

Judd did, too. "Plenty of shrubs and plants around," he said, following her thoughts. "Bones couldn't wash down here all of a sudden because of erosion."

"They've been brought here, probably by animals. The question is where were they to begin with…and how long have these pieces been in the woods?"

"Yeah."

"Has the site been photographed?" she asked.

"Yes. We have a full set of prints at the office."

"Well, let's pack up the evidence and see what else we can find. By the way, do you have an office I can work out of? I promised Uncle Frank the bones would be kept in a secure place. I'm not sure the cottage would qualify."

"There's a small conference room next to my office. You can use it if you like." He smiled grimly. "The department will bill the FBI for rent and phone use."

"Rent?" she demanded in disbelief. "For an unused room?"

"I didn't say it was never used. All right, no rent," he conceded when she started to argue. "But you pay for your long-distance calls."

"Agreed." She smiled, feeling relieved. They had established a working relationship. That was good. If they could keep their dealings strictly on a business level, all would be well.

And if they didn't?

She ignored the question. While Judd supervised the other two in gathering and sealing the evidence, she walked the area again, keeping to the same perimeter.

Tomorrow, she decided, she would widen the search

pattern until she found the rest of the skeleton or had to give up. Two weeks were all she'd planned for this case.

"Are you about through? I'm ready to lock up."

Tracy looked up from the table where the evidence was laid out on white paper. She laid the magnifying glass down. "Yes. I've noted every chip and scrape on these. The gouges were caused by animal teeth, as I thought. Tomorrow I'll start a systematic search of the area."

Judd frowned. She prepared herself for an argument.

"I'll assign someone to assist you."

"I'd rather you didn't."

"You're not going to wander around in the woods by yourself," he informed her. "Someone was murdered there."

"We don't know that," she said calmly.

He glared at her. She glared back.

After a couple of seconds, his lips relaxed slightly at the corners. "You're a stubborn cuss," he muttered.

She was reminded of times past. Their quarrels had never lasted for more than a few minutes. One or the other of them would start laughing at the stubborn look on the other's face, then they'd end up making love, or scooping Thadd up and going out for ice cream.

"I know." She smiled at him, then stretched her stiff muscles and yawned. "I'm going home. What time will you come in tomorrow?"

"Seven." He bent over the table and studied the small collection of bones.

She noticed the silver hairs threaded through the black locks—not many, but some.

Gray hair? Judd?

To her, he was the quintessential man, never aging, never changing, an archetype who served as the model for all the men she'd ever met. To observe signs that he was as vulnerable to aging as the rest of humanity disturbed her.

Not for the first time she wondered if she'd expected too much from this strong, silent man.

"What time will you arrive?" he asked, straightening and glancing at her in that sultry, devastating manner he was so unconscious of.

"The same as you."

Ignoring the lifting of his eyebrows that questioned her early arrival—she tended to be a night owl—she cast an eye over the small conference room to see if there was anything she'd forgotten to do. Everything was in order.

Picking up her purse and the hiking shoes she'd worn at the site on the reservation, she exited through Judd's office.

Judd locked the conference-room door, then followed her to the outer office. His secretary had gone home for the day.

Tracy started down the broad hall while Judd locked the office door.

"Do you want to go to dinner?" he called after her.

She stopped and glanced over her shoulder at him. "No, thanks. I thought I would visit Winona tonight. I called her earlier today. She's expecting me."

He nodded.

She rushed along the hall and out into the warm air. She drove to the cottage and changed clothes, replacing her slacks with a pair of white shorts dotted with blue-and-yellow butterflies, putting on the matching knit top and grabbing her Windbreaker for when the sun went down.

In ten minutes, she was speeding along Route 17. A few

miles from town she pulled off the road into what looked like a junkyard—and in reality was.

The sign that proclaimed the place to be the Stop 'n' Swap was barely legible. It swung from a signpost at an angle, one side an inch higher than the other due to the uneven lengths of chain that held it in place.

Below that sign was another that said wild honey was made and sold on the premises.

The entire front yard was filled with discarded household and auto items. Birds flitted around a feeder. A dozen cats snoozed in the sun. Two goats stood on top of a rusted station wagon and eyed Tracy as she parked by the open gate. The watchdog, an old blue tick hound, didn't raise an eyelid at her approach.

An eagerness to see the old woman she loved nearly as much as her own family propelled Tracy from the car, past an old bathtub filled with dirt and planted with moss roses and up to the door of the trailer where Winona Cobb lived. Winona stood in the door.

"Tracy!" she exclaimed warmly. She held the screen door open.

Tracy leapt up the concrete blocks that formed the steps and a small porch. She was enveloped in a hug.

Winona looked just the same—the same gray hair braided and wrapped around her head, a round, merry face with brown eyes sparkling with intelligence and wry wit, a short, rotund body that was sturdy and stout.

She'd put on a long flowered skirt and a faded blue blouse for the occasion, but she'd forgotten her shoes. Around her neck and dangling from her ears she wore polished stone beads and crystals of various colors.

To Tracy, she looked like an aging hippy. Most outsiders, upon meeting her, assumed she was one of the Northern Cheyenne. No one knew for sure where she'd come from, and Winona never told. Like the hills, she'd been part of the landscape forever.

Tracy and her father had visited frequently during their summer trips to the area. The old woman had served homemade wine and lemonade and sent them home with bags of fresh vegetables that she grew in a huge garden beside the trailer.

"Well, child, let me look at you," she said, moving back from Tracy, who was half-a-head taller. She clasped both Tracy's hands and studied her with a fond smile.

All at once an alarmed expression flitted over the lined face. Winona dropped Tracy's hands as if they'd burnt her. She crossed her arms over her chest and staggered back.

Blindly she reached out, found a chair and sank into it. She clutched the beaded necklace in a trembling hand.

"Winona?" Tracy said in alarm. She dropped to her haunches beside the padded rocker.

"Two faces," Winona murmured, her eyes closed, her tanned face going pale. "One woman…two faces." She shook her head slowly from side to side.

Tracy's heart was thumping. She'd forgotten about Winona's visions. The woman was a known psychic. She'd been the one who'd told Judd where to find Thadd when they were searching for him. Tracy didn't discount anything she said.

"Can you see anything else?" she asked quietly.

"A room. There's a man on a bed. Naked. He's asleep.

The woman is looking for something…she's going through his pockets…."

Tracy waited, but her old friend said nothing more.

Winona opened her eyes. She put a hand to her head. "Bring me a glass of blackberry wine, then put on a pot of chamomile tea."

Tracy did as she was told. She kept a keen eye on the older woman to make sure she didn't go into another trance and maybe choke on the wine. When the tea was ready, she prepared two cups and laced them generously with wild honey.

"Are you all right now?" she asked, pulling up the footstool where she'd loved to sit and listen to Winona's stories of bygone times for hours on end. She placed the cups on the end table and helped herself to a tiny glass of homemade wine.

"Yes. Who did you last touch before you came out here?" Winona asked after taking a swallow of the sweet, potent wine.

Tracy took a sip and let it roll over her tongue. She thought about her day. After returning to town from the reservation, she'd spent the afternoon in Judd's private conference room, poring over the bones.

"I haven't touched anyone since Frank Many Horses…no, I shook hands with Jackson Hawk when I left the res."

She tried to recall if she and Judd had touched. They hadn't. They'd both been very careful around each other all day. In fact, he'd left the office after showing her the room she could use and hadn't returned until shortly before five.

"That's all that I can remember," she finished. "Do you recall what you said?"

Winona nodded. "A woman with two faces. One over the other. I could see them both, but I couldn't tell who either was. It was one of the strangest visions I've ever had."

"You looked frightened."

"Not me. It was her…them. There was only one body. But two faces." Winona sighed and sipped the wine, slower this time. "I sensed she was angry…very angry…but also scared."

A frisson caused Tracy to draw her arms tightly to her sides. Winona's vision gave her a chill. "You think the vision came from me?" she asked, trying to find some clue to its meaning.

"Oh, yes," Winona said. She looked suddenly worried. "I just got another bit."

The hair crawled on Tracy's neck. "What?" she asked.

"You might…I think…there could be danger." She frowned and closed her eyes. After the silence stretched into a full minute, she shook her head. "It's gone. But I sense danger."

"Well, perhaps more will come later. Do you feel like showing me your garden? I loved those little cherry tomatoes you grew when I was a kid. And the sweet basil. It was like perfume to me."

After she admired the vegetables, especially the pumpkins and squash, they chose a big watermelon and cut it from the vine. Tracy carried it to the back of the trailer.

Natural stones formed a patio there. An oak tree provided shade over a picnic table. A line of stubby cedars formed a windbreak on the north side of the yard. The place was an oasis of flowers and fruit trees, as peaceful and pleasing as the front yard was cluttered and utterly disordered from Winona's trade.

They switched to iced tea with their meal, which was mostly vegetables, fresh bread and cheese made from the nanny goat's milk.

The goats, cats and hound joined them on the patio, but politely kept their distance. Winona didn't let them intrude on guests. Bees buzzed lazily among the flowers.

After polishing off big slices of watermelon for dessert, the two of them sat on lounge chairs and chatted. Winona called a cat to her and let it sit on her lap. Slowly she stroked its orange fur while the sun set in a brilliant display of fiery red. Tracy played with a black-and-white kitten.

"Tell me of your life," Winona ordered gently.

Tracy told of her travels and studies. "You wouldn't believe all the things a bit of research can tell about people nowadays, even those who lived thousands of years ago. I'll probably have to run a DNA check on the bones from the reservation."

"The tribal elders won't like that," Winona predicted without having to resort to psychic abilities.

Tracy wrinkled her nose. "They've made that clear. I promised I'd not do anything without their permission. Judd didn't like *that*. I'm going to search the area thoroughly first. I'd say by the depth of the dirt stains, the bones haven't been in the ground for more than twenty or thirty years. There should be other evidence. Of course, nature can fool you sometimes. I could be wrong."

She chatted on, drawn out by alert questions from her listener. Vaguely, she realized she hadn't talked to anyone like this in years, not since she and Judd used to plan their future.

"What is it?" Winona asked.

"What?"

"You had a thought that made you sad."

Tracy stared at the lined face. She sighed and took a drink of the spicy tea before answering. "It's hard…to come back to the place where all your dreams died."

"Are they truly dead?" Winona asked in a kind voice.

Tracy sifted through her memories. "Yes."

"But there are new beginnings. You're too young to give up on life."

"Well, I haven't." Tracy laughed, albeit a bit shakily. She pinched her forearm lightly. "Ouch! See? I'm still living."

Winona smiled at her foolishness. "Aren't there any men in California who have taken your fancy?"

Tracy's laughter faded. She stroked the kitten, which had curled into a ball in her lap. Its purr vibrated through her body. She suddenly felt the terrible ache of loneliness.

"No," she admitted. "I've dated some, but…"

"But they're not your true love."

Tracy pushed a strand of hair out of her eyes with an impatient gesture. She gazed into the distance, where night gathered behind the mountains to the west of the wide valley. The clouds had dried up during the night and no longer wreathed the far peaks. "Were you ever in love, Winona?"

"Everyone is in love at some stage of life."

"What was he like?" Tracy sat up straighter, curious about this woman's life. "Were you married?"

"No. He was a poet. He loved me, but he loved the world more. He went away to discover his Muse." She studied Tracy for a short spell before continuing. "He came back—I lived in the city then and taught English at the local college—but I was angry with him and sent him away. I regretted it afterward."

"Did you ever see him again?"

Winona nodded. She carefully smoothed the cat's fur. "Twenty years later, he returned. We were in our forties. Neither of us had married. He said he had to see me one more time. We lived together for a month. He died in my arms."

Tracy thought it the saddest story she'd ever heard. "I'm so terribly sorry."

"A month of memories isn't a lot to take a person through a lifetime...nor are a few years. The nights get lonely."

They sat in silence, each lost in thought.

"Well," Tracy said at last, "I suppose I should get home. I'm so glad I came. My father and I miss our summers here and the visits with you. He sends his love."

A smile lighted Winona's face. "I hear he may be getting married any day."

Tracy was startled. "Who to?"

"Lily Mae." The merry brown eyes twinkled. "She told everyone at the café she was going to nab him when he came back to town. She said two years was long enough to grieve."

Tracy didn't know whether to be amused or offended. "Dad won't be down this summer, but perhaps I'd better warn him of the widow lying in wait."

"Let him find out for himself," Winona advised. "Getting caught by Lily Mae isn't the worst thing that could happen to a man. She might be good for him."

"Funny, I thought the same thing when she and I were talking last night. Did you somehow listen in on the conversation?"

"My ability doesn't run to eavesdropping, although I sometimes wish it did."

They walked around the trailer to the front. The last dying rays from the sun lighted the western horizon to a paler blue than the rest of the sky, which was a deep royal blue.

"Have you missed the country since you've been gone?"

Tracy did a slow turn, looking in all the directions of the compass like a Cheyenne saying his prayers.

To the south of them, the Beartooth Highway ran over the high pass. The land dropped off a thousand or more feet on each side of the crest where the cars crawled along the narrow, winding drive. Most travelers found the Beartooth Pass a heart grabber.

To the west, Crazy Peak rose over eleven thousand feet. The Beartooth Creek ran east out of the mountains into the reservoir that gave Whitehorn its water supply. North and east of town the land was flat to rolling, not as rugged, but with its own beauty.

"Yes," she admitted.

"You must move back."

Tracy looked at her friend. "I can't."

"You will," Winona said with absolute conviction.

Four

Tracy walked the path to the site, her sneakers making no noise on the mossy ground under the thick stand of trees. Behind her, Sterling McCallum—Judd's top detective, according to the secretary—walked along, equally silent.

Judd and Sterling made a good pair, Tracy thought sourly. Neither spoke unless absolutely necessary. Sterling was helping her search the site for clues. Judd had told her Sterling was his best man for the search, that he had a "good eye."

She carried a paintbrush and dustpan, a pick, rock hammer and chisel, all tools of the archeological trade. She was going to dig for treasure…or in this case, bones.

No one was at the original location. The tribal elders had given her permission to do whatever she had to do. She set her tools out, tossed a cushion on the ground and plopped down.

Leaning over, she surveyed the ground where the other bones had been found. She formed a square with wire posts and string and began removing the top layer of dirt and leaf mold. No other site in her surveys had yielded so much as a clue, other than this one.

An afternoon of digging yielded the rest of the finger bones. She placed them in evidence bags with tweezers and wrote the location on a piece of paper and stuck it in the bag. She then recorded the information in her log book.

"You're good," McCallum said when she finally packed up her finds and indicated she was ready to leave.

"Thanks."

She gave him a curious glance as they returned to the police vehicle they'd come out in. He hadn't helped with the dig at all. Instead, he'd wandered around the area, peering at first one thing and then another as if he had nothing particular on his mind.

Once she'd seen him picking thimbleberries off a bush and eating them. He'd brought her a handful. She'd been grateful, for she'd forgotten to bring a water canteen with her.

She paused at the ridge and looked over the flat grassland below. "What are those?" she asked, pointing at some strange animals near the creek.

"Beefalo," McCallum said.

"Ah. I thought they were the strangest-looking cows I ever saw." She smiled. "A melding of the old and the new. I wonder if it will work."

He shrugged. He was a big man—big hands, big feet…a big heart? Hard to tell, but he *had* brought her the berries to munch on. He looked tough and had a military bearing. She was sure his nose had been broken at least once.

He wore a silver-and-turqoise ring and a wedding band. There had been some teasing banter between him and Judd that morning about the last big case he'd been assigned to…something about an abandoned baby. Apparently he and his wife had adopted the infant last fall.

Tracy couldn't imagine those large hands being gentle enough to hold a baby. But then, Judd had been incredibly wonderful with Thadd, even when the baby was a newborn and had weighed in at seven pounds, two ounces.

Her heart gave a squeeze, and she dropped that line of thought. Instead, she concentrated on what she'd learned during the past week. With tribal permission, she'd sent a small section of bone off to the forensic lab in California. When she got the results, she'd know how long the bones had been there.

On the way back to town, she decided to have a show-down with Judd. For three days—Wednesday, Thursday and today—he'd sent whatever policeman he could spare to stay with her at the site. She didn't need a baby-sitter, and she was going to tell him so.

"You like digging up bones?" McCallum asked.

"Yes." In her mind, she was rehearsing what she was going to say to Judd.

"How'd you get interested in that?"

She frowned at him. "What?"

"Never mind," he said. "I can see you're thinking of other things." He grinned, a slow, lazy smile that reminded her of Judd.

There seemed to be an understanding between the two men. They were kindred spirits, she decided. They shared certain, intangible characteristics…like being quietly stubborn when she'd insisted she didn't want anyone tagging along with her.

Pity the man's poor wife if McCallum were as much of a watchdog as Judd was proving to be, she thought waspishly.

When they arrived in town, the detective let her out at the police station and drove off. She carried the loot up to her assigned room. Judd had given her a key to his office, but she didn't need it. He was in, talking on the telephone when she went through.

She realized he had put her right where he wanted her. He or his secretary could keep on eye on her comings and goings with no problem whatsoever. She gave him a withering glance and sailed on by, closing the door after her.

Opening the bag, she laid out the new finds and compared the bones to the original ones George had found and to the bones found by the tribal police. They all fit together.

From the size of the hand, she assumed the person had been a male, twenty to forty years old. That was a rough guess. The hipbone was best for information on the sex and age of the person.

Getting out her magnifying glass, she studied all the bones for signs of breaks or thickening at certain places that could indicate the type of work he'd done. Bone density and wrist size indicated whether the person had been left- or right-handed.

Provided she ever found the other hand to compare the two.

The door opened. "How's it going?" Judd asked.

She laid the glass in its case. "Fine. I found some more bits." She glared at him. "While your watchdog stood around bored as all get-out."

The dark eyebrows jutted upward. "You sound tired."

"I sound irritated," she corrected. "Don't get in the way of my investigation, Judd. I'm ordering you to back off."

The tension in the small room escalated to tornado-warning velocity. Since the passionate episode, they'd stepped around each other with the caution of two cats who'd arrived in a new and strange territory at the same time.

But, she reminded herself, she was the top cat. And he'd better not forget it.

"All right. You're on your own." He spread his hands as if he were giving up. "The fair opened today. Winona called and wanted to know if you were going. She's entered several of the food categories, and they're being judged this evening. She wants to have supper at the fair afterward."

"I'll call her," Tracy murmured, the heat taken out of her anger by his cool acceptance of her authority.

She arranged to meet Winona at the main gate at six. She glanced at her watch after she hung up. It was already after five.

If she wanted a shower and change of clothes, she'd better get with it. She covered her work and laid her tool case on the end of the table. After clipping on her waist purse, she started out at a brisk walk.

Judd wasn't in his office when she left. She told the secretary good-night.

She'd left her car at the cottage, since it was as easy to commute on foot as by vehicle in the snug little town. On impulse, she walked around by the house she and Judd had built.

Strange, but she never saw a family there. In fact, she

never saw signs that anyone lived there at all—no lights in the house, no car in the garage…well, the garage was always closed, but surely they'd leave the door open once in a while.

However, the place was well kept up. The yard was mowed and weeded regularly. The rock garden she'd designed looked nice. She and Judd had planned it so very little maintenance was needed.

They both had liked the natural look of shrubs and pine needles and rocks, forming curving walkways among the many trees.

She rushed by and went on to her cottage. After a quick shower, she slipped on her favorite gold slacks and a gold silk shell with a white-and-gold-striped linen jacket for evening.

The gold loops she wore in her ears and the matching bracelet had been a gift from her father one Christmas years ago.

She glanced at the clock. Five to six. She considered, then decided her waist purse was the handiest to use. It left her hands free, yet kept her money and wallet right in front of her where she could keep an eye on them.

The county fairgrounds were five miles south of town. She arrived at ten after six, parked and dashed to the entrance. Judd was there, talking to an attractive woman.

It wasn't Maris Wyler—or whatever her name was, now that she'd married—but another woman who wasn't at all like Maris.

This woman looked very delicate. Her manner was demure. When she laughed and glanced up at Judd, then quickly away, she seemed shy.

And very attractive. A Laura Ashley type in a floral print skirt with a white lacy blouse and a bow holding her hair at the back of her neck.

Tracy felt a return of that odd emotion she'd experienced when she saw Maris pat Judd's cheek on Monday. Before she had time to define it, Judd saw her. His smile disappeared like spilled milk among farm cats.

She went forward, her shoulders squared as if going into battle. She forced herself to relax and smile calmly.

Judd made the introductions. "Mary Jo, this is Tracy Roper. Tracy, Mary Jo Kincaid."

Tracy shook hands with Little Bo Peep, as she named her in her mind, disliking the sweetly feminine woman on sight. Which wasn't at all fair or nice, but…

"Oh, you must be the FBI agent," Mary Jo exclaimed in a soft, almost breathless voice. "I just can't imagine doing dangerous work like that." She gave a delicate shiver and leaned against Judd's arm as if seeking protection.

"Dead people aren't dangerous," Tracy said bluntly. "Only the living." She ignored the ominous frown Judd gave her.

Tracy tried to place the woman. She knew the Kincaids fairly well. She and her father had collected their pioneer stories and read their great-great-great-grandmother's diary of the trip west. There had been two sons, one of which was dead. She didn't remember any daughters.

"Mary Jo was the children's librarian here. She and Dugin Kincaid were married last June."

"Oh." Tracy noticed the diamond rings on Mary Jo's left hand. A feeling like relief washed over her. Her smile became genuine. "I hope you'll be very happy."

"Oh, I am. Dugin is just wonderful to me. Well, I've got

to go. I'm supposed to judge flower arrangements in a few minutes. It was nice meeting you." She hurried off toward the gate, leaving a trail of expensive perfume to mingle with the scent of popcorn and hot dogs from a nearby stand.

Tracy glanced up to see Judd watching her with a definite look of hostility in his dark eyes. "Yes?" she said.

"Mary Jo has had a hard time this past year. First an abandoned baby was found on her fiancé's doorstep, then the body of a stranger was discovered during her wedding. And her father-in-law died two months ago. Jeremiah was a strong man and losing him turned the family upside down. Mary Jo is shy and doesn't open up to people easily. I thought you might be friends."

Tracy fumed at his censorious tone. "Why should she need me when she has *you* for her champion?" she asked acidly.

His eyebrows lowered like a thunderstorm about to start.

Tracy backed up a couple of steps. "I have to find Winona."

"She's at the vegetable-judging pavilion. She said to meet her there," he told her. He reached into his shirt pocket. "Here's your ticket." He handed it to her.

He, too, had changed clothes before coming to the fair. In jeans and cowboy boots, with a red shirt and denim jacket, he was incredibly attractive. He wore a Wind River hat, gray with a gray-and-black woven band. Not showy, but seductive just the same.

Her heart seemed to be beating against her ribs all of a sudden. Jealousy, she thought. She was jealous of any woman he smiled at. She swallowed and tried to ignore the painful beat.

"Who do I owe for it?" she asked, taking the ticket.

He looked annoyed. "No one. I had a couple of free passes." His smile was sardonic. "Perks of the office."

"Well, thanks." She paused, not sure what to do. "I'd better meet Winona." She hurried off without waiting for a reply.

Judd let her go. He watched her long, slender legs striding purposefully toward the gate. She handed over the ticket, got her hand stamped and went inside.

She couldn't get away from him fast enough.

He snorted cynically. Since that episode in the cottage, she stayed a cautious distance from him, as if she thought he couldn't be trusted around her.

He couldn't. That's what made him mad as hell. And another thing—he'd been flirting with Mary Jo, on purpose, knowing he was doing it and knowing that Tracy could see them talking while she crossed the parking lot and approached them.

His skin seemed too small for his body all at once, as if filling with needs too long denied. A clamoring hunger in him was growing and pushing to be let out. He clamped down on the unwanted desire. Not Tracy. No way. Never again.

Shaking his head, he walked more slowly toward the entrance. Winona had asked him to eat with her and Tracy. He didn't want to.

Tracy stirred up too much…tension in him. Yeah, his libido was real tense when she was around. He smiled grimly at the joke, but didn't find it all that funny.

Tracy saw Winona standing by an arrangement of gourds and pumpkins on a tray. The fall decorative display had a red ribbon for second place on it.

"Is this yours?" she asked. "It's lovely. Congratulations on the ribbon."

"It's only second place," Winona said grumpily. "I'm glad to see you. I'm hungry enough to eat a bear, hide and all." She smiled and reached over to straighten an ear of Indian corn.

Her hand brushed against Tracy's.

Tracy heard the gasp, then felt Winona sway. She put an arm around her. "Winona? What is it? Are you ill?" She wasn't sure if the psychic was having a vision or a heart attack.

"Rocks," Winona whispered, leaning heavily against Tracy, nearly making her stagger. "No, one rock... coming down hard...falling...falling...anger...furious anger..."

Tracy felt a strong arm slip under hers. Judd took Winona's weight easily and held the rotund body close until the spell was done. Their eyes met over the shorter woman's head.

"I have her," Judd said in a soft rumble.

Tracy caught Winona's hand in hers and rubbed gently.

Winona pulled away as if hurt. Her eyes snapped open. "Who have you touched?" she asked in a weak tone.

Tracy shook her head. "It must have been the bones. I found more of them this afternoon."

Winona nodded. She seemed to be okay.

"What did you see?" Judd asked.

"It was strange," Winona told him, her expression once more serene. "There was a rock, hitting something...or someone...I couldn't tell about that. Just this rock, flying through the air and hitting, then hitting again, only downward this time."

"Hmm."

The two women waited while Judd thought about it.

"The bones," he said to Tracy. "Maybe it was murder, after all." He turned back to Winona. "If you get any more visions, I want to know about them, no matter how remotely connected you think they are or how odd."

"All right. Now, about some supper."

Tracy noticed Winona didn't point out her second-place win to Judd. It came to her that the woman had a small streak of vanity of her own. She smiled and walked with the two back to the hot-dog stand.

The incident was forgotten as the three of them got their meal and found a table. The detective, Sterling McCallum, and his wife were in the food line behind them. Tracy knew Jessica Larson McCallum from before. Her father had tried to help Thadd when he was found. The couple was pushing a lovely, happy baby in a stroller. She looked eager to explore the world. Tracy smiled though she couldn't help remember another child so eager for adventure. Judd invited them to join him, Winona and Tracy at their table.

"Two women," McCallum mused after he and his wife sat down and introductions were made. "How do you rate that, Boss?"

"Just lucky," Judd said with that lazy grin that caused a shaft of longing to go through Tracy. When he shifted his chair to make room for the couple, his arm brushed hers.

"Don't get any ideas," Jessica McCallum told her husband. "You have enough going with the two women you've already got!" She took Jennifer out of the stroller and handed the toddler to her husband.

He cradled his daughter in one arm. She looked up at him and nestled sleepily. He smiled and tweaked a lock of her hair, but Tracy saw the tenderness in his eyes as he glanced from his daughter to his wife. She recognized the look of a man who was well satisfied with his lot in life. The tough detective had two soft spots, it seemed.

Tracy was touched by their happiness. Her gaze met Judd's. He looked at her so intently that she became flustered. She squeezed her hot dog. Mustard flew out the end and landed on her silk top.

"Here," Judd said. He picked up a napkin and dipped it in a cup of water. He slipped his fingers under the edge of the silk shell and rubbed the spot. His efforts only made it worse.

"Try spit. It might take most of it out," Winona advised.

Judd moistened the napkin with his tongue and went back to work.

Tracy felt the heat radiating from his hand into her flesh. Although he hardly touched her and his hand was a respectable distance from her breast, she kept getting hard, stabbing jolts of electricity all the way down her torso.

Her breath became jerky. In fact, her lungs were hardly working at all. She could feel sweat popping out on her forehead. "Don't."

Her protest apparently didn't register with him. He wore a frown of intense concentration as he worked on the stubborn spot.

When the tip of her breast clenched into a tight bead, perfectly visible under her bra and top, she grew desperate.

"Stop!" she said, the word coming out as a shrill cry.

Everyone stopped what they were doing and stared at her and Judd. His long fingers were still inserted under the edge of her blouse as he, too, went still. For a long second, they sat frozen into place.

She wished she could sink out of sight right into the ground.

A brick red flush swept up Judd's face. He released her blouse as if it were a hot coal.

"I think that's as good as you're going to get it," Jessica announced. She deftly changed the subject. "Sterling said you found some more bones today. Did they go with the others?"

Tracy was grateful for the new topic. "Uh, yes. I feel sure we'll find more. It looks very promising."

The conversation became general after that. Later, she and Judd went with the McCallums to the rides while Winona spotted Lily Mae Wheeler and went to talk to her. They all tried the Ferris wheel, then paused by the carousel.

Tracy was totally surprised by Jessica McCallum. She teased her husband unmercifully. "I'd like to ride the merry-go-round, but the horses will probably run off when they see you coming."

"I promise not to sit on one," he shot right back. "Although I might sit on you before the evening is over if you keep up the wise remarks." He gave her a menacing scowl that didn't frighten her in the least.

He bought five tickets and handed two to Judd. Judd looked at Tracy with a question in his eyes. She drew a deep breath and got in line behind the other couple. Judd stood behind her.

It was with trepidation that Tracy stepped up on the carousel platform. Jennifer chose a blue horse with a silver mane. Sterling lifted Jessica up on it so that she and their daughter sat sidesaddle. He stood beside them, his arms placed protectively on either side of his women. Jennifer laughed but waved at everyone.

"Let's take a swan boat," Tracy suggested.

Judd nodded.

They climbed in and sat on the wooden bench. In front of them, two girls, about nine, squealed with delight as they leapt upon two unicorns, which were white, with golden horns projecting from their foreheads.

"Beautiful mythical creatures," Judd remarked as the music speeded up and they started turning.

"Yes."

He had taken her to a carnival in July, nearly seventeen years ago to the day, a few weeks after they'd met. They had been on the merry-go-round when she'd suddenly become nauseated. He'd swept her off the unicorn she'd been riding and signaled the man to stop. In the privacy of his car, when she felt better, he'd questioned her gently. They had realized she was most likely pregnant.

"I should have taken better care of you," he'd blamed himself.

He'd gone with her to face her parents and tell them they wanted to be married right away. Six weeks after they'd met, they were married. Their son had been born in March.

For nine years, the marriage had been good.

Then one autumn a freak accident had destroyed their happiness. They had lived in the same house another year, but it wasn't the same. Unable to bear the mockery their lives had become, she'd asked for a divorce. Judd had moved out of the house while the legal arrangements were made. When the divorce was final, she'd left town, never intending to return.

The merry-go-round completed one full turn and started another. She thought of life, going around and around. Going nowhere, it sometimes seemed. That was her life.

Ahead of them, Tracy saw Sterling lean over and listen to something his daughter babbled. He laughed. Jessica kissed him on the cheek. He turned her face with a finger under her chin and claimed a quick kiss on the lips before tousling Jennifer's curls.

The tenderness between the other couple caused an ache to start deep inside Tracy. Once, she'd had that.

When she looked at Judd, he was staring off into the darkening sky, his jaw set in a hard line. Anger, raw and hurting, roiled in her. She wanted life to be different. She wanted all it had promised those many years ago. She wanted to start over….

Clenching her hands together, she forced her thoughts away from those lines. It didn't matter what she wanted. Life couldn't be lived over and adjusted to suit one's idea of happiness.

She would never hold another child in her arms. After Thadd's birth, she'd had a severe infection that had left her barren. She and Judd hadn't been able to conceive another child, although they'd both wanted a brother or sister for their son.

Judd touched her hands. He gently pulled them apart and held her right hand, rubbing it between both of his. "Don't think on it," he murmured soothingly. "Let it go, Trace."

Gradually, the feelings subsided, and she felt only the ever-present tinge of sorrow that colored her days. She stared at Judd in wonder. The harshness was gone from his eyes, and he looked at her in…pity?

She pulled her hand away. She didn't need pity from anyone. What had happened had happened. A person had to go on. She knew that. She was getting on with her life.

Was she?

Yes.

"I'm all right," she assured him. She smiled to show him. After the ride, she said good-night to the McCallums, having decided to return to Winona and talk to her for a while before returning to the cottage.

Lily Mae and several others sat at a large table where they'd left the older woman. The widow, wearing three-inch-long blue-and-purple earrings that matched her colorful knit pants and top, introduced Tracy to everyone and told her something of each person's life. "Tracy is the FBI expert investigating the murder on the reservation," she finished.

"Murder has not been established," Tracy hastily corrected.

"Well, everyone knows that's what happened," Lily Mae asserted with an authoritative air. "Why else would a skeleton be there?"

"People die of lots of things," Judd said, coming to stand beside Tracy. "A woman choked on a hot dog last week down in Big Timber and was nearly asphyxiated before the medics got it out."

Lily Mae peered at her hot dog, then shrugged. "There are worse ways to go." She finished off the last bite while the other women laughed or looked shocked, according to the way they viewed Lily Mae and her outrageous quips.

Tracy smiled. Maybe she'd have her father down next weekend for a home-cooked meal and invite the widow-divorcée, too. Her eyes went to Judd. No, she wouldn't invite him.

"Winona, I think I'll go home now," she said. "How would you like to go out to dinner tomorrow night? I thought I'd try the new pizza place I saw near the library."

"That sounds fine. I'll come by your house around six."

"Good. Well, good night. It was nice meeting all of you." She smiled at the group, then headed for her car.

Judd accompanied her. "It's dark," he said when she glanced at him. "A woman shouldn't be in the parking lot alone."

"I'm sure no crook would dare impose on your territory."

He lifted one black eyebrow at her mocking tone. "The fair brings in a lot of strangers."

They walked past the rows of cars. He was right, she realized. A dark parking lot was a lonely place. "How do people like Lily Mae come up with so much gossip, or in this case, the truth?"

"You have evidence of murder?"

"No." She paused at her car. "But Winona's vision—that rock hitting someone. I think she's seeing something connected with the bones. It's happened twice now, both times after I've handled the evidence. I think our mysterious victim was killed by getting bashed with a rock."

Judd drummed his fingers on the top of her car. "Well, if a rock did it, there's no shortage of weapons in the area. Or the county." He nudged a half-buried rock in the hard ground of the parking lot with the toe of his boot.

Tracy yawned. She hadn't been sleeping well that week. Maybe tonight she'd get a proper rest without waking and lying in bed for hours, thinking of the past.

"Judd, thank you for earlier. When we were on the carousel," she added when he looked at her questioningly.

His expression turned grim. He stared out into the night. It came to her that there was a blackness in his soul that matched the one in hers. Once there'd been such joy between them....

"It's hard not to remember," he said in a low tone.

"I know."

Sympathy stirred in her. Life could be unbearably hard for a man of Judd's temperament. He was a man of action, a person who got things done. But even he hadn't been able to save their son. Like her, he could only wait, pacing the hospital corridor while the doctor operated.

She climbed into her car, said good-night to him and drove off. Looking in her rearview mirror, she felt a wrenching pain inside as she observed him watching her drive off. If things had worked out differently, they would have been going home together.

Five

Tracy woke to bright sunlight streaming across her pillow. She'd slept fitfully the night before. Long after she'd arrived home and gone to bed, she'd lain there thinking of the past and the future she'd expected with Judd.

Impatient with this line of thinking, she flung the covers off and prepared to face the day. After dressing and making the bed, she ate a bowl of cereal, then carried her cup of coffee to the front porch to plan her day.

When the hardware store opened, she'd get a washer for the leaky faucet and fix that, she decided, settling into a wooden rocker with a cane bottom and back. She'd clean house, then go to the grocery store. Perhaps she'd go to the fairgrounds that afternoon and look over the livestock. She'd liked that as a kid. After that, Winona was supposed to come by and have pizza with her.

Satisfied that this was a workable plan that would keep

her moderately busy, she finished the coffee while the sun pushed higher into the clear morning air. It was going to be a hot day.

She glanced at her shorts and knit top. They were okay for a trip to the hardware store. She took her cup into the house and turned off the coffeemaker. Removing the worn washer from the faucet, she slipped it into her pocket. She clipped her purse around her waist and decided to walk downtown rather than drive.

At the hardware store, she bought a packet of washers that matched the old one. As she was leaving, a man walked up to her.

"Hello, Tracy, remember me?"

She looked into a familiar face. Dark eyes. Dark hair, worn rather long. Jeans. A blue shirt open to the waist. "Wolf Boy," she said before she thought.

A wry grimace briefly twisted the mobile lips of the good-looking young man who'd greeted her. "Smile when you say that, partner," he said with mock menace.

She grinned. "Rafe, how are you?" Memories leap-frogged over each other into her mind.

Her father had interviewed the Rawlings clan out on Whispering Pines Road about their early life in Montana, so she was familiar with the family history. Rafe had been adopted.

Tracy had been around eight years old the summer an abandoned child had been found in the woods north of the Rawlings ranch. That child had been Rafe.

The newspapers and TV stations had made a field day of his discovery, calling him "Wolf Boy," a nickname that stuck, and writing the most incredible stories about him growing up with the wild animals. What drivel. He'd been a baby at the time. No clues to his real parentage had ever turned up.

"Long time no see," he said. "I'd heard you were in town."

"Temporarily," she said. "Are you ranching?"

"Not entirely. I'm a detective here in Whitehorn."

"I didn't know that."

"You and Lily Mae didn't get to the folks who live on the west side of the county when you had dinner the other night?" His smile was wry. He'd been a topic of speculation all his life and had become a quiet, reserved little boy; he seemed the same as a man.

"I don't think we got outside the city limits."

"So what's happening with the bones?"

"Not much. I'd like to find the rest of the skeleton."

"You going to run DNA tests?"

"I don't know. The FBI doesn't like having its resources used without good reason."

"Meaning the budget is tight, so watch what you spend?"

"You got it. The local police department must operate like the federal government."

"Yeah. Things are tough all over." He glanced at the package in her hand. "You going into the repair business?"

"Just a washer on a leaky faucet."

She smiled fondly at him, remembering him as a toddler who'd followed her around when she had visited the ranch with her father. She'd played with him while the grown-ups talked. Twenty-eight years ago. Heavens, how the time did fly.

They walked outside and said goodbye. She started down the street on foot.

"Are you walking?" he called to her.

"Yes."

"Hop in. I'll give you a ride. I wanted to ask you a couple of questions, if you have time."

She sensed an edginess in his stance. "Okay," she agreed. She climbed into the pickup. He slammed the door and got in on the driver's side. He cranked up the engine and drove off.

They talked about the changes in the neighborhood on the way. It wasn't until he pulled into her drive that she realized she hadn't told him where she lived.

"It's a small town," was his comment when she mentioned this fact. "Besides, it's my job as a cop to know everyone's business."

"Hmm, maybe Lily Mae missed her calling. Perhaps I should mention the police department the next time I see her."

Rafe held up both hands. "I give," he declared. "Lily Mae would have the office running a lonely hearts club before the year was out. She's always trying to match people up."

"Yeah? Who has she chosen for you?" She led the way into the house and toward the kitchen.

He gave a snort of derision. "I keep a low profile where women are concerned."

Tracy studied him. She sensed a loneliness that matched her own. "Why would you do that? You're darned good-looking. The gals in the county must be real miffed if you never look at them."

"I never said I didn't look." His smile wasn't reflected in his eyes. "Marriage doesn't seem to work out. It's hard enough when you know a person, but someone like me… Who knows what my background is? I may be the son of the Son of Sam."

"You're not a killer," she told him sternly. "There's no such thing as bad blood. You're what you make of yourself."

"Enough. My past, or lack of one, is ancient history. Tell me how you got into forensic investigation."

"Like father, like daughter, I suppose. I spent my youth collecting old stories with him. Ancient ways interested me more than modern times. I also liked working puzzles of any kind. Put those two together. Forensic investigation is sort of like working jigsaw puzzles. You just keep moving things around until you get all the pieces to fit."

"Someone said the bones from the res weren't old."

Tracy rolled her eyes, exasperated with the local grapevine. "Coffee?" she asked.

"Got any iced tea? The day is already hot."

She checked the refrigerator. The tea pitcher was nearly full. She poured two glasses.

"Were the bones old?" he asked.

"No. My guess is they've been in the ground twenty or thirty years. No more."

"How can you tell?"

"Stain penetration into the surface. Also I'd say the bones have been in a protected place. They're in too good a condition to have been out in the open all this time."

"Animals would have eaten them," he suggested.

"Right. There are some fresh teeth marks, but no real damage. The bones are too old to be tasty." She removed the packet of washers from her purse and laid them next to the sink.

"Here, let me change those washers for you," Rafe said. He put his glass on the counter and checked the leaky faucet. "May as well do both sides. Got a screwdriver?"

"I found a box of tools under the sink." She bent and got them out. "There's no need. I know how to fix it."

"The independent woman, huh?" He gave her an assessing glance. "Come on. Let me feel I have some use in the world."

She laughed while he made sure the water was off and unscrewed the cold-water handle. He quickly and efficiently replaced the washers in both faucets.

"There," he said upon finishing. "Just in the nick of time." He held up the other one to show her it was worn almost through the rubber and would have started leaking soon.

"What do I owe you for this great service?"

He gestured toward the cabinets while he stored the toolbox under the sink again. "How about two of those chocolate-chip cookies I saw in there when you got the glasses?"

"Hmm, you are observant. I'd better watch what I let you see in the future."

They chatted while she got out cookies. Rafe retrieved his glass and headed for the table. She did the same. Into this comfortable idle another presence intruded, in the form of the sheriff.

Judd came to the back door. His furious gaze met her startled one just as she turned from the counter. Iced tea slopped out onto the floor. "Judd!" she exclaimed.

Rafe went over and opened the door. "Come in, Sheriff."

"Thanks," Judd said laconically. He smiled coolly.

Tracy wondered if that momentary glimpse of anger had been in her imagination. "We're having cookies. Would you like to join us?" she asked, placing the glass on the table.

"No, thanks. I gave 'em up when I outgrew my morning nap."

"Uh-oh," Rafe said in a loud whisper to her. "Me thinks the boss is madder than hell."

She realized Judd was throwing out a challenge and the younger man wasn't backing down. She wasn't sure what to do.

Judd scowled, then turned a deadly eye on Tracy. "I came over earlier to fix the faucet. No one was home."

"I was at the hardware store," she explained, then frowned. She didn't have to account to him. Irritated with herself, she used more vigor than necessary to wipe up the spilt tea.

"The faucet is fixed," Rafe announced.

Tracy noticed his keen gaze studying Judd, as if he were judging his reaction to this news. She looked at the older lawman. He was in control. Other than the remnants of irritation at the wasted trip, no emotion showed on his lean, handsome face.

Judd glanced at the leftover coffee in the pot, then at her. "I'll take some coffee, if it isn't too much trouble."

"Not at all." She poured a cup, heated it in the microwave and handed it to him. When she went to the table again, Judd joined her, holding her chair for her before taking the one on her right.

"Moonlighting as a plumber?" Judd inquired of Rafe after watching the young officer down two cookies and reach for another.

Tracy drank her tea. Her appetite had fled.

"No. I was curious about the bones from the res. Tracy was telling me about forensics. See?" Rafe inquired innocently. "All in-the-line-of-duty stuff. Nothing clandestine going on."

Tracy was both amused and appalled at his effrontery. She saw Judd give Rafe a glance from under his eyebrows that had always boded ill for Thadd when the boy did something wrong. She tried to think what she could do to head off a collision between the men.

"The res isn't in your jurisdiction," Judd remarked.

"Yours either, Sheriff."

The two men locked eyes in silent combat.

"I need to go to the grocery store, then I thought I'd go out to the fair to look at the livestock," Tracy put in hurriedly. "Thanks for fixing the leak, Rafe. Remember me to your mom next time you see her." She stood, causing the men to rise, and urged the younger man toward the door.

Rafe grinned at her, then winked. "I'll see you at the fair. Shall I look for you by the calf pens, say…about one?"

"Yes," she said, practically pushing him out the door. *Men.*

He left. In a minute, she heard his pickup fire up and back out of the drive. The sound of its engine faded as he drove off. She turned toward the table with a frown.

"What was that all about?" she demanded.

"What? These cookies are good. Did you make them?"

"No. Why were you rude to Rafe?"

Judd stopped concentrating on the cookie he was dunking in his coffee and stuck the rest of it in his mouth. He gave her such a falsely innocent look that it disconcerted her.

"Me? Rude?"

Their son had assumed the exact same expression when he was trying to wiggle out of trouble. Like father…

"What?" he asked, his voice suddenly deeper as if he sensed the stab of pain the thought had caused her.

"I...nothing. Just a thought."

He studied her for a long minute. "How did Rafe happen to drop by and fix your sink?"

She explained that they'd met at the store. "I used to play with him when he was a baby. I'd entertain him while my father went through the Rawlings family albums. It was such a long time ago, and now...now he's a policeman. It's hard to believe."

"You didn't seem to be thinking of him as a baby when you made a date for the fair," Judd commented.

"I'm eight years older than he is." She gave Judd a puzzled glance. "I didn't make a date with him."

"I'm eight years older than you," Judd reminded her. "He said he'd meet you at the calf pens at one."

"Oh, that. He was just riling you." She tilted her head at a slight angle and studied her ex-husband. "Did he succeed?" she asked and wondered why she was deliberately trying to needle him.

"Hardly." Judd took a drink of coffee, seemingly as cool as a mountain breeze, all emotion now gone.

She watched his throat work as he swallowed. Once she'd loved to kiss him there, the faint taste of salt on her tongue when she'd nibbled and licked his freshly shaved skin. She looked away.

"Well, I have to make out a grocery list," she announced.

Judd made no effort to leave after her broad hint.

She set about the task, ignoring the man who watched her as she went through the cabinets and refrigerator for supplies. She didn't want to get too many staples. She'd have to toss them out when she left or haul them all the way back to California with her.

"Are you going to the fair this afternoon?" he asked after a lengthy silence.

"Yes, I think so."

"I have to drive down to Billings to check on some stolen items that have been recovered. I thought you might want to ride along. You used to like that."

She stared at him, trying to figure out why he'd asked her. She knew he was keeping an eye on her because of the case, but was that the only reason?

The old attraction was still there, as strong as ever…maybe stronger. That could have been jealousy she'd seen in Judd's eyes when he'd arrived and found Rafe at her kitchen table.

Surely not. Other than the lingering traces of a passion too strong to be forgotten, there was nothing between them.

A tremor of unease went through her. At thirty-six, she found she wasn't half as sure of life and love as she'd been at nineteen.

"Well?" he muttered in a growl.

She glanced around the kitchen. "I have too much to do. I still have to clean house…and—and go to the store…."

A tumult of emotions hit her, so fast, so hard, she couldn't figure out the individual ones. She stole a glance at Judd.

He sat like a statue at the table, the planes of his face rigid, his thoughts unreadable. She wanted to ask him what he was thinking, why he'd invited her on the trip, but she didn't.

She'd learned long ago that Judd didn't share his deepest feelings with her. Once she'd needed him desperately. Once she'd begged him to talk to her, to help her get past the grief that ravaged her soul. He'd walked out.

It had destroyed something in her, having him turn his back on her…. She fought back the tears that burned her eyes. That had been long ago. It didn't matter now. Their lives had separated into two diverging paths.

He nodded and stood. "Here. I brought you a timer. Set it to turn a lamp on around dusk." He laid it on the table.

She was aware of his gaze running over her, dark, sensual, almost brooding. It made her feel tight and achy inside, and so full of longing the tears rose again. "Thanks."

He walked out, taking his toolbox and packet of washers with him. She felt the increasing distance between them as an abyss of utter darkness, too wide to cross, as he got into his truck and left.

Judd cursed all the way to the office. Why the hell had he asked Tracy to come along with him? Insanity, pure insanity.

Or jealousy? a part of him asked.

He didn't want to think about it. He unlocked his office and collected the inventory of the item he was to pick up. He studied the list. Truthfully, the trip could wait until Monday. Or he could send a deputy.

Hearing laughter on the street, he paused and looked out the window at a couple who'd stopped to let their two kids play. He watched them for several minutes while the emptiness inside shifted uneasily.

It was getting harder to maintain that vacuum, he admitted. Being around Tracy punched holes in his self-control.

Passion. He still wanted her. It burned in him like a steady flame, refusing to go out. Passion was all right, but a man would be a fool to get mixed up in all that emotional baggage again.

All he'd felt was an echo of male possessiveness. Seeing Rafe hanging around Tracy had stirred primitive urges he'd do better to ignore. Tracy wasn't his. He didn't want her to be.

He sat at his desk and went over the current cases on his agenda. There'd been a couple of car thefts, some vandalism involving spray paint, a couple of domestic-violence calls. All those were solved or under investigation.

The bones from the reservation were the biggest question mark. Winona's vision had convinced him the case was homicide.

That led to the problem of Tracy. She was so damned independent. She didn't want him interfering with *her* case.

Too bad. He was going to keep her under his watchful eye whether she liked it or not. This was his county, his people. He was responsible for them. And for her as long as she was in the area.

Darkness seemed to open within him when he thought of her leaving again. He cursed under his breath. He'd ignore the tension between them and keep his mind strictly on the law.

Restless, he checked the time and headed out the door. He'd go talk to Winona. Now *there* was a woman with a man's mind—practical and sane, not running on temperament, but logic.

Yeah, he'd go talk to her. About the case.

She was concluding a deal when he parked next to the lopsided sign out front. She and the Cheyenne shook hands and laughed, then the man departed, giving a quick nod to Judd when he passed on the way to his pickup with a wheelbarrow full of junk.

"Business looks good," he commented as he surveyed the new items in the yard.

"It is," she agreed. "Look at this blanket."

Judd admired the Indian blanket she held up, which was woven with a Navajo design. The tourists wouldn't know the difference, or care if they did, he thought cynically. "Nice," he said.

"I'm going to enter it in the fair for his wife." She nodded toward the road as the pickup disappeared around a bend. "It'll fetch a fair price whether it wins a ribbon or not."

"Good."

"You're in a foul mood," Winona said. "Come have some chamomile tea with honey. It'll soothe your nerves."

Judd followed her across the crowded yard, keeping a sharp eye out for the goats. They liked to sneak up on him and butt him from behind, hitting him right in the back of the knee, which caused his leg to buckle. He'd bashed his kneecap on a concrete birdbath the last time that had happened.

Winona led the way inside the trailer. It always surprised him how neat and orderly it was compared to the front yard. The backyard was an oasis of flowers and peace.

They chatted about the weather and the fair while she fixed the tea. When she handed him the cup, her fingers brushed his. She jerked back as if burned.

He set the cup down and prepared to catch her, but she shook her head, telling him she was all right.

"You've been with Tracy," she said.

"Yeah. I saw her briefly this morning."

"Why are you angry with her?"

"I'm not—" He stopped abruptly when she cast a penetrating gaze on him, reminding him of a teacher he'd had in the fifth grade who could detect mischief before it got started. He swallowed. "She was with Rafe Rawlings."

Winona sat in her favorite chair and motioned for him to be seated. He chose a straight-backed chair at the table, pulling it around so he could face his hostess.

"You shouldn't have let her go," Winona said, quite gently for her. She usually was pretty blunt with him.

He felt the emptiness whirl and waited for it to settle. "I'm not here to talk about that. It's…those days are gone."

"But not forgotten," she said with some asperity, sounding more her usual self.

He shrugged, unwilling to discuss it. What good would it do? The past was long gone. There was no way to get it back at this late date. Not that he wanted to.

"You want to know about Tracy," Winona guessed correctly. "You want to know if she's in danger. The answer is yes."

His pulse leapt like a startled rabbit. "What? Who?"

She shook her head. "I don't know. I sensed it on her. Did she tell you of the first vision I had, the one from the other night when she came out for supper?"

"No." Judd felt a chill crept over him. His lethal streak, Sterling called it.

When he was on a case, a certain coolness would sometimes come over him. His mind would become as clear as crystal. He would be able to make connections between facts that few others seemed to notice. However, in this case it felt more like fear. Tracy in danger…

Winona related the vision of the two-faced woman.

"A lot of people are two-faced," he mused when she finished. "They pretend to be one thing when they're really another. Or they say one thing when they mean something entirely different."

Tracy had acted as if she loved him more than life itself, but when the chips were down, she'd turned from him without a backward glance. Not that he blamed her. He was the one who'd encouraged Thadd to be independent and unafraid.

When the doctor had walked out of the operating room and shaken his head wearily, telling them their child was gone, her love had died, too. Sometimes he thought he'd never gotten over those twin blows—the loss of his son and the loss of his wife.

A hand touched his.

He glanced into wise brown eyes and saw sympathy. A pressure built behind his eyes. Hurriedly, he took a drink of the hot tea.

"Things will work out," Winona said. Her gaze took on a misty quality. "I see darkness ahead. Tracy…" She paused, frowned, then shook her head.

"What did you see?" he asked, his heart slamming against his breastbone.

"Nothing. Just a feeling." She studied Judd as they sipped the soothing brew. "You're going to have to confront your sorrow someday," she advised.

The cup jerked, and hot tea sloshed over his hand. He grabbed a napkin and mopped it up. "What sorrow?" he asked, keeping his tone neutral. Too many emotions were being stirred up nowadays. He didn't need an old woman that half the county thought was batty telling him about his emotions.

"There's an emptiness in your soul," she murmured, partially closing her eyes. A cat jumped into her lap, and she stroked it absently. "It can be filled. But the filling will be painful, and the cost high."

The chill shot right down into his backbone. "I like the

emptiness," he said in a low growl, feeling like a cornered wolf. "Life is easier that way."

"None of the pain?"

"That's right," he agreed harshly.

"But none of the joy," the wise woman reminded him gently. "Grab the joy while it's available. I let it go. In the end, I had only a month with the man I loved."

Judd looked at the old woman, startled. He'd never really thought of her being in love.

She smiled sadly. "Yes, even I was once in love. I'd never told another person until recently, and now I've told two."

"Tracy," he said, knowing at once who the other person had been. "There's something special between the two of you. Her mother commented on it once. She said she felt almost jealous of the bond you had with her daughter."

Winona merely nodded her head and rocked quietly back and forth, stroking the cat, whose purr filled the silence.

He sighed, then stood. "I'm going to Billings to pick up some stolen goods that have been recovered. Would you like to ride along?" He glanced around the neat trailer. "Or do you need to clean house, too?"

She laughed in delight at his irony. "So she turned you down. Don't be discouraged. Keep an eye on her. Twice I've sensed danger near her. Stay close."

"I will," he heard himself solemnly promise.

Later, driving back to Whitehorn from Billings, the crate of stolen guns in the back seat, he thought of his conversation with the psychic. God, he'd sounded as if he'd taken an oath to find the Holy Grail.

His feelings toward Tracy were the result of two things. One, since he was sheriff of the county, naturally he felt protective toward her. Two, there was a lingering passion between them.

Well, hell, nice to know some things in life never changed. Although desire wasn't one of the things he'd have voted for, given a choice.

After leaving the stolen loot with the officer in charge of the evidence storage room in the basement of the police station, he headed for the fairgrounds five miles south of town.

He found Tracy at the calf pens, laughing while she tried to pet a calf that was trying to suck her fingers. Rafe Rawlings stood beside her, one hand at her waist as she bent over the low fence.

White heat shot through Judd, followed by a coldness that left his mind crystal clear. He walked forward.

Tracy straightened up and glanced around, feeling suddenly uneasy. Her eyes met a dark and dangerous gaze.

"Hello, Judd," she said, her voice fairly steady.

"Lo, the lawman returneth," Rafe drawled, earning him a sardonic smile from the sheriff.

"In the flesh," Judd returned with cool nonchalance.

Tracy gave each man a warning frown. She was not going to be a bone fought over by two dogs…or cops, in this case. She didn't understand why men had to be so territorial in the first place.

She had decided that was the root of the earlier jealousy—if it had been jealousy she'd seen in Judd at her house. Anyway, she was going to choose her own companions.

Rafe had been asking her a million questions about forensic techniques and about the bones she was examining. She'd promised to let him see them and to explain some of the things she looked for when she was doing an investigation. As a local policeman, he was naturally curious about murder in his backyard, so to speak.

Judd, of course, thought the case should be his. It galled him that the reservation was in the county, but out of his jurisdiction. Tough. He would have to accept her authority just as the tribal council had had to.

"I'd like to see the rabbits now. The ribbons were supposed to be posted on them by noon," she said brightly.

The two men fell into step with her. They admired the rabbits, the pigeons, chickens, turkeys and ducks. She wandered over to the ring, where prize breeding stock was being judged.

She noticed Judd checking the security at the fair. Several deputies were in evidence. Their presence would do a lot toward ensuring a peaceful gathering. She saw him nod to each lawman they met. Most of them returned his greeting with a casual salute.

The two men were still with her when she spied Winona in the bleachers watching the judging. "Hello. I didn't expect to see you until tonight," she said, sitting by the older woman.

Rafe slid onto the bench beside her before Judd got a chance to. Judd's lips tightened fractionally, then he sat down in front of Tracy on the next bench and twisted around to talk to the other three.

"I got the honey collected, put in jars and labeled, so I decided to come in. I entered a pie in the fall-fruit-baking category—pumpkin and honey with wild nuts."

"My favorite," Judd muttered. "And you didn't even offer me a piece when I was out there."

"I didn't make it until later. Besides, I couldn't take a piece out of it and then put it in the contest." She gave him a grin that drew crinkles around her eyes in a merry fashion. She looked like an elf with her sun-browned face and plump figure.

"I wonder if the judges will leave any after they taste it," he grumbled.

"Leftovers go to the senior-citizen centers," Rafe put in.

"I made one to give to Tracy," Winona said with an innocent smile. "Maybe, if you're real nice, she'll give you some of it."

Judd glanced at Tracy. She saw him hesitate. "I'll buy that pizza you promised Winona for supper," he declared, "if you'll serve the pie for dessert."

"All right," she agreed.

"Great," Rafe said, counting himself in. "I'll get the ice cream to go on the pie."

Tracy choked back laughter at the look Judd gave the young policeman. Winona had no such compulsions. She cackled aloud.

After a second, Judd grinned and dodged a mock punch from Rafe, who was also laughing.

Sterling and Jessica McCallum joined them and demanded to know what the joke was.

"Two dogs and one bone," Winona told them.

Jessica glanced at the two men, then at Tracy. She grinned in delight and plopped down by Judd. "Looks like an even number of dogs and bones to me," she announced, clearly putting the men in the dog category.

Her husband groaned and demanded to know how much

of this stuff a man was supposed to take. That earned him a poke in the side from his wife.

The day ended with all of them going to the pizza place for dinner, then trooping back to Tracy's cottage for pie and ice cream. Jennifer played with several plastic bowls and a wooden spoon that Tracy gave her. After eating some ice cream, she went to sleep on the sofa.

The adults took their coffee out on the porch afterward and watched the sky darken from twilight into night. Rafe managed to stay at her side most of the time, which paired Judd with Winona.

Tracy felt a rush of pride as he escorted the older woman, who had to be in her late seventies, with all the gallantry of a knight of old guarding a princess.

After everyone left, she put the dishes in the dishwasher, then changed into her sleep set of satin tap pants and matching green top. She fastened a floral robe over it.

A knock at the back door startled her.

"Judd," she murmured, seeing his stern face beyond the small glass panes across the top of the door. She unlocked the dead bolt and let him in. "I didn't hear your truck. Did you forget something?"

"No." He thrust his hands into his pockets. "I walked over. There was something I wanted to talk to you about."

"Yes?"

"Why the hell didn't you tell me Winona sensed you were in danger?"

She stared at him in total surprise. "It wasn't a definite thing," she finally explained. "I mean, it was probably vibes she was getting from the bones."

Judd shook his head. "It's you. I talked to her earlier today. She said *you* were in danger."

"Did she see something?" While Tracy heeded the wise woman's visions, she wasn't sure about feelings. They could be deceptive. Once she'd thought Judd loved her more than anything, but since that time, she'd learned to distrust turbulent emotions.

"No," he admitted.

"Well, then…"

She stood in the middle of the kitchen floor, not sure what to say. Nervous flutters chased through her stomach at his silent stance. She tightened the tasseled belt of the robe.

He took a step toward her. His hands clenched and unclenched at his sides while his eyes devoured her.

She felt his gaze move over her, burning into every inch. A hot tide of longing ran through her. She might not trust her feelings, but she couldn't deny them. She still wanted him with all the wild yearning of long ago.

He must have seen it in her eyes. "Trace," he murmured.

For once he looked as uncertain as she felt. He took another step toward her. She witnessed his struggle with the force that had drawn them together from the first moment they'd met.

Bewilderment joined the other emotions that roiled in her. She didn't understand it—this irresistible magic that leapt into being whenever they met. She didn't want it.

She fought it and knew he was doing the same.

"No," she whispered, dredging up every ounce of willpower. "It's not…we can't."

The planes of his face abruptly seemed harsher, the bones pressing against his skin as if demanding to escape. "I know," he said with a bitter sigh. "Oh, God, I know."

He pivoted and crossed to the door in two long strides. She clutched the lapels of her robe, stifling the cry that rose in her, ignoring the part that wanted to ask him to stay.

He faced her, all iron control now. The tough sheriff in a tough situation. "You might be in charge of the case, but I'm still sheriff of this county. If your life is in danger, I'm going to do my damnedest to see that you aren't hurt…no matter what."

He went out, then stood on the other side of the door. When she didn't move, he rattled the knob impatiently. She rushed forward and locked the door. He nodded, then headed off into the dark, cutting through the woods in the moonlight.

Tracy turned out the inside lights, made sure the porch lights were on, then went to bed. She lay there a long time, worrying about the situation.

The pressure was building between them. When it got too great, what would happen?

Anxiety swept over her. She wanted to leave. She wanted to solve the case and get out of there…before it was too late.

Six

The Sunday paper arrived with a thud on the front porch. Tracy pushed her hair back and peered at the clock. Barely past seven. She groaned, tossed the covers off and headed for the bathroom. A shower would wake her up.

Later, after eating a breakfast of cereal and banana, she read the news from beginning to end. She folded the paper and stacked it neatly in the middle of the table.

She sighed. The sound seemed to echo through the empty house. Honestly, she never thought she'd see the day she missed the friendly *drip-drip* of a faucet!

Shoving back the chair, she stood and walked out on the front porch. It was almost ten. Down the street, she saw a family come out of their house and get in their car. The parents and two little girls were dressed in their Sunday clothes. Probably on their way to Sunday school, she thought.

She watched them until the car disappeared down the

lane. They'd looked so happy. With a soft gasp, she realized she was envious of their good fortune.

Stepping off the porch, she strolled around the yard, admiring the roses and daisies. Finally, the silence was more than she could take. She paused in her restless pacing and looked down the lane toward the south.

There was a place she'd been avoiding. She knew she'd have to go there before she left town. The psychologist had told her she had to face the past in order to get on with her life.

All right, she resolved, gathering her courage. She would.

Going inside, she clipped on her purse, rubbed sunscreen into her face and arms, donned a hat and started out.

She walked south along Pale Bluff Lane until she came to Willow Brook Road. She crossed the road and headed west until she reached a small chapel, which faced the street. The Whitehorn cemetery surrounded the natural-stone building.

Stopping, Tracy clasped the wrought-iron fence that surrounded the rolling acres and let her gaze roam from the stained-glass windows of the chapel to the delicate carving of twin angels set on the support columns at the entrance gate.

Past the entrance, benches were placed under shade trees in the cultivated lawn, and row after row of headstones marched over the rolling meadow.

Her hands trembled, but she opened the gate and went in. She walked down the path paved with river gravel, the sound of her steps carried away on the warm sigh of the breeze.

At last, in the newer section, she came to a site marked with four polished-granite columns at the corners. Inside the area, a small rectangle was squared off with granite posts set almost flush to the ground.

She sat on one of the taller columns and stared off at the mountains to the west. Part of a Bible verse she'd learned as a child came to her. *I will lift up mine eyes unto the hills.*

Sometimes the sight of mountains and far vistas offered comfort to her soul, but not today.

She swallowed hard, then looked at the low granite stone set at the head of the small rectangle and read the inscription.

Thaddeus Roper Hensley. Beloved Son.

The breeze sighed through the trees, and for a second she thought she heard his laughter, radiant with the delight he'd found in life, in the shear joy of living. She listened intently.

The crunch of gravel was the only sound that came to her. She pivoted on the narrow seat.

Judd stood on the path. He held a pot of golden-eyed daisies in his hand. He walked forward slowly as if he thought she might bolt if he came too close.

"I sometimes plant flowers," he said.

Her throat closed. She nodded and watched as he pulled a trowel from the back pocket of his jeans and planted a bright clump of flowers at each side of the headstone.

When he finished, he sat cross-legged on the grass near her feet and pulled a few tiny weeds from the grave.

"I wondered if you'd come." He looked at her then.

She saw the darkness in the depths of his eyes and knew it came from the soul. She lifted a hand, instinctively needing to soothe the pain with a caress. She let it fall back into her lap.

"I had to." She breathed deeply, carefully, holding on to a control that seemed intent on slipping if she didn't watch it. The need to weep rose in her until it became an ache.

He nodded.

"I still miss him," she heard herself confess, although she hadn't meant to mention it at all. "His laughter. His curiosity and endless questions. His love of all living things. I miss him. It's like…a cold and lonely place inside."

The tendons stood out in Judd's neck. She knew he didn't like to talk about it, but she couldn't seem to stop. The words, like the tears, pressed forward.

"I miss him, and…I'm angry with him." She clenched her hands together. "I'm angry with him for going off into the woods. He knew he wasn't allowed to go off like that by himself. I want him to come home with that sheepish look he got when he knew he was in trouble. I want to send him to bed without his supper. I want to ground him for a month—"

Judd stood abruptly, his fists clenched at his sides, his face as tight-looking as it had been the day before.

She stood, too.

He looked at her so long she began to feel they would turn to stone and stand there forever, locked together in mutual despair, yet apart, always apart.

"Trace," he said hoarsely. He made a movement with his hand, as if he wanted to reach for her, then dropped it.

The gulf of time and unshared grief stretched between them. A quiver of need fell into the darkness inside her like a stone into an abyss. She longed for warmth, for light in her soul.

Once she'd needed him, but he'd walked away. If he walked away now, she'd never forgive him….

No, she had no right to think that. Everything was over between them. They were strangers now, although they'd once created a child together.

She stared at the distant hills and swallowed against the ache inside. "I miss him," she whispered. "Our little boy. I miss him." She fought the darkness, but it closed over her.

Judd felt the blackness rise from the pit inside him. He'd thought the emptiness was safe, but that had been a delusion. He knew that now. The pain had been there all along, waiting for a chance to escape and consume him again.

He wanted to leave, to walk away and not have to think about the past. But he couldn't. Not this time. He was going to have to face her grief, and perhaps, in facing hers, he'd have to face his, too. The cold and lonely place she spoke of he knew lay at the bottom of the pit. It was where the pain dwelt.

Once, she'd asked him to tell her how to stop hurting, and he'd had no answer. He still didn't.

Not knowing how to comfort her, he'd left her to deal with the terrible grief on her own. Perhaps that had been the end of their marriage, not later, when she'd turned from his touch in loathing, as he'd thought. This time, he knew he couldn't leave.

She put her hands over her face. He realized she was weeping, although she made no sound. He lifted a hand, let it drop. He felt helpless in the face of her anguish.

"Trace," he said, searching for the words he hadn't been able to find in the past. "Don't. Crying…it doesn't do any good. It doesn't change things."

But she was beyond hearing him. Her hat blew off, and her hair gleamed like new pennies in the noonday sun, reminding him of the young girl he'd fallen instantly in love with.

She still didn't make a sound, but stood there with her hands covering her face, as if to hide the grief…from him, he realized. She didn't want him to see her cry.

He knew he couldn't walk away this time. He had to face the pain. He had to face it and deal with it…or damn her to the same emptiness he felt inside. She deserved more of life than that.

Swallowing hard, he stepped close to her. He touched her hair and gently stroked it, then down her back. She didn't jerk away.

He felt the tremors that ran through her slender body like shock waves through metal. He'd never seen her cry, not like this, as if her heart were dying inside her.

He felt a moment of panic as his own control slipped. The pressure that had been building inside rushed over him. He pressed his fingers to the bridge of his nose, trying to fight the weakness of tears. Tears…what good did they do?

And yet he knew they were needed…that Tracy needed them…. He had to help her, to save her from the dark hell that lived in his own soul….

God help him, he thought, and didn't know if it was a prayer for her or for himself.

He took her into his arms, cradling her grief against his body, trying to absorb it, to control it with his will. When she wrapped her arms around him and pressed her face against his neck, laving him with her own tears, he was lost.

"Trace, oh, God, Trace," he whispered, while blackness devoured him from the inside out.

Her arms tightened around him. He felt her warmth, the tremors that racked her slender body. The pressure built inside until he could no longer control it. He pressed his face into her hair and held her as closely as he could.

When the storm was over, she leaned into him as if exhausted by the silent weeping. For a while, she rested in his arms, and for those moments, a strange sense of peace washed over him.

"I miss him," she said again, quieter this time. It sounded like a final goodbye.

He had to clear his throat to speak. "I know."

She leaned back against his arms and looked at him. Her lashes outlined her eyes in wet spikes as she gazed up at him. He saw the trembling of her fingers as she reached up.

He held very still.

With the gentlest of touches, she traced the wetness on his lower lashes. He returned her gaze without looking away.

"You miss him, too," she said, rubbing the moisture between her fingers until it was gone.

"Yes." To his own ears his voice seemed far off, a distant rumble in his chest. He cleared his throat.

"Sometimes I wondered."

He dropped his arms and stepped back, too stunned to speak.

"You never…" She spread her hands in a helpless gesture. "You were always so…silent, so controlled."

The wind shifted, and patterns of dappled light danced over them. He studied the patterns, looking for answers to the silent questions between them.

The emptiness swirled uneasily inside him. It was no longer a haven from pain and hadn't been since her return. He realized the peace he thought he'd found had been but an illusion.

As for the control she spoke of, he'd lost that when

she'd covered her face and wept. Even thinking about her pain caused a tightening in his chest.

She dropped to her knees and plucked at some weeds among the grass blades. When she ran her fingers over the grass, he was reminded of how she'd once run her fingers through Thadd's hair to smooth it into place. She'd loved their son…and so had he.

He tried to find words to tell her how he'd felt. It was so damned hard to say it out loud.

"You didn't give me credit for loving him," he finally said, remembering that last desperate year together and some of the hurtful things they'd said.

She sat back on her heels and looked up at him. The sun lighted her hair into a glowing nimbus. Her eyes gleamed like green agates in her pale face. "What do you mean?"

"You seemed to think only a mother could hurt, that only a mother could miss her child until each day took more effort than it was worth to continue living." He paused and drew a deep, careful breath. "A father could never miss a child that much, hurt like that. Isn't that what you thought?"

"I never…Judd, I never thought that." She lifted her hand as if she wanted to touch him, but she didn't.

"You never forgave me." He gave a bitter snort and forced the words from a tight throat. "I can't say that I blame you. I never forgave myself."

She did touch him then. Rising, she caught his face between her hands and made him look at her. "I never blamed you." She said each word clearly and firmly. "Never."

"I was the one who laughed at your fears," he reminded her, bringing it all out in the open. "I was the one who took him hunting and let him roam the woods."

For an eternity, he stared into her eyes. She held his gaze, letting him look into her soul. He saw the truth in her. Or maybe he needed it so badly he thought he saw her forgiveness.

"Never," she repeated.

A light clicked on inside him, a dim one—the tiny flickering of a firefly seen through a storm—but it was there. He had needed to hear her say it. He'd needed her to forgive him....

It was a startling thought. He drew back from it. He'd made a life for himself that was bearable. He didn't need anything more. It was Tracy who'd needed comforting, not the other way around. Perhaps now that she'd faced this moment, she could get on with her life and find a future of happiness.

For a second, hope flared in him. He tamped it down. Not him. He wanted it for Tracy, not himself. His life was okay like it was. Not exciting, but...safe.

That is, it would be when she left again.

He turned his head, and she let him go. He looked at the mountains until the mist cleared from his eyes.

"I think I'll go now. I had to come." She paused. "I wonder if we would have made it, all those years ago, if we'd cried in each other's arms then."

Leaving him with this thought, she started along the path. He watched her, then knew he couldn't let her leave, not just yet. There was something else he had to say.

He picked up the trowel and empty flower pots, then spotted her hat. He retrieved it and hurried to catch up with her.

At the chapel, he opened the gate, then closed it behind

him. He saw her perusal of the sports car at the curb. "It's nearly time for lunch," he said. "There's this place I know that serves the best fried shrimp in the state. You interested?"

One hand went to her face as if checking for damages. Her eyes were a little red and her nose was pink, but she still looked beautiful. She glanced at her clothes. He could see the refusal forming before she spoke.

"You look fine," he told her, feeling stubborn about her joining him for some reason.

"If you're sure," she said hesitantly.

"We can stop by the house so you can freshen up," he offered.

"Your house?" The idea clearly startled her.

"I meant the cottage."

"Oh." She nodded.

He unlocked the car, and they climbed in. At the house, he waited outside while she went in. In less than five minutes, she was back. He'd always liked that in her. She never kept a man waiting for hours while she preened in front of a mirror.

Driving along the highway, soft music on the radio, he went over what he wanted to say to her, but it wasn't until they were far up in the mountains that he spoke.

"There was a time when you wanted to talk to me, but I walked out. I've wanted to tell you I'm sorry for that for a long time." He swallowed as the words balled in his throat. "It was just…I couldn't talk then, not about Thadd."

She didn't answer for a long time. "I understand," she said at last in a voice that told him she did.

Another load seemed to dissolve inside him. Funny, he hadn't realized he was carrying around such a heavy conscience. A sigh of relief escaped him.

"I knew you loved Thadd," she continued. "It showed in a hundred ways each and every day. I knew you had strong feelings. It was just that you never shared them with me. I needed…well, it doesn't matter now. We simply weren't at the same place at the same time, were we?" she mused aloud.

He suddenly wished they could go back to that day in the woods and start their lives over from that first meeting….

Tracy examined the slope of the bluff from the site where she'd found the new bones the previous week. If any bones had been buried farther up the slope and recently dug up and dragged down here by an animal, why didn't she see any signs of it?

Why take the bones to another place after digging them up?

Unless a bigger animal was in the vicinity and tried to take it, then the smaller one would head for cover with his prize.

She stretched her weary back. She'd spent most of the morning bent over, studying the ground for a clue. Bones didn't just appear from nowhere, unattached to the rest of the skeleton, without cause.

If she were to consider erosion, then she'd have to look further for signs of it. She started hiking up the hill.

A half hour later she emerged from the trees onto a grand escarpment of limestone that looked like the small end of a huge egg protruding from the ground. The limestone had cracked and buckled in several places, particularly along the tree line on the lower side of the slope.

She climbed to the top of the egg and sat down. From

there she commanded a magnificent view of the surrounding territory—the reservation on the north, the Kincaid place to the south, the mountains sweeping westward and northward, and finally, the ribbon of highway that led back to town.

The air seemed cooler up here. When the sun dipped behind a cloud, she decided to eat her lunch.

Swinging her fanny pack around to the front, she removed an energy bar and a banana. While she ate, she thought of her lunch with Judd on Sunday. Three days ago. She hadn't seen him on Monday when she and Winona watched the Fourth of July fireworks at the fair, but he'd been at the office yesterday and today.

Something had changed between them, she thought. She chewed a bite of energy bar and pondered the situation.

Like the rain, the tears they'd shed had cleared the air between them. Old questions had been answered or at least laid to rest. By the time he dropped her by the cottage that afternoon, they had been almost easy with each other.

Except for that smoldering hunger that wouldn't go away no matter how hard they tried to ignore it.

She swallowed, then sighed heavily. That hadn't changed, but he had managed to crack a joke about it when a couple had put some money in an old-fashioned jukebox and started dancing.

"If we danced to that, I'd have to arrest myself for indecent exposure," he'd murmured, listening to the theme from a movie they'd once seen together.

His disgruntled expression, as well as the complaint, had surprised her into laughing. Then he'd looked surprised that she'd found it amusing and had laughed, too.

"Such is life," she'd taunted.

So it is, she thought, sobering as she replayed the day in her mind. She'd done that often in the past seventy-two hours. There had been something sweet and poignant between them on the drive back to town.

At the cottage, she hadn't invited him in. Instead, he'd walked her to the door, handed her the hat she'd worn earlier, tipped his head and left.

But not before their eyes had met in a glance of mutual awareness. If he stayed much longer, they would end up making love. It was inevitable, like the ebb and flow of the tides. The forces of nature couldn't be stopped by the mere efforts of humans.

The worst part was she wasn't sure she wanted to stop it.

She sighed again and ate the banana and drank a small can of juice. She tucked the debris in a plastic bag and stuck it in the pack. Standing, she twirled the pack to her backside to keep it out of the way and started back to work.

Working around the limestone escarpment, she examined each nook and cranny of it, working in a spiral from the egglike top. Nothing in the cracks indicated a deeper opening underneath.

Slowly she moved lower, coming to the trees at the bottom edge where she'd first ascended. It looked like the accumulation of dirt and leaves had been recently disturbed. There were signs of erosion due to runoff from the limestone.

Finding a stick, she picked it up and poked at the buildup of leaves along an overhang. To her surprise, the stick went down a good ways.

After pulling her blue shirt off, she laid it and the pack aside, then started work in earnest. Little tingles of excitement went off inside her. She'd felt them before…when she was about to make a find.

She worked with a trowel and rock pick, carefully loosening the debris, then scraping it away. Sometimes it was hard not to rush right in, but she didn't want to damage any pieces.

Finally, she hit pay dirt…or rather, bone.

A femur, the long bone of a thigh. Now if she could just find the pelvis, she'd know for sure whether it was male or female and the approximate age.

She examined the femur before placing it beside her shirt and pack. From its thickness and length, it probably belonged to someone about five-ten to six feet. As she'd suspected from the thickness of the wrist bones, the skeleton was most likely that of a male.

DNA tests could tell her for sure, but so could the pelvis. She worked swiftly, removing the debris and placing it aside, making sure she wasn't overlooking any pieces. An hour passed.

She wiped the sweat off her forehead and took a break. It was while she was resting that she heard a "Hello-o-o" from below.

"Up here," she shouted.

A man came up through the woods. She recognized the broad shoulders and braids tied with leather strips before he emerged from the shadows under the trees a few yards away from her.

"Jackson, hello," she called to let him know where she was.

He spotted her and came over. "You've found something?" he asked, a tone of excitement underscoring the statement as he viewed her work under the ledge.

"Yes, a femur." She retrieved it and held it so he could visually examine it.

"Can you tell anything from it?"

"Um, yes." She became preoccupied with taking a closer look at the thick thigh bone. "I think it was a man, or a very tall, robust female. Young. There's no sign of deterioration in the joint. He was most likely a cowboy, or somebody used to sitting astride."

"Wow," Jackson said. "Anything else?"

She got out a bag from her pack and wrapped the bone, then turned back to the dig. "Not yet, but I'm hoping. The body was apparently concealed under this ledge...." She considered for a moment, then added, "Or he might have crawled in there for protection."

"Maybe he fell from his horse," Jackson suggested.

"And it was storming—"

"The wolves were after him—"

"Right. His leg was broken—"

"Could you tell that from the thigh bone? It looked okay to me."

She laughed. "No. I was just getting into the scenario." Sitting on the ground, she went back to work.

He dropped down on his haunches and peered under the shallow ledge. "Uncle Frank said to thank you for the reports you sent to the office. He was disappointed the bones weren't ancestors and said to tell you that you had permission to do any tests necessary to identify them, including DNA matching. He asked me to phrase this delicately, so here goes—could you have made a mistake about the age of the bones?" he asked bluntly, then grinned.

"You always did have a way with words," she remarked

dryly. "There's no mistake. The bones aren't fossilized, not even on the surface. They're not old. You knew that."

"Yeah, but as an official of the tribe, I had to ask. Now that that's out of the way, do you want to come to the house Friday night? Maggie and I are having a cookout."

She was curious about Jackson's new wife. "I'd love to…if you promise me fry bread with honey."

"Pick up some honey from Winona and you're on. I'll do the fry bread myself."

"Your wife isn't Cheyenne?" That surprised her, considering that Jackson had once been married to a white.

"She's a city Injun," he explained. "She doesn't know fry bread from buffalo chips." He shook his head, as if wondering why he'd ever married such an ignorant woman.

Tracy saw the warmth in his eyes when he spoke of his wife and suppressed a jab of envy. "I'm looking forward to meeting her. Now, enough socializing. My boss will fuss if he finds me talking instead of digging."

"I'll help. Tell me what to do."

She glanced at his clothes. He wore old jeans and scuffed boots. His shirt had seen many washings. "Okay. Block off a square and take off one even layer at a time."

They worked companionably for an hour. She was reminded of her childhood days on the reservation. Jackson had been her best friend. They'd both loved it there and wanted to stay, but both of them had had to leave.

Strange, the turns life could take. He'd left and married, apparently never to return, while she'd married and moved close by. Then he'd divorced and returned, apparently to stay. She'd divorced and left, meaning never to come back.

Longing washed over her in a sudden deluge. She

gripped her trowel and concentrated on digging until the emotion subsided.

"Hey," Jackson said. "Look."

She blinked away the memories and glanced over at his find. "The ilium! Don't move it!" she ordered when he tried to lift it.

He moved aside when she crowded in. Carefully, she dug out the debris around the bone. She lifted it out of the hole.

"It's complete," she murmured in satisfaction. She turned it, looking at it from every angle. "Yes...yes," she said, picking out clues as she examined the pelvic bone.

"Well?" Jackson demanded.

"Male. Less than twenty-five years old."

"Indian?"

She shrugged. "I don't know. Show me your thigh bone, and I'll make a comparison."

"Ha-ha," he said.

"Let's find the skull. It's bound to be here. With it, we can surely figure out who the cowboy was."

"I'll start a check of all the tribal missing-person reports," Jackson told her.

"Good. Now let's see what else we can find."

It was nearly dark before they gave up.

"Damn," Jackson said.

"My feelings, too." Tracy frowned at the hole.

They'd hit rock bottom. There was nothing else. She studied the area. He looked at his watch.

"Erosion," she muttered. "Look at the runoff patterns. This area under the ledge has eroded away where the water gushed through that crack." She pointed out the signs.

The shallow gully disappeared over the edge of the

bluff. She and Jackson walked over and peered fifty feet down into the creek that meandered along the cliff base.

"So that's the end of it."

"Heck, no. Now I'll search the creek," she said.

"We'd better leave. It's getting late."

"Right." She packed up and headed for her car, the bones wrapped in special paper bags, then in plastic.

Like a kid with a treasure she wanted to show, she was eager to get to town. She said goodbye to Jackson and drove down the steep trail. She had to see Judd right away.

Seven

Judd looked at the clock, then at the darkening sky. Where the hell was Tracy? She was usually back from her digging around on the res well before dark.

Not that she had to report in to him…as she'd made damned clear more than once.

Hell, she'd probably gone to the tribal chairman's house for dinner. Frank Many Horses seemed to think of her as a long-lost daughter. Jackson Hawk thought a lot of her, too. Of course, Jackson had recently married, so he wasn't a rival—

Judd broke off the thought and cursed aloud as he realized what he was thinking. He closed his eyes and leaned back in the comfortable executive chair, his heels on the desk, and idly rocked to and fro while he tried to get his head straight.

There was nothing wrong with him that a little sleep

wouldn't cure. *Or a long, satisfying tumble in the hay,* an insidious voice from some unbidden recess of his mind suggested.

Yeah, he admitted, that, too.

His dreams were a mixture of the old and the new—the old being the days and nights with Tracy when he'd been free to make love to her whenever he wished; the new being the days her perfume, her laughter, her womanly aura lingered in his office long after she took off for the res.

A hard pang whipped through him as his body reminded him all too forcibly that he was a man. The problem was Tracy. She was the one he wanted.

She'd been the most wonderful lover he'd ever had.

Not that there had been all that many. He was a naturally monogamous person. Maybe it was the way he'd been raised, or maybe it was something he'd learned from observing others, but he'd always felt that when two people were intimate enough to possibly produce a child, they owed respect to each other and that creative process.

He pressed his thumb and finger against his eyes, momentarily shutting out the headache that had plagued him all day, then looked at the clock again.

Where the hell was she?

Pivoting in the chair, he sat so he could see the street. Most of the parking spaces were empty. The stores didn't stay open past five o'clock on a weekday night. Farther along, there were two pickups and three cars in front of the local saloon.

He gave a snort of wry laughter. Sterling would have said he was being "bitchy." Maybe so, but, well, he was worried.

The courthouse clock chimed the hour. Seven. Maybe

her car had broken down. Probably a flat tire. Or she'd run out of gas.

Tracy tended to live in her own world and forget the basics, things like eating, putting gas in the car and so forth. It hadn't bothered him while they were married.

She'd pleased him in so many other ways, he admitted. When he came home, she was always delighted to see him. The way she'd look up, her eyes wide and shining, as if he were Prince Charming in person... God, what it did to a man to be wanted like that.

He gritted his teeth and tried to close out the troublesome thoughts. He couldn't.

The memory of their lovemaking filled his nights. She'd been so responsive, loving everything he did...so natural.

Images flashed into his mind. Her hair flowing around her shoulders as she turned the tables on him. Her teasing smile as she made him lie still and let her have her way with him. The little crooning cries she'd made. The low murmurs of delight, telling him what she liked.

Yes, like that...no, slower...lower...there...oh, yes... oh, love, love...

He leapt to his feet, his body as rigid as a steel beam. It was no good thinking of what had been. It was over. Over.

The ringing of the telephone halted him in his tracks as he headed for the door. He grabbed the instrument, nearly yanking the cord out in his rush to answer.

"Hensley," he said.

"Judd?"

He took a calming breath. "Winona. What can I do for you?"

"Is Tracy there with you?" she asked.

The hairs stood up on the back of his neck. He forced himself to be calm. Nothing had happened to her. He'd know it if she were in trouble. He didn't pause to figure out this last cryptic thought.

"No. Do you want me to take a message for her?"

There was silence at the other end of the line. "She wasn't home when I tried her house," Winona told him, worry in her tone.

"What's wrong? Have you seen something?"

"It's more a feeling. I can't describe it. I just sense…I don't know. Danger, I think. It came to me a couple of hours ago. Did she find more bones? That seems to trigger it."

"She's supposed to be at the reservation. Maybe I'll run out and check on her."

"Would you?" Winona requested. "I'd feel much better if I knew she was all right."

"Sure. She's probably had car trouble. I'll check it out."

They said goodbye. He locked his office and headed out the door. At the front steps, he stopped. A compact car, its metallic blue surface taking on a purple hue in the twilight, pulled to a stop across the street. Tracy hopped out.

He watched as she removed a package from the seat as if it were fragile and headed across, quickly glancing both ways. She saw him at the top of the steps and quickened her pace, a smile blooming on her expressive lips.

His heart rate speeded up, too.

There were dirt stains on the knees of her jeans and at her temple where she'd obviously pushed a wisp of hair out of her eyes. Her lipstick was gone, and her nose was pink from the sun. She was indescribably beautiful.

"Judd, wait till you see what Jackson found," she called out, holding her package out a little.

He waited for her, then fell into step with her as she headed for the building. "Jackson?"

"Um-hmm. He came by and helped me dig this afternoon."

Judd had to unlock the outside door to let them in. They went through the silent corridor and up the steps to his office. He opened the door. She went through to the conference room, where she set her package on the table. "Look at this."

She removed the two packages from the plastic bag, then laid her finds on the table. She smiled at him, her eyes wide and shining, filled with delight.

He bent over to hide the sudden sting of moisture in his eyes. Damn, but he'd have to get a grip on himself. The past was gone, and she wasn't in his future.

Her find was a femur and the pelvic saddle. He studied them for a couple of minutes. "Male?" he asked, venturing a guess.

He'd read a book on forensic anthropology once, not because her father had said she was studying it, he hastened to assure himself, but because it sounded like a subject a lawman ought to know a little about.

"Definitely. Early twenties."

"How can you tell?"

She picked up the pelvic bone. "See this Y-shaped junction here? The three main growth centers don't come together until the male is around twenty-five. The epiphyses are almost together but not quite. See?"

He studied the section she pointed out. Her hair brushed

against his cheek as he bent closer. He ignored the tingles that radiated from the spot. Concentrating fiercely on the pelvis, he peered at the Y-shaped line she'd mentioned.

"Can you give me a more definite age?" he asked, trying not to notice the tantalizing scent of her. She smelled of earth and sunshine, of mountain air and pine resin...of sweat and musk and perfume...of *woman*.

"Yes. He was twenty-four years, three months, two days and eighteen minutes old when he died. Would you like the seconds, too?" She replaced the pelvis on the table.

He inhaled the essence of her deep into his lungs. It was like filling himself with life. He realized she was staring at him, her eyes changing as she noticed his absorption with her rather than the conversation.

Heat seeped into his neck as he tried to remember what she'd just said. Her words finally registered in his brain.

"Very funny." He tried to sound amused. He pushed his hands into his pockets and walked away.

"He was closer to twenty-five than twenty," she told him in a softer tone.

"I see."

"I'm going to ask for another week here. I think we can make an identification. A young male, five-ten or so, strong, but lanky rather than bulky, a cowboy nearing his mid-twenties."

"Great. That only describes half the county, not to mention the state."

She shrugged. "Jackson is already checking the tribal missing-persons records. I'd suggest you get someone on the county files right away. Rafe Rawlings volunteered to check the city reports."

"Rawlings was at the site, too? What was it—a damned field day?" Judd snarled.

"Only Jackson was at the site. I saw Rafe patrolling the highway and flagged him down. He's interested in forensics."

"I'll bet," Judd muttered under his breath. He wished to hell people would stay out of what should have been *his* investigation.

"If I'm keeping you from an important date, please feel free to leave," she informed him coolly. "I'll lock up when I'm through here."

She placed her precious bones in their protective covers and stored them in the cabinet he'd assigned for her use. Her bearing was as stiff as a cactus and about as friendly.

"Winona called," he said, ignoring her dismissal.

"Oh?"

A smile tugged at the corners of his mouth. She'd always gone into her cool, barely speaking mode when she was miffed at him. He knew how to get her out of a snit.

He frowned. No, he didn't. Well, he did, but he couldn't grab her up in his arms and kiss that ticklish spot on her neck until her temper collapsed into a fit of giggles, then sighs, then moans as the kiss changed....

"What did she say?"

"Who?"

"Winona."

He gave her a blank look.

She heaved an exasperated breath. "You said Winona called."

The worry came back. "She said you must have discovered more bones. She had a feeling, she said. She thinks you're in danger."

Tracy nibbled on her lower lip while she thought. He wanted to take over the task for her. He watched her, the hunger growing stronger by the second. He saw her gaze drift over his face, down his body…. She looked startled, then her eyes flicked back to his face. He gave her a sardonic smile, acknowledging the erection he couldn't hide.

"Yeah," he said softly, "I've got a feeling, too. I think I know where the danger lies." He returned her steady gaze and forced himself to warn her. "With me."

"Us," she corrected with the honesty he'd always admired in her. "The danger is between the two of us." She managed to smile, but it was rather wobbly at the edges.

He shoved a hand through his hair, frustrated by the passion that just wouldn't give up and die. To get mixed up with her again was stupid. In another week, she'd be gone. And he'd have to face the emptiness all over again.

"Yes," he finally said. "But we're adults. The attraction is there, but we don't have to act on it. You were right. It's no good between us." He paused and tried to think of something to add to that. "It's no good," he repeated.

But once it had been the best. He went to the door, aware of the utter silence in this part of the building and that they were alone. "Call Winona so she'll know you made it back all right."

"I will."

He walked out, then sat in the truck until she left. He followed at a discreet distance until she was safely home.

The police station steps were jammed with reporters, television crews, photographers and spectators when Tracy arrived at seven the next morning. Questions were tossed at Judd faster than he could answer them. He smiled when he saw Tracy.

"Here's the person you should talk to," he announced, clearing a path up the steps for Tracy. "The FBI is in charge of the case, since the bones were found on a federally designated reservation."

"You louse," she muttered under her breath as he took her elbow and led her to the columned portico.

He gave her an oblique glance and smiled that slow, sexy grin that melted the heart. "It's all yours," he said and stepped back.

Flashbulbs went off in her face. Several microphones angled through the air toward her, supported on long poles, like some kind of prehistoric octopus.

For the next half hour, she answered questions about the "cowboy" and his mysterious demise. At the end of that time, she smiled and nodded—graciously, she hoped—and headed for the door of the police station. Judd opened it for her and ushered her inside.

In the conference room, she laid her purse on a table and fell into a chair. "Now I know how celebrities must feel. That was like facing a pack of starving hyenas."

Judd brought her a cup of coffee and set it on the conference table in front of her. The corners of his mouth were curved in amusement. "Such is fame."

She made a rude face while he laughed.

"So what's next on your busy agenda?"

"The missing-persons files."

He nodded. "I've got a man assigned to work with you on that." He paused and gave her a sardonic glance. "Guess who's been assigned to the task at city hall?"

"Rafe Rawlings," she promptly surmised.

"Right."

He drank from a mug that had holly and red ribbons painted on it. A Christmas present, she assumed, and wondered who had given it to him. Not that it was any of her business, of course.

"Who do I see?" she asked.

"I'll introduce you to the officer in charge of the archives."

She spent the rest of the day reviewing the missing-persons files for a ten-year period starting twenty years ago. She was surprised at the number of people who simply disappeared, even from a small county like Whitehorn.

Where did they go? she mused. Did they lie in unmarked graves like the young cowboy they'd found?

She shook her head at the unfairness of life. She thought of the people left behind, always wondering what had happened to their loved ones, never knowing. It was bound to have a profound effect on their lives.

"Tracy?" Judd stuck his head around the door. "It's time to lock up."

She closed the last folder in the file. The missing "person" in it was a dog named Bob White. Someone had realized this after the all-points bulletin had gone out. The dog had been found, but the folder had been left in the file. Some officer had probably thought that was a nice little joke to leave around for someone like her to find years later.

"Any prospects?" Judd asked.

"Not really. Mostly it's teenage boys or men in midlife crises who take off for parts unknown, it seems."

"No women?"

"Umm, there was one that sounded interesting." Tracy

rose and stretched her tired back. "A teenager named Lexine Baxter. She would be about your age now. I didn't know her, but I remember the old Baxter ranch. It was bought by the Kincaids, I think…yes, when Mr. Baxter died. His daughter had a reputation for being wild. The missing-persons report was filed by an aunt. I don't think she was very interested in finding the girl…."

She stopped as Judd smiled in his slow, sexy way.

"What?" she asked.

"You should write a book. Your childhood gave you a unique view of every family in the county, including the Cheyenne."

"You're right. I knew someone from every family who'd ever played a part in Whitehorn history. For instance, the original Baxter was a prospector looking for sapphires. Did you know that?"

"No, but I'm not surprised. Montana is known for sapphires, isn't it?"

She nodded. "I need to go back out to the site tomorrow. I want to check the soil under the ledge before it rains."

"For what?"

"Blood. Hair. Bits of material from clothing. It was getting late, and Jackson thought we should leave, so I didn't have a chance yesterday."

"Maybe he was worried about the ghosts of his ancestors getting mad about you being there," Judd suggested coolly.

"Maybe," she returned in the same tone.

He thrust a hand through the thick wave that had a tendency to fall over his forehead. "Sorry. It's been a long day…week… month." He grinned ruefully.

She could vouch for that. The ten days she'd been there

had been difficult, to say the least. She arranged the files neatly and retrieved her purse. "Well, I'm off."

"Good night," he said when she passed him.

She murmured a reply and walked swiftly from the office. Outside, she stood on the top step and looked out over the town she knew as well as Missoula, where she'd lived for the first nineteen years of her life.

A sense of being adrift came over her. She didn't feel she belonged anywhere. It was daunting to be thirty-six and feel she'd accomplished little, belonged nowhere, had no ties to the future. She'd once had such high expectations of life.

Unable to face the empty cottage, pleasant as it was, she headed for the café instead of her car. As she'd expected, Lily Mae was there.

"Tracy, come join us," the widow called across the room as soon as Tracy entered. The restaurant owner was with her, both of them drinking iced tea.

Tracy spoke, then asked, "Have you eaten?"

"Yes, but I'll stay while you eat," Lily Mae volunteered. "We've heard about the cowboy. It was all over the TV today. Tell us about it. Do you have any clues as to who he is?"

Tracy received a sympathetic smile from Melissa Avery.

"No," she replied. "We're searching the missing-persons files at present, but there're no real prospects." She repeated some of the information she'd given Judd earlier.

"I think it's terrible," Melissa said.

"Yes," Tracy agreed, thinking of the young cowboy, dying alone like that.

"Why is it mostly men who can't seem to stick with their responsibilities?" the waitress went on. "They run off and leave their wives and children all alone." She stopped abruptly. "Excuse me. I have to take care of the register."

When she left, Lily Mae leaned close. "Her father ran out on them years ago."

Tracy was at once curious. "How long ago?"

"Well, let's see, that must have been when I was married to my first husband. Yes…yes, it was."

Lily Mae counted time in three eras—husband number one, husband number two and husband number three. Was Samuel Thaddeus Roper to be husband number four?

"Melissa must be close to thirty," Lily Mae recounted. "She was just a baby when it happened."

"About thirty years? How old was her father when he left?"

Lily Mae studied Tracy, then understanding dawned in her eyes. She shook her head and leaned close again. "The bones don't belong to Charles Avery. He left town with that Baxter girl."

"Lexine?" Tracy couldn't keep the surprise from showing.

"Yes, that was the one." Lily Mae gave a disgusted grimace. "That girl was trouble from the word go, always wanting something more than she had, putting on airs and all."

Tracy wasn't interested in Lexine's sordid past. "I didn't see a missing-person report on Charles Avery."

"Well, I expect his wife was too embarrassed. Everyone knew he'd been carrying on something awful with Lexine Baxter. Then one day he climbed in his pickup and disappeared." Lily Mae leaned closer. "The cook that used to be at the Kincaid ranch—she was a cousin to my first husband, bless their souls—saw Lexine driving the truck that same day. So the whole county knew they'd taken off together. It was terrible for his wife, humiliated and left with two kids to raise…"

She shut up when Melissa joined them again and the conversation became general. After she ate, Tracy walked down the block in the evening air, which was cooling off nicely.

The story of Melissa Avery's father saddened her. People made such foolish choices, such stupid mistakes. *As she had done when she'd asked Judd for a divorce?* She didn't want to think about it.

She climbed into her car, stopped at the grocery store, then drove home. The sky was almost dark when she arrived. After putting the groceries away and changing clothes, she sat on the porch.

Deciding a walk would help her sleep, she started out. She'd gone a half block when she realized where she was heading. She kept on walking until she came to the house.

For the first time, there was a light on in the living room window and she could see inside. She stopped across the street, staying in the shadows. She waited, wanting to see the child who lived there, whether it was a little boy or girl.

The screen door slammed at the house next door to the one she and Judd had built. A boy dashed outside and peered around the yard with a flashlight. He looked to be nine or ten, a bit older than Thadd had been.

When he couldn't find what he wanted, he ran out the front gate, down the lane and through the gate next door. He went up to the front door and knocked.

The door opened. Judd stepped outside.

Tracy's heart stopped, started, skipped several beats, then pounded so hard her chest hurt. Breathing became difficult.

"Hi, Sheriff, did you see my soccer ball today? I can't

find it anywhere," the boy sang out. It was obvious he and his neighbor were on comfortable terms.

"Hi, Jimmy. No, I haven't seen it since that day it was by the porch steps. When was the last time you remember using it?"

"Um…uh, I think it was day before yesterday. Me and Mike were playing in the road. I had to go in…oh, I bet he took it with him 'cause I had to go to the dentist."

"Give him a call, why don't you? Let me know if you don't find it. I'll help you look tomorrow."

"Right. Thanks. I'll call Mike now. Will you help me over the fence?"

"Sure." Judd followed his young neighbor to the rail fence, which had "cultivated" blackberries growing along it. He easily lifted the boy across the barrier and set him down on the other side.

"Thanks," Jimmy called and ran toward his house.

Judd watched him go. The streetlight illuminated his smile for a second before he turned back to his own house. He stopped suddenly and tilted his head as if listening, then he swung around.

Tracy stepped from the shadows and walked across the road. At the open gate, she hesitated, then walked through.

Judd strode to her. They stood there in the whispery soft night, the rustlings of the pine needles, the sigh of the wind from the mountains surrounding them.

"You live here?" she asked.

She hardly recognized her own voice, it was so strained. Her throat ached with emotion she couldn't allow to escape.

"Yes."

"How…why?"

"It came on the market a couple of years ago. I decided to buy it back."

"I see." She didn't, not really.

"It was a good buy." His tone was hard, defensive. "I always liked the location. The privacy," he added, as if this explained everything.

She got her emotions under control, even managed a smile. "It's well built. I can vouch for that. Is it…has it changed much…inside?"

He stared at her, searching her expression with a closed moodiness in his eyes. "They finished the storage room upstairs and made it into a sitting room."

"Oh. That sounds nice. I'd like to see it, if I may," she said on impulse.

She didn't need a lot of light to see the stiffness in his shoulders. *He didn't want her inside.*

That hurt.

"Sometime," she quickly added. "Maybe before I leave, you'll give me the dime tour." She laughed to show she was joking and backed up a step. "Well, I'd better go. It's late."

She turned to leave, feeling his animosity like a whiplash against her back.

"You can see it now if you'd like," he said just before she stepped through the gate.

"It's too much trouble." She faced him, wondering why he so disliked the thought of her being there.

"It's okay." He sounded resigned. He gestured for her to precede him down the path.

At the front door, he reached around her and opened it, waiting for her to go inside before he let it slam softly behind them. She gazed eagerly around the entrance area.

The hallway that led to the kitchen was paved with natural stone that had been sealed and polished. To the right was a step down into the living room; to the left was a family room. Each could be closed off from the hall by double French doors.

A television was on in the family room. Judd crossed the polished oak floors and turned it off, then closed the oak cabinets they'd built into one end of the room to hold the TV, stereo and the many books they'd accumulated.

Someone had added plaid swags over the windows, which had wooden blinds for privacy. The material matched the green-blue-and-black plaid of the sofa. A braided rug defined the sitting area. When they'd lived there as a family, they'd given Thadd's room to the grandparents when they'd visited and put Thadd on the sofa in the family room.

The living room had a blue-velvet sofa with two velvet chairs in blue-and-green stripes. The swags over those windows matched the chairs. An oriental rug picked up the colors in jewel tones.

"It's well coordinated," she remarked.

He nodded.

She drifted toward the kitchen. It stretched the width of the house. The master bedroom opened off one side of it. Both rooms had views of the ten acres of woods behind the house. Outside, a deck made a nice place for cookouts and summer entertaining.

The stairs were located between the family room and the kitchen. She went up the treads, noting the carpet. She and Judd hadn't used carpeting because she was allergic to dust. Plain floors were better for her.

The upstairs bedroom held a queen-size bed, two tables, two lamps, a rocking chair and an old-fashioned oak dresser. A telephone and note pad were conveniently placed on one of the bedside tables. The wallpaper Thadd had chosen was gone, and the walls were a creamy white. The bed cover was the only spot of color—a deep green velour blanket, soft and luxurious looking.

The storage room was gone, its door removed and widened into an arch. The bathroom between the two rooms had been enlarged to include a shower stall. Bookcases had been added to the walls around the stair landing, transforming it into an attractive foyer. The whole of the upstairs made a private retreat.

"This is very nice," she murmured. "Very nice."

"Thanks."

"Did you do it?"

"I redid the bath to add the shower. I thought it would be better…for when there was company."

She wondered what company he had. His parents. His sister and her husband and two kids. A cousin he'd once been close to and the cousin's current girlfriend. She hadn't much liked having the cousin visit. He'd had a different woman each time.

"Very nice," she repeated.

She turned and nearly ran into him. She hadn't realized he was standing quite so close, one step down from her.

Their lips were nearly on the same level. She drew a shaky breath as the tension escalated to storm intensity.

Eight

Tracy moved first. She laid her hands, both of them, flat against his chest. She wasn't trying to ward him off. It was simply that the need to caress him, to feel his warmth, was more than she could resist at this moment.

It seemed the world stood still, listening, waiting to see what would happen. She waited, too.

A glance into his eyes informed her that he was fully aware of the escalating tension between them. She saw the tendons in his neck stand out as if he fought for control.

He removed his hand from the banister.

She felt it settle lightly at her waist, large and warm and somehow comforting. She sighed shakily, knowing they were on dangerous ground, but unable to force herself to retreat.

Longing poured into the molten core of her, then spiraled outward until she felt consumed by needs she'd denied for years. A harsh pulse of desire beat its way through her veins.

"I want you," she whispered. "I—I shouldn't…but I do."

His hand tightened on her. "A person would be crazy to get mixed up in all this again," he said in a husky tone that mixed mockery with a moody anger. "I've been bitten by the spider of passion before. It's a sure bet for misery."

She lifted her palms as if stung and tried to step back.

He held her in place with both hands. "No, don't pull away. It's something that has to happen. Perhaps when this—" his glance indicated them and the passion neither could deny "—this insanity is played out, then maybe we'll be free." He gave a brief, bitter laugh. "Or maybe we're doomed to stay in this circle of hell forever."

His bitterness hurt. "Walk away," she challenged. "Walk away now, and let it be finished."

He shook his head. "It's too late." He lowered his head.

She turned her face to the side. "I don't know where this will lead…or where it will end." That was the scary part.

"What does it matter?" He sounded weary and defeated, as if he were as tired as she was of fighting the attraction. "It doesn't have to lead anywhere. There's just now, this moment…."

She felt his breath fan over the side of her neck. They spoke without looking at each other, their heads close as if they were whispering secrets in each other's ears, but other than his hands at her waist and hers trapped between them against his chest, they didn't touch.

Invoking common sense didn't help at all, she found. Every part of her wanted what he promised—this moment and the completion it dangled before her like a long-desired gift.

He moved one hand, sliding it behind her, caressing the

small of her back, exerting the tiniest bit of pressure to propel her forward.

"And then what?" she asked softly. "There's always tomorrow to be faced." Sadness boiled up in her from deep inside. She wanted more than a moment. She wanted tomorrow and the next day and the next….

"Shh." His lips brushed her hair, her temple, her cheek.

She couldn't hold her lashes up. They were too heavy. She let her eyes close. He kissed them and her nose, her temple.

Against her hands, she felt his chest lift in a deep breath. A low, throaty sound of male need caressed her ears as he exhaled. Seemingly of their own volition, her hands slipped upward, removing the barrier between them. She wrapped them around his shoulders.

Flashes of heat lightning fused them together, her breasts against his chest. Willpower, good sense, caution went up in flames. She gave a little sob and sought his lips.

He positioned his head, letting her mouth touch his, then he opened his lips and gave her the kiss she yearned for.

It was as if they became locked in mortal combat. He moved his hands restlessly over her body. She did the same, striving to become closer and closer. But each new hold was ultimately unsatisfying.

There was only one closeness that would take away the painful hunger that racked them both, she realized…and fill the emptiness that had lived in her for years.

She moaned when his lips left hers. He kissed the hollow below her ear, then moved swiftly down her neck. He pushed her shirt collar aside and nuzzled her throat, then his hot, wet kisses burned a trail down the V opening to the first button.

He hesitated, but when she said nothing, he reached between them with one hand and flicked the button free. Then another. And another. His lips followed his hands.

At her waist, he pulled the cotton loose from her jeans. She clung to his shoulders when he slipped his hands up her back. The release of her bra caused strange sensations, like Fourth of July sparklers going off inside.

With her eyes closed, she experienced the removal of her clothing through the sense of feel—the whisper of cloth on flesh as the shirt was pushed off her shoulders and down her arms, the lighter sensation, like an echo, when he whisked the bra away.

And then the breathless anticipation as he bent his head toward her. He kissed her breasts, first one, then the other.

A shudder went through him.

She cradled his head against her and stroked through the thick, black waves of his hair, loving the tactile pleasure of touching him.

When he ran his tongue over her hardened nipple, she gasped aloud at the intense pleasure. "It's been so long," she murmured, her voice breaking as her senses were overwhelmed.

"Forever," he breathed against her. He drew spirals over her with his tongue, leaving a hot trail of moist desire behind.

He lavished attention on her breasts until she was weak in the knees. "I can't stand up," she murmured, clinging to him as her legs trembled uncontrollably.

She felt his arms close around her thighs. He lifted her from the floor, stepped up the remaining stair and proceeded into the bedroom. He laid her on the velour blanket and followed, lying half over her, his thigh nestled between hers.

"It hurts," she whispered, "to want...like this...." She moved her head restlessly back and forth against the blanket.

He slipped his hand into the hair at her temple and held her still. His eyes as he gazed into hers were haunted by visions she could only guess at. She clamped her teeth into her lower lip, wondering if he would leave her.

Then slowly...slowly...he lowered his head until their lips came together once more. She met the kiss with trembling ardor, eager for his touch. His tongue slipped between her lips, and he stroked her mouth until she responded with wanton demands of her own.

Wildfire enveloped her, and she moaned with ecstasy. He released her mouth and spoke against her lips.

"When you do that...when you moan and let me know how much you want me, it drives me to the wall, right to the wall. I want you, too, but you can tell that, can't you? A man can't hide his needs the way a woman can."

Her heart went all jumpy and nervous in her chest. She knew if they didn't stop now, they would make love... and then it would be too late to stop.

Too late?

It was already too late. A sob broke through the yearning. She felt his surprise when she wrapped her arms around him and went wild in his arms...simply wild.

She stroked and caressed with her hands and her body, moving against him until every part of her had been touched by him. She heard the whimpering demands that escaped from her parted lips and didn't care. It had been too long, much, much too long.

Through the red haze of wild hunger, she heard him

murmuring to her. "Easy, love, easy. We have plenty of time, hours and hours of time."

But the fierceness that glittered from under his half-closed lashes matched the ardor that consumed her.

"Now," she demanded. "Come to me now."

He drew a ragged breath, then cupped her face with one hand and settled his lips on hers again. He moved over her, rubbing his body against hers through the clothing that separated them. She tore frantically at his shirt until she had it open. He lowered his weight on his arms until his chest pressed like a solid sheet of fire against hers.

She closed her eyes again as savage heat poured over her and held on to him as tightly as she could.

All the bright dreams of her youth rose inside her, demanding notice, seeking satisfaction. No, no, she didn't believe in those anymore…but it would be easy…so easy to fall into those gentle delusions once more…so very easy….

"You're beautiful," he murmured over and over to her. "No other woman does this to me…makes me forget everything but the moment…makes me so wild I'd die before I let you go…."

"Yes," she whispered, barely hearing his words over the roar in her ears. "Oh, please…"

When his hand settled between their bodies, she twisted to the side to give him room. He unfastened the snap and zipper of her jeans. She held her breath as he slipped a hand inside, sliding under the lace band of her French bikinis, and caressed her abdomen.

"Judd," she said with a sigh. She ran her hands under his shirt and stroked all along his back, then pulled him hard against her.

"I've dreamed of doing this," he admitted harshly. "Every minute of every day. Thoughts of you tag along with me no matter what I'm doing. I think of your skin—how smooth it is, how pale, as pale as milk, and soft…so soft."

He pushed lower, cupping her mound in his palm. He stroked her intimately, causing her to murmur and writhe as the terrible need drove her toward completion with him.

"Come to me," she demanded. "Please, love, come to me."

He took a deep breath and pushed up from her with a powerful thrust of his arms. She opened her eyes and looked at him. Their gazes locked as he stood and tossed the loosened shirt aside. His hands went to his belt, but his eyes never left hers.

She waited anxiously, afraid it was all a dream, that she was going to wake and the moment disappear.

The telephone rang instead.

They both jumped. Judd cursed, low and eloquent. He glanced at the phone in irritation.

"I have to answer," he said.

She nodded.

He picked up the instrument and spoke his name, then listened. "Yeah," he said. "I'll be there in ten minutes."

The magic evaporated. A shiver passed over her. She sat up and crossed her arms over her chest.

"There's been a bad car accident. The hospital needs blood. I have to go." He reached down, picked up his shirt and pulled it on, fastening it with angry, impatient movements.

She looked around for her own clothing.

He brought her shirt and bra to her. "Will you stay?"

His voice was so low she had to strain to hear it. She hesitated, one part of her desperately wanting to say yes, another part glad of the reprieve and a chance to regain her senses.

She shook her head. "I think I'd better go."

A stark expression flickered over his face and was gone. He nodded. "I'll drop you by your place on the way."

"Do you think…should I go to the hospital? If they need blood…" she added at his quick glance.

He shrugged. "I suppose."

She slid from the bed and, with her back to him, pulled the undergarment on. She heard his footsteps behind her, then on the stairs.

"I'll meet you at the truck," he called over his shoulder.

"Fine." She finished with her clothing and ran quickly down the steps and outside. Judd waited in the truck, the motor running, the lights on, ready to go. She ran across the lawn and climbed in.

He turned the police lights on, but not the siren as he took Route 17 to Highway 191, which ran by the county hospital.

When they reached the hospital, she saw two ambulances already at the emergency entrance. Another could be seen in the distance, coming north on the highway, its siren wailing through the night.

She followed Judd inside.

Sterling McCallum was there, talking to a doctor. When Sterling moved aside, she recognized the sharp profile of Kane Hunter. She'd known Kane on the reservation. He was a couple of years younger than she was and completely dedicated to healing.

"What happened?" Judd asked when he came abreast of the two men. He left enough room for her to join the group.

"Drag racing," Sterling replied. "The cars sideswiped.

One flipped over, the other crossed the median into oncoming traffic."

"Kids," Judd concluded.

Sterling nodded. "Drinking. Whites and Indians."

Kane muttered under his breath. Tracy felt his frustration with his tribal members in particular and with youth in general. He ran an alcohol-prevention program on the reservation. "Can you guys donate some blood? We're going to need a lot."

Tracy said yes when the other two did.

"Hello, Tracy," Kane said. A smile warmed his face momentarily. "I knew you were back, but I haven't had time to look you up yet. It's good to see you again."

They had no chance to talk more. The third ambulance arrived and delivered its load of injured. Kane, head of the trauma team, went to check on a youth who looked about seventeen. Blood was all over him. A girl was helped out of the front of the vehicle. She held a compress to her head.

A hand closed over Tracy's wrist. "This way," Judd said.

A nurse took them along a corridor to another room. With quiet efficiency, she checked their vital signs, then settled them in reclining chairs rather like those in a dentist's office. In a few minutes, Tracy and the two men were hooked up.

Other people arrived as the news spread over the town grapevine. When Sterling was done, another donor took his place at once. Tracy smiled as she recognized her old friend.

"Tracy, Judd," Jackson Hawk greeted them. His dark eyes flashed from one to the other. "Everyone is turning out for the emergency, I see."

Tracy felt heat creep into her cheeks. She sensed that

Jackson saw much more. She had assumed everyone in the emergency room would be too busy to notice that she'd arrived at the hospital with Judd, but that was probably wishful thinking. In a small town like Whitehorn, the hospital staff would just file the information away until they got a chance to comment on it.

When she and Judd had separated before the divorce, the news had spread like a flash fire. Telephones had started ringing minutes after he'd packed and walked out the door.

"Okay, you're finished," the nurse announced. She removed the needle, pressed cotton and a bandage over the vein and cautioned Tracy about sitting up too quickly.

When she and Judd left the room, they went into the cafeteria, where orange juice, coffee and cookies were laid out for the donors to replenish their fluids and blood sugar. Other people—family members and those who couldn't give blood—were there, too. As in the past, an emergency drew the county together.

Tracy remembered coming to this room for cup after cup of coffee while the surgical team tried to save Thadd. The town had turned out for them, too.

Several people called to them. She stopped and talked to former neighbors she hadn't seen in years. A cup of juice was pressed into her hand. She glanced into dark eyes that observed her closely, but without discernible emotion.

"Thank you," she said to Judd. She quickly drank the juice down as a slight dizziness washed over her. She wasn't sure the dizzy spell was from the drop in her blood pressure or from the way Judd looked at her. The moment passed.

When he walked off, Tracy watched him go, aware

of a tug at her heartstrings. He was silent, as attentive as ever…and wary.

She understood the latter. They were daily becoming more entangled in the hot caldron of mutual desire. She was aware of him as she moved about the room, chatting with acquaintances and finally sitting to eat a piece of cake with Lily Mae Wheeler.

"That Judd," Lily Mae said in approval. "He's a rare type of man, he is." She sighed, then glanced at Tracy from the corner of her eyes. "I didn't see that little blue car you drive in the parking lot."

"I rode over with Judd," Tracy admitted, giving Lily Mae a bland, innocent look.

"Working late, weren't you?"

Tracy refrained from telling the friendly, nosy widow where to get off. "Um," she said noncommittally, not wanting to tell an outright lie. She patted back a yawn and realized how tired she was. She glanced around the crowded room.

Judd was talking to two couples, one Anglo, the other Indian. Parents of the injured teenagers, she assumed. They looked ravaged by despair and anger brought on by the helplessness of the situation. She knew the feeling.

"He's a handsome man," Lily Mae continued. "Some woman is sure to nab him soon."

Tracy forced a smile. "He's not a stray dog to be taken in and made a pet of."

"No, he's more like a mustang, smart and wary as they come. But he could be roped in by a sharp woman. He's lonely…and he's a man, the type who feels responsible for his partner. If he were lured into bed, he'd marry the woman…if that's what she wanted. Oh, there's the new teacher. Have you met her?" Lily Mae stood.

"No," Tracy said. "I think I'll head home."

She saw Sterling McCallum going toward the door. Maybe she could hitch a ride. She asked Lily Mae to tell Judd she was leaving, bade the woman good-night and rushed for the door.

"Sterling," she called, racing down the steps and across the drive to catch him before he left.

He paused at his car.

"Could I get a ride home?" She steadied herself with a hand on the vehicle. Running had made her dizzy.

"Be careful," he cautioned. "It'll take a few hours to build your blood volume back up."

"Yes, I keep forgetting. It's been awhile since I was a donor." She smiled at him. "I'm okay now. Do you have time to drop me by the cottage?"

His hesitation was brief. "Sure. Hop in." He opened the door for her.

She felt like a criminal sneaking away from the crime scene as they reached the highway and accelerated. A few minutes later he was pulling up at the cottage.

"Jessica wants to know if you'll come out for supper tomorrow night—"

"Oh, I just remembered. I'm supposed to go to Jackson's house. I've never met his wife."

"Um, I think Jessica was going to call them, too. Let me check with her."

"Okay. Thanks for the ride." She jumped out as soon as he stopped. With a wave over her shoulder, she dashed for the house.

Once inside, she locked the dead bolt behind her. She felt as if she'd just returned from combat. And was lucky to be back in one piece.

She washed and changed into her pajamas and robe, then sat on the sofa in the living room and turned the lamp off. In the dark, she contemplated the evening just past. She wasn't in one piece, she realized. She'd lost her heart to that wild mustang, the sheriff of Whitehorn County.

Tracy stood in the council office, a cup of coffee in her hand. Frank Many Horses—Uncle Frank to her—was seated at his desk. They were discussing the case.

"So you don't think the bones belonged to an Indian?" the tribal chairman asked, frowning thoughtfully at her.

"Well, I can't be positive," she admitted. "The thigh bone has a slight twist to it, which indicates Caucasian rather than Mongoloid, which usually has more of a twist. But those are generalities."

"Jackson tells me you could do DNA tests?"

She nodded.

"The parents are anxious to find out if the bones belong to their son. He disappeared fifteen years ago."

"If I can find the skull, I'll be able to tell more without running tests."

"They will pay," Frank Many Horses added. "Their son's remains, if it is their son, must have a proper burial."

"Kane can take blood samples from the parents to check against the sample from the marrow of the bones," Jackson interjected. "If you will approve the tests."

"Of course," she murmured.

She stayed another thirty minutes out of courtesy and

spoke of trivialities such as the weather, which was threatening rain. Jackson accompanied her outside to her car when she left.

"Jessica called Maggie and asked if we would come to her house tonight for dinner rather than trying to have a cookout. She said Sterling had already invited you."

"Yes, he mentioned it at the hospital last night."

"Good. Sterling said to tell you Judd would pick you up this evening around seven. Okay?"

Tracy murmured that it was, but her heart was jumping around in her chest. She hadn't gone by the office this morning because she hadn't wanted to face Judd after their tempestuous episode at his house. Now she was to be his date for the evening, apparently.

And would most likely end up in his bed.

After saying her farewells, she drove out to the site and went immediately to the ledge where she and Jackson had found the thigh and hipbones. She laid out her tools—tweezers, trowel, brush, magnifying glass and a small screen nailed to a wooden frame.

She began the laborious job of sifting through the dirt. Two hours later, she wondered if this was a good idea. Her back ached, her allergies were making her eyes and nose itch and the air was hot and ever more humid.

Hearing a noise, she glanced up. The clouds were spreading over the mountains like the gathering of a witches' coven.

It made her uneasy.

She went back to work. At last, finding a suspicious patch of darker soil under the eroded end of the ledge, she took some samples. After sifting more of the dark soil through the screen, she checked the debris left on top of the sieve.

A hair.

Using the tweezers, she carefully put her find in one of the small sample bottles and stored it in her pack. When she went back to the hole under the ledge, she heard a sound like a moan. The hair stood up on the back of her neck. She glanced all around.

A rumble of thunder sounded in the distance.

She studied the cloud formations, then went back to work. A squirrel chirred loudly, then went silent, the racket broken off as if the creature had been choked.

Tracy shook her head in exasperation. Nerves. Hers were reacting to every little thing today.

With her senses acutely tuned to her surroundings, she scooped another trowel of dirt onto the wire screen and sifted it. She found a few more hairs.

Curious, she took out her magnifying glass and examined the evidence. The hairs were short, dark brown to sandy blond. Male, she concluded. Caucasian. Sun-bleached hair. A cowboy, perhaps.

Now if she could only find the skull. Teeth were the most reliable visual method of identification.

Something hit the side of her neck and slipped down her shoulder to land in her lap. A stone.

She stared at it as if she'd never seen one before, then looked up at the sky. Strong updrafts could sometimes pick up rocks and debris and deposit them miles away.

Except there was no wind blowing up the lip of the bluff.

As she turned to look back at the woods, another pebble hit her. She gasped and put a hand to her cheek. It hadn't hurt, but she was alarmed. Who was throwing rocks at her?

She stayed low as she swung around for a full view

behind her. Nothing. She surveyed the woods, noting the absolute quiet.

Her heart began a fast, heavy pounding. It seemed like a warning. She clenched the sample jar as she tried to talk herself out of this foolishness.

Honestly, her imagination was running away with her. There was no danger here in the woods. She'd been working up here for days without any disturbances.

Yeah, but she was getting close to identifying the bones. And everybody in the country knew it after the TV and radio broadcasts yesterday, full of speculation about a break in the case at any time.

She was about to start back to work when a jingling sound started in the woods. Her breath caught. She forced herself to be calm.

The jingling came again, but to her left this time. She glanced that way. Then it came from the right. She swung her head around, but didn't see anything out of the ordinary.

Then the jingles started again, coming from both directions at once and increasing in volume.

Fear crawled down her back like a thousand-legged insect. Her skin seemed alive with them.

Without taking her eyes from the woods, she reached out and pulled her day pack toward her. She removed the rock pick, then slipped the container of hairs inside and zipped the pocket.

The jingling stopped all at once.

Tracy felt the silence as a threat. She got to her feet, her mind busy picking out an escape route over the rough terrain. Luckily, from her recent explorations, she knew every rock and cranny.

The bluff presented the greatest danger. The rocky out-cropping was the highest point above the creek below. If she fell from there—or was pushed—the fall would kill her.

The jingling started again, first left, then right, then both. Then came laughter. Raucous and cruel, it reverberated from the rocks and trees until it seemed to surround her.

Fear flew all around her, scattering her thoughts so that she wanted to cower under the ledge and hide from the terror that stalked the woods.

Judd, help! She instinctively sent the plea out, directing it toward the town and the man who meant safety to her.

As if his spirit were suddenly there, she felt calm return. A coldness came over her. Someone was trying to frighten her, and she was letting them!

She straightened up, pushing the day pack under the ledge with her foot. She didn't want anything to trip her if she had to move fast.

When the laughter and the jingling stopped again, she was prepared. Tightening her grip on the pick, she waited, alert and ready to bolt if she had a chance, willing to fight if she had to.

The creature leapt from the trees, a living kachina from Hopi lore, not Cheyenne. So it wasn't Indians trying to frighten her away from their sacred grounds.

The person wore a wolf mask. It reminded her of a werewolf face from a Halloween costume. Wild hair cascaded down to the shoulders, hiding any natural hair. The clothing was a mixture of doeskin leggings, vest and shirt, with feathers of various sorts and other Indian para-phernalia that made no sense.

None of that scared her, but the two skinning knives, one

in each hand, did. She'd seen Judd skin a deer with one of those and knew they were deadly sharp.

The monster stalked her. Tracy was aware of the cliff behind her and that the creature was trying to drive her in that direction. She edged up the egglike knob of limestone.

The monster followed, knives flashing over its head.

Lightning streaked across the sky, followed at once by a deafening blast of thunder. The creature started and seemed to cringe for a moment. Tracy grabbed the chance.

She bolted down the far side of the limestone slope and ran for the woods. She didn't look back. Heart pounding, she dodged among the trees, leapt over bushes and small boulders and found a path that led downward. She raced flat out along it until she came to the trail that led to her car.

Running a hand over her jeans, she felt the car keys tucked safely in her pocket. Thank God.

When she reached the clearing, she was relieved to see it empty except for her blue compact auto. She unlocked it, jumped in and locked the door. Her hands shook as she turned the key. The engine caught. She backed up without looking, then went forward, turning the wheel desperately. She took off in a spray of gravel and dust.

Behind her, a wild-maned, horrible-faced monster leapt out of the woods as she turned the car to head down the steep hill. The creature ran toward her, then threw one of the knives at the car.

The knife hit the rear window and skidded off onto the ground. Tracy plunged the accelerator to the floor.

"Judd, Judd," she whispered, a litany of safety in a world gone berserk.

Nine

Judd answered the telephone on the second ring. "Hensley."

A strained gasp came from the other end. "Judd…help Tracy," someone said.

He didn't recognize the voice. "Who is this?"

"Tracy…find Tracy…danger…"

"Winona?" he asked. Fear slapped against his spine like a wet rag. He glanced at the calendar. Friday, the thirteenth.

"Yes…danger…find her…"

He realized Winona was having one of her visions. She was fighting the trancelike state in order to call him.

"I will," he promised. "I'll find her."

"Hurry…wolf after her…running…wolf…"

"Winona, rest now," he said sternly, worried about the old woman's heart. "I'll find her. Don't worry."

"Yes…go…*go!*" She hung up.

Feeling like the hounds of hell were after him, he grabbed up his holster and belted it on his hips, then checked the clip in his gun. He selected several rounds of ammunition and a rifle out of a cabinet. Then he was off.

In the car, driving on the highway toward the reservation, he called Sterling and told him to get his butt over there. He wanted backup on the case, but he wasn't going to broadcast an all-points bulletin on the basis of a psychic's vision.

He'd hardly gone a mile from town when he spied a blue car coming from the opposite direction. It was doing at least ninety. He turned across the median and headed after the speeding vehicle.

After hitting the button to start the blue lights flashing, he pushed the pedal down. While he caught up with the small car, he called Sterling and told him Tracy was all right. He pulled up beside her and blew the horn.

Her face wore a startled look as she glanced out the window. Then she recognized him. She slowed at once, then pulled to the side of the road. She was out of the car and racing toward him before he'd opened his door and slid out.

Then she was in his arms. "Judd, thank God. Oh, thank God!"

He inhaled the sweet essence of her, felt the impact of her slender body in every cell in his. "Tell me what frightened you," he murmured in a soothing tone.

"A monster...a wolf—"

His low imprecation interrupted her as he recalled Winona's vision. "Go on," he ordered. He thought of Rafe Rawlings, the "Wolf Boy" who was now a policeman and asking a lot of questions. But he was much too young to be involved. "You were at the site on the reservation?"

"Yes." She took a deep breath and pulled away, looking embarrassed after her show of emotion. "I was sifting through the dirt under the ledge…where Jackson and I found the femur and pelvis?"

He nodded, indicating he understood where she meant.

She brushed a stray lock of hair back from her temple, leaving a smidgen of dirt there. "I thought I heard something, but then it thundered, and I realized we were in for a rain, so I went back to work. Then a rock hit me— actually, a pebble—then another."

A rock! Judd felt the crystal clarity coming over him. Winona had seen a rock hitting someone in her vision. Someone had thrown a rock at Tracy….

"Then this jingling started…like jingle bells used on sleighs or something."

"The Indians use bells in their dances," he reminded her.

She nodded, then licked her lips. "The bells seemed to come from two different directions. Then the laughter started."

Anger steeled over Judd—anger so cold it chilled his blood. When Tracy came to the part about the apparition with the knives, rage enveloped his senses, shutting out everything but the need to find the person who had frightened her.

"I left my knapsack," she ended, dismayed at its loss.

"I'll get you another," he promised absently, his mind going over all he knew of the case.

"It isn't that," she said impatiently. "I had found more evidence—several short hairs, probably belonging to the victim, *and* one long one—blond…with dark roots."

He almost smiled at the dramatic pauses she used to emphasize her find.

"I left them in the knapsack," she concluded. "I need to go back and get it before—" She broke off abruptly.

"Before the wolf monster destroys it?"

She nodded.

He shook his head. Thunder rumbled over the mountains. "You go home. I'll go back and get your things."

"You can't go alone. It's too dangerous."

"I put in a call to Sterling before I found you and told him to meet me at the bluff," he said, neglecting to tell her he'd cancelled it. "By the way, I ought to give you a ticket. You must have been going ninety when I spotted you."

"Well, actually, ninety-five. I'd slowed down some because of the traffic before I saw you." She gave him an insouciant grin.

He wanted to kiss her. "Get on home before the rain starts. I'll see you around seven tonight."

"Right." She returned to her car and drove off at a sedate speed while he watched.

Solemn, he climbed back in his truck and made a U-turn across the median again. He wanted to check out the site as soon as possible.

He thought of calling Sterling, then decided against it. The poor slob had been working overtime and was supposed to be off duty that afternoon. The detective needed some time with his wife and child.

At the reservation, Judd followed the road up to the bluff, parked and climbed out. He checked the area. The skinning knife that had been thrown at Tracy was gone. He'd figured it would be.

Using the tracking skills he'd learned since living in Montana, he quietly slipped into the woods. He picked up the tracks of two people. Tracy's he recognized by the print of her sneaker soles. The other tracks were indistinct. Moccasins, he deduced. He studied one clear print. Large. A man.

The cold settled in his soul. Someone had tried to hurt Tracy. He wanted his blood.

He followed the trail upward, found the deer path Tracy had followed. He could almost feel her fear as she'd run for her life. Thank God she hadn't tried to stand her ground. A sane person had no chance against a madman.

The woods were silent, just as Tracy had described. Judd's senses were so acute he could identify the faint rustling of the leaves as the wind moved in from the west. He sniffed the air. Ozone. The storm was approaching.

Near where the woods opened on the limestone knob, he found tracks around a shrub. Examining the bush, he saw a broken branch and found a piece of string. Here was where one set of bells had been tied, he deduced.

Moving on up, he left the trees and stooped by the ledge after surveying the area. Tracy's knapsack wasn't there. He spied it several feet away…or what was left of it.

The canvas tote had been slashed into ribbons. The tools of her trade were scattered about. The sample bottles had been smashed to smithereens, their evidence lost, the hairs probably blown away by the rising wind.

The coldness inside him became glacial fury as he thought of what might have happened to Tracy had she not had the sense to run.

He followed the trail of footprints to a second shrub next

to the bluff. He could easily see where something—more bells, he assumed—had been torn from a mangled branch.

The creature had been careful to take all evidence with it. A cunning monster, Judd thought.

After glancing around, he stood and looked out at the lush pasture fifty feet below. The tribe had refused to renew the lease with the Kincaids, who'd used the pasture for a hundred years. There'd been trouble brewing over the situation until Jackson's wife, Maggie, had testified before Congress. The ranchers had backed down, but they hadn't been happy.

He tried to figure out if this had any bearing on Tracy's fright, but couldn't see that it did. And she didn't think an Indian had been the culprit.

"After all, a Cheyenne should know his own culture," she'd said, rather indignant that the person hadn't dressed correctly.

A slight smile tugged at his mouth. That was Trace, a nit-picker for authentic detail. She'd learned that from her father.

The smile disappeared. He'd loved being a part of her family. They'd taken him into their closeness and kept him there. Even after the divorce, her mother had sent him gifts at Christmas and his birthday. She'd enclosed notes, too, but she'd never mentioned her daughter.

Somehow he felt he'd let go too easily. Maybe he should have confronted Tracy or fought harder for her.

But a man could only do what he could do. At the time of the divorce, he'd felt it was the only way to go. Now he wasn't so sure. There were still feelings between them. He just didn't know what the hell they were.

Well, back to the case at hand.

Before he could turn and head for the truck, something hit the back of his knee. His left leg buckled.

He tried to catch himself, but slipped on a loose piece of limestone, which flew outward as his weight slammed down on it. The shard of rock fell down the bluff. Judd realized he was going to follow it.

Instinct had him clutching the shrub desperately. It held for a second, but not long enough for him to get a toehold in the rough stone. The branch separated from the bush, and he plunged over the side....

Down, down, down, it was a long way down. He remembered the line from a book he used to read to Thadd. Dr. Seuss.

Then he started thinking about how the hell he was going to survive the fall. Maybe he'd land in the creek—one of the deep quiet pools where he and Tracy used to bathe the summer they fell in love.

He caught the stub of a dwarf tree growing from a crevice. It bent flat to the rock face with his weight, but it held.

Not for long.

When the stumpy tree started coming out by the roots, he wedged his hand in a crevice and held on while he felt around for places to put his feet. The rocky wall was shale here, loose stuff that wouldn't hold him. He felt a moment's despair as the tree slowly pulled free from the crack.

The last root gave way. He lost his grip on the narrow crevice. Then he was falling...falling.... His last thought was to wonder how Winona's goats had gotten up on the bluff.

Tracy reached for the telephone, then drew back. She glanced at the clock—7:10. Judd was late. Should she call and remind him?

What if Sterling had forgotten to tell him to pick her up? No, Judd had said he'd see her around seven. But maybe he hadn't realized he was supposed to stop for her. She'd leave...but she didn't know where Sterling and Jessica lived.

Jessica had called and confirmed that the dinner was to be at their house. Jackson and his wife would be there, too. "Jackson is going to do fry bread, and I got honey from Winona today. It's casual, so wear something comfortable."

Tracy paced to the front door and stared out at the evening sky. Where was Judd?

She chewed on her lower lip. He'd promised to retrieve her knapsack, with her tools and the evidence in it. Sterling was supposed to meet him at the site. But what if something had happened and Sterling had been delayed? Or hadn't shown up?

No, she was being silly. One thing she knew for sure—Judd could take care of himself. He was careful and alert.

A vision of the wolf-faced monster came to her.

She shivered as her fear increased a notch. She'd call Jessica and find out what time Sterling had gotten home. That was the sensible thing to do. It was stupid to stand around stewing over nothing. She crossed the room and dialed the number.

"Jessica? This is Tracy," she said when her hostess answered. "I, uh, was wondering—has Sterling gotten home yet?"

"He's been home all afternoon," Jessica said. "What's happening? Hasn't Judd stopped for you yet?"

"No. I wanted to check with you that he knew he was supposed to pick me up."

"He did. I reminded him when he called to tell Sterling to forget meeting him at the reservation."

Fear clutched at Tracy. "He told Sterling not to meet him?"

"Yes. He said he'd found you." Jessica laughed softly. "He was one worried man until then."

"Jessica, Judd went out to the site after leaving me," Tracy said, her own worry apparent in her voice. "Now he's late."

"And Judd is never late. Hold on."

Tracy heard Jessica calling to her husband. She heard Sterling's baritone voice as he joined his wife. Jessica told him what had happened.

"Tracy," he said into the phone. "The old man hasn't shown up, huh?"

"No. He was going to check out the person who frightened me. I thought you were going to meet him. It's dangerous. I've got to go—"

"Whoa, there. Tell me exactly what happened. He didn't mention any of this."

Tracy explained as quickly as she could. "I'm going out there," she added.

"Stay put," Sterling ordered. "I'll handle it."

When they hung up, Tracy ran to the bedroom and changed to jeans and a shirt, thick socks and her sturdy boots. She grabbed a raincoat and a flashlight, switching it on to make sure it worked. It did. She rushed out.

The rain was coming down in a steady drizzle as she retraced her path along the highway and onto the reservation. Sterling's truck was at the bluff when she arrived. She parked beside it and slid out. She decided she didn't need the flashlight yet.

Ducking under the police tape, she sped along the deer

track to the ledge under the limestone. There she found her knapsack torn to shreds. She felt sick with worry.

What if the monster had attacked Judd? Killed him?

She saw a shadow among the trees and hid behind a boulder.

"It's me," Sterling said. He came to her. "Did you see anything on the way up?"

"No." She showed him her slashed tote. "Look."

"Damn," he said. He bent to the ground.

She flicked her light on and held it so it would highlight any footprints.

"He was here," Sterling said. "This way."

They walked to a steep section of the bluff, found the broken limb on the shrub and followed skid marks over the ledge.

Sterling lifted a large, round rock, examined it, then put it down. Tracy noted there was no depression in the dirt under it. The detective peered at the edge of the bluff. The place where the fractured chip had given way was obvious. When he looked up, he gave her a probing glance.

"I'm all right," she said, knowing that Judd must have gone over the side. "How do we get down?"

"We'll take the main road. It's faster than the dirt trail. Stay close to me. I'll have my siren on."

Clutching the steering wheel of her car, she rode the bumper of the unmarked police vehicle. Its wail reminded her of a scream in the gathering dusk when Sterling used it to clear a path through the traffic. They followed a paved county road, then a short dirt track, then no road at all as they drove across a meadow. She stopped when he did.

"We'll have to walk from here," he said.

They jogged along the creek on a path worn through the grass and underbrush by generations of fishermen.

Tracy had gone through so many emotions on the drive that she felt numb as they searched along the base of the bluff.

"We're near where he went over. I'm going across to the other side," Sterling told her. "Stay close to the creek. Start calling. He may hear."

If he's conscious. If he's alive.

"All right." She waded through the twilight as if she walked through a strange medium, thick and cloying, instead of air. Each breath burned her throat as she ignored a need to cry.

"Judd," she called softly, over and over. She was afraid her voice would alert the madman who'd tried to kill her, if he was still around. Sterling didn't seem to think he was.

She skirted a section of high boulders, pushed into their present disorder by glaciers from long ago, she decided inanely as she searched. "Judd," she called, a bit more desperately.

"Here."

She stopped, listened. Nothing. "Judd?"

"Here."

"Where? Keep talking," she ordered. His voice had been so low and weak. Fear crawled along her spine. "Judd?"

"Here."

She found him lying on the bank between two boulders. One foot still in the water, as if the effort to pull it out had been too much for him. When she touched him, his skin was cold.

"You'll catch pneumonia," she murmured.

"Yeah. The water's cold."

She ran one hand over him while she held the light with the other. She couldn't find any injuries. "You fell from the cliff?"

"Yes. Caught a bush...but it wouldn't hold." He was plainly irritated by this fact. "A damned goat sneaked up on me."

She'd thought he was lucid until this last statement. Now she realized he must be delirious. "Don't try to talk," she soothed. "Save your strength."

"Trace, be careful. Winona said you were in danger." He pushed himself up on his elbows and glanced all around.

Tears filled her eyes as she realized he was concerned for her. "I'll be careful. Sterling is with me."

"Good," he muttered. "That's good."

She straightened and cupped her hands around her mouth. "Sterling!" she yelled as loudly as she could. She waved the flashlight in the air. "I've found him."

"Coming," he called at once.

She stripped out of her rain jacket and laid it over Judd. The drizzle went right through her shirt. "Hurry," she shouted.

"I'm here." He spoke near her, startling her.

"Thank God," she said. "He's hurt. I don't know how bad." Training the light on Judd, she waited while the detective pulled him onto the path and checked him over.

"His leg is broken. I'll make a splint. Then we'll get him to the hospital."

He found a stick and secured it to Judd's leg with their belts. They were going to carry him, but Judd insisted he could walk. After making a rude sound, Sterling lifted his boss to his feet. Tracy swung one of Judd's arms over her shoulder while Sterling did the same. They headed for the road where the vehicles were parked. It seemed to take forever.

Tracy's shoulders were burning by the time they hoisted Judd into Sterling's cruiser. The detective gave Tracy her coat and tucked a blanket around the patient.

"Follow me," Sterling ordered.

Reluctantly, she left Judd and got into her car.

They arrived at the hospital in record time. The nurse recognized her when she entered the emergency room and joined Sterling. The woman smiled reassuringly, then bent over Judd.

The trauma team on duty that night checked him over, then wheeled him into a curtained area. They were teasing Judd about taking a dip in the creek at his age. Tracy wished they'd get on with it. She'd seen the paleness of his skin despite his tan.

Sterling went to call Jessica to let her know what had happened. By the time Judd was taken to have his leg set in a cast, Jessica as well as Jackson and Maggie Hawk had arrived, Jessica after first dropping Jennifer at a sitter's. Lily Mae breezed in hot on their heels.

"I listen to the police band," she explained when Tracy stared at her in surprise. "I brought you some soup."

"Thank you, but I couldn't eat," Tracy said. She had no time for food now, not when Judd was hurt.

"For later." Lily Mae brought coffee and forced Tracy to drink it. "You're wet clear through, child," the widow scolded.

Tracy thanked her for her care. "I'd better call Winona," she murmured, feeling as if she needed to talk to her friend. She borrowed some money and went to the pay phone by the door.

Winona answered on the first ring. "Tracy?"

"Yes." Tracy told her what had happened.

"I saw the wolf," Winona said in confirmation, "and called Judd. I knew you were in danger and needed him."

"He's hurt because of me." Tracy was guilt stricken.

"No, because of some crazy person who's committed a crime and doesn't want to be discovered," Winona corrected. "Take care of him. He needs you."

Tracy swallowed as emotion tightened her throat. "I will," she promised solemnly. "I owe him."

Winona chuckled suddenly. "You may pay more than you mean to." She said good-night and hung up.

Tracy returned to the hospital cafeteria and joined the others. Lily Mae had gone to visit a patient. She'd left a container of soup with Jessica to give to Tracy.

Another patrol car arrived. Rafe Rawlings got out and came inside. "How is he?" he inquired of Sterling.

"He has a broken leg. That's all we know."

Kane Hunter entered through the hallway leading to the emergency room. "He's fine, grouchy as a spring bear and demanding to go home. He's had a painkiller and is a little groggy right now. Who's going to baby-sit him tonight?"

"I am," Tracy said.

Several pairs of eyes turned to her. Sterling nodded. "Good idea," he said. A smile appeared on the tough detective's mouth. "I'll help you get him home. His place or yours?"

The question was so suggestive—and Sterling, the rat, knew it—that Tracy blushed. Jessica frowned at her grinning husband. Maggie did the same with hers.

"Jessica, your dinner!" Tracy exclaimed, remembering suddenly. "It's ruined."

"Now don't you worry about that," the other woman soothed. "I'll bring you a plate over in a little while."

"I have the fry bread in the car," Jackson stated.

It ended that the two men took Judd home in the patrol car. At the house, they dressed him in pajamas, and put him to bed while Tracy found coffee in the kitchen and put on a pot.

Jessica and Maggie brought over the food, which consisted of Brunswick stew, plus a salad and dinner rolls.

"Do you feel like eating?" Tracy asked Judd, going into the master bedroom a few minutes later.

"Yes. I don't need a baby-sitter. Kane is worse than a mother hen. Tell everyone to leave."

"That wouldn't be polite. We're having dinner here."

She glanced around the bedroom as they talked. The furniture was made of golden oak. It had belonged to Judd before they were married. His parents had given it to him.

The room was the same as when they'd lived there. Even the family picture of Thadd, Judd and her hung on the wall in its usual place near the dresser.

"I looked for that," she said. "When I left."

"I took it to the office."

Their eyes locked for a long minute. She sensed the questions that neither of them could voice. It was too soon. The attraction between them was too compelling to ignore, but the old hurts were still too raw to examine at present.

She switched to a safer subject. "Were you injured anywhere besides your leg?"

"Some scrapes. Nothing major. The break was clean. It should heal without a problem." He glanced at his palms.

"Good." She moved closer and looked at them, too. "Oh, Judd, your hands."

The gouges weren't deep, but they were extensive. Kane had cleaned them with an antibiotic and sprayed on a medical coating of synthetic skin until Judd's own could grow back.

"How did you happen to fall?" she asked.

"Damned if I know," he responded with a grouchy frown. "I thought one of Winona's goats butted me in the back of my bad knee. Crazy." He shook his head.

"Not so crazy," Sterling corrected, coming in with a tray. "Someone could have hit you in the leg. I noticed a round rock there where the skid marks were—a hefty one about four inches in diameter. That would have done the trick."

Tracy recalled the rock that hadn't made an impression in the dirt, which indicated it hadn't been in that spot long.

"But why?" Jessica came in with a cup of coffee for Judd.

Jackson and Maggie joined them. Soon they were all sitting in the bedroom, eating their supper and discussing the case.

"Does this mean someone is afraid of the bones?" Maggie asked.

Everyone looked at her.

"You know, like if we find out who the bones belonged to, then we'd know who killed the person?"

"It must be someone local, someone still here," Jessica said, "someone who doesn't want to be discovered."

"Kane said something." Sterling paused and studied Tracy. "He said there's a hermit who roams the area, a man named Homer Gilmore. He's harmless, but he does look rather weird—long, gray hair that sticks out around his head, sharp facial features. He prospects around in the hills. He has been known to scare the life out of unsuspecting backpackers."

"It wasn't an old man," she said. "Not unless he was dressed in a variety of Indian clothes and something that looked like a Halloween mask with a werewolf face, plus a wig made out of buffalo hide. It was…very strange."

"To say the least," Jessica agreed. "To scare someone that way—the knives and all—was a terrible thing to do."

"The person may have meant to do more than scare Tracy." Judd scowled with visible anger. "He threw a knife at her."

"Well, at my car," she corrected with a faint smile. "I don't know that he was trying to actually hit me."

Sterling gave the three women a stern raking with his dark eyes. "When someone has a weapon, you always assume he means to kill you. Always, got that?"

"Right," Judd declared.

"Absolutely," Jackson stated unequivocally.

The three women looked at the three fierce, unsmiling men. They nodded solemnly.

Tracy studied the convivial group. A feeling of peace descended over her, in spite of the day's odd, dangerous events. She was among friends. She felt as if she'd come home.

A welter of emotions washed over her, destroying the brief contentment. Yearning so painful she had to clench her teeth to hold it back rose to her throat.

She looked at the two married couples, then at Judd. Once they had been like that—happy and in love. Once… She wanted it again.

Ten

"Call if you need anything," Maggie told Tracy as she and Jackson left the house. "I'll talk to you soon."

Tracy waved to the couple, then closed the door. It had been a pleasant evening. Even Judd, in spite of his painful leg, had laughed and chatted with ease.

He and Sterling McCallum were cut from the same cloth, she thought. Jackson was more open. Or maybe he seemed that way because she'd known him most of her life.

She poured a glass of water, glanced around the kitchen, which the three women had cleaned, then returned to the master bedroom.

"Where are the painkillers Kane gave you?" she asked.

"Who said he did?" Judd challenged. "Besides, I don't need anything for pain. I feel fine. You can go home."

She ignored his dismissal and rummaged through his damp clothing, which was hanging in the bathroom. She found several packets of pills. She opened one, dumped the two tablets on her palm and carried them to him with the water.

"I can tell you're hurting," she said softly.

"You can read minds?" he demanded. "Even Winona can't do that. You two should go into business together."

"Don't be a goose," she reprimanded mildly. "You get a tense look around the eyes when you're in pain." She held out the pills.

He snorted, threw the tablets into his mouth, took the glass and swallowed the medicine in one gulp. He finished off the water and set the glass on the lamp table. "There, all gone."

"Good. Do you want to sleep or shall I read to you?"

"Neither," he said, giving her a sour glance. "You can go."

"I'm spending the night."

"Like hell!"

"It might come to that." She grinned at him, feeling very much in control. He could hardly get up and throw her out...well, knowing Judd, he probably could, but he wouldn't.

He took a deep breath. "Look, I appreciate your TLC, but I'm all right. Really. You don't have to play nurse."

"I'm staying." She took his wet clothing from the bathroom and went to the laundry room, which was right off the kitchen. She tossed the clothes in the tub, saw a basket of other items, sorted them, added them to the load and started the machine.

While she checked the refrigerator and started a grocery list, she wondered if he did his own cooking and cleaning. Tomorrow she would bring over food from her place.

Hmm, perhaps she'd better go tonight. She needed her pajamas and toiletries.

She realized she was planning on staying for more than the night. But maybe not. There had been wariness and resentment in Judd's eyes whenever he'd looked her way during the evening.

Sighing, she rubbed the slight tension headache that had settled in the back of her skull and considered what to do. Well, she'd stay until Judd was up and about. Kane had said he'd drop off a pair of crutches in the morning.

With that off her mind, she checked on Judd, found him asleep or pretending to be, and left the house. At the cottage, she loaded up bags with groceries and packed a change of clothing along with her pj's and ditty bag. She returned to Judd's home.

When she went in the front door, she heard him cursing in the bedroom. She dropped her stuff on the sofa and rushed to the back of the house.

She found him hanging on to a chair with one hand and the wall with the other. "What are you doing?" she cried, angry that he would take a chance on hurting himself.

"Going to the bathroom. The damned floor seems to be bucking like a mustang," he complained. "I thought you'd left."

"I went to get my things. Here." She slipped an arm around his lean waist and drew his arm over her shoulder. "Come on."

He hopped while she steadied him. They reached the bathroom. She let him go and waited. He glared at her. "Waiting for the peep show? The admission is two dollars."

Heat flared in her face at his rude remark. "I've seen it all before. For free." She flounced out.

"It was never free," he muttered. "Woman always cost men a hell of a lot."

She closed the door, ignoring the sarcastic remark. Going to the bed, she fluffed up the pillows and straightened the covers, folding the sheet down so that all would be ready when he returned.

When the door opened, she hurried across the room and offered him her arm to lean on. He accepted her aid without a word.

"Thanks," he said when she pulled the sheet over him. "I'm sorry I snapped earlier."

She was surprised at his apology. Peering at his face, she saw that his eyes were closed, his brows bunched in an unconscious grimace of weariness. Her heart went out to him.

After turning the light low, she went to the guest room, made up the bed with sheets she found in the hall closet and changed into her pajamas and robe. She washed up and returned to his room.

Choosing a comfortable chair, she sat in it and watched the drizzle run down the windowpanes in zigzag lines. She sighed and wished she could see into the future. She very much wanted to know what tomorrow would bring.

"Trace."

She opened her eyes, realized where she was and sat up straight. Judd was restless on the bed. He said her name again, this time louder and in a worried tone. She went to him.

"I'm here," she said softly.

He opened his eyes and stared at her. "Be careful," he warned. "There's danger."

"I'm okay. I'm here with you," she reminded him.

She saw comprehension dawn in his eyes. He flicked a quick gaze over the room, sizing up the situation in that swift way he had. "I remember," he said. "I was dreaming."

"Yes." She checked the clock, then got more water from the bathroom and opened another packet of pills. "Here, you can take two more of these now. I think you need them."

"My eyes tense again?"

When she glanced up at the taunting remark, she saw the wicked light in his eyes. "You must be feeling better if you're up to teasing," she murmured, pleased.

"I feel like hell," he admitted. "My leg is throbbing and itching at the same time."

"I'll rub it," she volunteered.

After he swallowed the medicine and set the glass aside, she pulled back the sheet and pushed his pajama leg up. "Lucky for you, you landed in a pool," she told him.

"Not so lucky. I kicked out from the cliff in order to hit the deep part of the creek. If I'd been just another foot over, I wouldn't have hit a rock and broken my leg."

"Umm," she crooned sympathetically. She rubbed his toes, avoiding the areas that were a nice shade of purple. When she moved above the cast to his knee, he grunted as if her touch hurt.

"Sore there," he said when she looked at him.

"Let me see." She checked the back of his knee. "You have a bruise here, too. That rock on the bluff—remember, you thought one of Winona's goats had hit you? But it must have been the rock Sterling found."

"Yeah, I remember." He stopped her hands when she slid them under the pajama material and massaged his thigh. "You'll have me hurting someplace else if you keep that up."

"Huh," she said skeptically.

"My powers of recuperation are remarkable."

"They must be if you're up to bragging so soon after your fall." She spoke with some asperity.

He smiled slightly and lay against the pillows with his eyes closed while she rubbed his toes again.

"Tonight was fun, wasn't it?" she said a few minutes later. "It's nice to have friends."

"Don't you have any friends in California?"

"Yes, but..." She couldn't tell him it was different being part of a couple and sharing things with other couples, rather than a single as she was in her other life...her *real* life.

She let his foot go and covered him with the sheet. Sitting in the chair, she reminded herself that she was living in a fool's world to think of herself and Judd as a couple again.

"But?" he prodded when she was silent.

"Do you ever wish we could start over?" She bit down on her lip, but the words were out.

He met her gaze. "Yeah. But I know better. I'm not going to get mixed up with you again." He shifted about until he found a more comfortable position. "What would be the use? You'll be leaving in a few days."

She had nothing to say to that.

The next morning Tracy was awake shortly after dawn. She leapt up, washed and dressed, then went to check on her patient.

Judd was asleep. Normally, he was the one up at the first light of day. She noticed he'd put a pillow under the cast. That should help keep the swelling down and relieve the throbbing.

She went to the kitchen and put on a pot of coffee, then

decided on pancakes and sausage for breakfast. It was one of Judd's favorite meals.

A frown replaced the smile she'd been wearing. It was no good falling back into old routines. Judd had made his feelings plain last night. But he still wanted her.

Putting off useless brooding, she prepared the food, then left the plates in the warmed oven. When she peeked in his room, he was getting out of bed. She dashed across the room.

"Let me help." She looped his arm over her shoulders.

He sighed audibly and held on as he awkwardly walked on the thick cast. She saw him grimace, but he didn't complain.

When he was finished in the bathroom, she helped him back to bed and propped his foot on the pillow again. "I have breakfast ready. Would you like to eat now?"

When he said yes, she prepared a tray and brought it to him in bed. She found a TV tray in the family room and used it for herself. They ate in companionable silence.

At nine the calls started—local people checking on their sheriff. She screened them for him, feeling slightly jealous when he spoke to Maris—who was safely married, Tracy reminded herself.

He chatted with the rancher for several minutes before hanging up. It was obvious they were good friends and at ease with each other. He laughed more than once during the conversation.

Tracy went to the kitchen and poured them each another cup of coffee, then washed the pot. For a long time she gazed out the window at the woods. Next door, she saw the little boy—Jimmy?—and a friend playing near the trees.

She didn't look around when Judd thumped into the room.

He got his cup and stood beside her, drinking the coffee, which she'd made strong, the way he liked it. Gourmet coffee had been one of the small luxuries they'd indulged in as a newly married and very broke young couple.

"How old is your neighbor?" she asked.

"Jimmy is nine. That's his best buddy, Mark, who lives one block west of us. They'll be in fourth grade when school starts."

"You seem to know them well."

"Jimmy and I are pals. His parents are divorced. I'm sort of the regular male in his life. He helps me mow the yard and cut wood for winter."

"I see." Her voice quivered. She felt as if her heart were being torn out by the roots.

"Life does go on," Judd said harshly. He took his cup and went back to the bedroom.

"I know," she said to the empty kitchen, feeling alone and uncertain, and sure she was headed for heartbreak all over again.

Luckily, Kane Hunter showed up before she got into a serious case of self-pity. She welcomed him with a bright smile.

"Good morning, Dr. Hunter," she said in greeting.

"What's with the doctor business?" he demanded. He set a pair of crutches in the corner next to the pantry. "You and Jackson used to call me a little devil when I barged in on your games back at the res twenty or so years ago."

"All is forgiven," she assured him. "Coffee? I was just about to put on a fresh pot."

"Thanks, that would be nice. How's the patient?"

"Grouchy, but up and about. Go see for yourself."

Kane laughed and headed for the master bedroom with the crutches. She heard the men talking amiably while she waited for the coffee to finish. Judd's deeper voice ran over her ragged nerves like honey over a hot, buttered biscuit.

She suddenly remembered lazy mornings in bed, Thadd tucked between them while Judd read the funnies. She shook her head hopelessly. Remembering was *not* getting on with life.

After pouring the coffee, she took a cup to Kane and stayed while they concluded their conversation. When the doctor left, she asked Judd if she could do anything for him. "Run errands or something?" she suggested.

"Eager to be off?" he questioned, his dark gaze opaque as he studied her.

She realized she was nervously pleating and smoothing her slacks across her thigh. She forced her hands to be still. "Not particularly. If you don't need anything, I thought I would do some work."

"You should wind up the case soon, then you can leave."

"Yes."

They looked at each other. She felt herself being drawn into the dark vortex of desire he usually kept concealed. His gaze roamed over her hungrily. Her heart leapt as heat rioted through her entire body. She knew she would go to him if he but beckoned.

Before she gave in to that tempestuous yearning, she wanted one thing clarified between them. She hesitated, then gathered her courage. "Judd, when we married..."

His face took on a hard edge.

She doggedly persevered. "Was it…did you marry me because I was pregnant?"

He muttered an imprecation that shocked her.

"You never said…" She gestured helplessly. "It's something I've wondered about for a long time."

"Is that what you think?" he demanded harshly.

"I don't know." She faced him. "I don't know what I think, not anymore. You were always a quiet person. I assumed you felt the same as I did, but later, I decided I was wrong…."

He grabbed the crutches and got out of bed. He hobbled to the door, then stopped and gestured to indicate the house around them. "I built this house for you. Maybe you ought to think about why a man would do that for a woman." He stomped out, his *step-thump* mode of walking filled with anger.

Tracy let out a shaky breath. Maybe he had loved her as she'd loved him, but he didn't now. He wanted her, yes…and was furious with both of them for it.

Judd walked out on the front porch. He cursed fate for bringing Tracy back to Whitehorn. He cursed her for doubting his motives and himself for caring what she thought.

What the hell did it matter now?

He sighed as the anger cooled. What did anything matter anymore? Nothing had for a long time…at least, it hadn't until Tracy had returned, stirring up old memories he'd thought were dead, making him ache for her again.

All last night he'd thought of her in the house, sleeping only a few feet away in the chair or in the guest room. He'd awakened often and knew he'd been dreaming of her and him. Together. Making love.

A groan pushed its way out of his throat. He wanted her right now with a harsh need that drove all common sense from his mind.

And she wanted him.

He'd seen it in her eyes, the need…and the fear. She was afraid to come to him. Once she'd given herself to him with no doubts, no questions at all. She'd poured her pure, sweet love over him with no holding back.

He would have hung the moon for her if she'd asked. But she hadn't asked that. She'd asked him how to stop hurting. He'd had no answer to that question.

Moisture stung his eyes. He brushed it away impatiently. It was crazy to get involved. He wouldn't go through the pain again when she left.

Going inside, he called Sterling. "You're in charge. Contact the tribal police and go over the site with a fine-tooth comb. Tracy found some hairs. Sift through the dirt under the ledge and see if you can find some more. Bring in her pack and check it."

"Everything's under control. Jackson and I have men out there now," Sterling told him. "When will you be on your feet?"

"Kane brought me some crutches, so I'm mobile. I'll be at the office Monday. Try not to mess up in the meantime."

"I'll do my best," the detective promised. "Well, gotta go. There's trouble between the Kincaid ranch and the res. Jackson says they found Kincaid cattle in the pasture the ranch used to lease from the tribe. I'm going out to talk to Dugin now."

"Good. Then what?"

"After that we're planning a raid on the mayor's house.

Someone phoned in a hot tip that he was running a bawdy house on the third floor." With that, Sterling hung up.

Judd gave a snort of laughter. Sterling could be counted on to keep a level head—although there had been moments when Judd had questioned his wisdom in getting involved with Jessica and her do-gooder deeds.

It had worked out for them. They were happy.

He swallowed against the knot that formed in his throat. No use pining for what used to be. He would ignore the clamoring in his blood. Soon Tracy would be gone, and his life would return to normal. It couldn't come too soon for him.

Tracy swept off the deck and dusted the patio furniture. She jumped and turned around when a young voice piped up from behind her.

"Hi." The neighbor boy bounced up the steps onto the deck.

"Hello," she said. "You must be Jimmy."

"Yeah. How did you know?"

"Judd said you were a friend."

Jimmy peered around her. "I came over to see his leg. Is it in a cast?"

"Yes. Come on. He's watching a ball game." She led the way into the family room where Judd sat with the TV on. She saw he'd changed from pajamas to a sport shirt and a pair of cutoffs.

"Hi, Sheriff." Jimmy went over to admire the injured leg, which was propped on a pillow on the coffee table. "Wow, did it hurt when you broke it? How did they get the cast on?"

Tracy smiled as she went to the kitchen. Maybe Judd's

young friend would bring him out of his moody introspection. She'd certainly had no luck in cheering him up.

She poured two glasses of nonfat milk and arranged a variety of cookies on a plate. These she took to the family room and left for the patient and his guest to enjoy.

Grocery list in hand, she headed out, pausing to ask Jimmy to keep an eye on the sheriff.

"Sure," he said. "I can stay all afternoon. Mark has gone to visit his grandmother."

"Nice to know where I stand," Judd remarked.

Tracy laughed at his wry tone. "Number-two friend is pretty high on the totem pole, if you ask me."

His dark eyes roamed over her yellow slacks and bright-colored blouse. He opened his mouth, then closed it.

She was disappointed when he didn't speak. Scolding herself for wanting more than life offered, she hurried to the grocery store, then the bakery, then back to the house.

Jimmy was still there. He rose when she came into the house. "My mom called and said I had to come home when you got back. I'll come over tomorrow, if you like. I can bring a game to play. The sheriff likes checkers."

"That would be fine. Here, I bought too many of these apple turnovers. Maybe you and your mom would like some for dessert." She gave him a white bag.

"Thanks." He yelled a farewell to Judd, then bounded out of the house and across the yard. She saw him climb the rail fence.

She put the groceries away and straightened up the kitchen, then went into the family room. Judd was reading. The TV was on. The game was football instead of baseball. She smiled and settled in a chair with a magazine.

When she grew sleepy, she rested her head on the chair back and gazed at Judd. He'd gone to sleep.

His hair was thick, of a rich brown-black color. It waved smoothly back from his face. There was a suggestion of a widow's peak on his forehead.

She saw him draw a deep breath and exhale with a sighing sound. A storm grew in her, turbulent and demanding, until her body felt too small to hold it.

I love him, she thought, and knew the love had never gone away. It had lain dormant, like a seed in winter, waiting for the warmth of the sun to stir it to life. For her, Judd was that sun. She'd been back with him just a few days and her love had bloomed anew.

But what was she going to do with this love? It had no place in her future that she could see. Unless she could make Judd want her again…enough to ask her to stay.

She sniffed as tears pressed close to the surface. Judd opened his eyes and stared into hers. She knew the longing was there for him to see, and the love, if he cared to look.

The tears insisted on forming. She blinked them away as rapidly as she could.

"Don't," he said hoarsely.

"I'm all right. It's just…"

It was the hopelessness of the situation, of loving and not being able to do anything about it, but she couldn't say that. Her throat closed. She got to her feet, wanting to flee before she made a total fool of herself.

Judd stood, too. He took the three steps needed to bring him face-to-face with her. "Trace," he said and shook his head as if he, too, were in the grip of emotions too powerful to deny.

"I feel so lonely," she whispered.

He frowned as if in pain, then nodded slowly. "I know. God, I know." He reached out and touched her shoulder, then grasped her with both his hands. He drew her close.

She put her face into the groove of his neck and clasped her hands around his waist. For a while she was content to share the warmth of their embrace, then it wasn't enough.

Slowly, carefully, as if coaxing a wild creature, she ran her hands along his sides. Turning her head ever so little, she pressed her lips to the strong column of his neck.

She felt his breath catch. His hands tightened, then released her shoulders and slipped around her, pulling her against him.

"Trace," he said, a note of desperation in his voice.

"Hold me," she pleaded. "It's been so long."

He moved then, taking a seat on the sofa and pulling her across his lap. Her sandals hit the floor. His head bent, then his lips touched hers.

The kiss was so sweet it hurt.

She whimpered as the pent-up love crashed against the barrier of restraint she'd built inside. It had held too many years for her surrender to be an easy one. The ready tears burned her eyes as she fought for control.

"Oh, love, love," she murmured. She hadn't wanted to need to him like this, hadn't meant to let herself love him again.

The futility of fighting it swept over her. She couldn't give up the moment, no matter what tomorrow might bring.

"Make love to me." She remembered his leg. "Can we? Your leg…does it hurt?"

"Shh, no, it doesn't hurt," he soothed, his lips busy at

her eyes, her temples, her ears while his hands strayed all over her.

It felt so good to be touched and caressed. She loved the feel of him against her—big and strong and warm. With trembling hands, she unfastened his shirt.

"Take your blouse off," he requested in a low, husky tone that thrilled her with its urgency.

She stripped out of the bright silk print. Judd reached behind her and unfastened her bra with one hand. He hooked a finger at the front and pulled it from her. It whispered over her arms and disappeared behind her as he tossed it on the floor.

He brought her close, moving her from side to side so that her nipples brushed back and forth against the curly hairs on his chest. They beaded into hard, plump peaks at once.

Moving her so that she reclined against the arm of the sofa, he bent his head until he could reach one breast. He took the taut nipple into his mouth and ran his tongue around it, again and again. He remembered all the ways to drive her wild.

The sensuality that had always existed between them blossomed out of control. His hands touched her everywhere. When he unzipped her slacks, she twisted from side to side until he had them and the lacy underpants down her hips. They followed the rest of her clothing to the floor.

Against her hip, she felt the hard length of his phallus pulse against the denim of his cutoffs.

"The bedroom," he murmured. "I want to enjoy all of you without falling off the sofa."

When she opened her eyes, he smiled...so beautifully, it broke her heart. "I've missed that." She touched the corner of his mouth. "That slow, sexy smile…the way you look at a woman, as if she's the only one in your world…."

"You were. You were the only one," he avowed.

"But not anymore—"

He cut her off with his lips. When the kiss ended, he lifted her to her feet and pushed himself up from the sofa. He grabbed his crutches, hobbled a few steps, then paused and waited for her.

She stood there, rooted to the spot as love and fear collided inside her. She had no right to ask for anything from him—not his body, not his fidelity, not his love. But she wanted all of them.

"Are you coming?" he asked, a wariness in his manner.

He expected her to refuse, she realized. He thought she would turn from him as she'd done so long ago. He'd waited for her once, and she'd turned from him, lost in her own misery.

She took a step forward…then another. She felt she was on an ice bridge that might collapse beneath her at any moment.

When she came abreast of Judd, she walked past him and went to the master bedroom, feeling terribly exposed and vulnerable without her clothing. He fell into step behind her.

In the bedroom, she stopped beside the bed. She cast Judd an uncertain glance.

He bent and held the covers up with one hand, an invitation. She quickly climbed in. He propped the crutches against the wall.

Tracy watched as his hands went to the fastening of his cutoffs. He glanced at her, then turned his attention back to the task. His fingers trembled slightly as he worked the zipper.

Realizing he was as unsure of this moment as she was, she felt her own doubts ease up. They'd work it out, she decided. It would all work out.

"Hurry," she said. "I want you."

He pushed the cutoffs and briefs over his hips, then sat in the chair to work the clothing over the cast. When he rose and crossed the narrow space between the chair and bed, she laid her hand on his thigh, luxuriating in the feel of him.

"The first time I saw you, I thought you were a savage, wild and beautiful and free." She caressed his thigh, marveling at the hardness of the muscle beneath the taut skin.

When she touched him intimately, stroking the hard length of his erection, he made a low sound in the back of his throat, the sound of a man pushed beyond his limits.

With one mighty sweep, he threw the sheet aside. He pushed her down on the mattress and followed, dragging his injured leg up on the bed with a grunt of pain.

"Be careful," she said, worried that in their eagerness he might somehow injure it again.

"It's too late," he muttered hoarsely. He made a space for himself between her thighs. Then he pushed forward, his flesh hot and rigid against her as he sought entry.

She clasped his hips and drew him inside, pressing her hips upward to meet his downward thrust. Their bodies melded, sliding easily, snugly together. A perfect fit.

He took his weight on his elbows, his solid length covering her while he rested there. A shudder went through him.

"Don't move."

"I can't help it." She kissed his chest and nuzzled her nose through the crisp hairs. She flicked her tongue against his nipples and felt his body leap within her in response.

He tangled his fingers in her hair and angled her face up until her mouth was level with his. Then he kissed her. And kissed her. And kissed her.

It was wild and beautiful and desperate, each thrust of his tongue a sensuous prelude to the pleasure that would come later.

She clung to him helplessly, running her hands over his back and hips, along his thighs where the muscles were rigid with control. She vaguely realized she'd unleashed a tempest that wouldn't be contained until the final bolt of lightning jolted between them.

When he slipped a hand between them and stroked her lightly, an explosion of heat rippled through her. He rocked against her, then gasped and was still. She sensed he was fighting to hold back the climatic moment. There was no need.

She cried out as a great surge of tension coiled in her, then unfurled with the acute quickness of a whiplash.

Barriers fell by the wayside. Doubts were forgotten. There was only *now* and the pulsating intensity between them as he pounded into her, pushed over the edge by her climax.

Before she could think, the tension coiled again, then burst outward so that her entire body seemed to convulse around the point where he thrust so intimately, so pleasurably against her.

She clutched him desperately as the storm rode over her, blinding her, draining her. She heard him gasp, then his entire body went still. Inside, she felt the throbbing release of his seed. He started moving again, slower this time, until he at last rested, spent and panting, on her.

"So beautiful," she murmured, overcome by the intensity of their passion. "Oh, Judd, it was so beautiful." Tears slid down her temples into her hair.

Eleven

Judd thought beautiful didn't begin to describe what had happened between them. Mind-shattering, ecstatic…and, yeah, beautiful—all those terms applied, and then some.

He lingered, not wanting to break the connection between them, not wanting to think beyond the pure contentment of the moment.

And therein lay danger.

He'd been unable to deny the need between them, but he wouldn't become entangled with her again. He wouldn't let himself start thinking he had to have her in order to feel alive and whole, although that was the way he felt at the moment.

He'd been through that wringer once. When she'd told him she wanted a divorce, it had been like having open-heart surgery without benefit of anesthesia.

Her tears touched his cheek. He turned his head and sipped the salty moisture from her skin. Inside, something that had been hard and self-preserving went soft and mushy. He fought the need to comfort her.

Awkward with the cumbersome cast, he slowly eased away from her. The summer heat seeped into the house, but he felt the cold when he withdrew from the moist warmth of her body. He lay on his back and sighed as weariness riffled into every muscle.

He was aware of Tracy leaving the bed. He didn't open his eyes. He didn't want to see her go. She was a weakness he couldn't afford, he reminded himself. He had a job he liked in a town full of friends. He didn't need anything else.

A warm washcloth touched him in a sensitive place, causing him to jump in surprise. He heard her low murmur, reassuring him. Gently, she bathed him, then returned to the bathroom.

He lay there, feeling more vulnerable than he had at the moment of climax. A longing for the things they'd lost stalked his defenses. He felt exposed, his heart laid out raw and quivering on the primitive altar of…lust, he told himself, repeating the word until it felt hard and cold and pure in his mind.

Lust. That was all. Lust.

When Tracy returned to bed, she curled against him. She put one smooth thigh between his the way she used to and laid an arm over his chest. "Does this make your leg hurt?"

"No."

All pain had been burned away in the hot pounding of his blood through his body. He wiggled his toes, becoming aware of his injuries for the first time since he'd touched her. Caressing her hadn't bothered his sore hands at all.

Turning slightly, he eased an arm under her head and

rested the other on her side. With his thumb, he began stroking the side of her breast. The slow buildup of heat started inside him. He wanted her again.

Ha, when had he ever stopped?

Even making love to another woman hadn't erased the memory of Tracy's response— He broke off the thought as another came to him. He hadn't offered her any protection.

Between them, it had never been necessary. Their clumsy eagerness had resulted in their son's conception almost as soon as they'd met. During the years after that, there'd been no need for birth control. Tracy had never conceived again.

He wondered if he should mention it. He owed it to her. He cleared his throat. "I didn't use a condom," he said.

She raised her head. Her eyes held that sleepy contentment he remembered so well. They also held a question.

"In case you were worried," he explained. "I'm safe. I've never been…you're the only woman I've ever had without taking the proper precautions."

He wasn't going to tell her there had been exactly two women in seven years, each of short duration as a lover. With Maris, he hadn't even gotten that far. He'd realized early on that they were destined to be only friends.

"I'm safe, too," Tracy said.

For a second, the idea of her with someone else burned a hole in him, then he thrust it aside. He thought he heard sadness in her softly spoken words, but couldn't figure it out.

"Was there someone?" he asked.

Tracy stiffened for a second, then sighed. Judd, once he was on to something, was more persistent than a hound after a rabbit.

"There was a man who wanted to marry me. I thought I loved him, too. In a way. Except that I couldn't...each time he touched me, I...froze."

That was when she'd gone to the psychologist, who'd told her it was time to get over her grief and on with her life. Tracy wondered what the woman would say now, if she talked about going to bed with Judd and about her wild response.

Was this going forward with her life, or backward?

"That didn't seem to be a problem this time." Judd stroked the side of her breast some more.

She detected a hint of satisfaction in the words. She frowned at him, letting her irritation show. "I suppose you never had any such problem with the women you've dated."

The slight smile disappeared from his mouth. "No," he said truthfully. "There weren't many."

She seethed with jealousy, knowing she had no right to, but feeling it just the same.

He touched the frown lines on her forehead. "Two. Very brief, very unsatisfactory."

A sigh of relief escaped her. She gave him a frank look. "I'm jealous, terribly jealous." She paused. "I saw Maris touch you the day I arrived and I wanted to hit her."

"Maris is a good friend, nothing more. It just wasn't there for us, for either of us. She met someone later."

"I know. Lily Mae told me she was married." Tracy sat up in bed and combed her tangled hair with her fingers. "Speaking of Lily Mae, she gave us some soup. Are you hungry?"

"Yes," he murmured, reaching over and clamping both hands around her waist. "For you." He sat her astride his hips. "You're going to have to do all the work this time."

She bent to him and planted a fierce kiss on his smiling mouth. "Gladly," she whispered, feeling the fire start all over again. It was a long time before she prepared their dinner.

After they ate, they sat on the sofa and watched TV or read. They ended up making love there, too. Neither of them could get enough of the other.

Tracy held the doors for Judd. When he was settled at his desk, she went into the conference room she used as an office and opened the FBI report. She read it through.

The expert at the forensic labs agreed with her analysis of the age of the bones. He'd also run a blood test. She looked at the type, then picked up the phone and dialed.

"Jackson, I have some news," she said when she reached the tribal attorney. "Kane sent me the report on the blood samples from the family who think the bones belong to their son. I got word on the bones from the FBI labs today. The chances of that being their long-lost boy are practically zilch. They have no common blood factors."

"They'll be disappointed. It's easier to accept death than to face the fact that the boy doesn't want to see them."

They chatted a few more minutes, then hung up. Tracy sat there lost in thoughts of the weekend. Yesterday, she and Judd had spent the entire day together. Their lovemaking had taken place at several spontaneous moments throughout the day, much as it had during their early marriage before Thadd's birth.

She smiled and yawned. Jimmy had come over after church and played checkers with Judd. Fortunately, about the time Judd had grown restless at the youngster's prolonged visit, Jimmy's friend Mark had returned home and come looking for him.

Tracy had sent the two boys off with a sack of cookies to tide them over until their dinner. Over the fence, she'd chatted with Jimmy's mother about a camping trip the boys would be taking in a couple of weeks with their scout troop, then she'd gone back inside.

Judd had been waiting impatiently for her. As soon as she was inside, he'd locked the front and back doors, closed the shutters and taken her to bed for a nap. Well, they had slept. Eventually.

Yawning again, she admitted she was happy. Beyond that, she wasn't going to think at present.

A knock at her door brought her to attention. "Come in."

Rafe Rawlings entered. "Hi. I have something for you." He handed her a package.

She opened it and found her knapsack and tools. Carefully, she and Rafe sifted through the broken glass of the sample bottles, but the evidence was gone. "Well, I'm pretty sure the short hairs belonged to our cowboy and the long one to…whoever."

"An Indian?" he asked. "A lot of them wear their hair like Jackson Hawk—long and tied in braids."

"No, it was probably a wo—" She stopped. That was evidence she meant only Judd and Jackson to have for now.

"A woman?" Rafe jumped right on the tidbit like a crow on a june bug. "Can you tell that by its size or something?"

"An expert doesn't have to explain her methods," Judd said from the open door. He limped inside, glad that he'd interrupted when he saw Tracy's smile of gratitude. "Sara

Lewis called. She says she has Native American bones at the museum. Jackson thought you might be interested."

"Definitely." Tracy went to the cabinet. "I can compare the thigh bones to the one I have."

Judd observed the young policeman's interest as Tracy explained the bone characteristics of the three major human groups. When he left, Judd muttered, "I wonder what the hell he's up to?"

"I think he's looking for some clue to his parents," she said in a pensive tone. "It must be terrible to be totally abandoned by your family."

"Yeah." He eyed her as she prepared to leave. "Are you going to the museum?"

"Um-hmm."

"Don't go out to the site by yourself," he requested. He paused, then added, "I'm asking for your word on that."

She picked up the plastic bag with the femur tucked inside and went to him. "I promise," she murmured.

The scent of her cologne drifted around them. He remembered her splashing some at various places on her body after her shower that morning. The hunger rose in him.

Unable to resist, he caught her face between his hands and kissed her. A low growl of need escaped him. Every moment seemed to strengthen the bond between them.

When he let her up for air, they stared into each other's eyes, the passion plain to see. But there were other things there, too—the doubts and the questions.

Where was this going? When would it end?

The telephone on Tracy's desk rang. She reached out and flicked on the speaker, her eyes still dazed from their embrace. A sense of pride pushed its way into his consciousness. At least he did the same thing to her that she did to him.

He limped back to his office and sat down. Propping his foot on the desk, he picked up a report. But his mind stayed on Tracy.

She was talking to the FBI office, telling them what was going on with the case. "This week?" he heard her say.

His attention caught, he listened as she told her boss that she was sure they'd find more evidence soon. The man was against spending any more time on it.

"Okay, the end of the week," Tracy said. "Yes, I'll be off the case then. I'll tell the sheriff."

Judd realized he didn't want to know. Darkness hovered near, threatening to descend at any moment. When she told him she was leaving, what would he say?

Hell, he'd probably break into tears and beg her to stay. She had to know he wanted her. He'd accepted her into his house and his bed. Didn't that tell her how he felt?

He ran a hand over his face and searched for the emptiness that had saved him before. It wasn't there. She'd slipped in and filled every lonely crevice of his life. When she left…

Tracy finished her call. She walked into his office with her purse and bag in her hands. He noticed she didn't meet his eyes. Instead, she'd gone quiet…the way she had before she'd finally admitted the end of their marriage.

To his surprise, she knelt beside him and wrapped her arms around his neck. She kissed him. It felt like goodbye.

The secretary stuck her head in the outer door. "Hey, Boss, Sterling wanted to— Oh, excuse me."

Tracy let him go and stood. A flush crept into her cheeks. The secretary grinned.

"What was Sterling's problem?" Judd managed to ask in a level voice.

"He wanted to let you know the raid on the mayor's house went fine. They arrested this little old gray-headed woman who insisted she was the mayor's mother...as if we were stupid hick cops who'd believe that."

Tracy's mouth dropped open.

Judd closed it gently with a fist under her chin. "A hick cop's idea of a joke," he explained, a smile lighting his face. "Tell Sterling to use the rubber hoses on the little old lady. We're after a full confession."

Tracy was still grinning when she left, after promising Judd she'd be back promptly at noon. A short time later she pulled into the parking lot of the Native American museum.

Several other cars were there. She noticed the license plates. Lots of tourists on the road in August, apparently.

Sara Lewis was busy with a scout troop, but she stopped long enough to show Tracy where the bones were kept.

Tracy was impressed. The collection was housed in protective drawers the same as the Smithsonian used for their archives.

An hour of comparing thigh bones assured her she was right. Her bones belonged to an Anglo, a white cowboy who had trusted the other person enough to turn his back on him...or her, she mused, thinking of the long blond hair with the dark root.

The two-faced woman?

Tracy pictured the setting as she closed the last drawer and repacked her bone. A clandestine meeting...a lover's quarrel...anger...a thrown rock...then...

But women rarely displayed the type of fury that would result in bashing a person in the back of the head, even if they had knocked the victim down with a rock thrown in anger. Maybe some jealous husband had bashed the cowboy after seeing the young man with his wife. That was more likely.

Anyway, it was all speculation. A scientist was supposed to present the evidence, not make up wild stories.

"Did our collection help?" Sara asked when Tracy emerged from the back room.

"Yes. Thanks so much for letting me use it." She told the young curator what she'd found and headed back to the office. She needed to call Jackson and tell him the news so that the tribe could quit worrying about the bones. And the case. It was out of their hands.

In fact, it was now in Judd's jurisdiction. He'd be glad of that. She'd tell him over lunch. Maybe they would have a quiet meal together while they went over the case. Alone in the office while the secretary was at lunch. She smiled.

When she entered Judd's office half an hour later, she stopped abruptly. A woman was there with him. Holding his hand.

"You poor dear," the Kincaid woman was saying. "When I heard the news, I couldn't believe someone had tried to hurt you. This is all so strange. I thought small towns were supposed to be safe from all that."

"I guess people are the same the world over," Judd remarked.

Rather facetiously, Tracy thought. She noticed he wasn't trying to get his hand loose from the treacly female, whose name she couldn't recall. But she was married to Dugin Kincaid.

"Hello, Mrs. Kincaid," Tracy said brightly, bustling in and breezing toward her own office. She noticed the china plates, the silverwear and napkins on Judd's desk, all showing signs of a recent meal. She did a slow boil. "You brought lunch. How nice."

"The cook out at the ranch knows how much I like Cornish pies," Judd hurriedly said. "Mary Jo brought two in. I insisted she eat with me. We talked about the case."

"It's so interesting. I'd no idea a forensic detective could tell so much just by digging around and looking at old bones." Mary Jo gave her a gentle smile. "The news report said it was a cowboy. However could you tell that?"

Tracy felt like a heel. The woman was extremely nice. "By the shape of the pubic bone," she said.

"Oh," Mary Jo said. She actually blushed. "Oh, I see."

Judd covered a grin as Tracy stared in astonishment. She hadn't known anyone was that inhibited in this day and age.

"Well," Mary Jo said, getting to her feet. "I suppose I'd better go. I have some errands to run."

Tracy murmured a farewell and closed the door to her room. She replaced her evidence and went over all the reports, including her own, to make sure she hadn't missed anything.

Judd came in a few minutes later. He propped himself on the corner of the table. "Did you have lunch?"

She shook her head.

"I assumed you would eat before you came back. That's why I invited Mary Jo to share the lunch with me."

"And she was so interested in the case, especially your injuries, I noticed," Tracy replied sweetly.

"Jealous, Trace?"

She took a deep breath, aware of his dark gaze on her every second. "Yes," she admitted.

"Then you know how I feel about your old friend Jackson Hawk and your new friend Rafe Rawlings."

"Yes, I understand." She faced him. "Judd, where do we go from here?" It was an issue she didn't want to discuss, but she had to know.

"I wish the hell I knew." He lifted her hand and clasped it between his palm and his thigh. "I only know I don't want you to leave. I can't give you up, not yet."

To her, that implied he could give her up when he'd gotten his fill of her. She wondered how long that would take.

Tracy stretched her weary back. She and Rafe Rawlings, who'd volunteered to help her on his day off, had searched the area along the base of the cliff for hours. She'd spent the rest of the week combing the narrow bank in hopes of finding something.

Disgruntled, she sat on a boulder and ate an apple while staring at the creek. The water was at its lowest level now, but in spring, with snowmelt from the mountains, it turned into a dangerous torrent. No telling where or how far debris might be carried in the rushing current.

"Giving up?" Rafe asked.

She nodded. "This could take years."

He hobbled over, then plopped down beside her. He looked at the river. "Yeah."

"Yet I have this feeling…." She shook her head. She knew there were more clues, if only she could find them. She sighed, then laughed. "I'm like a prospector. I'm sure I'm going to find gold around the next bend."

"Why don't you ask Winona for help?"

"In case she can see where the other bones are?"

"Yeah. Why not?" he asked at her surprised glance. "What do you have to lose?"

"You're right." She jumped to her feet. "I'll take a bone to her." She laughed at how that sounded.

"Come in, you two," Winona called from the door.

"Help me watch for those damned goats," Judd told Tracy. She handed him the crutches after he'd maneuvered himself out of her compact car. Reaching in the back seat, she withdrew the bag with the pelvis inside, having decided that it was the most likely bone to invoke a sense of who the person had been.

"How's the missing-persons search going?" Winona asked, holding the door open so Judd could get inside.

"Well, we have a few possibilities. Judd has been checking the state and FBI lists through the computer for me this week." Tracy took the crutches and set them out of the way when Judd was seated. She pulled the footstool over and propped his leg up. "Is that comfortable?"

"Yes," he said grumpily. "You don't have to wait on me hand and foot. I'm fine."

"He's been on his feet way too much this week. Kane saw us at the café last night. He checked Judd's leg and told him to stay off it and keep it propped up until the swelling has gone down," she explained to Winona, ignoring his scowl as she put a pillow under the cast.

Winona sided with Tracy. "You should take care of yourself," she told Judd. "You'll end up with arthritis in that leg, then you'll be sorry."

"Is that a prediction?" he snapped. "I'm sorry," he went on before she could speak. "I'm in a hell of a mood."

"If you'd take the painkillers Kane gave you, you might feel better," Tracy put in with no sympathy.

"All right. Give me two. And don't complain when I fall asleep in the middle of dinner."

"We wouldn't think of it," Tracy told him coolly. "Winona, I brought the pelvis with me. Do you feel up to doing anything with it, or would you rather wait until after we eat?"

"Let's do it now."

Tracy nodded. She removed the evidence from the bag and carried it to the psychic.

"What do you want to know?" Winona asked, laying it in her lap and placing both hands on the bony structure.

"Who it belongs to?" Judd said dryly.

Tracy gave him a be-quiet-and-don't-be-so-cynical look. "Or where the skull is," she added. "That would help a lot."

Winona closed her eyes. Tracy pulled a chair close and sat down quietly. They waited.

A minute went by. Another. Five minutes. Six.

Winona opened her eyes. "Nothing is coming to me, except a few vague images. I can't force it," she apologized.

"I know." Tracy patted her arm.

Winona gasped and pulled away.

Tracy shot a questioning look at her, but the older woman's eyes were closed. "Tell me what you see, no matter how odd," she requested, bending close but not touching.

"A child, alone and frightened, crying…dark…woods all around…he's lost…falling…falling…you must save him…."

Tracy was disappointed. She knew the vibes Winona

was picking up came from Rafe Rawlings. His personal quest to find his parents was messing up her quest to find the rest of the bones, darn it.

She laid a hand on Winona's shoulder. "It's okay. You can let it go."

Winona moved away as if stung. Tracy hesitated, not sure what to do. She'd never seen her friend so pale.

"Leave her alone," Judd said quietly. "What do you see?" he asked the psychic.

"The woman, the two-faced woman. Two men, fighting." She shook her head. "Too many images…too hard to see…a child is crying…Tracy…crying…help her, Judd, help Tracy."

Tracy looked at Judd, but his attention was glued on Winona. She swallowed against the knot of emotion that had formed at the mention of a child. Her own memories must have interfered with the reading, even though she'd made her peace with the past. Or perhaps it was the future Winona was seeing.

Winona opened her eyes. She handed the pelvis back to Tracy. "I'll try and describe the images I saw as they came to me. First, I saw two men fighting, then they disappeared. Next there was a child lost in the woods. That was after you touched me. It wasn't Thadd," she quickly stated.

Tracy looked up to find Judd watching her with concern. The longing that had grown all week surfaced. She wanted another child with him. She wanted him to ask her to stay and make a new life. She wanted him to tell her how very much he loved her.

But he hadn't, and she couldn't ask.

"It was Rafe Rawlings," Tracy explained. "He worked

with me at the site today. He was probably the child you saw lost in the woods. That was where he was found, remember?"

Winona nodded. "But then the first image came back— the two men fighting. One of them was the person whose bones you found. I'm sure of that. The two-faced woman was there. But then the scene shifted and I saw you and Judd and many others." She frowned as she studied Tracy. "You were worried about someone. That was all. I don't know if any of the images were connected. They could have been entirely random events."

"Yes," Judd said sardonically. "There seems to be a lot of skeletons in a lot of closets in the county."

Tracy fetched him water and two tablets. "Let me help you with supper," she suggested to Winona.

It was time for a lighter mood. Judd was obviously tired and in pain. She didn't feel good either, in spite of a week of ecstasy in Judd's arms. It was only while they were making love that she could forget the distance between them. At those moments, they were of one mind, one body…but not one heart.

Judd was keeping his under lock and key.

"Is it that bad?" Winona asked softly when they were in the tiny kitchen.

Tracy glanced over her shoulder. Judd was catching the evening news on TV. He couldn't hear them. "What do you mean?"

"You sighed as if life were a burden you'd as soon put down." Winona checked the vegetable stew in the Crockpot. "From what I've heard, things are pretty cozy between the sheriff and the FBI lady these days."

"Lily Mae, no doubt," Tracy said with a wry smile.

"And others. Don't give up on him. You two shared something precious once. You can have it again. If you're not afraid to ask for it."

"He hasn't asked me to stay."

Winona gave an impatient snort. "Have you told him you want to? He's not a mind reader, you know." She grinned. "In fact, he's damned obtuse, if you ask me. He's waiting for you to make the first move."

"Do you think so?" Tracy wanted to believe her mentor, but uncertainty rose, jarring her confidence.

The rest of the evening passed in a pleasant blend of food and conversation. They sat outside while the sky changed from twilight to dark. At ten, Tracy herded Judd into the car.

Winona gave her a meaningful stare before they drove off.

The dark interior of the car held a quiet, intimate ambiance that Tracy didn't want to break. She'd wait until they arrived at the house before she said anything, she decided.

Fear ate at her. The seventeen-mile trip had never seemed shorter. Once home, she fussed over Judd, getting him inside and settled on the family-room sofa, then dashing off to bring him a glass of water and two of his pills. She knew he was hurting. He looked very grim and tense around the eyes.

"Will you stop fluttering around?" he finally snapped. "You may as well tell me what's on your mind."

She sat in an easy chair. The time had come to ask what his intentions were for their future.

What if he didn't want her to stay?

Twelve

"I talked to my boss on this project Monday afternoon," Tracy began tentatively. "As of now, I'm off the case. We agreed, if I didn't find anything else this week, to call it quits. As far as the federal government is concerned, it's your bailiwick now."

"Yeah, I heard the conversation." His face held no expression that she could detect. He kept his gaze focused on the TV, which he'd turned to a news channel, but with the sound off.

"The tough lawman who doesn't let emotion cloud his life," she muttered, feeling it was useless to talk to him. She'd felt that way before. She closed her eyes and pressed her thumb and finger against her forehead, where a faint headache nagged.

"What the hell does that mean?"

"It means I can walk out of here tomorrow and never

darken your door again…if that's what you want." She tried to smile, but her mouth wobbled.

The silence trembled between them. She recalled Winona's advice about speaking her mind and heart.

"Or I can stay…longer," she added, unable to ask for a lifetime. "I have some time before I report to a dig."

"A dig?" He glanced at her, then away.

"A Smithsonian fellowship to examine a find in South America. The bones may be Spanish. If so, the Conquistadors penetrated farther south during that era than previously thought."

"I see." His wariness was a barrier between them. Perhaps the chasm of distrust was too wide to ever be breached.

She hoped not. She was filled with so many wants. She wanted his love, his faith in their future. She wanted him to love her, to believe in her and her love. They'd had all that at one time, but somehow it had been lost, tragedy added to tragedy.

She knew now she wanted to go forward. She wanted a new life…with this man.

"Once," she said, "we needed each other, but we failed, both of us. You walked out when I needed you. I did the same to you." She stopped as sadness threatened to overtake her. "You told me, that day I went to the cemetery, that you were sorry. I'm sorry, too, for turning away when you came to me."

He closed his eyes. His face wore a stricken expression. "It doesn't matter now."

"It does to me." She gathered her courage. "I want to stay, at least for a while longer. Once we had something special. I'd like to find it again. If you want the same thing, then you must tell me," she said in a strained voice. She couldn't keep the tremor out of it. She stared at the man on TV, his mouth moving but no words coming out.

"What if we don't find it?" Judd asked. "Then what?"

"I don't know," she said truthfully.

She held the despair at bay. Somewhere in her heart, she believed he loved her, but the years of separation would take time to heal. If he never trusted her enough to let that love show, then she would have to accept that.

Uncertain and afraid, she nevertheless went to him, taking a seat beside him on the sofa. She needed the comfort of his nearness. He put an arm around her and held her close.

"Stay," he finally said. "We'll take each day as it comes."

"Yes." She'd have to accept that…for now.

Tracy walked along the bluff. Behind her, Rafe paused and inspected the spot where Judd had gone over the ledge. She stopped and waited for him. After wiping her face with a handkerchief, she took a long drink from her canteen.

"Who else has been up here?" Rafe asked.

"Sterling helped me find Judd."

"Um, this must be his print then."

"It couldn't be. It's rained since then."

"Then someone else has been scouting around. Here's where he stopped and looked at the place where the rock broke off."

She went over and examined the area, dropping to her haunches beside the young cop. When he pointed, she saw the prints, side by side, the boot heels digging deeper into the thin dirt beside the rocky outcropping.

"Whoever it was, he was sitting here just like we are, checking the evidence."

Goose bumps ran up her neck. She glanced behind them uneasily. It was unnerving that a killer might be on the loose and watching everything they did. He had already tried to put Judd out of the way.

Briefly, Tracy wondered if the wolf monster had thought the sheriff was more of a threat than she, the forensic expert. Or was the person merely in a panic and trying to scare everyone away from the spot?

She studied the land. There was more evidence to be found. She could feel it in her bones. She had to smile at her own play on words.

"I want to check around at the limestone knob. Somehow I think we're overlooking something."

"Right."

Rafe gave her a hand up, and they trudged along the steep slope to the "egg rock", as she'd dubbed it to herself. She knelt and peered under the jutting edge of the overhang. It formed a cozy little cave. High enough to sit in. For a short person. Such as a kid.

"Um," she said.

"What?"

"This would make a neat cave for a kid to play in. As an adult, they'd remember it."

Rafe nodded. "I follow you. Someone who found the cave when they lived in the area as a kid might come back to it if they needed a place to hide something."

"Right. Let's do some more digging." She took her rock pick and began testing the floor of the shallow cavern. To one side, where the crack in the overhead limestone admitted water, she found dirt. She realized that erosion had formed a runoff channel, which had filled with dirt and debris over time. She began excavating.

"Let me," Rafe requested when she grew tired. He took over the job of breaking the hard soil and moving it out from under the rocky overhang. She sifted through it, but found nothing.

"Be easy," she said. "If there is bone, I don't want to shatter it."

"No problem." He handled the pick almost tenderly.

Two hours later they took a break.

"So, looks like things are back on for you and the sheriff?" Rafe asked as they each drank a cold soda from a cooler he'd toted up from his truck.

She smiled. That was the question on everyone's mind, it seemed. The townsfolk weren't hesitant about voicing it, either. Lily Mae had announced the news for all and sundry at the Hip Hop Café when Tracy and Judd had joined the widow for dinner two nights ago.

"For now," she admitted.

"And tomorrow?" he asked softly.

She managed a smile. "Who knows what tomorrow will bring?"

"Yeah." He stared out at the lush valley, lost in his own thoughts, which Tracy thought were sad.

Before she had time to reflect on the man who'd been abandoned in the woods by his family, she detected a movement at the far edge of her vision. Every nerve in her body sprang to instant alert.

Without speaking, she reached over and touched Rafe's arm, then let her hand drop to the rock pick beside her.

He glanced at her in question. Seeing the warning on her face, he, too, became alert to possible danger. "Where?" he asked in a low, conversational tone.

She cut her eyes to where she'd seen the shadowy form behind a thicket of pine and chaparral. Picking up her cola, she drank from the can and let her gaze roam the woods to her left. She realized she and Rafe were totally exposed on the rocky knob.

A face appeared above the tangled brush under the trees. The man had tanned, leathery skin, with a hatchet of a nose, the bluest eyes she'd ever seen and the wildest hair— half gray, half russet, the shade of rusted metal. He looked like a madman.

She gasped.

Rafe whipped a glance at her, then in the direction she was staring. "Oh," he said. A smile turned the corners of his mouth upward. "Homer, come on out," he called.

The man emerged from the thicket, his manner suspicious of them, as if he considered them interlopers on his terrain.

His clothing was old. It fit loosely on his bony frame. Tracy had the impression of a man who was slowly fading away, until nothing would be left but a lonely spirit. It was an odd thought.

"Hey, Homer, I'm Rafe Rawlings. You remember me? We met when you were prospecting over on our ranch a few years ago."

The old man drew himself up with a show of dignity. "Of course I remember. I'm not daft." He grinned unexpectedly. His teeth were surprisingly white and even. "Although lots of folks would like to think that."

"This is Tracy…" Rafe paused and looked at her.

"Roper," she said. "Tracy Roper." She remembered him vaguely. She and her father had run across him in the woods a few times while they were looking for artifacts.

Homer nodded. "I knew your father. He still teaching?"

"Yes. What are you prospecting for—gold?" she asked.

His face immediately took on a secretive, wary expression. "Maybe, maybe not," was his response. He obviously didn't like the question and was suspicious of the person who asked it.

"Or sapphires," Rafe suggested. "There used to be a mine in these parts, but the stones weren't gem quality. Homer, were those your boot prints I saw over by the bluff where Judd went off?"

"I was just looking," the man said at once. "I didn't do it."

"I know. I just wondered—did you happen to be up here when that happened?"

Homer glanced around the woods, but didn't answer.

"Did you see anyone?" Tracy asked.

The old mountain man shook his head in denial. "It wasn't a person," he said in a near whisper. "It was… something else."

"What?" Rafe asked, his tone a little harder.

"One of the spirits," Homer informed them. "They don't like people in their territory."

"Is this their territory?"

Homer quickly scanned the area. "You know it is. It's sacred ground. You shouldn't be here. Sometimes I can calm them down, but not always."

Tracy wondered how long the old man had roamed the woods. He looked ancient, but age was hard to tell on a person who had spent a great deal of time outdoors. Exposure to the elements aged one excessively.

"You couldn't calm this one?" Rafe persisted.

"No." Homer came closer. He seemed worried. "It was a different one. I'd never seen it before."

She noticed his boots were new and wondered if someone had bought them for him. Indians had a special respect for eccentrics and such. Perhaps some of them watched out for the old prospector.

"You two had better be careful," he advised. He turned and walked back into the woods, disappearing into the trees.

"An oddball, but harmless," Rafe said.

Tracy hefted the rock pick. "Well, back to work." She didn't have much hope of finding anything. Her confidence in the project had evaporated. "This is the last day I spend on the case," she said.

"Hmm." Rafe clearly didn't believe her. "You're as dedicated to finding your artifacts, as you call 'em, as Homer is to finding that old sapphire mine."

"Nope, this is it. I've had it." She knelt and slammed the pick into the rocky crevice just beyond the rock overhang. When she pulled it free, a chunk of stone slid aside, revealing an eroded area underneath. Mostly out of idle curiosity, she dug the dirt out of the groove in the limestone.

The pick hit another object. Careful now, she scraped the dirt and leaf mold away. A white, rounded object became visible.

"I'll be damned," Rafe muttered beside her. He began working with her, removing the soil with his hands as she loosened it.

The object soon became visible. It was a skull.

They worked slowly, freeing the bone from the soil packed around and in it. When Tracy lifted it from its bed, it came out intact. She turned it over.

Chill bumps raced along her scalp.

The back of the skull showed a pattern of distinct fractures that radiated outward like a starburst. A few chips of bone were missing. "Here's where he was hit." She showed Rafe.

After emptying the dirt from the brain pan, she put the skull in a bag, then sifted through the soil. She found some short hairs similar to those she'd found before. That was it.

A crack of thunder had them scurrying to finish. "That's it," she said after they'd dug out the entire runoff channel.

They left at a trot, hurrying to beat the rain they could see in the distance like gray curtains obscuring the hills. At Rafe's truck, Tracy jumped in and laid her new knapsack—a gift from Judd—on the floor. She kept the bone bag in her lap.

In town, Rafe let her out at the police station. She dashed inside with her treasures, feeling much like she thought the old hermit might feel if he found his mine—buoyant of spirit and full of excitement.

The case was all but solved. The skull had a full set of teeth still attached. Now it was a matter of matching them.

She was assuming the cowboy was a local man, not a drifter who'd been passing through, and therefore had dental records in town. Another conclusion based on gut feelings rather than evidence, she acknowledged.

Judd wasn't in when she arrived. The secretary said he was out on a case with Sterling. A child was missing.

"A child? Who?"

"The little boy who lives next door to Judd."

"Jimmy? He was on a camping trip with his scout troop," Tracy said, recalling the fact. "He and his friend, Mark." A terrible fear seized her heart and wouldn't let go. It was the way she'd felt when they'd searched for Thadd those many years ago.

"Are you all right?" The secretary stepped closer.

Tracy nodded. "Yes. I need to call Winona." She went around Judd's desk, set the bone bag and knapsack on the corner and picked up the telephone. "Winona, have you heard about Jimmy?" she asked as soon as the woman answered. The secretary left the room.

"Yes. There was a news flash on the radio a moment ago."

"Can you come?" Tracy asked.

"Of course."

"Meet me at the house…Judd's place," she clarified. "The soccer ball is there. Maybe you can pick up something from it."

"There's no need. I already am," the psychic said.

Tracy realized Winona was getting something now. She waited, hardly breathing, until the vision was over.

"Yes, a hole, darkness," Winona said. "A mine… air…yes, the air shaft…wait, something else…the woman…the two-faced woman…" She was silent, then said, "It's hopeless. It's all mixed up. I can't sort through the images."

Tracy sighed in disappointment. Fear gnawed at her. Jimmy, with his sunny disposition, had entertained Judd so sweetly. The world would be a lesser place if he died.

As if echoing her worries, the thunder rumbled again. "Oh, no, the rain," she muttered. She said goodbye and ran to the outer office. "Where is Judd? I've got to go to him."

"He's out at the Kincaid spread. Here, I'll show you." The secretary got out a map. "That's where the kids are camping, near the spring that feeds the stock pond in this section. Take the mountain pass, then turn right at the old Baxter ranch. There's a sign."

"Thanks." Tracy rushed to her car and took off. She wanted to be with Judd. If Jimmy wasn't found—she wouldn't allow herself to think of him as dead—then Judd would need her. He'd feel responsible for finding the boy and seeing that he was safe.

It seemed hours, but finally she arrived at the Baxter ranch road. Several cars were already there, so it was no problem finding the spot. She found Judd and Sterling sectioning off a map for the search routine.

Mary Jo Kincaid was pouring coffee, made on a portable burner. She had boxes of cookies and doughnuts on a camping table beside the huge coffeepot. Two scoutmasters stood close by, wearing identical worried expressions. Dugin Kincaid was there, too, looking rather at a loss.

Tracy spoke to Mary Jo, accepted a cup of coffee and went to stand by Judd. He didn't speak, but rested a hand at the back of her waist while he finished giving orders for the search.

In ten minutes the search parties left, each squad commander carrying a walkie-talkie. Judd stayed by the radio to take their calls and give further orders. While the search was on, parents arrived to collect their sons and were asked to return home rather than stay and clog the access road.

As night and the storm drew closer, the desperation of the search-and-rescue team became quietly dogged. A horse-and-dog patrol scouted the ravines at the base of the mountains, while the other searchers formed a phalanx that moved steadily through the woods, each person in sight of the next so that no bit of ground was overlooked.

When night came, the workers were called in. It would be too easy to miss an unconscious child in the dark. Tracy prayed that the storm would hold off. So far, it had.

She milled around while Judd gave orders for the next day's search, which would begin at first light. He unrolled two sleeping bags in the back of the truck. He and Tracy slept there that night, curled together against the cold.

Lily Mae came out with bacon and eggs and biscuits the next morning. "You're a godsend," Judd told her.

"Nothing keeps the spirits up like hot food," the widow said, not missing a beat in her self-appointed duties. She handed him and Tracy steaming cups of coffee to go with their meal, then went to Jimmy's mother and forced her to eat. She looked as if she were staring death in the face. The Kincaids arrived with more coffee and doughnuts.

The search continued.

Tracy was more and more concerned about Judd. His face held a pasty grayness under his tan. His eyes were haunted by memories neither of them could keep at bay. They'd been through this eight years ago, and the pain was just as sharp now.

Sometimes she felt like railing at an indifferent God who would let a child be hurt; at other times she prayed feverishly. Mostly she sat by Jimmy's mother, quietly staying close.

"How did you stand it?" the woman asked at one point. "When it was your child…how could you bear it?"

"You just do. It's hard, but you do. Don't give up hope.

It's early yet." Tracy looked at the leaden sky and prayed hard that the rain would hold off another day.

They waited at the camping site, listening to the reports of sectors being covered by the searchers. It was noon on Saturday when they got word.

"He's here! He's alive!" a sector boss yelled from the radio.

Jimmy's mother put her hands to her face.

Judd listened to the report. "Okay," he said. "We'll move down there to plan the operation." He signed off and spoke to the waiting group. "Jimmy fell into an air shaft of an old mine while he was out exploring. One of the dogs took a point on it. The boy answered when the men called down the shaft. Now we have to get him out. Let's go."

They packed up and headed for the new site. The old mine was in one of the ravines, a rough area of steep-walled minicanyons and loose, rocky soil. Tracy felt her heart sink as she thought of cave-ins and various other dangers.

A mining expert was brought in by helicopter. "Too dangerous," he said in answer to a question on digging out the collapsed tunnel from the abandoned mine. "The ground is unreliable. The best bet is to have someone go down the shaft, tie a rope around the kid and haul him out."

"How?" One of the Boy Scout leaders asked.

"The person would have to be lowered headfirst into the hole." The engineer measured the width of the shaft.

Someone gasped. Tracy glanced up, to see Lily Mae clamping a hand over her mouth. The widow's first husband had been caught in a rock slide. His horse had lost its footing and fallen over, crushing the man as they slid down the mountain in a tumble of rocks.

"It would have to be someone small," the engineer continued, studying the diameter of the hole, "someone who can think in a dangerous situation."

"I'll go," Judd said.

Tracy gaped at him. "You can't," she said.

"I will," said the Scout leader, an older man with gray hair and a paunch.

The engineer shook his head, clearly considering the man unsuitable for the job.

"Make a rope harness," Judd told Sterling. "I'll need one for the kid, too."

"Don't be ridiculous." Tracy grabbed his arm. "You have a broken leg."

"I used to do some spelunking when I was younger," Sterling said, stepping up to volunteer.

"Both of you are too big. Your shoulders won't fit," the expert stated, dismissing them.

"I'll go," Tracy said. "I'm an anthropologist. I've been in some tight places digging out artifacts."

The engineer looked her over and nodded. "You'll do."

"No." Judd stepped between Tracy and the man. "Not her."

"She's our best bet. We'd have to shore up the ground every step of the way if we try digging the boy out."

"We can widen the air shaft," Judd decided. He looked at Sterling. "It would be dangerous."

Sterling didn't hesitate. "I can handle it."

"No!" Tracy exclaimed, anger forming a tight ball inside her. "The hole might cave in if you try to enlarge it. I'll go."

"Like hell," Judd said, flatly refusing.

She turned on him. "There's a child down there," she said in a quieter voice.

They stared eye-to-eye, neither blinking. Everyone watched the drama as if momentarily turned to statues.

"A child," she repeated in a low, intense tone.

At last he nodded. "You'll do exactly as you're instructed. If it starts to go, we'll yank you out. Don't fight me on this," he warned when she opened her mouth to argue. "Sterling," he snapped. "You'll handle the operation."

"I want you to," Tracy said stubbornly.

Judd looked at the clouds, then nodded grimly.

She turned to the engineer. "What should I watch out for?"

While he explained the composition of the loosely packed soil, Judd and Sterling planned the descent. Sterling made a harness from climbing ropes for her and another for Jimmy. All she had to do was snap it around the boy's waist and over his chest.

Judd buckled her into the climbing rig. He limped over to the mouth of the air shaft, where the mother talked soothingly to her son. He could hear Jimmy crying down below.

"Tracy is coming to get you," his mother said.

"Hey, Jimmy," Judd called. "It's the sheriff. I need to know something. Is your head up or down?"

"Down, sort of," he answered. "It's wider at the bottom. I'm sideways, sort of scrunched up."

"Can you tell if anything is broken?"

"Maybe my arm. It hurts something awful." He started sobbing again. "I want out. I want to go home."

"Right. Here comes Tracy. She'll get you."

Taking the rope for Jimmy in one hand, she indicated she was ready. The engineer adjusted the angle of the mining light on her head. She lay down on a tarp placed at the edge of the shaft and started wiggling her way inside.

Two strong hands caught her legs and lifted them into the air, hooking her toes into loops in the rope. "There," Sterling said. "That should help."

"Jerk on the rope when you're ready to come up," Judd told her. "Or if there's trouble."

She looked at him, her heart in her eyes. *I love you,* she silently told him. He gave her a harsh glance, then bent over the winch, checking the brake device. She pulled her arms in to her body and nodded for them to start.

It did give her a more secure feeling to have her feet anchored to something, even if it was the rope, which felt rather flimsy all of a sudden. Judd started cranking the winch that let her down into the blackness of the earth. Sterling guided her until he had to let go.

She was on her own.

Judd watched Tracy's feet disappear into the maw of the hole. He fought an urge to reverse the winch and bring her back to safety. A hand closed on his shoulder.

"Let me take over here," Sterling suggested. "You stay by the hole and keep a hand on the ropes. That way, you can tell if something is happening."

Judd nodded. He let his chief detective take the winch. He moved over to the hole and sat on the tarp, placed there to keep the loose soil from being dislodged into the hole. He put his hands on the two ropes and at once felt connected to Tracy.

This was their best bet for saving the boy, but it also put her in danger so real it was like a metallic taste in his mouth. Fear for her stuck in the back of his throat.

If she died...

God, he couldn't think about it—not now, when her life hung by this rope slipping steadily through his hands. He had to force himself not to close his fist and stop that downward drop. If anything happened to her...

He forced himself to finish the thought. If anything happened to her, then it would be over for him, too. It was that simple.

"Slow down," he said.

Sterling reeled out the rope at a slow, steady pace. Judd suppressed the need to yell down to Tracy and ask if she was okay.

"I'm almost there," she called out. "Slow. Slower," she directed. Her voice seemed miles away rather than fifty feet down.

He tested the tension on the line. She wasn't at the bottom.

"I see him," she cried, excitement in her voice. "Stop."

"Stop," he said to Sterling, although the detective had already stopped cranking. They could hear Tracy clearly.

From one side, he heard Jimmy's mother sobbing.

"A bit more," Tracy directed. "Let me down another foot. Do it slowly."

They fed the line out inch by inch.

"Hold," she called up.

Judd heard a different note in her voice. Something was wrong. He bent closer over the hole. His heart stopped. From far below, he could hear the tinkling sound of falling rock...a trickle of sound that sent a chill of fear into his soul.

"The ground is starting to go," he said tersely. "Get ready to haul her out of there." He called softly down the shaft. "Get ready, Trace. We're bringing you up."

She didn't answer.

"Trace?" he called again. The sounds from below grew more ominous. "Get her out of there," he ordered.

"No, wait," Tracy protested. "Judd, not yet…I'm almost…"

They heard a deep, low rumble, then a shock wave shook the ground under them.

"Jimmy!" his mother cried. "Oh, my God, *Jimmy.*"

"Pull," Judd shouted at Sterling. He moved to the winch and put his hands beside the deputy's. Together they worked furiously, winching the rope out of the hole as dirt caved in on the shaft that had provided fresh air to the mine long ago.

The earth around the mouth of the hole started falling in, tiny landslides that sounded as loud as thunder in the hearts of the people who watched.

No one spoke.

Another quake rumbled under their feet. Jimmy's mother cried out once more and buried her face against the Scout master. Tears streamed down his own face as he silently watched.

"Stop," the engineer warned, kneeling as close as he dared to the hole. He peered inside.

Instant silence prevailed.

"The walls are going," he said. "There's nothing we can do."

Tracy hung suspended, the blood rushing to her head as she swayed in her upside-down position. The world was collapsing all around her. *Judd,* she thought, and was filled with love and pity for him.

She knew then that she would never willingly leave him, no matter what he said. Maybe he wouldn't trust her again with his heart, but he needed her as much as she needed him. She realized that now. Together they were complete. Apart…life was nothing. It was the simple truth.

Rocks and dirt flew past her, pummeling her body as they fell into an endless darkness her light couldn't reach. Sometimes she couldn't tell if she were going upward or falling with the collapsing earth. Strangely, she wasn't afraid.

Because Judd was above her, taking care of her.

When their upward progress really did stop, she held on, waiting, knowing they were in safe hands…Judd's hands…his big, wonderful, tender hands.

When they didn't move for a minute, she grew a little worried. She didn't know how much longer she could hang on. Her shoulders were burning against the harness as she clung to consciousness.

The rocks stopped falling. The silence seemed to scream all around her. She breathed deeply. "Hold on," she tried to say. "Just hold on. Judd will get—"

The earth gave another rumble, a low growl of rage. The sides of the air shaft buckled against her and sent her swaying, banging from side to side. Then she was trapped as the ground started pressing against her, harder and harder.

What was going on? Why weren't they pulling her out?

She couldn't free her hand to jerk on the rope. But her feet could move. With all her might, she yanked her toes down and bent her knees at the same time.

Pull. Now.

She sent the thought to Judd, unable to speak as the earth

shifted and lurched, filling her mouth, eyes and nose with debris as it fell into the eternity of darkness.

Got to hold on. Judd, help.

She felt a gigantic heaving. It was the end, she thought, and regretted all the things she hadn't told Judd…like how very much she loved him. *Oh, love, my love, my dearest love,* she repeated as the suffocating dust filled her lungs.

Thirteen

"Trace!" Judd shouted. He grasped the rope, using every ounce of muscle he had to get Tracy free of the landslide. There was a second's resistance, then the rope began to move. He prayed it wouldn't break under the strain.

Behind him, Sterling winched in the slack, following his lead on the amount of tension to maintain. Judd pulled steadily, working hand over hand as the rope emerged from the dust cloud that rose from the collapsing air shaft. He stepped back when the edge where he was standing began to fall in.

Across from him, Jimmy's mother was screaming hysterically. Kane Hunter, who'd come out with the trauma team when Jimmy had been reported found, hurried over to her.

The roar increased. Judd couldn't tell if the sound was coming from the earth or from the frantic pounding of his heart. *Oh, God, not Trace,* he prayed. He couldn't bear to lose her a second time.

A foot appeared in the dust. Another. He reached for them, grabbing Tracy's ankles and yanking her out and to the side, away from the danger. The mining engineer helped him haul her to safety. A shout went up from those watching the drama.

Tears stung his eyes when he saw what had surprised the others gathered around the rim of the shaft. Tracy, unconscious, held on to Jimmy's ankles with a death grip. She'd brought the boy out with her.

"God, what a woman," Sterling said in admiration.

Judd dropped to his knees beside her.

Kane was already there. "Stay back," he ordered everyone. He freed her hands from the boy, then he and the paramedics got to work. First he did a Heimlich maneuver on her, while someone else did the same on Jimmy.

Dust puffed out from Tracy's mouth. She dragged in a breath of air, then was racked by coughs as her body tried to get rid of the debris she'd inhaled.

In a minute Jimmy, too, was coughing helplessly. Everyone cheered as if the two had won an Olympic event.

Oxygen masks were clamped over their faces. Their vital signs were checked, then both of them were loaded into the ambulance for the trip to the hospital. Jimmy had a broken arm to be set. Both of them would have to be watched for a few days, Kane explained, in case of complications.

Judd wanted to go to the hospital with Tracy, but he had other duties. "This area has to be secured and warnings posted about the danger of possible cave-ins." He looked at Dugin Kincaid, who owned the ranch now.

Mary Jo Kincaid touched Judd's arm. "Duggie said there used to be a sapphire mine somewhere on the old Baxter ranch. I understand they're used in medical research now and are quite valuable." She gave him a melting smile. "Wouldn't it be exciting if this was it…that something good came of a near tragedy?"

"It isn't." A member of the search team spoke up. Judd saw it was Rafe Rawlings. "Homer Gilmore has prospected this area. This was an old copper mine. It never produced anything worthwhile," the young cop explained.

Mary Jo looked disappointed. Judd frowned impatiently.

"I can finish up here," Sterling said. "Why don't you go on to the hospital? You might get your cast looked at while you're there," he advised with a puckish grin.

Judd gave him a grateful glance. "Thanks." He headed for his truck, but when a pain raced up his leg, he looked down. The cast had cracked from the pressure he'd exerted while pulling Tracy out, and had split nearly in two. He'd probably broken his leg again. It was a small price to pay, he thought, in exchange for two lives.

At the emergency department of the hospital, Judd found Tracy had already been taken to a room. She was in the shower. Kane took one look at him, shook his head and gestured toward the X-ray lab with his head.

"Let's get that leg taken care of, then you can see her. In fact, I'll put you both in the same room."

"I don't need to stay in the hospital," Judd growled.

"Tracy will want you close during the night. You may as well be comfortable."

After getting cleaned up and having a fresh cast put on

his leg, Judd was taken to Tracy's room in a wheelchair in spite of his protests.

"Judd!" she exclaimed. "Are you all right? Where are you hurt?" She had to stop her anxious questions when a cough overtook her.

Light rushed into his heart, making him feel warm and new. He got out of the wheelchair and went to her, needing to hold her. Not giving a damn if the hospital gown hiked up and showed his behind to the nurses, he bent over and took her in his arms.

"I love you," he murmured, for her ears alone.

The nurses giggled and hurriedly left the room.

Tracy looked stunned. She touched his face. He noted her hand trembled. Her expression was a little wary, her smile wobbly.

He'd done that to her, he realized. Maybe she'd never been sure of his love. He hadn't mentioned it. He'd thought deeds were enough—marrying her, building the house, making love. He saw that he'd been wrong. She needed the words.

"I love you with everything in me. I always have. Someday I hope you'll believe that." He kissed her gently, briefly, aware of the oxygen tube clipped to her nose. There were so many things to say, so many things he'd like to do with her.

"Judd," she said in wonder. Her voice was hoarse from the coughing. It hurt him that she'd been hurt.

"You were right. There's something special between us. Love, that's what it is. God, Trace," he whispered. "I thought I would die. To lose you again after just finding you…"

"Shh," she said. "I know. Oh, love, I know."

After that, he lay on her bed and held her close, content

to have her warm and safe beside him. He watched her become drowsy.

Just before she fell asleep, her eyes widened. "Oh, Judd, the most wonderful thing! I found the skull. It's in my knapsack on your desk. Can you start a check of the dental records right away?" She gazed at him earnestly before she started coughing.

Judd threw back his head and laughed. "I love you, you bone-crazy woman. I love you," he repeated, more softly this time.

Jimmy went home the second day, but Tracy developed pneumonia and spent five days in the hospital. Judd visited her each morning at six. He brought lunch each day at noon. He had dinner with her each night at five, then a snack at nine before he went home.

Her father came to visit. Lily Mae Wheeler invited him to her house for a home-cooked meal. Tracy giggled, then coughed for five minutes when her father, looking slightly dazed, and Lily Mae, smugly pleased, showed up for visiting hours the third evening of her hospital stay.

Tracy wondered if she should warn her parent that Lily Mae had designs on him, but decided against it. As Winona had noted, the widow wasn't the worst thing that could happen to a person.

Winona sneaked a jar of blackberry wine and another of chamomile tea up to her. Tracy's cough improved right away. Even Kane was impressed.

On Thursday, Judd took her home. He held her arm possessively as he guided her into the house, dragging his crutches in his left hand and limping on the new cast, which was covered with signatures of friends who'd visited him and Tracy that week. Jimmy's careful scrawl was included.

Once she was in bed, he served the supper Lily Mae had prepared and left in the oven. He'd already put out the word, through Sterling and Jessica for the townsfolk and Jackson and Maggie for the Cheyenne, that he didn't want company on their first night home.

"This is delicious," Tracy said, scooping up every bite as if they hadn't been swamped with wonderful homemade treats all week.

Every patient in the hospital had had fresh fry bread and honey for dessert that week, not to mention candy, cakes, cookies, fried chicken, sausage biscuits and everything else that Tracy had ever mentioned being fond of. She was the heroine of the hour with the news media and had received an award from the governor.

But now it was his moment, and he wanted no interruptions.

Judd removed the trays from the room and returned to sit on the bed beside her. He took her hand and cleared his throat.

"Do you know what next Tuesday is?" he asked, feeling almost reverent about the occasion.

"Yes," she answered, but said no more.

"Our wedding anniversary."

A flicker of emotion passed over her face and was gone before he could read it. She looked away. "Yes."

He cleared his throat again. He'd sort of *told* her they would be married the other time; this time he wanted to do it right.

"Trace. Tracy Roper Hensley," he said, starting over in

formal tones. "Will you do me the honor of becoming my wife again?"

Her smile, tremulous and beautiful, bloomed on her face. "I'd like that very much," she said solemnly. "Oh, Judd, I'd like that very, very much."

He reached for her then, unable to stop himself. The kiss was meant to be gentle, a reaffirmation of his love, his commitment to her, this woman of his heart, but she was having none of that.

As in their first wild coming together, she tugged at him, demanding passion, wanting him with the same hunger he felt for her. He went dizzy with the pure joy of it.

"Ah, Trace," he whispered, savoring her taste, the sweet enchantment of her skin as he kissed her throat, sucked at her plump nipples, making them hard under his tongue.

He moved down to her waist and circled her belly button with his tongue, then delved into that sensitive dimple. He heard her gasp, and her hands roamed restlessly through his hair. He found the wonderful delight of her womanhood, that tiny nub that brought such pleasure to her and such joy to him.

He chuckled as she writhed under his ministrations, knowing he was driving her mad. He found great happiness in the task, loving the scent and taste, the texture and heat of her body as he showed her his love in every way he could.

When she cried out and went still, he waited, barely touching her with his tongue, until she moved again. He rose and moved between her thighs.

"No," she said weakly.

He paused. To his surprise, she pushed him down on the mattress of the queen-size bed that they'd shared in married bliss so long ago. Her gaze filled with love, she bent over him and gave him the same pleasure he'd given to her. He closed his eyes as love and happiness too strong to contain burst over him.

"Now, my love," she said when he could take no more. She moved over him and took him into her. It felt like coming home.

He placed his hands at her waist and guided her, smiling when she arched back and climaxed again. The passion flowed like a river between them. He caught the current and went with the flow.

Tracy woke to the *step-thump* of Judd approaching her side of the bed. He had a tray in his hands. The Sunday paper was under his arm.

"You're spoiling me," she scolded, looking at eggs fixed just the way she liked them and English muffins toasted to perfection.

"Not for long." He grinned. "Monday I'll expect you back on the job. You still haven't identified those bones."

She wrinkled her nose at him. "Slave driver. Haven't the men been working on it this week?"

"Yes. I thought you might feel up to helping out. No match was found in the records of the two dentists who have been in town for thirty years and still have an office, but we found a box of records in storage from another dentist. Old Doc Webster was the only dentist in town for years. He was eighty before he retired."

"Oh, good. And yes, I'd love to look through his records."

They chatted about the case while they ate their meal. "What about your job?" he asked later. "You have a dig—"

"I'll cancel it."

"No, you can't do that. You've worked too hard to get where you are to give it up. I'll just have to be patient—"

"If you'll be patient now, I'd explain it to you," she told him. "My father and I have been trying to arrange our schedules so we can write some books together. I'd like to do that. I'd also like to continue to be a consultant to the FBI. They usually have all the bones assembled when I'm called in on a case. At my prices, they usually can't afford to have me digging around in the dirt. As for the dig, there are plenty of people who can fill in for me."

Judd laughed, then became solemn. "I want you to be happy. If you want to go on digs, then you should."

She kissed him. "Thank you, my love."

After he cleaned up the dishes, he read the funny papers to her. He paused once when he looked up and saw the tears she couldn't hide.

"Would you like me to stop?" he asked, fighting his own memories of Sundays with her and Thadd.

She shook her head.

He finished, then refilled their cups from the insulated pitcher he'd brought in and placed on the lamp table. "By the way," he said casually, "Kane did our blood tests while we were in the hospital. The mayor volunteered to perform the ceremony.

"Oh?" she assumed an air of casual interest.

"He'll probably insist on making a production of it in the middle of town on the courthouse steps with all the TV and radio stations in attendance. I thought Tuesday. What do you think?"

"Tuesday," she repeated. "That's our anniversary."

"Yeah, that way we won't have to remember two dates," he explained with great practicality. Then he grinned.

Tracy held the door for Judd while he maneuvered through on his crutches. She helped him into his chair and laid the crutches close by so he could reach them easily. Then she hurried into the conference room, leaving the door open.

The box of dental records was on the table. The skull was there, too, grinning morosely at her as she took a chair. She studied the fillings in the teeth, then lifted out the first record. It belonged to Lexine Baxter. She studied Lexine's dental chart and wondered about the girl who had disappeared.

No one had given a damn about her, it seemed. Tracy found that sad. She glanced at the skull. She wondered if anyone had cared about him.

The next record was for a man who would have been about the right age. She noted the last name was Thomas. The records obviously weren't in alphabetical order. Looking at the careless way they'd been inserted into the storage box, she realized someone had probably spilled the folders and stuffed them back again as quickly as possible.

She sighed. It was going to be a long day.

At noon, Rafe Rawlings showed up carrying three bag lunches from the Hip Hop Café. He gave one to Judd and joined Tracy at the conference table.

"How's it going?" He eyed the stack of records she'd already gone through.

"No luck so far."

"You sound discouraged."

She smiled. "I'm not, but this is practically our last hope. I really wanted to solve this case."

"Yeah."

"Are you looking for clues to your parents?" she asked.

He shrugged. "It would be nice to know where I came from," he admitted.

"A young woman in trouble," she told him gently.

His lack of biological roots had made him an outsider in many ways, she realized. He was wary of people and involvement. Lily Mae had said he didn't have a regular girl.

"That's almost always the case with an abandoned baby. The father usually doesn't know about the child."

"Or doesn't care if he does know," Rafe added, picking up his sandwich and taking a bite with stoic calm.

Tracy felt he hid much behind that placid exterior.

Judd spoke from his desk. "Did you think there might be a connection between you and the bones?"

Rafe shrugged. "I was found in the woods—not the same ones, but close enough. There was a possibility. When Tracy told me the blood type, though, I knew it was no go. I'm negative. The bones were positive."

"That doesn't mean anything," Tracy told him.

"Wouldn't both parents have to be negative for the child to be? Doesn't the positive factor override the negative one?"

"Yes, if those two genes meet in the child. But two positive parents can have a negative-blood-type child if they both carry the recessive gene."

"But the chance is less likely."

She nodded and bit into the thick sandwich of ham and sprouts with a savory dressing that was low-fat and delicious.

After Rafe left, Judd called her to him. She went and sat in his lap. They napped for twenty minutes. The secretary returned from lunch and walked in, waking them.

"Oh-oh," she said. "Look, Boss, you're going to have to start locking the door if you're going to make out in the office."

Sterling walked in behind her. He flashed his badge. "Vice squad. I'm investigating a hot tip about kissing and…" There was a dramatic pause "…other stuff going on in public offices. Looks like I caught you red-handed with the goods on you."

Tracy snickered as Sterling eyed her sternly. She liked being the "goods" found on Judd.

"You have the right to remain silent," Sterling intoned, reading from his wallet card.

Judd threw a pencil eraser at his best detective. "Get out of here, or you'll find yourself on night patrol up in the mountain pass for the winter."

"Hey, you don't have to take it personally," Sterling protested. He headed for the exit.

"By the way, you want to be my best man on Tuesday?" Judd called before he got out the door.

Sterling stopped at Judd's casual question. "Yes…*hell* yes," he said. He let out a whoop. "Wait till I tell Jessica. She and Maggie have a bet going about the wedding date. Jessica said before the month was over. Looks like she won."

After he and the secretary left, Judd turned to Tracy. "The whole town will know by suppertime. Who's going to be your best woman?"

"Winona. Or do you think I should ask Lily Mae, in case she ends up as my stepmother?"

"Winona. Though I think we're going to see a lot of Lily Mae in the future. God, I never thought she'd be a possible mama-in-law."

"Well, she hasn't wrestled him down the aisle yet."

A short while later Tracy returned to her task. She worked the rest of the day and got a bit over halfway through the long box. When Judd stuck his head in the door, she was ready to go. She put the file she'd just picked up back in the box.

On the drive home, she wondered how it was possible to be so happy…and yet sad. Judd had asked her to marry him, but he was holding back, too. He was still guarding his heart.

The next day, dressed in a hurriedly bought silk outfit in her favorite golden yellow color from a new boutique near the Hip Hop Café, Tracy stood on the courthouse steps with Judd.

The mayor stood between them and smiled at the press, his wife at Judd's side. Lightbulbs flashed and camera whirred as the news media took advantage of the photo opportunity thus provided of the heroine and the sheriff…who happened to be her ex-husband as well as her soon-to-be new husband.

"It's so romantic," Tracy heard one reporter exclaim.

"It'll make the national news," another predicted with great satisfaction. He stepped closer with a mike when the mayor opened the book of marriage vows and took his place.

Winona leaned close to Tracy. "I told you you'd stay."

"Nobody likes people who say 'I told you so,'" she whispered back. She kissed the older woman's cheek. "But I love you just the same."

Winona wore a blue silk dress the color of the Montana sky. Her hair was neatly braided and wrapped around her head. She wore shoes and stockings and a discreet crystal necklace. On her shoulder was an orchid, pinned there by Judd who also planted a kiss on her cheek.

On the white Bible Tracy held, a red rose and a white one, their stems entwined, were the only adornment.

When the vows were over, the entire county went across the street to the park for a cookout. The meal was followed by cake and punch and a few fireworks, which were illegal, but the sheriff didn't arrest his chief deputy or the young cop who helped set them off.

Lightheaded from champagne, Tracy held on to Judd when they were dropped off at their house by a grinning rookie cop, who left in a hurry when his boss scowled at him.

Judd decided he should carry Tracy across the threshold. He made it, but stumbled one step inside the door. They went down in a tumble. One of the crutches barked him on the shin of his good leg. He cursed soundly.

"A fine way to talk," Tracy scolded. "How will it sound to our grandchildren when they learn their grandfather dropped his bride and cussed like a Montana miner on his wedding day?"

He quit rubbing his leg. "What grandchildren?"

She drew a slow breath. "The ones our child will probably have." She gave him a sweet smile that trembled only a little and waited anxiously for his response.

Judd stared into Tracy's eyes and realized this wasn't a joke. Emotion roiled within him. Another child. A picture of Thadd, still and lifeless, rushed into his mind. He sat up and rubbed a hand over his face, shutting out the pain of that nightmare.

A child. He hadn't counted on that. He'd thought…if it was just him and Trace, with no other complications…he'd thought he could live with that, deal with it if anything happened to her. But to start over…to go through it all again…

"Judd?"

She touched him lightly on the arm and withdrew. He had to look at her then. Her skin, always pale as fresh milk, seemed whiter and drawn against the fine bones of her face. Her gaze was anxious…and pleading.

God, did she know what she was asking him?

"Are you sure you're pregnant?" he asked. He didn't recognize his own voice, it was so strained.

She nodded and visibly swallowed. Her hands plucked nervously at her wedding dress. She removed her hat with the net that covered half her face, laid it on a chair, then slipped out of her satin shoes and pushed them aside.

Without looking at him, she sat quietly, staring out the open door. Her face was still, as still as death…*no,* don't think that. Oh, God, to go through it again…to love a child.

"How…when? You've known…for how long?" He was stalling for time, for some insight to tell him how to deal with this.

"When I was in the hospital," she said. "I felt queasy, so I asked Kane to do the test."

"The pregnancy test," Judd mumbled, looking stunned.

"Yes."

"I thought…after Thadd…" He gestured helplessly.

"Yes. The doctors said it would be difficult, perhaps impossible, for me to conceive. And I didn't during all those years. Oh, Judd," she cried softly, "it's like a miracle. We'll be a family again, like we were…"

Tracy stopped at the grimace of pain that crossed his

face. She watched anxiously as he gripped one crutch like a lifeline. She hadn't realized it would be so hard on him to accept the idea of another family. It was too soon. She hadn't prepared him for fatherhood again.

"Please, say something." Fear ate at her, and she could hardly speak. "Please say you want it—our child…. I need you to say it…." Her world teetered on the brink of destruction.

He reached for her then. Pulling her close, he buried his face in her hair. She felt a shudder run through his hard, lean frame and she wrapped her arms around him, wanting to comfort him.

"It'll be all right," she whispered. "It will, Judd."

"I know," he said at last. "I know."

He took her face between his hands and gazed into her eyes. "I do want the child. It was…for a minute, I thought of the risk…."

"The risk of childbirth?" She'd had an easy birth. Judd knew that. He'd been with her throughout the labor.

"The risk of loving. I remembered how it felt to lose our son, and then to lose you. I thought of going through that again."

"You'll never lose me." She realized she couldn't give total guarantees for the future. "Life can be dangerous. I can't promise it won't be, but I'll never voluntarily leave you."

He laid a finger over her lips. "That day at the mine, when you went down for Jimmy, I thought if you died, then it would be over for me. The pain of it, Trace, God, the pain."

She made a little sound, trying to soothe and reassure him. She knew the anguish he spoke of.

He sighed. "That's a coward's way of thinking. There's always a risk in living. In loving, too."

His gaze held hers. She listened with all her heart while he sorted through his feelings, knowing this moment was vital to their future happiness. She wanted complete commitment from him now, for her and her love and for their child.

"Kids are curious beings," he went on. "They go off on their own to explore the world. That's natural."

"Yes." She realized Judd was accepting the past as she had that day in the cemetery. Like her, he was facing the sorrow, the pain, and letting it go. She held very still and waited.

"Things happen—car wrecks, cave-ins, fire, flood. The world is full of disaster. It's on the nightly news. But there are a thousand other moments, each one precious, each one blessed with love and joy. That's what I forgot with Thadd. The joy of knowing him. I remembered only the pain." He touched his forehead to hers. "Forgive me, my love."

"For what—being human?"

"I told you in the hospital I loved you. I've told you I didn't want to live when I thought you might die. But it wasn't the whole truth. You see, I thought I could love you a little bit. That it would be safe if things didn't get too involved. As long as it was just the two of us, without other complications."

"And then you learn about a new baby," she murmured, seeing what he was getting at. She'd sensed he was holding back, but she'd thought it was because he didn't completely trust her love yet. She'd thought, with time, it would come.

He gave a wry, husky laugh. "Life doesn't work in half measures, it seems."

"I'm sorry," she said, the words strained. "I didn't mean to make it so hard for you—"

"No," he said, cutting off her apology. "Don't be sorry. I want this child. I want you and our love and everything that love can possibly offer. I want it all, Trace. Everything."

Looking into his eyes, she saw he meant it. The barriers were completely gone. Love gleamed in those dark depths, bright as the rising sun…bright as all the tomorrows to come.

She lifted her face and felt his kiss on her mouth. A pledge, she realized, to the future, to their children.

Now…now she felt she was truly his wife, each of them part of the other and of the whole fabric of life.

"Where were we?" he asked. "Oh, yes, I was about to ravish you, Mrs. Hensley."

They made love there on the floor at eight o'clock on a late summer's evening with the door wide open. Fortunately, all the neighbors were still at the party.

Fourteen

Tracy woke at dawn. Judd was tickling her nose with the corner of the blanket. She laughed, pushed his hand away and scratched the offended part.

"What do you want to do today?" he asked.

"Well," she drawled, "what did you have in mind?"

"We've never had a honeymoon," he reminded her. He combed her tangled curls with his fingers. "The first time we couldn't afford it. But now we can. I'd like to take you somewhere special, to a place you've always wanted to go, but never had the chance."

"There's only one place," she said softly. "It's here, in your arms. From the moment I met you, this is where I've longed to be. Always." She caressed his strong jaw and ran her thumb over his lips. "For me, this is paradise."

They stayed in bed another hour, and Judd said all the things she wanted to hear, the special things that lovers say.

She loved it that he opened himself to her and expressed his feelings, and she told him so.

"If only we'd talked before," he said at one point.

She laid a hand over his mouth. "No regrets," she ordered. "We look forward from this moment on."

"No regrets," he agreed. His kiss was his promise.

"Well, look who's here—the folks who ran out on their own wedding party." Sterling laid a report on the secretary's desk and followed the couple into the other room.

"It was either that or arrest half the town, including the chief deputy, for disturbing the peace." Judd hung his hat on a peg and hobbled over to his chair.

Tracy grinned at the two and left them. Going into the small conference room, she plunked her purse on a chair, took her seat and picked up where she'd left off two days ago. Today she would finish the box of records.

A tingle of excitement shot through her as she lifted the next file, opened it, glanced at the macabre grin on the skeleton and looked at the dental record.

A filling in a molar matched, she saw. And another. And another. The root canal in a bicuspid was the same. The lower back molars had been extracted, according to the dental chart. The lower back molars were missing from the skull.

"Judd!" she yelled. "Sterling!"

The two men stopped their monthly planning session and peered through the open door at her.

"I've found him!" she said. "I've found our cowboy!"

Both men leapt to their feet and stampeded into the room. One on each side, they peered over her shoulders.

"Look." She pointed to each detail on the chart and on the teeth in the skull. Every one was the same.

"What's the name?" Judd demanded. "Who is it?"

She turned the card over and peered at the information side. "Charles Avery," she read. "Oh…"

"What just occurred to you?" Judd asked, his eyes narrowed on her as if she were the suspect in the case.

"He was the one…Lily Mae told me about him and the Baxter girl who used to live here. Everyone thought they'd run off together. That was about twenty-eight years ago. Oh, Judd, Melissa Avery from the Hip Hop Café—the bones…they belong to her father."

"Hmm," Sterling mused aloud, "did she kill him?"

"Melissa? She couldn't have. She was just a baby at the time," Tracy explained.

Sterling gave her a pained look. "I meant the woman he was supposed to have run off with."

"Lexine Baxter?"

"She would have had to be pretty strong to have killed him with a rock," Judd said.

"She wasn't an Amazon type, not that I remember," Tracy put in. "I don't think Avery was dead when he was pushed under the ledge. Remember, I found blood in the soil there? He could have been in a daze, then gone into a coma."

"And bled to death," Sterling concluded.

"Winona saw our cowboy…Charles Avery," Tracy amended. "She saw him fighting with another man. Maybe that was who did him in and left him to die."

"But who was that?" Judd frowned, then gave Sterling a wicked grin. "I know just the man to put to work on a twenty-eight-year-old murder mystery."

Sterling said a rude word.

The telephone rang. Tracy hit the speaker button. "Tracy Roper…Hensley," she said in her official voice, grinning at Judd's scowl.

"Tracy, I have some news for you."

"Winona," Tracy said warmly. She had news of her own. "We know who the cowboy was. I found his dental records. You'll never guess in a million years—"

Winona wasn't the least interested in the past. "It's a girl," she said smugly. "But the next one will be a boy."

* * * * *

SPECIAL EDITION

DIAMONDS, POWER AND PASSION…TEXAS-STYLE!

THE TEXAS BILLIONAIRE'S BRIDE

BY *CRYSTAL GREEN*

For nanny Melanie Grandy, caring for the daughter of gruff billionaire Zane Foley was the perfect gig…until she fell for him, and her secret past threatened to bring down the curtain on her newfound happiness.

Available June 30

Follow the biggest feud in Texas in these six titles:

SSE65463

Visit Silhouette Books at www.eHarlequin.com

Choose the romance that suits your reading mood

Home and Family

Harlequin® American Romance®
Lively stories about homes,
families and communities like
the ones you know. This is
romance the all-American way!

Silhouette® Special Edition
A woman in her world—living
and loving. Celebrating the
magic of creating a family and
developing
romantic
relationships.

Harlequin® Superromance®
Unexpected, exciting and
emotional stories about
homes, families and
communities.